ADA, THE BETRAYED;

OR,

THE MURDER AT THE OLD SMITHY.

———————

A ROMANCE OF PASSION.

———————

LONDON:

PRINTED AND PUBLISHED BY E. LLOYD, 12, SALISBURY-SQUARE,
FLEET-STREET.

PREFACE.

THE immense popularity which the present work obtained when brought out in a different form, led the Publisher to the belief that if reprinted in a style fit for binding, it would be acceptable to its readers, and he has not been disappointed.

The work has been eulogised by many (the press included) for which the Author feels justly proud.

The plot has been laid with great care, and worked out with the greatest circumspection, the Author having kept the incidents, as they really occurredd to him, in view.

The working of retribution upon the guilty, the self-congratulation and ennoblement of mind which always accompany a good action, and the degradation and misery to which vice subjects its possessor, have all been delineated in a natural manner.

With these few observatious, the work is left in the hand of the reader for his attentive perusal.

London, October, 1847.

ADA, THE BETRAYED;
OR, THE MURDER AT THE OLD SMITHY.
𝔄 Romance of Passion.

Around the winter's hearth the tale is told,
To lisping infancy and hoary age;
It is a story of strange passion—of grief and tears—
Of joy and love, and all the elements of mind
Which make us what we are.   SCOTT.

CHAPTER I.

THE STORM.—THE OLD SMITHY.—A DEED OF BLOOD.—THE DEATH CRY.—THE CHILD OF THE DEAD.—REMORSE AND DESPAIR.

IT was towards the close of the year 1795 that a storm, unequalled in duration and fury, swept over one of the most fertile districts of England, spreading consternation and dismay among the inhabitants of several villages, and destroying in

No. 1.

a few short hours the hopes of many an industrious family, who looked to the nearly ripened grain of the fertile fields for their means of subsistence through the coming winter.

The day had been lowering and overcast. An unusual sultriness had prevaded the air, and although more than sixty miles of hill and dale laid between the spot to which we allude and the Northern Ocean, which washes the eastern shore of England, several sea birds (a most unwonted sight) had flown, screeching and wailing, over the rich corn-fields and promising orchards.

The day had worn gradually on, and it was not until the sun was lost amid a mass of fiery clouds in the glowing west that any precise indications of the approaching tempest presented themselves. Then, however, when the long shadows from the trees began to lose their identity in the general gloom of the rapidly approaching night, a singular moaning wind began to blow from the north-west.

The cattle showed alarm and uneasiness—the birds flew low and uncertainly—horses trembled in their stables, and the hoarse scream of various large birds of prey as they flew over the farm-house, or settled on the roofs, had a peculiarly discordant effect. It would seem as if there was something in the air which enabled the inferior animals to know and dread the awful strife of the elements which was about to ensue.

The glowing clouds in the west rapidly disappeared, and the night fell over the land as if a black pall had been suddenly cast over the face of Nature. The wind momentarily increased in violence. Now it moaned like an evil spirit round the gable ends of the houses; then again, with a wild whistle and a rushing sound, it would sweep past the latticed windows like a wild animal seeking its prey

Occasionally there would be a lull in the tempest, and in one of these the heavens were lit up with a flash of lightning of such power and brilliancy, that all who saw it closed instantly their eyes in dismay, and trembled with apprehension. Then followed thunder—thunder that shook the houses to their foundations, and boomed and rattled in the sky with so awful a sound that many of the villagers sunk upon their knees to pray, for they thought the end of the world was at hand, and they should never see the blessed sun again. Mothers clasped their screaming children to their breasts, and wept in bitterness of heart. Strong men shook with fear, and when again the wind arose, and, like a giant's arm, levelled hedges, trees, haystacks, and some houses, a cry of dismay arose from the villagers, and the bells were rung in the rural churches. Some screamed—some prayed—some wept and rung their hands. All was horror, uncertainty, and despair!

The storm had lasted several hours, and still the forked lightning darted in livid streaks from cloud to cloud. The awful thunder filled the air with its hundred echoes, and the wind swept over a scene of desolation, for the smiling corn-fields were no more; the laden fruit trees were levelled with the soil, and many a cottage had its humble thatch torn off, and presented but its bare walls to the moaning blast.

The principle fury of the land storm seemed to have been levelled at a little village which occupied the gentle slope of a beautiful and fertile valley, some few miles from Ashby-de-la-Zouch, and through the lowest portion of which a branch of the river Derwent wound its serpentine course. The village was called Learmont, from the name of a noble family who, since the Norman conquest, had been the owners of the land.

There was scarcely a house, from the humblest cottage to the lordly mansion of the Learmonts, which had not suffered by the hurricane; and to add to the dismay of the inhabitants, who in fear and dread had rushed from their homes, there arose about the hour of midnight the dreadful cry of fire!

That fearful cry struck terror to every heart, and those who had breath to shriek joined the shout, and "fire! fire!" passed from mouth to mouth, in all the different tones and cadences of fear and hopelessness.

All uncertainty as to the precise locality of the fire was soon removed, for the flames from a large irregular building, standing somewhat apart from the other houses, quickly marked it as the spot of the conflagration.

"It's at the *Old Smithy*," cried a dozen voices.

The words had scarcely passed their lips, when a woman darted into the centre of the throng, shrieking wildly,—

"Aye—it is at the Old Smithy! The time has come—I knew. I have told you all; you, and you, and you, I've told. Ha! ha! ha! Heaven has at last forged a bolt for the Old Smithy! Do you stand aghast? Can you put out yon light? No—no—no! I know you cannot. The Old Smithy gone at last. Ha! ha! I am happy now—happy now! You do not stir. You are right—quite right. Let *him*, Andrew Britton—that's his name—let him roast and writhe in the flames—let his skin blacken in curling lights—let his flesh drop from him in the hissing, roaring fire—let his bones whiten, and glow, and crackle into long white splinters, as they will—as I know they will; but I want to see it, my masters—I want to see it. Live—live and shriek, Andrew Britton, till I come. Hark! now I hear him. Hark!—music—music— 'tis music."

She was about to bound off in the direction of the blazing house, leaving her listeners aghast at her terrible denunciations, when a man of forbidding aspect and Herculean build rushed into the midst of the throng of villagers round her, and with one blow of his clenched hand struck her insensible to the earth.

A cry of "shame! shame!" arose, and a young man stepping forward, exclaimed,—

"Unmanly ruffian! How dared you strike the woman? You know as well as all we that she is mad. Andrew Britton, you are a coward, and well you merit your name of 'The Savage.'"

"Down with the savage!" cried several.

"He has killed poor Mad Maud," said one.

"Is she not always crying out against me?" growled the ruffian. "Is there anything too bad for the old beldame to say of me, Andrew Britton?"

"Not dead! not dead!" suddenly cried she whom the villagers called Mad Maud, springing to her feet. "Mind ye all, Andrew Britton is to die before I do. Ha! ha!—not dead! To the Smithy—to the Smithy."

She darted off in the direction of the blazing house, and, as if by one impulse, the villagers followed her, shouting,—

"To the Smithy—to the Smithy!"

The building, which was in flames, had at one time evidently been of a much higher character than its present appearance warranted. It consisted of a large uninhabited house, with two wings, one of which had been converted into a smithy, and was in the occupation of Andrew Britton, the smith, who stood high in favour of the then Squire Learmont, whose property the old house was.

The fire was in the other wing to that which had been converted into a smithy, and when the villagers arrived they found it so enveloped in flames, that any attempt to save it seemed perfectly in vain.

"Blood—blood is spilling," cried Mad Maud, rushing close to the flaming building. "I heard it. A deed of blood! Hark!—hark!"

The villagers were horror-stricken by hearing piercing shrieks coming from the interior of the burning house.

"There!" cried the maniac exultingly; "that's a death cry Ha! ha! ha! Brave work—brave work. Andrew Britton, where are you?"

"Here," cried the smith. "Look at me, all of you, and swear hereafter you saw me here while—while——"

"While the murder was doing!" cried Maud.

"Murder?" said the villagers, as if with one voice,

"Drivelling idiot!" roared Britton. "By——"

Before the oath could escape his lips, there dashed from among the burning ruins a figure which might well strike terror into every heart. It was that of a man, but so blackened and scorched was he by the fire that he scarcely looked human.

"Help ! help !" he screamed. "Murder ! murder !"

Every heart was paralysed as he dashed into the centre of the throng, scream-ing with pain.

"The child! the child !" he screamed. "The child of the dead—save her ! save her !"

Many hands were immediately stretched forward to take from his arms an infant that the villagers now perceived he carried.

He resigned his charge, and then flinging his arms above his head, he cried,—

"Save me—save me from myself—from the glance of the dead man's eye—from blood save me. Oh, save me from conscience. The hell has begun."

His last words rung faintly on the ears of the horrified crowd, for having given up the child, he then bounded onwards, and was soon lost to sight and hearing in the darkness of a plantation which grew on the border of the stream that watered the valley.

Britton, the smith, glared with eyes of fury after the shrieking fugitive, then clenching his hand, he shook it wildly in the air, and breathing a bitter curse, turned from the burning portion of the house, and dashed into the wing in which was the Smithy.

———

CHAPTER II

THE LULL OF THE TEMPEST.—MORNING IS COMING.—THE CHILD OF MYSTERY.—THE NECKLACE.—A SURPRISE AND A DISAPPEARANCE.—THE INSCRIPTION.—THE LORD OF LEARMONT.

THE startling and singular events at the Old Smithy had the effect of distracting in some measure the attention of the affrighted inhabitants of Learmont from the fury of the tempest, which was still raging, although with diminished rage, around their humble dwellings.

The forked lightning was not so frequent in its flashes, and the thunder seemed to be passing away in the direction of the wind.

Still it was a night of terror, and it was not until the wind had sensibly abated, and a few heavy drops of rain fell splashing upon the ground, that the peasants ventured to re-enter their dwellings, with a hope that the storm had done its worst.

The child which had been brought from the burning house, in so awful and mysterious a manner appeared to be little more than one year old, and it was perfectly unknown to all in the village ; neither could any one give a guess as to who the strange man could be who with such frantic cries of pain and remorse, had appeared for a moment amongst them.

The wing of the ancient building in which the fire had originated, alone had suffered from the conflagration. It lay a heap of smouldering ruins, but the rest of the large rambling habitation, including the Smithy, was quite uninjured.

The child was surrendered by common consent to the care of a kind-hearted woman, by the name of Dame Tatton, who was a widow. She looked with an eye of trembling pity upon the little innocent who nestled in her bosom in sobbing fear.

The little girl, for such she was, shewed evidently by her attire that she had been in the care of those of a far higher rank in life than the kind-hearted, but humble cottager, who now strove to allay her childish terror.

Around the neck of the infant was a small necklace of pearls, and about its attire generally there were ample indications of wealth.

The little innocent soon sobbed itself to sleep upon the breast of Dame Tatton, and the village gossips, after resolving in the morning to go in a body to the

Squire Learmont and ask his advice, or rather commands, concerning the disposal of the babe that had been so mysteriously thrown upon their hands, dispersed to seek that repose they were so much in need of.

Every one naturally thought that Andrew Britton, the smith, knew something of the mysterious man and the child; but none would venture to the dwelling of "the Savage," as he was generally called, to make an inquiry, for his ferocity was too well known not to be universally dreaded.

The storm had nearly gone. A heavy fall of rain was splashing on the meadows, and beaten down vegetation, and all was still in Learmont till the morning's sun rose on the wreck which the tempest had made in the green valley that the day before was redolent of peace and plenty.

Young and old then sought the cottage of Dame Tatton. They knocked at first gently, then more loudly, but no one answered.

"My mind misgives me," cried the young man who had the preceding evening spoken so boldly to the smith—"my mind misgives me ; but there is something wrong. Let us force the door, my masters."

"Nay, Frank," said an old man. "The widow sleeps soundly after the storm. Ye are too hasty—far too hasty, Frank Hartleton."

"Nay to thee !" cried the impetuous youth. "'Tis but a broken panel at the utmost, an' we do force the dame's door, and that we can any of us mend again. What say you masters ?"

"Aye, truly," replied a little man with a red night-cap—"spoken truly—most sagely spoken."

"But will the squire approve of it, think ye ?" suggested one.

"By my shears I thought not of that," murmured the little man, who was the garment fashioner of Learmont.

"Knock again," cried several.

Frank Hartleton knocked loudly, and shouted,—

"Dame Tatton—Dame Tatton, I say ; hast taken a sleeping draught ?"

No voice replied. All was as still as the grave within the cottage.

Frank now placed his foot against the frail door, and with one vigorous push he sent it flat upon the earthern floor of the cottage, and immediately striding over it, he entered the humble dwelling.

The villagers hesitated for a moment, in order to be quite sure there was no immediate danger in following Frank Hartleton, and then they quickly thronged the little cottage, which could boast of but two small apartments, so that the whole interior was in a very few minutes examined.

The cottage was tenantless. Dame Tatton and her infant charge had both disappeared.

The simple rustics gaped at each other in speechless amazement. The bed had evidently been occupied, but there was no sign of confusion or violence—all was orderly and neat—nothing was removed or disarranged. A canary bird was singing gaily in a wicker cage; a cat slept on the hearth ; but the Widow Tatton and the mysterious child—now more mysterious than ever—had both disappeared.

"I cannot account for this," said Frank Hartleton. "By Heavens it's the most singular thing I ever heard of."

"The place has a strange look," cried one.

"A strange look !" said the rest in chorus. "So indeed it has."

"Strange nonsense," cried Frank. "So you are frightened all of you at an empty room are you ?"

"Master Frank," suddenly shouted one, "look ye here, you were always a main scholar."

Frank turned his attention to a part of the plaster wall indicated by him who spoke, and on it was traced, as if rapidly with a thumb or finger nail these words,—

"HELP—THE SQUIRE AND THE SAVAGE HAVE—"

and that was all. Whoever had written that hurried scrawl had not had time to finish the sentence which would probably have thrown some light upon the inexplicable affair.

"There has been some foul play, I am convinced," cried Frank. My friends let us go at once and confront the squire."

"You need not go far, insolent hind!" cried a hoarse voice, and Frank turned suddenly to where the sound proceeded from, saw Squire Learmont himself standing upon the threshold of the cottage.

Squire Learmont or Tearmont, only as he preferred being called, was a man far above the ordinary standard of height; his figure, however, was thin and emaciated, which, coupled with his height, gave him an ungainly appearance. His complexion was a dead white—there was nothing of the sallow or brown in it—it was ghastly white, and contrasting with his lank black hair which hung far down from his head straight and snake-like without the shadow of a curl, it had a hideous corpse-like appearance.

"I am glad," said Frank, when he had recovered his first surprise at the sudden appearance of Learmont, "I am glad we have not far to go, for the business is urgent."

Learmont waved his hand for him to proceed.

"Last night there was a storm," continued Frank.

"Indeed!" sneered Learmont. "That is news this morning."

Frank Hartleton felt his cheek flush with colour, but he controlled his passion and continued,—

"A wing of the old house adjoining the smithy was on fire—the house I mean that has been shut up so long because it is thought—"

"Who dared think?" cried Learmont, in a voice of violent anger. "Who dared think of me —?"

"Of you, sir?"

"Aye—who dared —?"

"It was of the house I spoke."

"But—but is it not my house, quibbler?" cried Learmont.

"Truly, sir."

"Then on with your speech, sir, and draw no inferences from idle gossips. The wing of my house was on fire. Enough—what followed?"

"A man rushed from it in mortal agony of mind and body, carrying a child —"

"Well—well!"

"That child was given to the care of Dame Tatton, who dwelt in this cottage. Now child and dame have both disappeared."

"I hear!" cried Learmont.

"What is to be done sir? You are the lord here."

"And so, I presume," sneered Learmont, "I must charge myself to bring back every old woman who disappears from her hovel?"

"Here is an inscription on the wall," said Frank, "which seems to refer —"

"Ah!" cried Learmont, striding forward, and reading the few words that had been scratched on the wall. "Well, what then?"

"That I ask you Squire Learmont."

"Then I reply, nothing. Will you finish that sentence?"

"Certainly not."

"Then what further have you to say to me?"

Frank was rather confounded by the manner of the squire and was silent.

"Young man," said Learmont, "your father did a service to the Learmonts."

"I know it," said Frank.

"In return for that service, the Learmonts gave him a patrimony, an estate, on the substance of which you live."

"'Tis well known," cried Frank. "The service was not overpaid. My father saved your father's life."

"True," sneered Learmont, "but beware!"

"Beware of what?"

"The house that was powerful enough to make a peasant an independent man can again convert the audacious son of a peasant into a hind he should have been. Beware I say. You know my motto."

"I do. 'Constant till death!'"

"Constant till death. Constant in all things, including—revenge!"

"I scorn your threats," cried Frank.

"Be it so," said Learmont, as with an angry frown he strode to the door of the cottage. He turned upon the threshold, and said, "this hovel shall be closed for ever. Once more I say beware!"

With a haughty step he left the humble dwelling and took the road to his princely mansion.

CHAPTER III.

TEN YEARS HAVE FLOWN.—THE OLD ROSE INN.—A SNOW STORM.—TOM THE FACTOTUM.—AN ARRIVAL TO THE OLD SMITHY.—THE MYSTERIOUS STRANGER.

TEN years had rolled away since the storm so memorable on account of the mysterious incidents connected with it, had swept over the village of Learmont. Ten weary years to some—to others, years of sunshine and joy—but of such chequered materials are human lives. But little change had taken place in the village. Some of the aged inhabitants had dropped into the silent tomb, and some of the young had grown grey with care—nothing, however, had occurred to cast any light upon the dark and mysterious occurrences of the well-remembered evening of the storm. The smith, Andrew Britton, still plied his hammer, and the mass of ruins which had once been the wing of the old house he inhabited, still lay as they had fallen—only they were overgrown with wild weeds, and coarse vegetation. The cottage of Dame Tatton remained uninhabited, for no one would live in what they considered an ill-omened and mysterious residence. It had, therefore, remained locked up since the unaccountable disappearance of its last occupant, and in course of time the villagers began to regard it with a superstitious feeling of fear—some even asserted that lights had been seen at night gleaming through the narrow casements—others reported that strange sounds of pain and distress had been heard proceeding from the humble dwelling—but whether or not these sights and sounds had really attacked the senses of the inhabitants of Learmont, certain it was that the cottage began by degrees to be regarded with as much dislike and dread as the large rambling habitation of Britton, the smith.

The child too—the infant who had been rescued from the flames was never heard of, and the storm—the fire—the burnt and shrieking man—the child and Dame Tatton, became all leading topics in the gossips of the villagers around their fire sides, as well as in the old oaken parlour of the "Rose," an ancient ale house, which stood in the very centre of Learmont, and had so stood for time out of mind.

It was in the depth of winter, ten years and some months after the storm, that a goodly collection of the village gossips—scandal-mongers and topers were seated around the cheerful, crackling, blazing fire in the before-mentioned oaken parlour of the "Rose." The hour was waxing late, but the room was so warm and comfortable, the ale so good, and the conversation so deeply interesting, that no one seemed inclined to move, but upon the principle of "let well alone," preferred the present good quarters to a turn out in the snow.

"How long has it snowed now, Tom?" said a jolly farmer-looking man, without taking the pipe from his capacious mouth.

"It *beginned*," replied Tom the waiter, ostler, and fag in general. "It *beginned* at half arter eleven, and here's a quarter arter ten. It's *snewed* all that time."

"Oh, that's nothing" said an old man. "Forty years ago, when I was a youngster, it used to think nothing of snowing for a week or a fortnight off hand."

"Ah!" said another old man, shaking his head. "Snow now isn't like the snow as used to be. It's not so white, I know, for one thing—"

"Mayhap, daddy, your eyes arn't so good?" said a good-looking young man, who was the very picture of health and strength.

"I can tell you," said the old man, with an air of indignation, "that in my days—that is my young days, everything was different, snow and all."

"You may say that," remarked another. "When now shall we ever hear of a storm, such as that happened only ten years ago, and a matter of three months or thereby—eh?"

"You mean the time when Savage Britton had part of his old Smithy burnt?"

"The fire wasn't near his Smithy," said the old man; "I saw it, and I saw the mad fellow rush out with the child too."

"We shall never know the rights of that business," remarked another, "and since Frank Hartleton has gone to London, there's no chance neither."

"And you know who has shut himself up more than ever since."

"The savage?"

"No—not he—some one else."

"The squire?" said the young farmer.

"I mention no names," said the old man, "mind I didn't say the squire shuts himself up. Did I, Tom?"

"Not at all," replied Tom. "Any ale wanted? Keep the pot a *bilin*."

"And if you did say the squire shuts himself up," cried the young farmer, "what then? We all know he shuts himself up, and room after room has been locked up, in Learmont house, till it's a misery to look at the dirty windows."

"That may be," said the old man, "but mind I didn't say so. Is it snowing still, Tom?"

"I believe ye," cried Tom, pulling aside a little bit of red baize that hung by the window, as fast as ever. "It *is* a coming now."

And so it was, for the large flakes of snow fell against the window with faint blows, and as far as the eye could reach, was one uninterrupted field of pure white which lent an unnatural colour to the night.

"I think we may venture to remark," said a little man who had hitherto sat silent in a corner next the fire-place, "that there won't be many out to-night that have got a chimney-corner to crawl to."

"That's uncommonly true," replied several in a breath. "Hark!" cried the young farmer, "there's the clank of Britton's hammer."

"Aye, aye," said the old man, who was so careful of speech. "In the worst weather he works hardest. I hear it—I hear it—and, friends, mind, I say nothing, but where does his work come from and when is it done, where does it go to—eh?"

"That's the thing!" cried several. "You've hit the right nail on the head."

"Mind, I said nothing—nothing at all," cried the old man, resuming his pipe, with a self-satisfied air.

"I'll say something, though," cried the young farmer, "my opinion is, that he forges chains for old Nick, and some day you'll hear—"

Several heavy blows upon the outer door of the ale house, which was closed to keep out the snow, stopped the young farmer in his speech, and attracted the attention of the whole company.

"Who's that?" said one, looking round him. "We are all here."

"House! house!" cried a deep hoarse voice, from without, and the blows on the door continued.

"Tom! Tom!" screamed the landlady, Mrs. Fairclaw, who was a buxom widow, fat, fair, and fifty. "Tom! you idle vagabond! don't you hear! there's some one knocking—if it's a tramper, tell him this is no house for him."

Tom, with a knowing wink, proceeded to the door, and, in a few moments ushered into the warm parlour a tall man, who was so covered with snow, that it was difficult to make out what rank in life his appearance indicated.

He cast a hurried and uneasy glance round him, as he entered the parlour, and then taking a chair in silence, he turned to Tom, and said in a tremulous voice,

"Brandy, if you please."

"Shall I take your hat and dry it by the kitchen fire?" said Tom.

"No," replied the stranger. "I—I must not stay long." So saying he turned his chair, so as to leave his face very much in the shade, and sat perfectly silent.

" A rough night, sir," remarked the young farmer.

" Eh?—yes—remarkably fine," replied the stranger.

" Fine?"

" Oh—the—the—snow you mean. Yes, very rough—very rough, indeed—I beg your pardon."

The company looked very eagerly at each other, and then at the abstracted stranger in great wonderment and intense curiosity.

Tom now entered with the brandy. The stranger eagerly clutched the little pewter measure in which it was brought and toss'd off its contents at once. Then he drew a long breath, and turning to Tom, he said :—

" Stay—I—I want to know—"

" What?" said Tom, as the man paused a moment.

" Is—Andrew Britton—still—alive?"

" Yes," said Tom.

" And does he," continued the man, " does he still live at—at the old place?"

" The old Smithy?"

" Yes.

" Oh, yes ; he lives there still."

" And—and is the squire—alive—"

" Ah! to be sure."

" The smith," said the young farmer, " still lives, sir, in his old place, part of which was burnt down ten years ago, or more."

" Ten years!" murmured the stranger.

" Yes ; the night there was a storm—"

" The stranger rose, saying—

" Indeed! you talk of *a* storm as if there never had been but one."

So saying he threw down a shilling to Tom, and hastily left the room.

The occupants of the parlour looked at each other in silence, and those who had pipes smoked away at such speed, that in a few moments the room was full of dense blue vapour.

CHAPTER IV.

THE OLD SMITHY.—A LONE MAN.—THE ALARM.—THE MYSTERIOUS CONFERENCE.—
GUILT AND MISERY.

It was the hammer of the smith which had sounded on the night air, and the clangour of which had reached the ears of the frequenters of the snug oaken parlour of the Rose Inn.

The Smithy was of great extent, for it occupied nearly the whole ground floor of the wing of the dilapidated mansion in which Britton resided.

There were about the stained windows and carved oaken chimney-piece ample evidences of ancient grandeur in the place, and it was not a little singular to notice

No. 2.

the strange effect produced by the mixture of the rude implements of the smith, with the remains of the former magnificence of the ancient hall.

A blazing fire was roaring on the hearth, and by it stood Andrew Britton, the smith, or the "savage," as he was called, in consequence of the known brutality of his disposition. There was no other light in the large apartment, but what proceeded from the fire, and as it flared and roared up the spacious chimney it cast strange shadows on the dusky walls, and lit up the repulsive countenance of the smith, with unearthly-looking brilliancy. A weighty forge hammer was in his hand, and he was busily turning in the glowing embers a piece of iron upon which he had been operating.

"Curses on his caution," he muttered, as if following up some previous train of thought. "And yet—yet without the work—I think I might go mad ; drink and work. Thus pass my days ; aye, and my nights too. He is right there ; I should go mad without the work. I drink—drink till my brain feels hot and scorching—then this relieves me—this hammer, and I fancy as I bring it clashing down upon the anvil that—ha ! ha ! that some one's head is underneath it. And most of all, is it rare and pleasant to imagine it his head, who turned a cowardly craven when he had work to do which required a cool head, and a quick hand. Curses on him ! curses !"

He lifted the immense hammer which no ordinary man could have wielded, and brought it down upon the anvil with so stunning a sound, that it awakened startling echoes all over the old house.

Suddenly the smith stood in the attitude of attention, for as the sounds he had himself produced died away, he fancied there mingled with them a knocking at the door of the smithy.

For a few moments he listened attentively, and then became confirmed in his opinion, that some one was knocking at his door.

"A visitor to me ?" he muttered, "and at this hour—well, well—be it whom it may, he shall enter. Whether he goes forth again or not is another consideration. Men call me a savage. Let those beware who seek my den."

He walked to the door of the smithy, and removing an iron bar which hung across it, he flung it wide open, saying, "who knocks at Andrew Britton's door?"

The mysterious stranger who had created so much sensation at the "Rose," stood on the threshold. His form was clearly defined upon the snow, and the smith started as he said,—

"Andrew Britton, do you know me?"

"Know you?" said Britton.

"Aye ! look at me."

The man took off his hat as he spoke, and stood in the full glare of the flickering fire light.

A dark scowl came over the brow of the smith, and he still continued silent while the man repeated,

"Andrew Britton, do you know me?"

"Know you ?" cried Britton, with a voice of rage almost goaded to fury. "Yes, I do know you—robber—thief—paltry wretch that had not courage —"

"Hush, Andrew Britton," said the stranger. "I have travelled many weary miles to visit thee. From the moment that a stranger told me that the clank of your hammer still sounded through the village of Learmont, I guessed how you had been requited. I resolved to seek you, and tell you how to better your condition. I am here with such a purpose. Am I welcome? or shall I turn from your door in anger, Andrew Britton? Speak at once."

Owing to the position in which the man stood, the red glare of the smith's fire fell full upon his working features, and after regarding them attentively for some moments, Britton spoke in a calmer tone than he had used before.

"I think I understand you now," he said. "Come in—come in."

"One word before I accept your hospitality," said the stranger.

"Such conversation as ours," remarked the smith, "is safest carried on within."

" But what I have to say is safest said now, and more to the purpose, as I stand here upon your threshold."

" Say on," cried Britton, impatiently.

" 'Tis three days' journey by the quickest conveyances and the nearest road to where I have hidden my head for ten years—ten weary years. In my chamber lies a sealed packet, on which is written the date of my departure, and accompanying it are these words : " If I return not, or send no message with assurance of my safety by the time eight days have expired, take this packet to the nearest justice and bid him open and read its contents."

The dark countenance of the smith turned to a allid hue, as the stranger spoke and his gigantic frame perceptibly trembled, as he said in a low husky whisper,

" And that packet contains—"

" A confession."

" You are cautious ; but, you were safe without so deeply laid a plan."

" I may have been ; nay, I think I should have been safe when I explained to you, Britton, the motive of my journey hither ; but the mind is never so free to act as when safety is doubly assured."

"Come in—come in," said Britton, "the night air is chilling, and the snow flakes dash upon the floor. Come in at once."

" Freely," said the stranger, stepping into the smith's strange abode.

Britton carefully barred the door, and without speaking for a few moments, he threw coals upon his forge fire and stirred up the glooming embers until a cheerful blaze of light illuminated the whole interior of the smithy.

The stranger, from the moment of his entrance, had fixed his eyes upon a large oaken door at the further end of the ancient hall, and he continued to gaze at it, as if under the influence of some fascination which he could not resist.

" Britton" he said at length, while a shudder for one instant convulsed his frame, " have you ever passed through that door since--since--"

" Since the night of the storm?" said Britton. " Yes, I have passed through it."

" You are bold."

" I had a motive, and since your candour has been such as to tell me of that little contrivance of yours about the packet you have left with such urgent directions, I will tell you my motive, and ha ! ha ! we--we--shall better understand our relative situations."

" What was the motive ?"

" Can you form no guess ?"

" I cannot ; how--how should I Britton ?"

" Did you lose nothing, ten years since ?"

" Yes--yes--I did lose a knife--but not here--not here !"

" You did lose it here."

"And you found it, good Britton, and will give it to me. 'Twas an old keepsake from a friend. You will give it to me, Andrew Britton ?"

" Ha ! ha !" laughed the smith in his discordant manner. " You know the mind is free when safety is doubly secured."

" The knife--the knife !" cried the stranger, earnestly. " My name is--is--"

" On the handle," added Britton, " which makes it all the more valuable. You say it was a keepsake. It shall be a keepsake still. I will keep it for my own sake. I would not barter it for its worth in gold."

" Perhaps you have not got it."

" Do not please yourself with such a supposition, I will show it to you."

Britton walked to an old press which stood in an obscure and dark corner of the room, and then returned with a large knife in his hand, the blade of which opened and remained fast by touching a spring.

" Do you know that ?" he said, holding it to the eyes of his visitor. The man groaned.

" Give it to me. Oh, give it to me, Britton," he said.

" No," said the smith. " You have taught me a lesson, I shall write a confession and wrap it round this knife with ample directions to the nearest justice, in case anything should happen to me. Do you understand, my friend ?"

The man's lips became white with fear, and he faltered—

"If—if you will not give it me—take it away—out of my sight with it. It makes my blood curdle in my veins, and a cold perspiration hangs upon my brow. Curses! curses! that I should have come thus far to be so tortured."

"Nay," said the smith, in a tone of sneering exultation, "you shall be convinced. Look at that name upon the blood-stained haft."

"Away! away, with it," shrieked the stranger, covering his eyes with his hands.

"Joseph Gray!" said Britton, reading the name on the knife. "Ha! ha! Master Gray, is not this a damning evidence?"

"Away! I say--oh, God, take it away."

" Nay, your curiosity shall be amply satisfied," continued the smith, appproaching his mouth closer to the ear of him who we shall henceforth call Gray. " It was a week before I—even I, savage Britton, as they call me, ventured to unbar that door, and when I did it was at midnight."

Gray shook with emotion and groaned deeply.

" I knew the spot," continued Britton, and he lowered his voice to a whisper, while deep sighs of anguish burst from the labouring breast of his listener. The snow pattered against the windows of the smithy—a howling wind swept round the ruined pile of building, and not more wild and awful was the winter's storm without than the demoniac passions and fearful excitement of those two men of blood who conversed in anxious whispers in the Old Smithy, until the grey tints of morning began to streak with sober beauty the eastern sky.

CHAPTER V.

THE MORNING.—A VISIT.—BLASTED HOPES.—THE ARRANGED MEETING.—THE PACKET.—AND THE KNIFE.

THE snow storm had ceased, and a clear cold winter's sun rose upon Learmont, making even stern winter look most beautiful. The snow hung in sparkling masses upon every tree and shrub, and in the valley where the village nestled, it was in some places many feet in depth. The little streamlet which ran through the village in the summer time, with a happy murmuring sound, was now still and voiceless and scarcely to be distinguished from the surrounding land. Curling masses of dense smoke arose from the chimneys of the thatched cottages. The robin sang his plaintive ditty on the window sills, and occasionally might be seen a group of children with their scanty garments repairing to the frozen stream to gambol on its slippery surface.

Far above every other habitation in the place, towered the feudal residence of the Learmonts. It was an ancient residence built in Gothic style of architecture, and its blackened walls and time-worn towers looked more than usually stern and desolate now that they were contrasted with the pure white patches of snow that had lodged on every projecting stone and window ledge.

In a chamber situated nearly in the very centre of the mansion, the windows of which were provided with painted blinds, representing the most beautiful and glowing Arcadian landscapes, and the temperature of which was raised fully to that of summer, sat the same tall, dark-browed man, who ten years before had visited the deserted hovel of the Widow Tatton. Time had not swept harmlessly over Squire Learmont. His raven locks were largely mixed with " hoary grey." The deep olive of his complexion had given way to a sickly sallow tint, which was peculiarly disagreeable to look upon—but in all other respects the man was the same. There was the same contemptuous curl of the lip—the same angry contraction of the brow, and the same ever-shifting glance and restlessness of manner which betokened a heart ill at ease with itself.

An open letter lay before him which he occasionally referred to, as if to guide the wandering current of his thoughts, and after perusing several times he rose from his seat, and for a time walked backwards and forwards in the room in silence—then he spoke in indistinct and muttered sentences. "Surely," he muttered, "I may at last venture to enjoy what I have plunged so deeply to obtain. What a vast accumulation of wealth have I not now in my grasp, and shall I longer hesitate? Have I not now the means to sit down by royalty and outvie its grandeur? I have—ample—ample. Again let me read the dear assurance of unbounded wealth. Truly, this money scrivener has done his duty with the large sums I have entrusted to his care. Let me see."

He stood by the table, and again perused the letter in an audible voice.

"NOBLE AND HONOURED SIR,—Agreeable to your most kind instructions I send an account of the disposal of all the moneys from time to time entrusted by your most noble worship, to the care of your most humble servant. Your honour will perceive by the annexed schedule, that like a river augmented by a thousand little streams, your honour's real property has swollen to nearly one million sterling."

"A million!" cried Learmont, drawing himself up to his full height and casting a flashing glance around him. "A million pieces of those golden slaves, that are ever ready to yield enjoyment. A million of those glittering sprites which are more powerful than the genii of old romance. Can I not now triumph? What refinement of life—what exquisite enjoyments can now be denied to *me*?"

The door now softly opened, and an old servant appeared.

"What now?" cried Learmont abruptly.

"Britton, the smith, comes for your worship's orders," said the servant.

A gloom spread itself over the countenance of Learmont.

"Shew him this way," he said, as he sank into a chair with his back to the light.

"He brings one with him, too, who craves to see your worship."

"No! no!" cried Learmont, springing to his feet. "'Tis false—false as hell. Has he dared to—to—. The villain!—his own destruction is as certain."

The domestic looked amazed, but before he could make any remark, Britton, the smith, accompanied by Jacob Gray, stood on the threshold of the door.

The hand of Learmont was plunged deep beneath the breast of his coat, as he said.

"Well? what—who is that?"

"A friend," said Britton, in a low voice.

For a moment Learmont regarded the face of the smith with attentive earnestness, and then slowly withdrawing his hand, which had doubtless clasped some weapon of defence, he said to the servant,

"Leave the room. Well, Britton; I—I am glad you have come about the—the—steel gauntlets. Leave the room, I say."

The servant who had lingered from curiosity, reluctantly left and closed the door.

His curiosity, however, was far from satisfied, and after lingering a moment or two, he fairly knelt down outside the door and placed his ear as flat against the key-hole as it was possible so to do. A confused murmur of voices was all that by his utmost exertions he could hear.

"A plague on them," he muttered. "If they would but get in a passion now and speak loud."

His wish was gratified, for at the moment Learmont's voice rose above its ordinary pitch, as he said,

"A thousand pounds upon the assurance of the fact, beyond a doubt."

The reply was too indistinct to hear, much to the torture of the servant, and in another moment his curiosity received a disagreeable check by his master exclaiming,

"I'll get it, and return to you immediately," and before Oliver, which was the old domestic's name, could rise from his knees, the door opened, and his master nearly fell over him on the threshold.

"Ha!" cried Learmont, drawing back.   "Fool, you have ensured your destruction."

"Mercy, sir! oh, mercy!" cried the old man.

Learmont took a sword from a corner of the room and unsheathed it.

"Hold, sir, a moment," said Gray.   "I do not think it possible he could hear much."

"Dotard!" cried Learmont, to the trembling Oliver.   "What could induce you to throw away the remnant of your worthless life by such folly?"

"Oh, sir, I heard nothing—I know nothing," cried the old man, "I—I was only passing the door to—to go to the picture gallery, and stooped to pick up—a nail—that's all, upon my word, sir."

"Where is the nail?" said the smith.

"Here," said Oliver, pointing to the oaken floor.   "I thought it was loose, but found it fast."

"It matters not," said Learmont, suddenly casting the sword from him; "I don't like even the most trifling affairs to be pryed into; but since you know all, Oliver, will you assist us?"

"Sir, I am at your service," said Oliver; "but, on my soul, I heard nothing but your honour say you would get something."

"Pooh,—pooh!" cried Learmont.   "I forgive thee listening.   Would money tempt you, Oliver?"

"To what, sir?" said Oliver, with such a look of real innocence, that Learmont turned aside, saying,—

"Enough—he knows nothing.   Begone!"

With precipitation the old servant left the apartment, and when he was fairly gone, Learmont turned to his visitors and said,—

"Rest quiet till to-night.   I will then meet you at the smithy."

"That may scarcely be," said the smith, "for this gentleman—this considerate Master Gray, must get hence again with all expedition."

"There will be time, then," said Gray, "and a day to spare."

"Be it so, then," said the smith.

"To-night at the Smithy," again said Learmont.

"At what hour?"

"After midnight.   I will tap thrice at your door.   Reflect upon my offer, Gray; 'tis a large sum.

Gray turned his small cunning eyes upon Learmont as he replied,—

"There is an old fable, of the Goose and the Golden Eggs.   You cannot expect me to kill my goose so soon."

"Nor can you expect me to comply constantly with extortionate demands," replied Learmont, trembling with passion,

"We will settle all to-night," said the smith.   "Do not fail us, sir."

"Be assured I will not.   But recollect, I come to purchase the silence, not of a well kept secret, but of *the grave*."

They parted, and once again the Squire of Learmont was alone with his own thoughts.   He threw himself into a chair, with a deep groan, saying,

There must be more blood--more blood, ere I can dream of safety."

CHAPTER VI.

NIGHT AGAIN.—THE RUINS.—THE CONFERENCE.—THE OLD OAKEN DOOR.—THE RESOLVE.

GREAT was the surprise in the village of Learmont, at the non-appearance of the stranger, who had arrived during the snow storm at the village.   He had been seen with the smith proceeding to Learmont House, but that one should willingly ake up even a day's residence with Savage Britton, at the Old Smithy, was quite beyond the comprehension of the simple villagers.

But such appeared, however, to be the fact, for every one was confident the stranger had not left Learmont, so it was quite clear he was with the smith.

Such was the terror which Britton and his house were held in, that none ventured to go sufficiently near it to ascertain the fact, and the day passed away in endless conjectures as to what the stranger could by possibility want at Learmont, first, with the smith, and then with the squire. Night came without, in the least assuaging the general curiosity, or adding any new food to it, and as the sun sunk in the far west, and the cold evening wind swept moaning and sighing among the leafless trees, the heavy clank of the smith's hammer was heard as usual at intervals till near midnight.

Then when the clock in the high tower of Learmont struck twelve, a tall figure enveloped in an ample cloak, stalked through the village, and took the direct route to the Old Smithy.

The night had set in very dark, there was no moonlight, for masses of heavy clouds obscured its light, although it was nearly at the full, and the long straggling building, one wing of which was inhabited by the smith, showed but faintly against the black sky.

The Squire of Learmont, for it was he, who at the silent hour of midnight, had stolen out to keep his appointment, paused when he reached the wing of the house which had been burnt down on the night of the storm, and the crumbling ruins of which remained by his orders just as they had fallen.

A shudder came over his frame as he regarded them, and he muttered,

"Can I? dare I leave this spot with the knowledge of what it conceals? and yet, I am surely safe now. If these men—these tools by which I have hewn my path to wealth; if these could be safely disposed of—then—ah, then, I might know peace. At least this anxious fever of wild apprehension that gnaws at my heart would subside, and if I had a pang it would be for the past and not from a dread of that which was to come."

He folded his cloak closer around him, and with hasty steps passed onwards to the smithy.

Thrice he struck the heavy door with the hilt of his sword, and in a moment the smith's voice from within called loudly,

"Who knocks?"

"Learmont," was the answer; the door was flung open and the squire stood as the stranger had stood the preceding evening in the glare of the fire from the smithy.

"You are punctual, sir," said Gray, advancing with an air of mock ceremony.

Learmont waved his hand in reply, and stalked into the old hall.

"Now," he said, when Britton had barred the door, "I am here. Make your proposition."

"Are you not afraid, sir," sneered Gray, "to trust your worshipful person alone with two such old acquaintances?"

"No," answered Learmont fearlessly, "I know you both too well. You calculate. My life is valuable to you. My death, in the accomplishment of which you might get some chance injury yourselves, would be a perfectly gratuitous act."

"Enough of this folly," growled Britton. "Let us to business."

"I persevere then in my offer," said Learmont, with a slight trembling of his voice. "A thousand pounds."

The smith was silent, but Gray spoke.

"We have decided, worshipful sir," he said.

"And your decision is—"

"This. We think, with your worship, that London is the most delightful of cities, and we purpose to follow you thither; to live ever near you, and to trust to your liberality for our wants."

For a moment it seemed, by the convulsive working of the countenance of Learmont, that he was about to burst into an uncontrollable fit of passion; but if such was his feeling he succeeded in suppressing it, and replied with an affectation of calmness,

"Preposterous! you must think me weak, indeed, to be thus dictated to, Master Gray."

"Then I must to London," said Gray, "and my only regret is that I have wasted valuable time."

"Look ye, Squire Learmont," said Britton, folding his huge arms across his breast, and glaring with his ferocious eyes in the face of his patron. "I was to have been well paid for a black job. You know I have been ill paid, on the plea that it was not completed."

"I have constantly supplied your wants," said Learmont, shrinking under the savage gaze of the smith.

"I have not starved, truly," continued Britton. "But now I will have wealth."

"Wealth? How can I divide sufficient among us three to make you wealthy?"

"Master Gray," continued Britton, "has a ready wit, and the news he brings shall enrich us."

"If I absolutely refuse?"

"Then we bargain for impunity for the past, while we——"

"Denounce me?"

"Exactly."

' And to what extent, most considerate gentlemen, do you contemplate making me your banker?"

"More or less as the case may be," said Gray; "but we will be moderate in a gentlemanly way. Eh, Britton?"

"Certainly," growled Britton, with the laugh of a hyena.

"The sum! the sum!" said Learmont, impatiently.

"Five hundred pounds each as a start," said Jacob Gray, with the most unblushing effrontery.

"Enormous!" cried Learmont.

"As you please, sir. Our conference then is over."

"Britton, answer me one question," said the squire.

"A dozen, if you please," replied the smith.

"Have you been through that door-way, since—"

"I have, Squire Learmont."

"And in what state—"

"Can you venture to look for yourself?" said the smith, with a sneer.

Learmont hesitated, and then said,

"I can. Give me a light."

The smith lit a lamp and handed it to the squire, along with a key.

"Can you give me any directions?" said Learmont.

"Take the second passage to your right and look closely on the ground as you go on."

Learmont took the lamp and advanced to the old oaken door. His hand trembled as he turned the rusty lock, and in another moment he had passed through, and was lost to the sight of the confederates in the smithy.

In less than two minutes, he returned and staggered to a seat.

"You have seen it?" said Britton.

"No," answered Learmont. "I—I thought I had the nerve—but for my life I could not proceed three steps in that awful place."

"Do you consent now to our conditions?" asked Gray.

"Who has the—the papers?"

"I," replied Britton.

"And I a more dreaded secret," still whispered Gray.

"I—I consent," said Learmont. "I consent."

CHAPTER VII.

THE CONFERENCE, CONTINUED.—MUTUAL SECURITY.—THE OAKEN DOOR AND THE STRANGE APPEARANCE.— MYSTERIES THICKEN.

For several minutes neither of the three men whose crimes had brought them into such strange fellowship, spoke. They regarded each with the most strange and mixed emotions. Upon the face of the haughty Lord of Learmont were pride, hate, and fear, each struggling for mastery. The smith looked, as he always looked, brutally ferocious, but upon this occasion there was an air of exultant villany upon his swarthy visage, which made him like a fiend in human shape. Gray, the cautious and politic villain, with just sufficient relenting in his cold heart to make him stop short at the consummation of some dark deed, while he waded recklessly through all the preliminary proceedings to it ; he, too, wore a triumphant look, but it was one strangely mingled with suspicion and doubt, whether or not some sudden occurrence would damp his joy, and turn his self-congratulations to laments.

He was the first to break the silence.

"Had we not now better separate ?" he said. "We can see you on the morrow, squire."

"There i yet one thing which remains to be considered," said Learmont, in a low voice.

"What is that ?" cried the smith.

"When we are all gone, may not some one's curiosity be prompted to visit this house ?

"That is true," said Gray, turning pale.

"If they do," cried Britton, "they shall find nothing ; I will see to that."

"Let it be so, then," said Learmont, rising.

"Before we separate now," interposed Gray, "there is one thing which we should all feel thoroughly assured, and that is, that our mutual safety depends upon our mutual preservation ; that is, I mean, if one falls the others are in danger."

"We understand that, most politic Master Gray," sneered Learmont, as he clasped his cloak, preparatory to leaving the smithy.

"Perhaps, not fully," said Gray.

"I am sure, not fully," cried Britton, with a hoarse laugh. "I have a hold upon our good friend the squire, which I will not even trust to the good-keeping of Master Jacob Gray."

"Ha !" cried Learmont, turning ghastly pale. "What—what mean you ?"

"This way," said the smith, beckoning the squire to the further end of the apartment. Learmont obeyed the invitation, and whatever was the communication he received, it was conveyed very briefly, for he suddenly exclaimed—

"Enough ! enough !" and strode to the door.

"Your worshipful squireship," said Gray, "will always please to recollect that my little packet, that is at home, would be an exceedingly awkward revelation, should anything happen to me."

"Hear me, both of you !" cried Learmont, turning with flashing eyes upon the two men who so mocked him with their power. "I know—I admit that you both possess secrets that would prove my destruction : aye, my death. We do understand one another, and we may as well speak openly. What you would say is this, Jacob Gray, that I dare not, for my own safety, take your vile life ; and you the same, Britton ; you have me in your toils, I grant it ; there needs no insinuations. We have waded through too much blood to feel any delicacy of speech towards each other. You have power, but beware how you use it, or you will rouse a devil that you cannot quell again. Be moderate and faithful, and it will not be worth my while to seek for safe means for your destruction. Drive me too far, and you perish, though I call on hell to aid me !"

So saying, without waiting for an answer, he strode from the smithy with his face distorted by passion, leaving the two confederates, who had not expected

No. 3.

such a burst of fury, abashed, even in spite of their deep villanies and abounding craft.

"Gray !" said the smith, after a few moments' silence.

Jacob Gray started and cried,

"What shall we do now? Squire Learmont is a man of wild passion."

"What is his wild passion to us?" said Britton ; "we have the means of stripping him of his wealth, and leading him to a scaffold."

"But you forget, Master Britton, that upon that same scaffold you and I would be accommodated with prominent situations."

"Pshaw !" cried the smith. "That is a thought that does not haunt me. We are as adventurous miners, Gray, who have suddenly hit upon a vein of wealth, which it requires but ordinary skill to work to our mutual profit."

"True," said Gray, "and we will work it, always my friend, Britton, remembering that we are so situated that we stand or fall together."

"Agreed," cried the smith. "If I fall I care not who stands ; only thus much I will take pains to do—drag all I can within the sphere of my own ruin."

"You are very considerate," said Gray. "And now you must recollect that my absence from London must be limited. There is danger in a longer stay."

"Away, then, with you at once."

"What ! leave Learmont with nothing but sounding promises, and an empty purse ? No, Britton. I must again see Squire Learmont, before I take my leave of this place, which I hate."

"True," said the smith. "And before you go, there is another small matter in which I claim your assistance."

"What is that?"

"Beyond that ancient door is a sight which must be placed beyond human recognition."

Gray turned ghastly pale, as he said,

"Britton, your nerves are strong. You will feel little in—in—disposing securely of whatever is there that would blast the gaze of another."

"Jacob Gray," said Britton in a determined tone, "you share the advantages. You have by your cunning so hedged yourself in with precautions, that I, even I, feel how impolitic it would be to scatter your brains with yon forge hammer."

Gray started to his feet, as he exclaimed :

"You surely did not mean to murder me ?"

"I did !" roared the smith. "And now, Jacob Gray, we understand each other, and you know you are safe with me. But I will have no flinching, there is a work to be performed which you shall aid in, although you shrink from it as you would from the mouth of hell. If it turn your blood to liquid flame you shall do it. If your reason fail you at the ghastly sight, for ghastly it is, you shall do it ; nay, should you die in gasping terror, and involve me and Learmont in one common destruction by the wily narrative you have left in London, you shall do it."

"Spare me ! spare me !" said Gray.

"Ha ! ha !" laughed the smith, with a discordant yell that echoed through the lofty hall. "Spare you? spare Jacob Gray ?"

"I implore you," cried Gray. "Spare me this task and I will pay you handsomely."

"You forget," said Britton "that I have a better-filled purse than yours to apply to. I love money, because it is enjoyment and power, but I have my fancies, and one of them is, that you shall do your full share of this necessary work. Your safety, as well as mine, demands that it should be done. Any prying rustic who could so far call upon his curiosity as to master his fears and penetrate from this hall through yon door, would find food for gossip and inquiry, that would raise a spirit, even all the wealth of Learmont could not quell. It must be done, I say, and by the infernal powers you shall do it."

Gray shuddered, and he said in a low voice,

"When shall we again see Learmont ?"

"By the morning's light," answered the smith, "I will take you to the mansion by a secret means, known only to myself. You can then procure the means you immediately require. He dare not refuse you, and post-horses will carry you to London, in ample time to take possession of the little document you have so providentally left behind you."

"Yes—yes," said Gray. "Oh, yes, there will be time and—and Britton, I will hand to you one-half of the sum that I procure from Learmont's fears, if—if you will do this work that must be done alone."

"No!" cried Britton. "A hundred times, no! the world's wealth, Jacob Gray, should not tempt me to let you off."

He took a flambeau from a corner as he spoke, and lighting it by the forge fire, he held it high above his head, and while its flickering light cast many dancing shadows upon the time-blackened walls of the Old Smithy, he pointed to the oaken door, and exclaimed to the trembling Gray:—

"Come, now, at once. 'Tis a work should be done at such an hour as this."

"Mercy! mercy!" cried Gray, clasping his hands.

"Rare sport! rare sport!" shouted the smith, in an ecstasy of mirth. "Come on."

"Britton, you do not mean it; I beseech, I implore."

"Come on!" roared the smith.

"On my knees, I beg—"

"Coward! come on! I could revile thee, trembling wretch, but that it delights my very soul to see you suffer such mortal agony. Come on; you knew him once. Come on, I say, and see if you could recognise him now."

Holding the torch in one hand, so as to throw a red glare of light over the vast apartment, the smith clutched with the other the trembling companion of his guilt, and dragged him with irresistible force towards the oaken door. In vain did Gray beseech for mercy. In vain did he beg and implore, and pray to be released. And now they reached the door, and he clung to the damp wall and screamed, but the smith heeded him not; he answered him but with shouts and wild laughter, and lifting his foot he, with one heavy kick, dashed the door open.

About two paces within the entrance stood a figure, tall and erect. The glare from the torch fell upon it for one moment; with a shriek of the most horrifying description, Gray fell insensible to the ground, and even the iron nerves of the smith were shaken: the flambeau dropped from his hand, and with a cry of surprise and horror he rushed from the spot, trampling in his way upon the prostrate form of Gray, nor stopping till he stood at the further end of the now gloomy hall, with the outer door in his hand.

CHAPTER VIII.

THE MANSION.—OFFERS OF MAGNITUDE.—THE DOUBLE PLOT.

WHO or what the form was that so unexpectedly met the terrified gaze of the savage smith, and his more nervous and timid companion in the Old Smithy, we must leave to be discovered in the progress of our eventful and strange narrative.

By the first gray tint of morning light, there sat three persons in a small room of the mansion of Learmont: they were the smith, Gray, and the squire himself. A quantity of money lay upon the table before them, upon which Gray's eyes were fixed with eager expression. The smith was evidently not indifferent to the sparkling treasure before him, but he did not exhibit his feelings so openly as Jacob Gray, while the Lord of Learmont himself sat with his back to the dim light in moody silence.

"I shall be off," cried Gray, "before another cock can proclaim the day is coming."

Learmont merely inclined his head.

"And I," said Britton, "leave here for London in the course of the day."

" Once more," said Learmont, in a deep hollow voice—" once more I offer you the large sum I have mentioned, if you will accede to my two propositions."

" No sir," replied Gray, " I say no."

" And you, Britton ?"

" I say no, likewise," replied the smith.

" I double my offer," cried Learmont.

" Double ?" echoed Gray.

" Aye, double. Let me but be sure that he is no more, and upon your arrival in any part of America you may choose, you will find an order there for the amount."

" No ! no !" cried Britton.

" 'Tis a large sum, a very large sum," murmured Gray.

" Hark ye !" cried Learmont, his face glowing with excitement. " Hark ye ! your presence will be my curse. Every time I see you will blast my eyes with the remembrance of what I intend to forget in the vortex of pleasure. My double offer amounts to no less a sum than two thousand pounds to each of you. Once more, I raise your price, I will make those sums three thousand each."

" It is useless," said Britton. " A night at the gaming table, and we are beggars again. No, Learmont, there is nothing like a constant resource."

" Very true," said Gray. " That is exceedingly true ; besides, my feelings would not allow me to take the life of—of—"

" Your feelings ?" cried Learmont. " Wretch ! if among us three there be one more doubly damned by crime than another, that one is Jacob Gray. If there be one villain more coldly calculating than another, it is thou. Talk of thy feelings? thou sneaking ruffian—thou shrinking cut-throat !"

The smith threw himself back in his chair, and burst into a peal of uproarious laughter.

" Capital! oh, capital !" he cried. " That's you, good, politic Master Gray. Ho ! ho ! how well we all understand each other ! There are no needless delicacies. Ho ! ho ! ho !"

Gray rose from his chair without saying a word, but his very lips were pale with suppressed rage. He hastily collected the money that lay before him, and having bestowed it away in safety, he cast a malignant scowl upon Learmont, and said,—

" We shall meet again soon, sir, when, should you happen to raise your voice so high, there may be listeners, who will say we judge of Learmont by his company.' Now to London."

So saying, without waiting for a reply, he left the room.

The dark eyes of the Squire of Learmont flashed with rage, as Gray gave utterance to this taunt, and when the last echo of his retreating footsteps had died away, Britton broke the silence that ensued, by saying,—

" Yon knave knows his power."

" Aye, does he !" cried Learmont, striking the table with his clenched hand. " But we, Britton, are not altogether powerless."

" What can we do ?" said the smith.

" Jacob Gray and his secret must perish together."

" With all my heart, squire ; but the fellow's caution is so excessive, that we are more interested in his preservation than his destruction."

" True," replied Learmont. " His caution is great, as you say, but there are times when the most cautious are off their guard. Remember this, Britton, that every guinea that finds its way into the purse of Jacob Gray, is a guinea torn from you."

" I know it," cried the smith, " and I would have scattered his brains upon the hearth-stone of the Old Smithy, but that he averred he had taken the precaution of leaving the written statement of all he knew at home, to be opened if he returned not within a given time, and although I doubted that he had done so, even to the verge of positive disbelief, yet was the risk too great, and I let him live."

" For a time—only for a time," said Learmont.

A grim smile crossed the face of Britton, as he said,

" Should Jacob Gray die suddenly, and leave no trace behind him, shall I be entitled to the whole of what is now divided?"

" You shall," cried Learmont, eagerly. " Assure me of the death of this man, who, from my soul, I abhor, and I will add to rather than diminish the sum, which will now be divided between you, and further, mark me, Master Britton. Should you find it in your way to dispose quietly and surely of—of that one being who stands between me and the assurance of my safety—"

" You mean the boy?"

" I do."

" It would be worth a large price, Squire Learmont, to rid you of Jacob Gray— the boy, and place in your hands the document which the wily Jacob has composed."

" It would be worth a price," cried Learmont, " so high a price that—that, Britton, you should yourself name it, and then, be it what it might, couple it with but the condition that you leave England for ever, and it is yours."

" 'Tis a tempting offer," said the smith.

" I mean it to be such," replied Learmont. " Insinuate yourself, Britton, into the confidence of this man, Gray; steal his very heart's inmost secrets; make common cause with him; get inmates at his home, and then—then take some propitious moment to possess yourself of his written confession, if he have really produced one, and crush him at a blow."

" I should name thousands as the price of such a piece of work," said the smith.

" Name thousands, if you will. You shall have them."

" Agreed, then, Squire Learmont. I accept the work. We shall meet in London."

" Yes, in London."

" And in the meantime these shining pieces will make a gentleman of Britton, the smith," said the ruffian, as he took from the table a number of gold pieces. " Fare you well, squire! You are liberal at last."

" Farewell," said Learmont. " To-morrow evening I shall be in London."

" And I likewise. Whenever I seek your worship's presence I will send a message to you in these words—'A message from the Old Smithy.'"

A dark scowl passed over the face of Learmont; but before he could object to the pass-words which the brutal smith had adopted, he had left the room, and the wealthy but ill-at-ease owner of Learmont and its huge possessions was left to the communion of his own brooding thoughts.

For a time he sat in silence, with his head resting upon his hand. Then he rose and paced the apartment with unequal strides, muttering to himself in disjointed sentences.

" Yes—yes," he said, " this is politic—most politic. If Britton can be so far wrought upon by his love of gold as to destroy this Jacob Gray, and bring me his written confession, all will be well. Ha! ha! good Master Britton, I will be well prepared for thee on that auspicious and eventful day. You shall have your reward. You shall assure me, convince me, past a doubt, that I am rid of Gray, and then a dagger shall be found to reach your own heart. 'Tis well—exceedingly well. These knaves will destroy each other in this way—Britton destroys Gray —and I destroy Britton, so all will be well. That child will then be innoxious. No one can know who it is: it will be a child of mystery; and if I, in my abundant charity, support it, my praises will be in the mouths of all good men. By the fiends! it shall be my slave—shall tend me—wait upon my every nod and beck. What a glorious revenge! Let me consider—those papers which Britton says he has, and which he likewise asserts prove me—what?—illegitimate? I know I am illegitimate, but is there proof, and has he such proof? Let me recollect what he said—that Gray had taught him more craft, and he took care of the papers he had. Yes, that was it. Shall I employ Gray to do by Britton even as I have urged Britton to do by Gray? I will—I will—it is a master-stroke. I cannot well deal with the two, but whichever succeeds in being the destroyer of the other will, at least, rid me of one-half my trouble. It shall be so—it shall be so."

So saying, with a smile of anticipated triumph in his face, Learmont left the room.

CHAPTER IX.

THE course of our narrative compels us now to leave the little village of Learmont and all its mysteries to direct the reader's attention to the great metropolis, not as it is now, crowded with costly buildings, and its shops vieing with palaces in splendour, but as it was a hundred years since, before Regent-street was thought of, and when we were still enjoying that piece of wisdom of our dear ancestors which induced them to make every street as narrow as possible, every house as dark as possible, and everything as inconvenient as possible.

In a long narrow street, which began somewhere about where the County Fire Office now stands, and terminated Heaven knows where, inasmuch as it branched off into a thousand intricacies of lanes, courts, and alleys, there stood one house in particular, to which we wish to call attention. It was a narrow, gloomy-looking habitation, and stood wedged in between two shops of very questionable character.

The person who rented this house was a Mistress Bridget Strangeways, and she did not belie her name, for her ways were strange indeed. This lady (from courtesy) professed to be a widow, and she gained a very comfortable subsistence by letting to anybody and everybody the various furnished apartments in her house. With the curious collection of lodgers which Mrs. Strangeways had in her house on the occasion to which we refer—namely, the winter of 1742—we have little or nothing to do. The only one of her lodgers to whom we shall at present introduce the reader, was sitting alone in a back room boasting but of few comforts, and the walls of which were of a deep brown colour from age.

Still, if the furniture and appointments of the room were few, mean, and scanty, everything was arranged with great neatness and order. The hearth was cleanly swept, the little fire that blazed in the small grate was carefully tended, the windows were scrupulously clean, and it was clear that the most had been made of the scanty means of comfort which the place afforded.

Seated in a high-backed, ancient-looking chair, was a boy reading. His face was inclined towards his book, and a mass of raven curls, which he held from covering his face with his hand, fell, however, sufficiently over his countenance to hide it from observation. His figure was slight in the extreme, and the long taper fingers which held back the tresses of his hair, were exquisitely white and delicate. The dress of the period was ill-suited to set off the figure to advantage, but still, cumbrous and ungraceful as was the long-flapped waistcoat, broad-skirted coat, and heavy shoe-buckles, no one could look for a moment upon that young boy without confessing him to be eminently handsome.

He was most intently engaged upon his book, and he moved neither hand nor foot for many minutes, so absorbed was he in the narrative he was reading. Suddenly, however, he lifted his head, and shaking back from his brow the clustering hair, he cried in a voice of enthusiasm,—

"Oh, what a dear romance! How these treasures of books cheat the hours of their weariness."

As he spoke he turned his head to the window. What a world of intelligence and gentle beauty was in that face! It was a face to gaze at for hours and speculate upon.

"Five days my uncle has been gone now," he said—"five whole days, and what should I have done without these dear books? How kind of Albert Seyton to lend them to me! I do love Albert Seyton, and if—if,—no—no, I must not breathe that even to myself. Oh, Heavens! that I should be so unfortunate. When—oh, when will my uncle, who is so stern, and yet tender—so cruel, and yet sometimes so kind—when will he explain to me the awful mystery he hints at when with tears I urge him to let me—"

A low knock at the room door now attracted his attention, and the boy cried cheerfully,—

"Ha! I know that tap. 'Tis Albert. Come in—come in, Albert, I am here, and all alone."

The door was immediately opened, and a boy of about fourteen or fifteen years of age, whose long flaxen hair and ruddy complexion proclaimed him to be of true Saxon origin, bounded into the room.

"Your uncle still absent, Harry?" he cried.

"Yes," replied the lad who had been reading.. "Five days now, Albert, he has been gone. What should I have done without you?"

"You know I love you, Harry Gray," said Seyton. "You are very young, but you, are a great deal more sensible than many lads of twice your age."

"I'm past eleven!" said he who was called Harry Gray.

"That's a great age," said the other, laughing. "If you don't think your uncle would pop in unawares, I would sit with you an hour. My poor father is out again. Ah, Harry, he still hopes to procure a recompense from the count. He lost his all in the cause of the present royal family, and now you see they have left him and myself to starve. It's too bad!"

"It's wicked," said Harry Gray.

"So it is," replied Albert. "But we won't talk about it any more now."

The lad who was the occupant of the apartment was silent for a few moments, then he said sadly,—

"Five days gone—five days. Albert, I think I will tell you a secret."

"A secret, Harry?"

"Yes; it is a very strange one, and has made me very unhappy. Come here."

He took the hand of his companion and led him to a corner of the room where there was a large, old-fashioned oaken chest, and taking from his breast a key, he opened it, and lifting the lid, disclosed lying at the bottom of it a roll of paper, and under that a large sealed packet.

Harry Gray lifted out the roll of paper and handed it to Albert, saying,—

"Read what is written there," pointing to a few lines on the wrapper.

Albert read with surprise the following words:—

"WEDNESDAY.—HARRY,—If I am not with you by twelve of the clock on next Wednesday, take this roll of papers to Sir Francis Hartleton, who lives in the Bird-cage Walk by the Park. Do not let any hand but his own take it from you. "J. G."

"That's very odd," said Albert. "Sir Francis Hartleton is a great man. The king knighted him lately, I heard, and he is a magistrate. This is quite a mystery, my dear Harry. I dare say you are some prince, really."

Harry looked up with a beaming smile in the face of his young friend, as he said,—

"Be I who or what I may, I shall never forget Albert Seyton."

"You have a good heart, Harry," cried Albert, throwing his arm affectionately round his young friend's neck, "and when my father gets his own again, I will get him to ask your uncle to let you stay with us."

"That would be joy," said Harry, clasping his hands—"oh, such joy!"

"You are a little delicate thing, you know," continued Albert, "and you want somebody to take care you are not affronted nor imposed upon; and woe be to anybody who dared so much as to——"

The door was at this moment suddenly flung open, and, livid with rage, Jacob Gray stood on the threshold.

Harry gave a faint cry of alarm, and Albert started to his feet from kneeling by the box, and boldly confronted Gray

"So," cried Gray, striding into the room, and shutting the door violently behind him—"so, it is thus I find you engaged!"

"Sir," said Albert Seyton, "if you have any fault to find, find it with me and not with Harry. If he has done wrong, it was my fault, and—and——"

"And what, young sir?"

"I suppose I must fight you," added Albert.

"Brat! beggar's brat!" shrieked Gray, rushing towards the box. "What have you seen—what have you done?"

"Seen very little, and done nothing," said Albert.

Gray aimed a blow at Harry, which was warded by Albert, who cried,—

"For shame, sir—for shame to strike him. By Heavens! Mr. Gray, if you hurt Harry I'll just go to Sir Francis Hartleton, and tell him there is something that concerns him in your big box here."

Jacob Gray stood with his arm uplifted, as if paralysed at this threat. He trembled violently, and sank into a chair. Several times he tried to speak, and at length he said, with a forced smile, which sat hideously upon his distorted features,—

"Well—well, it's not much matter. Never mind, Harry, I—I have come back, you see, so there need be no appeal made to the kindness of Sir Francis in your behalf. It was—that is, the papers merely say you were an orphan, and ask him to do something for you; but no matter—no matter."

"Then you forgive Harry?" said Seyton.

"Yes, yes—oh, yes."

"Thank you, sir—thanks; he meant no wrong. Good-bye, dear Harry. Your uncle will say no more about it now."

Harry Gray 'raised his head from the edge of the box, and his eyes were filled with tears. He took Albert's hand and pressed it to his lips.

CHAPTER X.

THE DISAPPEARANCE.—MRS. BRIDGET STRANGEWAYS AND THE OLD OAKEN CHEST.—ALBERT'S GRIEF AND DESPAIR.

THERE were cries of pain and deep sobs heard proceeding from the room occupied by Jacob Gray long after Albert Seyton had left them. None of the inhabitants of the house thought it necessary to interfere, although it was shrewdly suspected that Master Gray was not very kind to his poor, delicate little nephew.

It's a true adage that what is everybody's business turns out to be nobody's. Surely it *was* everybody's business to interfere and prevent ill-usage in any shape, and yet no one did interfere; and Albert Seyton had left home in search of his father, so that poor Harry Gray had no friend.

The night set in cold and dreary, and before the evening had far advanced, Jacob Gray left the house, locking Harry in while he was gone, and presently returned with several bottles of wine under his arm. The neighbours then heard him alternately cursing, laughing, shouting, and singing till past midnight; then all became suddenly still, and those who had been kept awake by his voice went comfortably to sleep, while Mrs. Bridget Strangeways made a mental determination and a strong vow that the next morning she would give Mr. Jacob Gray notice to quit forthwith and at the same time take the opportunity of telling him "a piece of her mind," that she would.

Now M... Strangeways enjoyed nothing better than telling people "pieces of her mind," and, by some strange fatality, such mental extracts were never of a complimentary character, and whatever charms the mind of Mrs. Strangeways might possess as a whole, it was quite well known that, given forth in "pieces," each piece was enough to set a city by the ears, and would have most surely come under the cognizance of that clause in the New Police Act which punishes people for using language calculated to excite a breach of the peace. But there was then neither a New Police nor a New Police Act, so Mrs. Strangeways made up her mind very composedly and comfortably to give Mr. Jacob Gray such a

'hearing" as he never had in his life, and never would have again, except h provoked Mrs. Strangeways on some future occasion to an equal pitch of wrath.

The morning came, and Mrs. Bridget Strangeways having communicated her intentions with respect to Mr. Jacob Gray to a select few of her lodgers and neighbours, fortified herself with a tolerable dose of "cordial," and setting her arms a-kimbo, she walked majestically up to the room of her troublesome lodger. She knocked and knocked, and knocked again; but Jacob Gray was obstinate, and

No. 4.

would no t say "come in;" so at length Mrs. Strangeways opened the door with a rush, and entered the room, exclaiming,—

"Muster Gray, I'd have you to know, Muster Gray, as this house is——"

The lady had got so far when she saw that there was no Muster Gray to hear the "piece of her mind," and her eyes dilated as she glanced round the room and saw nothing but vacancy.

On the table lay a little piece of paper, and on the little piece of paper lay some money. Mrs. Strangeways clutched at both, and, as she afterwards declared, "you might have knocked her down with a small feather" when she read,—

"Mrs. Strangeways' rent. Her lodger, Jacob Gray, is going to the other end of the world, and he has taken his nephew with him."

The lady gave a great shriek (after pocketing the money), which roused the house, and in a few minutes the room was full of company, among whom was Albert Seyton, with apprehension in his looks.

"Good Heavens !" he cried, "is anything the matter with Harry?"

"What is it—what is it ?" cried a dozen voices at once.

"Oh, that villain, Jacob Gray !" gasped Mrs. Strangeways.

"Where is he ?" cried everybody.

"At the other end of the world," replied Mrs. Strangeways.

"Harry! Harry!—where are you ?" shouted Albert, at once rushing into the little closet which had been the sleeping-chamber of the delicate and sensitive boy. All was still and empty. Harry's little bed had evidently never been slept in. Jacob Gray's was in the same state. Every little article that had belonged to them was removed. There was nothing in the rooms but what was the lawful property of Mrs. Strangeways, except the old oaken chest.

"That chest," said Albert—"he has left that."

"It's mine," cried Mrs. Strangeways. "The villain has run away, as you all see, and cheated a lone and defenceless, delicate female out of her lawful rent. Oh, the wretch !"

Albert Seyton sprang to the box. It was locked.

"I think we ought to see what's in here," he cried.

"Do you, Jackanapes ?" screamed Mrs. Strangeways, who by no means wished, should there be anything worth having in the chest, to let every one know it. "I'd have you to know, Master Albert Seyton, as it's no business of yours."

"It's locked," cried Albert ; "but the poker, I dare say, will open it."

"Do you dare say the poker will open it,!" screamed Mrs. Strangeways. "Let anybody touch it if they dare."

So saying the lady, to make sure of her real or fancied prize, rushed forward and sat herself down on the old chest with such a thump, that the crazy lid gave way, and with a shriek Mrs. Strangeways fell in a singular position into it.

When she was hauled out by the united exertions of everybody, it was satisfactorily discovered that the chest was empty. Albert Seyton saw at a glance that it was so, and he immediately left the deserted rooms in grief for the loss of his young friend Harry, to whom he felt warmly attached. He went to his father's apartments, and throwing himself into a chair, he burst into tears, exclaiming—

"My poor Harry, I shall never see you again !"

Albert Seyton's father had been a gentleman of considerable property, but he had lost all by his adherence to the royal family, who, now at the end, as they thought, of a civil war, were seated on the throne of England. In vain he had sought compensation. A scanty pension just sufficient to keep him and his only boy Albert from actual want, was a l he could wring from the government, and now, day after day, he haunted the court with the hope of calling attention at some fortunate moment to his just claims.

He was out when all this conversation took place in the house, where circumstances had compelled him to take up his humble home.

While Albert was still suffering from the first real gush of heartfelt sorrow which had dimmed the brightness of his early youth, his father returned home, and seeing his son in tears, was at once alarmed and afflicted, nor could he be convinced that something had not happened until Albert had related to him the history of the oaken chest and what it had contained. This, coupled with the sudden and mysterious disappearance of Jacob Gray, led Mr. Seyton to think that there was a great deal more in the matter than met the eye.

Moreover, he had another reason which he did not disclose to Albert, but which the reader will know in its right place, for suspecting that a great mystery was connected in some way with Jacob Gray and his young nephew. Full of these thoughts, Mr. Seyton debated with himself whether it was his duty to inform Sir Francis Hartleton of all the circumstances; but then when he came to consider how bald and disjointed a narrative he had to tell, and how he must terminate it by saying that he had no clue whatever to the whereabouts of the parties who he suspected of he knew not what, he gave up, the idea as premature, and turning to his son, he said,—

"Albert, did young Harry Gray ever confide to you a r particulars of his early life?"

"Never, father," said Albert. "He always told me he was the child of mystery, and that his life was a romance. Then he would sigh and weep, and hope that the day would come when he could confide all t me. So, sir, I could not press him."

"Press him!—certainly not. To have wormed his secret from him unwillingly would have been unjustifiable in the extreme. In truth, he was a gentle boy."

"Oh, father, I loved him, dearly loved him."

Mr. Seyton was silent for some moments, then beckoning his son to him, he whispered a few words in his ear, which brought the eloquent blood in a full rush to the cheeks of Albert, and he gasped rather than said;

"Indeed, no father; I—I—never thought—"

"Then never mention what I have suggested, just now," said Mr. Seyton, "till I give you leave, and Albert, depend upon my using my utmost exertions to endeavour to discover the mystery which envelopes the fate of your young friend."

Albert listened to his father with rapt attention, when he threw himself into his arms, crying,

"Oh, find them! find them, and I shall be happy."

"This very day shall be devoted to inquiries," said Seyton. "I am greatly interested by all that has occurred, and perchance it will withdraw my mind from sorrows and disappointments of my own, to turn my mind and energies to unravel the mystery connected with your pretty playmate."

Albert looked his gratitude, and after the morning's scanty meal was despatched, he saw his father depart upon his promised expedition with a heart elate with hope and expectant joy.

For a time the youthful Albert remained at home in deep thought; then he suddenly rose, saying,

"Why should I be idle? I may do something in this matter. Just Heaven! if that bad man should have murdered him? alas! my poor—poor Harry. My mind misgives me, that he loves you not. Oh, had I but some clue—some means of commencing in the right path of inquiry, I should then have some hope."

So saying, with a desponding air, the youth left the house and wandered onwards without any definite idea of whither he was going or how he was to set about his self imposed task of endeavouring to discover the retreat of Jacob Gray and the young Harry.

CHAPTER XI.

LEARMONT IN LONDON.—THE ENDEAVOUR TO DROWN THOUGHT.—LIFE IN 1742.—
ALL IS NOT GOLD THAT GLITTERS.

MANY spacious mansions which adorned the old city of Westminster at the date of our story, have long since been swept from the ground to give place to more modern structures, and where the stately home of the noble or wealthy commoner reared its lofty walls, are now to be seen but lines of streets, and the busy hum of commerce has superseded the stately aristocratic silence which used to reign undisturbed in many parts of the ancient district.

In a mansion of princely splendour which has long since been pulled down to build some approaches to Westminster Bridge, dwelt the head of the house of Learmont, whenever business or inclination called him to the metropolis. In that house, however, as yet, the present Squire of Learmont had never resided. He had resided in deep seclusion ever since he had been acknowledged as the head of his house. A small part of his history was well known, but there were darker portions which the public eye might in vain attempt to fathom. He was a younger brother of the house he now represented, but his senior, from deep distress at the loss of a young and lovely wife in the first year of his marriage, had resolved by travelling in foreign countries, to endeavour to forget his irreparable loss, leaving the present squire in undisputed authority over his domains and extensive property. Then shortly came news of the decease, at Rome, of the elder brother. The present squire entered on his own account into undisputed possession of the vast accumulated property, for the relatives of the family were very few and very distant. This was all that was really known of the history of Squire Learmont, and his sudden determination, after nearly fourteen years of seclusion, to visit London, and launch out into a style of expensive living which, although it was well known he could afford, yet astonished everybody, were the themes of very general gossip. The old mansion had been hastily put in order for his reception. The complement of servants was greatly increased; an immense sum was spent in costly liveries and interior adornments; expectation was on the utmost stretch, and when Learmont did arrive and stalked into his ancient house, he created a scarcely less sensation, than as if he had been some petty monarch.

No one liked the dark penetrating eye that scowled around, as if suspicious of everything and everybody, but there was no absolute stain upon his character; moreover he was immensely rich, and reported, of course, to be a great deal richer than he really was, so that when it became known that he intended to give a series of entertainments, unequalled in effect and magnificence by any commoner, numbers of old friends of the family sprung up from all quarters, and had his spacious halls been ten times as spacious he would have found no difficulty in filling them with glittering throngs whenever he chose.

Certainly Learmont seemed to be at the height of his ambition. The possessor of a princely revenue which had been allowed to accumulate, first by his elder brother, who was a man of frugal habits, for several years, and then by himself, for a number of years more, until he found himself possessed of a sum of money in actual cash, which had the worthy associates, Britton and Gray, but fancied to be a third of its real amount, would materially have assisted them in putting a high price upon their services whatever they were.

On the evening of his arrival, Learmont sat alone and silent for a considerable time in the magnificent library of his mansion; then, when he could no longer look upon the gorgeous hangings and superb decorations of the apartment, in consequence of the rapidly darkening sky, he rung a small silver hand-bell which was immediately answered by a page, attired in crimson and gold livery, who waited respectfully for orders.

"Bid my steward," said Learmont, "with my chamberlain and the officers of the several departments of my household, attend me with lights. I will walk through the house."

The page bowed and retired.

"Yes," muttered Learmont, when he was again alone, "I will sate my eyes with gazing upon the glorious magnificence I have panted for so long; I will see the glitter and the beauty of what I have so dearly purchased. Attended by those who are taught to watch the slightest indication of my pleasure, I will traverse the stately and gorgeous mansion, which years since I used to wildly dream might once be mine, and smile when I awoke to think of the extreme improbability of the vision."

The door was now thrown open and the same page who had before attended upon

Learmont, respectfully announced that his commands had been obeyed, and that his servants were in waiting to escort him over his mansion.

He rose from his seat and strode with a haughty air to the door.

"Lead the way," he cried, "I'll follow."

The servants bowed, and while some preceded him, conveying large wax lights, others again followed, so that a full glare of light was thrown upon the path of the proud man, who had purged his very soul for the purpose of procuring such perchased and empty homage.

Saloon after saloon was traversed, and in each Learmont paused and ordered the chandeliers and clustering lamps to be lighted, in order that he might judge of the effect by night of the gorgeous decorations of those noble apartments. Everything rich or rare that money could produce was there congregated. The walls were hung with the most superb tapestry; the ceilings were freshly and vigorously painted by artists of celebrity, and the highly-polished oaken floors shone like mirrors, reflecting all the brilliancy and lustre of both roof and walls.

The heart of Learmont swelled with pride and triumph, as he glanced round upon all this luxury and refinement, and whispered to himself "it is mine—all mine."

"Lead on," was his only cry as room after room was lighted and examined.

Now the mansion had been nearly traversed, and the chandeliers and lamps being left lighted, the whole house shone and glittered with unparalleled brilliancy. There was but one other state apartment which Learmont had not visited, and that was a spacious ball-room, upon which an enormous sum had been lavished. He wished, he hoped to be greatly struck by the splendour of that noble room, and he sent the domestics on before to light its numerous lustres, in order that he might judge of its first effect upon the eye as any one entered it.

The steward of the household returned to say that all was ready, and preceding his master with a long white wand in his hand, tipped with gold, he led the way to the ball-room.

"Perfect!" was the exclamation of Learmont, when he stood in the centre of that hall. To attempt a description of it would be in vain. It was one gorgeous glitter; all that mirrors, gilding, hangings, painting, lights and flowers could do to render it a scene of enchantment was done.

Learmont's colour deepened with pride as he looked around him and could see nothing that he would have altered. All was as he wished, and he felt conscious that such another apartment was not to be found in London.

"This is the broad path to honour and distinction," he muttered to himself. "If you would be regarded among men as little short of a divinity, you have but to throw gold-dust in their eyes, and through that glittering medium they will see you are a very god."

Now there suddenly burst upon the air from a balcony at the further end of the hall, a strain of exquisite music. The lofty room echoed with the melodious strains, and when the gay and spirit-stirring strains were over the steward advanced with a self-satisfied air, and said,

"Sir, those are the musicians you are pleased to order should be engaged to wait upon your pleasure, as part of your household. I thought your worship might be pleased to judge of their skill and the effect of their music in this apartment."

"'Tis well," said Learmont, inclining his head. "Bid them play again."

Obedient to a signal, the musicians again filled the air with joyons sounds, and Learmont stood and listened with delight, forgetting in those moments everything but his own present greatness and wealth.

"Yes," he said, when the strain ceased, as if pursuing a previous train of thought: "this is the way to forget. Steep the senses in enjoyment, and the conscience will have no room for action; wine, music, the dance, the smile of beauty, all shall contribute to my enjoyment, and life shall be—"

"May it please you, honourable sir, some one desires speech of you," said a domestic.

"Say I am occupied," replied Learmont, and he again resumed his glowing meditations. "Nobility," he muttered, "will crowd to my *fêtes*, even royalty might borrow new grace and dignity from the halls of Squire Learmont. But tha shall not long be my designation. Wealth in England can purchase anything, and titles are easily procured where the price is of little moment. I will be ennobled and—"

"Your pardon, sir," said the servant, returning, "but the stranger will not take a refusal."

"Ha! he will not?"

"An' it please you, sir, he will not go."

"Have I not idle knaves enough about me to drive an insolent intruder from my doors?"

"'Tis a rude knave, your worship."

"Cast him into the street. How dare he say he will see the master of Learmont?"

"It shall be done, sir. To come here talking about an Old Smithy."

Learmont caught the muttered words of the man as he was hurrying from the hall, and a cry of pain and horror escaped him as he rushed forward, and seizing the terrified servant by the arm, he cried—

"What —what manner of man is he who seeks me with such pertinacity?"

"A rough knave, an' please you, sir; coarse of speech and appearance."

"And—and he said—what?"

"He said, he brought 'a message from the Old Smithy!'"

A deadly paleness came across Learmont's face, as he said in a husky whisper,

"Show him into a private room and tell him I will be with him soon. Begone, knave, nor stand gaping there.'"

The terrified servant darted from the hall, and Learmont turning to the throng of domestics who were standing at a respectful distance from him, cried—

"Lead on. To my chamber, and bid yon knave bring me word in what apartment he has placed this—this—visiter."

The servants hastened to throw the doors wide open for their imperious master to pass out, but his mood was changed. The glow of triumph and gratified pride no longer lent a glow to his sallow cheek, nor lit up his deep-sunken eyes with brilliancy. There was a load of care and anxiety, almost amounting to agony, upon his face. His contracted brow bespoke deep and anxious thought, and his limbs trembled as he left his hall of light and beauty, to seek an interview with the man who, he had always dreaded, would exercise the power he had of stepping between him and his moments of forgetfulness and consquent enjoyment.

CHAPTER XII.

THE CONSEQUENCES OF CRIME.—A FAMILIAR FRIEND.—A CLOUD UPON LEARMONT'S FELICITY.

BEING informed by his servants that his visiter had been shown into a small room adjoining the library, Learmont took a lamp from his table, and with a frowning brow and compressed lips, walked towards the room to demand of Britton, for he guessed too well it was he, the cause of so early a visit.

When he entered the room he found the smith lolling, at his ease, upon a costly couch, and although he did rise at the presence of Learmont, it was with an air and manner of extreme insolence.

"To what am I indebted for so early a visit, or rather I should say intrusion?" asked Learmont in a low hollow voice.

"Principally," said Britton with an air of perfect indifference, "to assure you that I had arrived in London, perfectly safe.

"Well?" said Learmont.

"Aye and well too," answered the smith, purposely mistaking the other's meaning. "I wish to know likewise, if you have seen Jacob Gray?"

"I have not," replied Learmont.

"Know you, squire, where in London he is to be found?"

"I do not. Has he not confided that to you?"

"In faith, he has not. In vain I urged him to tell me his place of abode, and if I know not where to find him how can I carry out the project we have decided upon?"

"True," said Learmont. "There must be found some means. Listen to me: when next Jacob Gray seeks me for money, I will put him off to a particular hour the next day. Be you then, at that hour, lurk about here, and follow him to his home, whither he will most likely go directly, having a sum of money with him."

"That may do," said Britton, after a moment's consideration. "You can send to me at any time, by my real name, addressed to a little hostelrie, called The Old Chequers, by Storey's Gate hard by. You see, squire, I thought it handy to live near at hand."

"Promise me—swear to me, you will take this man's life!" cried Learmont, with sudden vehemence.

"I have no particular objection to take his life," replied Britton.

"And the boy?"

"That's as circumstances turn out, squire. If the boy knows nothing—suspects nothing—"

"Aye, there's the doubt. Britton, dispose of Gray, and your reward, as you know, is most ample. Bring, then, that boy to me."

"Agreed. You shall have him."

"Thanks, good Britton; and—and when you bring him you shall not be five minutes without your just reward."

There was a peculiarity of tone and manner about Learmont as he uttered these words, which startled the smith, and he looked for a moment or two suspiciously at his employer, then he said,—

"Squire Learmont, I have been taught an useful lesson by Jacob Gray. I, too, have written a confession, and lodged it in a place of safety."

"What mean you?" said Learmont.

"This—that if I should die suddenly, a packet of papers will be found, which will do no good to the Squire of Learmont. You understand me."

"I do understand you," said Learmont; "but your suspicions are groundless."

"Be it so," said the smith. "It's best to be cautious."

"Take what precautions you please," replied Learmont; "but keep your promise."

"I will keep it," cried the smith; "for I hate this Jacob Gray, although he has made me know my own value."

"Know your value—what mean you?"

"It was Jacob Gray who told me there were documents of some importance about the body of——"

"Hush—hush!" cried Learmont; "name him not—it is enough. But tell me, why did Gray inform you of the existence of those papers instead of securing them himself?"

"He lacked the courage to seek them where they were to be found."

"And yet I must take your word that they do prove what you say?"

"Squire Learmont, these papers distinctly prove your illegitimacy. Among them is a letter from your mother, urging your father to marry her on account of her infant—that infant was yourself, for you know she died before you were one year old."

"Enough—enough," said Learmont—"I will believe it is so."

"So you perceive, squire, admitting your brother to——"

"Cease—cease!" cried Learmont. "I want not these details."

"I was only about to remark that you were not the heir-at-law," said Britton.

"Heir to hell!" cried Learmont. "Now begone. You have delivered your message. I will send to you at the pot-house you mention when a fitting time comes. Now, away!"

"Not so fast," said Britton.   "I have made a resolution."

"What resolution?"

"Never to leave this house empty-handed."

"Pshaw! You forget the large sum you have received of me within these three days."

"No, squire, I do not; but I have told you my resolve—I shall charge for my visits here."

"And pray how much do you expect to receive whenever I am honoured by your presence?" sneered Learmont.

"I shall leave that to your generosity," said Britton.

"And how often do you purpose coming?"

"As often as the humour takes me, or my wants require," replied the smith, insolently.

Learmont evidently made a great effort to subdue his rage, and he said, in half-choked accents,—

"Name your price."

"Ten pieces," said the smith.

Learmont took his purse from his pocket, and, without a word, counted out the required sum, and then stood with his lamp in his hand waiting for the other to leave the place.

"You won't show me your house, I suppose?" said Britton, in an aggravating voice.

The dark eye of Learmont flashed with rage; but he said nothing.

"Oh, very well," cried Britton; "another time will do just as well. Recollect the sign of 'The Old Chequers.' I shall be very glad to see you whenever you may choose to call, and we can always find something interesting to talk about."

"Away with you—away!" cried Learmont.

'Let me see," said Britton, with great deliberation, counting on his fingers, "this is Tuesday—Wednesday—Thursday—Friday,—well, say Friday."

"Friday for what?"

"My next visit."

"So soon?"

"I don't call that soon.   Friday it shall be, squire."

The lamp trembled in the hand of Learmont as he thought—"Oh, that for my own safety's sake I dared plunge a dagger to the hilt in his heart!"

Britton, however, seemed fully to feel his entire safety, and he evidently felt an exquisite enjoyment in the agony he was inflicting upon Learmont. He lounged slowly to the door, and nodding then in an insolent and familiar manner, he crossed the hall to the outer door, while Learmont, nearly bursting with rage, sprung up the marble staircase to the upper apartment of the house.

"This is brave work," muttered Britton when he had passed out into the street. "Humph! For ten long years did Master Learmont get the better of me in cunning, and I could not drag him down without placing a halter round my own neck; but now, thanks to the cunning of Master Jacob Gray, I have the means of toppling the squire from his height of power and grandeur without doing myself the least harm in the world. Ho! ho! 'tis brave indeed. And now for this Gray. I don't see why I should not have charge of that young scion of an ancient stock, who is so great an eye-sore to Learmont. We shall see—we shall see, Master Gray, whether you or I will succeed best in a contest of cunning in the long run, and now for wine and jollity."

The smith had now arrived at the door of "The Old Chequers," where, as the place most congenial to his disposition, he had taken up his abode, and where, showing that he had plenty of money, he was welcomed accordingly.

"Hilloa!" he roared.   "Landlord, some of your best. Quick—quick, I say; I am thirsty, man."

The landlord needed no second bidding, but placed a tankard of foaming ale before the smith, who immediately took a deep draught of its contents,

" Hurrah !" he cried; "I am Andrew Britton, the smith, and I don't care who knows it."

" Certainly not, most worshipful sir," said the landlord.

" Ah," cried Britton, " worshipful sir. That's a very good name, and I'll be called that for the future. Here's a quart of the best to whoever calls me worshipful sir, and whoever don't I'll wring his neck."

" Hurrah ! for the jolly smith" cried a chorus of topers who were around. " We'll drink your health, worshipful sir."

" So you shall," cried Britton. " Here's gold, and there's more, too, where that comes from. Landlord, do you hear? quarts all round. The best—the humming ale, recollect, that makes a man sing."

No, 5.

CHAPTER XIII.

A WALK IN THE PARK.—A RECOGNITION.—THE QUESTION.—A DEFIANCE.—JACOB
GRAY'S FIRST VISIT.—THE DREAM.

THE Squire Learmont's first night in his splendid mansion was by no means an agreeable one. He retired to rest vexed and enraged at Andrew Britton, and his mind in a chaos of conflicting thoughts how to rid himself of the insufferable torment of the threatened visits from that man whose very name would have been sufficient, at any time, to bring a chill to Learmont's heart, and dash the brimming cup of joy from his lips.

His restless slumbers, too, were haunted by the visionary creations of his excited fancy. One moment he would be plunging a poniard into Britton's heart, while he dragged from his breast the papers so important to his peace. Then again, at the moment of his fancied triumph, the scene would change to a court of justice, and a voice arraigned him for murder! In such fearful and disordered fancies was his night passed, and he rose in the morning pale, haggard, and unrefreshed. Hastily attiring himself, he drew aside the curtains of his chamber-window, which commanded an extensive and pleasing view into St. James's Park. It was yet very early, but Learmont thought that he should be able to withdraw his mind from disagreeable and horrible reflections by healthful walk in the shady Mall.

He accordingly took his hat and sword, and walked from his house by a garden-gate, opening into a narrow lane of trees, which terminated in the park itself. The air was very cold, for frost was on the ground, and the trees were stripped of their beautiful verdure; but it was exercise that Learmont wanted, and he rather rejoiced than otherwise at the necessity of active walking, inasmuch as he hoped exertion of body would control the excitement of his mind.

The canal was then, and for many years afterwards, a mere straight cutting, strongly resembling a wet dock, for the repair of ships, and as little ornamental as it could possibly be. The walks, however, in St. James's Park, were then preferable to what they are now, for many old trees were then in existence that have now perished, and their places are, of necessity, occupied by saplings, which the present generation have been kind enough to plant for their successors.

Learmont walked very quickly over the frozen ground, which crackled like glass under the feet. There were but few persons at that early hour abroad, although the day gave promise of being one of those clear, cold, frosty ones which are admired by a great many persons.

Approaching, however, from the direction towards which he was proceeding, Learmont observed a gentlemanly-looking man enveloped in a large cloak. By some sort of instinct, Learmont seemed to feel a dread of this stranger's approach, although he could not at all recognise in him, at the distance they were apart, the gait or aspect of any one that he knew. Nearer and nearer they approached each other; and, so strong was the feeling of dread in the breast of Learmont, that, had it not been for his stronger curiosity to ascertain who it was, he would have turned from the open pathway among the trees, whose huge trunks would have effectually hidden him from observation. As it was, however, he pursued his walk until he and the stranger with the cloak came nearly face to face. Then, as the stranger lifted up his eyes, which had been fixed on the ground in a meditative manner, Learmont knew him.

It was the young man, by name Frank Hartleton, who had been so curious and suspicious at the period of the great storm at Learmont, when the wing of the building, in which was the smithy, had been burnt down.

The recognition was evidently mutual; indeed, no one who had once seen Learmont could easily again forget him; and, although a great personal change had taken place in the appearance of Hartleton, yet the features of all who had taken any part in the proceedings of that eventful night at the little village of Learmont, were too indelibly impressed upon the memory of the squire, for him to find any difficulty in recognising in the staid, and somewhat grave, gentlemanl person before him, the Frank Hartleton who had always held him at open defianc and laughed at his power.

Hartleton stopped short when he saw Learmont; and his first exclamation was,—

"This is strange, indeed!"

"Sir," said Learmont; "did you address me?"

"Scarcely," replied Hartleton; "but your name is Learmont?"

"Well, sir?" replied the other with considerable *hauteur*.

"Do you know me, 'Squire Learmont?"

"I recognise the features, and know the names of many, sir," said Learmont, "that still are not upon my roll of friends or acquaintance."

"You do know me," said Hartleton. "I have no desire to be rude to you, 'Squire Learmont; but our sudden meeting took me somewhat by surprise, and the exclamation that I uttered arose from the curious coincidence that I have been all night dreaming of you and the village of Learmont, and was in deep thought about the mysterious occurrences that took place three years ago when I suddenly came upon you."

If his hatred and dread of Hartleton would have induced Learmont to treat him in such a manner that he could not address him, his guilty fears urged him to prolong the conversation, in order to discover, if possible, the complexion of Hartleton's thoughts with regard to him, that he might know if he had anything really to dread from that quarter. It was, therefore, with more courtesy that he said,—

"The coincidences are curious. I—I believe I speak to Sir Francis Hartleton now?"

"Yes," replied Hartleton; "I was, you recollect, destined for the law, which my small patrimony just enabled me to enter with credit. I am now a justice, and a knight, as you say."

"I give you joy, sir, of your advancement," said Learmont.

"You are very kind," replied Hartleton, fixing his eyes upon the countenance of Learmont in a manner that it required all the firmness of the latter not to quail under.

"Might I presume so far," said Learmont, "as to ask what were the thoughts concerning me that engaged Sir Francis Hartleton even now?"

"I was thinking of the mysterious man," said Hartleton, "who rushed with such wild gestures and shrieks from the burning house."

Learmont strove to command his features to indifference; but the effort was almost beyond his power, and he spoke to endeavour to cover his agitation.

"It was very strange," he said; "most singular!"

"And the little child, too, that he had in his arms," continued Hartleton; "what can have become of that?"

"Ay—what?" said Learmont.

"Did you never get any clue, 'Squire Learmont, to these mysterious circumstances, which must have greatly interested you?"

"Interested me? How?"

"Inasmuch as they occurred upon your estate, and among your own tenants."

"True—most true, sir. I—I was—and am much interested; but I know nothing—have heard nothing, and have no clue to unravel the mystery."

"We must only hope," said Hartleton, "that some of these days, accident as it generally does, will throw a light upon the subject, and give it to us in all its details."

An awful expression came across the face of Learmont as he replied:

"Yes—yes. As you say, it will be an accident. May I ask what your impression is?"

"I have scarcely an impression upon the subject," replied Hartleton; "we lawyers, you know, are particularly cautious how we take up impressions upon subjects unfounded upon evidence."

"Exceedingly proper is such caution," said Learmont; "otherwise the innocent might be the victims of endless mistakes."

"Exactly," replied Hartleton; "but I have no particular objection to tell you my dream without founding any impression upon it."

"I am all attention," said Learmont.

"I dreamt first that that smith, o   me of Britton, was a desperate villain, and for gold would—"

"Would what?" gasped Learmont.

"Do anything," said Hartleton.

"Well, sir, is that all?"

"Oh, no; my vision changed, and I thought I saw a gloomy passage, mouldy with the damps of time, and dripping with unwholesome moisture—creeping slimy things were all around, and in the midst I saw——"

"Yes—yes," gasped Learmont. "W—what saw you?"

"A mouldering skeleton."

"Indeed!"

"Yes, and the most curious circumstance of all was, that in the midst of it I constantly heard the clank of the smith's hammer. I knew the sound in a moment."

"'Tis very strange!" muttered Learmont.

"Most strange!" said Hartleton; "but again my vision changed."

"What saw you then?"

"A hall of judgment."

"Yes—yes."

"It was densely crowded, and some important and interesting proceeding was evidently pending; then suddenly I heard a voice cry your name."

"My name?"

"Yes, and you were asked to plead to a charge of murder!"

A cold sweat broke out upon the forehead of Learmont, and he could not answer, when Hartleton added,—

"It was but a dream, though. I wish you a good morning, and a pleasant walk, 'Squire Learmont."

CHAPTER XIV.

THE DARK THREAT.—THE BITER BIT.—ANOTHER MURDER PROJECTED.— LEARMONT'S REASONING.

LEARMONT stood for a few moments gazing after the retreating figure of Sir Francis Hartleton; then, shaking his clenched hand in the direction he was proceeding, he muttered between his teeth,—

"Beware—beware, Sir Magistrate!—beware! You may rouse a spirit you cannot quell again. I am not the man to allow such as thou to be a stumbling-block in my path."

So saying, with a dark scowl upon his brow, the 'squire retraced his steps towards his own house. The morning sun was now gilding with beauty the house-tops, and the icicles, which, pendant from every tree, shone like gems of the purest water and brilliancy. Unheedful, however, of the beauties of nature around, the wealthy Learmont passed onwards, his thoughs, dark and painful as they were, fully absorbing all his attention. He passed up the little lane which was the nearest route to his own house; and, as he was about to emerge from it, he was startled (for the guilty are ever timid) by some one touching his shoulder. Turning quickly round, he saw Jacob Gray, with a sickly, disagreeable smile upon his face, standing close to him.

"Your worship rises early," said Gray.

"Yes; you—you have been seeking me?"

"I have, 'squire. Your servants sought you, it appears, and found you were not within; and, as I knew it was much the custom of the great gentry, such as your worship, to gather an appetite for breakfast by a stroll in the park, I made bold to seek you.'

"I am now proceeding homeward," said Learmont. "In half an hour from now I shall be at leisure."

"As your worship pleases," said Gray; "but methought there was an inclination on the part of your lackeys to deny me speech of you. Now, 'squire, if you would have the goodness to leave a message in your hall to the effect that your old and trusty friend Jacob Gray was always to be, admitted, it would save us both trouble."

Learmont was exceedingly impatient during this speech, and, at its conclusion, he said, in a vexed tone,—

"Well—well—I will leave proper orders. In half an hour I shall expect you."

"Your worship shall not be disappointed," said Gray, with a bow which had more of burlesque mockery in it than respect.

Learmont turned haughtily from him, and in a few moments he entered the gardens of his mansion, by the same private door through which he had proceeded to the park. He ordered a sumptuous breakfast to be immediately prepared for him, and took an opportunity to say, in a careless manner, to the servant, whose special province it was to answer the silver bell which always was at Learmont's elbow,—

"Tell them in the hall that I expect one Jacob Gray. Let him be admitted."

The servant respectfully retired to communicate the message, and Learmont, after a pause of thought, said, in a low voice,—

"Yes, Jacob Gray, you shall be admitted as often as you call; but it will go hard with me if I do not take thy life soon. Assuming wretch!—oh! can there be a state of more abject slavery than his, who, after carving the way to his ambitious height, then finds himself at the mercy of the mean and despicable tools he has used, and would fain throw aside, and forget for ever! We shall see: we shall see. Surely I, who have already done so much when so little seemed possible, am not to be scared through life by such two ruffians as Britton and Gray. They must destroy each other! Yes; that is the true policy, and now to work on the fears and cupidity of this Jacob Gray!"

He had scarcely whispered to himself these reflections, when the object of them was announced.

"Bring him hither," said Learmont, and in a few moments Jacob Gray was introduced. The moment the servant had left the room, and closed the door behind him, Gray seated himself with an air of insolent familiarity, which, under any other circumstances, would have produced a storm of passion in Learmont; but he felt the necessity of temporising; and, severe as was the struggle to him, he nevertheless succeeded in keeping down his passion sufficiently to address Gray calmly.

"You reached London in safety, of course?"

"Even so," replied Gray. " Permit me to congratulate you upon your house. It really is——"

"Yes, yes," cried Learmont, impatiently. "Let us to business, Master Gray. You found the papers your extreme prudence had left in London, when you favoured me with a visit, quite safe, I trust?"

"Perfectly safe, and untouched, "said Gray; "and—and—permit me to add, that I have placed them again under such circumstances as must ensure their delivery to one who has power and will to use them, should anything sudden—you understand—happen to your humble servant, Jacob Gray."

"May I ask whose hands you consider so peculiarly adapted for those papers?"

"Oh, certainly; a neighbour of yours, Sir Francis Hartleton."

"Sir Francis Hartleton ?" exclaimed Learmont.

"Yes," replied Gray ; "one of the most acute lawyers and active justices in London."

"As you please," said Learmont. "Now, with regard to the—the—child ?"

"He is quite well, 'squire, and likely to continue so."

"Humph ! Is he tall ?"

"Not over tall, but slim and active."

"Enough of him at present. I wish to speak to you of another matter. The sums demanded of me by Britton are large."

"Doubtless, 'squire ; 'tis an extravagant knave."

"Now those sums, Gray, added to what you yourself receive, would make a goodly income."

"In faith you speak truly, 'squire."

"Now, Gray, I will deal frankly with you," continued Learmont. "This Britton is fond of wine, and in his cups some day he may hint or say enough to—to hang you, Master Gray."

"Eh ?" cried Gray. "Hang me ?"

"Even so."

"Oh, I understand, along with your worship, of course."

"I don't know that, Jacob Gray," remarked Learmont, calmly and firmly. "I have a long purse, you see, which you have not."

"There—is—something in that," muttered Gray.

"A man of your acuteness must perceive that there is a great deal in that," continued Learmont.

"Yes, truly ; but still there would be danger, most imminent danger, 'squire."

"That I grant you, but yours, Jacob Gray, would far exceed mine. Be that, however, as it may, you must see how very desirable a consummation it would be if this swilling drunken knave, Britton, were some day to choke himself."

"Or be choked by Jacob Gray ?" added Gray, with a smile of dark meaning.

"Exactly," said Learmont. "It may be done easily. Invite him to your house ; feast with him, plan and plot with him ; give him wine ; and then, some day, when time and circumstances are fitting, I will give you a drug of such potency, that, if ever so slightly used in his wine-cup, will seize upon the springs of life, and at once, you will see, Master Gray, you are rid of this dangerous man."

"And rid you likewise of him," interposed Gray.

"Of course ; but I gain little—you everything—by his death—safety and wealth !"

"It might be done," murmured Gray, "if it could be done safely."

"With your caution," suggested Learmont, "with but a little of the admirable cunning you have as yet displayed in this business, methinks it might be possible, Master Gray, for you to overreach in some way so dull-witted a villain as this Britton, who, you see, stands so much in the way of your fortunes."

"If," muttered Gray, "it can be done at all by me, that poison draught you mentioned is, to my mind, the most ready, and—and—"

"Safe," added Learmont.

"Well, safe be it," said Gray. "There is no occasion for a greater risk than necessary."

"None in the least," sneered Learmont : "you will then do your best, Master Gray, to rid yourself of this sot, this incubus upon you, this villain, whom I hate as—as——"

"As you hate me !" said Gray, twinkling his small eyes, and peering in the face of Learmont.

"No," said Learmont ; "you are not so dangerous, because you are more cautious ; but, Jacob Gray, is it not possible that, hould you succeed in ridding yourself of this Briton, you may think it worth your while to name some price for the only thing I dread ?"

"The child ?"

"Yes : think of my words."

"I will think," said Gray ; "but now I must be gone."

Learmont placed in his hands a purse of gold, and with a shifting, low-cunning glance of his little grey eyes, the wily villain left the place muttering —

"Humph!—He wants to kill my goose, to get all the golden eggs at once! Indeed!—we shall see!"

CHAPTER XV.

THE CHASE.—A LONG RACE, AND ITS RESULTS.

WHEN Gray left the splendid mansion of Learmont, he stood for a few moments in the street, turning round him cautiously to see if he was watched, for his suspicions had been awakened by Learmont, once during this interview, ringing for an attendant, and giving some order outside the door in a very low whisper.

Now Jacob was extremely cunning. He refined upon ordinary duplicity, and now, as he stood in the street casting cautious glances up and down its silent extent, he muttered to himself,—

"Humph! my way is westward. Now, your ordinary clever fellow would go westward, for fear of being watched; but I—I, Jacob Gray, have got beyond such cunning. Learmont knows well I am a careful man. Should he have set a spy upon me, it will be with the certainty that I will not go directly to my home; and to defeat that I will go—not directly home, but in the direction of home. Ho! ho! Squire Learmont, you are not yet a match for Jacob Gray!"

Continuing muttering to himself, and peeping into every door-way that he passed, Gray then betook himself to the river side, and, ordering a boat, he desired the waterman to take him across the stream.

Well did Jacob Gray's cunning teach him that the difficulty of following a person crossing the river was immeasurably greater than on shore, for, if followed by a boat, concealment of the person pursuing would be nearly out of the question, and to make a palpable *detour* for the sake of crossing a bridge would most probably ensure the complete escape of the watched party. Jacob Gray did not know that he was watched, but he knew that, had he been Learmont, and Learmont, Gray, he would then have been watched with the keenest of eyes that could be procured for that duty.

When the boatman neared the centre of the stream, Jacob Gray desired him to pause upon his oars for a few moments, ostensibly that he, Gray, might admire the bright sunshine on the frosted spires of the various churches, but really to see if any other boat was about leaving the point from which he had started. Nor was he disappointed; for scarcely had the wherry floated idly in the stream for a few brief seconds, when Jacob observed a boat push off, in which were two rowers, and a third muffled in a cloak, and seated very low in the stern of it.

The waterman was now upon the point of urging his boat forward again, when Gray said quietly :—

"Hold still a moment, my friend. Your time shall be paid for. Surely yon boat is making speed through the water."

The waterman looked in the direction of the wherry with the two rowers, and exclaimed :—

"Some one is in haste. Yet, no,—they are pulling but lazily suddenly."

Gray's small eyes twinkled as he replied :—

"I have altered my mind; row easily up the stream."

The boat's head was turned in the required direction, and the waterman, with regular and long sweeps of his oars, propelled the wherry towards Westminster Bridge, and presently glided beneath one of its gloomy arches. For a few moments the rowers in the boat in which Jacob Gray suspected was some one upon his track, appeared quite undecided what to do ; then, in obedience to some order apparently from the cloaked figure, they gently followed in the wake of Gray's wherry.

"So," muttered Gray to himself between his clenched teeth ; "I am followed; —and with what intent ?—my safe destruction, of course. Waterman," he said, in a louder tone, "we are going with the tide?"

"Scarcely," replied the man ; "it is just on the turn."

"When it is fairly running down," said Gray, "I will go back. Keep on, however, as you are for a short time."

The waterman now shading his eyes with one hand from the sun, while the oar idly played in the rollocks, said :—

"It seems to me, master, that yon skiff is following us for some reason."

"Indeed!" says Gray. "What have you been doing, that you should be followed on the Thames ?"

"I doing!" cried the man.

"Ay.—You suspect you are followed."

"Mayhap it's yourself, master, they follow," remarked the man, rather surlily. Gray smiled as he replied :—

"Oh, no ;—they suspect you of being one of the notorious pirates of the Thames we have heard so much of lately."

"The tide has turned," said the waterman, looking into the stream as it appeared, in preference to making any reply to this vague charge.

"Hark ye !" said Gray, as if a sudden thought had struck up in his brain. "If you are inclined sometimes to earn more money at once than a year's plying as waterman on the river could produce you, it is possible I may throw a job in your way."

The man glanced uneasily at Gray, as he replied in a low tone,—

"Your lordship might trust me—if——"

"If what, my friend?"

"If I might trust your worship."

"You may, or rather the trusting is all on my side. All I want of you is this: when I shall some day give you notice that I shall want a wherry at a particular hour and at the stairs I shall name, will you be there?"

"Certainly," replied the man, "But that is not quite all ?"

"You are right," said Gray. "I shall bring one with me; we will take with us wherewithal to make us merry. I am abstemious, but my friend is not, and I have often told him that some of these days, when drinking in a wherry, he will become so confused, that he will accidentally fall into the Thames. Do you understand ?"

"I—think—I—do."

"I am sure you do," added Gray.

The man nodded.

"Your reward shall be ample," continued his tempter.

"I don't see why I should turn away a job," said the man ; "if I wasn't to take it, some one else would, of course."

"A very true remark," cried Jacob Gray. "You consent then to do this little service ?"

"I do, master."

"Give me your name and address then."

"Sheldon is my name, and I am always at the stairs at which you hired me, unless away as might be now, when I return again as soon as possible."

"That will do," said Gray. "Now turn your boat's head and go back with the stream."

The wherry, with the two rowers, had kept at a considerable distance in the rear ; and now that Gray's boat was suddenly turned and rapidly going down the stream, there seemed some little confusion on board the other wherry; but before the two boats could meet or pass each other, the pursuers had shot off on one side, as if with the intention of landing near Westminster.

"Follow them," cried Gray; "and wherever they land, do you land me."

The waterman was a powerful man, and he bent to the oars with such effect, that the wherry shot through the water with amazing speed.

It was curious to see the pursued become the pursuers, for such seemed to be the state of things, as no sooner did it become evident that Jacob Gray's waterman was making fast for the boat with the two rowers, than in obedience to a violent gesture from the person in the cloak, they pulled vigorously towards the shore.

"I must see that man in the cloak," said Gray, "if it be possible."

The waterman said nothing, but with his long sinewy arms, he took tremendous sweeps with the oars, and sent the boat forward at each pull with a force that astonished Gray.

The two wherries were not now above a quarter of the width of the river apart from each other, when the foremost one ran upon the muddy beach, and the man in the cloak springing up, made an effort to jump on shore, in which he fell over

No. 6

the seats of the boat.   In the next moment the other wherry was within two boats' lengths of the shore.

With an oath the choked man scrambled to his feet, and without turning, rushed on shore, and was soon lost to sight among the mean habitations that crowded the banks of the river.

"It is the smith!" muttered Gray.   "I see it all now, he has a commission for my destruction, as I have for his, and in either case, Squire Learmont betters his condition.   Waterman, row me across now, as I originally asked you."

Again the wherry shot into the stream, and with his eyes fixed upon the water, Jacob Gray appeared absorbed in deep thought.

The boat's head grated against some stone steps that were on the opposite landing, and Gray sprung to his feet, and stepped on shore.

Handing the waterman then a liberal gratuity, and whispering in his ear the word "remember," he walked at a rapid pace in the direction of the ancient suburb of Lambeth.

<hr>

CHAPTER XVI.

THE LONE HOUSE IN ANCIENT LAMBETH.—THE BOY.—A SOLITARY HEART.

IN a district of Lambeth, which is now the mart of trade, but which at the period of our narrative was scarcely inhabited, and consisted but of a mass of old melancholy-looking buildings, which had been long since condemned as dangerous, there stood one house in particular, the exterior of which presented to the eye an appearance of such utter decay, that it would have required an adventurous person to venture within its crumbling walls and mossy prisons, who, for the sake of a short cut to some of the high roads, passed the old building, would walk out into the road-way, rather than run even the momentary risk of walking close to its dilapidated walls.

The world, however, is ever being taken in by appearances.   Not only was this house much stronger and more substantial than its neighbours, but within it there was a degree of comfort and even luxury which no one could for a moment have surmised.   It is true the windows were either broken, or so much begrimed with dirt that it was impossible to say if they were glass or not, and here and there a brick was displaced so naturally, that it seemed to have fallen out by the natural decay incidental to the age of the structure.   Such, however was not the case, for these signs and tokens of insecurity had been manufactured in the silence of the night for the express purpose of deterring any person from entering the gloomy house, or supposing for a moment that it was inhabited by other than rats and mice.

There were no persons living very close to this wretched-looking residence, and the poor squalid creatures, who did occasionally seek a shelter for a few nights in some of the "condemned" houses, never approached that one, for it had the reputation of being haunted, inasmuch as twice had strangers, in passing through the locality after nightfall, called attention to lights dimly observable in the house, and once a man had entered a little hostelry in the immediate neighbourhood, and while his tongue clove to the roof of his mouth with fear, and he trembled in every limb, he said he had seen a sight at one of the lower windows of that particular house, which he would not see again for his soul's sake, and after fortifying himself with a bumper of spiced canary, he had taken his leave, being firmly believed, and leaving behind the character of the house, which lost nothing by being repeated from mouth to mouth, and which produced so powerful an effect upon the superstitious inhabitants of the vicinity, that it is doubtful if any bribe of sufficient magnitude could possibly be offered to induce any one of them ever to pass it even after at sunset.

Into this mysterious house we will conduct the reader. The room to which we would direct attention was small, but by no means destitute of comforts ; a wood fire burnt within the grate, and its low flickering light disclosed several articles of domestic convenience about the apartment. The only coarse appearance the place had was owing to some rough ragged edged planks being nailed across the window on the inside, so as effectually to close it against the egress of any wandering stream of light from the fire.

The room was consequently dark, for the process of preventing the fire-light from showing through the window, likewise excluded the daylight, and, although it was mid-day without, that apartment presented the appearance of midnight within.

Stretched on the hearth before the fire, was a large gaunt-looking dog, apparently in a deep slumber, and sitting on an old-fashioned chair, with his head buried in his hands, and resting on the table, was the young boy, who has been already introduced to the reader as Harry Gray, and who passed as a nephew of wily Jacob Gray. His remarkable long and beautiful hair fell in masses upon the table, and the fine light glistened on the glossy ringlets as they strayed in wild luxuriance over his hands.

So still was that young creature, that he might have been thought sleeping, and, perhaps, he had been, and had awakened from some dreams of happiness to weep, for a deep sob burst from his heart, and looking up, he cried, in accents of deep misery and despair,—

" I am very unhappy—I wish I could die."

The dog, upon the sound of the voice, immediately rose, and with a low whine, placed his fore paws upon the knee of the boy, and looked in his face with an expression of sagacious affection, which of all the inferior animals dogs alone are capable of.

For a moment the boy did not heed him, but wept bitterly, and kept repeating,—

" If I could but die—if I could but die !"

Then passing his delicate hands across his brow to part back the clustering hair, he looked in the face of the dumb animal, that again with a low whine claimed his attention.

" You love me," he cried ; " yes—yes—I know you love me, my poor dog. I found you starving in this lone house, and made a friend of you. I called you ' Joy,' because it was joy to me to find you, and I can talk to you, and fancy that you understand me as you gaze thus at me with your honest face of dumb intelligence. There are two have loved me ; you are one, my poor dumb Joy, and the—the other—I shall never—see—again—it was Albert Seyton, and he has left me— even he. Oh, Albert, if I were free as thou art, and thou wert hidden—"

Sinking his head upon his hands, again the beautiful boy burst into tears, and sobbed so bitterly that the dog howled piteously, in unison with its master's grief.

" Hush—hush, Joy, hush !" said the boy. " My faithful kind friend, if he had heard you, you would have an unkind word and a blow for this. It is weak of me to give way thus to tears, but my spirits are subdued, and my heart is nearly broken—broken—broken," he repeated.

Then suddenly starting to his feet, he stood for a few moments in a listening attitude.

" 'Tis he," he suddenly exclaimed. " Too well I know that step."

In another moment the door opened, and Jacob Gray stood on the threshold of the apartment.

His look was ferocious, and he pointed to the dog as he said, or rather growled, in an angry tone,—

" I heard that cur."

Harry laid his arm over the dog's neck, but made no answer.

" I told you," continued Gray striding into the room—" I told you that I would knock out the brains of that creature if ever I heard it bark, or even whine too loudly."

The boy held the dog tighter as Gray advanced and said,—

"Uncle, spare him this once—'twas my fault."

"Pshaw!" cried Gray, "I tell you the cur shall die."

A flush of colour came across the face of the boy as Gray spoke, and pushing the dog behind him, he drew his slim figure up to its full height, and confronted Gray with his dark, lustrous eyes, flashing with unusual brilliancy.

"Then I tell you he shall not die!" he cried firmly.

Gray for a moment quailed beneath the glance of that singularly beautiful child, and twice he tried to summon courage to meet that look of proud defiance ere he could accomplish it, then he said slowly,—

"So you are bold. How long is it since you have plucked up so much spirit?"

"From the moment that it was necessary to protect the only friend I have against your violence," replied the boy,

"Indeed!" answered Gray.

"Aye indeed!" said the boy, trembling with excitement.

"Your only friend?" continued Gray. "Humph! you think more, then, of that dog than of me?"

"The hound," said Harry, in a lower tone, "is kind, affectionate, and faithful—'tis in its way, poor thing, tender and devoted; Uncle Gray, are you all that?"

Gray laughed hysterically, as he replied,—

"Ha! ha! is that all? Have you quite summed up the virtues of your hound?"

"Its virtues," said Harry, "are much to me, for they are the only ones I have now an opportunity of noting. Its kindly instincts and dumb affection appear to me so great and estimable because I have no human ones with which to contrast them. I do love the dog, for I have nothing else to love."

"Now," cried Gray, "by hell——"

"Hold, uncle—for shame!" said Harry. "Love the dog, and the dog will love you. They never betray their masters."

A livid paleness came across Gray's face as he held by the table, and gasped,—

"Wh—what—do—you mean by that?"

"I say," repeated Harry, "that dogs never betray their masters."

"Never betray—their—their masters!" said Gray. "Oh, that is what you mean—that is all?"

"Nay, uncle, what do you mean?" said the boy, surprised at the awful and convulsive agitation of Gray.

"Mean?" echoed Gray—"what can I mean—I—I have said nothing. Recollect—I know I said nothing, I am quite sure."

"I know not the cause of your agitation," remarked Harry; "but I cannot have my poor hound injured."

"He shall die!" shrieked Gray. "Heaven nor hell shall not save him. You don't know how or why, but you have sealed his fate."

"I sealed his fate?"

"Yes, you—you, by your prating of his virtues."

"Impossible, uncle; you do but jest. This noble creature is a safe-guard to you as well as to me. Dogs have been known to famish by the murdered body of their master."

"Cease—cease!" cried Gray. "Do you want to drive me mad?"

"Mad, uncle, because dogs are faithful?"

"No more, I say. Stand aside."

"I will not forsake my dog. Joy, defend yourself."

The dog uttered a low growl, and showed rather a formidable row of glistening teeth.

"Harry," said Gray, "do you know who and what you are?"

A mantling flush colour crimsoned the pale brow of the boy, as he said,—

"You have told me."

"You know your utter dependance is upon me?"

" I know it, and I feel it."

" You are base born."

" You have not omitted to let me know that before," said the boy, proudly.

" So that, although I am your father's brother," added Gray, " you call me uncle but by courtesy."

The boy was silent, and Gray continued,—

" Stand aside, then, and baulk me not in such a matter as the life of a hound."

" No," cried Harry; " were you ten times my uncle from courtesy, you should not harm him !"

Gray clutched his hands convulsively, as if he felt an inclination to rush upon the weak, defenceless boy, and crush him in his fury. He, however, restrained himself, and said,—

" You are mad—quite mad. How can you hope for a moment to resist my will?"

" Uncle," said the boy, " I have done much to please you; I immure myself here alone with you, and you are not always kind, as you know. Once, then, rouse my suffering heart to resentment, and I will leave you but one of two resources."

" What are they?" cried Gray eagerly.

" Touch with an unkind hand my poor dumb companion here, and I will fly from window to window of this ill-omened house, shrieking for aid."

" You would?"

" Ay, would I, uncle, and you should not stop me by the other alternative."

" And what is that?"

" My murder !"

" Pshaw !" cried Gray; " you are ill, your mind is deranged. Go to rest."

" God knows I have need of rest," said the boy. " Come, Joy—come with me."

The dog followed closely upon the heels of the boy as he slowly left the room. When he had quite gone, Gray lit a lamp, and without speaking, stole into the passage and listened attentively. Then returning, he threw himself into the chair in which the boy had been sitting, and commenced a murmuring colloquy with himself.

" The sight of this young thing," he said, " always freezes my blood, and yet I dare not murder. Oh, if by some grand stroke of fortune now I could be revenged on the whole of them for the disquiet they have caused me, I think I should be happy. What am I now? Am I even calm? There was a time when I fancied gold had but to be possessed to bring joy in its train. 'Twas a great mistake. I have gold. A large sum is in my hands, and yet, by some damnable train of circumstances, I dare not use it. I must think and contrive some means of freeing myself from the shackles that bind me. Well may Learmont hand me the glittering price of my silence with a smile. 'Tis so much dross to me. I dare not for fear of my life, which I know he thirsts for, even let him know where I lay my head at night. I am still a fugitive, although rich! And—and that smith, too, is on my track like a blood-hound. If I could get a large sum from Learmont, and then dispose of this young creature I have here, I might fly to some other country and use my wealth. It must be so. More—blood—more blood—blood ! bloo—bl——"

His head dropped upon his breast, and yielding to the fatigue he had undergone and the somnolent influence of the fire, he dropped into a deep slumber by the dull red embers that still smouldered in the grate.

CHAPTER XVII.

"THE CHEQUERS," AT WESTMINST   —RRITION'S NOTIONS OF GREATNESS.—
"WHEN THE WINE IN, THE WIT IS OUT."

JACOB GRAY was quite right when he averred that the smith was on his track like a blood-hound. Britton had entered heartily into the scheme of destroying Gray. It was not that he particularly wished to appropriate to himself Gray's portion of what was wrung from the fears of Learmont, nor did he particularly see or care for the destruction of Gray as a matter of policy; but he hated him personally. His assumption of superior address was especially annoying to Britton. He felt that Gray was more than a match for him in cunning, and moreover, he despised him for the cowardice of his character, and over his cups thought it would be a rare thing to outwit Jacob Gray, which, translated, meant kill him with safety—not personal safety in the act of killing, but safety from the consequences of Gray's extreme precautionary measures for his own preservation.

The smith familiarised himself thus with the thought of overcoming the wily Jacob, and his ferocious fancy indulged itself in glutting over some violent and bloody death for the man who had presumed to assume greater address than he. By some curious train of thought, too, the smith always considered himself as personally injured by Gray, because the latter, when he visited him at the smithy, had so fenced himself round with precautions, that he, Britton, could not but see the extreme impolicy of knocking him on the head with his fore hammer, which he had fully resolved to do whenever he had an opportunity.

"Curse him!" Britton would growl over his cups, "I will have his life yet. Despite his cunning I will have his life!"

Britton's scheme of operations was more in accordance with his violent nature than any which Learmont could suggest to him. It was to dog Gray to his house, and then finding some means of admittance, either wring from his fears the secret of where he kept the written confession he talked so much of, and then kill him; or should that plan not succeed, take his life first, and trust to his powers of search to find the dangerous document somewhere in his abode.

With this project in view, Britton had kept an eye on the house of Learmont, and followed Gray upon the river, as we have seen.

Great was the rage of the smith at the utter failure of this, his first attempt to ferret out the hiding-place of Master Gray, which he began to think was by no means so easy a job as he had supposed. In fact, should Gray pursue the plan he had commenced so successfully, of turning upon his pursuer, the scheme would be fraught with the greatest difficulties. Moreover the smith could not conceal from himself that by his unsuccessful attempt he had put Gray upon his guard, which was the very last thing he should have risked. All these reflections put the smith in no very pleasant mood, when he repaired from the water-side to "The Chequers," and it was not until he had quaffed at two draughts a huge tankard of humming ale that he felt his equanimity at all restored.

He then began to swear awfully, which unburthened his mind very much, and calling for another tankard, he shouted —

"Landlord, come hither, man. Dip your red nose in the tankard."

The landlord, nothing loth, took a hearty draught of the ale, after which he smacked his lips with a knowing air, and looking intently at a fly-cage that hung from the ceiling he said in an abstracted tone,—

"This ale is splendid—glorious. I must keep it for the worshipful Master Britton's own drinking. I ought to do it—and I will do it."

"What are you muttering about?" roared the smith, taking up the empty flagon, and bestowing a hard rap with it on the landlord's head.

"Bless us!" cried the host, rubbing the afflicted part. "I—I do believe I was in deep thought."

"Deep lies you mean," cried Britton. "You'll keep the ale for me, will you?

Again the flagon touched not over gently the landlord's head, and the smith was mightily amused at the wry faces he made.

"Come—come, sit down, man," he cried, "and don't try to deceive me ; you'll keep the ale for me, will you ?"

"In a moment I will attend your worship," said the landlord, bustling off as some one knocked furiously at the little wooden bar.

"Now, by the Holy Well of Penscross, which they say was pure Rhenish wine," muttered the landlord, when he was out of hearing of the smith, "I could see that rascal hung with as much pleasure as—as—as—"

"Timothy !" screamed a female voice at this moment, which could be likened to nothing but a tin trumpet with a bad cold—"Timothy, I say."

"My wife !" said the landlord, finishing the sentence and rushing into the bar with a "here my love—here I am."

The abundance of money possessed by Britton made him perfectly welcome at "The Chequers" notwithstanding the rough nature of many of his practical jokes. The landlord lived in the full expectation of finding some day that the smith's funds were exhausted, and his object was to keep him in good humour, and put up with him so long and no longer, for the wiseacres at "The Chequers" had made up their minds that the gold which Britton spent so freely was the produce of some great robbery, and their only surprise from day to day was that they did not hear a hue and cry after Britton, with an accurate description of him appended to it.

The smith now took up the massive poker appertaining and belonging to the fire-side of "The Chequers," and commenced beating upon one of the oaken tables so lustily, that the landlord rushed into the room in wild fright and amazement, crying,

"The saints preserve us, Master Britton ! What does your worship want ?"

"Sit down," roared the smith. "Hurrah ! I'm going to treat everybody."

The landlord lifted up his hands and exclaimed, —

"Worshipful Master Britton, my humble opinion is of very little moment."

"That's true," said Britton.

"But I assert," continued the landlord, "that you ought to have been a king."

"And how do you know I ar'nt a king, eh, numskull ?" cried the smith.

"This was certainly a poser to the politic landlord, and he only muttered that he ventured to suppose he was not.

"Then you're a fool !" cried Britton, to the great amusement of the company, who had pricked up their ears wonderfully since Britton had talked of a general treat.

"The landlord's a fool !" repeated the smith, looking round the room with a half-intoxicated stare.

"So he is," cried several voices.

"No he aint," roared Britton.

"N—n—not quite a fool," said a little punchy man, with a pipe in his mouth.

"But you are !" added Britton, which at once silenced the little punchy man, who very wisely made no reply whatever.

After the applause of this sally had subsided, the landlord ventured to suggest that mugs of spiced canary all round would not be amiss to begin the evening with.

This suggestion met with universal approval, and Britton waving his hand, consented, whereupon the landlord heaved a deep sigh, and remarked, that if all the world was like him, the worshipful Master Britton, what a different world it would be to what it really was.

"Off with, you," shouted Britton. "The canary—the canary, and we'll have a song. I've got a toast, too, to propose."

The canary was not long in appearing, and Britton rising, proposed as a toast,— "Damnation to Jacob Gray !"

The landlord looked aghast. and the guests looked aghast, till the punchy man volunteered his opinion in the following terms,—

" Gentlemen, we don't know Jacob Gray, but there can be no doubt he's a very bad man—(Hear, hear.) Master Britton stands spiced canary all round, and, consequently, it's my humble opinion it must be right."

The topers looked at each other in amazement at this splendid piece of reasoning ; and one remarked that he, the punchy man, was the person to get over a knotty point, which was universally responded to in the affirmative, and the toast was drunk with acclamation.

" A song," cried Britton—" a song."

The landlord looked imploringly round him for some one to sing, but no one seemed inclined, therefore he said,—

" The worshipful Master Britton calls for a song, and there must be a song."

" Of course," cried Britton, " and you must sing it."

The landlord hemmed thrice, and after taking a deep draught of the canary, he fixed his eyes on the fly-cage hanging from the ceiling, and chaunted the following Bacchanalian strains,—

> " Care mantles not in brimming cups,
>   It cannot enter there ;
> Within the bowl there's nought but joy,
>   Without, but grim despair.
>
>   Hurrah, boys !
>
> " Care shuns the wine cup, boys—for why ?
>   Because its blushing hue
> Forbids the fiend to enter there,
>   Lest he be lost to view.
>
>   Hurrah, boys !
>
> " Drink—drink, and let the gushing stream
>   Of life boil through our veins,
> While sober fools seek chill content,
>   And find care for their pains.
>
>   Hurrah, boys !
>
> " They lie who say that rosy wine
>   Can ever breed a pain,
> For when the joy of one day's o'er,
>   We drink and live again.
>
>   Hurrah, boys !
>
> " They tell us that when once the fire
>   Of wine has gone away,
> Our hearts will beat in dull despair,
>   Nor be so calm as they.
>
>   Hurrah, boys !
>
> " But we a cure for such an ill
>   Can find in every glass ;
> And, boys, we know that life is short,
>   Catch pleasure ere it pass.
>
>   Hurrah, boys !"

" Bravo !" cried Britton. " That's good—mind, that's good."

" Very good, indeed," cried everybody.

" Hurrah !" shouted the inebriated smith—" Hurrah ! boys. Three—ch—ch—cheers. I—I say—I—I'm a k—k—king !"

After an ineffectual attempt to stand, he dropped on the floor in a state of unconsciousness.

CHAPTER XVIII.

THE LONE MAN.—THE VOICE OF CONSCIENCE.

ALONE, and still, as a sculptured image, sat the 'Squire Learmont, in one of his stately halls. He was surrounded by magnificence, but he was alone. The closely-fitting casements admitted, but in subdued murmurs, the various voices of the city, but there was no one, save himself, to enjoy the luxury of the calm that reigned in that gilt and gaudy saloon. The choicest hangings depended from the

walls, half concealing, yet rendering more effective, the glowing paintings that were hung in the most favourable lights; but Learmont was alone. A chandelier, shaded by coloured glasses, shed a sweet and chastened light upon every article in that costly room, but who was there to admire, to gaze in rapture upon the splendour of that magical scene? Learmont was alone, and the deep sense of his

No. 7.

utter loneliness crept across him with a chilling influence that seemed to penetrate even to the very marrow in his bones.

How many, in the selfish pride of their hearts, suppose it possible to extract joy from merely selfish pleasures! How many have cast from them all the endearing associations of kindred and fellowship to wrap themselves up, as it were, in their own hearts that they might share no delight with another, imagining that they might, by such a process, concentrate in themselves all the diffused happiness of many. This has been the dreary delusions of many, but a time has come when all have awakened to the truth that man must borrow his greatest joy from the reflected happiness of others. To such a mind as Learmont's, this immutable and holy truth was long in coming, but now as he sat alone in his princely hall, surrounded with light and splendour, he would have felt relieved could he have turned to any one upon whose countenance he could have read with pleasure and delight—aye, the veriest beggar that ever asked for alms of rich and proud, would, at that moment, have been welcome, for Learmont's very heart felt lonely and desolate. Did he enjoy the exquisite covering of that lofty ceiling? Did he exult over the rich gilding which lay like plates of massive gold on the elaborate cornices? Did the soft, beautiful light, which seemed in its rare excellence to belong to the sunrise of a better world, fall upon his heart with joyful brilliancy? Alas, no! he was alone! the first proud flush of gratified pride, in having created, and being the master of all this, had died away and left behind it but a sensation of loneliness and desolation of spirit, such as he had never before experienced.

In vain the Lord of Learmont battled with his own feelings. They would not be resisted; and, at length, half mad with the mental struggle he was enduring, he rose from the chair on which he had been sitting, and stood up to his full height, in the centre of the saloon, while one deep groan burst from his heart, sounding strangely awful in the midst of all that glitter and display.

Then his dark eye flashed fire, and he made a great effort to rouse himself from the deep dejection that had stolen over him.

"What have I striven for?" he cried. "What dipped my hands in blood for, but for all this? This pride of wealth—this glory of magnificence—and does it now pall upon my senses? Can I not enjoy what I have striven so hard to obtain? Away, vain shadows of remorse—born in superstition, and fostered by prejudice —away—I will—I must enjoy what I have wasted the better part of life to obtain. My gilded saloons, I love you—my house—my retinue—my jewels—all are what men struggle for, even to the grave's brink, because the universal opinion of mankind has proclaimed, that to have these things is to have the means of happiness. I have them; and yet what serpent is it that now gnaws at my heart, and forbids the enjoyment of what is mine own? There is, perhaps, too much silence in my glorious house. I must fill my saloons with the young and the beautiful. I must have joy reflected on my own face from the sparkling eyes of beauty. I—I will not be alone!—no—no. I will be seldom alone! 'tis the silence of this spacious hall has bred and nursed gloomy fancies in my brains. I was foolish to sit here—because I was alone."

His voice sounded hollow and distinct in the large space around him, and the word "alone" seemed to catch some strange echo in the saloon, and to be whispered back to him from the high ceiling, with a mournful tone.

'Squire Learmont paused, and a sneer curled his lips, as he said,

"Now, were I weak and superstitious, how well could busy fancy people this large space with grinning gliding shapes, such as haunt ordinary men and drive their weak brains to distraction. I hear yon echo, but I will not be alone. Ha! ha! 'tis your concave roof that throws back my words. Now if, as I say, I were superstitious—but I am not."

Even as he spoke, he repeatedly turned to look behind, and it was evident that the guilty man was battling with his fears.

"This hall," he continued, "is very large—and—and cold withal. I will make some smaller room suffice me."

He rang for a domestic, and, in spite of himself, he could not help averring to his own heart, that it was a relief to see the face of a human being in his magnificent solitude.

"Light up the small room with the yellow hanging," said Learmont, "I will sit there."

The servant bowed and retired.

"Yes," continued Learmont, in a low tone, as he seated himself in a chair, the back of which touched the wall. "A smaller room to sit in is more agreeable and much warmer than this saloon." He would not own to himself that the large space around him had frightened him, and that he was really trembling with a terror of, he knew not what—such an awful terror as commonly creeps over the hearts of the guilty in solitudes.

In a very few moments the servant returned and announced the smaller room as ready for his master's reception.

Then preceding him, with two wax lights, he showed the trembling 'Squire into a room of about one-third of the size of the saloon, and which was furnished more plainly, but quite as richly as regarded the costly nature of its hangings and various appointments.

Oh, let the innocent of heart and single of purpose lift their eyes to Heaven, and thank it for their great happiness. Let those who can challenge their deepest memories, to picture to the mental vision one deed of wrong, lie down in blessed repose, for they are rich beyond the wealth of kings—powerful beyond the power of the mightiest conquerors—happy beyond any happiness that this world can afford, as the price of that peace of mind, which so many barter for a bauble.

It was not the extent of his saloon, that had come across the soul of the crime-steeped Learmont, with a shuddering horror. It was not that his voice echoed in his lofty house. It was the undying worm, conscience; that takes no rest, knows no peace, but will be heard amid the din of battle—the hilarity of the banquet—that will float upon the wine-cup—mingle with every strain of noise, and make a hell of the human heart more maddening than the wildest fanatic can promise to the wicked.

Learmont could not sit—he could not rest—the air around him seemed thick and heavy—his first impulse was to ring for more lights, and more were brought—more and more, until the apartment was one blaze of illuminations; but all was in vain, and just before the midnight hour sounded from the various churches, the lord of all the beauty and magnificence of that costly mansion seized a hat and cloak, and rushed into the streets to seek relief by violent exercise from the agony that tortured him.

Without aim or object, save the one of endeavouring, by sheer bodily fatigue, to seek repose for the overwrought mind, Learmont walked onwards through the various streets that happened to present themselves at convenient junctures to his notice, and as he walked with a quick step, he muttered to himself the anxious reasoning that was crossing his fevered brain.

"I will never be alone!" he muttered; "never—never. Why should I be alone?—I who am revelling in wealth? From this moment I resolve to cram my saloons. The brilliant decorations of my home shall be admired by all; I will move amidst a throng of youth, beauty, and nobility, as the presiding genius of a place which shall be little short of a fairy palace of romance and beauty. I—I will intrigue with the intriguing—quaff goblets of rich wine with the voluptuous. Ha! ha!—I will lead a life of enjoyment that shall leave no time for thought. I will have pleasure after pleasure—excitement after excitement, succeeding each other with such rapidity that they shall only occasionally cease when the wearied frame calls loudly for repose, that it may awaken with renovated strength to undergo a routine of new pleasure!—I will never be alone!"

He walked on now for many minutes, only now and then muttering the words "Never alone!" Then a new train of thought seemed to come across his mind, and he whispered :—

"These two men, this Britton and the crafty Gray! they, indeed, are thorns among the flowers with which I would surround myself. If either could but safely destroy the other, I could then find an opportunity of getting rid of the survivor. My deepest hatred light on Gray! May the curses——pshaw! what boots it that I curse him?—I must have his blood! 'Tis he, and he only, who by his craft preserves his own life, and teaches Britton how to preserve his. What devil whispered to the villain to write a confession of his crimes for his own preservation? Time was when a master-spirit such as mine could with small pains rid himself of the base lowly tools with which he built his fortune and his fame. The grave closed over the hateful secrets that embittered the road to power and greatness, leaving that power and greatness, when once achieved, undermined by the black shadows of the past. Unbounded wealth is at my command—a crouching herd at my feet, because I am the master of the yellow dross for which mankind will barter Heaven! And—and yet I—even i am to be haunted by two ruffians, who with a subtlety undreamt of, have hedged themselves in with precautions. By hell, I will not—cannot bear it!—I'll pluck these papers from their very hearts, if they should hide them there!—I will no longer be scared by this awful phantom of fear that shadows my heart!—They shall die!"

———

CHAPTER XIX.

LEARMONT'S ADVENTURE.—A DISCOVERY.—THE HAUNTED HOUSE.—EXULTATION, AND A RESOLUTION.

IN the wild excitement of his passions, Learmont had walked onwards, heedless of whither he was going, and now that he had in some measure found the relief he sought for in fatigue, he glared anxiously round to find if possible what part of the town he had strayed to in his deep abstraction.

The night was very dark, not a star peeped forth from heaven to light with its small twinkling lustre the massive black arch of the firmament. No moon shed its silvery radiance on the gigantic city;—a darkness, so intense that sky, houses, trees,—all seemed merged into one chaotic mass.

" Where should I be?" muttered Learmont; " I must have walked far, for I am weary. Ha! is that the hour?"

The clock of St. Paul's struck three as he spoke, and from the direction of the sound, Learmont guessed that he was somewhere southward of that edifice.

"Some chance passenger," he muttered, "will direct me to Westminster; yet I hear no footfall in these silent streets. How still and solemn now is the great city; one might imagine it a vast cemetery, in which the dead alone dwelt."

He paced slowly down a long straggling street, and his own footsteps were the only sounds that disturbed the solemn stillness that reigned around.

Learmont walked on slowly, for he knew not but he might be in some dangerous quarter of the city, and his suspicions that the locality in which he was did not possess any great claims to fashion or respectability, were much increased by a door suddenly opening in a house some dozen yards in advance of him, and a man being flung from it with considerable force into the centre of the street, while a loud voice exclaimed :—

" Go to the devil, an' you will. Are we to sit up all night to attend to one sot? No, that will never suit the Old Mitre; an' there were a round dozen of you, we might think of it."

" It's d—damned ill-usage," remonstrated the man who had been turned out so unceremoniously from what appeared to Learmont a little tavern, and the door of which was immediately flung close, and barred from within.

" That's the—the way of the world," remarked the drunken man, as he slowly gathered himself up on his feet, and shook his head with tipsy gravity. " There's no such thing as—as consideration in the world, and the street even is turning round—and round in a most ex—ex—extra—ordinary manner. That's how I never can get home prop—properly. The streets keep a moving in that ex—ex—extraordinary manner;—that end comes round to this end—and that's how I'm led astray. It's too bad—it is indeed; it's enough to—to make one weep, it is. But no matter, I—always suffer;—I am a ex—ex—a double extraordinary man, and a greatly injured character."

The drunkard had evidently reached the sentimental stage of intoxication, and he staggered along weeping and lamenting alternately.

"I may gather from this sot some information of where I am," thought Learmont, and in an instant he strided after the reeling man.

When he reached him he touched him on the shoulder, and said,—

"My friend, can you tell me where I am?"

"Eh?—pon my w—w—word, that's a funny question. Why, you—you've just been turned out of the Mitre."

"Pho! pho!" cried Learmont, impatiently. "Can you tell me what part of the town we are in?"

"The o—open air, of course," replied the man. "Hurrah! that's my opinion. My opinion's hurrah! and all I mean to say is, if somebody else—no, that isn't it—if I didn't take somebody else's job—no, that aint it."

"What do you mean?" said Learmont.

"I'll do it—I'll do it, I tell you."

"Do what?"

"Do what? Come, that's good of you. You know what. All I mean to say is, that if somebody else is to do it, why I am sure nobody—no, that isn't it either. How very ex—ex—extraordinary!"

"Idiot!" exclaimed Learmont, striding away; but the man called after him, and his voice echoed through the deserted street, as he said,—

"Don't be—be—offended. I'll do it, I tell you. No, no—nonsense, now. I know you—mind I—know you: it's only a mur—murder! Ah! ah!"

Learmont paused in astonishment, not altogether unmingled with dismay, at these words, and he was by the man's side again in a moment.

"You know me?" he said.

"Yes, yes, I believe you," replied the man. "I'll do it."

"What can this mean?" thought Learmont; then he said, aloud,—

"Who am I—you say you know me?"

"You—you didn't think it," said the man, with much drunken cunning; "but I watched you home."

"You watched me home?"

"Yes,—to be sure. Don't be frightened; I—I saw you go in. Oh! oh!"

"Indeed!" said Learmont, who was determined to humour his singular companion.

"Yes, I believe you. I—I thought you'd be surprised; and so you are: it's ex—extraordinary, aint it?"

"Oh! very."

"Well, I'll do it—you recollect my name?"

"Perfectly."

"Of course you do. Sheldon, you know."

"Sheldon is your name?"

"Yes, you know. There isn't a waterman on the river as—as—can drink like me."

"You are a waterman, then?"

"You—know I am."

"Of course. Oh, yes, of course I do," said Learmont.

"Well then, you know—I—can keep my own counsel—it's extra—extraordinary how clever I—am."

"Quite remarkable."

"Well—I—I—watched—you home, and I heard you—a talking to—the—boy—'

"The boy?"

"Yes. You keep him shut up — in the haunted—house—oh! oh!—I've watched you—you—see."

"The boy?" repeated Learmont.

"Yes, yes, the boy. I climbed up at the back of—of the old house, you see."

"Yes, yes," said Learmont, eagerly, "and you saw—"

"Nothing."

"Nothing?"

"D—d—damned a thing—but I heard you—"

"And—the boy? You heard the boy? A boy's voice?"

"No, I didn't."

"You said so."

"No, I didn't—don't in—in—insult me!"

"My good friend, I would not insult you on any consideration. I am mistaken—I thought you said you heard a boy's voice."

"The—the—then—you thought wrong."

"Exactly."

"You are—a—f—f—fool—a ex—extraordinary fool."

"Well," said Learmont, in an oily voice, "you *saw* the boy?"

"Ah, now," cried his drunken companion, "now you have hit it. I'll just tell you how—I—I cir—circum—navi—no, that aint it, circum—*ventated* you."

"Do," said Learmont. "You are exceedingly clever."

"I know it. Well, I heard you talking to some one, and I went from window to window to try to see in, you know, and at one of 'em I saw him."

"The boy?"

"Yes—to—to be sure."

"Did you hear him speak?"

"I—I believe you—".

"Well—well."

"Says he, in a mournful kind o' way, says he,—what do you think now?"

"Really, I cannot tell."

"Oh, but it's ex—extraordinary, because you see that's how I—I found out your name, you see."

"My name, Master Sheldon?"

"Yes, your name."

"No, you don't know it. You cannot know it."

"N—n—not know it?"

"Well, what is it, then, if you do know it?"

"Gray, to be sure."

"Gray!" cried Learmont, with so sharp a cry, that the man jumped again, and would have fallen had not Learmont clutched him tightly by the arm.

"Ye—ye—yes," stammered the drunken man, in whom the reader has already recognised Sheldon, the waterman, to whom Gray had proposed the murder of Britton.

"You are sure? on your life—on your soul, you are sure the name was Gray?"

The man looked in the countenance of Learmont, as well as the darkness would permit him, and answered, not without evident trepidation,—

"Gray—yes—Gray—it—it was. I shouldn't have known it—but, you see, the boy stopped at the window to cry—"

"To cry?—well—and then?"

"Then, he said, ' Can this man, Gray, really be of my kindred? Do we think alike?' says he, ' do we'—now, hang me, if I recollect what he said."

"Ha, ha, ha!" suddenly laughed Learmont. "You are brave and acute. Ha, ha! you have found me out, I see. I am Gray. Ha, ha!"

"I—I—beg—your pardon, Mister Gray," hiccupped the man, "but was that y—y—you that laughed in that odd way? Eh?"

"I laughed," said Learmont.

"Then—d—don't do it again. It's the most uncom—com—comfortable sort o' laugh I ever heard; an ex—ex—extraordinary laugh."

"Good master a—a—"

"Sheldon," said the man.

"Ay, Sheldon," resumed Learmont. "I will have no secrets from you. You shall come home with me. You know the way?"

"Of—of—course I do."

"Then, come on," cried Learmont, with difficulty concealing his exultations at the chance that had thus thrown in his way a guide to Gray's house.

"Ay, you—you're right," said the waterman. "Come on—come on. We'll have a cup together."

"Ha, ha!" cried Learmont, "we will."

"Now didn't I tell you," said Sheldon, with drunken gravity, marking off each word on his fingers, and making the most ludicrous efforts to speak very clear and distinct, "didn't—I tell—you—to—keep—those laughs—to yourself?"

"You did," said Learmont; "but I forget. Come on, we will have brimming cups."

"Hurrah for everybody!" cried Sheldon. "We — we are jolly—fellows. Hurrah!

'Hurrah! hurrah for the vine,
    When its sparkling bubbles rise,
Call it divine—divine,
    For God's a dainty prize.

Hurrah!'"

"By heavens, a brave ditty," said Learmont, "and well sung. You are an Apollo, Sheldon, with a little mixture of Bacchus."

"D—d—don't insult me," cried Sheldon. "I—I won't bear it, Master G—Gray."

"Not for worlds," muttered Learmont.

"Eh?" cried Sheldon, "was that you?"

"What do you mean?"

"Mean? why—I—I—heard an uncommon odd voice say, 'N—n—not for worlds.'"

"'Twas some echo, my good friend. Is this the turning?"

"Oh! ah!" laughed the waterman. "Now that is good. Is—is—is this the turning—and—you going—have—ho! ho! you know it's the turning—perhaps you want to in—in—sinuate that I'm drunk?"

"Certainly not," replied Learmont. "I was only surprised at your amazing knowledge of the road. I only meant to try you, good Master Sheldon."

"Try me? try me? I—I know every inch of the road—i—follow me, and I'll take you to your own door."

"Is it possible?"

"Come on and see. Follow, I—say—follow."

"I will," cried Learmont, his dark eyes flashing with unholy fire, as he thought how gigantic a step towards the accomplishment of Gray's destruction would be the knowledge, unknown to him, of his secret abode.

Cautiously he followed the devious track of the drunken man, who, with mock gravity, marched onwards to show the way. "Now, Jacob Gray," he thought, "you are in my grasp; you shall die—die—some death of horror which in its bitter pangs shall give you some taste of the heart-sickness you have given me."

CHAPTER XX.

THE GUIDE.—THE OLD HOUSE.—THE MURDER.

Sheldon continued singing snatches of rude songs, and staggering onwards, while Learmont followed closely upon his heels, and judiciously kept up a conversation with him that prevented him from giving any further thought on the object of his present undertaking.

It was strictly true what Sheldon had stated. After landing Jacob Gray, he had left his boat in charge of one of the idlers who are always plying on the banks of the river, and cautiously dogged his customer home. This was a circumstance which it had never for one moment entered into even Gray's over-suspicious imagination to conceive. He had, as he felt well assured, scared Britton from pursuing him for that time at least; and he fancied himself, therefore, quite free. Hence was it that the waterman, who wished to know something more of the man who had made to him a proposal amounting to murder, succeeded in so successfully following Jacob Gray.

At that period the Thames was infested with the worst of characters, and scarcely any proposition, let it involve what measure of guilt it might, could be made in vain to many of the desperadoes who were ostensibly watermen, but really robbers and cut-throats of the vilest description. That Sheldon was a man not tortured with many virtuous scruples, the reader will readily conceive; but he *did* shrink from the cold-blooded murder so calmly proposed to him by Gray, and he felt well inclined to sell that gentleman to justice, only he was very anxious to have a good price for his virtue, for Master Sheldon was fond of sack, doted on canary, and idolised all manner of strong drinks; so that a good reward in gold pieces for *not* doing a decidedly disagreeable job, presented itself to his mind in lovely and agreeable colours. So elated had he been with the bare supposition of such an event, that instead of going back to the stairs at which he had left his wherry, he had repaired to the "Mitre," and tasted so many different enticing and delicious compounds, that, as the reader is aware, the calculating and considerate landlord was compelled to turn him out at three o'clock in the morning, because, being only one drunkard, he was not worth attending to any longer.

With eager steps Learmont followed his guide till they came to the range of miserable habitations, in one of which Jacob Gray had concealed himself and his precious charge.

"Ah," said Learmont, "I begin to think you do indeed know the way."

"Know the way!" cried Sheldon—"I could find it blindfold. Come on, I—I'll take you to your own door."

"What astonishing acuteness!" remarked Learmont.

"Yes," said Sheldon, wonderfully flattered. "I—I believe you there, Master Gray. You are no fool yourself, because you—you see you've found out how ex---ex—extraordinary clever I am—you see."

"Exactly," cried Learmont. "This is a lonely district."

"Here you are—ah! ah!" laughed Sheldon. "I—I know it—this is the house. Bless you, I know it by the painted windows."

Learmont walked to the middle of the roadway, and by the dim morning light, which was just beginning to shed a faint colour across the dusky sky, he gazed earnestly at the ancient building, in which he had no doubt were the objects of his hatred and dread.

"Well," said Sheldon, "aint—aint you going to ask a fellow in, just to take a drop o' something?"

Learmont heard him not, or if he did, he heeded him not, but stood intently gazing at the house, and treasuring up in his memory every little peculiarity he could by the faint light detect, in order that he might again recognise it without doubt or difficulty.

"Hilloa!" cried Sheldon. "What are you staring at--d--d—did you never see your own house before?"

Learmont started, and advancing to Sheldon, he laid his hand upon his shoulder saying,—

"My good friend, in that house I have not one drop of liquor, good or bad, to ffer you."

"The d—d—devil you haven't," said the waterman.

"Not a drain; but if you will walk with me till we come to some really

good hostel, I will make you the partaker of the value of a couple of gold pieces melted down into humming ale, spiced canary, sack, or choice Rhenish—ay, what you will you shall have, if you will now take my arm, and let me be your guide."

"You—you are the prince of good fellows," cried Sheldon, " d—d—damme you are—humming ale, did you say?"

"Certainly, such as will be music in your ears."

"And—and spiced canary?"

No. 8.

" Even so ; deep draughts that will shut the world from your eyes and your thoughts."

"Sack---s---sack, and Rhenish too ? "

" All—all. You shall steep your senses in delight, drown your soul in a delirium of pleasure.   Come on—come on, good Master Sheldon—do you not see the morning is breaking ? "

" D—d—d—n it, let it break.   I mean to say that you are my best friend. Bless you---I aint a-going to cry---no---no."

"Come—come, say no more—say no more."

Learmont took the arm of the waterman, who was rapidly becoming sentimental again, and, passing it through his own, he led him away from Gray's house at a quick pace.

The morning light was now each moment increasing, and Learmont did not fail to note every particular building he passed, in order that, when he came again, he should need no guide.

Suddenly, as they turned the corner of a street, they came in sight of the square tower of the Bishop's Palace, at Lambeth, and as Learmont knew that well, he felt quite assured that he could from that, as a land-mark, walk with certainty to the house of Jacob Gray.

He now threw his whole thoughts into a consideration of what was to be done with his intoxicated companion.   That he had been in some sort of communication with Jacob Gray he could not doubt, and moreover, he shrewdly suspected that the destruction of Britton was the object hinted at by Sheldon—that, however, was a far inferior object in Learmont's mind to the destruction of Gray himself, and the possession of the boy he held in his power.   Therefore was it that Learmont fell into a train of anxious and horrid thoughts as to whether Sheldon after he had left him might not, by his relation of having brought some one to his secret abode, alarm the cautious Jacob Gray into an immediate removal, and so baffle him, Learmont, again.

If there be any crime more awful than another, it is a cool and deliberate murder founded upon calculation ; but Learmont was just the man to commit such an act, and while the thoughtless Sheldon was hanging upon his arm and murmuring disjointed snatches of songs in praise of good fellowship and glorious wine, Learmont half resolved upon his death.

" This drunken idiot can be of no use to me," he reasoned with himself, " because I could never depend upon him ; but he may, if I let him escape, warn Gray, and I lose the rare chance that kind Fortune has thrown so strangely in my way.   He must die."

They now passed the ancient entrance to the Bishop's Palace, and entered upon the well-known walk along the banks of the Thames, which was then much more shadowed by lofty trees than it is at present ; and although those trees, in consequence of the season of the year, were now leafless, yet their gigantic trunks cast broad and obscuring shadows between them and the wall of the Bishop's garden.

A cold piercing air blew from the Thames, and Sheldon shuddered as he remarked,—

" I say—my—my good fellow, the—sooner we get to some place where we can have this same ale, and—and sack—and Rhenish—the better—on my faith it's c—c—cold."

" Come this way, close to the palace wall," said Learmont, " and the old trees will save us from the cool air that blows across the river."

So saying, he led his doomed companion close to the ancient wall, then he paused and listened attentively, in case any one should be within hearing ; all was as still as the grave—not the most distant sound indicative of human life, met his ears.

" He must die !" muttered Learmont.

"You may say it's cold," remarked Sheldon ; " w—w—what are you waiting for—

> " Ha ! ha ! ha ! who would not drink
> When the cup is brimming over,
> Be it Rhenish—be it—sack—
> Or burning old—Oc—Oc—October !

that's a—b—b—brave song—a ex—extraordinary brave song—a—w—w—wonderful song."

Learmont laid his hand on his sword as he said—

"There is more light now, Master Sheldon. Look at me."

As he spoke he raised his cap, which previously had been drawn close over his eyes, and raised himself to his full gaunt height.

The waterman fixed his wondering eyes upon him, and muttered :—

" I—I—think—you—you aint Master Gray."

" Do you know me ?" cried Learmont, fiercely.

The man trembled and seemed all at once half-sobered by terror as he stammered—

" I—I—have seen—"

" Seen what ?—who ?"

" Your worship at Westminster."

" Ah ! My name—know you that?"

" They called you 'Squire Learmont."

Learmont suddenly turned his back upon Sheldon, and casting an anxious glance around him to satisfy himself that they were still alone, he suddenly drew his sword and faced the trembling man.

" Mercy ! mercy !" cried Sheldon, dropping on his knees.

" Idiot !" cried Learmont, " you are in my way. Curses on your worthless life !"

" Oh, God, mercy !" cried the man.

Learmont shortened his arm, and plunged his sword through the body of the defenceless man.

With a wild shriek that rung through the Bishop's-walk, Sheldon sprang from his knees ; he grasped wildly at the air, and spun round and round in his frantic efforts to stand.

" Help ! help ! murder !" he shrieked.

" Damnation !" cried Learmont, and again he passed his reeking sword through the heaving chest of Sheldon.

Again the wounded man tried to speak, but a low, gurgling sound in his throat was all he could produce, and he fell with a deep groan at the feet of the murderer.

CHAPTER XXI.

A SUNNY MORNING.—THE CHAMBER IN THE OLD HOUSE.

THE morning gathered each moment strength and beauty, for it was beautiful, although the trees were stripped of their summer verdure, and the earth no longer sent forth sweet flowers to

> ———— " Load with perfumes
> The soft dreaming idle air
> That steeped in sunshines.
> Music, and all dear delight,
> Hung tranquilly 'twixt heaven and earth,"

The sun, however, was bright, and the air, although the soft voluptuous warmth of summer, was full of health and life. The little waves on the river sparkled like silver broken into fragments and strewed upon the surface of the stream. For miles the clear cloudless sky reflected nothing but pure sunshine, beautiful although cold; it shone upon the palaces, the churches, and the bridges, and upon the meanest hovels pregnant with squalid proverty; it shone upon all alike. It found its way in floods of beauty, softened by rich colouring of glass and drapery, into the chambers of the rich and great, and it struggled through the dingy panes of the cottage windows, making, perchance, more happiness there than in the lordly mansion, which more frequently is the habitation of an aching heart.

There was one small room into which that clear morning sun shone in all its dearly-welcomed beauty, and there was one heart that was cheered by its presence, and smiled gladly in its radiant light; that room into which it shone was the sleeping chamber of the young boy, Harry, and that heart that welcomed its rays was his—a heart that ever beat in unison with all that was good—all that was beautiful.

The apartment was a small one adjoining a spacious room that was on the second floor of the house, and communicating with it by folding doors. It contained little else than a small couch and a few necessary articles of the toilette. A large mat lay at the door, on which reposed the dog, which was poor Harry's only companion—his only friend.

The boy was up and leaning upon the window-sill, gazing earnestly through a small chink that was left in the beading (for the window was blocked up from without) which enabled him to see, and without danger of being observed by any one in the street, and likewise was quite of sufficient width to allow the morning sun to stream into the little room.

With a deep sigh he turned from the window, and the dog at the same moment rose, and with grateful gestures approached its kind master.

"The sun is shining, my poor Joy," said Harry, mournfully; "but you and I may not gambol in its beams. The world without this gloomy house seems bright and beautiful, but we are prisoners. 'Tis very, very strange; Gray tells me he is my uncle, and that there is a fearful secret connected with the family that forces him to shut himself and me up in this mysterious manner. Uncle Gray, I doubt you. Such a tale might suit the ears of a child, but—I—I am one no longer. Can this man be my uncle? His behaviour is so strange to me, alternately harsh and kind, affectionate and cruel. Alas! I know not what to think. Oh, how my heart yearns for the bright sunshine, the open sky, and the green fields! How long am I to be thus immured? Heaven only knows. I—will—I must seek some other explanation. I know he fears me. I have seen him shrink before my eyes. I have marked him tremble and turn pale at a chance word I uttered, and yet I had no clue to such feelings, because I knew not which word it was that moved him so; and this disguise, too, which he persuades, begs, implores of me to wear, as he says, for my life's sake; 'tis very strange. These are not the garments of a young maiden as I am. What have I done that I should thus forswear sex, liberty, sunshine, joy, all that makes life rich and beautiful to the young? Alas! alas! what have I done to be a dreary prisoner? In all my weary years, short, but oh, how long to me! but one face beamed with kindness on me, that face was Albert Seyton's; but one voice spoke to me in accents of love and pity—that voice was Albert Seyton's; but one heart seemed ever to really feel for me a pang of sorrow, and—and—that heart was Albert Seyton's."

The young girl, for such she was, sunk into a chair and wept bitterly. Then suddenly dashing aside the tears that obscured her beautiful eyes, she said,—

"No—no, I will not weep. No, uncle Gray, if such you be, you shall not wring another tear from me. You have made me a lonely being; you have been harsh, unkind—nay, you have struck me; but you shall not see me weep, no—no, I will not let you see a tear. You have torn me from the young heart that in my solitude found me and loved me as an orphan boy, supposing me such. Oh, uncle—uncle, you are cruel! Another day shall not pass without an explanation with you, uncle Gray. I—I—will have reasons—ample reasons—full explanations from thee. And he wanted to kill my poor dog, too, because it loved me—because I had found some living thing that looked fondly in my face. Oh, uncle! uncle! you have raised a spirit in my breast—a spirit of resistance and opposition, that in happier circumstances would have slumbered for ever."

For a few minutes the young girl stood in deep thought, then, with a remarkable alteration of tone and manner, she said, snddenly,—

" Come, Joy, come ; we will go to *uncle* Gray, our breakfast should be waiting."

She opened the door which led into the larger room, and crossing that, closely followed by the dog, passed out of it by another door that opened upon the staircase. Slowly, then, she descended the creaking, time-worn steps, and pushing open a small door at their feet, entered the room which has already been described to the reader, and in which we last left Jacob Gray.

Gray was in the room, and he cast a suspicious glance at the young creature who entered the room, as if he would read from her countenance in what mood she was in that morning.

" Oh," he said, " you have risen early, Harry, and—and Joy, too, is with you—poor dog!"

Joy's only answer to this hypocritical pity was a low growl, and getting under a chair, he exhibited a formidable mouthful of teeth as a warning to Jacob Gray not to attempt any familiarity.

" Do not call me Harry," cried the girl, " you know it is not a fitting name for me, *uncle*."

Gray's face assumed a paler shade, as he replied, in a low tone,—

" Wherefore this sudden passion—eh ?"

" Uncle Gray, I have been thinking—"

" Thinking of what, child ?"

" Call me child no more," replied the girl, pushing the dark ringlets from her brow, and gazing steadily at Gray. " Call me child no more, uncle Gray, and to prove to you that I am something more, I tell you now that the poor tale that frightened the child will not now do for me."

" W—w—what do you mean ?" gasped Gray, his lips trembling with ghastly fear.

" I mean," continued the other, " that the time has come when I must know all. Who am I—my name—my lineage—my friends— kindred—where, and who are they? Why am I here an innocent victim to the crimes, perchance, of others? The reasons of this solitary confinement, its duration, the circumstances that would rescue me from it—this—all this I want to know fully—amply, and I must know it, *uncle* Gray."

To describe the wild stare of astonishment and dismay that sat upon the face of Jacob, as the fragile and beautiful creature before him poured forth with earnest firmness this torrent of questions, would be impossible : rage, fear, dismay, all seemed struggling for mastery in Gray's countenance, and the girl had done, and stood in an attitude that a sculptor might have envied, bending half forward with a flush of excitement upon her cheeks, awaiting the answer of the panic-stricken man before her. It was several minutes before that answer came. Once, twice, thrice, did Jacob Gray try to speak in vain, and when he did produce an articulate sound, his voice was hollow and awful to hear.

" W—what devil," he said, " has prompted you to this? what busy fiend has whispered in your ears? Speak—speak !"

" I have spoken," said the girl. " I ask but that I have the right to know."

" The right ! How know you that ?"

" How know I that ! My heart tells me. 'Tis a right of nature, born with the lowest, and no greater with the highest."

" Then—you would destroy me !"

" No, I would destroy no one ; give no one even a passing pang ; but oh ! uncle, I am young, and life is new and precious. I have read of sunny skies, and smiling happy flowers; I have read of music's witchery, until my heart has sighed to create its own dear melody. I have read of love, pure, holy love, such as could knit together young hearts for ever in a sweet companionship; and oh! how my heart has yearned for the sunlight, the flowers, the music, the sweet murmuring sound of moving waters, the dear love that gilds them all with more than earthly beauty, because it, and it alone, is the one gift that clings yet to man from Heaven! How my heart has leaped upwards, like a living thing, to read of kind words softly spoken, of purest vows breathed from heart to heart, making as it were sweet music, and its still sweeter echo! Oh! how I have clasped my hands and cried aloud for music, to shroud in its elysium a sound, filling the sunny air with a mild embroidery of tones! I have asked of Heaven to send me warm hearts to love me; to place me on the mountains, that I may look around me and adore the God that made the valleys look so beautiful! I have prayed to wander through the verdant valleys, that I might look up to the mountains, so lifting my thoughts to the great Creator. I have wept—sobbed aloud for all the dear companionships of youth—the thousand sparkling, glowing charms that lend life its romance, and make the world an Eden, Heaven a dear inheritance! The dreary echo of my own voice alone has answered me! My own deep sobs have come back to my ears in endless mockery, and I was alone; a chill would then gather round my heart, for I was alone! The smile of a father never—never gladdened my heart! A mother's gentle kiss never rested on my brow! I—I am a lonely thing; a blight and a desolation is around me; no—no one loves me!"

To describe the exquisite intonation of voice with which these words were uttered would be impossible. The gushing tenderness, the deep pathos, the glowing tones! Oh, what must be the construction of that heart that could listen unmoved to such an appeal? Gray trembled like an aspen leaf, his eyes glared from their sockets, and he stretched out his hands before him as he would keep off some spectre that blasted his sight, and seared his very brain.

"Peace! peace!" he shrieked; "peace! You want to—kill me, to drive me mad; but that voice—that manner—those speaking eyes!—Peace, ADA, peace, I say!"

"ADA!" cried the girl; "that, then, is my name?"

"No, no, no, no!" cried Gray. "God of Heaven!—no, no, no, no!—I—did not say Ada?"

"You did, and something tells me that it is my name—the name you have concealed from me so long. I am Ada. Uncle, some strong passion, some awful fear at your heart overcame your caution. I am Ada; but Ada what? Tell me, for the love of Heaven, all, and if you have done me wrong, uncle, I will forgive you, as I live!"

Jacob Gray's voice trembled, and the perspiration stood in cold drops upon his brow, as he said, faintly,—

"Water! water! water!—I—I am faint!"

Ada, for henceforward we will call her by that name, filled a glass with sparkling cold water, and handed it in silence to the trembling man. With a shaking hand he raised it to his lips, and drank deeply of it; the glass dropped from his nervous grasp, and lay in fragments on the floor.

"I—I am better now," said Gray.

Ada stood before him—her dark eyes bent on his with a scrutinising glance, beneath which he shrunk abashed.

"Now then, uncle Gray," she said, "now that you are better, will you answer me?"

Gray looked at her for a moment or two in silence before he replied; then he said slowly,—

"What if I refuse to answer the question you ask?"

"Then is our compact broken," cried Ada.

"And—and—what will you do? What can you do?"

"What can I do? I can toil, work, attend upon those who may perchance repay my service with a smile, ample and dear wages to the poor, desolate child of harshness and misfortune. I will leave you and this gloomy abode for ever, and trust to the mercy of that Providence that finds food for the merest insect that buzzes in the evening time !"

"Humph!" muttered Gray. "I never knew Providence feed anything yet. Providence will let you die on a door-step, and rot in a kennel !"

"Peace," cried Ada, "and profane not that you cannot comprehend. I repeat I will leave you, without sufficient reason for my stay be given me. Blind obedience to you is past. There was a plan which would have ensured its continuance."

"Indeed! what plan?"

"A simple one," said Ada, mournfully: "uncle Gray, you might have bound me to you by the ties of such dear affection, that I should have smiled upon my bondage, and obedience without inquiry would have seemed to me a pleasant virtue."

"I—I have used you well," stammered Gray.

"Well!" cried Ada; "uncle, you have scoffed at my childish tears. I have felt even your blows : you would kill even my poor dog. Used me well ?"

Gray looked down for a few moments ; then he said,—

"To-night—or—or—say to-morrow morning. Yes, let it be to-morrow morning, and I will tell you all."

"To-morrow morning? Well, be it so!"

"Yes," continued Gray, "give me but till to morrow morning, and you shall ask me no more questions."

"Tell me, though, now," said the girl, kindly, "is Ada my name ?"

"It is."

"And what more ?"

"Wait—wait till to-morrow. I—I have breakfasted—take yours. I have business abroad."

Jacob Gray rose, and keeping his small, keen, grey eyes fixed on Ada, he left the room. Outside the door he paused, and, raising his clenched hand, while his face was distorted with passion, he muttered,—

"To-morrow, to-morrow, you shall be a stiffened corpse !"

CHAPTER XXII.

LEARMONT AT HOME.—HIS EXULTATION.—THE SMITH.—THE PLOT.

LEARMONT, after committing the cold-blooded and brutal murder in the Bishop's Walk, hastily wiped his blood-stained sword, and walked quickly onwards till he came to the further extremity of the avenue. He then darted down a narrow opening, which led him first away from, and then by a circuitous route, to the back of the river.

"Boat !—boat !" he cried, impatiently, and from a mean habitation a boy immediately emerged.

"Can you row me across ?" cried Learmont.

"Yes, your worship," replied the boy. "This way, an' it please your honour."

He led the way to a wherry which was moored close to some little wooden steps, and Learmont, seating himself in the boat, said,—

"Quick !—quick ! I am in haste."

The boy handled his skulls with dexterity, and the boat soon reached the Middlesex shore. Throwing him a piece of silver, Learmont strided over the boy, and was soon at his own house in Westminster. Without deigning the slightest notice to his servants at the hall of the mansion, who made obsequious way for him as he entered, he strode onwards till he came to the room in which he had sat the preceding evening, when his thoughts had been so great a torment to him, and, flinging himself into a chair, he began to think over the singular events of the night, and to arrange the plan that he had already conceived for the destruction of Gray, and the possession of his young charge.

" This is indeed a stroke of good fortune," he said. " By Gray's destruction I gain much. The dull-witted sot, Britton, is not half the annoyance that this Jocob Gray has proved to me. I hate—I abhor him. Let me consider how the case stands.—He lives in a solitary, miserable abode, out of the way of note or observation. Oh, Master Gray, you have outwitted yourself here ! With him, of course, is the great object of all my fears. My worst enemy is that boy, whose existence I am so far sure of, from the s atement of the babbling fool who has paid with his life for meddling with affairs beyond his comprehension. So far, so good. Those papers containing Gray's written confession that he speaks of, let me consider well of them. The object of writing them was, that they should be found, in case of his death—found where ? In his home, of course, and easily found, too, most easily ; because they were to fall into the hands of persons not searching for them ; so they must be in some place easy of discovery, and most simple of access. How easy then will it be for me to find them, knowing that they are there, and determined to leave no nook or corner unsearched till I do find them. Good, good ; and the result, Gray dead—the boy is in my power, and the confession, which was to preserve him so well, to be my torment—in the flames. Yes, all is clear, quite clear ; and now for the immediate means."

For several minutes he paced the apartment in silent thought, then suddenly pausing, he exclaimed:—

" Certainly : who so proper as Britton ? It is a great and important principle in all these matters, to confine them to as few hands as possible. Britton already knows enough for mischief, and his knowledge, being a little extended, cannot make him much more noxious. He shall aid me. He and I will storm your garrison, Master Jacob Gray ! cunning, clever, Jacob Gray ! And then why then, I have but one more object to accomplish, and that is the death of Britton ! The boy, too—By Heavens, I always had my doubts if it were a boy ! This drunken fool, who I have been compelled to put out of the way of mischief, saw him though, and doubt vanishes. He shall either die, or be rendered innoxious ! Oh, clever, artful, Jacob Gray, I have you on the hip !"

A servant now opened the door slowly, and Learmont turning quickly on him with a frowning brow, cried,—

" How now, sirrah ? Why this intrusion ?"

" An' it please your worship," said the man, " there is one below would have speech of your worship."

" Speech of me ?"

" Ay, truly ; an' it please your ——"

" Psha !" cried Learmont. " Use fewer words ! Who is it waits to see me ?"

" He says he brings a message from the Old Smithy ; but I thought, your worship ——"

" You thought," cried Learmont, making two gigantic strides, and seizing the trembling domestic by the throat. " You thought ! Wretch ! if you dare to think about any of my visitors, I'd give your brains to a dog, and if your tongue but wags of aught you see or hear in this house, I'll tear it out by the roots !"

" The—the—Lord have—m—mercy upon us !" groaned the servant. " I—I—I'll never think again, your worship, as long as I—I live !"

" Begone ! and show him who asks for me to this room."

The terrified man made haste from the apartment, and in three or four minutes Britton, the smith, staggered into the room, with an air of the most insolent and independent familiarity.

His face was bloated and swollen from his deep debauch of the previous night, and his eyes looked sleepy and blood-shot. His attire hung loosely on his huge form, and he was altogether the picture of ferocity and sensuality.

" Good morning to you, 'squire," he said, as he threw himself into a chair. " By G— you are well lodged here. You haven't a spare room, have you ?"

Learmont stood with his back to the light, so that he was not in a favourable position for the smith to notice the working of his countenance, where indignation hatred, and policy were battling for pre-eminence

"Away with this nonsense," cried Learmont. "What brings you here?"

"What brings me here? Why, my legs, to be sure. It's too short a distance to think of riding."

"Your errand?" cried Learmont.

"Money!" bellowed Britton, in a still louder voice.

"Money! again so soon?"

"Ay; so soon. I have found a mine, and I don't see why I should not work it, as that infernal Jacob Gray says."

"Oh! Jacob Gray says that, does he?" sneered Learmont.

"On my faith he does. 'Tis a shrewd knave, but I hate him. I hate him, I say!"

"Indeed!" says Learmont. "He says you are a beastly sot, good Britton."

"Does he?"

No. 9,

"Ay, does he. A thick-skulled, drunken idiot."

"Ha ! he says that of me ?"

"Even so ; a mere lump of brutality—savage beast !"

"Now curses on him !" muttered Britton.

"How much money do you want ?" said Learmont, very suddenly.

"Twenty pieces."

"Twenty ? Pshaw, make them forty or fifty, provided you have likewise your revenge on Jacob Gray."

"Revenge on Jacob Gray ? I tell you, squire, I'd go to hell to have revenge on Jacob Gray."

"Have you traced his abode ?"

"No—no—curses on him. I watched him, but he doubled on me, and I lost him."

"Indeed ! then you know not where he lives, or rather, hides ?"

"No ; but I will though. I——"

"I will show you."

"You—show—me—squire——"

"Yes. I will take you to his house, where he hides alone ; with, at least, none but the boy."

"You—you can, squire ?"

"I can, and will, to give you revenge, Britton ; and when you have killed him—when you see his heart's blood flowing—then—then, Britton, come to me and ask for unbounded wealth."

Britton sprang to his feet—

"I will tear his heart out," he cried. "Kill him ? I will torture him."

"To call you a muddle-headed beast," said Learmont ; "a thick-skulled sot ! a brute ! a savage ! a drivelling drunkard !"

"Enough ! enough !" cried Britton ; "he dies—had he a hundred lives I'd take them all."

"Now that's brave," cried Learmont ; "that's gallant, and like you, Britton. He *shall* die."

"Die ! of course he shall," roared Britton. "When shall I seek him ? Tell me when ?"

"To-night."

"To-night ? shall it be to-night ?"

"Ay, shall it. Meet me on the bridge at midnight, and I will take you to the bed-side of Jacob Gray ; you shall have your revenge."

"On the bridge, hard by ?"

"Yes, Britton. At the hour of midnight. Do you not fail. I shall be there."

"Fail ! I would be there, 'squire, if ten thousand devils held me back."

"Away then, now. Drink nothing till that is accomplished. Speak to no one—brood only over your revenge ; and when it is done, come to me for any sum you wish. It shall be yours. Jacob Gray now robs you of what you ought to have, Britton."

"I know it, curses on him ! But he shall do so no longer."

"He kept you poor for years at the smithy."

"He did."

"And now calls you drivelling idiot."

"Oh, he dies ! he dies !"

"Away then now with you ; be careful, sober, and trust no one."

"At midnight, 'squire, on Westminster-bridge."

"Yes ; midnight."

The smith shook his clenched hand as he left the room, muttering,—

"I shall have my revenge ! I shall have my revenge !"

Fortune now, indeed, appeared to have favoured the 'Squire of Learmont, beyond his most sanguine expectations. What was there to stay his progress up

"The slippery steep of his ambition ?"

Who was there to say to him, " Thus far shalt thou go and no further ?" Did not every circumstance conspire to favour his greatest—his most arrogant wishes? Nay, even the very fear and disqniet of the last ten years of his life had unconsciously, as it were, conspired to place him on the proud height he so much panted for, and fancied he should enjoy so truly, for by such circumstances the revenues of the broad estates of Learmont had accumulated to the vast sum which he now had in his hands; a sum so large, that, in a country like England, where even crime has its price, there was no refinement of luxury or vice that he could not command.

———

CHAPTER XXIII.

THE PROJECTED MURDER.—THE UNCONSCIOUS SLEEPER.—A NIGHT OF HORROR.

It wanted but one hour of midnight, and silence reigned about the ruined and deserted street, in which Jacob Gray resided. Heavy clouds hung in the sky, and not a star peeped forth to look with shining beauty on the darkened world. A misty vapour, betokening the breaking of the frost, arose from the surface of the Thames, and occasionally a gust of wind from the south-west brought with it a dashing shower of mingled rain and sleet. A clammy dampness was upon every thing both within doors and without; the fires and lights in the barges on the river burnt through the damp vapour with a sickly glare. It was a night of discomfort, such as frequently occurs in the winter seasons of our variable and inconstant climate. It was a night to enjoy the comforts of warm fire-sides and smiling faces; a night on which domestic joys and social happiness became still more dear and precious, from contrast with the chilling prospect of Nature in the open air.

In the room which has already been described to the reader, as the one in which Jacob Gray usually sat in his lone and ruinous habitation, he now stood by the window listening to the various clocks of the city as they struck the hour of eleven.

A bright fire was blazing on the hearth, but still Jacob Gray trembled and his teeth chattered, as he counted the solemn strokes of some distant church bell, the sound of which came slowly, and with a mnffled tone, through the thick and murky air.

In a few minutes all was still again. The sounds had ceased. Nothing met the ear of Jacob Gray but the low moaning of the gathering wind as it swept around his dilapidated dwelling. Then he turned from the window and faced the fire-light, but even, with its ruddy glow upon his face, he looked ill and ghastly. His step was unsteady, he drew his breath short and thick, and it was evident from the whole aspect and demeanour of the man that his mind was under the influence of some excitement of an extraordinary nature.

In vain he strove to warm the blood that crept rather than flowed in healthy currents through his veins. He held his trembling hands close to the fire. He strove to assume attitudes of careless ease. He even tried to smile, but produced nothing but a cold and ghastly distortion of the features of his face.

"Surely," he muttered, " the—the night must be very cold. Yes, that is it. It is a chilling night. Eleven—eleven o'clock. I—I—meant to do it at eleven; at—at least before twelve. Yes, before twelve—there is time, ample time. 'Tis very—very cold."

With a shaking hand, he poured from a flask, that was upon the table, a quantity of raw spirit, and quaffed it off at a single draught. How strange it is that the mind can, under peculiar circumstances, so entirely conquer the body and subvert, as it were, the ordinary laws of nature! Such was the frightful state of excitement which Jacob Gray had worked himself up to, that he might as well have swallowed an equal quantity of water, for all the effect that the strong spirit had upon him. Still he trembled, still his teeth chattered in his head, and his very heart appeared to him to be cold and lifeless in his breast. He heaped fuel upon the fire, he paced the room, he strove to think of something else than the one subject that filled his brain, but all was in vain. He had determined that night to murder the hapless girl whom he had wronged so much, and he had passed a daya nd evening of unspeakable agony in working up his mind to do the deed calmly and surely.

Ten o'clock he had pitched upon as the hour, then half-past ten, then eleven, and still he trembled with dismay, and could not for his life command his nerves to do the dreadful deed.

He now flung himself into a chair by the fire-side, and covering his face with his hands he rocked to and fro, in agonising thoughts. In a low tone then he held unholy communion with himself.

"I—I must do it," he said. "I must do it. I always thought it would come to this. When she became of age to inquire I was sure to be tortured by question upon question. What resource have I? I dare not do her justice, and tell her who she is. No—no. She has been my safeguard hitherto, she may now be my destruction; should she leave me she may either fall into the hands of Learmont, in which case I lose my chief hold upon him, or, what is worse, she tells her strange tale to some one, who may hunt me to force an explanation of her birth. There is but one resource; she—she must die. Yes, she must die. Learmont still fancying 'tis a boy, must still be tortured by the idea that such an enemy lives, and requires but a word from me to topple him from his height of grandeur to a felon's cell. Yes—yes. That must be the course. There is no other—none—none. Then I will accumulate what sum of money I can, and leave England for ever— for—for well I know the savage smith thirsts for my blood, and—and—should he discover my place of concealment, my death were easy, and the packet containing my confession, which, while I live, is equally dangerous to me as to Learmont and Britton, would fall into their hands."

He rose and paced the room again for several minutes in silence; then taking from the table a small-hand lamp, he lit it, and clutching it with a nervous grasp in his left hand, he muttered,—

"Now—now. It is—time. Ada, you will not see another sun rise. Y must die. 'Tis self-preservation, which even divines tell us is the first great law of nature, that forces me to do this act. I—I do not want to kill thee. No—no; but I—I must—I must do it; I cannot help the deed. Ada, you must die—die —die."

He placed the lamp again upon the table, and approaching with a stealthy step a cupboard in the room, he took from it a double-edged poniard. With a trembling hand he placed the weapon conveniently within his vest, and then casting around him a hurried and scared glance, as if he expected to find some eyes fixed upon him, he walked to the door of the room.

There he paused, and divested himself of his shoes, after which, with a slow, stealthy movement, he began ascending the stairs to the chamber in which reposed, in innocence and peace, the unconscious Ada.

Suddenly he paused, and staggered against the wall, as a new thought struck his mind.

"The hound! the hound!" he gasped. "I—I had forgotten the dog."

Here seemed at once an insurmountable obstacle to the execution of his murderous intention, and for several minutes Jacob Gray sat down on the staircase in deep thought, while his face was distorted by contending passions of hate—fear— and rage.

"Curses—curses on the dog!" he muttered, as he ground his teeth together and clenched his hands in impotent malice. "To be foiled by a half-starved hound! I, Jacob Gray, with my life hanging as it were by a single thread, to be prevented from taking the secret means of preserving myself by this hateful dog! Curses! curses! I—I—yes—yes. There is a chance—one chance, the poison that Learmont placed in my hands, for the purpose of drugging Britton's wine cup!

That—yes, that may rid me of the dog! I will try. Let me recollect. The animal sleeps by the door, sometimes on the mat on the outside, and sometimes within the chamber. We shall see—we shall see—the poison! ay, the poison!"

Cautiously he descended the few steps he had gained, and going to a drawer in the table, which he had the key of, and which stood close to the blazing fire in the room he had so recently left, he took from it the phial of poison which he, Learmont, had given to him. After a moment's thought, he repaired to the cupboard, and taking from it the remains of some meat, upon which he had dined, he poured at least one-half the contents of the small bottle of poison over it.

"This deadly liquid," he said, "has a grateful smell. If I can induce the hound to fasten on this meat, his death is certain and quick, for Learmont is not a man to do things by halves. Poison from him I should assume to be deadly indeed! Ay, deadly indeed!"

Jacob Gray's hatred for the dog seemed to have got in some degree over his extreme nervousness, and it was with a firmer step now than he could command before, that he cautiously again ascended the narrow staircase conducting to Ada's chamber.

Still, however, in his heart, he quailed at the murder—the deliberate, cold-blooded murder of that innocent and beautiful girl, and he presented the ghastly appearance of a resuscitated corpse, rather than a human being who had not passed the portals of the grave. The feeling of honourable humanity was a stranger to the bosom of Jacob Gray. He did not shrink from the murder of the poor and persecuted Ada, because it was a murder—no, it was because he, Jacob Gray, had to do it, unaided and uncheered in the unholy deed, by aught save his own shivering and alarmed imagination. Jacob Gray had no compunction for the deed; his only terror arose from the fact that he could not shift its consummation on to some one else's shoulders.

He would gladly have held a light to guide the dagger of another assassin, but he did shrink from the personal danger and the personal consequences of doing it himself. He was one of those who would watch the door while the murder was doing—hold a vessel to catch the blood—anything but do the deed himself.

His little accession of strength and confidence now only arose from the fact that owing to the intervention of the circumstance of the dog, the murder was, as it were, put off for a little time ; he must first dispose of the dog, then the murder itself, with all its damning train of fears and agonies, would take its former prominent place in his mind, and again would Jacob Gray tremble to his very heart's core.

Stealthily he moved his way up the staircase, his great object being to ascertain if the dog was within or without the chamber of Ada.

His doubts were soon resolved, for suddenly a low growl from the faithful animal smote his ears.

Jacob Gray gave a malignant smile, as he said in a low whisper, "The dog is outside the door."

The growl of the hound now deepened to a louder note, and just as that again was shaping itself to a short angry bark, Jacob Gray threw up the piece of poisoned meat on to the landing on the top of the staircase.

Folding his lamp then under the lappels of his coat, Jacob Gray sat down on the staircase, with a feeling of gratification on his mind, that, in all human probability, he was at length revenged on the poor animal, whose only crime had been too much affection and fidelity towards the hand that fed and caressed him, and the voice that spoke to him in kindly tones.

All was as still as the grave after the meat had been thrown, and after several minutes of suspense, Jacob Gray began to feel anxious for some indication of the success of his scheme. Cautiously, he then ascended a step or two, and paused—no sound met his ears. A few steps more were gained—then a few more, and finally, by stretching out his arm with the light, he could command a view of the landing-place, but he looked in vain for the dog: the animal was nowhere to be seen.   Jacob Gray now stood fairly upon the landing, and peered carefully around him, with the hope of seeing the body of his foe, but such was not the case.

The open door of the outer room which led to Ada's smaller sleeping-chamber now caught his eyes, and at once afforded a clue to the retreat of the dog.

With a soft footfall that could not have possibly disturbed the lightest sleeper, Gray entered that room, and moving his hand slowly round him, so as to illuminate by turns all parts of the apartment, he saw, at length, the object of his search.

Close up to the door leading to Ada's room was the hound quite dead.   The faithful creature had evidently made an effort to awaken its gentle and kind mistress, for its paws were clenched against the bottom of the door, where there was a crevice left.

For a moment Jacob Gray glanced at the fixed eyes of the dog, then he spurned it from the door with his foot, as he muttered,—

" Humph ! so far successful, and now for—for—"

" The murder," he would have said, but in one moment, as if paralysed by the touch of some enchanter's wand, all his old fears returned upon him, and now that there was no obstacle between him and the commission of the awful deed he meditated, he leaned against the wall for support, and the perspiration of fear rolled down his face in heavy drops, and gave his countenance an awful appearance of horror and death-like paleness.

" What—what," he stammered, "what if she should scream?   G od of Heaven, if she should scream !"

So terrified was he at the supposition that his victim might, in her death-struggle, find breath to scream, that for a moment he gave up his purpose, and retreated slowly backwards from the room.

Suddenly now the silence that reigned without was broken by the various churches striking twelve.

Gray started as the sounds met his ear.

" Twelve! twelve !" he exclaimed.   " It—it—should have been done ere this. To-morrow.   The to-morrow that she looks for is come.   I—I thought not 'twas so late.   It must be done! it must be done !"

CHAPTER XXIV.

THE ATTEMPTED ASSASSINATION.—A SURPRISE.—ADA'S SURMISES.—
THE AGONY OF GRAY.

THE last faint echo from the slowest clock had died away upon the midnight air, when Jacob Gray started from his position of deep attention, and placing his small lamp on one of the window sills, he drew from his breast the knife with which he intended to take the life of the hapless Ada.

" She—she surely sleeps sound," he muttered through his clenched teeth, " or all these clocks with their solemn and prolonged echoes must have awakened her. Yes ; I—I—hope she sleeps sound.   I—would not have a struggle—a struggle. Oh, no, no, not for worlds.   I—can fancy her clinging to the knife and screaming— shrieking even as—as—her—father did—when he had his death wound.   That would be horrible.   Oh, most horrible—and yet I must kill her.   I must kill her. Did she not brave me to my face ? did she not tell me that she suspected me and my motives, and that no more would she keep herself immured for my sake ?   I— she—she did, and more than this, far more, she taunted me with.   Yes—I—I am quite justified—she must die !"

The door which led into the inner chamber was in two compartments, and when Gray gently pushed against them, they both opened slightly, and the dim, sickly light of a lamp from the interior room, to his surprise, gleamed through the crevice, meeting the kindred ray of the one which Jacob Gray had placed so carefully out of the way of, as he thought, the eyes of the sleeping girl.

He crept into the room, and stood motionless for many minutes, regarding the sight that met his eyes. Seated by a small table, on which was the lamp dimly burning and near its expiration, was Ada, completely dressed, but fast asleep. Her face rested partially upon an open book, which she had evidently been reading before retiring to rest, when sleep must have come upon her unawares, and sealed her eyelids in forgetfulness.

Her long hair fell in beautiful disorder upon the table, and the one eyelash that was visible hung upon her fair cheek wet with tears. She had been weeping, but whether from some vision that crossed her slumbers, or from lonesome and unhappy thoughts previous to dropping into that temporary oblivion of sorrow, could not be known.

Jacob Gray stood like one spell-bound by some horrible apparition, for to the wicked can there be a more horrible apparition than youth, beauty, and innocence?

"She—she sleeps," he gasped; "but by some strange fatality has not retired to bed. My—my task is now ten times more difficult. I—I know not what to do."

The knife trembled in his grasp, and he shook vehemently; then, as a low murmuring sound escaped the lips of Ada, he sunk slowly down, first crouchingly, then on his knees, and lastly he grovelled on the ground at her feet in mortal agony, lest she should awaken and see him there, with those starting eyes, those livid lips, and that knife, which he came to bury in her innocent and gentle heart.

Some fearful vision was passing over the imagination of the sleeping girl. Fancy was busy in the narrow chambers of the brain, and pictured to her some scene of sorrow or terror; deep sobs burst from the breast—then she spoke, and her words thrilled through Jacob Gary like liquid fire.

"Spare, oh, spare him!" she said; "he is my father—my own father. Spare him; oh, spare—spare——"

She awoke not even in her agony of spirit, but wept bitterly; then the tears decreased and sobs only were heard; the vision, like a thunder-storm, was passing away, low moans succeeded, and finally all was still again.

It was, however, many minutes before Jacob Gray again rose from his crouching position of abject fear, but at length he did so, and with the glittering knife in his hand, he stood within a pace of his innocent victim.

Then arose in his mind the awful question of where should he strike? and, like a vulture, he hovered for a time over his prey, with the fatal steel uplifted, doubting where he should make the sudden swoop.

By an accidental parting of the silken curls that floated upon Ada's neck and shoulders, he saw a small portion of her breast; it was there then he determined to strike. He glanced at the blade of the knife, and he thought it long enough to reach even to her heart.

"Now—now!" he groaned through his clenched teeth. "Now!"

The steel was uplifted; nay, it was upon the point of descending, when one heavy knock upon the outer door of the lone house echoed through the dreary pile, and arrested the arm of the murderer, while the blood rushed in terror like a gush of cold water to his heart.

There was then an awful silent pause, when again that solemn heavy knock awakened the echoes of the empty house.

Slowly, inch by inch, as if his arm worked by some machinery, Jacob Gray brought the knife by his side, and still bending over the unconscious Ada, he listened for a repetition of that knock, as if each melancholy blow was struck upon his own heart.

Again it came, and then again more rapidly, and Jacob Gray trembled so violently that he was fain to lean upon the table at which Ada slept for support.

That movement awakened Ada, and starting from her position of rest, she suddenly, with a cry of surprise, confronted the man who had sought her chamber with so fell and horrible a purpose. One glance at the knife which Jacob Gray held in his hand, and then a searching look at his face, told her all. She clasped her hands in terror as she exclaimed—

"You—you—come to kill me?"

"No—no," stammered Gray, trying to smile, and producing his usual painful distortion of features. "No—no—I did—not—no—-no ! Ada, I did not."

"That knife ?" said Ada, pointing to it as she spoke.

"The knife," repeated Gray. "Hark, some one knocks, Ada, at our lonely home."

"Those looks of terror," continued the young girl, "those blanched cheeks, those trembling hands, all convince me that I have escaped death at your hands."

"No ; I say no," gasped Gray.

"And my hound too," added Ada ; "my fond, faithful dog, where is he, uncle Gray ?"

"Yes ; the dog," cried Gray, eagerly catching at the hope of persuading her that it was solely to compass the destruction of the hound he had thus stolen to her room. "I admit I did seek the dog's life ; you vexed me about the animal."

The knocking at the door sounded now more loudly than before, and the knocker was evidently plied by an impatient hand.

"Hark, hark !" cried Gray. "Ada, hear me ; whoever knocks without can be no friend of ours."

"Indeed ?" said Ada.

"'Tis true ; I am the only friend you have in the wide world."

"You mean, I suppose, since you have killed my poor dog," said Ada, pointing through the open doorway to the inanimate body of the animal.

"The dog is dead," said Gray.

"Uncle," replied Ada, mildly, but firmly ; "now hear me. You have broken the compact. Let those who knock so loudly for admission enter, I will not avoid them. Were they ten times my enemies they could not be more cruel than thou art."

"Ada, you know not what you say," cried Gray. "They cannot be friends, and they may be foes. 'Tis light enough for me to note them from a lower window. Yes, I will see, I will see. Remain thou here, Ada. Stir not—speak not."

"I promise nothing," said Ada. "You shall no longer prescribe rules of conduct for me, uncle Gray. I tell you I will promise nothing."

Gray made an impatient gesture with his hands, and quitted the room. He repaired to a window on the ground floor, in one corner of which he had made a clear spot for the express purpose of reconnoitering the door-way, and applying his eye now close to this, he could by the dim light trace the forms of two men upon his threshold. Too well were those forms engraven on his memory. It needed not a second glance to tell him that the savage smith, Britton, and Squire Learmont, were his unwelcome and most clamorous visitors.

Now, indeed, the measure of Jacob Gray's agony appeared to be full. For a moment he completely surrendered himself to despair ; and had Learmont then forced the door, he would scarcely have made an effort to escape the sword of the man of blood.

"Ha ! ha !" he heard the smith say ; "I like to knock thus, it alarms poor, clever, cunning Jacob. It shatters his nerves. Oh, oh, oh !"

"Can you depend on the men you have placed at the back of the house to intercept his escape that way ?" said Learmont.

"Depend upon them ?" replied Britton. "Of course. They ain't paid, and are quite sober, as you see ; they are ready for any cut-throat business. Let's knock again. Oh, oh, how Jacob Gray must be shaking !"

The taunts of the smith seemed to act as a stimulant to the sickened energies of Gray. He roused himself and muttered, as he shook his clenched hand in the direction of the door—

"Indeed, Master Britton. Do not even yet make too sure of cunning Jacob Gray. He may yet prove too cunning for the sot, Britton. You think you have me so safely that you can afford to tantalize me by knocking, when a small effort of your united strength would burst yon frail door from its frailer hinges. We shall see—we shall see."

He bounded up the staircase to the room in which he had left Ada. She was standing by the body of the dog with the lamp in her hand.

"Ada! Ada!" cried Gray; "we are lost—lost. We shall be murdered, if you will not be guided by me."

Ada only pointed to the dog.

Gray was thoroughly alarmed at her decisive manner, and another loud knock at the door at that moment did not tend to pacify his nervous tremors.

"There are those at the door who come purposely to seek your life!"

"*Your* life, most probably, Uncle Gray."

"Ada! Ada!" cried Gray. "Each minute—nay, each moment is precious There is no escape, none—none!"

"You are alarmed, Uncle Gray," said Ada.

The perspiration of fear—intense fear, was standing upon the brow of Gray, as he felt that each fleeting moment might be his last. From exultation at the thought of still deceiving Britton and Learmont, he dropped to a state of the most trembling, abject terror.

No. 10.

" God of Heaven !" he cried ; " you—you will not, cannot refuse to save me !"

" Our compact is broken," said Ada.   " I do not believe that I have so much to fear from those who seek admittance here as from him who but a few minutes since stood over me as I slept——"

" No—no !" shrieked Gray.   " It was not I——"

" It was you," said Ada.

" I did not mean to—to kill you."

" The knife was in your hand, uncle ; you had destroyed my faithful guard ; you trembled ; your guilt shone forth with an unholy and hideous lustre from your eyes.   Uncle Gray, God can alone see into the hearts of men, but, as I hope for heaven, and—and to meet there my dear father, whom I never knew, I do suspect you much, Uncle Gray."

" Mercy !—Have mercy on me, Ada."

" Ask that of Heaven."

" In your chamber, you have clothing befitting your sex ; for such an emergency as this I provided it. Go, oh, go at once, and you may escape as a girl from those who come here to murder a boy."

Ada glanced at the trembling man, who, with clasped hands and trembling limbs, stood before her, and then with a firm voice she said,—

" No, no, I cannot."

With a loud crash at this moment the street-door was burst from its hinges.

Gray gave one frantic scream, and threw himself at the feet of Ada.

" Save—oh, save my life !" he cried.   " Have mercy on me, Ada ! You shall do with me as you please ; I will be your slave,—will watch for you when you sleep,—tend upon you, discover your wishes ever by a look.   But oh, save me— save me.   I cannot—dare not die !"

Ada shuddered at the wild frantic passion of Gray. She struggled to free herself from his grasp, for he clung to her with a desperate clutch.

" Mercy ! mercy !" he shrieked.

In vain she retreated backwards from him ; he crawled after her on his knees, shrieking " Mercy ! mercy !"

Now Ada had gained the door of her own room, and, with loathing and horror, she tried in vain to disengage herself from Gray.

" They come ! ah, they come !" suddenly cried Gray, springing to his feet. " Now, Ada, hear the secret you pine to know !"

" The secret ?" cried Ada.

" Yes, *I am your father*.   These men will apprehend me for murder ; but *I am your father !*"

For an instant Ada passed her hands upon her eyes, as if to shut out the hideous phantasma of a dreadful dream, and then, with a cry of exquisite anguish, she rushed through the folding doors and closed them immediately after her.

" That—that will succeed," gasped Gray, wiping from his brow the cold perspiration that hung there in bead-like drops.   " The lie is effective ; she may not believe it, but now she has not time to think.   She will save me now !"

He rushed to the door of the room which led to the staircase, and in a momen locked it.   Then he stood with his arms folded, and an awful demoniac smile played upon his pale and ghastly face, awaiting the issue of the next few minutes, which comprised to him the fearful question of life or death.

CHAPTER XXV.

THE ESCAPE.—TAUNTS.—THE CONFESSION.—LEARMONT'S RAGE AND DISCOMFITURE.

But few moments remained to Jacob Gray for sad or exultant communion with his own thoughts.   A heavy blow from without dashed the door open, and Learmont, with a drawn sword in his hand, closely followed by Britton, carrying a lighted link, entered the room.

"Well met, Jacob Gray," cried Learmont. "Your cunning is now at fault. You are scarcely a match for 'Squire Learmont, who you thought you had so safely in your toils."

"Ho! ho!" sneered Britton, holding the torch close to the pale, agitated face of Gray. "So we have unearthed the fox at last. Cunning—clever Master Jacob Gray—amazingly artful Master Gray."

"You have triumphed but for a short time," added Learmont. "Your own cunning has been your destruction. Jacob Gray, your life is not now worth five minutes' purchase."

"Taunt on," said Gray. "I know not what you mean or what you want."

"Well you know," cried Learmont, angrily, "you had a double hold upon my fears, Jacob Gray, but that double hold depended upon a slender foundation. So long as you could keep your hiding-place secret you were safe, but no longer."

"I—I still do not understand you," said Gray, who was anxious to give Ada time to complete the change he did not doubt she was making in her apparel.

"Ha! ha!" laughed Learmont. "It were a thousand pities you should die in ignorance of what had been the result of your extreme cleverness, Jacob Gray. Suppose me, as I shall be now, possessed of the boy, and the confession, which, of course, must be somewhere handy, else it is objectless."

"Well—well," said Gray, trembling, "suppose all that."

"Ho! ho! ho!" chuckled the smith. "Upon my soul that's good, cunning Jacob—clever, artful, deep-designing Jacob. Why, supposing all that we mean to cut your throat."

"We waste time," cried Learmont. "Where is the boy?"

"Ay, the boy, the cherub, the boy!" cried Britton.

"He is not here," said Gray, with as much boldness as he could assume.

Learmont gave a smile of contempt as he said,—

"Indeed, he is not here, and yet Jacob Gray is here. That is very probable. Now I tell you he is here, and what is more, he cannot escape. The back of the house is guarded by persons who have orders to cut down whoever attempts to leave it that way. Britton and I came in at the front. We have well searched the lower rooms, so you see we have taken our measures almost as cleverly as Jacob Gray took his when he came to Learmont to whisper in his ear that the boy still lived!"

"Ho! ho! ho!" roared the smith, patting Gray on the back. "How feel you, Master Jacob? Does your blood dance merrily through your veins, or have you still some stroke of cunning unplayed off that shall put us yet to shame? By hell, if you have, Jacob Gray, I'll—I'll give you my head!"

"Agreed," said Gray.

"Give me the light," cried Learmont.

He snatched the link from the hand of Britton, and made two strides towards the inner room.

Gray with difficulty suppressed a scream of alarm, but before Learmont could lay hand on the lock, Ada flung the door open, and walked composedly forth.

She was attired in a plain, but neat girl's dress. A small hooded cloak was clasped round her neck; and now that she was attired in the proper costume of her sex, she looked several years older, and the change in her general appearance was so great, that even Jacob Gray would scarcely have recognised her.

She showed no nervousness, no haste, no sign of trepidation as she stepped from the room, and her voice was soft, and musical, and quite calm as she paused and said,—

"Good evening, Mr. Gray. I have put all Harry's things in order."

Then curtseying to Learmont, who stood almost directly in her way, she passed across the outer room, and disappeared through the broken doorway.

For several minutes not a word was spoken by either of the three men there assembled. Oh, what precious minutes they were to Jacob Gray!

Learmont then, without a word, entered the inner room. In a few moments he returned with his face distorted by passion, and placing his sword's point against the throat of Gray, he said,—

"Where is the boy ?"

"Not here—on my soul not here !" cried Gray, trembling with fear that Learmont's passion might get the better of his prudence, and that by one thrust of his weapon he might shed his life blood.

"Where is he ?"

"Where is he ?" echoed Gray, to whom each moment gained for Ada thoroughly to escape, was equal to a drop of blood to his heart.

"Answer me !" shrieked Learmont.

"I repeat the boy is not here."

"One moment more I give you," added Learmont, "to declare to me where the boy is, or you die, as sure as—as that I hate you from my soul !"

"Pause yet a moment, 'Squire Learmont," sneered Gray. "If my life has hitherto been valuable, and my safety precious to you, they are doubly so now."

"No, Jacob Gray," cried Learmont, "that tale will do no more. We have hunted you down. It is not probable that the cautious Jacob Gray has trusted the boy we seek with the secret of his birth."

"You are right," said Gray, "I have not."

"And you are candid," sneered Learmont.

"Ho! ho !" laughed Britton. "Poor Jacob Gray has forgotten even to lie—"

"Exactly," snarled Gray; "because the truth will do as well. That is a piece of philosophy which the muddled brains of savage Britton would never have conceived."

Britton made a furious rush at Gray, but the latter stepped behind Learmont, saying,—

"It is still the interest of 'Squire Learmont to protect Jacob Gray."

"Hold, Britton," cried Learmont. "Stay your arm yet a moment. We—we will hear him."

"You need not be alarmed, 'squire," said Gray. "Our relative positions are still the same."

"How mean you? Your retreat is discovered."

"True, but—"

"And the confession which has hitherto ensured your safety, must be here, and easily found, else it were valueless, and would defeat its object."

"Indeed !" said Gray. "Now, hear me. The boy is not here ! The confession is in his hands."

Learmont trembled as he slowly dropped the point of his sword, and fixed his eyes upon Jacob Gray's countenance, as if he would read his very soul.

"Go on, go on," he said.

"I repeat, the boy has the confession. He knows not what it is. It is sealed."

"Well. Go—go—on."

"But he has express instructions, which, be assured, he will fulfil to the letter; that if he and I do meet at an appointed spot, by an appointed hour, he is to hasten to Sir Francis Hartleton, and deliver the packet. You understand my position, 'Squire Learmont ? and even your dull-pated Britton may now see the expediency of being careful of your dear friend, Jacob Gray. Fancy any delay being thrown in my way now, which should prevent me from meeting the boy. How disagreeable it would be to me to see hung, kind Britton, while I had my free pardon in my pocket for being evidence against you. Do you understand ?"

There was a most remarkable difference in the expression of the smith's countenance and that of Learmont's, while Gray was speaking. The former became nearly purple with suppressed rage, while the 'squire turned of an ashy, ghastly paleness, and seemed scarcely equal to the exertion of standing erect.

"Gray—Jacob Gray," he gasped. "You do not—you cannot mean that—that—"

"That what, squire?" said Gray. "Why do you hesitate? I will answer any question candidly."

" Have you," continued Learmont, " indeed set all our lives in such a chance as your meeting a boy at an appointed hour in this great city ?"

" I have," answered Gray; " or rather I should say you have."

" I—I ?"

" Yes. 'Squire Learmont, you thirst for my blood! You would hunt me to death could you do so with safety to yourself! Beware ! I say, and give up the chace !"

Learmont attempted to sheath his sword, but his hand trembled so excessively, that it was several moments before he could accomplish it. When, however, he had succeeded, he turned to Gray, and said,—

" At what hour—are—you to meet the boy ?"

Gray smiled, as he said,—

" Perhaps your next question, sir, may be where I am to meet him ?"

" I—I merely asked the hour."

" Whatever the appointed hour may be," said Gray, " be assured I shall not meet him, let the consequences be what they may, until I am assured that you and this angry smith are not dogging my footsteps."

" Let—us—go, Britton," said Learmont.

" Jacob Gray," said Britton, striding up to him, and grinding his words through his set teeth, " there will come a time for vengeance."

" Exactly," said Gray, calmly.

" An hour will come when I shall have the pleasure, and I would pay dearly for it, of cutting your throat."

" You shall pay dearly for it when you do," said Gray ; " and, in the meantime cunning, clever, extremely artful Master Britton, I bid you good morning."

" Wretch !" cried Britton.

" Oh ! very cunning Britton," sneered Gray ; " amazingly clever, artful, deep Master Britton—ha ! ha ! ha !"

" Now, if I dared !" cried Britton, half drawing a knife from his breast.

" But you dare not," cried Gray. " You are too cunning, far too cunning, clever Britton—ha ! ha !"

" Away ! away !" said Learmont. " Come, Britton, we waste time."

" Ay, and precious time, too," added Gray, " only Master Britton is so very —so extremely cunning and clever."

" Come, come," cried Learmont, seizing Britton by the arm.

" Nay, do not hurry away," sneered Gray. " Shall I offer you refreshments? 'Tis some distance to Westminster. Will you go by water, cunning Britton ?"

Britton's passion was too great for utterance, and he walked to the door, which he kicked open with a violence that split it from top to bottom.

" You will like to hear, 'Squire Learmont," said Gray, " that all is right. I will do myself the honour of paying you a visit to-morrow."

Learmont turned at the door, and cast a glance at Gray, that even he quailed under, and then followed Britton down the staircase.

CHAPTER XXVI.

THE MORNING.—THE BODY OF THE MURDERED MAN.—THE OLD INN.— JACOB'S REFLECTIONS.

When Learmont and the smith had left the house, and Jacob Gray felt that his great and inevitable danger was over, he sunk into a chair, and a fit of trembling came over him that he was many minutes in recovering from.

" They are foiled this once," he muttered; " but they may not be again— 'twas a rare chance, a most rare chance. I—I must leave here now. I am hunted

—hunted like a wild animal, from den to den.   Oh ! how they would have rejoiced in my destruction. This is a sad life to lead—and—and if, before they came, I had taken her life, I should even now be lying a stiffened corpse on these boards—yet, what can I do?   She is my torment : she will be my destruction !"

He then rose, and paced the room for some time with hasty and unequal steps. Suddenly pausing, he trembled again with the same awful intensity that he had done before, and in a hoarse, husky whisper, said,—

"What if she come not back ? She suspects me. It is time she were here again. Oh! if she should seek protection elsewhere !   More danger !—more danger !—into what a tangled web of horrors am I placed ! Can I fly ? What money have I ? A large sum, but yet not enough.   Oh ! if Learmont would give me at once a sum of money which would suffice me in a foreign land, and trust my word to go, and—if I could trust him to let me live to go.   Ah ! there it is ! —there it is ! We cannot trust each other—not for a moment—no, not for a moment."

Jacob Gray muttered these gloomy meditations in a low, anxious tone, and almost at every word he paused to endeavour to detect some token of the return of Ada.   None, however, met his ears, and, after two hours of mental agony of mind had thus passed over the head of Jacob Gray, he crept down the stair- case, and stood at the door looking anxiously about him by the dim morning light that was beginning, with its cold grey tints, to struggle through the darkness of the sky.

"She does not come," he muttered—"she does not come.   What shall I do— whither seek her ?   Yet—I—I must endeavour to find her."

He now turned his attention to the broken lock of the door, and after some time, succeeded in closing it after him tolerably securely, then searching in the road till he found a piece of chalk, he wrote on the door,—" wait—J. G."

"Should she return during my absence," he thought, "she will recognise my writing and initials to wait my return. She is most probably near at hand, waiting for me to search for her."

Casting again a cautious, scrutinising glance around him, Jacob Gray walked slowly down the ruined street, peering into each doorway as he went, with the hope of seeing Ada.

His search was unsuccessful.   He could see no trace of Ada ; and a thousand feelings of alarm and suspicion began to crowd upon his mind. He paused irresolutely at the end of the street, uncertain which way he should shape his course.   At last, with a sudden resolution, he walked in the direction of West- minster Bridge.

As he neared Lambeth, he observed that the watermen who plied at the different stairs by the side of the river, seemed particularly engrossed by some subject of importance, for they were congregated together in knots of two, three, and four, discoursing earnestly and vehemently.

He approached one, and touching his arm, said,—

"What is the matter, friend?"

"Murder's the matter," replied the man.

"Murder !"

"Ay, murder.   There has been a murder done in the Bishop's Walk."

"In the Bishop's Walk ?"

"Yes ; the body was found cold and stiff—the body of a waterman ; but we will have justice."

"What was his name?" said Gray.

"Sheldon.   He plied at the bridge stairs opposite."

"I thank you, friend," said Gray, as he walked on muttering to himself,—

"Now, I'd lay my life this murder is Britton's doing. Oh, if I could fix him with it—and yet there might be danger.   At the gallows he might denounce me— yes, he would. It must have been by means of this man somehow that my retreat was so quickly discovered—yet how, I cannot divine."

He now observed a small public-house, at the door of which was a throng of persons, and pressing forward, he soon learned that there the body of the murdered man lay.

Impelled by a curiosity that he could not resist, Gray entered the house, and calling for some liquor, commenced a conversation with the landlord, which somewhat altered his opinion concerning the murderer.

"I saw Sheldon," said the host, "and intend to swear to it solemnly, pass my house at an unusual hour, in company with a stranger. I was looking out to see the state of the night, when I saw them pass on towards the Bishop's Walk."

"What kind of man was he with?" said Gray.

"A tall man."

"Thin and dark?"

"Nay, as for his complexion I can say nothing, for in the dark, you know, all cats are grey."

"True; but you could swear to the man being tall and thin, Master Landlord?"

"In faith I could, and your tall, thin men are just what I dislike—bah! They seldom drink much."

"Most true—I thank you. 'Tis a barbarous murder."

"Would you like, sir, to see the corpse?" said the landlord, in an under tone.

"The corpse?" echoed Gray.

"Ay; he was a fine fellow. You must know that Sir Francis Hartleton has been here——"

"The magistrate?"

"Yes. He is here, and there, and everywhere; and no sooner did he hear of the body of a murdered man being found in the Bishop's Walk, than he had a cast across the Thames from his own house in Abingdon-street."

"Yes—yes," said Gray, abstractedly.

"He had the body brought here," continued the loquacious landlord, "and he says to me,—' Landlord, allow no one to see or touch the corpse or it's clothing until you hear from me.'—'No, your worship,' says I;' and I've kept my word for excepting neighbour Taplin, the corn-factor, Mrs. Dibbs, next door, Antony Freeman, the hosier, John Ferret, the bishop's steward, Matthew Briggs, who keeps the small wareshop at the corner, Matthew Holland, the saddler, Dame Tippetto, the old midwife, and just a few more friends, no one has crossed the threshold of the room the corpse lies in. That I could take my solemn oath of, sir, I assure you."

"No doubt—no doubt," said Gray. "I—I will, if it so please you, see the body."

"Come along, then," said the landlord, placing his finger by the side of his nose, and keeping up a succession of winks all the way up the staircase, till he came to the room door in which the body of the murdered waterman was lying.

Jacob Gray entered after the landlord, and closed the door behind him.

"Now, sir, you will see him," said the host. "Just let me move a shutter, and you will have a little more light. There, sir—there he lies. Ah, he was fond of his glass—that he was—a fine fellow."

A stream of light came from the partially unclosed shutter, and Gray saw the corpse of the man whom he had tempted to commit a murder upon Britton himself, lying cold and stark in the bloody embrace of death.

The body lay upon a table, and the warmth of the house had caused the wound to bleed slightly again. The face was ghastly and pale, and the wide open staring eyes gave an awful appearance to the fixed rigid countenance.

"See there, now," cried the landlord. "You may note where he has been run through the breast; don't you see the rent?"

"I do," said Gray.

"There are two such wounds."

"Don't it strike you," remarked Gray, "that these are sword wounds?"

"Of course it does."

"Then who but a gentleman accredited to wear a weapon, could have killed the man?"

"That's true.   I'll solemnly swear to that," cried the landlord.

"The tall, thin, dark man," added Gray, "must be some gentleman, residing, probably, hereabout, or directly across the bridge."

"No doubt; I'll swear."

"Most properly," added Gray.   "Good day to you, sir,   I may perchance look in again."

"Come to the inquest, sir," said the landlord.   "There you shall have it all out, I'll warrant.   There you shall hear me solemnly swear everything."

"Perchance, I may," said Gray, as he descended the staircase.   "Will it be to-day?"

"To-morrow, at noon, as I understand, sir."

"Thank you.   Thank you."

Gray left the house, and when he was some paces from the door, he muttered,—

"So, Master Learmont, I have another hold upon your kind generosity.   That by some strange chance, which I cannot conjecture, this waterman found out my place of abode, and thus communicated it to you, 'Squire Learmont, I am convinced. Humph! He has got his wages. I could accuse you now of a crime, good, kind, considerate Learmont, that would not in the least compromise my own safety.   We shall see—we shall see.   I—I must now make my way homewards again.   Surely by this time Ada has returned.   She must be waiting ; home! home! and then to think of another place in which to hide my head from my worst foe, and yet my only source of wealth."

CHAPTER XXVII.

ADA'S FLIGHT AND DESPAIR.—OLD WESTMINSTER BRIDGE AT DAYBREAK.—THE SMITH.—MAD MAUD.

WHEN Ada, the beautiful and persecuted child of the dead, passed from the room in the garments befitting her sex, she thought her heart must burst with the suppressed feelings which were conjured up in its inmost recesses.   One awful question occurred to her to be traced in letters of liquid fire upon her brain, and that was " Is it true that Jacob Gray is my father?"   His assertion of the fact had come upon her so entirely unawares that, as Gray had himself exultingly supposed, she had not time to think—but the doubt—the merest suspicion that it might be true, was madness. Ada did not—she could not, even at the moment that Gray declared himself her father, believe his words ; but still the doubt was raised, and although all reason—all probability—all experience gave the lie to the assertion, there was still the awful intrusive thought that it might be so.

Upon the impulse of that small possibility, that in that moment of despair and agony of soul Jacob Gray had spoken truly, Ada acted.   She could not run the dreadful risk of sacrificing even a brutal and criminal father, and with a speed that in her state of mind was marvellous, she altered herself in her girl's clothing, and, as we have seen, for the time, saved Jacob Gray from death.

As she descended the narrow, dilapidated staircase, she pressed her hands convulsively upon her heart to still its tumultuous beatings.   Her position in life appeared to her to be all at once strangely altered.   If—and oh! that horrid if,—if, conveying as it did a possibility of the fact—if Jacob Gray was really her father!— What was she now to do?—How think of him?—How address him?   Could she ever bestow upon him the smallest fraction of that dear love which flows in so easy and natural a current from a child to its parent?—Could she call him father?—No, she felt that she could not.   She examined her feelings to endeavour to detect some yearnings of natural love and duty—some of that undefined, mysterious instinct she had read of as enabling the parent to single out the child—the child the parent, from the great mass of humanity; but the search—the self-examination was in vain. Jacob Gray was to her but the cruel, vindicative tyrant, rioting in oppression and brutality when unresisted, and shrinking from her like a beaten hound when she dared to confront him, and question his acts.

" God of Heaven !" she said, when she had reached the street.; " there should be some similarity of thought, some community of feeling between a father and his child. Do I and Jacob Gray think alike in anything? Have we one feeling in common ?—No,—not one."

As the probabilities of his not being her father crowded upon her mind, now that the intense excitement of the minute was over, Ada became more happy and composed, and she slackened her pace, seeing that she had already placed a considerable distance between herself and the house which had been to her a prison for so long a period.

" I will not, cannot believe it," she said to herself ; " that man is no father of mine. 'Twas a trick—a last master-stroke in the extremity of his fortunes to bend

No. 11.

me to his wishes, for some reasons which I know not, and cannot even hazard the wildest guess of. My father? Jacob Gray, my father? Oh, no, no, no! Rather never let me look upon a father's face, than feel assured of such a horror as that! It cannot—cannot be. Oh, what would I not give to be assured of the lie! Had I worlds of riches in my grasp, I would unloose my hold and let them fly from me to be assured, past all doubt—past all hesitation, that Jacob Gray was to me neither father nor uncle.

The dank fog that hung upon the Thames was now slowly clearing from before the face of heaven, and by the time Ada had reached Westminster Bridge, she could see through several breaks in the sky, glimpses of the starry host looking down upon the rapidly departing night.

The excitement the young girl had gone through had hitherto supported her against the intense coldness of the raw air, but now she trembled in every limb, and as she stood upon the silent bridge, trying to pierce with her dark, lustrous eyes, the heavy fog, and to catch a glimpse of the rushing stream below, she felt the cold to her very heart, and all the miseries of her homeless, friendless situation, rushing at once like a full tide upon her mind, she shrank into one of the little alcoves of the bridge, and sinking upon the rude wooden seat, she burst into tears, and sobbed aloud in the deep anguish of her heart.

Suddenly then she started to her feet, as she heard a heavy footstep approaching. Her first impulse was to leave her place of refuge, and walk quickly onwards, but a second thought caused her to shrink back, with the hope that the stranger would pass on, and she should escape his observation.

Nearer and nearer she heard the heavy measured tread approaching, and an undefinable sensation of fear crept over her as the sounds echoed from one side of the old bridge to the other.

Now and then the person, whoever it was, would pause in his walk, and indistinct mutterings, as if he were communing with himself, reached the ears of Ada.

As he came near she could detect the words he used, and her ears were shocked by oaths of the most awful character, coupled with invectives and horrible imprecations against some one. Involuntarily Ada shrank still closer within the alcove, and now the stranger paused nearly opposite to where she was concealed, and she could hear his words distinctly.

"Curses on him," he muttered; "I swear, I, Andrew Britton, swear by all the furies of hell that I will have that man's blood! He shall bitterly rue his taunts, most bitterly. By Heaven, I would like to tear his heart out. I—I could set his blood flowing like a torrent. I could exult in any agony inflicted upon him. Cunning Britton am I? Taunt on—taunt on; every dog will have his day."

There was now a dead silence for some moments, and Ada strove to recollect where and when she had heard that voice before.

"Can this be one of those from whose visits my—my—no, no, not my father—my uncle shrank from in so much terror? It surely is—or else I have heard his voice in some dream. Ha! he comes—he comes!"

Britton, for it was he, advanced a pace or two and leaned upon the parapet of the bridge, still muttering deep and awful curses. He was so close to Ada that she could have touched him with her small white hand, had she chosen, but she stilled the very beating of her heart as much as possible, in instinctive terror of that man.

"It's all to do over again now," he said: "all over again—with the additional difficulty that he is upon his guard. Oh, could I but light on that boy; I—I'd wring his neck—and then—then Jacob Gray, I would invent some method of burning you to death painfully; some method that would take long in doing this—I should see you writhe in your agony. By the fiends there's comfort in the thought. Oh, that I had him here—here clinging to the parapet of this bridge while I—I, Andrew Britton, was slowly—yes, very slowly, sawing his fingers till he loosed his hold and fell. Then he would strike against yon projection. Ha! ha! that would be one pang—I should him shriek—what music! then down—down he would go into the water, mingling his blood with it! I should see him rise again, and his heart would break in another shriek. Ha! ha! ha! I—I am better with the very thought. He—a step—I will to the Chequers, and drown care in a flagon!"

A strange wild voice was now heard singing in a kind of rude chaunt. The tones were feeble and broken, but Ada, with a feeling of pleasure, recognised in them those of a woman. Her attention, however, was in a moment again turned to Britton, who all at once exclaimed,o

"What voice is that? I—I know that voice, although I have not heard it for some time now."

The voice became more distinct as the singer approached, and there was a wild earnestness in the manner in which the following words were spoken, which touched Ada to the heart:—

"The winter's wind is cold,
    But colder is my heart,
I pray for death full oft,
    Yet may not now depart.
I have a work to do,
    The gentle child to save,
Alas! that its poor father
    Should want a shroud and grave."

"Now I know her—now I know her!" cried Britton. "Damnation, it's—it's Mad Maud! Shall I fly from her—or—or kill her?"

Before he could decide upon a course of action, the poor creature was close to him. She laid her hand upon his arm—

"Found—found," she shrieked, "ha! ha! ha! found at last. Andrew Britton I have travelled many miles to find thee out."

"Away, cursed hag!" cried Britton.

"I have sought you," continued the poor woman, "oh, how I have sought you and Learmont too. You see I am mad, and so I know more than ordinary people. The day is coming—the day of vengeance, and I have come to London to see it. I have asked often—often for you, Andrew Britton, and now you are found."

"Devil!" cried Britton, "why do you haunt me?"

"Haunt you! Yes, that is the word, I do haunt you! I will haunt you to the last."

"Indeed! Perhaps you may meet with some accident."

"No, no; I will tell you who I asked for you. You will not be surprised."

"Who!—who dared you ask for me?"

"There was a man hung last Monday——"

"Well, w——what is that to me, if there were fifty men hung? What is it to me, I say?"

"Nothing—oh, nothing, Andrew Britton; but I asked if he knew your hiding-place."

"Why ask him?"

"Because the good and just cannot know you; you belong not to them; I asked the man who stood beneath the gibbet if he had been tempted to crime by Andrew Britton, the savage smith of Learmont; I asked the hangman if he knew you, and when he said he did not, I described you to him, that he might recognise you, when his cold clammy hands are about your neck!"

"Prating idiot!" said Britton, "if you tempt me to the deed, I'll cast you over the bridge!"

"You dare not, Andrew Britton; you dare not," cried Maud. "Savage as you are, you dare not do that! Strange, too, as you boast yourself, you could not?"

"Indeed!" answered Briton. "Now, by Heaven——"

"Hold—hold! Whatever you do, swear not by Heaven;—that Heaven you will never see! What have you to do with Heaven, that you should record your blustering oaths in its pure annals? Swear not by Heaven, Andrew Britton, or you may provoke a vengeance that may be terrible even to you."

" Tell me," said Britton, in an evidently assumed tone of mildness, " what brought you to London ?"

" A holier errand, Britton, than that which has brought you. God knows I came to save, but you came to destroy."

" Save who ?"

" The child ! the child !"

" You speak in riddles, Maud. What child ?"

" I am mad !" replied the woman. " I know I am mad, but I have not forgotten—no, no. I cannot tell how long ago it is, but I saw the child of the dead brought forth by the bleeding man !"

" You rave," cried Britton.

" No—no; I had no clue to that young child. To wander in search of it was hopeless till—till I found that you, Andrew Britton, were on the move. So long as the sound of your hammer rose on the night air at Learmont, I stayed there,—I hovered round your dwelling."

" You played the spy upon me ?" cried Britton.

" I did—I did; and wherefore should I not ? I have followed you to this city. You came to seek the child ; so have I. But you came quickly, with gold to urge you on your way; I have been many weeks begging from door to door. I asked two things wherever I went ; one was a morsel of broken bread, and the other was to place my face towards London ; now I am here,---here, Britton, I came to save the child."

" Wretch !" cried Britton ; " your madness may be feigned for all I know. Swear to me that you will at once return to Learmont."

" Return ?"

" Ay ; you shall not dog my steps. I know not what you mean. You rave, woman---you rave."

" Do I rave ? Well, well, perhaps 'tis true. But I saw the child."

" Tell me one thing, Maud. Do you know who that child is ?"

There was a pause of a moment and Ada's heart beat with tumultuous emotion, as she thought that now she might hear by this strange accidental meeting the secret of her birth.

" Yes," said Maud ; " yes—I know."

" You are sure ?" said Britton.

" I know, I know," repeated Maud.

" Then, if there is a heaven above us, or a hell beneath us," cried Britton, " you shall not leave this bridge alive !"

" Hush---hush !" cried Mad Maud, " I have dreamt it often, and believe it. You are to die before I do ; it is so arranged, Andrew Britton."

Ada looked out with trembling apprehension from her place of concealment, and she saw, by the rapidly increasing light of the coming day, the savage smith casting rapid glances around, as if to assure himself that no one was within sight of the deed of blood he was about to commit. For a moment an awful apathy crept over the heart of Ada, and she felt as if she were condemned to crouch in that little alcove without power of voice or action, and see the murder committed.

Mad Maud did not appear to have comprehended the last muttered threat of Britton, for she stood with her arms folded across her breast, murmuring in a low tone to herself, and apparently unheedful even of the presence of her enemy. Ada then saw the smith fumble awhile in his breast, and then he drew forth a knife. She saw it glitter in the faint light.

" Yes, yes," said Maud, in a low tone, " I recollect all, or nearly all. How difficult it is to separate the dreams from the reality. The spirit of the dead man still haunts the place ! Yes; that is real ! He cries for his child !—his little child !—and there is a garb on his breast ! Let me think. How has he lived so long after his murder ? Oh, yes—I know now : it is by drinking the blood continually from his own wounds ! Ay, that would preserve him !"

Britton made a step towards her.

" The child !" she cried, suddenly.

"You shall torment me no longer," he cried.

"Ha!" shrieked Maud, as she saw the knife uplifted, "you dare not—cannot do it!"

She shrank back, but Britton followed close upon her. Ada again saw the knife uplifted, and by a violent effort, like a person recovering from a nightmare, she screamed.

The sound seemed to Britton so great a surprise, that he staggered, and dropped the knife from his trembling hand.

Her own voice appeared to have broken the spell of horror that bound up the faculties of Ada, and now, by an impulse which lent her strength and courage, she rushed from the place of concealment, and, snatching the knife from the ground, she fled quickly along the bridge, crying, "Help!—help!"

She had not proceeded many paces when she was caught in the arms of some one who cried,—

"Hilloa!—hilloa! What now, little one?"

"Help!—murder on the bridge!" cried Ada. "Oh!—haste!—haste!—save the woman!"

It was the watchman going his rounds, and he hurried onwards, as fast as his chilled limbs would permit him, towards the spot indicated by Ada, who closely followed him.

"He has killed her!" exclaimed Ada, as she saw Maud lying apparently lifeless on the stones.

"Murder done!" cried the watchman.

Ada cast an anxious glance around her, and she thought that at the further extremity of the bridge she caught sight of the flying figure of the man who she believed had done the deed.

"There!" she said, pointing in the direction—"pursue him!—there flies the murderer!"

The watchman immediately threw down the lantern, and with a great clattering of his iron-shod shoes, rushed across the bridge.

"Alas!—alas!" cried Ada, clasping her hands, "what can all this mean? Who is this poor mad creature?—and who that fearful man? The mystery in which my birth, name, and fate is involved, grows more and more inexplicable. Was it of me she talked so strangely and so wildly? Oh! if she could but breathe to me one word, to assure me that Jacob Gray was not my father, how richly would the terrors of this fearful night be repaid!"

Ada knelt by the body of Maud as she spoke, and placed her hand upon the heart, to endeavour to trace some sign of vitality.

"She lives!—she lives!" suddenly cried Ada, as she felt the regular beating of the organ of life. "Perchance the villain has only struck her. He may not, after casting away his knife, have had the means of harming her very seriously.'

A deep groan now came from the lips of the insensible woman.

"Speak—oh, speak!" cried Ada.

Maud opened her eyes. They glared with the wild fire of insanity on Ada.

"Do you know me?" said the girl.

"Know you?"—know you? Are you an angel or a devil?"

"Alas!" cried Ada, "there is no hope.'

Maud passed her hand across her eyes for several moments as if trying to clear the mist that beset her memory and mental faculties. Then she said,—

"Where is he?"

"The man you were talking with?"

"Yes, Britton, the savage smith of Learmont."

"He has fled,"

"Yes—yes—fled. He was pursued by the dead man asking for his child."

"What child?" said Ada, in a voice trembling with anxiety.

"I saw its little arms cling round its father's murderer. I heard him shriek—I heard him say the hell of conscience had began its awful work within his guilty breast."

"The child—the child," cried Ada,—"what was its name? Oh, tell me, if you can, its name?"

"Its name," repeated Maud. "It was the child of the dead. It—it reminded me of my own. Listen! When I was young—for I was young once—and my hair hung in long silken rights from my brow, when my eyes danced in the pure light of heaven, and my heart mounted with joy, singing like the lark that carries its sweet notes even to the gates of heaven. Long—long ago I clasped to my breast such a dear child as that. So you see it reminded me of my own dear infant."

"And you knew not its name?" said Ada.

"Its name!—no, I cannot tell you its name! but I will tell you a dream."

"Answer me one question," said Ada. "The child, I heard you say, you came to London to save. Was its name Gray?'

"Gray—Gray. Who is Gray?"

"There is hope even," sighed Ada, in the want of confirmation of a terrible doubt. If I am the child she raves so strangely of, she knows me not by that most hateful name."

"Will you hear my dream?" said Maud, endeavouring to rise form the cold stones.

Ada saw that blood was trickling from her head, but whether she had struck it in falling, or the man who had attempted her destruction had inflicted the wound, was doubtful. Ada, however, assisted her to her feet, and as she did so she heard the tread of the wathcman as he returned slowly from his pursuit.

"He's off," cried the mon. "Hilloa!—aint the woman dead?"

"Dead!" shrieked Maud, suddenly confronting the watchman. Is Andrew Britton dead?'

"Who?"

"Andrew Britton, the savage smith; because he is to die before me. Ha! ha! Yes, Andrew Britton will die before I do.

With wild laughter she flew rather than ran across the bridge in the direction of Lambeth, and her voice echoed in the still morning air, as she shrieked,—

Andrew Britton—Andrew Britton—I am not dead!—not dead yet!

The watchman stared after her in amazement, and Ada took the opportunity, while he was thus fully engaged, of walking quickly onwards until she had cleared the bridge and the solemn spires of Westminster Abbey came upon her sight.

CHAPTER XXVIII.

ADA'S WANDERINGS.—THE PEARL NECKLACE.—A KIND HEART.—THE PARK.—A JOYOUS MEETING.—THE ARRANGEMENT.

Cold and hunger now began to exercise a sensible influence upon the fragile frame of Ada. Her step became languid and slow, and she began to feel that her strength was fast deserting her. Her dislike to return to Jacob Gray was very great, and yet where else in that great city could she find a place whereon to lay her aching limbs? The sense of her own extreme destitution came vividly across her imagination, and had it not been for the curious gaze of the early passengers she met, she could have wept freely in her bitterness of heart. Listlessly she walked onwards, and thought, from its very intensity, became at last a positive pain. Money she had none; and, in fact, so secluded from the world had she been kept by the fears of Jacob Gray, that she would not have known how to procure the means of supporting life, even had she possessed valuable property about her.

A cold, glaring winter"s sun shone forth from a clear sky, mocking the earth with an appearance of warmth, which made the sharp wind that whistled round the corners of the streets seem doubly keen and piercing.

"Must I return to that dismal house," thought Ada—"must I again throw myself on the mercy of that man who calls himself my father?"

She paused in doubt and irresolution, and no one who passed could fail to mark the air of deep dejection which sat upon the pale anxious face of the young girl.

It so chanced that she stopped opposite to the shop-door of a jeweller and dealer in precious stones, in Parliament-street, and as she clung to the little wooden rail that guarded the window, she saw the keen, sparkling eyes of an old man fixed on her from within. His beard and general appearance proclaimed him a Jew, and scarcely had Ada shrank from his gaze, and paused a step or two onwards, when she heard a voice behind her saying,—

"My dear, will you sell that necklace?"

Ada turned quickly. The old man from the shop stood before her, and repeated his question.

"Will you sell that necklace?"

"Necklace?" said Ada.

"Yes ; the little necklace you have round your pretty little neck, my dear."

Ada now recollected that among her female attire she had found the necklace, and hastily clasped it on when dressing, to elude the search of Jacob Gray's furious visitors.

"I am tired and hungry," said Ada.

"Are you indeed. Bless me!" cried the old man. "Walk into my shop. You see I am an old man. Walk in—do walk in."

Ada suffered herself to be led into the little shop, and unclasping the necklace, she said—

"Will it fetch me a meal?"

"A meal?" said the jeweller, and his eyes sparkled as he took the necklace. "A meal? Why it's real—no, I mean mock—mock pearls——"

"And valueless?" said Ada.

"No—no—not quite—not quite, my dear. Here is a new guinea—a brigh new guinea!"

Ada took the coin, and said, languidly—

"Alas! I am so strange here, I know not even how to dispose of this to procure me food."

"Indeed?" said the jeweller. "Do you know nobody? Have you no friends?"

"Do you—can you," said Ada, and a radiant blush suffused her cheeks as she spoke—"can you tell me, if you know where a Mr. Seyton lives?"

"Does he know you had a necklace?" said the Jew.

"No, I scarcely knew it myself."

"Indeed!" cried the jeweller, lifting up his eyes and hands. "My dear, I don't know the gentleman you mention."

"I thank you," said Ada, rising.

She left the shop, and looking back after she had gone a few paces, she could not derive how it was that the Jew was putting up his shutters with nervous haste. She little knew that her necklace was of Indian pearls, and worth a very large sum indeed.

To her joy, after she had proceeded a few paces further, she saw that the second house down a small turning to her left, was a little dairy—and immediately entering, she requested of the old woman who served, a draft of milk.

It was handed to her, and she drank it off with great pleasure and laid on the little counter her guinea.

"Would you like the rest, miss?" said the old woman ; "you do seem tired, to be sure."

"I am tired," said Ada, "and would gladly rest myself, if I am not in your way."

"Dear heart, no," said the old woman. "Come in here, it's warmer than the shop. What weather we do have to be sure."

Ada accompanied the woman to the little parlour at the back of the shop, and the good dame placed before her some rolls and more milk, of which the wearied girl partook with more pleasure than she ever made breakfast with before.

"You are too young to be out by yourself," said the dame; "and a great deal too pretty too."

Ada shook her head, as she said,—

"Do you know where resides a Mr. Seyton?"

"No," replied the woman. "This London is such an immense place, that it's like looking for a needle in a bottle of hay to find anybody."

"If I could find him," sighed Ada, "he would be my friend. Is there a gentleman named Sir Francis Hartleton?"

"Indeed there is; and if you want him, he lives close at hand. He is a magistrate, and as good a man as ever breathed."

"Indeed," said Ada. "'Tis very strange!"

"What's strange, my dear?"

"Oh, nothing—nothing. Can you show me his house?"

"Yes; if you come to the door, I can point it out to you, though he's very likely to be at his office, and that's across the park."

Ada accompanied the old woman to her outer door, and she pointed out to the refreshed and much revived girl, a large handsome house, as the residence of Sir Francis Hartleton.

She again tendered her guinea, but the kind-hearted woman replied,—

"Pho, pho, my dear. You sha'n't change your guinea for a sup of milk."

The tears gathered to Ada's eyes at this trifling act of kindness, and she grasped the hand of the good dame, warmly, as she said, in a voice of emotion,—

"I am not used to kindness."

"Not used to kindness? Ah, well, poor thing! If your friend, Sir Francis Hartleton, aint in the way, come here again."

"If I live," said Ada, "I will visit you again."

She then, with a sweet smile, walked from the little dairy, and slowly approached the house of Sir Francis Hartleton. She paused as she neared it, and many anxious doubts and fears crossed her mind, concerning the result of an interview with the magistrate to whom Jacob Gray's mysterious bundle of papers was addressed, and above all, rose like a spectre, the still clinging horrible supposition, that Jacob Gray might possibly be her father. She could not positively swear that he was not. In defiance of all probability he might have spoken the truth.

She stood by the portico of the magistrate's house, and her irresolution increased each moment that she strove to reason with her fears.

"Dare I," she thought, "run this dreadful risk? Heaven knows what that paper may contain which Gray sets such store by. Some awful history of crime and suffering, perchance, which would bring him to a scaffold and proclaim me the child of a murderer. Can I make conditions with the magistrates? Can I say to him, I will direct you to a packet addressed to yourself, containing, I know not what, which you can send a force, if necessary, to possess yourself of, but which you must act upon only so far as may be consistent with my feelings? Alas, no! I feel that such would not be acceded to, and I am tortured by doubts and anxieties —dreadful fears—Jacob Gray, what devil tempted you to raise so dreadful a supposition in my mind that you might be my father? And yet I do not, cannot believe you. No—but I doubt—ay doubt. There lies the agony! the fearful irresolution that cramped my very soul—cripples my exertions to be free, and makes me the unhappy, wretched thing I am. No, I cannot yet betray thee to death, Jacob Gray, although you would have taken my life, even while I slept unsuspectingly beneath your roof. I cannot, dare not yet betray thee."

Scarcely, in the confusion of her feelings, knowing whither she went, she passed the door of Sir Francis Hartleton's house, nor paused till she found herself in the Bird Cage Walk, in St. James's Park. It was still very early, but the fine bracing morning had attracted many pedestrians to the park, and the various walks were beginning to assume a gay appearance, the fashionable hour of promenading being then much earlier than it is at present.

Many an admiring glance was cast upon the beautiful Ada, as she slowly took her uncertain way beneath the tall ancient trees which have now given place to young saplings, the full beauty of which the present generations will never enjoy. The cool air that blew across the wide expanse imparted a delicate bloom to her cheeks, that many a court beauty would have bartered a portion of her existence to obtain. The hat she wore but partially confined the long dancing black ringlets, that fell in nature's own freedom on her neck and shoulders; and, withal, there

was a sweet pensiveness in her manner, and the expressions of her face, which greatly charmed and interested all the gentlemen, and greatly vexed and discomposed all the ladies, who, with one accord, voted it to be affectation.

How little they dreamt of the deep sorrow that was in the young girl's heart.

No. 12.

She walked on till she reached the Great Mall, and then, feeling somewhat weary she sat down on one of the wooden seats, and seeing nothing, hearing nothing, she gave herself up to her own thoughts, and tears trickled slowly from her eyes, as all her meditations tended to the one conclusion that she must starve or go back to the lone house and Jacob Gray.

She was aroused from her reverie by some one repeatedly, in an affected drawl, pronouncing the word,—

"Delicious ; de—licious ; oh, de—licous !" immediately in front of where she sat.

Ada looked up, and balancing himself before her nearly on his toes, was an affectedly dressed person, who was staring at her through an opera-glass, and repeating the word delicious, as conveying his extreme admiration of her. When Ada looked up he advanced with a smirk and a bow, and laying his hand on his embroidered waistcoat, said, in the same drawling, affected tone—

"My charming little Hebe—what unearthly change—what glorious concatenation of sublime events have procured St. James's Park the felicity of beholding you ? Eh, eh, my delicious charmer ?"

"Sir," said Ada, annoyed by the tone of the remarks, the substance of which she scarcely heard or comprehended.

"Charming simplicity !" cried the beau ; "permit me."

He seated himself with these words by the side of Ada, and attempted, in an affected, apeish manner, to take her hand.

Ada shrunk from his touch, and rising with an innocent dignity, that appalled for a moment the fine gentleman, she said—

"I do not know you, sir," and walked onwards, leaving him the questionable credit of having turned her out of the seat.

"Charming ! charming !" she heard him say, after a few moments, as he pursued her along the Mall.

Ada was excessively annoyed at this most disagreeable intrusion, and she quickened her pace in the hope of distancing the gallant ; such, however, was not the event, for he was nearly close to her when she arrived at the next seat, which was occupied but by one gentleman, who was reading a book.

"One stranger," thought Ada, "may protect me from the insults of another," and she paused close to the seat on which was the gentleman reading.

"'Pon honour," cried the beau who had followed her ; "you walk most vulgarly fast. Ah ! ah ! really now, a delicious little creature like you ought to glide, not walk—to glide—positively glide. Ah ! ah ! that would be delicious."

The gentleman who was reading looked up, his eyes met Ada's.

"Harry !" he cried.

"Abert !" she replied, and bursting into tears, she clung convulsively to the arms of Albert Seyton.

CHAPTER XXIX.

THE YOUNG LOVERS.—THE GALLANT OF A HUNDRED YEARS SINCE.—HOPES AND FEARS.—THE DREAM OF A TRUE HEART.

It was several moments before Ada or Albert Seyton could speak from excess of joyful emotion, and it was then the drawling, affected voice of the beau that recalled them to a consciousness of where they were, and that some one besides themselves was in the world.

"'Pon honour—really—damme !" cried Ada's persecutor. "This is extraordinary."

"Sir," said Albert Seyton.

"Well, sir," said the beau.

"I thought you spoke to me."

"'Pon honour no; I wouldn't condescend on any account. Oh, no, 'pon honour."

"I have no desire for your conversation," said Albert, turning his back to him.

"My dear, my charming, delicious damsel," said the beau, smiling at Ada.

"Do you know, sir," said Albert, rising, "that it is a high crime to commit an assault in the Park?"

"Well, 'pon honour what then?"

"Only this, that if you will come outside the gates, I'll cane you within an inch of your life."

"Eh, oh—a perfect savage—a wild beast, 'pon honour," said the beau, making a precipitate retreat.

"Oh, Harry; dear, dear Harry!" said Albert; "by what kind mercy of Heaven are you here?"

"Albert, do not call me Harry."

"My own girl, I know you by no other name. I am not surprised to see you in these becoming garments."

"You—you did not know——"

"That my playmate, Harry, was a beautiful girl," interrupted Albert. "No—I did not—my father it was who first breathed the suspicion that such was the fact. And now tell me some dear feminine name to call you by."

"My name is Ada."

"Ada? A charm is in the sound. My own dear, dear Ada. How came you here—have you thought of me? Where is your uncle? are you happy—dear Ada, are you glad to see me?"

"Albert," said Ada, smiling through her tears, "I will answer your last question first—I am glad to see you, so very glad that I could weep for joy."

"Nay, dear Ada, weep not. You shall never weep again if Albert Seyton can save a tear from dimming your eyes."

"I know it," said Ada; "you were ever kind to the poor persecuted Ada."

"I loved you, Ada."

"Oh, Albert; I have passed through such horrors since we met."

"Horrors, Ada?"

"Yes; and even now I shudder to think of my situation. I am destitute, homeless, hopeless."

"No, Ada," said Albert; "there you wrong yourself and my love; destitute you cannot be while I have an arm to labour for you—homeless you shall not be, for my father, who is an honourable gentleman, will love you as his adopted daughter. Can you then call yourself friendless, Ada?"

"Albert, I am—I am."

"What, Ada; what can you be but what I know you are—all truth, all innocence and virtue?"

"Suppose—suppose," gasped Ada, looking beseechingly in Albert's face, as if her whole existence hung upon his reply—"suppose my name was a disgrace."

"A disgrace?"

"Yes; suppose I had found a father whose hands were stained with blood."

"Oh, no—no—Ada. This is some chimera of your own over-wrought fancy."

"Suppose it's true, Albert Seyton; could you—dared you then call me your Ada?"

"I could—I dared."

"If—I were—the child of a—a——"

"A what?"

"A murderer!"

Albert took her hand gently and tenderly.

"Ada," he said, "crime is not hereditary. You are sinless, spotless, and if I desert you because you may have the misfortune to be the child of one who is guilty, may God desert me in my utmost need."

"Albert," sobbed Ada, "I—I do not believe it; but it is a remote possibility that Jacob Gray is my father."

"Nor do I believe it," said Albert. "'Tis against all nature—depend upon it, Ada, it is not true."

"But—but if it were?"

"My Ada," was his only reply, accompanied by a smile that fell like sunlight upon the young girl's innocent heart.

"You would not, even then, despise me, Albert?" she said.

"Despise you? oh, how can you associate that word with yourself? Despise you, Ada; if you knew the weary miles I have traversed in search of you, you would then feel how truly my happiness is wound up in yours. Not a street, court, or lane in the great city, has been untrodden by me to look for you since your sudden departure from Mrs. Strangeways."

"My uncle hurried me from there to a more secret place of concealment. We have now for some time inhabited a dilapidated house in Lambeth, which you might pass a hundred times, and never guess that aught human lodged within its crumbling walls."

"And still you know not the cause of all this mystery?"

"No; all is dark and mysterious as ever, Albert, except my name, my Christian name, and that in a moment of unguarded passion, Jacob Gray let slip from his lips. Oh, you know not what a pleasure it was to me, in my desolation, to find I had a right to a name."

"My poor Ada."

"Yes, Albert, I am your poor Ada."

"But rich in all true wealth, beauty, innocence, and dear virtue, such as no gold can buy."

"The kind words of those who love are so very grateful," sighed Ada, "and they are so new to me."

"Tell me all that has happened to you since we last parted," said Albert. "My own history is very shortly summed up. My father remained some few weeks longer at Mrs. Strangeways, and then having by dint of earnest applications and remonstrances, procured some portion of what was his due from the Government, we have come close here by Buckingham House, and I am myself in the hope of procuring a situation as private secretary to a man, they say, of enormous wealth and great liberality."

"I joy in your prospects," said Ada. "Alas! mine is a darker retrospect—a gloomier future."

"Nay, Ada, our happiness must go hand-in-hand; or farewell to it for Albert Seyton."

Ada sighed.

"You forget, Albert, that I am beset with difficulties—strange mysteries are around me; who and what I am, even, I know not; although perhaps my ignorance is my greatest joy, while it is my constant source of anxiety, for I have hope now which might by a knowledge of the truth be extinguished for ever."

"Your hope shall become a bright certainty," said Albert, fervently; "and now, tell me, Ada, of your present situation. You have more freedom, or you would not be in the Great Mall of St. James's Park."

"My freedom is but transitory," sighed Ada.

"How so?"

"Last night there came with furious knocking at our house, two men. My uncle said they came to take his life and mine, but that, not finding me, they would allow him to escape."

"'Tis very strange."

"He urged me then to change my boyish clothing for these garments. I resisted his request; he implored me—begged of me to do so, saying that those who sought me knew me but as a boy, and would allow a girl to pass out unmolested. Still I refused, for he had taken the life of a poor dog that loved me, and my mind was sore against him. He kneeled to me, wept, and at the last moment declared himself my father and a murderer!"

"Good Heavens!"

"Yes; the words fell like a thunderbolt on my heart. The men were at the door; there was not time to think. With frantic speed I did his bidding."

"And the plan succeeded?"

" It did. With wondering looks they let me pass. I wandered I know, not where ;—to some bridge I came at length, and there, as I lay crouching from the cold of the raw morning, one of the men passed over."

" One of those who sought Jacob Gray ?"

" Yes, the most violent. There, within my hearing, he had an altercation with a poor mad wanderer, from whom I heard his name."

" His name, Ada ?—It may afford some clue."

" It may. She called him Andrew Britton."

" Andrew Britton!—I will not forget."

" He attempted her murder. My screams, I believe, saved her life."

" And their discourse, Ada ?—What said they ?"

" There speech was of some child to whom great wrong had been done years since. Oh, Albert, my heart told me it was of me they spoke."

" Could you learn nothing of the woman ?"

" Alas! no. Her wits were gone. She wandered strangely in her speech ; madness had taken possession of her, and she, who seemed to know the mystery which envelopes me, could not shape her thoughts to tell me."

" Heaven, Ada, will work out your deliverance in its own good time from this tangled web of guilt and mystery that is cast around you. I still think as I thought before, that the packet which Gray keeps so carefully concealed would unravel all."

" And perhaps destroy him !"

" It might be so."

" Then, Albert, arises the terrible doubt that bad, wicked, cruel as he is, he may be the father of the wretched Ada."

" I cannot for one moment think so," said Albert ; " and yet, I own the thought is terrible."

" If we err, Albert, oh, let us err safely. I cannot call down upon him the vengeance of the laws he has outraged. If some proposal could be made to him, by which he might be induced to tell the truth, upon an assurance of safety from the consequences, I might be saved the bitter pang of betraying my own father, guilty though he may be."

" You are right, Ada," said Albert ; " that is the best, the surest, and the most merciful course. My father will undertake to make such terms with Jacob Gray. He will be mild, yet firm."

" That would be joy indeed," said Ada.

" It shall be done. Dear Ada, a happier future is brightening before you. The past will seem like an envious dream, that has only robbed you of a few hours of sunshine and joy."

" Oh, would I could think so !" said Ada.

" It will—it must be so !" cried Albert, with a full face of animation. " Come with me now to my father, and we will concert all necessary measures."

" I think," said Ada, " that if this matter can be arranged with Gray, as we wish, he must be taken completely by surprise, or all will be lost. If he have time time to hide the papers, or to concoct some deception, we shall gain nothing."

" That is true, Ada, but how can we do as you wish ?"

" Thus," replied Ada. " I will show you the house, and expecting you and your father at a particular hour, I can direct you. Then there can be no time for Gray even to think of any but a straightforward course of action."

" But—but," said Albert, " that involves your return to—to—Gray—and—"

" Oh, heed not that, Albert. A few short hours, blessed as they will be by the conviction that they are the last, will seem nothing in that house, where for so long I have been immured secretly during the light of day, and with no companion to cheer my solitude but a poor dumb creature, that could but look its kindness and gratitude."

" And yet, Ada, my heart is very sad at the mere thought of your returning."

" And so would mine be, Albert, were it not with the assurance of so soon bidding adieu to those gloomy walls for ever."

" I suppose it must be so," said Albert, with a sigh. " I will only just see you so far as to enable you to point out the exact place to me, and then depend upon my father and I being with you in another hour."

" But one hour ?"

" But one, dear Ada."

" That will be easily supported," said Ada, with a grateful smile.   " Oh, let us go at once."

They rose from the Park seat, and the young lovers, arm-in-arm, walked down the Great Mall.

" Are you sure you know the way, Ada?" said Albert, anxiously.

" If I saw the bridge again, I could find it, I know, although I might not discover the most direct route, Albert."

Thus affectionately, and dreaming of future happiness, which, alas ! was still not close at hand, the young guileless beings pursued their course to the old house at Lambeth.

CHAPTER XXX.

JACOB'S RETURN HOME.—AN UNEXPECTED VISITOR.—THE LONELY WATCH.

WHEN Gray left the public-house in which lay the body of the murdered waterman, ne took a rapid route by the edge of the river to his own gloomy home, and very soon reached the cluster of condemned houses, in one of which he resided.

Looking very cautiously around him, as was his invariable custom before gliding into his abode, to see if any one was observing him, he took a key from his pocket, and, opening the frail door, quickly entered the passage.

Then applying his eye to the window, through which he had reconnoitred Britton and Learmont, he took a long look up and down the street to see if he could detect the form of Ada lurking in any of the door-ways, awaiting his return.

" She is not here," he muttered.   " Well, she knows nothing—can guess nothing, or, what little she does know or guess, she dares not utter to human ears, for she will be tormented by the supposition that I may be her father.   Let her die in the streets—let her rot, so she trouble not me ; and yet I wonder she has not returned. She must have lost her way."

Gray then opened the door again, and wiped off the words he had written, then, carefully closing it, he had ascended about half way up the creaking staircase, when his ears were suddenly saluted by a noise that made him tremble, and convulsively clutch the crazy banisters for support.

The noise was of quite a new character to Jacob Gray, and he could not divine how or in what manner it could possibly be produced.   It was not a walking, it was not a fighting or a struggling—a dancing ; but it was a singular and wonderful admixture of them all.   Then there would be a shuffling scramble across the floor, then a hop, step, and a jump, apparently, which would be followed by a continued bumping that threatened the existence of the crazy house, and shook it to the very foundation.

The perspiration of intense fear broke out upon the aching forehead of Jacob Gray, and he sat down melancholy upon the stairs, to try to think what could be the cause of the singular uproar in his commonly so lonely dwelling.

Suddenly the noise approached the stair-head, and it assumed the form of the pattering of naked feet, accompanied by the heavy tread of some one in clumsy shoes.

Jacob Gray's superstitious fears, and they were tolerably numerous, got the better of his prudence, and he raised a cry of terror at the idea of something of an unearthly character having taken up its abode in his solitary dwelling.

The moment he spoke, the sounds rapidly retreated from the stair-head, and for a few moments all was still as the grave.

Jacob Gray listened attentively for a long time before he would venture up the staircase, and when he did so, it was step by step, and with the utmost caution.

When he reached the top, he stood for a time, and listened attentively. Not a sound met his ears. Then he gathered courage, and advanced to the door of the room from whence the noises had seemed to proceed.

All was still, and Jacob Gray summoned his courage to turn the handle of the lock and peer into the apartment.

" There is no one here," he muttered. " What could it have been ? Imagination could not so deceive me !"

As he glanced round the room, to his surprise, he saw that several of the articles which it contained were displaced ; and his apprehensions were still further increased by seeing on the floor several prints of feet, of a character he could not define, and was quite certain he had never seen before.

Scarcely had he time to think upon these strange and startling appearances, when a low growl met his ears, and immediately upon that a voice exclaimed,—

" There, now, you've done it ! Oh, cuss you, Popsy."

Gray gave a jump to the door, and he could scarcely believe his eyes when a man's head appeared from beneath the sofa, and confronted him with a mixed expression of effrontery and apprehension.

" How—came—you—here ?" gasped Gray.

" Popsy come out," was the man's only reply to his interrogatory ; and, to Gray's surprise, an immense shaggy bear made its appearance from the same place of concealment.

" Who are you ?" cried Jacob Gray.

" Why don't you answer the gentleman, you brute ?" said the man, dealing the bear a heavy blow with his fist ; " affectionate ways is lost upon you, that they is——"

" How dare you come here ?" cried Gray.

" Don't ye hear ?" screamed the man, still addressing the bear. " How dare ye come here ?—Eh ?"

" Spy !—villain !" cried Gray, drawing from his breast the same knife with which he would have stabbed Ada to the heart.

" Hilloah !—hilloah !" cried the man. " Do you hear, my Popsy, what he calls ye ?"

The bear commenced a low growling, and displayed a formidable row of blackened fangs at Jacob Gray.

" Who and what are you ?" shrieked Gray to the man.

" Barbican Tibbs, the bear warden, but common people calls me Tipsy Tibbs, and nothink else."

" What in the name of hell brought you here ?" cried Gray.

" Oh ! I'm confidential," replied the man, " and I don't mind telling you."

" Quickly then, quickly."

" Why, you see they say as there isn't to be allowed more than three bear wardens in Westminster, and as I've only just come from Canterbury, I makes faces and a parsecutor."

" Faces, and a what ?"

" A parsecutor—that is, they parsecutes me, and I gives them a dodge through the streets, you see ; and they, coming rather quick, I bolts down this here street, and the first thing I sees is ' wait, J. G.,' on your door."

" Well, what then ?"

" Why, then Popsy and me, we gives the door a drive and we gets in, then we shuts it again, and we've waited here ever since."

" And it was you who made the noise I heard just now, as I was ascending the stairs ?"

" Very like ; and it has quite alarmed poor Popsy, and shattered his nerves by squeaking out in the passage."

" How long have you been here?"

" A matter of half an hour."

" What have you stolen ?"

" Stole ! stole !"

" Yes: tell me, for there are some things I value, and some I do not."

" Popsy, does ye hear what a opinion he has of your morals ?"

Gray walked across the room, and opening a door that led to an inner apartment, he entered it and remained absent some minutes. During that absence he took from a chest (the key of which he had about him) a large sum of money, being the bulk of what he had, from time to time, received of Learmont, and he stowed it carefully about his person ; the greatest care, however, he bestowed upon a packet of papers that were at the bottom of the bag. These he placed carefully in his breast, and then returned to the room in which was the bear warden and his shaggy associate.

" Hark you, friend," said Gray, " I am going to leave this house."

" Good morning," said the bear warden.

" You seem a—a deserving man."

" Do I ?"

" Yes: I will give you the furniture you see about here, if you will defend it against all comers ; and should a young girl come here, will you detain her for me ?"

" Well, that's odd," said Tibbs, " but I don't know you, my master."

" Nor will you. I will take my own time and opportunity of calling upon you."

" Well," said the bear warden, " I don't mind obliging you, particularly as I haven't anything of my own. Is there anything worth having up stairs, old fellow ?"

" There is," said Gray—" and recollect one thing."

" What's that?"

" Should a man come of burly frame and bloated aspect, be assured he comes to take from you, if he can, all that I have given to you—be assured of that."

" The deuce he does !"

" You will know him. He is rough of speech, and coarse and bulky. Beware of him !"

" But what shall I do with him ?"

" Kill him—slaughter him. Take his life how and when you will—or maim him— do him some deadly harm, for, on my soul, I do not believe he has has written any confession. Stay, I had forgotten."

Gray hurried to the cupboard, and took from it the remainder of the poison he had given to Ada's dog ; then turning to the astonished bear warden, he said,—

" Remember, we shall meet again."

He rapidly then descended the staircase, and was out of the house before the man could answer him.

" Well, if ever I knew the like o' that !" said the bear warden. " Popsy !"

The bear answered with a growl.

" We're dropped into a furnished house, and nothing to pay. The blessed world's a beginning to find out our merits, it is !"

CHAPTER XXXI.

ADA'S FATE AGAIN AGAINST HER.—THE THREAT.—THE NEW HOME.

JACOB GRAY was not acting with his usual caution when he left such directions to the bear warden ; but the attempt which had been made upon his life by Learmont and the smith had filled him with rage, and he would, in the heigh of his passion, willingly run some risk to be revenged upon them.

" There is an ancient uninhabited house," he muttered, " nigh to Battersea-fields, that I have several times noted. Its walls are crumbling with age. The bat screams around its tottering chimneys. I have marked it well. There will I now take up my abode, until I have wrung from Learmont a sum sufficient to induce me to leave England for ever ; and when I do—ay, when

I am safe in another land, then will I bring destruction upon him and Britton. They shall find that Jacob Gray]has yet a sting to reach their hearts."

As he spoke, he cast an habitual glance of caution up and down the street, ere he emerged from the doorway of the house he was about to leave for ever.

Some distance from him, the flutter of a white garment caught his eye, and he retreated back into the shadow of the door-way, from where he peered forth, to note who it could be that was approaching that solitary and ill-omened district.

Suddenly he clutched the door-post for support, and a deadly paleness came over him. He saw Ada taking leave of Albert Seyton at the corner of the street. He saw her hands clasped in affectionate pressure. Then, with a
No. 13.

lingering step, Albert Seyton turned away, looking, however, many times back again to smile another brief farewell to Ada.

The deadly feelings of hatred that Gray entertained towards Albert Seyton now all returned in their full force, and he muttered curses, deep and appalling, against both him and Ada.

"That boy again," he growled between his clenched teeth. "How in the name of hell met she with him? In this large city what cursed fate has caused them to meet? I will have his life. Something tells me he will be a stumbling block in my way. I will take his life. Some means I will devise to safely put him in his grave. Yes—yes—smile on, young sir. You fancy now you have tracked Jacob Gray to his lair. You are mistaken. You have found a clue but to lose it again. Ha! she comes. Now, there is some deep-laid plot between them to surprise me ; but I will foil it—I will foil it."

Ada now rapidly approached the door-way, in the shadow of which Gray was concealed. There was a smile of joy upon her face—the pure light of happiness danced in her eyes—and her step was agile as a young fawn.

"Another hour," she whispered to herself—"but another hour of misery, and life commences, as it were, anew for the poor forlorn Ada. My existence, as yet, presents me with nothing but dim shadows ; the dear radient sunshine of the life which Heaven has bestowed upon me, is now at hand. Gray must see his own interests and safety in making terms with Albert and his father. He will tell all—he will absolve me from the fancied ties of friendship, and I will forgive him for all he has made me suffer. If he be very guilty, in another land he may find security and repentance—nay, make his peace with Heaven."

Such were the glowing thoughts of the young girl, who was hastening to separate herself from those who loved her, while in her guileless heart she fondly imagined she was taking the surest means of securing her happiness.

Jacob Gray saw her approaching. Eagerly he watched her steps, and when she paused at the door of the house, he shrunk back into the passage, and allowed her to enter its gloomy portal. Then stepping forward, he closed the door, and said in a low tone,—

"Ada, is there anything in this house you value?"

Ada started, and glanced at Gray with surprise, as she replied,—

"Why do you ask? You see I have returned.'"

"Ay. You could not desert your father!" smiled Gray.

Ada shrunk back as he laid his hand upon her shoulder, and he could not but note the shudder of dislike that came over her.

"Listen to me," he said. "I will give you your choice of one or two alternatives."

"What mean you."

"You recollect the young man, Albert Seyton?"

A deep blush came over Ada's face, as she said,—"I do."

"Well—he had a father——"

"He has a father still!" cried Ada.

"In—deed!" sneered Gray. "You know that."

Ada looked confused.

"Nay," contiued Gray, "you need not blush. Think you, Albert Seyton loves you?"

"Loves me?" echoed Ada.

"Ay. You have read enough to tell you the meaning of the term."

Ada was silent.

"Attend to my words," continued Gray. "I have another home besides this."

"Another home?"

"Yes, Ada ; and in that other home there are domestics which would place you in so proud a station, that Albert Seyton would, in calling you his some few years hence, be acquiring a rank and fortune beyond his or your wildest dreams."

Ada's eyes sparkled as Gray spoke, and she involuntarily moved a step towards him. The thought of enriching, perhaps ennobling, the poor dependant Albert Seyton, was delightful to her heart.

"Oh!" she cried, "if you can do this, I will forget all the past."

"At my house," said Gray. "'Tis near at hand."

"I will count the minutes till you return," said Ada. "Oh, go at once."

"Yes, but not alone. You go with me, or I go not at all. Come, Ada, quick. We shall be back very soon. You are equipped for walking. We will go together.'"

"No—I—wish not to leave here," said Ada.

"Not leave here? Has your love for this place suddenly grown so strong?"

"I am weary," said Ada.

"Then we part for ever! Farewell! Ada. I go now to destroy—to burn those papers! Carry with you through life the doubts that now harass you!"

"Why force me to accompany you?" said Ada. "I am very weary."

"Decide! The distance is but short. The next half hour fixes your fate for life!"

"Half hour!" said Ada. "Will it consume but half an hour?"

"Scarcely so much. A boat will take us where we are going in half the time."

"Jacob Gray," said Ada, solemnly.

"Well—well," replied Gray, avoiding her eyes.

"On your soul, are you speaking truly?"

"On my soul!"

"You swear you are not deceiving me?"

"I swear!"

"We shall return here?"

"We shall, assuredly. Then my task shall be to find out this young man— this Albert Seyton."

"I—I will go," said Ada. "Let us hasten—but half an hour?"

"Nay, not so long a time."

Still Ada hesitated.

"You will know all then," remarked Gray; "who and what you are, you will know; but if you come not now, I leave you this instant for ever! You'll never see me more! and in losing me, you lose all clue to the solution of mysteries that will torture you through life."

"I will go—I will go," said Ada. "Within the hour we shall return."

"We shall. Come, Ada, come."

"The papers that were above in the chest, where are they?"

"In my safe keeping," cried Gray.

"I am weary. Will you not wait until sunset?"

"Not another moment."

"Then I—will—go."

Gray took her by the arm, and they left the house together.

A thousand conflicting thoughts rushed through Ada's mind. The prominent one, however, was the pleasure it would give her to meet Albert Seyton, no longer the child of mystery, and perhaps of guilt, but the proud discendant of some pure and unsullied house. If she let Gray depart now, with him all chance of unravelling doubts and mysteries which, as he truly said, would torture her through life, would be lost. Albert and his father would come but to encumber themselves with a nameless, destitute girl. That she could not bear, and although she doubted, yet she trusted Jacob Gray.

Ada, when she made up her mind that she would accompany Gray, quite astonished him by the nervous haste which she showed in urging him along, and his naturally suspicious mind at once surmised that there was some especial reason in the mind of the young girl which induced her desire to return to the house they were leaving within the hour.

"She has betrayed me to yon boy," he thought. "'Tis more than likely that within the hour I should be a prisoner suing for mercy to him, and my confessions in his hands."

They soon reached the river side, and Gray, addressing a waterman said,—
"Can you take us to Battersea, quickly?"

"Yes, master," said the man ; "the tide serves."

Without another word Gray handed Ada into the boat, and they were soon gliding swiftly along the Thames, towards the marshy fields of Battersea.

As the time progressed, Ada's uneasiness became more and more apparent, and when the waterman landed them at a craggy flight of wooden steps that merely led to the open fields, a tremor came over her, and she began to repent trusting Jacob Gray.

"I see no house," she said. "Whither are you leading me?"

"There—to your left," said Gray. "Yon low building is the place of our destination."

"Let us be quick," said Ada.

With a sneering smile Jacob Gray led the way by the side of the scanty hedges till they reached the gloomy desolate mansion he had long fixed upon as his next place of concealment, should his lone dwelling at Lambeth be discovered.

Ada looked upon the damp crumbling walls and shattered windows with a feeling of dread she could not conceal.

"What place is this?" she falteringly asked.

"'Tis an old deserted farm-house," said Gray, "in which a murder, they say was committed."

"A murder?"

"Yes ; by a man named Forest. It is called now Forest House, and no one will willingly approach it."

They stood now in the shadow of the deep overhanging porch, and Jacob Gray for a moment gazed around him upon the wide expanse of marshy ground. A smile of triumph lit up his face with a demoniac expression.

"Ada," he said, "you would have betrayed me—you may shriek now—no one will hear you ; you may struggle—no one will aid you. This house is your prison —perhaps your tomb."

Ada clasped her hands in terror and despair. "Betrayed—betrayed !" she cried, " oh, Albert——" and sunk in a state of insensibility on the door step of Forest House.

CHAPTER XXXII.

ALBERT'S DISAPPOINTMENT.—TIBBS, THE BEAR WARDEN.—THE SEARCH.—A CONSULTATION.

WITHIN the hour he had named as being the extreme limit of his absence, Albert Seyton and his father arrived at Gray's house at Lambeth. They knocked at first quietly, and finally loudly, for admittance. Here, as they had predetermined, they burst upon the frail door, and, calling upon Ada, Albert flew from room to room of the dismal house.

No voice responded to his, and he was about to give up the search in despair, when a low rumbling sound met his ears from a room he had already visited, and which was immediately followed by a heavy crash of some fallen body.

He and his father instantly rushed into the room, and there, amid the ruins, a table, several bottles, glasses, &c., lay Tibbs, the bear warden, who was evidently far gone in intoxication.

The bear was licking its paws on the spot which would have been under the table had that article of furniture preserved its perpendicularity; but it now lay on one side, and it is to be surmised that Tipsy Tibbs had hidden under it upon hearing the sound of footsteps, and then upset it in his clumsy efforts to emerge from his temporary concealment.

Mr. Seyton Albert looked with undisguised astonishment on the strange spectacle of a drunken man and a bear, where they expected to find a young girl and a cool designing villain.

"How are you?" said Tibbs. "So, so—you're come back, have you? Hurrah—hurray—that's my op—opinion."

Albert stepped up to him, and shaking him roughly, cried in a loud voice:—
"Who are you?"

"Who—who—am—I? why, everybody knows me—I'm—Tip—Tip—Tipsy Tibbs, the bear warder."

"Tell me, have you seen a beautiful girl here? Speak at once."

"A w—w—what?"

"A young girl, with black eyes; sparkling as diamonds—long dancing ringlets."

"Whew!" whistled Tibbs; "don't I wish I had? Oh, the little charmer."

"Wretch!" cried Albert, "have you seen her?"

"Do—do—you mean—Mrs. Tibbs?"

"Albert," said Mr. Seyton, "we shall get no information from this man by angry questioning. Allow me to speak to him. Are you alone here, my friend?"

"No, I aint."

"Who else inhabits this house?"

"Popsy. Hurrah—let's have another bottle—never get drunk—don't make a beast of yourself, old gentleman."

"How long have you been here?"

"Two bottles!"

"How long a time, I say, have you been here?"

"Well, I say—two—two bottles."

"The villain Gray has been more than a match for me, father;" said Albert. "My poor Ada is not here!"

He sunk upon a chair, and gave way to a violent burst of grief as he spoke, and Tibbs gazed upon him in speechless astonishment.

"Albert," said his father, "this is childish of you. Let us thoroughly search this house. We may still find some clue to the object of our search."

"True," said Albert, rising, "I will not despair. We may, perchance, light upon the mysterious packet of papers which Jacob Gray thinks so much of, and which were addressed to Sir Francis Hartleton."

"Take another bottle," suggested Tibbs, making various ridiculous efforts to get on his feet, in all of which he signally failed.

"Sot," said Albert, "I will force more intelligent answers from you yet before I leave this house."

"Take another bottle," said Tibbs. "My dear, here's your health. You have a rare voice. Bless you, you want to stay because I'm here. Don't let him persuade you; d—d—d—n his important papers."

"What do you mean?" cried Albert.

"Why, she's gone, to be sure. They didn't know I was listening on the stairs. Ho! ho! ho!—they're off, and the furniture's all mine. Take another bottle."

"From the ravings of this drunkard," said Mr. Seyton, "we may gather what has happened, Albert. Jacob Gray, on some pretence, having his suspicions awakened, has induced Ada to leave this place with him."

"I fear it is so, father," said Albert; "but here I vow to Heaven that I will not know more rest than is needful to my health and strength till I have found where this bad man has hidden the fairest, best—"

"Control your feelings, Albert," said his father. "God knows how willingly I would have taken this persecuted young girl to my home, and done a parent's duty by her; but Heaven has decreed it otherwise."

With a saddened and dejected air Albert again searched the house. He found no vestige of Ada, save her male attire and the dead dog. An open book was upon the table of her room. That he placed next his heart, with the fond thought that she might have owned and prized it.

"Let us leave this place," said his father, "and the more quickly the better. I will employ some one to watch the house for some days in case Gray should return, and in the meantime, we will ourselves make every inquiry, and use our utmost endeavours to discover his retreat."

With a heavy heart Albert left the house ; he lingered long at the door and in the street, and it was only his father's arguments that induced him at length to quit the spot.

"Father," said Albert, "I will make an application to Sir Francis Hartleton !"

"You forget," replied Mr. Seyton, "that Sir Francis Hartleton is a magistrate, and has a public duty to perform, from which he is not the man to flinch. We wish to temporise with this man Gray, and not drive him to extremities. The more heartily Sir Francis might enter into this business, the more misery we might be laying up for the persecuted girl it is our wish to rescue. Recollect, Albert, there still lives the awful doubt that Jacob Gray may still be the father of Ada."

"It is an awful doubt," said Albert.

"We must not then embitter her existence, wicked as Gray may be, by executing upon him the full measure of justice until that doubt is solved. It would be coldly right to do so, I will grant; but we look more to Ada's happiness, Albert, than the vengeance of the law upon a guilty man."

Albert grasped his father's hand as he replied, in a voice struggling with emotion,—

"Guide me, father—tell me what to do. Your words bring truth and conviction with them."

"Then, Albert, if you succeed in getting the situation you have been endeavouring to obtain, as private secretary to this gentleman, who is reported to be so rich and liberal, there may arise some opportunity of interesting him in the matter, and, through his means and influence, much might be done to unravel the whole mystery without endangering Gray, should he turn out to be Ada's father, of which, however, I have the strongest doubts."

"Yes," cried Albert, with renovated hope ; "they tell me this gentleman, 'Squire Learmont, is rolling in wealth."

"Ay, that is his name. He is comparatively unknown, I hear, in London; but if you become his secretary, he may take a pleasure, if he be a good man, in assisting you."

"It shall be tried, father," said Albert.

Learmont had been inquiring of several persons since his arrival in London for some young man as private secretary, and Albert Seyton, who never in his wildest dreams imagined that the rich 'Squire Learmont, whose wealth was the theme of every tongue, could possibly be in any way connected with the fortunes of the poor persecuted Ada, had applied for the situation, and met with a favourable although evasive answer.

CHAPTER XXXIII.

LEARMONT AT HOME.—DARK REFLECTIONS.—THE SUMMONS.—THE CONFEDERATES.—SUSPICIONS.

IN the small room which he had fitted up specially for himself, sat the 'Squire Learmont, in an attitude of deep thought. His lips occasionally moved as if he were repeating to himself the subject of his meditations. The colour went and came upon his agitated face, according to the uneven tenor of his thoughts. For more than an hour he thus sat, and then suddenly rising, as if with a violent determination to shake off completely

"The thick coming fancies',

that disturbed his brain, he went to the window and looked out upon the court-yard of his mansion.

The uneasy thoughts of Learmont were not, however, to be thus laid aside. In a few moments he again threw himself into the chair from which he had risen, and commenced in a low, anxious, trembling tone, muttering half aloud, the subject of his gloomy thoughts :—

" Was ever a man," he said, " so circumstanced as I ?   With all the will to act, yet so hemmed in by strange circumstances as to be powerless—completely powerless.   In truth, the wily Jacob Gray has had a triumph.   Can the smith have played me false, and warned him of his danger ; yet, no—I cannot think so. Britton hates him, and would gladly take his life.   He could not, with such consummate art, act the passion he exhibited at that lonely hovel, wherein I thought I had entrapped this Gray.   There is yet another supposition.   Does the boy live?   Ay, is there a young heir to Learmont's broad acres and princely revenues?   That is a grave doubt ; but let me doubt ever so strangely, I dare not act.   Jacob Gray—Jacob Gray, the arch-fiend himself could not have woven a better web of protection around a human life, than you have cast around yours ! I dare not kill you.   No! Jacob Gray, you are very safe."

Learmont clenched his hands and ground his teeth together, in impotent rage, as he felt the full conviction upon his mind that he dared not, for his own life's sake, interfere with Jacob Gray.

" There is no plan but one," he said, after a long pause.   " I must try to purchase from him, by some large and tempting offer, both the boy and the confession —then, should he be attracted by such a bait, he shall die for the disquiet he has given me.   If I slaughter him here in my own house, he shall die.   I shall know no peace till that man is a corpse."

A small time-piece in the room now struck the hour of twelve.

" Twelve o'clock," muttered Learmont.   " 'Tis the hour the smith said he would be here ; but punctuality is not one of his virtues.   He knows I must wait for him.   Curses on him—curses !"

A servant slowly opened the door at this moment, and said, in a timid voice, for the household had had several specimens of Learmont's wild passions and violence,—

" An it please your wor hip, here is Master Gray."

" Show him here," said Learmont, quickly, and the man was out of the room as expeditiously as if he had been pulled from behind with a sudden jerk.

" They will meet here," muttered Learmont.   " Well, be it so.   Three persons so strangely knit together, as these two men and myself. were surely never heard of.   Hating them with that hatred which requires to be glutted with blood to calm its fury ; yet I am obliged to supply their wildest extravagancies and most insolent demands.   Oh, if I, dared, if—oh, you are here, Jacob Gray ?"

As you perceive, most worshipful sir," said Gray, as the closed the door behind him, and fixed his keen, ferret-looking eyes upon the 'Squire.

For a few minutes they regarded each other in silence.   Learmont at length, uttered the word,—

" Well ?"

" I am rejoiced to hear you are well," sneered Gray.   " The fog last night was very damp."

" Jacob Gray," said Learmont, " I sought your life."

" Your worship was so kind," said Gray, " and since my connexion with your worship has grown so dangerous, it shall bear a higher price."

" What mean you ?"

" I mean," said Gray, striking the palm of his hand with his fist—" I mean that where I have had one guinea, 'Squire Learmont, I will have ten ; where ten, a hundred.   Thank yourself for raising my price.   My nerves are weak, and yet I prize them.   I like my blood to keep its even pace.   If I am to be tortured-—if I am to be threatened—broken in upon at midnight, and cold steel held to my throat, I will be well paid—extremely well paid.   You understand me, 'Squire Learmont, I have raised my price."

There was a strange mixture of cunning, rage, and ferocity in Jacob Gray's tone and manner as he made this speech. Every other word that he spoke showed a disposition to shout with anger, but then it was as quickly subdued again by his habitual caution and timidity. When he had finished he glared at Learmont with a pale and distorted countenance awaiting his reply.

"Jacob Gray," said Learmont, "I did seek your life, but it was not for your life's sake I sought it."

"Indeed!" sneered Gray.

"No," continued Learmont. "What is your life to me? But the precautions that you have taken to protect yourself keep me in continual and imminent danger. What's so uncertain as human life?"

"Ay—what?" said Gray.

"Suppose your sudden death—by accident or illness—what though I had poured into your coffers half my income?—what though I had satisfied your wildest demands, still might I be exposed to danger most imminent, nay, to death, without your meaning so to involve me."

"Well I know," said Jacob Gray, "that life is uncertain—too well I know it. 'Squire Learmont, you have coined for yourself the danger you describe. While you live, it will haunt you."

"But wherefore should I?" said Learmont. "You talk of increasing your demands by tens and hundreds—why not name thousands at once as the price of——"

"Of what?"

"The boy, and your absence for ever from England."

"I—I—had thought of that," said Gray.

"And a wise thought too," urged Learmont. "What is your life to me, were it not that you have surrounded me with danger? Do I thirst for your blood for its own sake? Certainly not—have your own price—bring me the boy, and destroy your writtten confession."

"And leave England for ever?" muttered Gray.

"Yes—seek safety and enjoyment somewhere else in another land, where the finger of suspicion can never be pointed at you, and where you will only appear as the wealthy stranger."

"'Tis tempting," said Gray; "but——"

"But what?—Why do you hesitate?"

"Would there be no danger, even between the threshold of this house and the deck of the vessel which was to convey me and my fortunes from England for ever?"

"Danger?—a—what danger?"

"The assassin's knife," said Gray. "Hear me, 'Squire Learmont; if we could trust each other for so brief a space as half an hour, it might be done; but we cannot—you know we cannot!"

"You refuse upon danger," said Learmont, trying to smile, and producing a ghastly distortion of visage. "You are over cautious, Master Gray."

"I think not," said Gray, "and yet I will think upon your offer, 'Squire Learmont. I will not deny that some scheme of the kind has already dawned upon my own mind. I will think upon your offer; and should some means occur to me by which safety can be so well assured as to be past a doubt, I will accept it, for I loathe the life I lead."

"'Tis well," said Learmont.

"And now I want a hundred pounds," said Jacob Gray, in an affectedly submissive voice.

"A hundred pounds!" exclaimed Learmont.

"Yes, a hundred! and I will have them."

"Jacob Gray," said Learmont, "why have I plunged myself into crime, and leagued myself with such men as you and Britton, but for this gold which your and his insatiable demands would wring from me?"

"Agreed," cried Gray. "But now 'tis done, and to keep the gibbet——"

", The gibbet!"

"Ay, the gibbet, 'Squire Learmont. To keep that without its victim, you must, and will pay the last farthing, if needs be, of that gold you talk of as your tempter. Why, it tempted me, and I will riot in it! A hundred pounds, good 'squire."

"Ten thousand are yours, if you bring me the boy and your written confession."

"Ten thousand! You may safely make it twenty, 'squire, or thirty."

"What do you mean?"

"You call me cautious—cunning—wily as a fox, and am I all that; and because I am, I will not sell my life for five minutes at the utmost possession of any sum."

"Sell your life!"

No. 14.

"Yes, my life. How many paces from this room would suffice to carry Jacob Gray to his grave, provided he gave up his two most rare securities—the boy and the confession?"

"You wrong me by your suspicions," said Learmont, with difficulty suppressing the rage that was swelling in his bosom."

"A hundred pounds!" said Gray.

"Jacob Gray, hear me——"

"Hear me first. A hundred pounds!"

Learmont went to a cabinet in the apartment, and without another word counted out the sum.

"Have you moved Jacob Gray?" he said, in a calm voice.

"Nay," replied Gray, "why need you ask?"

"A message from the Old Smithy," announced a servant at this juncture.

"'Tis Britton," whispered Learmont to Gray.

"What, cunning Master Britton!" answered Gray. "Ho! ho! I shall be glad to see him."

"Admit him," said Learmont to the servant; then turning to Gray, he added,—

"Will you leave me, now?"

"No," said Gray.

"Wherefore?"

"Because I do not want the smith again upon my track, like a blood hound!"

"Oh, Jacob Gray," said Learmont, "if you could destroy Britton, securing at the same time the dangerous papers he has—bring me the boy—commit your own confession to the flames, and share my fortune!"

"Humph!" said Gray, "If I could."

"You might."

"Well, that'll do," roared Britton, as the servant held the door open for him to enter the room. "Oh—oh—you here?"

"Yes, cunning Britton," said Gray, "I am here."

"Curse you, then!" said Britton, flinging himself into a chair.

"Bless you!" said Gray. "Ho, ho! clever Britton."

"Perhaps, gentlemen," sneered Learmont, "you will condescend to carry your quarrels to some pot-house, when you have said what you wish to say to me?"

"Yes," said Gray, "we shall anger his worship."

"Damnation take——"

"Hold, Britton," cried Learmont. "You come here for money. Name the sum, and go."

"Oh, name the sum!" said Britton. "What's to-day?"

"Friday, my dear Britton," said Gray. "It's generally considered an unlucky day. I pray you to take care of yourself, cunning Britton."

Britton cast a savage scowl upon Gray, as he said,—

"I shall, and mind you be as careful. Friday, is it? Twenty pounds will last me till next Monday, 'squire."

"Will they, indeed?" sneered Learmont. "Here they are, then. May I now be indulged with the privacy of my own house?"

"There now," said Gray, "you hear his worship; why don't you go, Britton?"

"Because I intend staying out, Jacob Gray," cried Britton, fiercely.

"Well," said Gray, rising, "be it so, but hearken to me, 'Squire Learmont. If I find this ruffian upon my track, I will be revenged with safety to myself—bitterly revenged—now beware!"

So saying, Jacob Gray left the room, with an expression of countenance perfectly demoniac.

Britton made a movement to follow him, but the 'squire laid his hand upon his arm, and said,—

"No—not now, Britton. We must devise some better means yet of destroying with perfect safety, this Jacob Gray."

"Curses on him!" growled Britton. "Did you hear how he taunted me?"

" I did."

" Then, I say I must have his blood."

" You shall."

" I will—I have sworn it—I will take the hateful life of Jacob Gray."

" Britton, we understand each other. This Gray is as great an enemy to you as he is to me."

" I know he is," growled Britton. " You need not tell me that. And who, think you, is in London, and raving through the streets to every one she meets, about the Old Smithy, and a murder?"

" She ? Who mean you ?"

" Mad Maud, who used to haunt the village, and ever vented her bitterest curses upon me."

" Mad Maud ! she must be secured. Even her clamour might arouse suspicion in some quarter, and many a prying knave would be glad to pick a hole in the reputation of the rich and proud 'Squire Learmont. When did you see her, Britton ?"

" On Westminster-bridge, after you and I had parted last."

" The—water—was—near."

" It was, but the old beldame raised a clamour that brought help. When next we meet, she may not be so near assistance."

" True. How true is the lesson taught by Jacob Gray, that safety is best doubly assured. You stay still at the Chequers ?"

" Yes—you know I do? Why do you ask ?"

" From no special motive."

" Yes ; I am still at the Chequers. Ho! ho! ho! money flies there. Mine host is about to build a new front to his house and it's all with your money, 'squire. By G—d, they sell good liquor at the Chequers, and there's a merry company— a good song and a silver tankard on purpose for good Master Britton. Ho! ho! ho!"

" You sleep there?"

" Yes ; but mind ye, 'squire ; drunk or sober, at home or abroad, those papers are well secured. Don't try to play any tricks with me, 'squire ; you would rue the hour."

" Pho! pho!" interrupted Learmont, " we understand each other—our interests are mutual—but, as for this Jacob Gray——"

. " Ah! curse Jacob Gray!"

" To which I devoutly cry—Amen!" said Learmont. " And now, Britton, it is our policy to let matters sleep for a time, until Gray's newly awakened caution is somewhat calmed. Go, now, good Britton, and—mind you, when you are inclined to set a price upon the papers you have, tell me and we will talk about it."

" Oh, very well," said Britton. " I shall be glad to see you at the Chequers any time. I will say this for you, 'Squire Learmont, that you pay very well, indeed. I lead the life of a gentleman now—nothing to do, and so many people to help me—drink—drink from morning till night. Damme, what could a king do more."

CHAPTER XXIV.

THE GIRL IN HER MELANCHOLY HOME.—THE PRISON HOUSE.—A DUNGEON'S LGOM.—UNAVAILING SORROW.

WHEN Jacob Gray pitched upon the lone house, at Battersea, as his place of abode, he could not have resolved upon a house less likely to be visited by the curious, although seen from the river at a considerable distance: it was always pointed out by the watermen to their customers, as " Forest's haunted house."

The fact was, that a most awful and cold-blooded murder had been committed in the house, since which it had been allowed to fall into decay, and the land around it, which had been at one time well drained, had subsided into its old character of a marsh. The fall of a stack of chimnies had impressed every one with a belief of the extreme danger of venturing within its crazy walls, lest they should fall and engulf the rash intruder in their ruins.

It was with great caution that Gray first visited this place, that he was long in discovering that the signs of decay were more superficial than otherwise, and, inquiring diligently and cautiously concerning it, he heard the character of the deserted house, which induced him mentally to resolve upon making it his next abode, should he be hunted out of his miserable residence in the ruined street at Lambeth.

The only risk he considered he ran of discovery, was in conveying Ada there by daylight; but, after that, he resolved upon never leaving, or approaching his gloomy abode, except by night, or early in the morning, when he was quite sure no one was observing him, save upon special occasions, such as his recent visit to Learmont, whom he was anxious to see after the stormy meeting in his former residence.

When Ada recovered consciousness, she at first felt all that sensation of relief which comes over any one, awakening from a horrible dream; but this feeling of satisfaction lingered but for a few fleeting moments in the breast of the persecuted, betrayed girl. The gloom that surrounded her—the damp air that imparted a chill to her very heart—the dim ray of light that proceeded from a candle, the wick of which showed that it had been some hours unattended, all convinced her that she was a prisoner.

With a cry of despair she started to her feet: she clasped her hands, and called on Heaven to protect her, as she hastily glanced round the gloomy place in which she found herself.

The dismal echo of her own voice only answered her wild and incoherent appeal.

"Oh! Heaven," she cried, "I shall be murdered here. No one to hear my cries! No one to aid me! I am lost—lost! Oh!—Albert, Albert!"

She sank upon the ground, and wept long and bitterly as the thoughts of how foolishly she had allowed herself to be deceived by Gray crowded upon her oppressed mind.

"No hope!—no hope!—now there is no hope!" she cried, bitterly. "Oh! why was I preserved for this dreadful fate! 1 thought it hard to endure the cold air from the river, while crouching on the bridge. O God! O God! what would I not give now to be as free beneath the canopy of Heaven as I was then!"

After a time the native energy of Ada's character overcame her first bursts of bitter grief; and raising her head, she strove to pierce, with her tear-filled eyes, the dim obscurity by which she was surrounded.

"What can this place be?" she asked herself. "Let me recollect. He brought me across swampy fields to a ruined house, and there, at that point, recollection ceases—memory fades away in a confused whirl, none of which are sufficiently distinct for the mind to grasp and reason upon.

She now approached the light, and, carefully trimming it, she held it as high as she could, and, turning slowly round, took a long and anxious survey of as much as she could see of her dungeon, for such she considered it.

The floor was of earth merely, and the walls seemed to be composed of the same material, mingled with stones and broken bricks, to give them some degree of solidity and strength. The place altogether appeared to be of considerable extent, and, by the various refuse matter that lay about, it would seem to have been a cellar for strong vegetables, wood, &c. during the winter season. A quantity of rough sacks and baskets lay in different corners mouldy and moist, with the accumulated damp of many years, and the air, too, was loaded with unwholesome moisture, and pernicious exhalations.

With a slow and cautious step Ada traversed the whole of this gloomy place, and what surprised her much was, that she could see no means of ingress or egress from it.

"How have I been placed here?" she asked herself. "There is no food. Good Heaven! Am I doomed to starve in this wretched place? Alas! is this the awful mode which the fears of Jacob Gray have suggested to him as the easiest and safest of compassing my death?"

So terrible did the dread of death in that damp, gloomy dungeon become to the imagination of Ada, that she could scarcely hold the light for trembling, and she placed it on one of the mouldy baskets, while with clasped hands, and upon her knees, she breathed a prayer to Heaven for protection and safety in her extreme peril.

How calming and sweet is the soothing influence of prayer! As the trembling words, wrung from the pure heart of the gentle and beautiful Ada in her deep anguish, ascended to that Heaven which never permits the wicked to prosper, but always interposes to protect the innocent and virtuous, a holy balm seemed to fall upon her blighted spirit, and the benign influence of some air from the regions of eternal bliss seemed to fill the gloomy dungeon with a brightness and a beauty that deprived it of its horrors.

For many minutes now Ada remained silent, and her fancy strayed to the last kind words of Albert Seyton. Then she pictured him and his father seeking her in the house at Lambeth. In her "mind's eye" she saw his despair when he found her not, and she thought then that her heart must break to think that she should never see him more.

"Albert—Albert!" she cried,—"oh save me—save—seek for me! Oh, could your eyes but cast themselves upon this gloomy abode and know that I was here, how happy might I be—far happier than before, for now I feel convinced this dreadful man Gray is not my father. No—no, he could not thus before Heaven have betrayed his child! Albert—Albert!"

She dropped her head upon her breast, and again the tears blinded those beautiful eyes, and rolled gently down her cheeks, thence falling upon a neck of snowy whiteness, and losing their gem-like lustre in the meshes of her raven hair. Suddenly she ceased to weep. She ceased to call on Albert, and a chill came over her heart, as she heard Gray's voice, cry,—

"Ada—Ada!"

She looked up, and from a square opening in the wall far above her reach, she saw a streaming light enter the dungeon.

"Ada!" again cried Gray, and she saw him peering into the gloom below, and shading his eyes from the glare of the light he carried. "Ada!" he cried, impatiently.

"I am here," said Ada.

Gray immediately disappeared from the opening, and all was again darkness whence the light had issued.

"What can he mean?" thought Ada. "Did he suppose that already my spirit had yielded to this gloomy prison, and is he disappointed to find that I still live?"

While Ada was pursuing these reflections, Gray suddenly re-appeared, and placing a ladder from the opening into the dungeon, he said, in a voice intended to be conciliatory,—

"Ascend, Ada—ascend."

"I can meet death here," said Ada.

"There is no death to meet," said Gray. "I mean you no harm."

"Because you have done me as much, short of taking my life," said Ada, "as lies in your power. By what right—by what flimsy shadow of justice am I immured here?"

"Ascend I say," cried Gray. "There is warmth and comfort above here."

"I may as well," thought Ada, with a shudder, "meet my death from his hands above as by starvation in this place."

She placed her foot upon the ladder, and slowly ascended. When she neared the top, Gray reached out his hand, and assisted her into the room in which he was.

" You tremble, girl!" he said.

" And so do you," replied Ada, fixing her eyes upon Jacob Gray's pale face.

" You—you think I mean you harm," he said, in a hesitating tone, and avoiding Ada's gaze as much as possible.

" Think !" repeated Ada,—"think, Jacob Gray !"

" Jacob Gray !" he cried. " You speak strangely. I thought you now me."

" I do—too well," said Ada.

" I have told you I am your father, girl."

" You have told me."

" And you believe——"

" No," said Ada, with sudden energy; " on my soul, no—as I hope for heaven, no !"

" Indeed !"

" Yes, Jacob Gray, for the honour of all fathers—for the credit of humanity, I cannot—will not believe myself your daughter. No, no, Jacob Gray, I am no longer scared by that dreadful thought—thank God !"

" Girl, you know not what you say."

" My words may be incoherent—not aptly chosen—but the sense is the same. Jacob Gray, you are neither father, uncle, kith, nor kin of mine. No, no !"

" Who—who—told you so ?" gasped Gray.

" There—there !" cried Ada," your fears speak the truth; you have confessed he cheat. Jacob Gray, I could forgive you all, now that that dreadful weight is removed from my heart. '

" Know you where you are, since you know so much ?" said Gray, after a pause.

" I do not, save that I have been deceived by you, and lured by false promises to this dismal place."

" You are in my power. Still, likewise, I assert you are my daughter."

" In your power I grant myself, as far as Heaven will permit you; but you are no kindred to me, Jacob Gray."

" By hell, if you call me Jacob Gray again——"

" Jacob Gray," shouted Ada, her face kindling with excitement, and her delicate form appearing to dilate as she pointed to the abashed and writhing countenance of the villain who trembled before her.

" Be it so." said Gray; " we understand each other now. You defy me."

" I ever defied you, Jacob Gray !"

" Be it so," he repeated. " Follow me."

" It is my heart that defies you, Jacob Gray," said Ada. " You are a man, and I a weak girl. You are strong enough to enforce me to accompany you."

" Come on !" cried Gray.

Ada slowly followed him from the room. Gray passed out at a large doorway into a smaller apartment, in which was a table, some baskets, similar to those Ada had seen in the cellar, turned up for seats, and a small fire dimly burning on an ample hearth; before which a bullock might have been roasted, and perhaps had been in days gone by.

" Ada," said Gray, " look around you."

Ada did so, and Gray continued,—

" This is a place of discomfort; there is little to recommend it, but it is preferable to yon gloomy dungeon from whence you have but now emerged."

" I grant it," said Ada.

" Your secret existence here is necessary for me; nay, my very life depends upon it. It may be but for a very short time. You may imagine that I am not in love with this mode of life. I have gold—store of gold—but I want more, and each day shall add to the glittering mass. When it has reached the amount I wish, you shall be free."

" Free ?"

" Yes ; free as air."

" When you have the gold you wish ?"

" Even so, Ada."

" I have read that the love of gold is one of those passions that increase as they are fed."

" Not with me; I have fixed in my imagination a sum which I must have. Then, Ada, I leave England for ever, and you are free !"

" But wherefore is my captivity essential ?"

" Ask no questions," interrupted Gray. " Circumstances make you valuable ; but mark me, you are equally valuable, dead as alive. Nay, start not—I wish you to live, if possible. I do not want to take your life—because—because——"

" Because, what ?"

" I can use you as such an implement of revenge that—that—but no matter, no matter, your fate is in your hands ; you shall yourself decide your destiny."

" Myself ?"

" Yes ; swear to me that without my permission you will not leave this place. Swear to me you will aid me in keeping you in silence and secrecy. Swear this, and you return no more to yon loathsome dungeon, and perhaps, in a short time, I may place you on a dazzling height of power, and wealth shall make all England ring with your name ! You could be the admired of all ; your beauty, your wit, your gold would be the themes of every tongue, if you will but swear."

" How can I believe you ?" said Ada.

" If ever words of truth passed my lips," said Gray, " these are such."

" On what pretence was I lured hither ?" '

" Ada, by force or fraud I was compelled to bring you here. 'Twere better the latter than the former."

" And now," said Ada, " by force or fraud I am to be kept here. Jacob Gray, I will not swear faith to thee."

" You will not ? '

" I will not."

" Girl, you are mad—you know not what you do. This is a device of mine to save your life—to place you above the reach of fortune's malice."

" Answer me one thing, and call on Heaven to witness your truth," said Ada. " Are you father, uncle, or nothing else ?"

" Will you swear as I bid you ?"

" I cannot resign the dear hope of escape," said Ada.

" Escape," replied Gray, " is impossible. The dungeon from which I have even now brought you is inaccessible save by the means in my power. For my own safety, I must keep you a prisoner, or—or——"

" Or murder me, you would say. Jacob Gray, I think you dare not kill me."

" Dare not ?" said Gray, trembling.

" Yes ; dare not were my words. Now, I will make to you a proposal. Trust me ; tell me all, who and what I am. Tell me all, and I will forgive injuries, and perchance do your bidding."

" No, no, I cannot tell you yet," said Gray. " I wish you one day to know all —when I have my gold."

" Am I to be the slave of your avarice ?"

" Call it so, if you will."

" Who am I ? '

" I cannot tell you."

" Who were those men who sought your life ? Was the name of one Andrew Britton."

Gray absolutely shrieked as Ada pronounced the name of the smith, which it will be recollected she had heard from Mad Maud on Westminster-bridge.

" A—what is this—what do you mean ? Who—what devil told you—speak— Ada—speak. Have the—the dead risen ? Speak, or you will drive me mad !"

CHAPTER XXV.

ADA'S APPEAL.—THE PROMISE.—ADA'S DESPAIR.—GRAY'S TRIUMPH.

ADA had seen too often the nervous terrors of Jacob Gray to feel much alarm at his present emotion, and she merely replied,—

"The man I mention—Andrew Britton by name—was one of them who came to you at our late house. That he is in some manner connected with the mysterious circumstances which envelope me, I am convinced. Oh, Jacob Gray, bethink you now of the evil of wickedness; you cannot gain more, nay, not half so much by deceiving and persecuting me than you would gain by trusting me with every secret. Besides, there is one possession which would then be yours, which is beyond all price—that dear inheritance we all have from Heaven as its best, most costly gift, and which is too often bartered for a bauble. You would have peace of mind, Jacob Gray, which you have not now. He who tries may read pain and disquiet in your face. You are haunted by the fearful creations of your own over-burdened conscience. I—even I—can see that some hideous spectre of the past is ever rising, perhaps in bloody guise, before your appalled imagination. Oh, I am weak, young, and unknowing in the ways of life, but I can tell you, Jacob Gray, that guilt is misery. You are wretched—most wretched—you lead a life of apprehension. Your own fears will carry you to an early grave. Oh, do some solitary but great act of justice, and it will stand as a shield betwixt you and your trembling soul—will plead with Heaven for you, and by its brightness so dim the record of your guilt that you may cherish such dear hopes of mercy as shall in themselves be happiness. Release me—trust me. Tell me, Jacob Gray, who and what I am. Justice, though tardy, is justice still. I will invent causes for you up to this moment—I will pray for you, Jacob Gray. Oh, end at once this life of horror, suspicion and distress!"

Gray waved his hand several times while Ada was speaking, as if he would implore her to cease, but wanted power of speech to stop her in her appeal. When she had ceased speaking, she stood with clasped hands gazing in his face, and waiting with a deep and holy anxiety the words that would pass his lips in reply.

"Girl!" he gasped, " you know not what you ask! I wish you well, but—dare not—dare not—dare not tell you a tale would drive you mad! Enough—enough—urge me no more! All this will have an end—it must—but not as you ask. Have patience, Ada, and I will do great things for you! Yes, great things, when I am far away in another land, and safe—safe from those who would take my life—who would spill my blood like water! Have patience, girl! Have patience, and all will be well."

"I am your prisoner, then, Jacob Gray," said Ada—" still your prisoner?"

"For a time—only for a time. Promise me, by the faith you have in Heaven—swear that you will abide here without an effort to escape, and such a freedom as you can safely have, you shall have."

" If I refuse?"

" Then you must take the consequences. My safety—my life, I tell you, depends upon your security. I will not trifle with my own existence! Night and day you cellar shall be your home!"

" But how can my being your unknown, solitary, and unseen prisoner avail you?"

" Ask me not," cried Gray. " There is but one other alternative."

" And that is —— "

" Your death, Ada!"

" Ay—my death! such was my thought."

" But I—I do not want to kill you," cried Gray, hurriedly. " On my soul, I do not! Understand me, girl; your existence is equally valuable to me as your death!

perhaps more so, although it has its risks. Promise me that you will not increase those risks, and on my oath, you shall live unharmed by me."

Ada sank into a seat, and a feeling of despair came over her heart.

"Jacob Gray," she said, "let me promise to go far away—I will be unseen—unknown."

"Not yet," cried Gray. I tell you I have not gold enough for that yet. There will come a time when to proclaim who and what you are will be so sweet to me, that it is only my love for that gold which brings in its train the means of every enjoyment that can stifle pangs that spring from the past, that induces me now to put off the dear gratification of that deep revenge!"

"Still a bad and unworthy motive," said Ada. "You will only do justice to me for the gratification of your own malignant passions,"

"Say what you will, girl," cried Gray. "Call me what you will, I care not You are to me now a mine of wealth! When my love of gold is glutted to the full, I can make you an instrument of such revenge, that I shall wish for no greater

No. 15.

gratification! You understand your position now—you may baulk me of my revenge by forcing me to kill you! Save yourself, Ada, by your solemn promise to remain here!"

Ada felt that all further appeal was useless, and she wept bitterly as the dreary future presented itself to her as a protracted imprisonment, or a speedy and cruel death.

Gray watched her keenly, and advancing close to her, he whispered in her ear,—

" Ada, life is sweet to the young! A world full of beauty and enjoyment is before you—if you promise what I ask—you shall have wealth—and wealth is power. You shall be able to raise the lowly—to crush the proud, if you promise! Those whom you love, you may do wonders for! He too—that youth who has wound himself around your girlish heart—he you can enrich! He will owe all to you! It will be Ada that will lift him from his low estate, and make him great—perhaps noble! But you must promise! How hard it is to die so young! Think of the last bitter pang! None to pity—none to love you! But I need not point such agony to you, you will promise?"

" Jacob Gray," said Ada, dashing the tears from her eyes, " the allurements you hold out to me are not sufficient; but I will not cast away the life God has has given me."

" You promise?"

" On condition, I will. But hear me, Gray. I do not believe the tale you tell me, that you will take my life some time when I am sleeping, for awake you dare not —if I promise not, I do believe, for already have you attempted the deed."

" You—you will promise?" cried Gray, impatiently.

" Not unconditionally," replied Ada. " For one month from now I do promise.

" To make no effort to leave here?"

" I will be passive merely. I will repel no one."

" But you will remain?"

" Unsought by any one, I will not leave this place."

" You swear?"

" No, Jacob Gray, I will not swear."

" Well! I—I will take your word. You have made a wise decision."

" Heaven knows I am helpless," said Ada. " The decision is scarcely mine."

She burst into tears, and wept bitterly. The name of Albert mingled with her sobs, for she felt now that she was separated from him for an indefinite period.

" Heaven help me," she sobbed. " I am now desolate, indeed."

" Hope," cried Gray. " Hope, Ada. The time may come sooner than you think. The time for my revenge, but I must have more gold yet—much more gold; then, Ada, begins your triumph. You shall find yourself raised to a height you dream not of. Jacob Gray's revenge shall be your fortune. You need not weep. You will cause tears of blood—yes, the blood of those who would have murdered me, but they dare not. Ha! ha! they dared not; and Jacob Gray is still too cunning—far too cunning to fall their victim."

Ada sat silent and spirit-broken in that lonely house. A weight seemed to hang upon her heart, and even hope, that one dear solace of the unfortunate, appeared to have flown from her breast.

Gray had brought food with him, which Ada partook of in silence, and when the night had come, and the short-lived winter's sun had gone to rest, he took his hat and cloak, and prepared to go forth.

" Ada," he said, " attend to nothing—heed nothing while I am gone. If danger —that is, I mean, if any one should venture here, extinguish your light, and seek some hiding-place, for be assured, your life is the object sought by those who would visit the dwelling of Jacob Gray. You understand me. Be cautious."

Ada answered not, and Gray slouching his hat over his face, and drawing his cloak closely around him, left the lone house with a slow and stealthy step, taking his route towards the river's bank, from where he took a boat to Westminster.

CHAPTER XXVI.

HE SQUIRE.—THE LIFE OF A CAPTIVE.—A STRANGE FATALITY.—THE ASSOCIATES

VICE, by the decrees of Providence, seems to have its allotted span. Truly may we say, "The wicked triumph for a season," and by some strange combination of circumstances, notwithstanding the turbulence, the anxiety, and the danger of Learmont's early days in the metropolis, matters so arranged themselves, or were arranged for wise purposes by the great Dispenser of all things, that from the day on which Ada made her promise to Jacob Gray, Learmont had prospered in his career of villany. His natural sagacity had told him, that now Jacob Gray was put upon his guard, any further open attempt against his life would be attended with great danger, and might possibly have the effect of driving him to some desperate measure of retaliation and revenge, which might involve both. From a deep and careful review, therefore, of the whole of the circumstances by which he was surrounded, the criminal and unscrupulous 'squire decided upon a safer, although more expensive and protracted course of action, than he had hitherto pursued; that was, to continually tempt Gray by large offers to give up the supposed boy, together with his own confession, and go to some foreign land to spend the earnings of his criminality.

Jacob Gray, with the cunning which formed such an ingredient in his character, favoured this idea on the part of Learmont, by apparently always hesitating upon his offers, while at the same time he had thoroughly and entirely made up his mind not to accept them; feeling, as he did, that his life would not be worth a minute's purchase after he had declared Ada's sex, and given her up together with his written confession.

Learmont at the same time was not neglectful of the chance that continually presented itself of discovering Gray's place of abode, and pouncing upon him some night unawares, and wresting from him both the boy and the confession, at the same time that he glutted his hatred by putting him to death.

Jacob Gray for once in his life had been injudicious when he told Ada that he only waited for a certain amount of gold before he gratified his revenge by declaring who and what she was. He really had decided upon such a course. The taunts and undisguised contempt of Learmont had awakened a revengeful spirit in his breast, while the attempt to murder him in the old house at Lambeth inflamed to perfect fury, and made, as it were, part of his very nature.

Learmont laboured under considerable difficulty in any attempts he might make to trace Jacob Gray to his abode, in consequence of the impossibility of trusting any one to do the office of spy upon him, except the smith or himself. To the smith, Britton, there were many weighty objections now. Intoxication was doing its work, and moreover Grey knew him so well. Learmont therefore felt that henceforward Britton could be no useful agent in any attempt to discover the retreat of Gray.

Then for him, Learmont himself, to dog the footsteps of the cautious villain from his own house, was an undertaking full of difficulty. The very haste with which he would have had to attire himself for the street had its objections; and were Gray to come some day by appointment, and find him ready equipped to follow him, would not his extremely suspicious mind at once conclude the object?

Thus the task of following Jacob Gray became one of no ordinary difficulty, and Learmont wasted many months in trying to dissuade himself from persevering in his present course, and take a large sum at once; expatiating himself immediately afterwards, which, by-the-by, Learmont never for one moment intended to permit him to do, for he would have slaughtered him upon his own marble steps rather than allow him to escape the moment he could do so with no other danger than that to be encountered from the mere fact of taking a life, in justification of which he would easily have found some plausible excuse, if questioned concerning the act by the laws.

Not a week passed without a visit from Gray, and at each he always carried away as much as he could wring from Learmont's policy or his fears.

But how truly did poor Ada say, that the love of gold was a passion which grew as it was fed. Already had Gray received from Learmont a sum far exceeding that which he had first fixed in his mind as what would content him ere he sought his revenge. Still, however, he lingered, and as each visit to 'Squire Learmont's mansion added something to his store, he could not bring his mind to stop in time. Day after day—week after week—month succeeding month—he still hoarded, saying over to himself,—

"Not yet—not yet! I will have more gold ere I have my revenge."

The smith, too, was to Learmont ever a sight of terror. He still lived at the Chequers, close to Learmont's mansion; and he, too, paid periodical visits to the proud 'squire, although his demands were insignificant in comparison with those of Jacob Gray.

While a few guineas sufficed for the coarse vices, the drunkenness, and the debaucheries of the smith, Jacob Gray was not satisfied unless he increased his hidden store by a large sum.

Thus, although the smith's eternal "message from the Old Smithy" grated upon his very soul, Learmont did not feel that intensity of hatred to Britton that he did to Jacob Gray.

Nevertheless he made frequent offers to Britton to quit the country, and give up to him certain papers which, on the night of the murder at the Old Smithy, had been by Britton taken from the corpse of him who met his death within that ill-named pile.

These papers were of as much importance to Learmont as any could well be; for if they did not prove his illegitimacy, they raised the point so strongly that had he stood alone as the last and only heir to the vast estates of Learmont, he could scarcely have established his claim.

Of this he was assured by Gray, who would himself have gloried in the possession of such a document, but he dared not take them from the body; hence they fell, knowingly by him, into the hands of Britton.

It was likewise constantly urged by Britton that he, too, had a confession written, and, in pursuance of his word, had rolled it round the knife of Jacob Gray, which the latter had left behind him at the smithy in the body of his victim.

For a long time it had become an object with Learmont to discover from Britton where he kept such important documents, determining, should he find out, to make some desperate effort by fraud or violence to possess himself of them; but the smith constantly and pertinaciously eluded the most artful inquiries, and Learmont could obtain no clue to where they were concealed, although by Britton's manner he felt satisfied they were not at the Chequers. Still he feared to do violence to Britton, lest he might have adopted some means of bringing them to light after his decease.

Never probably were three persons placed by a curious train of circumstances in such strange relation to each other.

Learmont hating the two accomplices of his guilt, and not deterred by the slightest compunctions of conscience from taking their lives if he dared, yet placed in so singular a position with regard to them, that he trembled at the idea of any accident or sudden illness depriving either of them of existence, as such an event might bring to light the documents by which they held themselves safe from assassination at his hands.

Jacob Gray received large sums of money which he dare not use, and trembled with apprehensions from day to day lest his miserable retreat in the marshes of Battersea should be discovered, yet with a species of insanity lingered on with an unquenchable thirst of adding to his store of gold before he began the enjoyment of a single guinea of it.

Britton, the reckless savage smith, was the only one of these three men who in his own brutal manner enjoyed the fruits of his crimes. He feasted, drank, and led a life of awful and reckless debauchery from day to day—defying the future and drowning the present in a sea of intoxication.

And now let us speak of Ada—the young, the beautiful, the persecuted Ada—who now for many weary months had endured the solitary and miserable life of a captive in the little house at Battersea.

From time to time Jacob Gray had enforced a renewal of the girl's promise not to escape from her state of bondage; and who, under similar circumstances, would have refused the pledge when death was the only alternative? Life to all is dear and precious—it is the one possession to which mankind fondly clings under all privations—all sufferings. Rob life of all its joys—clothe it in misery—attack the frame in which it lingers by disease and unceasing pain; still, while the brain retains its healthy action, there will be a clinging to life—to mere vitality, which is in human nature a feeling altogether independent of all that makes up the pains or joys of existence. But if life is thus clung to with a desperate reluctance to quit it by the aged, the diseased, and the hopeless, how much greater must be its charms to the young, healthful, ardent, and enthusiastic spirit that in its young existence seems almost immortal!

Ada was unhappy—miserable, but she had not yet done with hope; she could not say, take my life, Jacob Gray, for I will promise no more; that would have been a species of moral suicide from which she shrank aghast; and feeling, from Gray's manner, a firm conviction that he did speak the truth when he declared that her death or life were alike indifferent to him, except so far as the former placed him in a less dangerous position, and the latter would eventually gratify some wild feeling of revenge against some one, she did go on from month to month promising that she would make no effort to escape, and still hoping that a day of deliverance was near, till the hue of health began to fade upon her cheeks, and she felt that dreadful sinking of the heart which ever waits on hope deferred.

We have now another person in our *dramatis personæ* to speak of, and that is the gallant, young, and enthusiastic Albert Seyton.

The sudden and mysterious disappearance of Ada had struck deeply upon his heart, and after about a fortnight's hopeless search through London, during which he endured immense fatigue, and scarcely took any nourishment to sustain his exhausted frame, he was seized with an illness which brought him to the point of death, and from which he recovered but very slowly, although a good constitution and the affectionate solicitude of his father at length triumphed over the disease.

CHAPTER XXVII.

LEARMONT AT HOME.—THE BARONETCY.—A VISITOR.—THE REJECTED OFFER.

A RICH, glowing summer's sun was shining through the stained glass in a large window of one of the principal rooms in the mansion of Learmont. The very air seemed filled with glorious tints, rivalling in hues of gorgeous beauty the brightest refulgence of the rainbow. The songs of birds from the gardens came sweetly to the ear: a dreamy stillness, such as is often to be observed towards the close of some delicious summer day, seemed to pervade all things. He, however, who sat in that richly-decked apartment had no ear for the melodies of nature; for him the glorious sunlight had no romantic charms. His brow was knit with anxious care—deep furrows were on his cheeks, and a nervous irritation of manner betrayed the heart ill at ease.

It was 'Squire Learmont himself who thus sat at the close of that summer's day, and the change in his appearance since we last presented him to the reader was so great, that it might have been supposed many years had passed over his head instead of the comparatively short time that had actually elapsed. His lank black hair was thickly mingled with grey tints, and the sallow of his complexion had changed more and more to a sickly awful white, such as might be supposed to sit upon the countenance o fone risen from the grave.

He sat for a long time silent, although his lips moved as if he were muttering o himself something that formed the principal subject of his meditation.

"Well," he suddenly said, half aloud, "if I have made so great an inroad in my accumulated wealth as to reduce it by one-fourth of its whole amount, I have achieved something—ay, a great deal, for I have made the first step up the ladder of nobility. This baronetcy that is promised me is what I suggested to myself long since. Yes, that is the commencement of power, the limit of which who shall define—then a marriage—one of those marriages of convenience on one side and ambition on the other. My wealth will make me a most acceptable suitor to some branch of a noble family, whose peerage will look all the better for a new coat of gilding. Humph, what says the minister?"

He took from the table before him a note which lay open, and read it lowly and distinctly. It ran thus :—

"There can be no doubt of his Majesty's most gracious inclination to confer a baronetcy upon you, without the slightest reference to your patriotic and disinterested offer to purchase the means of occupying six seats in the lower house. The matter may be well concluded this present week."

"May it?" muttered Learmont; "it shall. I am not one who brooks delays. I have paid dearly for my baronetcy, and I will have it. Those six seats have cost me thrice their sums in thousands—ay, more than that. There can indeed be no doubt of the gracious intentions of his Majesty; that business is settled. I am to all intents and purposes even now a baronet—I have paid the price, and, thank the Fates, this is a country where all things have a price, nobility included; and now, how much longer am I to be tortured by these rascals, Gray and Britton? My bitterest curses on them both. Gray's demands increase each time he comes here; his love of gold is insatiable, and he never relaxes in his caution. How on earth to cope with that man I know not. Must I ever be the victim of his avarice until some day he dies, leaving behind him that which might condemn me? No; this must, cannot last. Too long already have I groaned under the weight of this man's hideous presence, and frequent visits. Some bold or hazardous scheme must rid me of him; and, too, he peremptorily refuses aught to do with the destruction of Britton. He thinks the job too dangerous, and taunts me with the sneer that he gets of me already what gold he chooses to demand. Jacob Gray, beware. Some accident may yet arise to place you at my mercy—my mercy? Ha! ha! Oh, if I could invent some torture—some—Ha! what now?"

"Master Gray desires speech of your worship," said a servant.

In a moment Gray entered the room. Anxiety of mind, and the necessity of constant caution, had had all their effect upon Jacob Gray. He stooped considerably, and moved along with a slow, silent, shuffling tread, as if he feared the very sound of his own footsteps would betray him. He peered into the face of Learmont from his half-closed eyes, and then gently sliding to a seat, he said, in a half whisper,—

"Well, 'squire, how fares it with you?"

"Indifferently well, Jacob Gray," said Learmont. "You look pale and ill."

"No, no!" said Gray, quickly, "I'm very well, quite well and strong. I shall have many years to live yet, I am quite well and strong."

"Your looks belie you then; your hands tremble; you are weak, Jacob Gray."

"And yet so strong," said Gray, trembling, his small eyes fixed at Learmont, "that those who would destroy me dare not lay a finger on me in violence!"

"I understand your taunt," said Learmont; "it has long been settled between us that I dare not take your life, Jacob Gray. But even now, will nothing tempt you to conclude a business which is slowly but surely hurrying you to the grave?"

" 'Squire Learmont," said Gray calmly, " it may be hurrying me to my grave, but I do not wish to avoid the hurry by being at once placed in it; I may be ill, but I am not yet disposed to take death as a remedy. You understand me, 'Squire Learmont?"

" 'Twere needless to affect to be ignorant of your meaning; you think that I would be so foolish as to run the great risk of not letting you go in peace."

" I know it."

" You are wrong, Jacob Gray. There was a time, I admit, when I panted for your destruction—I longed to be revenged upon you for your hints and instructions to Britton; but that time is past—personal safety is now all I care for."

" Humph!" said Gray; " revenge is such a long-lived passion. 'Tis sometimes like a blazing fire craving fiercely for its prey, and then it moves to something desperate and dangerous; but at others 'tis like a smouldering combustion, scarcely telling of its existence, but still slowly and surely burning on till the end of time, as if it were by some mysterious means fed by its own ashes. 'Squire Learmont, I do not say absolutely nay to your offer. There may come a day when I shall wish for freedom of action in another land; then I will bring the boy perchance to you, reserving the confession until my foot is on the shore, or some other safe method which I have not yet matured: at present, however, we will wait; yes, we will have a little patience, 'Squire Learmont."

Learmont bit his lips, and bent a scowl of such fierce hatred at Gray, that if he had for a moment doubted the flame of resentment still lived in Learmont's breast or not, such doubt would have been at once dissipated, and he would have felt convinced that their relative positions had not altered one iota.

" Well, well," said Gray, after a moment's pause, " we will talk of other things. The boy improves exceedingly."

Learmont bent on him a glance of peculiar meaning as he said—

" Gray, that boy would be to me a dainty sight in his coffin."

" No doubt—no doubt," said Gray. " The time may come, when you may enjoy such a sight; but not yet—not yet."

" I must needs wait your pleasure in this matter, Master Gray; but you are not serious in refusing to exert your skill in the destruction of the besotted knave, Britton? Ah! Jacob Gray, you stand in your own light most grievously."

" Do I?" said Gray. " Hem! 'Squire Learmont, some time since I listened to your proposals for the death of Britton, the savage smith. I agreed with you that his love of drink should be the means used to lure him to destruction. The plan was this—to stultify his judgment and never very active caution, by the strong stimulants he so dotes on, till I wound from him the secret of where he kept the papers, you know, and the confession, if indeed he had written one—a fact I always doubted; and then a subtle poison in his cup would remove him for ever. Two things prompted me to the deed, 'Squire Learmont."

" What were they?"

" The one was, my love of gold. Look ye, sir; had I obtained the papers which prove, as I well know, your illegitimacy, and bar you for ever from possessing the estates of Learmont, be assured I should have kept them."

" Kept them, Gray?"

" Ay, kept them."

" But you had—you have—sufficient hold on me already, in the person of that boy."

" A hold I had, but scarcely sufficient, 'squire. I am as a careful mariner who in the calmest sea, would like two anchors to hold his bark. The boy is a great thing; a valuable property; but human life is uncertain, and the 'Squire of Learmont deep and bold."

" What mean you?"

" I mean that I have lived upon the rack!" said Gray, his pale face quivering with emotion. "Was I not by you watched, hunted like a wild beast to my lair. You know I was; and the possession of these papers would have made me sleep more soundly at night, for it would scarcely have been prudent of you to hunt a man who possessed such certain means of disinheriting you, even although you had paved your path to wealth with oceans of blood. I tell you I would possess these papers."

"And what benefit would the death of Britton have been to me, then?"

Gray smiled hideously as he replied,—

"It is always better to consolidate debts, 'Squire Learmont; you would have had one creditor then, instead of two. Then, likewise, I would have sold you the boy and left England for ever."

"Indeed?"

"Yes; with the papers."

"And yet," said Learmont, after a pause, "with all these advantages to you resulting from the deed, you refuse to prosecute the enterprise of removing Britton safely, which I am quite sure that you can do."

"Hem!" said Gray, and his small eyes twinkled as he fixed them upon the countenance of the 'squire. "There is an old fable of two dogs fighting for a bone, while a third walks off unscathed with the object of contention. 'Squire Learmont, you are scarcely yet a match for Jacob Gray!"

Learmont was silent, and Gray laughed, and then started in alarm at the unwonted sound of his own mirth.

"You spoke of two reasons for the death of Britton," said Learmont, after a pause of several minutes' duration.

"Ay," said Gray, "I did, and there I was indiscreet. My second reason was, revenge. I hated Britton. I still hate him. I—I loathe him; and my deep hatred, the direful spirit of my revenge, urged me to run some little risk to gratify it. I knew your policy—I saw it as clearly as the sun at noon-day. But I was a little blinded by my revenge, and I did make an attempt to get the savage smith in my toils."

"You failed?"

"Yes, because you were too hasty in your wish to get rid of Jacob Gray. You recollect the Bishop's-walk on a certain frosty morning some time since?"

"The Bishop's-walk?"

"Yes. There was a man who would have assisted me in the destruction of Britton. You, 'Squire Learmont, left that man a mangled, bleeding corpse in the Bishop's-walk."

"I!" exclaimed Learmont.

"Yes you! I did not see you do the deed, but after some thought I could stake my life upon the fact that Sheldon, the Thames waterman, came by his death from your sword. Thus it was 'squire; that man was tempted by me to assist in the murder of Britton. Curiosity, or breach of faith, induced him to dog my footsteps to the lonely house in which you and I and Britton had the pleasant interview at midnight."

Learmont made a gesture of impatience, and Gray proceeded.

"You note how candid and explanatory I am; it is not worth my while to lie or conceal aught from you. By some means then, which I own I know not, you met with this Sheldon. He told you my place of abode, and for the information you murdered him."

Learmont bit his lips with passion.

"That circumstance awakened me," added Gray; "oh! it did me a world of good. I then saw on what slippery ground I stood. I let my revenge sleep, and had its proper time for awaking. You taught me an useful lesson, 'squire, a lesson on prudence."

"Jacob Gray," said Learmont, gravely, "you have great talent. Think over my offers. If you can, procure me Britton's papers. Give me up the boy, and spend your life in any other land you choose. I will charge my lands with an annuity of five thousand pounds per annum."

" But the smith ?"

" I will; you having rendered him innoxious by depriving him of the papers, undertake to destroy him.   He shall not live four-and-twenty hours after that event.'

" I—will—think," said Gray, rising.

" You had better," cried Learmont. " Here is more money now; but you had
better take my offer.   It is a large one.''

" Hem !" said Gray.

"And before you go, now," added Learmont. in a tone of excitement, "since you
have been so candid with me, know that I am not altogether so much in your
power as you, in your great cunning and admirable wisdom, may imagine."

" I am all attention," answered Gray.

" Then I tell you there is a point of endurance beyond which even I may be
   No. 16,

goaded : pass that by your demands; and I collect all my portable wealth and eave England for ever, first handing you over to the tender mercy of the laws."

"Indeed!" said Gray; "I have too much faith."

"Faith in what?"

"In your love."

"My love?"

"Ay—for yourself. I wish you a good evening, and pleasant dreams. Hem!"

CHAPTER XXVIII.

ADA'S LONE HOME.—THE SUMMER.—AN ADVENTURE.

"BLESSED," says the simple 'squire of Don Quixote, "is the man who first invented sleep." What would the spirit-worn—the persecuted—the heart-stricken—and the desolate do without sleep? Oh, if there be one heavenly seal set upon the pure and innocent heart, it is that dear impressive slumber—deep and dreamless as infants, which, like a soft south wind in dreariest winter, lays for a time the wearied senses in a blessed repose. Then is the imagination freed from earthly dross, and clinging cares, carried far, far away to happier times. The poor prisoner then escapes from his dungeon—his fetters drop from his benumbed limbs, and he lives again in the glorious sunshine, with the blue heavens alone looking down upon him, and the green earth in all its wondrous beauty stretching far before him. The wave-tossed mariner,

"Absent so long from his heart's home,"

will, in the dreamy watches of the night, revisit the loved ones that are far away. The freezing winds of the "blustrous north" will lack their power to chill his blood—the lashing surges will, by

"Some strange magic,"

be converted into sweet gentle sounds, such as perchance surround his young home; a home to which his affections still cling, the more distant he may happen to be from it. It was a beautiful idea of the Italian poet, who likened the yearning for home of the Swiss exiles to the tightening of the invisible strings that bound their hearts to their native lands as they increased in distance from it. The tired soldier too,

"When the night cloud has lowered,
And the sentinel stars set their watch in the sky;"

on his pallet of straw, he dreams of his home and all his dear associations. He dreams of his native vale far away, and in imagination he looks for the familiar objects of childhood, each associated with some dear reminiscence that makes perchance a wild flower to his heart a dearer object than the richest gem! What is cold, hunger, wounds, and pains then to him? He returns "weary and wan," yet, oh! so happy to those he loves.

"He hears his own mountain goats bleating aloft,
He knows the sweet strain which the corn-reapers sing."

He sees his home—the cottage embowered 'mongst crawling honey-suckles. Every sight and sound is to his ears delightful. The wild flowers breathe delicious perfume. Then he reaches the well-known door. There is a cry of welcome!

"His little ones kiss him a thousand times o'er
And his wife sobs aloud in her fulness of heart."

Oh, what a magic is in that scene conjured up by the fairy power of imagination!

The visions may fly at the first faint blush of the coming morn. The sleeper may awaken with a sigh and a tear; but he *has* been home again ; he *has* kissed his children ; oh, he *has* been happy, although 'twas but a dream. Soldier, may such dear visions ever haunt thy pillow!

May sleep—gentle sleep—

"Nature's soft nurse,"

ever haunt the couch of innocence ! If the persecuted and the unhappy had nothing but that oblivion from care to thank Heaven for, it should be sufficient to fill the heart with holy thoughts and deep thanksgiving.

What would our poor Ada have done, but for sleep? and she could sleep, although Jacob Gray could not. The weary months were reduced more than one-half, and Heaven sent visions of joy and gushing tenderness to uphold and comfort that young and beautiful girl in her solitude. The day might be gloomy, and the old lone house dispiriting and cheerless, but the fancy, when the body slept, took its airy flight, and, Heaven-directed, laid in stores of beauty and food for waking thoughts.

Ada had kept her word with Gray. She had never once passed the threshold of that lonely abode, and she had renewed her promise from time to time, although with many tears ; but she would not throw away the life that God had given, so she lived on, illumined in her heart by the hope that the day would come when her dreams would become reality, and her present reality seem to her but as the fevered imaginings of a dream !

From some hidden place in her prison-house, she would sometimes look out for hours together upon the blue sky, and envy the wild birds as they winged their free and happy flight far, far away in the liquid depths of the blue arch that spanned the world. She would listen, too, to the song of the aspiring lark as it flew up—up towards heaven, until it became but a small speck in the sky. This was a delight to Ada; and to her imaginative mind nothing could be sweeter music than the slowly decreasing cadences of that wild, happy song of the lark as in its very recklessness of joy it leaves the earth so far behind.

Far away sometimes in the open fields she would see some one picking his or her way along the swampy ground, and she blessed the sight of any other human face than Gray's.

Then in the old house there were insects—crawling things, which in the great world are despised and put to death because we cannot see their beauties, nor appreciate their pains ; but Ada, with a simple and beautiful theology, taught her by her own heart, and culled from the few books she had read, feared not these creatures, for she looked upon them all with a kindly spirit, as being the creations of the same Great Being who had made the mountains, the wondrous ocean, and all the living, breathing things of earth, sea, and air.

So in course of time the very mice would come forth at the sound of her voice and eat from her hand, peering at her from their bright twinkling eyes, without fear.

Ada shrunk from no living thing but Jacob Gray, and him she avoided as much as possible. He always brought home with him food enough for their wants, and Ada took her portion in silence. There was one small room which she had appropriated to her own use, and into that room she forbade Jacob Gray to enter. Wicked and ruthless as he was, that young girl had acquired a kind of moral control over him which he could not shake off. They never conversed. They had no discussions. Their whole intercourse resolved itself to this:—That he would murder her if she did not promise to abide where she was without making an effort to escape, and she, having promised so much, was otherwise a free agent, and under no sort of control from him.

Thus the seasons had rolled on, and Ada had marked the subsidence of winter, and the budding beauty

"Of the sweet spring-time,"

from her lonely home.

Sometimes Jacob Gray would be absent for a whole day, and Ada was glad he stayed away, for she would then sing to herself old ballads which were dear to her, because the book from which she had learnt them had been lent to her by Albert Seyton. But when she heard his well-known signal of return, she went to her own room, and sung no more. Thus, to a certain extent, Ada enjoyed the glorious summer, although she could not wander in the green fields, or lose herself among shady trees. The soft genial air, however, visited the ill-omened house at Battersea, as freely as it blew its sweets in at the windows of a palace, and these were moments when Ada felt most happy.

Gray, when he remained out the whole day, never mentioned to Ada his intention of so doing ; but she knew that if the day fully dawned and he came not, that he would wait until the shades of evening rendered it safe for him to cross the fields without the risk of observation.

On these occasions it seemed to Ada as if she was half liberated from her prison, so grateful to her was the absence of Jacob Gray ; and after seeing the day fairly commenced. and rambling through the old house without encountering the object of her dread and dislike, she would feel comparatively happy.

It was on one of these occasions that we purpose conducting our readers to the Lone House at Battersea.

Gray had gone out the preceding evening at sunset, and the morning came without bringing him back again. A glorious morning it was—full of life, beauty, and sunshine. The summer air blew sweetly into the chamber of the lovely girl ; but the very murmuring of the soft breeze was company to her, and the twitter of the happy birds as they flew past the old house fell like Nature's own music, as indeed it was, upon her innocent heart.

Hastily dressing herself she rose, and with a slow, cautious step, descended to Gray's sitting-room. He was not there. Here she stood for a few minutes upon the principal staircase, and listened attentively. No sound disturbed the repose that dwelt in that house. Ada smiled.

"He has not returned," she cried; "I shall have a whole day to myself. A wholetday, in which to sing over my old songs, to converse with the birds, to feed the mice and insects that abound here ; and I think they have learnt to know me now, and love me in their way, and according to their several natures."

The day wore on, but it was scarcely wearisome to Ada, 'Tis true she sometimes wept when she thought how cruelly she was situated ; but then she would soon smile again, and sitting opposite to an open window, she would gaze for a long time upon the clear blue sky, and speculate upon the various forms of the light fleecy vapours that imparted an additional charm to the sky, by partially concealing some of its beauties. Then she thought of those who were dear to her—of Albert Seyton—of his father—of the poor woman who had spoken a few kind words to her at the little milk-shop at Westminster. To those who have been accustomed to harshness, with what a freshening joy the recollection of a few words kindly spoken comes upon the mind ! Oh, if the rich and powerful—those who are living in high places, and revelling in luxury—did but know how delightful to the bruised heart but a few simple words of common courtesy are, they would themselves feel a pleasure in speaking them, such as all the adulation of their flatterers— all the glitter of their homes,—all the gaudy insignia of their rank can never bestow upon them. Ada wept with grateful joy because that poor woman spoke but a few short sentences of kindness to her !

CHAPTER XXIX.

THE ALARM.—THE PURSUIT.—A MOB IN THE LAST CENTURY.—THE FUGITIVE.—
MAUD, THE BEGGAR.

As Ada sat in an attitude of deep musing, and her long silken eyelashes were wet with the tears starting to her eyes, a confused murmuring sound from afar off came faintly to her ears. She started, for in that solitude any direct or tangible sounds from the great world without were strange and new.

Bending forward in an attitude of listening, the young girl endeavoured to catch the purport of the unwonted disturbance.

Still nothing but faint mingled cries and shouts came to her ear; she could hear no words distinctly, but, from the general tone of the cries, she guessed they were those of derision and contempt.

So faintly were they borne across the fields, that had not the light winds blown steadily in that direction, no sound of all the uproarious voices, that were so mingled together in strange confusion, would have reached the ears of the solitary prisoner.

Nearer and nearer, however, came the sounds; and Ada went to the highest floor in the house, the windows of which commanded an extensive view in all directions. Close down by the river's side she could now discern a disorderly rabble, apparently pursuing another object. She saw the action of casting stones, and shouts, shrieks, loud laughter, and every kind of noise which the human voice is capable of producing, came each moment more distinctly to her ear.

That the crowd were pursuing and pelting some object of popular scorn or hatred she could easily perceive. Foremost, there appeared a strange cowering mass of rags and squalid poverty, against which the indignation of the rabble of Lambeth seemed to be directed.

Ada watched the scene with a pitying eye; she could not imagine any circumstances which could justify the hunting down of a fellow-creature in such a manner; but Ada did not know enough of human nature to be aware that one of its recreations is persecution in all forms and shapes.

Now she saw the fugitive take to the fields, and, to her surprise, make directly for the Lone House. Ada's heart beat quick with the idea that the mob would follow, and her promise to Jacob Gray would become nugatory by persons discovering her, and forcing her from her imprisonment, instead of she herself contriving the means of escape.

Too soon, however, was this hope dissipated, for the yelling rout, after pursuing the fugitive a short distance further, gave up the sport, and retired with shouts and execrations from the pleasures of the chase.

Still Ada saw the fugitive rushing wildly onwards, and from the looseness and ragged plight of the apparel, she could not decide whether it was a male or a female, who was evidently making with speed towards Forrest's house.

To obtain a nearer view of the stranger, Ada descended to the lower portion of the house, and, by the time she had reached a window on the ground floor, the persecuted one was so close to the building that she, with a cry of surprise, recognised her as the mad female she had met on Westminster bridge, and whose features and general appearance the extraordinary events of that night had evidently impressed on her memory.

For several moments after making this discovery, Ada's mind was in such a whirl of conflicting emotions, that she could decide upon no particular course of action; and it was not until the poor hunted, bruised, and bleeding woman had sunk upon the door-step with a deep groan of anguish, that Ada felt herself at once roused to exertion, and determined to dare all, risk all, in the sacred cause of humanity.

In another moment the compassionate and warm-hearted Ada was at the door. She hesitated not a moment; but flinging it open, stood, for the first time for many weary months, from under that miserable prison-house.

The sound of the opening of the door seemed at once to strike alarm into the heart of the poor creature, who sat crouched upon the steps and sobbing bitterly. She sprang to her feet, and then, as if she lacked the strength to fly, she sunk upon her knees, and in low, heart-broken accents, she cried,—

"Mercy—mercy! Oh, spare me! Mercy—mercy!"

It is impossible to describe the tone of exquisite anguish in which these words were spoken; but Ada felt them keenly, and the tears rushed to her eyes, and her voice faltered as she said,—

"I am myself a child of woe and persecution. Come in, for some few hours yet you will be safe here."

With a shriek the poor maniac threw herself at Ada's feet, and attempted to kiss them.

"How I love to hear a word of kindness! Is there a human heart can feel for poor Mad Maud?—Is there a human voice can speak to me in tones of pity?"

"There is," said Ada. "God knows I pity you; but you are hurt—come in—come in—I dare not myself stand here."

"Hush—hush!" said Maud, holding up her finger and smiling. "Do not speak—you are young and beautiful; but do not speak, for I heard just now the voice of one of God's ministering angels. The tone was low and sweet; but I knew it—Ha, ha! I knew it—'tis comfort to poor Maud."

"'Twas I that spoke," said Ada.

"Hark—hark! There again! Is it indeed you?"

"It is."

"Shall you stay long?"

"Stay where?"

"From your house."

She pointed to the blue sky as she spoke, and gazed earnestly upwards.

"See—see—yon cloud is waiting for you," she said suddenly. "So you have come from your own house of light and everlasting joy, to speak words of comfort to poor Mad Maud? I bless—bless you."!

The poor creature covered her face with her hands, and wept aloud in her fulness of heart.

Ada gently laid her small hand upon Maud's arm, and led her unresistingly into the house, closing the door after her.

"Do not weep now," she said; "I saw you the sport of many from a window in this house. What you may have done to anger those who so hotly followed you with shouts and cries, I know not; but it is sufficient for me that you are faint and weary. You shall have refreshments, and as long a rest here as I dare, for your own safety as well as my own, offer you."

Maud withdrew her hands from before her eyes, and gazed earnestly at Ada.

"Are you indeed mortal?" she said. "Must I once more, for your sake, love my kind?"

"I am as you see me," said Ada, "a poor helpless girl. Here, take refreshment, and deem me not inhospitable if I tell you then to go from this place, and forget you ever saw it."

Ada placed before the poor, half-famished being, such food as she had in the house, and, while she ate of the meat and bread voraciously, Ada amused herself with conjecture as to who and what this singular creature could be, who seemed, in some strange and confused manner, mixed up with her own fate.

"Your name is Maud, I heard you say?" remarked Ada, kindly.

"Mad Maud, they call me," was the reply—"but I am not so mad as they think me. Do not tell them that though, for the Savage Smith would kill me, and then I should not die, as I ought to do, before he does."

"Alas," thought Ada, "it is in vain to question this poor creature, her wits are tangled; she may know all, but can tell me nothing; and should she tell me my own story, how can I unravel her strange discourse, or separate the truth from the strange web of fiction which her mental alienation mingles with it."

"You are thinking," suddenly said Maud, "so am I, so am I,—do you recollect the burning of the smithy ? ha, ha! That was brave work."

"What smithy ?" said Ada.

"And do you know," continued Maud, unheedful of the question, "do you know, the crackling roaring flames would not touch the body ? No, no, the smith tried that, but the flames would not touch it! Like long fiery tongues they licked round and ronnd it; but, ha, ha! it could not burn, it would not burn. No, no, it would not burn !"

There was a wild insane exultation about the poor creature as she uttered these words that almost alarmed Ada.

"The man you call the smith," she said, "was he you met one night on Westminster-bridge,? heard you address him by that title."

"On a bridge ?"

"Yes, you must recollect, he would fain have taken your life."

"That was a dream," said Maud, shaking her head ; "a long wild dream."

"The sun is in the west," said Ada, mournfully ; "before it sinks I pray you to go, I have no power now."

"They called me a witch, and hunted me," suddenly said Maud, shivering and drawing her tattered garments closely around her; "'tis very hard for I am only poor Mad Maud; I follow Britton the smith, and he cannot kill me, because the Almighty has doomed that he shall die first—did you ever see that child again?"

"What child? said Ada, earnestly, "of what do you speak?"

"Ha! ha!—'twas brave work! brave work!" muttered Maud. "Was not that an awful death, eh? It came from the Smithy, but they could not burn the body! No, no,—God! how the man screamed—he was torn and bleeding—his shrieks were music to me—music! music! to me, because I knew he was a murderer! and Andrew Britton was plunged deeper, deeper in crime! so I follow him —I must see the smith die—that is my task for life!"

"Poor creature!" sighed Ada.

"Who's that," cried Maud, "who pities me?"

"I do, from the bottom of my heart," said Ada; "oh! tell me, if you can, what has driven you to this state—this fearful state? Had you a house, kindred, were kind looks ever bent upon you ; did the sweet echo of soft words ever ring in your years? Tell me all."

Maud convulsively clutched the arms of the chair upon which she sat, and she trembled violently as Ada spoke—once, twice, thrice, she tried to speak, then with a violent effort she gasped the words,—

"House—kindred—love—oh, Heaven! Oh, Heaven, spare me—spare me !"

She then burst into such a violent and frantic fit of weeping, that Ada became much alarmed, and entreated her to be composed, in the most moving and tender accents.

Gradually the deep anguish of Maud subsided, and when she again looked on the face of Ada, the wild glowing expression of her eyes had given place to a mild lustre, and she said in a low soft voice, exceedingly different from that in which she usually spoke,—

"Where am I ?"

"Alas!" said Ada, "I can scarcely tell you ; but till sunset you are welcome to what shelter and food I can give you."

"Give !" said Maud ; "God's mercy has granted me just now, for the second time, the calmness and rationality of my happier days—this will pass away soon, and I shall become what I know I am—mad again !"

"Nay," said Ada, "hope that Heaven is not so stinting of its mercy"

Maud shook her head and sighed deeply.

"You wish me to go at sunset ?"

"For your own safety."

"Well, be it so; I was guided hither for I know not what—I believe only because I am poor and wretched, and my wits wander sometimes."

"Can there be any so wretched?"

"Ay," said Maud, "many, many—be poor, houseless, and mad, from deep grief and injury, and there is scarcely a human hand but what will not be raised against you."

"Horrible!" exclaimed Ada. "'Tis very wicked."

"'Tis very true," said Maud. "But hear me—my tale is very short—my brain again will throb and beat—my blood will boil, and strange shapes will again goad me to madness."

She compressed her head tightly for several seconds, and rocked to and fro as if in pain—then suddenly she laid her long skinny hand on Ada's arm, and said—

"Listen—you shall hear what drove me to this—haply it may save you from the like."

CHAPTER XXX.

THE TALE.—A BLIGHTED HEART'S DESPAIR.

Poor Maud spoke in a low earnest voice, and Ada became deeply interested in her story, as with many tears she poured it into the hears of the lovely and persecuted girl.

"You are young and very beautiful," she commenced. "I was young, and they told me I was beautiful. Look at me now, and smile at the idle boast. Still there was one who loved me—one who listened to my voice, as though it had a magic in it—one who followed me where I led. My heart was touched by the purity of his devotion, and I loved him even as he loved me, next thing to Heaven. It might be that we each made too much of our earthly idols, and so turned the face of Heaven against us both; but I scarce can think so, for He who made His creatures with fond and faithful hearts, must surely look with pleasure rather than anger upon their deep and holy affections. Well, girl, the future lay before us like a summer's day—all sunshine, joy, and delight. We asked each other what could mar our happiness; and in the ecstasy of our own dear truthfulness we answered, Nothing.'

"Where our mutual parents lived, there came one day a man of coarse and ruffianly aspect. He said he came to settle in the place, and seek a helpmate among the village maidens. None welcomed him, for his manner was harsh and brutal—an index of the mind. This man's name was Andrew Britton.'

"Indeed!" said Ada.

"Yes, Andrew Britton, a smith. With unparelleled insolence he said he had fixed on me for his wife. I scorned his suit. He jested at my indignant refusal. I wept, for we were alone. He laughed at my tears. Then I threatened him with the resentment of him to whom I had already plighted my young heart, and Andrew Britton swore then a fearful oath that I never should be his.

"He whom I loved found me in tears, and after much solicitation, got from me the particulars of the interview that had just terminated with the Savage Smith. I would not tell him, though, until he had promised me he would not endanger himself by resenting—men heed not such promises. His young blood boiled with anger. He met the smith, and from words they came to mutual violence. Britton was much hurt, and he whom I loved came off the conqueror, to the joy of all.

"Britton then came, and asked my forgiveness. He said he was an altered man. He swore he repented of his passion, and we believed him. But, oh, girl! when a bad, wicked man speaks, you may fairly mistrust him. 'Tis the glitter of the eyes of the serpent that fascinate but to betray.

"The day of my union was at length fixed. There were no regrets—no grief—all was happiness. We wandered hand-in-hand the evening before to look at the last sunset ere we should be bound together in those holy ties which none dare impiously to break asunder.

" We wondered what could happen to make us unhappy. We saw no cloud in the clear horizon of our joy! Oh, what an hour of bliss was that! 'Tis needless to dwell on what we said or how we looked into each other's eyes to see our own reflected happiness.

"The sun sunk to rest, and in the east uprose the silver moon ere we parted. With many lingering regrets, we said adieu. Oh, God! we never met again!"

Maud sunk on her knees, and, hiding her face upon her chair, she again gave way to a similar wild, awful passion of grief to what had before affected her.

Ada had been deeply impressed with poor Maud's simple and affecting narrative, told as it was with a pathos which defies description. She did not speak, but let

No. 17.

the woman have her way, and after some minutes, the violence of her grief, as before, subsided, and she rose to outward appearance calm again.

"Bear with me yet a brief space," said Maud. "I shall not weep so much again."

"I hope indeed you never may," said Ada. "But it would be a harsh and unfeeling heart that could not bear patiently the tears springing from a bruised heart."

Maud took Ada's hand, and pressed it to her lips in silent gratitude, and then resumed her narrative.

"The morrow came, and brought with it a cloudless sky and a bright sunshine, which never to me seemed so bright and beautiful. We were to meet at the village church, to part no more! and, when I and my friends arrived, and we found that we were first, they were inclined to chide my lover's delay, but I only smiled, for no doubt crossed my mind. Not the smallest speck appeared to me as yet in the heaven of my happiness.

"An hour passed, and still he came not. Then, indeed, there was a flutter at my heart—a mingled feeling of alarm and anger. Then some went to seek him, and returned unsuccessful. He could not be found! My anger vanished, and I began to tremble. Two more hours passed away—the last was one of agony.

"Then came one into the church, and whispered to my father. I saw his cheek grow pale! I saw him clutch at the altar rail for support! At that moment, I thought I should have died, for I knew that something had been whispered which was too horrible to speak aloud.

"By a violent effort, I preserved myself from fainting, and rushed to my father.

"'Tell me—tell!' I shrieked. 'What has happened? Father, suspense will kill me.'

"'He is dead!' was the reply.

"I heard no more—I saw no more! For many months they told me I lay a breathing senseless form, and then I awakened, and my first words were, 'Take me to him!'

"They told me then that the grave had long since received its tenant, and by degrees I learned from them that my lover—my husband in the sight of Heaven, had been found a mangled corpse at the foot of a deep precipice.

"He must have fallen over, they told me, but I knew better; something whispered to me that Andrew Britton did the deed.

"Since then I know not what has happened. Once I awoke and found myself chained to a stone wall in a gloomy cell; then again I was thrust out from somewhere, and a voice told me to be gone, for I was harmless. So I became Mad Maud as I am, and I follow Britton the Savage Smith, because he is to die before I do, and then I shall meet my lover again—and do you know that some sunset, by the great bounty of Heaven, he will come again—when the murder is found out; yes, yes, when the murder is found out. Ha! ha! ha!"

Again the maniac's eye glanced with the wild fire of insanity, and poor Maud was lost once more in the wanderings of her imagination.

The sympathies of Ada had been so strongly excited by the narrative of poor Maud, that she had allowed the lucid interval of the poor maniac to pass away without questioning on the subjects nearest and dearest to her. With a hope that even yet it might not be too late to glean some information from her, she said,—

"What murder do you mean?"

"The murder at the Old Smithy," replied Maud. "You saw the man as well I—we all saw him."

"When was that?" asked Ada.

"Last night! last night! Hark, the wind is still around the Old Smithy."

"'Tis all in vain," sighed Ada. "The time is past."

It now suddenly struck Ada that there would be extreme danger to the poor creature should she stay till Jacob Gray came home; and as the sun was just dipping into the western horizon, she said to her,—

"Take with you all these victuals,—I have no power here to prolong your welcome."

"The child of the dead! the child of the dead!" muttered Maud, totally unheeding what Ada said.

"Let me now entreat you to go," said the alarmed girl. "There will be one here by sunset who has no feeling, no mercy."

"That must be Britton, the Savage Smith," cried Maud.

"No, 'tis one Jacob Gray. Heard you ever that name before?"

"Jacob Gray!" repeated Maud, evidently with no sort of recognition of the name. "I will sing to him and you."

"Go; let me entreat you to go," cried Ada.

Maud heeded her not, but began to sing in a wild but sweet voice,—

"'Who loves the bleak night wind,
That roars 'twixt earth and sky,
Say, is its loud voice kind?
Not I—not I.'

That's a brave song, but cheerless. I love the day and the sweet sunshine. Here's another for thee, maiden; 'twill suit thy young heart:—

"'Love's like a rainbow,
Why, maiden, why?
It opens from the earth
Up to the sky!
A young heart's passion
Is all as bright
As that purest arch
Of Heaven's own light.'

Like ye that, young heart? Alas! 'tis long since I learned the ditty. Hark ye, here is one more sad and sombre, for I see the tear-drop in your eye. Hark—hark:—

"'The storm bird may scream
O'er the desolate moor,
And the north wind blow wide
The poor cottager's door.
The snow drift may level
Mountain with plain,
But the sunlight will come,
And the birds sing again.
But, oh! the fond heart
Which one storm has swept o'er,
Can ne'er know the peace
It rejoiced in before.'"

As the last sound of the poor creature's voice ceased, Ada clasped her hands and uttered a cry of terror, for she heard without the low whistle which she had been taught by Gray to recognise as the signal of his return.

CHAPTER XXXI.

THE INTERVIEW.—JACOB GRAY'S MEDITATIONS.—THE SLIP OF PAPER—THE NAIL.—THE GUILTY CONSCIENCE.—THE DEPARTURE.

For perhaps the space of a minute, Ada lost the power of action; but the stern necessity of doing something to save the poor creature from the death which Jacob Gray's fears would, she doubted not, induce him to put her to, braced the nerves of the young girl.

She took Maud by the arm, and looking her earnestly in the face, she said,—

"What was the name of him you loved?"

Maud pressed her hand upon her brow for a moment as if striving to comprehend the question; then she replied,—

"His name was William Heriot."

" Then follow me, and speak not for his sake, as you hold his memory dear."

" To the world's end! to the world's end!" said Maud.

Ada heard the outer door now close, and she was sure that Gray was in the passage. He might, or he might not, enter the room in which she and Maud were, the door of which was within a few paces of the steps. Oh, how dreadful to poor Ada were the few short, but to her awful moments that elapsed before she felt convinced that Gray had passed the door. He always trod slowly and stealthily even in that lone house, for caution and suspicion had grown so habitual with him, that even in security he could not shake off the actions which rendered those feelings manifest.

It was difficult, therefore, for Ada to trace his footsteps, or come to any positive conclusion as to what part of the house he had proceeded towards.

One thing only she could feel certain of from the duration of time, and that was, that the immediate danger of his entering the room in which she and Maud were was past, unless he were lingering in the passage, which she had never yet known him to do.

A few more minutes of great anxiety now passed, during which Maud did not speak, but rocked to and fro in her chair, sighing deeply, as if the sound of her murdered lover's name had affected her deeply.

" Maud," said Ada, " Maud, attend to me."

" I hear the voice," said Maud, "the voice of the angel that has come from Heaven to speak words of kindness to poor Mad Maud."

" By the memory of William Heriot," said Ada, " do not speak or move till I come to you again."

Ada then left the room for the purpose of ascertaining in what room Jacob Gray was staying. With an assumed carelessness of step and manner she walked into the rooms on the ground floor, but in none of them was Jacob Gray; she then ascended the staircase, and as she neared the top of the crazy flight, a door was suddenly opened upon the landing, and Gray appeared.

Ada paused, and they regarded each other for a few moments in silence. Then Gray said, in a low tone,—

" Nothing has happend, Ada? No alarm?"

" No alarm," said Ada, answering his last question; " wait for me below, we must have some talk to-day."

" To-day?"

" Yes, I promise but from month to month—to-day the month expires," said Ada.

" It does, but the promise will be renewed."

" Stay where you are," said Ada, " I will come to you in a short time."

"Nay, not here," said Gray, "go to the room below. I will be with you shortly."

" I am even now proceeding to my own chamber," said Ada; " in a quarter of an hour I will meet you here."

Without waiting for a reply, Ada ascended to her own room.

Gray stood for a minute with the door in his hand, muttering to himself,—

" She braves me thus ever—if I were to remark that the sun shone, she would declare 'twas very cold—sometimes I doubt if I hate her or Learmont most; yet I must spare her to be revenged on him! Curses on them all!"

He flung the door to, which shut with a bang that Ada heard with thankfulness. Gray then unlocked a cupboard in the room, and proceeded to deposit in a sacred place he had constructed at the back of it, the last sum of money he had wrung from the fears of Learmont.

In the same place of safety, likewise, was the written confession addressed to Sir Francis Hartleton, but that was not concealed; it lay openly in the cupboard, a prominent object to any one who should force the door. A smile of self-satisfaction came across Jacob Gray's face as he took the paper in his hand, and fixed his keen eyes upon its superscription to the magistrate.

" It would, indeed, be a glorious revenge," he muttered, " on both Britton and

Learmont to accumulate an ample fortune first, and then, when my foot was on the very deck of the vessel that was to bear me from England for ever, to hail some idle lounger on the quay, and bid him take this to Sir Francis Hartleton, and ask his own reward. Yes, if I had half a million, that would be worth as much again. The time will come—yes—it will—it must come—when I have got enough money first, and then my revenge. Ye taunt me, 'Squire Learmont, and you, Britton, too, with my cunning—ha! ha! I am cunning, it is true—I am too cunning for your dull wits. Jacob Gray will be too much for you both : when he has enough money !"

Suddenly then he now dropped the paper, and started ; a slight noise outside his door met his ears, and his guilty soul trembled.

"What—what noise was that ?" he whispered. "Ada—yes—Ada,—ah ! it must be Ada !"

In order to explain the sound that disturbed the gleeful cogitations of Jacob Gray, we must follow Ada to her chamber, whither, as the reader will recollect, she repaired after her very brief conversation with her gaoler, Jacob Gray.

The moment Ada found herself in the privacy of her own room she burst into tears, and a fervent " thank Heaven!" burst from her lips.

The necessity of instant action and self-possession, however, rushed simultaneously across her mind, and dashing away the tears with the brief exclamation of,—

" My promise no longer binds me—I am free to act," she hastily wrote on a slip of paper, the following words :—

" To Albert Seyton,—Ada is betrayed—seek her in a Lone House by the river."

She then concealed the paper in her bosom, and, commending herself to Heaven, with a beating heart she descended the staircase.

Her object now was to pass the door of the room in which was Gray, without arousing his attention ; but this was a matter of no ordinary difficulty in that old house, for the staircase was so ancient and dilapidated that it creaked and groaned under the slightest pressure.

Taking, however, as much of her weight off the stairs as possible, by clinging to a stout rail, which was supported firmly by the wall, Ada slowly descended.

She reached the landing, from which opened the door of the room in which was Gray, in safety. To pass that door was dreadful, and Ada thought each moment that her strength would desert her, and all would be discovered. The life of poor Maud, she felt certain, hung upon the slightest thread, and this thought nerved Ada more than any consciousness of personal danger would have done.

Creeping cautiously along, she reached the door—one moment, then she paused, and the sound of Jacob Gray's voice, as he muttered his unholy thoughts, came clearly upon her overstrained senses.

With her hands pressing upon her heart to still its wild tumultuous beating, she passed the door ; now the flight of stairs leading to the house was gained in safety. She laid her trembling hands upon the banisters, and at that moment it was that Gray heard the creaking sound, that alarmed him in the midst of his wicked rejoicing over the treachery he meditated.

Ada turned slowly round, and faced the door. To fly she knew would tempt pursuit ; and without, in her confusion, being able to reflect further than that the best plan would be to face Jacob Gray should he come from the room, Ada stood for several minutes enduring the most torturing and agonising suspense.

All remained still ; Gray did not appear, and once more Ada turned to descend the staircase ; one step she had taken downwards, when a loose nail from the crazy banisters fell into the passage below, making, in the solemn silence that reigned in the house, an alarming noise.

Ada paused.

" Now, now," she thought, " I shall need all my firmness. Heaven help me now !"

The door of Gray's room opened, and he stood in the entrance with a pale and anxious face : Ada turned as before, and met his gaze. It would have been difficult that moment to have decided which face bore the palest hue—the beautiful and innocent one of Ada, contrasted as it was with her long jetty ringlets, to the disturbed, haggard countenance of the man of crimes and blood.

"There—there was—a noise!" said Gray.

"I heard it," replied Ada.

"W—where was it?"

"Above."

"'Twas nothing, Ada—nothing—I suppose quite accidental, Ada; you are going down—I—I'll follow you—I'll follow you."

He closed the door behind him with a trembling hand, and made a step towards the staircase.

"Jacob Gray," cried Ada, "stop."

He paused, for there was an awful earnestness in her manner that greatly added to his alarm. Yet Ada knew not what to do or how to act. The words she uttered were almost involuntary. Then it might be that Heaven whispered to her mind a course of action; but it came across her mind that Gray might be alarmed still more, knowing the lurking superstition of his character, and she suddenly said,—

"Did you not tell me once this house was haunted?"

"Haunted!" echoed Gray, suddenly descending several stairs, and showing by his rapid changes of colour the craven fear that was at his heart's inmost core.

His fears, however, had prompted him to the very course which Ada so much dreaded, namely, to descend to the lower part of the house, and on the impulse of the moment she laid her hand on Jacob Gray's arm, and said,—

"I was following it—it has gone down!"

"It!—who?—what?" cried Gray, as he sprung back again to the door of his room in an instant, trembling exceedingly.

Ada's pure and innocent heart detested all kinds of duplicity; but if ever such was justifiable, it was surely then; and to save the life of the poor creature who had sought shelter with her, and had suffered so much wrong and unmerited persecution, was a justification which, with the rapidity of thought, came to Ada's relief.

"There is some one below," she said.

"You—you saw—it?"

"I did."

"And—and—followed it?"

"I did."

Gray licked his parched lips, as after a pause he added,—

"Ada—a—what manner of appearance was it?"

"Will you follow it with me?"

"Not for worlds—not for worlds," cried Gray. "Tell me, Ada, was—was—was it a man of—tall stature?"

"It was," said Ada.

"Of—of noble bearing—hair—slightly silvered?"

"Even so."

"I—I thought—'twas he. I—I saw him once at the door—in that—that smithy. Yes, that has began now. I—shall be haunted now—for ever. Oh, horror! horror!"

The word "smithy" struck upon Ada's ears, and for one moment she could not recollect why it came as if it were an old recollection to her. Then she remembered that Mad Maud had spoken of a murder at an Old Smithy, and she asked herself, can there be any connection between all these dark hints of things long past and my own fate? There must be—I will probe your heart, Jacob Gray.

"I will tell you," she said, turning suddenly to Gray. "Listen! A wild bleeding form has appeared in this house."

"Bleeding?" gasped Gray.

"Yes, bleeding."

"And—and—it is—" Gray pointed down the staircase.

"It is there," said Ada.

Gray shuddered, as he said,—

" Can you—look on it, and live ?"

" I can."

" God help me !"

" Come with me, and we will together question it further," said Ada.

"No! no! no!" cried Gray. " The sight would blast me for ever. Ada! Ada! if you have one spark of pity, one yearning of heavenly mercy in your heart, you will pray for—me—pray for me!"

" For you—my persecutor?"

" Implore that hideous form to visit here no more. I shall go mad!—mad!—mad !"

Gray hid his face in his hands, and groaned bitterly.

" In his anguish he may confess all," thought Ada, and hastily calling to her memory the words spoken by Maud, she said in a solemn whisper,—

" Jacob Gray, the bleeding form that has visited is not terrible to me."

" No, no," said Gray, " because——"

" Because what ?"

" Nothing—nothing—I have said nothing."

" Then hear me," added Ada. " Strange things have been spoken to me."

" By—it ?"

" Yes. Do you recollect an Old Smithy?"

Gray removed his hands from before his face, and sinking on his knees, he crawled towards Ada.

" Mercy! mercy!" he said, in a husky whisper.

" There was a murder," continued Ada.

" Ada! Ada !" shrieked Gray. " Child of the dead, spare me! Oh, spare me !"

" Child of the dead!" cried Ada. " Speak, Jacob Gray. Am I that child? Tell all now that conscience is awakened, and soothe the pangs of your own seared heart by relieving mine of worlds of agony. Speak, Jacob Gray—oh, speak. Tell me who I am now at this moment of awful and bitter repentance. I will forgive all—I will, as you ask, pray for you, Jacob Gray. Heaven will pardon you. Speak —speak to me. Tell me, am I that child?"

" Bid—bid—him go !" crawling towards the room.

" And then——"

" Then—you shall hear—all—all. The sight of him would overturn my reason! Even now my brain reels. Bid him go—implore him not to haunt me—not to drive me mad by a glance!"

Ada's object was more than accomplished.

" Wait for me," she cried, and glided down the staircase, leaving Gray crouched up by the door of the room, with his glowing eyes fixed upon the staircase, in awful expectation of seeing each moment a dreadful form, that would drive him to insanity by one look from its glazed eye.

The period of trembling and nervousness was now passed with Ada, and with the lightness and speed of a young fawn, she bounded into the room where sat poor Maud.

The poor creature's eyes brightened as Ada approached, and she said,—

" I have not stirred—I have not spoken."

" Hush! hush!" said Ada. " Speak not now. Here, take this paper. Fly across the fields. Look not back, but get away from this place."

" Yes, yes," said Maud.

"Moments are precious," continued Ada. " Wherever you go, I conjure you by the remembrance of him you loved, and who you will meet again in the presence of God, to show that paper—but never, never part with it."

" Never, never !" cried Maud. " Oh, never !"

" Now follow me. Heaven speed you on your way!"

Maud thrust the paper into her bosom, and allowed herself to be led by Ada to the door.

" God bless and help you," cried the girl.

Maud kissed her hand and sobbed bitterly.

" Away—away !" said Ada. " Oh, pause not a moment. For my sake hasten."

Like a hunted deer, Mad Maud flew from the Lone House. Ada watched her for a few minutes across the swampy waste, then, the excitement being over, she burst into a passion of tears, and dropped into a state of half insensibility in the passage of the old house.

CHAPTER XXXII.

JACOB GRAY'S FEARS.—THE PROMISE.—ADA'S MEDITATIONS.

How long she remained in the passage of the house, Ada had no means of distinctly knowing, but, when she recovered from her insensibility, she found herself in the parlour alone, and nearly in total darkness.

A few moments sufficed to bring to her recollection all that had occurred, and she sprang to her feet, looking anxiously around her, as well as the dim light would permit, to see if Jacob Gray was in the room.

An instant inquiry satisfied her that she was alone, but scarcely had she made this discovery when a gleam of light came in from the passage, and the door was gently and cautiously pushed open. Ada did not speak, but she shrunk into a corner of the room, and saw Gray enter, carrying with him a dim light.

" Ada ! Ada !" he said.

" I am here," she replied.

He set the light on the table, and she saw that his face looked harsh and haggard.

" We cannot stay here," he said, after a pause. " This place will be hideous now."

" Not stay here !" cried Ada, and her heart sunk within her at the thought of being again removed at the very time when there was a chance of her being rescued by Albert Seyton, should he or any one knowing his name chance to see the paper she had given to Mad Maud.

" No—no," added Gray, " I—I would not sleep here. The very air of this place smells of the grave ! We must away, Ada !"

" How came I in this room ?" said Ada !

" After a long time when you returned not to me," replied Gray, " I descended the staircase, and found you lying in the passage just by the door which you had evidently been trying to escape by."

Ada was deeply thankful that Jacob Gray himself put this interpretation on the circumstance of finding the door open, and she said,—

" My feelings overcame me."

" Ay—Yes. The sight must have been terrible !" said Gray. " Come, Ada ; 'tis a very dark night—attire yourself in the less cumbrous and safer garments of a boy, and let us leave here."

" You forget your promise," said Ada.

" My promise ? What promise ?"

" You said you would tell me all."

" And so will I at the proper time and season, which, believe me, will be the sooner for what has chanced this night."

" And so am I deceived again," said Ada.

" Girl," said Gray, " you are young enough yet to wait a short time. There will come a day when justice shall be done you, and the cup of my revenge will be filled to the overflowing ! It will be very soon, Ada."

Ada felt that to urge Gray now that his great fear had passed away, to fulfil any promise he might have made while under its influence, would be quite futile.

Moreover, her great object—the escape of poor Maud—was accomplished, and she had no new spectre wherewith to frighten Jacob Gray."

"For that brief time you speak of," said she, "let us remain here. Think you the spirits of another world cannot follow you wherever you go, Jacob Gray.

"Follow me?" echoed Gray.

"Ay; are not all places alike to them? Why remove from here?"

Gray seemed to remain silent, then he said in a low, agitated voice,—

"Girl, what you say may be true. I will think of it again. To-morrow I will decide! Yes, let it be till to-morrow! You are not weary?"

"Wherefore do you ask?" said Ada.

"Because," faltered Gray, "I do not wish to be alone."

"And can you ask me to save you from the horrors of that solitude which your conscience peoples with hideous forms?"

No. 18.

"Question me not," cried Gray, impatiently. "I—I would have desired your company—but will not enforce it."

"You cannot," said Ada.

"Cannot? You know not what you say."

"You dare not!" added Ada.

She had learnt by experience that she could defy Jacob Gray to his face successfully. Her only fear of him was that he would murder her while she slept, or mingle poison with her food! She could not look on him.

"Leave me, then! Leave me if you will," he said. "I will not invade your chamber."

"If you were," said Ada, "you might perchance be frozen with horror by meeting the form you have described, with so much dread—a form which the voice of nature hints must be that of my murdered father!"

As she spoke, Ada walked to the door of the room, but ere she reached it, Gray called to her.

"Ada, stay yet a moment!"

"You forget!"

"Forget what?"

"That I must this day again receive your promise to exert no contrivance for your escape from me. At twelve to-day your word expired."

"Oh!" cried Ada; "then I was free."

"No," said Gray, "you were not free! I knew that if you meditated escape, you would seize the first moment! I watched this house from twelve till two. Then as you came not forth, I knew I was safe."

"And you departed?"

"I did."

Had Jacob Gray watched another hour he would have seen Maud hunted to the old house.

"Your promise, girl," he cried. "Before we part to-night I must have your solemn promise!"

"On the same condition," said Ada, "to preserve that life which God has given me, I will give you my promise."

"Be it so," said Gray.

"Then in the name of Heaven, I promise from one month from now that if aid come not to me—if no one comes here to take me hence, and offer me liberty, I will remain a prisoner! so help me Heaven!"

"Enough," said Gray, "I am content. I know you will keep your word, Ada."

"How is it," said Ada, "that you can trust thus to my word, Jacob Gray? Have you not taught me deceit? Were I to deceive you as you have deceived me, could you blame me?"

"Question me not," cried Gray. "I have said I would trust to your word. Let that suffice."

Ada turned away, and sought the solitude of her own room. She always wept bitterly after renewing her promise to Gray—it seemed like pushing hope to a further distance from her heart, and on this occasion, when she was alone, the tears dimmed her eyes as she reflected another month—another month! but then even upon the instant, a small still voice within her heart seemed to whisper to her that there were now better grounds for hope than ever. She had made an effort by the slip of paper that poor Mad Maud had taken with her—and her promise to Gray was expressly conditional, so that if Albert Seyton should seek her, she was free! How delightful did that word sound to the desolate heart of the young girl. She clasped her hands, and a smile played over her face like a sunbeam on a lake.

"Oh!" she cried, "if kind Heaven has indeed joy in store for the poor, persecuted Ada, surely it will be more delightful by the contrast with what has passed! Friends will be dearer to me, because I have known none! The sunshine will to me possess a greater charm than to those who have always been so happy as to revel in its beams! The charms of music will entrance me, where they present but ordinary oints to others, for I shall contrast them with the echoes of th is dreary house

The voices of those who will love me, and use kindly phrases when they speak to me, will ring in my ears with an unknown beauty! Mere freedom—the dear gift of being able, at my own free-will, to seek the leafy glade of some old forest—or walk in the broad sunlight of an open plain, will be a rich reward for all that I have suffered! Oh! how can the world be unhappy while Heaven has left it youth, sunshine, and love?"

Thus the young, ardent, enthusiastic girl beguiled the tediousness of her imprisonment. She lived in a world of romance of her own creating, a romance too, that was mixed up with a pure and holy system of natural theology culled from her own heart, and those mysterious impulses which tell all, but those who wilfully shut their ears against the solemn glorious truth—that there is a great and good God above all—a Being to be loved more than to be feared.

Ada would now sit for hours picturing to herself the meeting of poor Maud with Albert Seyton. She would frame all the dialogue that would pass between them, until Albert had, piece by piece, extracted from the wandering mind of the poor creature the exact situation of the old houre in which Ada was immured; then she would imagine his joy, his rapture, until busy Fancy almost conjured up the reality of his voice in her charmed ears.

The dull sons of system and calculation—the plodders through life without the capacity to look beyond the present, or reason on the past, may condemn the airy freaks of the imagination, because of their unreality; but what would the lonely, the persecuted, and the unhappy do, if Heaven, in its great mercy, had not laid up within the chambers of the brain, such stores of joy and extatic thought ready to be drawn forth infinitely to cheat what is real of its terrors, by contrasting it with the rare creations of the ideal. Oh, is it not a rare and amiable faculty of mind, that can thus shift, as it were, the scenes of life, and with a thought, change a dungeon to a sweet glade in some deep forest, where birds are singing for the pure love of song? Let then the dreamy "castle builder" pile story upon story of his æriel fabric,—he will be the nearer Heaven.

CHAPTER XXXIII.

BRITTON AT THE CHEQUERS.—THE VISIT.—A MYSTERIOUS STRANGER.— THE GOOD COMPANY.

BRITTON, the smith, was in truth a great man at the Chequers, in Westminster, His love of liquor suited the landlord amazingly, and his custom, when the whim took him, of treating every-body who happened to be present, turned out an exceeding good speculation for mine host. Sots and topers came from far and near to the Chequers, upon the chance of a treat from "King Britton," as he was commonly called, and they would wait patiently drinking at their own proper costs until the smith got intoxicated enough to act the great man, and order drink for all at his own expense.

This acted well for the landlord, whose liquor was constantly kept flowing at some one's expense, and he put up patiently with the brutal jests of the smith, many of them being accompanied with personal ill-usage, rather then turn the tide of prosperity that was pouring into his house.

Many were the conjectures as to the source of Britton's ample means; but although all supposed them to proceed from some not over honest means, all were so much interested in their continuance, that the curiosity excited produced no further result than whispered expressions of wonder and wise shakes of the head.

It was true that Britton had been watched to Learmont's house, but it never for a moment entered the heads of the busybodies at the Chequers that he visited the great 'Squire Learmont himself, and whether or not he had some accomplice at Learmont's house which enabled him to rob the wealthy 'squire, was the only thought suggested by tracing him more than once to the hall door of Learmont's princely and much-talked-of abode.

Daylight was commonly shut out of the old oaken parlour of the Chequers before it was all necessary, by the orders of Britton, who found himself more at home and enjoyed his liquor better by candle or lamplight [than with a bright setting sun streaming in upon his drunken orgies.

It was upon one of these occasions that the shutters had been close by the obsequious landlord at least an hour earlier than necessary, and for which he had been rewarded by a crack on the pate with a pewter ale measure, and that made him dance again, that a more than usually thronged company filled the parlor of the ancient house.

Britton sat in an arm-chair in the first stage of intoxication. His eyes were inflamed and blood-shot, and his whole visage betrayed the debasing influence of habitual drunkenness. He wore a strange mixture of clothing; a richly-laced coat which he had bought from the window of a tailor, who had only charged him double price for it and a kick, contrasted oddly with a coarse red nightcap that he wore, and the pipe stuck in the buttonholes of the rich laced waistcoat, presented a strange anomaly of elegance and vulgarity.

The company were some smoking, some drinking, and some talking; but it was easy to see that the general attention was fixed upon Britton, who there sat, as he considered, in his glory.

"Landlord!" he roared, in a voice that made the glasses ring again. "Landlord! I say, curse on you for a sluggish hand, come hither! Where's your respect for your king, you keeper of bad butts—you thief, you purloiner of honester men's sack?—come hither, I say."

"Ha!—ha!" laughed a man, who had come a long way to chance a treat at the Chequers—"ha!—ha!—that's good. Ho!—ho!"

"Who are you?" roared Britton.

"I—I—oh—I—I—am—a cordwainer from the Borough, sir."

"How dare you call me, 'Sir'?"

"Why—a—a—really——"

Some one here charitably whispered to the cordwainer the fact of Britton's kingly dignity! and with many winks and nods he corrected himself, and said,—

"I humbly beg your majesty's most gracious pardon."

"You be d—d!" said Britton. "You are a cordwainer, are you?—a cobbler, you mean—a patcher of leaks in bad shoes. Hark ye, Mr. Cordwainer, the next time you presume to laugh at anything I say, I'll make a leak in your head."

"May it please you, King Britton," interposed the landlord, "I am here!"

"No you aint," cried Britton, tripping up the landlord, who forthwith fell flat on the floor, "you are there!"

This was a stock joke, and was perpetrated nearly every evening; so the company laughed accordingly, particularly those who had seen and heard it before, the new-comers not being fully up to the wit of it.

Here the landlord rose, and, rubbing the injured part of his person, said with a groan,—

"Well, gentlemen, did you ever know the like of that?"

"Here, come back with a bowl of punch," cried Britton; "and, do you hear, some spiced canary—come, quick!"

"May I venture to ask!" said the landlord, still affecting to writhe with pain, "if the spiced canary is to be all round?"

"No, you may not ask!" said Britton; "off with you!"

"We'll drink your majesty's health," said a pale thin man, with great humility.

"Oh, you will, will you?" said Britton.

"We will—we will," cried many voices.

"Drink away, then!" roared Britton.

"Your majesty has not yet ordered anything for us to drink," said one.

"No, no, his majesty don't mean," said Britton. "You are a set of rascals—thieves all."

"Ah," said the cordwainer, casting his eyes up to the fly-cage that hung from the centre of the ceiling, "there is a great deal of dishonesty in the world."

"There aint, and you are a liar!" cried Britton.

At this moment the door was flung open, and a wild figure stood in the entrance taking up the laugh of the guests in a strange discordant tone, and pointing the while at the smith with exultant look.

Britton started from his chair, but he was scarcely able to stand, and staggering into it again, he muttered,—

"Mad Maud, by all that is damnable!"

"Britton—Andrew Britton!" shrieked Maud, clapping her hands together, "I have found you—ha!—ha!—ha!—I have found you!"

The perons assembled in the parlour looked at each other in speechless amazement, and the majority of them in the excitement of the moment finished at once whatever liquor they had before them.

"Britton!—Britton!" shrieked Maud, "are you not glad to see me? I heard your voice—too well I know it! Oh, oh, I was passing—I was crawling past this door when your voice struck upon my ear. Andrew Britton, I won't leave you now! Stop, stop—yes, I must do my errand. I had it from one of bright things that live among the stars—I must do my errand."

She fumbled for a time among her strange mass of many-coloured clothing, and produced at length a small piece of paper. She gazed at it for a moment, and then kissed it devotedly.

"It saves me from horror," she said, in a low, unusual tone. "It saves me from cramp and colds, from the frost and the scorching heat, but I am bound to show it to you—all of you shall see it. It is blessed, and was given to poor Mad Maud by the bright spirit. Look, do—you, and you, and you. Are they not brave words—words to save and bless?"

She glided among the guests, and held for a moment before the eyes of each the slip of paper that Ada had given her, till she came near the smith, when she replaced it in her bosom, saying,—

"Not to you, man of blood—not to you. Ho!—ho! Andrew Britton, not to you!"

The smith had sat till now as if paralyzed; but, when Maud was making for the door, he suddenly cried with a tone of anger, while his face swelled with wild passion,—

"Hold—stop that witch! kill her—tear her to pieces—curses on her!"

He rushed forward as he spoke, and would most probably have done the poor creature some fatal injury, had he not been suddenly stopped by a tall, stout man, who rushed from a corner of the room, upsetting several persons in his progress, and placed himself before Maud.

"Stop!" he cried, in a voice of command—"touch the woman at your peril."

For a moment Britton paused, while his face worked with fury, and he more nearly resembled some wild animal at bay than a human being. Suddenly, then, collecting all his energies, he sprang forward with a cry of rage; but the stranger adroitly stepped on one side, at the same time that he threw a chair, on which he had his hand, across Britton's path, who fell over it with great violence. Britton lay a moment as if stunned by the fall, and several of the company began to cry shame upon the stranger, who stood quite calm awaiting the rise of his foe.

The landlord, however, who had witnessed some of the affair from the bar, now rushed in in a state of great indignation with the stranger, for not allowing King Britton to do just what he liked.

"Troop out of my house," he cried. "How dare you insult a customer of mine? Troop, I say. Go after your pretended mad woman. You want to rob the house, both of you. Troop, I say."

"Suppose I won't go?" said the stranger.

"Then suppose I make you, you vagabond?" cried the enraged landlord.

" You can't," said the stranger.

" Now, by the mass, that beats all the impudence ever I heard of," cried the landlord. " Here, Gregory—Gregory! my staff—quick—my staff! we will have this fellow out in the king's name. My staff, I say! Was there ever such a rogue, to assault my best customers; and then not run away."

The stranger laughed in spite of himself at this last remark of the landlord's and turning to the company, he said,—

" Every one here present can witness that I only interfered with this drunken ruffian to prevent him from committing an assault upon a maniac, and his present condition arises part from intoxication, and partly from falling over a chair in an attempt to attack me."

" You are a scoundrel," said the landlord.

" Out with him! turn him out!" cried the company, with one voice.

" My staff! my staff!" roared the landlord, gathering courage from the unanimous support he seemed likely to receive.

" You need not trouble yourself for your staff," said the stranger, " I am going, and if you required a staff, I could lend you mine, friend."

The stranger took from his pocket, as he spoke, a small bright silver staff.

" W—w—what! who—who are you?" stammered the landlord.

" It matters not just now who I am," said the stranger, " but look to your house, sir—it has grown disorderly of late."

With a slow step the stranger then left the room, amid an universal stare of astonishment from the company.

" Well, I never—" cried the landlord, " a silver staff! He belongs to the office of the High Bailiff of Westminster, as I'm a sinner."

" And yet you wanted to turn him out," said the cordwainer.

" Landlord, you are an intemperate man," said another.

" The landlord's a fool," cried a third.

" Not to know an officer!" cried a fourth.

" Ah—ah!" chimed in three or four more.

" Why—why you all called turn him out," said the discomfited landlord.

" Ah—yes," said the man who had prepared to drink Britton's health—" but we meant you."

" Yes—yes! Hear—hear!" cried everybody; " we meant turn out the landlord."

" The deuce you did."

" Where—where—is she? Curses on her—where is she—is it a dream?" murmured Britton, recovering from his mixed state of insensibility, produced by drink and a blow of his head against the floor.

" Was—it true—eh?" continued Britton; " where the devil am I now? Can't you speak, none of you?"

The landlord turned to the company, and placed his fingers confidentially and knowingly against the side of his nose, in intimation that he was about to perpetrate some piece of extreme cleverness not quite consistent with truth. Then, turning to Britton, he said, in a commiserating tone,—

" Good luck, Master King Britton, your majesty certainly took forty winks in a chair, and by some sudden move, it has upset your majesty."

" Is—is—that it?" said Britton, looking around him with heavy eyes.

" Yes; all these honourable gentlemen can bear me out in what I say."

" Curse me, then, if ever I had such a dream," said Britton.

" All dreams are very disagreeable," said the landlord.

" Oh, very!" said the company.

" D—n you all," muttered Britton.

The landlord now turned again to the company, and favoured them with another bit of facetiousness, which consisted in rubbing his left elbow and going through the motion of drinking in dumb show; and having so bespoken their kind and considerate attention, he turned to Britton, and added,—

" Your worship's majesty had just ordered cans of spiced canary all round, as you went off to sleep like a babe."

" Had I," growled Britton ; " I suppose they all had it then ?"
" No, no, no !" cried a chorus of voices.
" Quite sure ?"
" Oh, quite."
" Then I'll be d—d if you get it !"

The landlord looked rather taken aback by this, and rubbed his chin in an abstracted manner with his apron, while the guests looked at each other in consternation.

" What are you staring at, all of you?" cried Britton. " You have seen a gentleman before, I suppose ?"

" Oh, yes—yes," said everybody.

" Then go to the devil while I go for a walk !" added Britton, staggering to the door, and as he passed out, he muttered to himself,—

" A dream ! No, no—no dream. She will do me some mischief yet. I must kill her—curses on her ; and he too. What did he want here ? I know—it was Hartleton ! But curse them all—I'll be even with them yet ! I should like to cut all their throats, and treat those beasts I have just left with cans all round of their blood ! I'd make them drink—damme, I'd make them drink it !"

CHAPTER XXXIV.

THE FETE.—VILLANY PROSPERS FOR A SEASON.—AN INTERRUPTION.—THE DANCE.

THAT night the halls of the princely residence of Learmont presented to the eye one blaze of light, brilliant costumes, costly decorations, and everything that his imagination could suggest as calculated to entrance the senses, and convey a notion of his boundless wealth and unlimited prodigality. Learmont was now in truth carrying out to its utmost the mode of life he had so often proposed to himself as that alone which could smother the stings of conscience, and by not allowing him time to think of the past, enable him to extract some enjoyment from the gaudy glittering present.

To the entertainment which he now gave, he invited scores of persons whom he knew only by name, but who scrupled not to accept the bidding of a man who was supposed to be rich beyond all comparison.

There were members of Parliament—of both houses, holy ministers of the church, high legal functionaries. In fact, Learmont, from the mere rumour of his enormous wealth—a rumour which he had himself originated, and to which he lent countenance by his great expenses, found no difficulty in filling his saloons with all that were considered illustrious or great in the metropolis.

Learmont was not a man to allow anything to be wanting at such an entertainment as that he was now giving. He possessed education, talent, and taste, although all were perverted by the utter absence of all moral feeling in his mind.

The most delightful music, breathing low dulcet sounds, mingled sweetly and harmoniously with the hum of conversation among his courtly guests. The saloons rivalled the mid-day splendour of a summer's day, by the colour and profusion of the lights, which lent a charm to everything within their glittering influence.

There were beaufets loaded with costly luxuries, to which the guests helped themselves at discretion ; and all this, heightened as it was by brilliant costumes, civil and military, created a scene of magnificence that astonished and delighted every one there to witness it.

The guests would congregate together in small knots,—those who knew each other, to wonder at the glory and enchantment around them, and many were the whispered surmises as to how the owner of such riches had spent his early life, when now he manifested so prodigal a spirit, and showed such rare taste and royal magnificence in his mode of life.

Some of the more superstitious would have it that he was an alchemist, and had discovered the transmutation of metals, by which he could turn lead and copper to gold. Others looked upon it with the jaundiced eye of party politics upon the scene, and whispered to a friend that the lord of so much wealth must be a spy in the service of the dethroned family, whose rights, real or fancied, were not at that period, set at rest in this realm.

It was strange that but one of all the guests of Learmont suggested a probable and creditable mode of accounting for his great wealth, and sudden freak of spending it ; that was that he had lived many years in melancholy seclusion, making mercantile ventures secretly with his large revenues, which proving successful, had placed some enormous sum at his disposal, the possession of which had dazzled his brain, and induced him to fly from the pecuniary economy to that of profuse and lavish expenditure.

This supposition was, however, far too common-place and reasonable to find many supporters, and the majority decidedy inclined to the more marvellous opinion.

Learmont himself, attired in a handsome dress, which set off his tall figure to the best advantage, seemed upon this occasion to have cast off his habitual gloom and asperity of manner. He mingled freely with his guests, jesting with one, discussing some knotty political point with another in forcible and lofty language, cautiously complimenting a third, and in fact, winning from all those golden opinions which ever wait upon a known cold, proud, and haughty man, when he chooses to unbend himself, and make an effort to become agreeable.

By degrees, however, he confined almost all his attention to a few well-known political characters who were at the fete, and who were the agents of ministers in the barter of a baronetcy for a certain sum of money invested in parliamentary seats with Learmont. This baronetcy to procure which Learmont had lent all his abilities of intrigue, he fairly considered as the first grand step up the ladder of ambition; for even supposing the remote probability of his legitimate claim to the Learmont estates to be disputed successfully, he would still have higher dignities of his own acquisition to fall back upon.

Thus it will be seen that the wily Learmont was playing a complicated game of public ambition, while at the same time, he was privately tortured by doubts and fears, concerning the fidelity of his accomplices in crime—the crafty Jacob Gray, and the dissipated and ruffianly Britton.

The fete was to conclude with a ball in a style of unparalleled splendour : one of the largest of the saloons had been fitted up as the ball-room, in a style of costly and rare elegance ; the chalked flooring alone costing five hundred pounds in execution, it being designed by some of the first artists of the day.

This room was kept carefully closed, until Learmont himself should perceive that his guests were desirous of some changes of amusement, when upon a signal given by him, the folding doors were to be thrown open.

This signal he did not give until late ; and he had been assured of the baronetcy in the following week, before he fancied it time to change the scene.

" Your exceedingly patriotic conduct, sir," said an eminent political personage present, " has been represented to his majesty, who at once acceded to the proposed baronetcy, which he was gracious enough to say should be but the prelude to much greater things."

" I trust that my future patriotism will be equally appreciated," replied Learmont, courteously, and with the smallest dash of satire in his manner ; " the next step up the ladder of nobility, I am quite aware is not so easy of access."

" Real patriotism," replied the political personage, with a low bow to Learmont, 'will accomplish wonders."

" Would three more seats in the Commons be of service to the minister ?" said Learmont, in a low tone.

"I should say, decidedly," replied the other in a suppressed voice; "and a-hem, Baron Learmont would sound well."

"There is nothing like patriotism," said the 'squire.

"Oh! nothing," replied the political personage.

"And it should be rewarded."

"I quite agree with you, sir."

London : Printed and Published by E. Lloyd, 12, Salisbury-square, Fleet-street.

Learmont then took another round of his saloons, and conversed gaily and appropriately with several groups of his guests.

A new arrival was now announced, which Learmont had been most anxiously looking for. Not the least important of the schemes of Learmont was to unite himself by marriage to some noble and influential family, who would feel their own dignity and importance interested in upholding him against any untoward circumstance that might occur, of a nature to depreciate him; and the announcement that

No. 19.

now greeted his ears, of the arrival of Lord Brereton, Lady Brereton, and the Honourable Georgiana Brereton, their only daughter, was the most welcome one that had yet occurred. This family had all the mean, proud vices of the aristocracy, with scarcely any of their redeeming virtues; but they were of an ancient race, and numbered among their connexions all the principal nobles of England, claiming likewise a distant alliance with royalty itself.

Her father was one of those men who fancy they and their extravagancies have somesort of claim upon society at large for support, and all thoughts of usefulness or prudence were with him quite out of the question, and derogatory to his dignity. The family estates were mortgaged to the last farthing; the family plate and diamonds were only in their possession on hire from the money scriveners. Still the income of Lord Brereton was immense, for he was in various shapes quartered upon the public purse as a holder of sinecure appointments with large salaries, on account of his high birth.

His lady was silly, weak, and egotistical—the Honourable Georgiana Brereton, it was well understood, was for sale to the highest bidder; she was proud, supercilious, and handsome.

Lord Brereton, it was understood, would settle upon his daughter an estate worth ten thousand pounds per annum, always provided the happy man who made her his wife was in a condition to advance the sum necessary to redeem the title-deeds from the money-lenders. Therefore was the Honourable Georgiana Brereton, with all her pride and all her insolence, put up for sale at the goodly sum claimed by divers lords as mortgagees of the estate which was to be settled upon her.

Into this family Learmont thought it policy to enter. They had all the influence of high rank, and were unscrupulous in using it. For the Honourable Georgiana he cared no more than for the feathers that danced in her head-dress. She might be proud, haughty, insolent, silly, but her pride was nothing to his; her haughtiness must cringe before his, associated as his was with intellect of a high order. Her indolence, too, he could treat with contempt. She was, in his eyes, merely one of the props to his ambition, and he approached the family, that he despised in his heart, with a smile of welcome of the most engaging character he could assume.

"Welcome to my humble house," said Learmont; "no longer humble, however, when graced by your presence, ladies."

Lady Brereton bowed, and agitated all her feathers, while the honourable daughter took no notice whatever of the courteous salutation of the master of the house.

"You are well lodged here, sir," remarked Lord Brereton. "I hear it is his Majesty's intention to create a baronetcy for you."

"His Majesty is very gracious," replied Learmont.

"I think it judicious," added the lord; "wealth should never be allowed to remain in the hands of untitled persons. Either they, if fitted, should be raised to rank, or the wealth should be by some means taken from them."

"There is much sound philosophy in what your lordship says," answered Learmont.

"It is my opinion," said Lord Brereton, with affected dignity.

"Certainly," added Learmont; "and that should be sufficient to settle the question for ever, my lord."

Lord Brereton bowed stiffly.

Learmont now cast his eyes around the saloon, and fancying he saw an air of satiety creeping over his guests, he resolved upon opening the ball-room, which he felt sure would give an impetus to the flagging spirits of his company, who were really getting tired of the incessant glitter of all around them.

CHAPTER XXXV.

THE BALL-ROOM.—A NOBLE FAMILY.—THE INTERRUPTION.—UNEXPECTED END OF
LEARMONT'S FETE.

CLAPPING his hands as a signal to the attendants, who were in waiting, the whole of one end of the saloon vanished, as if by magic, being slid away like a scene at a theatre, and disclosed the magnificent ball-room, brilliantly illuminated, and adorned with the most exquisite plants and flowers. A murmur of delight and astonishment at the suddenness of the change arose among the guests, and then the younger portion eagerly pressed forward to enjoy the delight of the dance.

A choice band of music struck up in an enlivening strain, and in a few moments, scarcely a guest remained in the first saloon, in which the numerous domestics began to lay a costly supper.

Even the apathetic Georgiana Brereton condescended to remark to her noble mother that the poor man, meaning Learmont, ought not to be blamed or despised, for he was evidently doing his best, to which the mother replied, in an affected languid tone,—

"Certainly, my dear. They say he is very rich. I declare it's quite sinful for people with no names at all to have the means of doing these things."

"Papa says," added the young lady, who, by-the-by, was thirty years of age, "papa says that the Learmont family came in with the conquest, as a Learmont was a standard-bearer to William."

"Indeed, my love! Well, there is something in that, and should he propose, we can make inquiry."

"Exactly," drawled the daughter.

The ball-room was now filled with the guests, and altogether, a more brilliant spectacle could scarcely be conceived.

Learmont made a signal to the musicians to cease playing, while the partners were chosen for the dance. With a gallant air, he stepped up to the Brereton party, and offered his hand to the Honourable Georgiana, which was graciously accepted, so far as the tips of that young lady's fingers extended.

All eyes were upon him and his patrician partner as he led her across the richly-chalked floor. There was an impressive silence for a few seconds, when from a side-door a servant appeared, and gliding among the guests, approached Learmont, and stood for a moment as if he had something to say to him.

"Well, knave!" cried Learmont, his face slightly flushed with anger, at being interrupted at that moment.

"An please you, sir, there—there—is——"

The Honourable Georgiana tossed her plumed head with a look of great displeasure, and Learmont forgetting everything on the impulse of the moment, cried angrily,—

"Speak your message, sirrah!"

"A message from the Old Smithy," said the trembling servant.

Learmont's cheek blanched in an instant, and his lips quivered with agitation.

"How dare you!" he gasped.

"An please your honour," said the man, in a submissive tone, "your honour ordered that—the—the—message from the Old Smithy should be always brought to your honour, and—he—he won't go away—he—has knocked out two of Timothy's teeth, your honour, besides, he—he——"

"Peace!" cried Learmont. "Peace, I say. No! music there—music!"

The band immediately struck up an enlivening air, and the guests gazed at Learmont with bewildered looks, for he presented more the appearance of a madman than the high-bred courteous gentleman he had seemed during the evening.

The servant slowly retreated, but Learmont could not, dared not, let him go without some answer to the savage.

"Will your ladyship excuse me one moment?" he said to the Honourable Georgiana Brereton, in an agitated manner.

"For as many as you please, sir," answered the haughty damsel, with a tone of pique and insolence.

Learmont strode after the servant, and just as the latter reached the door, he caught him, and said,—

"Tell him to wait."

"Yes, your honour," said the servant.

Learmont hurried back to where he had left the honourable lady, but she was not there. He glanced hurriedly around him, and saw her with her noble relatives at a distant part of the room. In a minute he was with them.

"Pardon my rudeness," he said, "in leaving you. I am a bachelor, and have so many troublesome domestic matters to arrange that I am compelled sometimes to appear rude where I would most of all wish to be otherwise."

"The interruption," said the young lady, "was so very extraordinary."

"Yes—a—a—rather an ill-bred knave," said Learmont. "My servants want a mistress sadly."

"Such a strange thing in a ball-room," added Georgiana.

"Eh!" said Lord Brereton. "If it be pronounceable, my dear, what was it?"

"Oh, a mere nothing," said Learmont; "an absurd mistake. Is not that a divine strain they are playing?"

"Delightful!" said the lady; "but the words were a message from the Old Smithy!"

"The old who?" exclaimed Lord Brereton, with a shrug.

"The Old Smithy. I cannot pretend to know what it means."

"Frightful!" exclaimed Lady Brereton.

Learmont tried to smile, but the distortion of his features looked as if occasioned by some acute pain rather than any sensation approaching to the mirthful.

"It was most absurd," he said, "and might make one angry, but that it is too laughable."

As he spoke a voice behind him said in a tone of trembling apprehension,—

"An it please your honour—he—he——"

Learmont positively gasped, and clutched the back of a chair for support, as he turned and faced another servant, the former one being afraid to venture into the presence of his fiery master again.

"W—what now?" he said.

"He won't go, an it please your honour."

"Won't go?" echoed Learmont, in such a confusion of mind that he scarcely knew what he said, and the servant, emboldened by the apparent placidity of his master, added,—

"No, your honour, and he says he won't wait either."

"Thrust him from my door," shrieked Learmont; "kill him—no—no—tell him to come to-morrow—yes, to-morrow."

Learmont's noble guests looked at each other in mute surprise. The voice in which Learmont had spoken was loud and strange, and attracted all eyes to the spot on which he stood. A glance around the ball-room at once showed him that he was the observed of all, and he felt the necessity of controlling his passion.

"The dance, the dance," he cried; "the most precious hours of gladness and joy. The dance! the dance!"

These words were scarcely spoken, when his attention was arrested by an unusual commotion at the further end of the saloon, accompanied by cries, the trampling of feet, and a few oaths, which sounded strangely in that gaudy scene.

Learmont's heart sunk within him, and at that moment he suffered a pang greater than any he had ever power to inflict, as the conviction came across his mind that Britton was forcing his way into the ball-room, despite of every obstacle.

This was an event which could not have happened under ordinary circumstances, but the whole of Learmont's household were aware that the strange man who came with the message from the Old Smithy had some sort of power over their master, and their ignorance of its extent, paralysed their exertions in opposing his entrance to the ball-room, although had they felt themselves free to act, he would never have reached beyond the hall of the mansion.

Thus it was that the proud, wealthy, and haughty Learmont, surrounded by troops of servants, and evidently exercising the most despotic sway over them, appeared to his assembled guests in the curious and anomalous position of being unable to keep a drunken brawler from the very penetralia of his mansion.

Too well the 'squire kew the voice of the smith not to feel convinced that it was he, who in some freak of wilfulness or drunkenness was thus invading his gay saloons. Defy him, he dared not; kill him he dared not; nay, it was questionable if he dared even be rude to the burly, and perhaps infuriated savage. A deep groan burst from Learmont's labouring breast, as the conviction came across his mind quicker than we can relate the various steps of thought that led to it, that he would always be subject to these visitations, even in his hours of greatest enjoyment, when he was making the attempt to drown reflections in a crowd of the gay and the trifling.

None of the guests seemed disposed to place themselves in the way of Britton, and when the contest ceased between him and the servants, which it did at the door of the ball-room, he found himself free and unimpeded.

With a reeling gait he walked to the very centre of the splendid apartment, and for the space of about a minute he seemed confused and half stupified by the glare of light around, and the brilliant costumes and decorations that everywhere met his drunken gaze.

"Hulloa!" he cried at length, "the squire's coming out at last. A dance, by h—ll! I'm your man—I'll dance with the best of you; I tread on no one's toes if they avoid mine; I've had a little drop, but what matters! there are lights enough here to make a sober man's brain dance again; what do you all stare at me for? I came with a message from the Old Smithy—tell that to the 'squire, and then hear what he says. Ho—ho—ho! We are old friends, very old friends, but he didn't invite me to-night: it was d—d shabby; but here I am—the messenger from the Old Smithy, at ten guineas a visit. What do you think of that? If anybody says I'm drunk, I'll take his life—his life I say—Hurrah for a dance! a dance! hurrah!"

Britton had all the ball-room nearly to himself, for the guests shrank from him on all sides, and Learmont seemed for the moment completely unmanned and powerless.

Shaking off, however, by a violent effort the confusion of his senses, he suddenly advanced and confronted Britton.

The smith shrunk for a moment before the pale face of Learmont, in which was an expression of concentrated rage and hate that might well have appalled even a far bolder man.

Britton, however, was not in a state to admit of any moral control; drink was inflaming his brain, and there was a recklessness about him that, if not carefully treated, might involve both Learmont and himself in one common destruction.

The haughty 'squire felt fully the precarious situation in which he stood, and therefore was it, that in the midst of a wild passion that made him tremble, he felt obliged to temporise with the man whose life's blood flowing at his feet would scarcely have satisfied his feelings of awful hatred.

"Andrew Britton," he said, in a half-choked voice, which he wished no one to hear but the smith.

"Well, 'Squire Learmont," replied the ruffian, endeavouring to stand steadily the fixed gaze of the other.

"For your own life's sake go away from here—you are drunk, and know not what you do."

"Drunk, am I? Well, there's many a better man been drunk before to-day?"

"What do you want?"

"Ten—ten—guineas and—a (hiccup) dance; I tell you what it is—it's infernally unfriendly of you not to invite me. You know I'm a gentleman now. Never—never—never—to show me—your nobles—curse me if I—stand it. In—introduce me to the rest of the gentlefolks, can't you, and be d—d to you. I—I aint such a sneak as that cursed Jacob Gray. No—no, I'm a gentleman every—every inch a gentleman. Hurrah! hurrah!"

"Are you mad?" said Learmont.

To his agony the 'squire now observed that, impelled by curiosity, his guests were slowly creeping closer around him and the savage smith. He raised his voice suddenly and cried—

"My noble and honoured guests, this is a poor mad fellow, who from motives of charity, I support. I do not like to commit violence on one so afflicted by Heaven. Here, take this purse and go."

"Oh, yes," hiccuped Britton; "that's all very well as regards the purse, but I don't mean to go yet. I'll have a dance. Let me see—I've got something to say to you, 'squire."

"Another time," cried Learmont.

"No—no—time like the present. Life is so very un—uncertain. I tell you what—you—you recollect that infernal Frank Hartleton?"

"Mad,—mad—quite mad," said Learmont, striving to stop the smith.

"Beware," said Britton, with drunken solemnity. "I say beware. He's on the look-out—curse him—and that infernal mad woman too—curse her! they want to hang us—curse all the world. Beware, I say, that's all—never mind me, ladies and gentlemen—I'm a gentleman—I live on my means—I'm King Britton, and hope to see you all at the Chequers. Thank you ma'am."

This last observation was addressed to the Honourable Georgiana Brereton, who having given her head a toss of disdain upon meeting the anxious eye of the confounded Learmont, imparted such a nodding reaction for some seconds to her feathers that the intoxicated smith took it as a complimentary acknowledgment of his invitation to the Chequers.

Some of the guests now began to laugh, and others to complain to each other in no very measured terms of the intrusion among them, of so very questionable a character as the smith appeared to be; while several, among whom were the Brereton family, made a move to depart, fearful how the singular scene would end.

For a moment Learmont had his hand on his sword hilt, and the turn of a hair would have induced him to plunge the weapon, at all risks, into the heart of Britton, but the latter seeing the Honourable Georgiana Brereton, who he supposed had been so civil to him, about to depart, made a sudden rush forward, and before any one could be aware of his intentions, he clasped her round the waist with one arm, and commenced dragging her along in a wild dance, entirely of his own invention. A general rush now took place to rescue the shrieking female, and a scene ensued of the greatest confusion.

Britton grew absolutely furious, and dealt blows and oaths about him with equal liberality. In the midst of all this Learmont was in a state of mind bordering on distraction. He rushed into the midst of the throng, and seizing Britton by the throat, tore him from among the guests, nor relaxed his hold till he had dragged him through the outer saloon, and flung him into a small ante-room, the door of which he locked and placed the key in his pocket. Partly with the fumes of what he had drunk, and partly with the heavy fall Learmont had given him, the smith dropped into a lethargic state of half insensibility and half sleep, so that at all events he was for a time quiet in the room where he was thrown.

Dispirited, angry, and his apparel disarranged, Learmont returned to his ball-room. His guests would not, however, be persuaded to remain, and despite all his protestations that the "madman" was properly secured, he could not restore the confidence or hilarity of the company.

Upon one excuse or another, they one and all departed, and not a single dance took place in the elaborately and expensively prepared ball-room of the ambitious and mortified 'squire.

With a forced civility he saw the last of his numerous guests to his door. The lights were still blazing in his saloons, but there was silence and loneliness in the midst of all his splendour, which now looked such a mockery of gaiety.

He sunk upon a chair, and buried his face in his hands for many minutes, in an agony of painful reflection.

Learmont's first grand fete was over, and a signal failure.

CHAPTER XXXVI.

ALBERT SEYTON.—THE LONELY SEARCH.—A SUGGESTION.—AN IMPORTANT VISIT.

WE will now conduct the reader to one of our *dramatis personæ* that we have unwillingly been compelled to neglect for some time—we mean the gallant and enthusiastic Albert Seyton. As we have recorded the prostration of spirits which ensued, when he lost all trace again of the unfortunate and persecuted Ada, after so providentially, as it were, encountering her in St. James's Park, terminated in a long and dangerous illness---an illness which brought him to the brink of the grave; but thanks to the tender nursing of his father, and an excellent constitution, he successfully battled with his sickness, and after some months, was able, although but the shadow of his former self, to walk abroad, by the assistance of his father.

His deep dejection concerning Ada, however, still clung to him like a blight, and it became clear to his deeply affected father that he should never again see the bloom of health upon the cheek of his son, unless the hiding-place of the deceitful Jacob Gray was once more discovered.

The old house at Lambeth had been soon deserted by Tibbs, the bear-warder, The gloom and solitariness of the situation by no means suited the habits of the roving vagabond, who had been so long without a fixed home of any kind, that now he had become possessed of one, such as it was, he soon hated it, and looked upon it in the light of a prison. All that Jacob Gray had left in the house he sold off and once more the ruined building was tenanted only by the rats and mice, who scampered along its deserted rooms and echoing corridors.

Twice Learmont himself had visited the house, and explored every nook and corner ; and once the savage smith, in a state of semi-intoxication, had burst open the door, and rushed from room to room in the vain hope that Jacob Gray might have returned to his hiding-place.

After that it was the haunt of any desperate character who chose to enter it, for the door swung loosely by one hinge, and the winter's wind, hail, and sleet, found free entrance to the crazy building.

Albert's father, too, had been often, and lingered about the ruined street, until he could no longer cherish the remotest hope of being enabled to find a clue to the place of confinement of the beautiful girl, with whose weal or woe the happiness or sorrow of his dear son was so much mixed up.

Then he besought Albert to be patient, and trust in Heaven to send succour to her whom he loved ; and when Albert himself could walk so far, he went with his father to the old house, and wandered for hours from room to room, pleasing himself with the thought that he was treading upon the spots oft trodden by Ada, and looking upon the objects most familiar to her eye.

The situation of secretary to Learmont, which Albert Seyton, little dreaming how closely he was connected with the fate of Ada, had endeavoured to obtain, was filled up long before he was convalescent, and the state of health of the unhappy youth gave his father far more uneasiness than any consideration of his present prosperity in life. d

Daily, however, the strength of Albert returned, and once again he commenced the search throughout London and its suburbs for the lost Ada. When wearied with some long perambulation, he would bend his steps to the Park, and sit melancholy thought upon the same seat on which he had been sitting when he heard the voice of Ada. There, chewing the cud

> " Of sweet and bitter fancy,"

he would recline for hours, endeavouring to devise fresh schemes for the discovery of Ada, and trying to recollect some part of the city that he had omitted to visit. He would then wander homewards, listless, dispirited, and fatigued, to relate to his father the particulars and non-success of his toils.

It was upon one of these occasions that poor Albert was more than usually dispirited and weary, that his father said kindly to him,—

" Albert, it does appear to me that we can have no further scruple how we commit this man Gray. He cannot be the father of the persecuted Ada."

" He her father!" exclaimed Albert. " I would as leave think that the tiger could be sire to the lamb. Oh, no! there is some dark, mysterious villany at the bottom of all. My poor Ada is the innocent victim of some intrigues and enemies, with which this Gray and others are mixed up. Alas! alas! the villains may have killed her. Oh! would that kind Heaven would direct me where to seek her!"

" Do not despair, Albert," said his father soothingly, " the time will come when all this must be made clear and apparent."

" I hope it may, father," said Albert, despondingly, " but I am very wretched."

" It strikes me," continued Mr. Seyton, " that we are not justified, Albert, in the course we are pursuing."

" Indeed! father."

" No, Albert. What I advise is, an immediate communication of the whole of the circumstances to the magistrate, Sir Frederick Hartleton. The fact that a mysterious packet was actually addressed to him, and set such a store by this man Gray, will be sufficient to interest him in the case."

Albert remained in thought for a few moments, and then springing from his seat with energy, he exclaimed,—

" Yes, father, let us do so. There is hope in that. Sir. Frederick Hartleton must have means of inquiry, and sources of information that no one but a person in his situation could have. Let us go at once."

" You are wearied now, Albert."

" No, no ; I am never wearied in the cause of Ada."

" Wait till you are invigorated ; you can then tell your fate better, for in truth you must know a geat deal more than I."

" Oh! ather, come with me now. You have made this suggestion, and it may be a most happy one. Come now!"

" I will not baulk you," said Mr. Seyton, rising. " I do not think it a proper course ; but do not build too much upon it, Albert : only look upon it as a chance that should not be thrown away."

Sir Frederick Hartleton's office was across the Park, somewhere close about the spot now occupied by the gardens of Buckingham Palace, and Seyton lived in the neighbourhood of Soho ; so that the father and son proceeded to Charing Cross, and entered the Park by the gate in Spring Gardens.

The sun was setting ; but the great mall of the Park was thronged with promenaders—St. James's being then a much more fashionable place than it is now.

Albert and his father paid but little heed to the careless throng they passed among ; their thoughts were intent upon the object of their search, although it was with a sigh that the elder Seyton marked the hopeful countenance and tone of his son ; for he himself had been used to disappointment, and expected but little from the visit to the magistrate. It grieved him therefore to think that Albert should hope much from the application, because he knew that his disappointment, should it result in nothing, would be proportionately great.

" Albert," he said, " this step I consider more a matter of public duty than anything else. We must still trust to Providence to protect Ada, only we place ourselves in a little better position by the co-operation of a magistrat so much respected and esteemed as Sir Frederick Hartleton, in what we do."

"He may find me, my Ada," said Albert, "and so entitle himself to a gratitude from me that shall be boundless."

"You had better let me tell the tale," said his father, noticing the agitated spirits of Albert—"should I omit anything, you can put me right, Albert."

"As you please, father," he replied. "I am too much agitated to speak what I know."

No. 20.

" Your sincerity will be the more apparent to Sir Frederick by the emotion you cannot subdue, Albert. All men, but those who are evil-doers, or live on the fruits of crime, speak well of this gentleman, as an upright magistrate and a feeling man."

He had now crossed the park and emerged at the little gate leading to Pimlico. They then inquired for the office of Sir Frederick, and were directed down a narrow street, called Buckingham-place, which was but dimly lighted by the inefficient oil lamps of the period.

Over an open doorway was a lamp, with the words " Magistrate's Office," boldly enamelled upon the dirty glass.

" This must be the place, father," said Albert, hurriedly.

" No doubt," replied Seyton. " Come in, Albert."

They stooped under the low arched doorway, and were immediately confronted by a man of coarse heavy build, who demanded to know their business.

" We have a private communication to make to Sir Frederick,'" said Mr. Seyton.

" Oh, private?" muttered the man.

" Yes, strictly private."

" Is it anything about Bill Soames ?"

" Bill who !"

" Bill Soames—he's nabbed for robbing the Bishop of Ely, crossing the open waste opposite Tyburn Gate."

" No, its quite private business of another kind," said Mr. Seyton. " There is my card—this is my son. Please to tell Sir Frederick that we have a private communication to make to him alone."

The man took the card and passed through a doorway, growling as he went.

In a few moments he returned, and taking a key from a bunch at his girdle, he opened a door at the further end of the passage, at the same time saying,—

" This way."

Albert and his father stepped forward after their guide. In a moment another door opened, from which issued a stream of light, and they found themselves in the presence of Sir Frederick Hartleton, the magistrate, the terror of highwaymen; several of whom he had himself captured on Hounslow and Barnes' Commons.

He rose courteously on the entrance of the Seytons, and invited them to be seated. Before they could speak, he said rapidly,—

" Gentlemen, I trust you will not take any offence at my saying that my time is very much occupied, and begging you to be brief."

" The time of public affairs, sir," said Mr. Seyton, " should never be heedlessly wasted. Do you know a man named Gray ?"

" Gray—Gray ?" repeated Sir Frederick Hartleton. " No, sir, I do not."

" There exists, however, a man of that name, who, without authority, keeps prisoner a young girl, if he has not destroyed her."

" Where is he ?"

" That, sir, we do not know."

" Where is the girl ?"

" We are equally ignorant."

" What's her name ?"

" Ada."

" Ada what ?"

" I know not, sir."

" You do not bring me many particulars," said the magistrate. " What do you wish me to do ?"

" In this man Gray's possession, sir," added Mr. Seyton, " is a sealed packet carefully addressed to you ?"

" Indeed !"

" Yes—and with a superscription attached, that is only to be forwarded to you, should he, Gray, be absent from home without note or message for a certain time."

" Then you may depend that this Mr Gray has always found his way home in good time, for I have received no such packet."

" We," continued Mr. Seyton, " from once living in the same house with her, have warmly interested ourselves in the fate of the girl, who is as vrtuous and amiable as she is beautiful."

" Is this Gray in London?"

" We believe he is. He has twice shifted his residence, to ensure the better concealment of the girl."

" There is most probably some c'ime at the bottom of this business," said Sir Frederick ; " but I cannot help you. If you can find the girl, I will of course grant a warrant to bring Gray here, for keeping her a prisoner without her will. At the same time, you had better tell me the minutest particulars as rapidly as you conveniently can."

Mr. Seyton then related all that he knew of Ada and Gray, comprising what he had gathered from Albert, and comprehending the meeting in the park, and the particulars which Ada had related of the midnight attack upon Gray's house."

" What names were mentioned accidentally or otherwise, during all this business ?"

" But two, sir," said Albert. " Ada told me in the park that one of the men who sought the life of Gray, was called by him Britton !"

" Britton ?" said Sir Frederick. " Are you quite sure that was the name?"

" Quite."

" I do know that name !"

" You—you do, sir !" exclaimed Albert, with sudden animation—"then you will save her !"

" Oh—you are in love with this imprisoned young lady," said Sir Frederick, with a smile.

Albert drew back, abashed.

" Nay, my young friend," the magistrate added, " you need not be ashamed of an honest attachment, which, in the case of this persecuted girl, must be disinterested."

" You know Britton, sir ?" said Albert, confused.

" I know a person of that name—in fact, I am watching his proceedings."

" There was another name too mentioned," said Albert, " it was that of a poor maniac called Mad Maud. She seemed to know this Britton."

" She has cause to know him," remarked Sir Frederick Hartleton.

" Stay—1—"

The magistrate paused, and it was evident that something had crossed his mind of an important nature. He covered his eyes with his hand, and seemed to be musing over some train of circumstances in his mind that wanted some connecting links.

" Be so good," he said, suddenly, " as to answer me as exactly as you can, what I shall ask of you."

" We will, sir," said Mr. Seyton.

" What kind of man is this Gray?"

" He is rather above the middle height, of spare habit, and very pale."

" His eyes ?"

" Shifting and inconstant—looking here, there, and everywhere, but in the face of any one he addresses."

" You never saw Britton ?"

" Never."

" Now tell me as nearly as you can the age of this young girl you call Ada ?"

" She cannot now be above seventeen," said Albert.

" Seventeen ?"

The magistrate took a scrap of paper, and made some slight calculations in figures upon it—then he said,—

" During all this business, did you never hear another name mentioned as a prime mover or important personage, connected with it ?"

' No," said Albert, " those were all."

' Well, gentlemen," remarked Sir Frederick ; " you have said enough to interest me. Pray come here again this day week, if I should not send to you ; for which purpose be so good as to leave your address. You may depend upon my utmost exertions to solve the mystery in which this affair is at present so strangely enveloped."

Albert and his father returned their warm acknowledgments to the magistrate; and, leaving their address, they were escorted through the same door they had entered from the private room of the magistrate.

CHAPTER XXXVII.

THE PURSUIT.—THE ATTEMPTED MURDER.—A PROVIDENTIAL INTERFERENCE.— THE PAPERS.

For some moments after the departure of his visitors, Sir Frederick Hartleton remained in deep thought, then he commenced a diligent search among some memoranda that he took from an iron chest imbedded in the wall, and, selecting one paper, perused it attentively more than once.

"Surely," he suddenly exclaimed, "this is the clue at last. Well do I remember the awful night at Learmont, when the storm spread confusion and dismay among the peasantry, and Britton's ill-omened house was in flames, while he dreadful cries that even now seem to ring in my ears, so forcibly does memory recal them, issued from the burning mass. Let me see. The time. Yes, that is sufficiently near,—between fourteen and fifteen years since. Learmont in London, and Britton, the smith, living near him, in a style of coarse extravagance and debauchery befitting his coarse nature. Who supplied the funds ?—Why the rich ambitious money-loving 'Squire Learmont, to be sure! and wherefore ?—Aye, that's the question. For one of two reasons, I'll swear. Either as a reward for present services, or to purchase silence for the past. Humph! Learmont is by no means scrupulous. He would murder the smith. Ay surely would he. There is something then in progress which makes Britton's life valuable to the 'squire. And this man, Gray, too. Who is he ? Was he the man who rushed with such frantic gestures from the fire with the child in his arms ? And is that child, this girl—this Ada, as they call her ?—Surely the whole fits well together. But still there is no proof—all is circumstantial as yet, and involved in mere conjecture. 'Squire Learmont may maintain Britton if he please, and who shall question him ?"

Sir Frederick now again remained in silent thought for a long time, then he said in an assured voice,—

" I must trust this affair to no one. It is too intricate for any ordinary scouts to trace. I must see to it myself. The smith, I am aware, holds his drunken orgies at the Chequers. Thither I will myself go, and watch him. 'Squire Learmont, the time will come when the crimes that I suspect you of, may be made apparent; but cunning devil that you are, I must be cautious or I shall alarm you, and defeat myself."

The magistrate now rose, and disrobing himself of his upper clothing, took from a cloth-press in his room the apparel in which he afterwards appeared at the Chequers, where the little scene occurred between him and the smith, Britton, of which the reader is already cognisant.

We will now, therefore, follow the proceedings of Sir Frederick Hartleton after he left the Chequers. His object was to procure poor Maud, and get from her as much information as he thought he might, by comparing with what he himself knew, rely upon.

He walked very quickly down the street; but the object of his search was nowhere to be seen, and he felt convinced that she must have gone in the opposite direction, although he felt almost sure likewise that he had noticed a figure somewhat resembling hers in the way he was proceeding. While he was standing in a state of doubt, the smith reeled past him, and, Sir Frederick stepping into the shadow of a doorway, escaped recognition from the drunken and infuriated man.

He then resolved to follow him, to see whither he went, as Mad Maud he could easily discover by his police agents on the morrow.

Dogging, therefore, the unequal footsteps of Britton, the disguised magistrate followed him closely and safely.

The smith paused at the corner of the street, and asked a drowsy watchman if he had seen a beggar woman pass. He was at once answered in the affirmative, and in the same breath asked for something to drink, which Britton, being at the same time more savage than hospitable, refused with the addition of a curse.

Sir Frederick now congratulated himself upon following the smith; for he doubted not that, should he encounter poor Maud, he would inflict upon her some fatal injury, unless he, Sir Frederick, was at hand to protect the poor creature.

Britton blundered on, cursing and muttering to himself, but in so low a tone that, although the magistrate came as close to him as he could with safety, he could not shape any intelligible phrases from what was thus uttered.

Britton walked on in the direction of the Houses of Parliament and Westminster Hall, still very closely followed, and almost every passenger he met he asked if a beggar woman had been seen. Some answered one thing and some another, until a lad affirmed that an old beggar woman passed him near to Millbank, and then sat down on a door-step nearly facing the river.

With a shout of triumph Britton rushed onwards; but Sir Frederick kept as close as prudence would dictate, until they cleared Abingdon-street, and came upon the then dark and straggling purlieus of Millbank.

There were but few lights in this quarter, and the inhabitants were not very favourably known to the magistrate as the most moral race in London.

Britton now proceeded more cautiously, and kept peering about him to endeavour, as it appeared to Sir Frederick, as well to discover Maud as to note if any one was near. By gliding along close to some black palings the magistrate entirely escaped observation, and Britton seemed satisfied that he was alone.

Close to the river was a low wall of not more than four feet high, and the night was so dark that it could scarcely be distinguished from the dark stream that rolled by on the further side of it. Directly over the wall was a kind of parapet of about three feet in width, which was about level with the decks of the small river craft that came to disengage gravel, wood, logs, &c., at the wharfs, and was very convenient for them. Immediately, however, below this parapet, and, in fact, partly washing under it, was the black muddy tide of the river.

Dark as was the water, the wall was still darker, and Sir Frederick Hartleton could plainly see the upper part of the bulky form of the smith in slight relief against the water, as he walked slowly along close to the wall.

Once or twice he looked back; but his pursuer was on the other side of the way, and quite well backed by the black paling which, when he stooped a very little, was above his head.

This was the state of things, when suddenly a wild plaintive voice broke the stillness of the night air; and, with a mockery of gaiety, that had in it the very soul of pathos, sang or rather chaunted the words of a song of joy, hope, and mirth, which was then popular in the metropolis, and was the composition of one of the most distinguished wits of the day.

There was a wild abandonment of manner about the singer, that would have commanded the attention of Sir Frederick at any time; but now that he saw the smith suddenly pause, he paused likewise, and the strains with all their melancholy pathos came full upon his ear.

TO THE BRIDE! TO THE BRIDE!

To the Bride! To the Bride,
  I sing,
And away to the winds the strain
  I fling.
There's a tear in her gentle eye,
  I trow—
She weeps, and her heart is sad,
  I vow;
Her hand like a leaflet shakes,
  I see,—
That hand which never more
  Is free.
She leaves her happy home
  Of light,
Where her happiest days were past
  So bright:
She has trusted all to one,
  The bride.
Shall her young heart's joy e'er know
  A tide—
Shall her bliss flow on for aye
  Or not?
When distant far, shall ever
  The spot,
Where she lived and loved so long,
  Be forgot?
To the Bride! To the Bride,
  I sing,
And away to the winds my strain
  I fling!

The voice ceased. A solemn stillness reigned for a few brief seconds, and then Sir Frederick saw the shadowy form of the smith glide forwards—the gruff voice of the savage drunkard came to his ears as he stooped and exclaimed,—

"So Maud—we have met again. D—n you, we are alone now!"

A half-stifled scream followed that speech, and the magistrate bounded across the road. He paused, however, when he was within a few paces of Britton, for he heard the poor mad creature speak, and the thought crossed his mind that her cry had proceeded from sudden surprise, and not from any injury inflicted by the smith, and knowing his power to save her he thought that if Britton wished to procure any information from Mad Maud previous to offering her any violence, he might as well hear it, as in all probability it would be important and correct.

Acting upon this supposition, he crouched down close by the wall for some few seconds—then suddenly recollecting the parapet on the other side, and the facilities it afforded as sufficiently close to aid poor Maud in case of the most sudden emergency, he crept some twenty yards or more away, and then clambered over the wall in a moment, on to the parapet. To draw himself along this noiselessly until he actually faced Britton, was the work but of another minute, and laying flat down was quite secure from observation, while he was ready for action, and must hear the slightest murmured word that passed.

CHAPTER XXXVIII.

THE MEETING AT MILLBANK.—THE KNIFE.—ADA'S FATE HANGS ON A
THREAD.—THE BOLD PLUNGE.

"What do you mean?" exclaimed Britton, as Sir Frederick Hamilton halted on the parapet. "Speak, Maud, or by hell I'll throw you in the river!"

"What do I mean, Andrew Britton!" replied Maud, "I mean pain and death here and torture everlasting in a world to come for you. Ay, for you, Andrew Britton—you cannot kill Maud. The Almighty has written our names in the book of mortality—but yours comes first. Yes, yours comes first, Andrew Britton!"

"Idiot!" muttered Britton. "Tell me at once—did you bring that Hartleton to the Chequers?"

"Hartleton!—Hartleton?" repeated Maud. "Oh! he was one of the spirits I knew long ago, before I dropped from among the stars."

"Answer my question!" cried Britton, fiercely. "Did you bring Hartleton to the Chequers?"

"Answer my question, Britton," said Maud, "If your seared black heart will let you. Why does not my husband come to his bride?"

"What do you mean?"

"We waited for him, but he came not; then they whispered he was dead—yes, dead, and I asked Heaven who had killed him, when a voice whispered—Andrew Britton!"

"Peace," cried Britton. "You are mad."

"Yes, mad—mad," said Maud; "but not so mad as Andrew Britton, for he has murdered—murdered the innocent. There's blood on your hands!"

Britton started and involuntarily glanced at his hands.

"Ay blood—blood," cried Maud; "you may wash away the outward stain, but then it clings to your heart; and when you are asked at the last if you are guiltless or not of shedding man's blood, you will hold up your hand, and it will drip with gore!"

"Beldame, peace!" cried Britton. "You tempt me to do a deed before the time I intended. Hear me, Maud; you have but a chance now for your life. Answer me what I shall ask of you truly and I may spare you. Refuse, or tamper with my temper in any way, and yon river receives you in its black and rolling tide. We are alone; there is no one to hear a cry, and I will take care you shall have breath but for one. No one is at hand to aid—I have you at my mercy."

"Your mercy, Andrew Britton?" said Maud. "Oh! profane not the word. When did you show mercy? Savage—the spirit of God is above and around us. The fiat has gone forth, and Heaven has said, thus far shalt thou go and no further—but your questions?—your questions? I will hear your questions, although I am a widow."

"What paper is that you have?"

"Paper?"

"Yes; you have a paper with something written on it."

"Well?"

"Give it to me or you die."

"An angel gave it me. I dream of her now sometimes when my sleep is blessed and happy.

"'Tis not for you, Andrew Britton. It belongs to the angel. I must only show it, and that not to you. No—no—not to you with your blood-stained hands."

Britton was silent for a moment. He was hesitating whether by violence, at once, to tear the paper from the poor wandering creature, or endeavour first to procure such other information as he expected she possessed.   He decided on the latter course, as violence could be resorted to at any moment.

"Maud," he said, "when did we meet last?"

"In a crowd," she replied.   "I recollect there were many men, but none so bad as Andrew Britton.   They held up their hands, the one after the other, and none had blood upon them save his alone."

"What brought you there?   Tell me, or this moment is your last!"

"How far is it to the Old Smithy?" said Maud, as if she had not heard or understood his question.

"Curses!" muttered Britton, whose passion and fear together had tended to sober him ; "is she mad, or cunning?"

"The Old Smithy, where the murder was done, I mean," added Maud.

"I'll tell you," said Britton, in a tone that he intended should be artful and temporising, "if you will answer me what I ask, and give me the paper you have?"

"Britton, where's the child?" said Maud.   "How came you to spare the child? Did it lift its little hands in prayer to you? and was there one spot in your heart that shuddered at the deed of blood?   Did conscience for once stay your arm? or did Heaven interpose, and strike you powerless, when you would have slaughtered the babe?   Tell me that, Britton.   Where have you put the child?—where is Dame Tatton?—speak, Andrew Britton!   I have travelled many, many miles to seek you.   You killed him who loved me,—nay, scowl not, your brows are darker than the night, and I see them frowning on me.   Oh! there is nothing in nature so dark and terrible as thy heart, Andrew Britton.   Even at midnight, when people call it dark, and say you cannot see your hand, the smile of heaven still lingers on the world, and there is the faint light of its love still beaming through the mists of night!   Andrew Britton, give me the child, and I will teach it to pray for you to Heaven.   Oh, give it to me!   It must be cold and weary.   Give it to me, Britton, and then hope to be forgiven!"

"I have no child," said Britton ; "you know that years have passed, and the child who was brought by—by—a man from the burning smithy, must be now a child no longer."

"You would deceive poor Mad Maud, because she hunts you—ay, to the death, hunts you.   You cannot escape me, Britton—you are d——d !"

"D——d! how—what mean you?"

"I am to see you die."

"Pshaw! tell me now, Maud, didst ever see the man again who rushed forth bleeding, with the child, from the Old Smithy "

"What man was that?"

"Didst ever hear the name of Gray?"

"Gray! Gray!   The angel asked me that."

"Ha!"

"Yes—yes—Gray.   Who is Gray?"

"You could take me to the angel," said Britton, in soothing accents.

Maud laughed hysterically, and pointed to the sky, as she said,—"Take you! take you! with the weight of so much blood upon you!   No, no.   Were you lighter you could go.   Andrew Britton, what did my husband say when you killed him?   What was his last word?   You could not forget it.   It must be scorched on your heart.   Tell it to me, Andrew Britton."

"You rave," said Britton ; "do you know that Frank Hartleton, who used to live at Learmont, has become a magistrate?"

"Do you know," cried Maud, "that there's blood wherever Andrew Britton goes?   If the soft dew of Heaven falls upon him, it turns to gore—he dips his hands into a pure streamlet, and the limpid waters turn to blood—his drink is blood, when it touches his lips—spots of thick clotted gore fall on him wheresoever he goes—it is the ancient curse of the Egyptians that is upon him!   Ha! ha! ha! Blood—blood, Andrew Britton!—blood!"

"Devil!" muttered Britton.

"I will haunt you!" continued Maud—"I will shout after you as you go—
There steps a murderer! I will proclaim your calling to all—'tis one of deep iniquity—you are branded by the mark of Cain—you have sinned before Heaven in
taking the life which thou could'st not restore or even comprehend! Wretched—
scared—cursed Andrew Britton! I will be with you when you lie writhing in
your last agony—when you try to pray, 1 will clap my hands and shout 'The

Smithy!' in your ears. When you gasp for water to quench the fever that shall
then be consuming your heart, I will answer you by 'The Smithy!' When you
shriek to Heaven in your dark despair, I will answer you shriek for shriek, and the
words of my vengeance shall be 'The Old Smithy!' Ha! ha! ha!—The murder
at the Old Smithy! When the day comes, that the graves give up their dead, then
will appear a sight to blast you from the Old Smithy! 'Tis hidden now; but the

No. 21,

earth will crack, and with a hideous likeness of what it once was, the form of your victim will pursue you to accuse you before the judgment-seat of God! Then—then you will shriek—yell for mercy!—you, who showed none,—and the blue sky shall open to let you go down—down!—encircled in the loathsome embrace of slimy awful things, that will lick your shivering form with tongues of flame!"

"Peace, wretch!" cried Britton.

At the same moment he lifted his arm, and in his hand gleamed a knife.

"Hold!" cried Mand, " you dare not!"

Sir Frederick Hartleton raised his hand. Britton slowly dropped his murdering arm.

"Woman," he said, "do you wish for death, that you tempt me thus to kill you?"

There was a trembling fear in Britton's voice that re-assured Sir Frederick; and, congratulating himself that the sudden movement he had, on the impulse of the moment, made, had escaped observation, he again lay perfectly quiet, but prepared to aid poor Maud upon an emergency.

"Maud," said Britton, after a pause, "give me the paper you have, and leave London."

"Leave you," said Maud, "I dare not; I have a duty to do,—it is to follow you. Wherever you go, Andrew Britton, there will you find me. No, no! I cannot leave you; I sometimes think I am dead, and that there is my spirit haunting you."

"We shall see," muttered Britton; "spirits have never troubled me yet. The paper, I say!—the paper that you set such store by! I must and will have it."

"Never!"

"Then take the consequences."

He again raised his knife, and was in the very act of bringing it down to plunge it into the breast of the hapless creature, when his eyes fell upon the form of Sir Frederick Hartleton, who rose up on the parapet between him and the water.

This sudden appearance, rising apparently from out of the river, had all the effect which Sir Frederick expected it would. Britton, for the first time in his life, was affected by superstition. He could, on the spur of the moment, imagine the tall dusky form that thus rose before his very eyes, and, as it were, from the bosom of the Thames, to be no other than some supernatural being interposing between him and his victim.

He started back in horror, then, dropping the knife, he rushed precipitately from the spot.

Maud burst into a wild laugh, and before Sir Frederick Hartleton could speak a word to detain her, she fled in a contrary direction to that which Britton had taken, with great speed.

Hastily springing over the wall, Sir Frederick, as well as he was able by the dim light, pursued the flying woman, his object being the same as Britton's, namely, to possess himself of the paper in Maud's possession, and which, he doubted not, was in some way near or remotely connected with the chain of mysteries that enveloped the crimes of 'Squire Learmont and his associates in guilt, the savage smith and the man named as Gray.

Now and then he could see the flutter of her garments, as she rushed along by the wall; and as often as he did, he redoubled his speed with the hope of overtaking, while she was compelled, from the nature of the ground, to go forward in nearly a straight line; for he well knew, that after passing the river wall, which did not extend much further, from the broken nature of the open country, and several hedges and plantations that were close at hand, he might be completely foiled till daylight in his attempt to follow the poor creature, who most probably fancied she was flying from Britton.

"Maud! Maud!" cried Sir Frederick Hartleton, with the hope that she would recognise that his voice was not that of the savage smith.

His call, however, seemed to alarm her still more, and, in fact, notwithstanding her wild and superstitious confidence in the probability of her outliving thes   i h the fear of death from his ruffianly hands had come strongly upon her, and she fled, shrieking from the magistrate, with the full confidence thar Britton was pursuing her, armed with the knife she had seen gleaming for an instant above her devoted head. Her fleetness astonished Sir Frederick Hartleton, for swift runner as he was, he could not come up with her.

"Maud!" he cried again, and the poor creature answered him by a scream, which at once convinced him that he inspired her with terror, rather than confidence, by calling after her. He therefore abstained from doing so, and began evidently to gain upon her just as she neared the part of the river's bank where the low wall terminated.

Now she looked back and screamed again, as she saw his figure dashing onwards through the gloom.

"I am a friend!" cried Sir Frederick Hartleton, but his voice was weak from the violence from which he had been pursuing Mad Maud, and she heard him not.

Now she reached the end of the wall, and looked round again.—A cry announced her terror, and she turned toward the river instead of the land.

There was a heavy splash, and as he heard it, the awful conviction came across the mind of the magistrate, that the unhappy creature had thrown herself into the Thames to escape him.

He gained the spot in an instant. A lighter stood moored close to the bank. With a tremendous spring Sir Frederick gained the deck, and leaning anxiously over the side, he gazed earnestly into the stream as it rippled by. A stifled cry met his ears. He looked in the direction from whence it came, and saw a dark object hurried on by the water.

It was but the act of a moment to dive from the deck of the lighter, and in the next the athletic Sir Frederick Hartleton touched the bottom of the Thames.

He was an admirable swimmer, and rising to the surface, just as the watchmen on the Surrey side began to spring their rattles, and give an alarm by calling out that some one had fallen in the river.

Some few hundred yards in advance of him, he saw the dark object still hurrying on. Assisted by the tide, and his own vigorous swimming, he soon neared it. A few more sweeps of his arms brought him within arm's length, and he grasped poor Maud, for it was she, indeed, by her long raven hair which had escaped from its confinement, and floated in a dark mass upon the surface of the water.

"Help!" cried Sir Frederick in a clear voice, and turning towards the Surrey shore, which was now much nearer to him than that from which he had come.

Several boats had now pushed off, and in one a man stood up with a link that cast a lurid glare over the stream.

"Hilloa!" cried the man. "Who's in for a ducking now? Hilloa there."

"Hilloa!" cried Sir Frederick, and the rowers at once pulled towards him.

"Back water!' cried the man with the light—"I see him—here ye are."

The magistrate grasped the side of the boat, and said—

"Now, my lads, take in the woman."

Maud was lifted into the boat, and Sir Frederick himself clambered after her."

"Fifty guineas, my brave fellows," he cried, "if we get to shore in time to recover this poor creature."

"Fif—fif—fifty?" ejaculated the man with the light.

"Yes—fifty guineas."

"Pull, you devils!" he shrieked out to the rowers, "pull—pull."

The men bent all their energies to the task, and in less than three minutes more the keel of the boat grated on the shore.

Wet and cold as he was, Sir Frederick Hartleton seized the inanimate and light form of Maud, as if she had been an infant, and springing from the boat, he ran to a public-house called "The King's Bounty," that was celebrated at the time, and declaring who he was, had poor Maud immediately properly attended to, while he himself ran to a surgeon, and procured his instant services to restore her if possible to consciousness.

CHAPTER XXXIX.

THE SMITH'S ANGER.—A DRUNKEN TOUR THROUGH WESTMINSTER IN THE OLDEN TIME.—THE WATCH.—A SCENE AT THE CHEQUERS.—THE DETERMINATION.

WHEN Britton fled in sudden fright from the low wall by Millbank, he took his rout up Abingdon-street, and turning into the first house of entertainment he saw, he ordered a quantity of brandy that made the landlady stare again ; but when he lifted the measure to his mouth, and then after a dead silence of about a minute, laid it down empty, the aforesaid landlady's eyes became much larger than before, and she looked again and again in the measure, as if she imagined the brandy might still be only lurking in some corner, and would suddenly make its appearance again.

When Britton then struck his own head, which he did with his clenched fist, the landlady gave a great jump, and exclaimed,—

" Bless us, and save us !"

" I am a fool ! an ass !" cried Britton, " to be scared by a shadow—curses ! what's to pay, woman ? Don't stand staring at me !"

" You—you've had a—pint, sir," gasped the alarmed landlady.

" Take your money out of that, and be quick," cried Britton, throwing down a guinea, the ring of which on a little bit of marble, which the landlady kept behind the bar door, being quite satisfactory, she turned round to hand her customer his change, but to her surprise he was gone.

Half maddened by rage and drink together, Britton now rushed back to where he had left Maud ; but both she and Sir Frederick, from the pace at which they had immediately left the place, were out of sight and hearing ; muttering, therefore, imprecations on his own head, the smith returned towards Westminster in a fit mood for anything.

" Fool that I am !" he roared, for the tremendous dose of brandy he had taken made him quite reckless of who might be within hearing. " Idiot ! I who have made the clang of my hammer heard by midnight, when within a dozen paces of me was a—sight—sight that would—d—n the lights ! they stand in my eyes— and the houses are toppling. Fool—fool to let her go. Would Jacob Gray have done as much ? No, no, not he. It was the idiot Britton. Oh, if I could find them out—Gray and the boy—ay, the boy—I'd dash his brains out against Gray's politic skull. Curses on them all. The—the very pavement is mocking me. The houses reel, and the lamps seem—dance—dancing—from earth to sky—as if they were all mad. It's to annoy me—I know it is."

He reeled on, the liquor he had drunk so recklessly each moment exerting greater effect upon him. The few chance passengers whom he met heard his wild ravings before he reached them, and some had the prudence to cross to the other side of the street, while others would stand in a doorway until the evidently furious man had gone past them.

One watchman, who had just awakened from a sound nap, and walked out of his box, eager to show his efficiency upon somebody, had the temerity to hold up his lantern in Britton's face, and make the simple and innocent remark of—

" Hilloa, friend !"

Britton was, however, in no humour to be spoken to at all, and with one crashing blow of his herculean fist he sent watchman and lantern into the middle of the road, where they lay a dirty mass, consisting principally of a great coat of a dingy whity brown, with the letters W. L., signifying Westminster Liberties, on the back of it.

This little adventure calmed, in a slight degree, the animal irritability of Britton; and although he shouted and reeled along in a stage of intoxication only one degree removed from the last, he spoke more joyously, and even condescended to alarm the neighbourhood by some snatches of Bacchanalian songs, roared out in a voice loud enough to arouse the celebrated Seven Sleepers. In fact, divers of the indignant and infuriated inhabitants opened their windows, and called "watch!" but as no watch answered, they closed them again, wondering where the watchman was, and remarking, as testy old gentlemen do now of the new policeman, that he is never to be seen when he is at all wanted,—although, in this case, the watchman might have been seen by any curious inhabitant who chose to walk into the middle of the road in Abingdon-street.

In about half an hour the guardian of the night recovered; and as Britton had hurried on, and the neighbourhood was restored to quiet and serenity, he roused it all up again, by springing his rattle, and crying "murder!" for about five minutes incessantly.

The good folks of Abingdon street and its vicinity had therefore two alarms that eventful night, the one by Britton himself roaring through the streets when there was no watchman, and the other by the watchman when there was nobody to apprehend.

In the meanwhile Britton went on until he reached, more from habit than design, the door of the Chequers. There he paused, and as it happened to be shut, by way of saving himself the trouble of knocking or lifting the latch, he flung himself against it with such force, that he rolled into the passage, as if he had been suddenly discharged from a cannon.

The landlord was not slow in recognising his Majesty King Britton, and stooped to assist him to rise with all humility, which piece of kindness was rewarded as kings very often reward thier subjects, at least as far as principle went, for the smith seized the unhappy landlord by the hair of his head, and then bumped the said head against the floor, with a reiteration of blows that alarmed the house.

"That will teach you to shut your doors in the faces of your best customers," stammered Britton, rising.

"Ye—ye—yes," said the landlord, rubbing his head, and making a variety of wry faces, "I—I—really—good Master King Britton—you—are quite—facetious. I declare I never had such knocks on the head in my life. I'll see you hung some day." This latter sentence was uttered aside, and with an air of candour that left no doubt of the deep sincerity of it.

"Stir yourself," cried Britton. "Who's here?"

"Who's here, King?"

"Yes—Have you any croaking spies here! Who was yon vagabond in the grey coat?"

"The—the—villain who stood in your worship's way awhile ago?"

"Ay, the same: do you know him?"

"No, no, your Majesty."

"So much the better. I do know him; and if you had, I'm not sure but should have been under the ne—ne—necessity of smashing you—do you hear?"

"Yes—most humbly—Oh, I shall see you at Tyburn yet!"

"What's that you mutter?"

"I—I was arguing that—all villains ought to be at Tyburn, your worship."

"Oh, ought they? Then why aint you there?"

"I—I—really don't know."

At this juncture, when the courteous host felt himself rather at a loss to give a reason why he should not be hung, there entered the house a little bustling man, exclaiming, as he came,—

"Well, they are coming it—there's nothing but lights here, there, and everywhere. You may hear the music in the park. Ah! no doubt, 'tis a right merry scene."

"What do you mean?" roared Britton. "Ex—ex—plain yourself, you bad-looking—piece of—of—bad—clay, you gnat—ex—explain, or I'll give you a blow—shall—shall—Curse me, if—I know."

"Ah, explain yourself, Master Sniggle," said the host, winking at the little man.

" Why," said the little man, " there's lights everywhere—there's lights above— lights below—"

" Ex—ex—plain !" roared Britton.

" Well, I am explaining. There's lights—"

" If—you—you say lights again, I'll be the death of you."

" The—the—death of me for saying lights ?"

" You are an idiot," said Britton, gravely.

" Ah, a rank idiot," cried the landlord, winking again at the little man, who, however, was too much enraged to notice the telegraphic regard of the politic host.

" I an idiot !" he exclaimed. " Well, I never heard the like of that before. I tell you what it is, master landlord, I—I—I won't drink any more of your ale —d—e !"

" You—you can't drink much, you wretched little midge," said Britton.

" Sir," cried the little man, giving his hat a fierce cock. " Sir, I never enter your house again, and my wife shall get her ratifia from the Blue Cat and Frying Pan, or the Crocodile and Crumpet, d—e !"

The landlord now winked so dreadfully and so incessantly, that it seemed quite doubtful whether or not he would ever leave off again ; but the little man was not to be winked into good-humour, and shook his head in great indignation.

Britton reeled towards the bar, exclaiming, " Give me a half-pint measure, and if I don't put him into it, my name an't King—King Britton !"

The landlord now took the opportunity of whispering to Master Sniggles—

" Do for Heaven's sake be an idiot."

" I—I—the devil !" cried Sniggles.

" Say, you are a midge," added the landlord, at the same time enforcing his argument by a poke in the regions of Master Sniggles' ribs.

" He'll be desperate if you contradict him. Be an idiot just for old acquaintance sake, and to oblige me."

" It's not very pleasant," suggested the little man.

" Now," roared Britton, returning with a pewter measure in his hand. " Are you going to ex—explain yourself."

" Ye—yes," stammered the little man. " The lights, good sir, were at the large house belonging to the rich 'squire, whose floors, they say, are paved with dollars, and his walls hung with gold leaf."

" Who—do—you mean, Learmont ?"

" Ay, marry do I—that's his worshipful name ; they say he eats off gold plate, and cuts his food with a diamond.

" But what about the lights ?" roared Britton.

" Why, that's what I asked a knave that was lounging at the door, and he, a burly knave he was, he says to me—he was a stout fellow to—'"

" What did he say ?"

" Why, says he, the 'squire gives an entertainment to-night to the court and nobility."

" Oh, cried Britton. " He does, and he has not invited me."

The landlord winked at Master Sniggles, and Master Sniggles this time winked at the landlord, both the winks signifying how very far gone was Britton in drunkenness to make so very absurd and preposterous a remark.

Britton was silent for a few moments. Then a half-drunken, half-malignant smile covered his swarthy visage.

" I will go," he cried, " I will be the only uninvited guest, and—and yet the most free. Ha, ha! Learmont would as leave see the devil himself walk in as King Britton, the smith. I'll go !"

" Does your majesty really mean," suggested the landlord, " to kick up a royal row at the rich 'squire's ?"

" Do I mean ?" said Britton. I will have a dance in his halls, I say. There's not a knave in his household dare stand in my way. Hurrah! hurrah ! I'm a gentleman. I do nothing but drink, so I'm a gentleman. Ha! ha! ha! Learmont don't expect me, but there's nothing like an unlooked for pleasure. I'll visit him to-night, if the pit of hell should open at his threshold to stay my progress."

So saying, he dashed from the Chequers leaving the landlord and Master Sniggles gazing at each other in speechless amazement.

What occurred at the drunken smith's visit to Learmont's *fete*, we are already aware.

CHAPTER XL.

THE OLD HOUSE AGAIN.—ADA'S ALARM.—GRAY AND HIS GOLD.

ADA felt that after the experience of the recent interview with Gray, she had a power over him which, were she free from her promise not to escape, she might use for the purpose of restoring herself to liberty. That power was grounded on the superstition of his character—a weakness which had grown with his crimes, and been increased by the constant pangs of remorse, which even he could not stifle entirely. The solitude likewise, and the constant state of trembling anxiety in which he lived, had shattered his nervous system to that degree that he was indeed a melancholy and warning spectacle of the mental and bodily wreck to which crime is sure to reduce its unhallowed perpetrators.

His eyes were sunken and bloodshot, his lips never bore the hue of health, his step was stealthy and trembling, and his hands shook like an aspen leaf. He would lock himself in the room which contained his hoarded wealth, and recount the glittering mass for hours together; but still he could not think it enough. The demon of avarice had got a clutch of his heart, and the larger the amount of his gold became, the wider range his love of the bright temptation took, and constantly fixed a sum far beyond what he had as that which would content him and enable him to put in practice his scheme of departure from England, and vengeance upon Learmont and Britton.

" I must yet have more," he would mutter. " 'Tis but a short delay, and Learmont cannot refuse me the gold. Yes, two hundred more of those pieces shall satisfy me. That will make up a goodly sum ; and then, in some other land, I shall get some sleep undisturbed by the awful visions that here crowd upon my trembling imagination ;—but two hundred more. Perhaps I may get so much before this month is past, and then I shall be saved the trouble of extorting a renewal of the promise of this wilful girl. Yes, it shall be so. I will raise my demands upon Learmont. He cannot—dare not say me nay, unless I were to become outrageously unreasonable in my drafts upon his purse.—Two hundred.—Let me think ;—five visits at twenty pounds each will be half the money. Pshaw ! I will have forty each visit. Ay, forty ; that will not alarm him. If I insist on more he might, in his cautious brain, think upon the scheme I mean to practise, and take some means of most effectually preventing such ruin to himself. I will lull his suspicions. Oh ! what a day of triumph will it be to me when I sail from England with the conviction that, within four-and-twenty hours after I am gone, Learmont and Britton will each inhabit a prison. They will then confess that Jacob Gray is cunning. The sneer will turn with an awful fact to them. There is but one drawback.—I shall not see them hung. No ;—I cannot—dare not—stay to see them hung. Ada will be rich and great; but she will know who I am. Will she use her wealth in hunting me through the world ? or will she forgive in the flush of her prosperity ? If—if—I thought that the firm, untameable spirit which this girl evidently possesses, and which, I may confess it here in secret, daunts me,—if I thought it would induce her to hunt me down, as she might, for her means would be ample for such an object, were I hidden even in the bowels of the earth, I'd—I'd—kill her ere I went. Yes, some night when she slept I could do it; but not till the hour before I meant to go ; for I—I could not stay in this lone place without her. She scorns me,—treats me with a haughty contempt ; will scarcely condescend to address me : but still she is here, and there is company in the thought that I know I am not quite alone in this gloomy place. She may load me with opprobrium,—she may heap scorn upon my head ; but she is here, and I could not lie down for one night here, without the conviction that there was some one else within these walls. So, Ada, you are safe now—very safe ; but ere I go I must seek some subtle means of knowing what will be your course of action when you know all, and the name of Jacob Gray is linked with a crime that will rouse your nature, and bring an angry flash to your eye. Ha !—what noise was that ?"

Gray sprang to his feet, and he trembled violently, for some slight noise, such as old decayed houses are full of, came upon his ear in the stillness that reigned around.

" I—I thought I heard a noise," he muttered : " but I have thought so often, when 'twas nothing. Ada is here ; I am not quite alone ; should I see anything, I—I could scream, and then she might come, perchance, to exult in my agony ; but there would be protection in her presence—because—because she is—innocent.—Innocent !—Oh, God ! why am I not innocent ? Is all this world and its enjoyments a gross delusion, for which I have bartered all the essence and foundation of all joy—peace !"

For many minutes he remained silent, and the nervous twitching of his countenance betrayed the disturbed condition of his mind. Then he spoke quickly and nervously.

" I must not give way to thoughts like these," he said ; they will drive me mad. Yes, murder lies that way. I must go on now ;—the path I have chosen is one which there is no retracing. 'Tis as if a wall of adamant followed close behind, to prevent one backward step. I am committed to the course I have taken ;—to pause is madness. I must go on—I must go on ! but I will spare you, Ada, if I can."

The sound of a distant clock sounding the hour of twelve, now came upon the night air, and Jacob Gray listened to the faint moaning tones of the bell until all was still again, and no sound broke the solemn stillness but the agitated beating of his own heart.

" Midnight !" he said. " 'Tis midnight ! I will now endeavour to snatch a few hours' repose ; I have fatigued myself now for many hours, with the hope that the body's weariness might lull the mind's agony. Agony ! I—do I call it agony ! is that all I have purchased by—crimes ?"

He lifted the light as he spoke, and its feeble rays fell upon the glittering heap of gold that lay before him. A ghastly smile played across the pale countenance of Jacob Gray.

" I have gained something," he said, as he laid his thin, cold hand upon the gold. " Yes, I have gained these—these pieces of bright metal, that will exchange for honours—service—gay attire—enchanting music—nay, they will buy what men affect not to sell—opinion. There may be some pure state of society, in which, when speaking of a man, the question may be, ' What is he ?' but here—here, in civilized, moral, intellectual England, the question is, ' What has he ?' These," he continued, running his hand among the guineas ; " these even will purchase prayers to Heaven—petitions to God from the good, the saintly, and the pious. Gold, I love thee—but now to bed—to bed !"

He carefully placed his treasure in its recent receptacle at the back of the cupboard, and then with a faltering step, and a shifting glance of fear, he repaired to his own chamber, which was near to Ada's room.

In his progress he passed the door of the dormitory of his victim—he paused a moment, and listened attentively. Then in a voice of deep anguish, he said,—

" She can sleep—she can sleep—no ghostly vision scares slumber from her eyes —while——"

He shuddered, and passed a step or two on, then pausing again, he said,—

"Oh, if she, the young and innocent—the loved of Heaven—if she would but bid me a 'good night,' I think I could sleep—I asked her once, and she would not—no, she would not give me so much peace : she would not say good night to me!"

These words were spoken by Gray in a tone of great mental anguish, and he passed on silently to his own chamber.

A silence, as of the grave, reigned over the old house, and an uneasy slumber crept over Jacob Gray.

Well might the man of crime dread to sleep ; for, although exhausted nature sunk into repose, the busy fancy slept not ; but, ever wakeful, conjured up strange ghastly shapes to scare the sleeper.

The imagination, unchecked by reason, began its reign—a reign sometimes so full

No. 22.

of beauty and joy, that we sigh to awaken to a perception of that which is, instead of remaining in the world of dreams.

Jacob Gray's visions, however, took the shuddering ghastly complexion of his waking thoughts and recollections.

From memory's deepest cells would these creep forth one by one in hideous distinctness—remembrances that were maddening, and scenes would be enacted over and over again within the busy chambers of the brain, that in his waking moments he would shun the faintest reminiscence of, as he would the terrors of a pestilence.

The smithy at Learmont rose up before him, black and heavy as it appeared among the drifting snow. Then he would hear the howling of the wind even as it howled on that eventful night, when the storm was just commencing—momentarily it increased in fury, and Jacob Gray felt that all the awful events of that night were to do again; why or wherefore he knew not.

Then the smith, he thought, took him by the throat and threw him down upon a ghastly rotting corpse, and the long bony arms closed over him, while he felt his own warm living face in hideous contact with the slimy rottenness of the grave. He heard then, as he had heard it on that dreadful night, the cry of fire! and he strove with frantic efforts to free himself from the embrace of death—but 'twas all in vain.

*   *   *   *   *

The flames then waved around him like a sea, and the skeleton arms grew to a white heat, and burnt into his flesh, and a hot pestilential breath seemed to come from the grinning jaws of the dead—still he could not move. His struggles were as those of an infant in that awful clutch, and he prayed for death to terminate his agony.

Then a voice said, " No! you will remain thus till time is no more."

With a scream Jacob Gray awoke, and starting wildly from his couch, he sunk on his knees, shrieking—

" Mercy—mercy! spare me, Heaven !"

CHAPTER XLI.

A HUMAN VOICE.—THE DEPARTURE.—AN UNEXPECTED MEETING.—THE DECEPTION.

THE dim, cold, uncertain light of morning was faintly gleaming in long sickly streaks in the eastern sky, and the trembling, half-maddened Jacob Gray crawled to the window of his room, and hastily tearing down some paper that patched a broken pane of glass, he placed his scorched and dry lips against the opening, and drank in the cool morning's air as one who had crossed a desert would quaff from the first spring he met after the horrors and thirst of the wilderness.

On his knees the wretched man remained for some time, until the mad fever of his blood subsided, and calmer reflection came to his aid.

"I cannot sleep," he said, " I cannot sleep—'tis madness to attempt it; my waking thoughts are bad enough, but when reason sleeps, and the imagination, unshackled by probability commences its reign, then all the wildest fancies become re-realities and I live in a world of horrors, such as the damned alone can endure, endurance must constitute a portion of their suffering, for if they felt so acutely as to decrease sensation, they would be happy. Alas ! what can I do, I must rest sometimes. Exhausted nature will not be defrauded of her rights; but while the body rests, the mind seems to take a flight to hell! Oh, horrible! horrible! I—I—wonder if Ada be awake—methinks now the sound of a human voice would be music to my ears. I will creep to her chamber door, and speak to her the slightest word in answer will be a blessing. Yes, I will go—I will go." Jacob Gray then, with a slow and stealthy step, left his chamber, and as he glided along the dim corridor of that ancient house, he might, with his haggard looks and straining eyes, have well been taken for the perturbed spirit that popular superstition said had been seen about the ill-omened residence of crime and death.

He reached Ada's door, and after a pause, he knocked nervously and timidly upon the panel. There was no answer. Ada slept—she was dreaming of happiness, of joy, that brought pearly tears to her eyes—those eyes that are the blissful overflowings of a heart too full of grateful feeling. Again Jacob Gray knocked, and he cried Ada! in a voice that was too low and tremulous to reach the ears of the sleeping girl, but which startled Gray himself by the hollow echoes it awakened in the silence of the gloomy house.

Again he knocked, and this time Ada started from her sleep—Gray heard the slight movement of the girl.

"Ada!" he said, "Ada, speak!"

"Jacob Gray!" said Ada.

"Ada—I—I am going forth—speak Ada, again."

"Wherefore am I summoned thus early?" said Ada—"what has happened?"

"Nothing, nothing!" replied Gray. "Be cautious, Ada; I shall not return till night."

He waited several minutes, but Ada made no reply. Then he crept slowly from the door muttering,—

"She has spoken—I think there is some magic in her voice, for I am better now, and the air in this place does not seem so thick and damp. It may be that there are evil spirits that, at the sound of the voice of one so pure and innocent as she, are forced to fly, and no more load the air with their bad presence. I am relieved now, for I have heard a human voice."

Gray then proceeded to a lower room of the house, and enveloping himself closely in an ample cloak, he cautiously opened the door and went forth secure in the dim and uncertain light of the early morning.

The air was cold and piercing, but to Jacob Gray it was grateful, for it came like balm upon his heated blood, and the thick teeming fancies of his guilty brain gradually assumed a calmer complexion, subsiding into that gnawing of the heart which he was scarcely ever without, and which he knew would follow him to the grave.

He skirted the hedges, concealing himself with extreme caution, until he was some distance from Forest's house, for notwithstanding the great improbability of his being seen at so early an hour, Jacob Gray was one of those who, to use his own words to Learmont, always wished safety to be doubly assured.

Walking rapidly now, along a pathway by the river's side, he soon neared Lambeth, and the sun was just commencing to gild faintly the highest spires of the great city, when he arrived near the spot which is now occupied by the road leading over Vauxhall-bridge.

Gray began now to look about him for some place in which to breakfast, for such was his suspicious nature and constant fear, that he never from choice entered the same house twice. As chance would have it now, he paused opposite the doorway of the public-house called the King's Bounty, and while he was deliberating with himself whether he should enter or not, he started and trembled with apprehension as the figure of Sir Frederick Hartleton passed out.

Jacob Gray had made himself well acquainted with the magistrate by sight, for curiosity had often impelled him to take means of seeing the man to whom he had addressed the packet containing his confession, and from whom he expected his revenge against Learmont and Britton, and at the same time that he, Gray, had personally to dread Sir Frederick most of all men, while he should remain in England.

Gray drew back as the magistrate advanced, although a moment's thought convinced him of the extreme improbability of his being known even to the vigilant eye of Hartleton, who had almost grown proverbial for his skill and tact in discovering who any person was, and for recollecting faces that he had only once in his life seen.

Gray was so near the doorway that he had to move in order to allow Sir Frederick to pass, and at that moment their eyes met.

The magistrate looked earnestly at Gray for a moment, and then passed on. During that brief look the blood appeared to Jacob Gray to be almost congealing at his heart, so full of fear was he that some distant reminiscence of his countenance might still live in the remembrance of Sir Frederick Hartleton. Such, however, appeared not to be the case, for the magistrate passed on, nor once looked behind him, to the immense relief of Gray, who now made up his mind on the moment to enter the house from a feeling of intense curiosity, to know what business his greatest foe could have there at such an early hour.

When he reached the small sanded parlour of the little hostel, he found several persons engaged in earnest discourse, among whom he had no difficulty in selecting the landlord, who was talking earnestly and loudly.

"Ah, my masters," cried the landlord, "he's a brave gentleman and a liberal one, I can tell you. He said to me—'Landlord,' says he—'let her have of the best your house affords, and send your bill to me'—that's what he said—and it's no joke, I can tell you, for a publican to be on good terms with a magistrate. Oh, dear me! then you should have seen how cold and wet he was; and when I offered him my Sunday garments, he took them with a thank ye, landlord, that was worth a Jew's eye—coming as it did from a magistrate, mind you."

"Bring me a measure of your best wine," said Gray, "and whatever you have in the house, that I may make a breakfast on."

This liberal order immediately arrested the landlord's attention, as Gray fully intended it should, and mine host of the King's Bounty turned instantly all his attention to a visitor who ordered refreshments on so magnificent a scale for the house.

"Di—rectly, sir," cried he, "your worship shall have some wine such as the bishop has not better in his cellars, and they do say that he keeps his Canary cool in an excavation that goes from his palace some feet under the bed of the Thames."

"I wish for the best of everything in your house," said Gray. "By-the-by, was not that Sir Frederick Hartleton whom I saw leave your house a few minutes since?"

"An it please your honour, it was," said the landlord. "Mayhap your worship is a friend of his, and comes to speak to the poor creature above?"

"Eh?—a—yes—yes."

"By my faith, I thought as much."

"Yet, stay," said Gray, for he was cautious to the extreme. "Do you know when Sir Frederick will be here again?"

"Not till to-morrow, sir."

"Humph! then I will see the poor creature you mention."

"Certainly, sir. This way, sir. Your breakfast will be ready by the time your worship comes down stairs again."

"Who can this be that he calls the poor creature?" thought Gray, as he followed the landlord up stairs.

"This way, sir," exclaimed the loquacious host. "It was touch and go with her, poor thing, they say; but Sir Frederick saved her. I dare say, however, your honour knows all about it. That room, sir, if you please."

The landlord now opened a door, and, popping his head in, cried, in a very different tone to that in which he addressed Gray, upon the supposition of his acquaintance with Sir Frederick Hartleton,—

"Hilloa! here's a gentleman come to see you, old 'un."

Gray did not hear the reply; but he entered the room at once, and confronted Mad Maud, who was sitting in a chair, looking more like a corpse than a human being.

CHAPTER XLII.

GRAY'S CUNNING.—DANGER THICKENS.—THE HOUR OF RETRIBUTION HAS NOT COME.

"Who are you," cried she, "that seeks poor Maud?"

"Maud!" exclaimed Gray, "I have heard Britton speak of you."

"Britton, Britton, the savage smith!" cried Maud, rising, and trying to clutch Gray with her long skinny arms. "He speak of me? Have they hung him, and I not there? Tell me, have they dared to hang him without my being there to see it? Ha! ha! ha!"

Gray shuddered. He had heard that wild and fearful laugh before. On the night of the storm at Learmont he had heard it, and he had never forgotten it."

"You—you lived once far from hence?" he said.

"Far—very far. 'Twas a weary way to walk. Sometimes I slept in a barn; and they hooted me out in the morning, because the frown of God was upon my soul, and I was mad—yes—I was mad, so they who had sense and judgment cast me out."

"You know Sir Frederick Hartleton?" said Gray.

"Frank Hartleton I know," she replied. "He was always kind to poor Maud. When the smith hunted me into the river, he saved me. Yes, I know him and the angel."

"And who?"

"The angel who fed me, and spoke kind words even though I was mad. Those kind words made me weep; an angel spoke them."

"Mad as she can be," thought Gray, "I do not like her acquaintance with Hartleton, however. There may be danger."

"The savage smith hunted you, did he?" he then said aloud.

"He would have killed me," replied Maud, with a shudder; "but the water came up to where we were, and saved me."

"I am a friend, a dear friend of Hartleton's," said Gray; "and he wishes you to say to me all you know about things that happened long ago."

"What things?"

"Oh, you recollect the Old Smithy?"

"The Old Smithy!" repeated Maud. "Yes—I do—I do. Why should I not? The murder was only done last night, and the death-cry of the victim still lingers in the air. The storm is lulling, but the wind moans like an infant sobbing itself to sleep upon its mother's breast. The distant shrieks of him who rushed forth with the child still echo through the valley. Do I remember?—yes— 'twas brave work—brave work for the savage smith. Hush! hush! Tell me now, if it be true that they will bring me the child? I will tend it for I have nothing to love now; Britton killed him—him that I loved. Oh! give me the child of the dead, and I will be a mother to it for its orphan state!"

"Indeed! who has promised you the child?"

"He—the good—the brave."

"Who?"

"Frank Hartleton. 'Be patient,' he said, ' and you shall see that child agai.n"

Gray trembled as he said,—

"You—you are sure he said this—he—Sir Frederick Hartleton? Tell me what more he said, and if you love gold, you shall have it. Tell me all that has passed in your interview with him, and then ask of me what you will, it is yours. You seem poor—nay, wretched; I will give you money if you will tell me all you know of this—this murder you mention."

"Gold! gold!" muttered Maud; "that is man's enemy; for that he betrays trusts—robs—lies—murders!"

Jacob Gray groaned.

"Yes," continued Maud, "the red gold is Heaven's worst foe. It robs the realms of light and glory of many mortal souls. I will not have your gold. Tempter, away! Give me the child, the sweet, smiling babe that Heaven made the bad man save from the burning smithy. Give me that, and then tell me where Britton is, and I will do your bidding,—you shall know all!"

"I accept your terms," said Gray; "you shall have the child. Tell me who did this murder at the smithy, and what Hartleton says about it."

"Ay, Hartleton!" exclaimed Maud; "he, too, has promised me the child; but he says I shall not know it."

"Indeed!"

"Yes; he says that years have passed away; that the child has grown to be a maiden of rare beauty. But I shall see it. Yes, poor Maud will see it yet; and I shall know it, because its hands have some blood upon them."

Gray absolutely reeled, and mechanically sunk into a chair as Maud spoke, and a conviction crossed his mind that by some means Sir Frederick Hartleton was on the scent for him. A short interval of confused and agonising thought now followed. Then it shaped itself into a course of detail that he felt was the only one presenting a chance of escape, and that was to discover, if possible, in what particular manner the danger threatened, and whether it was near or remote—if it consisted of positive knowledge, or only surmise.

"Go on," he said, making a great effort to speak calmly, and communicate his feelings. "Go on, I pray you."

"I shall have the child?"

"You shall! Be assured you shall!"

"Ah, then Britton will soon die. I shall live till then—to see him die, and then poor Maud is willing to die. I am to remain here till he comes again."

"Who?"

"Frank Hartleton, blessings on him! He says that the career of the wicked is now over. Who is this Gray, they all speak to me about?"

Jacob Gray started, and fixed his eyes intently upon poor Maud's face, for an awful doubt, suggested by his shivering fear, came across his mind, that he might be falling into some trap laid for him by the cunning of the magistrate; and that she who asked of him so strange a question might be only aping the malady she seemed to suffer under.

"Don't you know Gray?" he said sharply, at the same time fixing his keen, ferret-looking eyes upon the door, and then suddenly turning them to her.

Maud shook her head; and there was something so genuine in her negative, that Gray drew a long breath, and felt reassured that he was at the moment safe.

"Oh, Gray!" he said. "Who mentioned him? He is dead—dead long ago."

"Dead?"

"Yes; there is now no such person. So Sir Frederick—I mean Frank Hartleton, mentioned this Gray?"

"All have mentioned him," said Maud. "'Tis very strange, but I am asked by all if I know Gray?"

"Indeed! By—by Hartleton?"

"Yes, by him. He says that Gray is the worst villain of all. The Lord of Learmont is scarce worse than Gray. Where is he, with his dark scowl? I have not seen him for some days, that is, since he would not have the fire put out. They said he and the savage smith killed Dame Tattan, and took the child away; but I know better, ha—ha—ha! poor Mad Maud knows better."

"Then Learmont did not do so?" said Gray, in a soft, insinuating tone.

"How could he, when I met her by the mill-stream, weeping?"

"You met her?"

"Ay, did I, by the mill-stream. It was early dawn, and the birds alone were awake, as well as Mad Maud. Ha—ha! I met her, and, I will tell you, she had the child; and she wept while I kissed and blessed it."

"But, about this man, Gray? Speak more of him—I pray you, speak of him."

"I know him not, but Frank Hartleton, who always had a kind word for poor Maud, which makes me believe him—he says, that before sunset, Gray shall be in prison, and that he is a villain."

Gray rose with his features convulsed with rage and fear, and approaching Maud, he said, in a husky whisper,—

"Woman—on your soul, did he say those words?"

"He did. It will be brave work!"

"How is this?" cried Gray, clasping his hands. "God! how is this? Am I betrayed—lost—lost!"

He sank in a chair with a deep groan, at the moment that the landlord opened the door, saying—

"An it please your honour, your breakfast is hot. There be new-laid eggs, and buttered buns; a chine, the like of which is rarely seen at the King's Bounty. Then we have some confections, your honour, which would be no disparagement to the bishop's own larder, which, they do say, keeps up a continual groaning from the heap of niceties collected therein. Then, as to wine we have, I will say it—who should not—the very creamiest, rarest——"

"Peace—begone!" said Gray.

"Your honour!"

"Begone, I say!"

"I humbly——"

"Peace! Is it thus you torment your guest? Do not interrupt me until I call for you. I have a private conference to hold with this poor creature. Here, pay yourself as you will for the cooling of your most precious viands."

Gray threw a piece of gold to the landlord, who picked it up, and vanished with a profusion of bows, to tell his company below what a nice gentleman, a friend of the great Sir Frederick Hartleton, he had above stairs, who not only paid for what was cooked for him, but requested he might be charged for the cooling of the various delicacies!

"Now, that's what I call a real gentleman," added the landlord; "and one as makes a virtuous use of his money."

When Jacob was once more alone with poor Maud, he approached her and said,—

"As you value your life, tell me all."

"My life? Is Britton dead?" she replied.

"What do you mean?" said Gray, impatiently.

"Because I cannot die till he does."

"Listen to me," said Gray. "You say that this Hartleton talks of imprisoning Gray. Was that all he said?"

"I wept, and he would not then take from me what the angel had given me. I promised her by a name, as sacred to me as that of Heaven, and I could not even let him have it,—no, no! he pitied my tears, and let me keep the angel's paper."

"Paper!—paper!—What paper?"

"Oh! it is precious!" continued Maud; "I think it is a charm against sickness,—it is, truly, as coming from an angel."

"Let me see it."

"Yes, of course; I am to show it to all,—that was what the angel said. You shall see,—but you will not take it—promise me you will not take it."

"I promise."

Maud then dived her hand in her breast, and produced, with an expression of intense pride and satisfaction, the scrap of paper which Ada had given her, with the faint hope that it might meet the hands of Albert Seyton. She held it out to Gray to read, and as he did so, and fully comprehending the few words it contained, his lips turned to an ashy paleness, and his brain grew dizzy with apprehension.

"He—he has seen this?" he gasped.

"Who?"

"Hartleton!"

"Oh, yes: I tell you he wanted it, but he would not tear it from me."

Gray made a snatch at it, and tore it from the grasp of the poor creature. Maud uttered a loud scream, and Gray, drawing a pistol from his pocket, stood in an attitude of defence, as he heard a confusion of steps upon the stairs.

"Give it to me!" shrieked Maud—"oh! as you hope for heaven, give it to me!"

A moment's reflection assured Jacob Gray, that not only was he acting indiscreetly, but that he had no time to lose. Hastily concealing the pistol, he handed the paper to Maud, saying—

"Hence, hence; I did but jest."

The door was immediately flung open, and several heads appeared.

"This poor creature is mad, friends," said Gray, " she—she thinks she has seen something."

"The Lord preserve us!" cried the landlord. "An it please you, sir, I see Sir Frederick crossing the river."

"Who!" cried Grey.

"Your honour's good friend, Sir Frederick Hartleton—ah, I'll warrant he has some sport in view, for he has Elias and Stephy, his two runners, with him."

Gray darted to the door.

"Your honour—honour," cried the landlord, "an' it please you, what did the poor crazy creature fancy she saw?"

"The devil!" cried Gray.

In a moment he was outside the house. He cast one glance towards the river. In the middle of the stream was a two-oared cutter, pulled rapidly by two rowers, while a figure that he at once recognised as the magistrate, sat steering.

With a stifled cry, Jacob Gray set his teeth, and darted off towards his solitary home, like a hunted hare.

CHAPTER XLIII.

THE PROPOSAL.—GRAY'S REASONING.—THE VAULT.—ADA'S TEARS.—A GUILTY
HEART'S AGONY.

Oh, what a fearful race home that was to Jacob Gray. He knew he had the start of the magistrate by some quarter of an hour, or probably more; but still that was not time sufficient to pause upon, and he relaxed not his headlong speed till he came within sight of the lone house that was his home; then, for the space of about a minute, he turned and looked back to see if he were followed, and to strive to think what he should do when he did reach the house, which he now felt could shelter him no more. That the scrap of paper in the possession of Mad Maud was written by Ada, he did not entertain a doubt, but it utterly foiled all conjecture to think how she could have found the opportunity, confined as she was, of giving it to the poor creature, who set such great store by it.

Forward, then, Jacob Gray rushed again, after ascertaining that there was no one within sight. It was yet very early, and but few persons were out, so that Gray hoped he might be able to cross the fields without being seen; but how to drag Ada away and leave Forest's house in safety, before Sir Frederick and his party arrived, defied his thoughts, and he groaned and struck his breast in the bitterness of his anguish and despair.

w

"The time has come—the time has come!" he muttered. "I am lost—lost! —no chance!—no hope! If—if I kill Ada—what then? I only exasperate my pursuers, and my death is certain. I have, if taken, but one solitary gleam of hope for mercy, and that is, that I have done no violence to her. No—no—I dare not kill her, unless she would betray me. We must hide. Aye that is a remote chance."

He bounded over the swampy fields and gained the door. Without pausing to make his accustomed signal, he drew from his pocket the key which he had fitted
No. 23.

to the rusty lock, and in another moment he had entered his house of dread and danger, and closed the door behind him.

"I have yet some time," he said or rather panted, for his violent rush homeward had quite exhausted him. He reeled rather than walked to his own chamber, and took a copious draught of spirits. The ardent liquor in his excited and agitated state of mind appeared to have but little more effect upon him than would so much water—at least so far as its power to intoxicate went. He felt refreshed, however, and now he rushed to the window, which commanded an extensive view across the fields, and he drew a long breath, as he said to himself with a sensation of relief,—

"I do not see them yet—I have time—yes, still some time! Now for Ada—for Ada! I have a task before me!"

He crossed the corridor to see if Ada was in her own room. The door stood partially open.

"Ada! Ada!" cried Gray. There was no answer; and, looking into the chamber, he saw she was not there. Suddenly he started. The sweetly clear and natural voice of Ada emerging from an upper room met his ears. She was looking out at the blue sky, and watching the soaring larks, totally unconscious of the sudden return of Jacob Gray, and fondly anticipating the pleasure—for all our pains and pleasures are comparative—and it was a pleasure to Ada of being alone for a whole day.

Gray was in no mood for singing, and with a step very different from the cautious stealthy one with which he usually crawled about the house, he ascended the staircase, and presented himself before the astonished eyes of Ada.

"Returned!" she exclaimed.

"Yes—returned," echoed Gray. "Ada, you have broken your vow."

"So help me, Heaven, no!"

"You have," cried Gray, in a high, shrieking voice that decreased to a hissing sound, as if he were afraid of his own violent outcry.

"I have not," repeated Ada, fearlessly, and meeting Gray's eyes with a clear and open gaze that he shrunk from.

"The—the scrap of paper," said Gray. "The note to the—the—what shall I shall I call him?—Albert Seyton— I have seen that. Ah! well may your colour flit. Ada, you are detected—you have tampered with your vow. No more prate to me of your innocence and high virtue—no more taunt me with your purity. Ada, we understand each other better now."

"Liar!" cried Ada, with an energy that made Gray start. "I will still taunt you—still prate to you of my innocence, which only can gall you in proportion as you yourself are guilty. I have tampered with no vow, and you know it. I still stand on a pinnacle, from which you have fallen, never, never to rise again. Bend not your brows on me Jacob Gray—you are my slave and you know that too!"

Gray quailed and trembled before the flashing eye of Ada, who, as she spoke, assumed unconsciously an attitude of such rare grace and beauty, with the fire of heavenly intelligence and truth beaming in every feature of her face, that it was with mixed feelings of fear, hate, and admiration, that Gray replied,—

"You have made an indirect attempt to escape from here."

"And why not?" said Ada. "If I have the power and opportunity, I will make a hundred—ay, Jacob Gray, and a hundred more to back them. My vow contained a special reservation, that I would accept of aid if it came to me. Moreover, Jacob Gray, when I made the attempt, of which, by some accident, you have become aware, I was as free as air—my promise had expired."

"Ha!"

"Yes: it was made in the brief time that elapsed between one promise and another, Jacob Gray."

"Damnation! why do you reiterate my name so constantly?"

"Because it angers you, Jacob Gray."

"What if I were to kill you?" growled Gray.

" 'Twould be another murder," said Ada.

"Ada, I do not believe your exculpation. Why did you not escape, if you had the opportunity you speak of?"

" That I had a special reason for, which I will not tell you, Jacob Gray."

" I do not wish to kill you."

" That I know—you have some highly politic reason for preserving my life, else it had been sacrificed long since."

" But now it has become politic so to do," added Gray.

" Indeed ?"

" Ay—indeed."

" Then, God help me. If I must die now by your hands, may Heaven forgive you for your deep sinfulness."

" Hear me, girl," cried Gray. " There is yet a chance of saving you."

" Say on. You have some proposition to make, from which you guess I will revolt, or you would not preface it with such murderous looks."

Gray walked first to a window, which commanded a view in the direction of Lambeth. He saw as yet no traces of the magistrate and his party, and he returned to Ada.

" Attend to what I say," he cried. " There are those coming here who, as it happened once before in our former place of abode, seek mine and your life."

Ada started.

" Yes," continued Gray. " By an accident little short of a miracle, I have discovered their intentions—they are now on their road here. There is not time to fly."

" They may be foes to you only," said Ada. She then suddenly clasped her hands and uttered a cry of joy. " I see it now," she said, " Albert—Albert is coming."

" No !" thundered Gray. " You are wrong—on my soul, you are wrong. It is not he. If you hear his voice, act as you please—I will not restrain you."

" Who are these men then ?"

" That I cannot, will not tell you. Suffice it, they seek your life. We must die or live together in this emergency ; or else if you, with fatal obstinacy, will not be guided by me, and embrace the only chance of escape, in self-defence I must silence you."

" By murdering me ?"

" Yes, although reluctantly. Ada, you have sense, knowledge, discretion, beyond your years."

Ada sat down, and deep emotion was evident in her countenance.

" Jacob Gray," she said, " death is frightful to the young. Let me believe the reasons you urge, or believe them not, it matters little. You will kill me if I do not do your bidding in this case. Those who are coming may be my friends or they may be my enemies, I cannot tell, and your statements carry not with them the stamp of truth to my mind. The heart once thoroughly deceived, trusts no more. You need not seek to delude with untruths—it is enough that you will kill me if I do not hide from those whom you dread—but you have said that, should I hear the voice of him—him who—why should I shrink from the avowal ?—him whom I love, you will not stay me."

" I swear I will not," cried Gray.

" Your word is quite as weighty as your oath, Jacob Gray," said Ada. " Both are worthless. But you would not make such a promise even if you thought that *he* would be one of those you expect."

" Time, Ada—time is precious!" cried Gray.

" To you probably—but I must obey you."

" You have chosen wisely," said Gray. " Hear me. My own life hangs upon a single thread. If you had persevered in obstinately refusing to side with me, I should have killed you for my own preservation, and cast your lifeless body into the same place of secrecy where we will soon repair to."

" Where mean you ?"

" That dark cell in which you have passed some gloomy hours.   The entrance to it is by a panel in the wainscotting of the room below, which fits so truly that none, not previously aware of it, would suspect its existence.   When I came first here I found it by an accident.   If we are found there, we shall be found together, and by any crying to me, you would benefit nothing.   All I require of you now is silence."

Gray now again walked to the window, and this time he started back with a loud cry.

"'They are coming," he said ;   "look, Ada, be satisfied that neither of these men in any degree resemble him you so much wish to see."

Ada sprang to the window, and at some considerable distance off, crossing the fields, towards the house, she saw three men who were strangers to her.

" You see they are armed," said Gray.

" They are—I know them not.   How can they be enemies of mine ?"

" Follow me!" shrieked Gray.   " There is not time for another word."

As he spoke he took a pistol from his breast, and turned to Ada.

" You know the use and powers of this weapon.   So much as stir, unless I bid you, when we are hiding, or speak even in the lowest whisper, except in answer to me, and I will assuredly take your life."

Ada did not answer, and after regarding her fixedly for one moment to see what impression he had made upon her mind, Gray hastily left the room, saying,—

" Follow quickly.   We have time enough, but none to spare."

He led her to the crevice in the wall of which the aperture opened, leading to the damp vault, in which she had been before.

" The ladder is on the inner side," he said, as he placed a chair to assist her in reaching the opening.   " Descend, while I make some other arrangements in the room."

He hastily left the room, locking the door behind him.

Ada stood upon the chair and looked into the dismal vault, from whence a damp earthy smell arose, and sighed deeply.

" Alas !" she said, " must I obey this man ?   Is he so desperate that he would really take my life, or does he only threaten that which he dare not perform?   No —he is a villain, and he would kill me.   I am sure that my life is of value to him, but with such a man the feeling of self overcomes all other considerations.   He will kill me if I obey him not now.   My heart tells me he will.   Albert, for thy sake I will do what I can to preserve my life.   Just Heaven, direct and aid me !"

She passed through the opening in the wall, and slowly descended the ladder into the dismal darkness of the vault.

CHAPTER XLIV.

THE SEARCH.—THE CONFESSION.—THE STRANGE REPORT.—AN AWFUL DILEMMA.

Jacob Gray's first care, when he left Ada, was to repair to the room in which he concealed his money.   Hastily collecting together the really large sum he had from time to time wrung from the guilty fears of Learmont, he bestowed it about his person, and then carefully placing his written confession, with its dangerous address, in his breast, he hurried to the street-door, upon the back of which he wrote with a piece of chalk, " J. G. and A. left here June 2nd," thus endeavouring to paralyse the magistrate's exertions in the way of search by inducing him to think that the house had been deserted by Jacob Gray for some time.

He then with wild haste ran through the house concealing everything in the shape of provisions which would undeniably indicate a recent occupancy of it. Ada's bed and his own he cast into a dusty cupboard, and altogether succeeded in producing a general appearance of litter and desertion.

Then, without daring to cast another look from the windows, for fear he should be seen, he rushed to the room in which he had left Ada, and getting through the opening in the wall, he closed the panel and stood trembling so exceedingly on the ladder, that had he wished he could scarcely have commanded physical energy sufficient to descend. His object, however, was to remain there, and listen to what was passing, which he could not do below.

"Ada, Ada," he said, in a low tone, "you—you are safe?"

"I am here," said Ada.

"Hush! hush! not another word, not even a whisper; hush, for your life, hush!"

A heavy knock at the outer door now echoed fearfully through the spacious passages and empty rooms of the house. To Gray that knock could not have been more agonising, had it been against his own heart.

By an impulse that he could not restrain, he kept on saying, in a half-choked whisper, "Hush—hush—hush!" while he clutched the sides of the ladder till his nails dug painfully into the palms of his hands, and a cold perspiration hung in massive drops upon his brow. Ada meanwhile was getting a little used to the darkness of the place, and feeling cautiously about, she found one of the baskets she recollected to have seen there before. This she sat down upon, and burying her face in her hands, she gave herself up to gloomy reflections, while tears, which she would not let Jacob Gray see for worlds, slowly and noiselessly trickled through her small fingers.

In a few moments the knock at the door again sounded through the house, and Gray, although he was expecting it, nearly fell from the ladder in the nervous start that he gave.

Then followed a long silence, after which a voice came to his ears in indistinct tones, saying something which terminated with the words,—"In the King's name."

There was then a slight pause, followed in a moment by a crash; and Jacob Gray knew that the doors were burst open.

A sensation of awful thirst now came over Gray—such thirst as he had read of only as being endured by adventurous travellers in crossing hundreds of miles of sandy desert. His tongue seemed to cleave to the roof of his mouth, and his parched lips were like fire to his touch. Still he clutched by the ladder, and each slight noise that met his overstrained attention added fearfully to the pangs of apprehension that tortured him thus physically and mentally.

He could hear the sound of heavy footsteps through the house, and occasionally the low murmur of voices came upon his ears, although he could not detect what was said. That they would, however, come to the room from which he was only separated by a thin piece of wainscotting he knew; and if his dread and agitation were great now, he thought with a shudder what would be his feelings when each moment might produce his discovery and capture.

Then he strained his ear to listen if he could hear Ada moaning, and a low stifled sigh ascended from the gloomy vault.

"Yes, yes," he thought. "She will be still—she will be still. The fear of a sudden and violent death is upon her young heart. 'Tis well, 'tis very well, now she thinks me the unscrupulous man—the—the murderer that she taunts me with being. She—she does not suspect that if I were taken, my only hope of mercy would be in having preserved her life—and, and my only plea would be that not a hair of her head was injured. No, no, she guesses not the value of her life. I—I have been cunning, very, very cunning. Besides, if they find me, what evidence—"

Jacob Gray very nearly uttered a cry of terror as this thought passed through his mind, for he immediately then recollected his own written confession that he had in the breast pocket of his coat, and which, if he were taken, would be his destruction.

He struck his forehead with his clenched hand, and uttered a deep groan. What means had he there, situated as he was, of destroying the damning evidence of a guilt which otherwise would only rest on conjecture and surmise, 'and from the consequences of which, it not being distinctly proved, the money and influence of Learmont, exerted for his own sake, might actually free him. The written confession was an admirable weapon against Learmont, so long as he, Jacob Gray, had the control of it, and lived ; but now, when there was a fearful chance of his own apprehension, it was at once converted into a fearful weapon against himself, and a damning evidence of his guilt.

For some moments he was incapable of anything resembling rational thought, and his reason seemed tottering to its base. This state of mind, however, passed away, and how to destroy his confession became the one great question that agitated and occupied his throbbing and intensely labouring brain.

If he attempted to tear it into fragments, he must either cast these fragments on the floor of the vault, from whence they would easily be recovered, or he must keep them in his possession, which would avail him nothing.

He thought of descending the ladder, and digging a hole with his hands, in which to bury the dangerous document, but then Ada was there, and would by the dim light of that place see what he was about, and it was not to be supposed that she would keep a secret she was so strongly and personally interested in revealing.

There was but one other resource that occurred to the maddened brain of Jacob Gray, and that was one which, in his present state, nothing but the abject, awful fear of death by the hands of the executioner could have brought him to—it was to tear the confession into small pieces, and eat it.

With trembling hands, while he stood upon the ladder as well as he could, he drew the paper from his breast, and notwithstanding his awful and intense thirst, he began tearing off piece by piece from it, and forcing himself to swallow it.

Thus had this written confession—this master-stroke of policy, upon which he had so much prided himself, become to him a source of torment and pain.

Occasionally he could hear a door shut in the house, as Sir Francis Hartleton and his two officers pursued their search, and he went on with frantic eagerness devouring the paper.

Now, by the distinctness of the sounds, he felt sure those who sought him were in the next apartment. In a few short moments they would be there. His danger was thickening, and the confession was not half disposed of. With trembling fingers, that impeded themselves, he tore off large pieces, and forced them into his mouth, to the danger of choking himself.

Now he really heard the door of the room open, and the heavy tread of men upon the floor. In a few moments there was a death-like stillness, and Jacob Gray stood in the act of suspending mastication, with a large piece of the confession fixed in his teeth.

Then Sir Francis Hartleton's voice, or what he guessed to be his, from the tone of authority in which he spoke, came upon Gray's ears.

"This is very strange," he said. "To my thinking, there are evident indications of recent inhabitants in this house. Go down to the door, and ask your your comrade if he has heard anything."

" Yes, Sir Francis," replied another voice, and the door closed, indicative of the man proceeding on his errand.

" Now—now," thought Gray, " if we were alone—if there were no other, a pistol would rid me for ever of his troublesome and most unwelcome visit."

Sir Francis spoke, as if communing with himself, in a low voice—but in the breathless stillness around, Gray heard distinctly what he said.

" Is it possible that the man Gray has left here?" he said. " Are we, after all, as far off the secret as ever? And yet I cannot think so. What could be the motive of such an inscription on the door as that which states his departure more than a month since ? It is some trick merely. By Heavens, that must have been Gray who left the King's Bounty so soon before me. The fates seem to be propitious to the rascal, and to aid him in every way. I made sure the information was good, and that I had him here safe for the fetching merely."

Sir Francis now walked to and fro in the room for some minutes; then he paused and said,—

"He can't be hiding here anywhere. The old house is full of cupboards and closets, but they are very easily searched. Learmont, Learmont! are you still to tr umph in your villany for a time? I could stake my life upon the fact, that some crime of black hue was committed that night of the storm at the Old Smithy at yonder village. The issues of the crime are still at work, but they are not revealed. Humph! It's of no use apprehending Britton on mere vague suspicion. No, that would be very foolish, for it would set the whole party on their guard, and that which is difficult now might become impossible."

"Please your worship, he aint heard nothing," said the man, at this moment entering the room again.

"No noise of any kind?"

"No, nothing, your worship."

"No one has crossed the fields within view since he has stood guard?"

"Not a mouse, your worship."

"Very well. Now go and search the lower rooms thoroughly, and then come back to me here. I shall rest on this chair awhile."

So saying, Sir Francis Hartleton sat down on the chair which Ada had stood upon to enable her to reach the panel that opened to the vault.

How little the poor, persecuted Ada imagined that a powerful friend was very near to her.

Jacob Gray was now almost afraid to breathe, so close was the magistrate to him. Had the wainscotting not intervened, Gray could, had he been so minded, have touched Sir Francis's head without moving from where he stood.

At length he spoke again.

"I wonder," he said, "if this girl that the Seytons speak of, and yon poor creature, Maud, raves of as an angel, be really the child that was saved from the Smithy on the night of the storm and the fire? I have only one very substantial reason for thinking so, and that is, that the name of Britton is mixed up with the business. To be sure, the dates correspond pretty well with what the young man, Seyton, says he thinks is her age. It's rather strange though, that no one except Maud mentions Learmont at all in the matter, and her mention of him is nothing new. 'Tis a mysterious affair, and, at all events, this man, Gray, is at hide and seek for some very special reason indeed."

The man who had been sent to examine the lower rooms now returned.

"Well," said Sir Francis.

"There aint not nothing, your worship, by no means," he said.

"You have searched carefully?"

"Yes, your worship. I'd take my solemn 'davy as there's nothing here."

"I know I can rely upon you," said Sir Francis, in a tone of disappointment.

"Ex—actly, your worship."

"Do you think there are any hiding-places about this house?"

"Can't say as I does. Your worship sees as it's a house a standing all alone, and there aint no great opportunity to make hiding-places, you see."

"I will make one more effort," said Sir Francis; "it is a forlorn hope; but if the girl be hiding anywhere in this house under the impression that I am an enemy, she may hear me and put faith in my words. I will call to her."

Sir Francis rose as he spoke; and Jacob Gray, upon whom this determination came like a thunder-clap, dropped from his trembling hands the remnant of the confession he had been eating, and curling his feet round the ladder, he slid in a moment to the damp floor of the vault. His great dread was, that on the impulse of a moment, Ada might answer any call to her by name; and he knew that, close as Sir Hartleton was, the least shrill cry of hers must inevitably reach his ears, when instant discovery and capture would be certain to follow.

Drawing then his pistol from his pocket, he felt about for Ada.

" Ada, Ada," he said, in the faintest whisper.

" Here," said Ada.

" Hush," said Gray, as he grasped her arm ; "speak above the tone I use, and you seal your own destruction."

He placed, as he spoke, the cold muzzle of a pistol against her forehead. Ada shuddered as she said,—

" What is that ?"

" A pistol ! make the least noise—raise the faintest cry, and I will pull the trigger. You will be a mangled corpse in a moment. Hush, hush, hush !"

A voice now reached the ears of Ada, and thrilled through the very heart of Jacob Gray. It was the voice of Sir Francis Hartleton, which, now that he raised it to a high key, was quite audible to Ada, while before, from the low position she occupied at the bottom of the vault, she had only heard a confused murmuring of voices, without being able to detect what was said.

" Ada!" cried the magistrate ; " Ada."

The girl clasped her hands, and an answering cry was on her lips, but the cold barrel of the pistol pressed heavily and painfully against her brow, and Gray, with his lips close to her ear, said,—

" Hush, hush !" prolonging the sound till it resembled the hissing of some loathsome snake.

" Ada !" again cried Sir Francis. " Ada! if you are concealed within hearing of my voice, be assured it is a friend who addresses you."

A low gasping sob burst from Ada, and Gray again hissed in her ear,—

" A word, and you die. You are a corpse if you speak ; and all hope of seeing Albert Seyton in this world will be past."

" Ada," again cried Sir Francis: " speak if you be here. A friend addresses you, I am Sir Francis Hartleton, the magistrate."

Ada made a slight movement, and Gray pressed her quite back with the violence with which he held the pistol against her temple.

There was a dead silence now. Sir Francis said no more. Ada's hope was past. Still, however, Gray stood close to her with the pistol ; and as the murderer and the innocent Ada remained thus strangely situated, it would have been difficult to say which suffered the most mental agony of the two. Ada to know that relief had been so near without the power to grasp at it—or Gray to know that one word from her would have consigned him to a prison, from whence he would never have emerged but to ascend the scaffold to die a death of ignominy and shame.

CHAPTER XLV.

THE LONELY WATCHER.—GRAY'S CUNNING.—THE CUPBOARD ON THE STAIRS.

NOTWITHSTANDING the search which Sir Francis Hartleton had made—a search that satisfied him that Ada had been removed from Forest's house by the cunning of Gray—he could not divest himself of the idea that one or both might return to the old mansion, if for no other purpose than to remove some of the articles, which in the course of his researches he had found in various closets and cupboards, into which they had been hastily thrust by Jacob Gray.

In case such a thing should be, after some consideration, he resolved to have one of his men there for several days, and he accordingly turned to him who had been guarding the door. and said,—

" Elias, you must remain here for a few days."

" Here, Sir Francis ? In—in this old house, your worship?"

"Yes, here, in this old house, Elias. You are strong, fearless, and well armed. Arrest any one who comes here."

"Yes," said Elias, looking about him, not over well pleased with his commission, as it did not promise much comfort or sprightly company—two things that Elias was rather partial to.

"I expect a thin, sallow man," continued Sir Francis, "to come here, of a pale and anxious cast of countenance. Arrest him by all means."

"Yes, your worship."

"And should a young girl come with him, or by herself, mind, Elias, she is a lady, and take care you treat her respectfully."

"A lady!" ejaculated Elias, in astonishment. "Your worship, is she a real lady, or like Moll Flaherty?"

"Pshaw!" cried Sir Francis; "treat her, I say, with respect, and bring her to me."

No. 24.

" Oh ! bring her to your worship—oh !"

"Now you have your instructions. It's warm, so you can do without a fire, and it's light, and smoke would scare away the people I wish to come. When you sleep, Elias, shut your door lightly, so that you may hear if any one comes. Upon consideration, however, you had better sit up all night, and sleep a little in the day time, for those that I seek are not likely to venture across the fields, lest they should be seen."

" Your worship's unkimmon considerate, and very kind," muttered Elias.

" You have your lantern, Elias ?"

" Yes, your worship, and lots of little wax ends put in it."

" Very well. Now, good day. Keep a good watch, Elias—and, do you hear ? there's fifty pounds reward for either the man or the girl."

" Fifty !"

" Yes, from me ; so you know you are sure of it if you earn it."

" Oh !" cried Elias, looking round him, with a very different expression, upon the old house, "it's a very comfortable place, indeed, your worship."

" By-the-by," said Sir Francis, " I forgot one thing—the girl may come in boy's clothing."

" Oh, the dear !" said Elias.

" So, if what you think a boy comes, you may assume that that's the girl."

" The pretty cretur !" exclaimed Elias. "Fifty pounds! Bless her."

The magistrate then reflected a moment, and not recollecting anything else that it was necessary to impress upon the sensitive mind of Elias, he was turning away from the door, when that gentleman himself suddenly thought of something of the very greatest importance in his eyes.

" Your worship," he said, " my victuals—my victuals, your worship."

" What ?" said Sir Francis.

" Am I to be starved, your worship ? How am I to get my victuals ?"

Sir Francis smiled, as he replied,—

" I should not have forgotten you. You must do the best you can till sunset, when I will send Stephy to you with plenty to last you."

" Well," exclaimed Elias, " it is a mercy that I tucked in a tolerable breakfast." Sir Francis now left the house with his other companions, and Elias, who was remarkable for his size and great personal strength, closed the door, and began to bethink how he should amuse the leisure hours until sunset, when the welcome provisions should arrive ; after which time he did not contemplate that the time would hang at all heavily upon his hands.

In the meanwhile Jacob Gray remained in the vault, threatening Ada, until he thought all danger must be past, from the extreme quiet that reigned in the house. Not the most distant notion of Sir Francis Hartleton's leaving any one behind him to keep watch in the lonely mansion, occurred to Jacob Gray, and after half an hour, as he guessed, had very nearly passed away, he began to breathe a little more freely, and to congratulate himself that for that time at least the danger had blown over his head.

During that half hour he made a determination to leave the house, and for the short time now that he would stay in England—for he was thoroughly scared, and resolved to be off very soon—he would take some lodging for himself and Ada, at the same time binding her by a solemn promise, as before, not to leave him, which promise he would now render less irksome to her, by representing that in a short time she should be quite free to act as she pleased, as well as knowing everything that might concern her or her future fortunes.

With this idea, and believing the danger past, he spoke in a more unembarrassed tone to Ada.

" Ada," he said, " be not deceived—the voice you heard calling upon you was not that of Sir Francis Hartleton. That name was assumed merely to deceive you to your destruction. You, as well as I, have escaped a great danger—so great a danger, that I shall hasten my departure from England, and you may rest assured now that within one month from this time you will be rich and free."

" Indeed !" said Ada, incredulously.

" You may believe me," said Gray ; " on my faith, what I say is true."

" 'Tis hard to believe him who would murder one moment, and promise wealth and freedom the next."

" I was forced to threaten your life, Ada, for my own, as I tell you, hung upon a thread; you will not repent this day's proceedings when you are happy with him you love, and surrounded by luxury."

Ada started ; and had there been light enough in that dismal place, Gray would have seen the mantling flush of colour that visited the cheek of the persecuted girl, as the words he spoke conjured up a dream of happiness to her imagination, that she felt would indeed pay her for all she had suffered—ay, were it ten times more. She did not speak, for she would not let Jacob Gray guess, from the agitation of her voice, the effect that his words had produced, and after a pause he said to her,—

" Remain here while I go into the house and see that all is safe. They must be gone by this time ; Jacob Gray has foiled them once again, but he will not incur the danger a third time, I assure you. Ada, as I live and breathe, your thraldom shall not—cannot last another month."

He ascended the ladder as he spoke, and after listening attentively and hearing nothing, he slid open the panel and looked into the room. All was still, and the glorious bright sunshine was streaming in upon the dingy walls and blackened floor.

Again Gray listened—all was still, and he got through the opening with a lurking smile of gratified cunning upon his face. He, however, could not forget his habitual caution, and it was with a slinking, cat-like movement that he walked along the floor of the room.

He intended to walk through the entire house, to see if his unwelcome visitors had left behind them any traces of their presence. Opening the door of the room very carefully, he began to descend the stairs ; he muttered to himself as he went,—

" 'Twas an hour of great danger. I have been saved by what good and pious people would call a miracle, had it happened to them, but I suppose it's merely an accident in Jacob Gray's case ; well, well, be it so—accident or miracle, 'tis all the same to me ; and I am not sorry too, to leave this old house ; it has grown hateful and loathsome to me : I would not pass such another night in it as I have passed for—for—much money. No, no—it would indeed require a heap of gold to tempt me."

Now he reached the door of a large cupboard on the staircase, which was wide open, as Sir Francis and his men had left it in the course of their search.

" So," sneered Gray, " they have looked for me in the cupboards, have they ? Well, the keener the search has been, the better ; it is less likely to be renewed, far less likely. I wish I could think of any plan of vengeance upon this magistrate, for the misery he has caused me ; oh, if I could inflict upon him but one tithe of the agony he has made me suffer within the last hour, I should be much rejoiced. Curses on him—curses on him and his efficiency as a magistrate : a meddling cursed fiend he is to me—I must think, Master Hartleton ; some little plan of revenge upon you may suggest itself to me by-and-by."

Jacob Gray rubbed his hands together, and gave a sickly smile, as he said this. He was about the middle of the staircase, and it was fortunate for him he had his hands on the banisters, or in the intense horror and surprise that suddenly overcame him, he might have fallen down the remaining portion of the crazy stairs.

He heard a door open, leading into the passage, from one of the lower rooms, and a heavy careless step rapidly approached the staircase, while a common street melody, whistled with a shrillness and distinctness that was more horrible to Jacob Gray than would have been the trumpet of the angel at the day of judgment, fell upon his ears.

Jacob Gray gave himself up for lost. The blood rushed to his heart with frightful violence, and he thought he should have fainted. How he accomplished the feat he afterwards knew not, but he stepped back. Two paces brought him to the cupboard. It seemed like the door of heaven opened to him. He doubled himself up under a large shelf that went across the middle of it; and, clutching the door by a small rim of the panelling, he drew it close.

Mr. Elias, with his hands in his pockets, and whistling the before-mentioned popular melody, passed on up the staircase, leaving Jacob Gray almost distilled to a jelly with fear.

Then, when he had passed, Gray thought at first that his best plan would be to rush down the stairs, open the outer door, and make a rush across the fields, leaving Ada to her destiny—but this was hazardous—he would be seen—hunted like a wild beast, and taken! No. That was too bold a step for Jacob Gray. He listened, with heart and soul, to the footsteps that sounded so awful in his ears, and the question arose in his mind, of—should the man, whoever he was, enter the room where he, Jacob Gray, had just left, so heedlessly as he now thought, with the panel open, or would he pass on? That was a fearful question. He thought he heard him pause once, and his heart sunk within him. No, he passed on. He was ascending the second flight of stairs leading to the second story.

CHAPTER XLVI.

THE DEATH OF THE ELDER SEYTON.—ALBERT'S GRIEF.—THE PROPHECY.

It is necessary now that we should, although unwillingly, leave the fortunes of the beautiful and persecuted Ada to proceed by themselves for a short space, while we acquaint the reader with what the other important personages in our story have been and are about.

First, we will turn to Albert Seyton, who, with his father, returned from the office of Sir Francis Hartleton, rather dispirited than otherwise at the result of the interview with him.

It was in vain that Albert reasoned with himself on the folly of his having had any immediate expectations of news of Ada through the interposition of the magistrate. He did feel depressed and disappointed, and the words indicative of the difficulty that enveloped the business which Sir Francis Hartleton had used, made a far greater impression upon the mind of Albert, than anything else that had transpired at the interview.

Had Sir Francis Hartleton not been a magistrate, but a mere private gentleman, knowing what he did, and suspecting what he did, in all probability the interview with the Seytons would have been more satisfactory to them, and more productive of beneficial results to Ada; but as it was, Sir Francis felt that, in his official capacity, he could not be too cautious as to what he said, or what opinion he suggested, in any criminal undertaking. Thus he did not (and so far he was quite correct) feel himself justified in mentioning the name of Learmont, unless the Seytons had heard it previously, in connexion with any of the mysterious circumstances surrounding Ada.

As yet all was mere suspicion; and there was no direct evidence on which to found an open accusation against the acts of 'Squire Learmont; for although he, Sir Francis, by putting together all the circumstances in his own mind, felt morally convinced that there had been some great crime committed, in which Learmont, Britton the smith, the man Gray, and possibly others were implicated, still the evidence of that crime were to be sought; and it would have been highly inconsistent with him, Sir Francis, as a magistrate, to have brought a loose and unsubstantiated charge against any one—much less a man with whom it could be easily proved he had previously quarrelled, and who might, by the very indiscretion of making an improper charge against, be so far put upon his caution, as to succeed in effectually destroying all evidence that could ever militate against him.

Taking, therefore, this view of the case, and being satisfied that the Seytons had communicated to him all they knew; and having their promise to bring him any fresh information they might become possessed of, he resolved to prosecute the matter quietly and cautiously, until, by getting some of the parties in his hands, he would be able to put together something distinct in the shape of a charge against Learmont, or ascertain his innocence.

The magistrate had seen much of human nature, and he very soon came to the conclusion, in his own mind, that brave, ardent, and enthusiastic as Albert Seyton was, he would be very far from an efficient assistant in a matter that required the utmost coolness, caution, and *finesse*. Thus it was that he acted entirely independent of Albert, and said as little to him as he could upon the subject, at the same time that he, Sir Francis Hartleton, would not have lost a moment in communicating with Albert, had any discovery really taken place at the old house at Battersea.

While all this was going on, Albert Seyton pursued his inquiries, although with a languid spirit, for there was no place he had not already several times visited. Twice or thrice he had actually looked at the house in which Ada was a prisoner, and once he thought of crossing the fields from curiosity to visit it, but was told that it was in ruins, and in fact dangerous to approach, as it was expected to fall to the ground very shortly ; and considering it as a most unlikely place to search in, standing as it did so very much exposed to observation in its situation, he abandoned the notion of crossing the marshy fields to the old ruin.

Pale and languid, he would return to his father in the evening, and it was some time before he noticed that there were perceptible signs of rapid decay creeping over the only earthly tie he had, save Ada.

In truth, Mr. Seyton was near that bourne from whence no traveller returns, and in the midst of his other griefs, the absorbing one sprang up, of the loss of his father.

Every other consideration was now abandoned by Albert in his anxious solicitude for his father's health. It seemed, however, that a rapid decay of nature was taking place, and in less than three days Mr. Seyton lay at the point of death. Medical advice was of no avail; the physician who was called in declared that neither he nor any of his brethren could do anything in the case. There was no disease to grapple with—it seemed as if nature had said, "the time of dissolution has come, and it may not be averted."

It was early dawn, and the stillness that reigned throughout London had something awful and yet sublime in it, when Albert, who had been watching by the bedside of his father, was roused from a slight slumber into which, from pure exhaustion, he had sunk, by the low, faint voice of his dying parent feebly pronouncing his name.

"Albert, Albert!" he said.

Albert started, and replied to his father.

"Yes, father, I am here."

"You are here, my boy, and you will remain here many years—here in this world, I mean, which I hope may teem with happiness to you ; but I am on my last journey, Albert; I shall not see another day."

"Father, say not so," replied Albert, endeavouring to assume a tone of cheerfulness that was foreign to his feelings. "Say not so; we may yet be together many years."

"Albert, do not try to delude me and yourself with false hopes—listen to what I shall say to you now."

"I will, father."

"They are my last words, Albert, and it is said that when the spirit is about to quit its earthly tenement, and is hovering, as it were, upon the confines of eternity, is permitted to see things that in its grosser state were far above its ken, and even to obtain some dim glimpse of the future, so that it may to the ear of those it loves hazard guesses of that which is to come."

Albert listened with eager attention to his father's words ; and it seemed to him as if there were something of heavenly inspiration in his tones.

After a pause, Mr. Seyton continued,—

"Albert, for two days now I have known no peace on your account,—"

"On my account, father ?"

"Yes, Albert. By my death, the pension which my just claims have wrung from the government, for which I suffered so much, ceases, and you know I have not enjoyed it long enough to leave any sum that will do more than supply your immediate exigencies."

"Think not of me now, father," said Albert ; "dismiss all uneasiness from your mind on my account. I am young, and can labour for my bread as well as—as——"

"As what, my boy ?"

"As my griefs will let me, father."

"Listen to me, Albert. I say I have suffered much on your account, because the thought haunted me that I was leaving you to struggle unaided in a cold, selfish, and too—too frequently, wicked world ; but now that feeling, by some mysterious means, has left me."

"Indeed, father ?"

"Yes, a kind of confidence—surely from Heaven—has crept over my heart concerning you, and, without knowing how or why, I seem to have a deep and thorough conviction that you will be happy and prosperous."

"Father," said Albert, "for your sake do I rejoice in your words, not for my own. If you must be taken by God from me, let me see you thus even to the last, free from care and that cankering anxiety which has now for some time afflicted you."

"Yes, I am comparatively happy," said Mr. Seyton. "You will wed her whom you love, and there shall not be a cloud in the sky of your prosperity and happiness. All shall be achieved by Heaven in its own good time."

"Father, your words sink deep into my heart," cried Albert ; "they come to me as if from the lips of the Eternal One himself."

"I—I would fain have lingered with you, my boy, yet awhile, even until I could have seen and rejoiced in all this that I now foretel to you. But it may not be—it may not be."

"Oh, yes! there is still hope."

"No, no! my mortal race is nearly run."

Albert wept.

"Nay, Albert, do not weep," said his father ; "we and all we love—all who have loved us—will meet again."

"'Tis a dear hope," said Albert, endeavouring to control his tears.

"And now, my dear boy, when you do see this young and innocent girl—this Ada, whom you love—tell her I send her my blessing, and beg her to accept it as she would a father's. You will tell her, Albert?"

"Tell her, father? Oh yes!—your words will be precious to her, father."

"I know her gentle nature well," continued Mr. Seyton. "Cherish her, Albert, for she is one of those rare creatures sent among us by God, to purify and chasten the bad passions of men. Cherish her as a dear gift from Heaven to you."

"As Heaven is my hope, I will," said Albert. "I will live but for her."

"'Tis well, 'tis well. I would have joyed to see her ; but no matter. The spirit may be allowed to look with purer eyes upon those it loved on earth, than it could through its earthly organs."

"Your love, father, will cling for ever round us, and we will rejoice in the fond belief that we are seen by you from above."

Albert's voice became choked with tears, and he sobbed bitterly.

"Nay, now, Albert," said his father, "this is not as it should be. We were talking cheerfully. Do not weep. Death is not a misfortune ; 'tis only a great change.   We leave a restless, painful scene for the calm repose of everlasting peace and joy.   Our greatest thrill of happiness in this life is like a stagnant pool to the ocean, in comparison with the eternal joy that is to come.   Do not, therefore, weep for me, Albert, but do your duty while you remain here behind me, so that we may meet again where we shall meet never to part, without the shadow of a pang.''

" Father, your words are holy, and full of hope ; they will ever be engraven on my heart."

Mr. Seyton was now silent for many minutes ; and Albert, by the rapidly increasing light of the coming day, watched with painful interest the great change that was passing over his countenance.

" Father," he murmured.

" Yes, Albert, I am here still," was the reply.

" You are in pain ?"

" No, no.   Bless you, my boy !"

Albert sobbed convulsively, and took his father's hand in his.

"And bless you too, Ada,'' added Mr. Seyton, after a pause.   Then he seemed to imagine she was present, for he said,—

" You love my boy, Ada ?   Blessings on you !—you are very beautiful, Ada, but your heart is the most lovely.   So you love my boy ?   Take an old man's dying blessing, my girl."

Albert was deeply affected by these words, and in vain he endeavoured to stifle his sobs.

" Albert !" said his father, suddenly.

" Yes, father, I am here," he replied.

" Do you recollect your mother, my dear boy ?"

" But dimly, father."

" She—she is beckoning me now.   Farewell!   Bless you, Albert—Ada !"

There was one long-drawn sigh, and the kind-hearted, noble Mr. Seyton was with his God.

It was some moments before Albert could bring himself to believe that his father was no more; and then, with a frantic burst of grief, he called around him the persons of the house, who with gentle violence took him from the chamber of death, and strove to soothe his deep grief with such topics of consolation as suggested themselves to them.   But poor Albert heard nothing of their sympathy.   His grief was overwhelming; and it was many hours before his deep agony subsided into tears, and the last words of his father came like balm to his wounded spirit.

Then his grief assumed a more calm and melancholy aspect.   He shed no more tears ; but there was a weight at his heart which even the bright and strangely earnest prophecies of his father, concerning his happiness with Ada, could not remove.   Time alone, in such cases, heals the deep and agonising grief which ensues in a fond and truthful heart, after such a disseverment of a tie which, while it exists, we cannot imagine can ever be broken.

CHAPTER XLVII

THE SMITH AT LEARMONT HOUSE.—THE BREAKFAST.—THE THREAT, AND ITS RESULTS.—THE CAUTION.

WHILE these events were taking place, Learmont was ill at ease in his stately halls.   Well he knew that the visitation of the smith at so inopportune an hour at his *fete* would be related throughout that circle of nobility and power into which it was the grand end and aim of his life to force himself ; and it added one more damning argument to those already rapidly accumulating in his mind towards the conviction, that after all he had made a grand mistake in life, and mistaken the road to happiness. At the same time, however, he felt that having chosen the path of guilt he had, there was for him no retreat, and with a dogged perseverance, compounded of mortified ambition, he continued his career of guilt.

Take the life of Britton he dared not, although he lay such an inanimate, helpless mass in his power, and it was not the least of Learmont's annoyances that he was compelled to see to the personal safety of the drunken brute who had produced confusion and derangement among his most ambitious schemes.

It was many hours before Britton slept off the intoxication under the influence of which he had acted in the manner described in the ball-room, and when he did recover, and open his heavy eyes, it was with no small degree of surprise that he found himself in the same dark room into which the squire had thrown him to sleep off his debauch.

His first thought was that he was in prison, and he rose to his feet with bitter imprecations and awful curses upon the head of Learmont and Gray, whom he supposed must have betrayed him in some way. A second thought, however, dispelled this delusion.

"No—no; d—n them—no!" he cried. "They dare not! ¡Well they know they dare not!—I have them safe!—My evidence would destroy them, while it would not place me in a worse position. Where the devil am I?"

The room was very dark, the only light coming from a small pane of g ass at the top of the door. Britton, however, was not exactly the kind of person to waste much time in idle conjecture, or imaginative theories as to where he was; but, ascertaining that the door was locked, he placed his shoulder against, it and with one heave of his bulky form, forced it from its hinges.

A loud cry arrested the smith's attention as he accomplished this feat, and, to his great amusement, he saw lying amid the confusion of a tray, glasses, and decanters, a man who happened to have been passing at the moment, and, alarmed at the sudden and violent appearance of the smith, had fallen down with what he was so carefully carrying.

This was a piece of sport quite in Britton's way—one of those practical jests that he perfectly understood and appreciated. In order, however, to add zest to it, he gave the astonished man a hearty kick, which induced him to spring to his feet, and make off with frantic speed, shouting " Murder! murder!" at the top of his lungs.

Britton immediately turned his attention to one decanter which, in a most miraculous and extraordinary manner, preserved its position of perpendicularity amidst the universal wreck of every other article. He seized it instantly as a lawful prize, and plunging the neck of it into his capacious mouth, he withdrew it not again until it presented an appearance of perfect vacuity, and the bottle of wine which it had contained was transferred into his interior man.

"That's good," gasped Britton, when he had finished his draught. "I was thirsty. Upon my life that's good. Curse the awkward fellow! he has broken the other. I wonder how the d—l I came—by G—d! this is the squire's, now I look about me. I must have been drunk. What the deuce has happened? my head is all of a twirl. Let me think,—humph! the Chequers—d—n it! I can't recollect anything but the Chequers."

Britton's cogitations were here interrupted by the appearance of Learmont with a dark scowl on his brow that would have alarmed any one but the iron-nerved and audacious Britton.

"Well, squire," he said, " I suppose I'd a drop too much, and you took care of me, eh? Is that it?"

"Follow—me," said Learmont, bringing out the two words through his clenched teeth, and making a great effort to preserve himself from bursting out into a torrent of invective.

"Follow you?" exclaimed Britton. "Well, I have no objection; I'll follow you. Our business is always quite private and confidential."

He followed the rapid strides of Learmont along a long gallery, during the progress of which they encountered a servant, when Britton immediately paused, and roared out in a voice that made the man stand like one possessed,—

"Hark, ye knave!—you in the tawny coat, turned up with white—bring breakfast for two directly."

"Andrew Britton!" cried Learmont, turning full upon the smith, with his eyes flashing with resentment.

"'Squire Learmont!" replied Britton, facing him with an air of unparalleled insolence and bloated assurance.

There was a pause for a moment, and then Learmont added,—

"You—you are still drunk!"

"No, I am hungry; a drunken man never orders victuals, 'squire."

"I have breakfasted," said Learmont.

No. 25.

"Very like, but you don't fancy I meant any of it for you. Curse me ! I always make a point of ordering breakfast for two, now that I am a gentleman and can afford it ;—I'm sure to have nearly enough then. Breakfast for two, I say ! You can get it ready while your master and I settle some little affairs connected with the Old Smithy. Do you hear ?—what are you staring at ?"

The servant looked at Learmont evidently for orders, and the 'squire, almost inarticulate with rage, said,—

"Go—go ! you may get him breakfast."

"Ah, to be sure," said Britton ; "of course you may. I'm a particular friend of your master's ; and mind you are more respectful another time, you beast, and use polite language, and be d—d to you, you thief !"

The amazed domestic hastened away, for he shrewdly guessed that, if he delayed much longer, he might be favoured by some practical display of the excessive freedom which the messenger from the Old Smithy evidently could take with the proud, haughty, Learmont, and everything that was his, or in any way connected with him,—a freedom which puzzled and amazed the whole household, and formed the theme of such endless gossiping in the servants' hall, that without it, it would seem impossible they could found any materials for consideration, conjecture, and endless surmise.

Learmont now stalked on, followed by Britton, until he reached the small private room in which the conferences with both Gray and the smith were usually held. The 'squire then closed the door, and turning to Britton with a face convulsed with passion, he said,—

"Scoundrel ! are you not afraid to tamper with me in this manner ? Drive me too far by your disgusting conduct, and insolent, vulgar familiarities, and I would hang you, though I had to fly from England for evere befor I denounced you ;—nay, hear me out, and let my words sink deep into your brain, if it be capable of receiving and recording them. If you dare to thrall me by untimely visits, I will, though it cost me thousands, lay such a plot for your destruction, that your life shall not only be forfeited, but I will take care to associate your name with such infamy, that no confession nor statement of yours would be received with a moment's credence. You earn from me the wages of crime—deep crime, and you know it ; but were those wages millions, and were those crimes of ten times blacker hue than they are, you have no right, nor shall you be, a torment to me. I am your master, and I will make you know it, or rue the fearful consequence."

Learmont paused, and regarded the smith with an air of haughty defiance.

"Oh !" said Britton, "so you've had your say, 'Squire Learmont—you threaten to hang me, do you? Ho! ho! ho!—the same length of cord that hangs me will make a noose for your own neck. You will lay a plot to destroy me, will—beware, 'Squire Learmont! I have laid a mine for you—a mine that will blow you to h—ll, when I choose to fire the train. I don't want to quarrel with you; I've done a black job or two for you, and you don't much like paying for them; but then you know you must, and there's an end to that. Now for the familiarity business : I give in a little there, 'squire, D—me ! justice is justice—give every dog his day ! I have been cursedly drunk, I suppose, and made an ass of myself. I came here, though, now I recollect, with a good motive,—it was to warn you. But mind you, 'squire, don't call me any ugly names again—I won't stand them. Be civil, and growl as much as you like—curse you ! be genteel, and don't provoke me."

"Solemnly promise me that you will only come here at stated times, from visit to visit, to be arranged," said Learmont, "and I am willing to forget the past."

"Well, that's fair," cried Britton. "When I've had a drop, I'm a little wild or so,—d—n it ! I always was."

"You consent ?"

"I do. Now give me my fee."

"Your fee ?"

"Yes ; ten pounds."

Learmont took out the sum required from his purse, and handed it to Britton, saying as he did so,—

" And when shall I be honoured again with your next visit ?"

" What's to-day, 'squire ?"

" Thursday."

" Then I'll see you on Saturday morning. If I've been sober on Friday night, we'll say eleven o'clock ; if drunk, make it two or three."

A low tap at the door now announced some one, and Learmont went to see who it was.

" The—the—breakfast — for two, your honour—is—is—laid in the south parlour," stammered a servant, with a frightened aspect.

" Oh, it is, is it ?" said Britton. " Then you may eat it yourself, for I aint going to stay to breakfast with his worship."

" Yes, yes," said the servant, disappearing.

" There now," cried Britton, " aint I respectful? You see I aint going to touch your breakfast, I dare say I shall get a d——d sight better one at the Chequers. Ha ! ha ! ha ! I'm a king, then. Who'd have thought of that—King Britton, the jolly smith of Learmont."

" You said you came to warn me of somebody or something," suggested Learmont.

" So I did," replied the smith. " That cursed Hartleton has got some crotchet or another in his head, you may depend. He came in disguise to the Chequers to watch me. Beware of him, 'squire. If I catch him prying into my affairs, and listening to what I say over my glass, I'll meet him alone some dark evening, and there will be a vacancy in the magistracy. Perhaps, 'squire, you could step into his shoes. That would be glorious. I'd have a row every night, and you could smother it up in the morning, besides paying all the expenses. Good morning to you, 'squire. Take care of yourself."

CHAPTER XLVIII.

THE ESCAPE.—A SONG OF THE TIMES.

It was several minutes after Gray felt perfectly assured that the man, whoever he was, that had passed whistling by the cupboard door, had gone up to the highest story of the house before he could summon courage to leave his temporary hiding-place. The urgent necessity, however, of doing so while there was an opportunity, came so forcibly upon his terror-stricken mind, that although he trembled so excessively as to be forced to cling to the banisters for support, he crawled from the place of shelter which had presented itself so providentially to him in such a moment of extremity, and treading as lightly as he could, while his whole frame was nearly paralysed by fear, he succeeded in reaching the room from which opened the small aperture to the vault where Ada awaited his coming.

Jacob Gray's mind at this moment embraced but one idea, indulged in but one hope, and that was to reach the vault in safety, and close the opening in the wall which had already escaped the scrutiny of Sir Frederick Hartleton.

The extreme caution that he thought himself compelled to use in his movements made him slow in attaining his object, and each moment appeared an age of anxiety and awful suffering.

Now he mounted the chair, and as he did so he heard, or fancied he heard, the descending footsteps of the stranger as he came from the upper story. Jacob Gray then trembled so excessively that he could scarcely contrive to put himself through the small panelled opening ; and when he did, his anxiety was so great, and his nervousness so intense, that it was several moments before he could place his foot securely upon one of the rounds of the ladder.

The shrill whistle of the man now sounded awfully distinct in his ears, and he fancied that he must have closed the panel scarcely an instant before the stranger entered the apartment.

Then Jacob Gray laid his ear flatly against the wainscot to listen if more than one person was in the room, and gather from any conversation they might indulge in what were their objects and expectations in remaining so long in the ancient and dilapidated house.

For some minutes the whistling continued, for that was an innocent amusement that Mr. Elias was fortunately partial to, and one to which he invariably resorted when anything of a disagreeable character absorbed his mind ; and as now he could not withdraw his thoughts from the fact that he must fast until sunset, he whistled with an energy and a desperation proportioned to the exigency of the case.

At length, however, from want of breath, or that he had gone through every tune he was acquainted with three times, he paused in his whistling, and uttered the simple and energetic apostrophe of,—

" Well, I'm d—d ! "

This did not convey a great deal of information to Jacob Gray, and he waited very anxiously to hear what further remarks concerning his thoughts and objects in this world might fall from the speaker who had so cavalierly and offhandedly settled his destination in the next. Nor was he disappointed, for Mr. Elias, having no one to talk to, addressed himself, in the following strains :—

" Well, here's a precious old crib to be shut up in. Upon my soul, it's too bad of the governor. And no dinner—not a drop of nothing, nohow, whatsomedever. How would he like it, I wonder ? Why, not at all, to be sure. The fifty pounds is something—but it's all moonshine if the fellow don't come, or that ere gal as he talks on, as may make her blessed appearance in a masculine sort o' way. Well, I only hopes she may, that's all. Won't I give that Stephy a precious nob on his cocoa-nut, if he makes it very late afore he comes ? Curse this place, it's as dull as a sermon, and about as pleasant and lively-looking as mud in a wine-glass. I don't like these kind of goes at all. Give me fun, and a hunt after such a rollicking, slashing blade as Jack Sheppard. Ah, he's the fellow for my money. I love that blade. He's got a voice, too, like a flock o' nightingales, that he has. Shall I ever hear him sing that song again as I learnt of him by listening to him in quod, and all the while as I was taken up with the tune, he was a filing away at his darbies, bless him ! Oh, he's a rum un ! "

Elias then delighted himself and astonished Jacob Gray, by singing the following song, which was in great vogue at the time :—

"WHAT KNIGHT'S LIKE THE KNIGHT OF THE ROAD ?

" What knight's like the knight of the road ?
  Who lives so well as he ?
The proudest duke don't lead
  A life so brave and free.
Heighho ! how the maidens sigh,
  As he dashes proudly by !
And there's not a gentle heart of all—
  Let weal or woe betide—
That would not leap with dear delight
  To be his happy bride.

" The day goes down on Hounslow-heath,
  The night wind sighs amain ;
Hurrah ! hurrah, for the road !
  For now begins his reign.
Heighho ! how the ladies cry,
  As they see his flashing eye.

And there's not a pair of cherry lips,
    Of high or low degree,
Would scorn a kiss from the knight of the road,
    Who's welcome as he's free."

As Mr. Elias, between the stanzas of his song, whistled an accompaniment, in which there were a great number of shakes, trills, and what musicians call variations, which means something which is not at all connected with the tune, the whole affair took some considerable time in execution; and Jacob Gray stood upon the ladder in a perfect agony of annoyance until it was over.

"Bravo!" cried Elias, when he had completed the last few notes of his whistling accompaniment. "Bravo!—Encore!—Bravo! Well, I do hate these long summer days, to be sure. Why, it will be half-past eight, if it's a bit, before Stephy comes. There's a infliction. I wish this cursed fellow, or the gal, or both of them, would just trot over the fields, and save me any further waiting. Let me see—a thin, pale covey, the governor said, with a nervous sort o' look. Very good; I shall know him. Just let him show his physiogognomi here, and I'll pop the darbies on him before he can say Jack, to leave alone the Robinson. Well, I'll take another walk through the old den. They say there's been a murder here. I wonder if the fellow got much swag? I never heard o' any gentleman being hung for a murder here. I 'spose as that affair never put forty pound into a runner's pocket. Some fellows is such beasts when they does slap-up murders; they commits suicide, and so cheat somebody of the blood-money. Curse 'em!"

Having uttered this sentiment, Mr. Elias struck up an intense whistle, and walked from the room.

Jacob Gray could hear him descend the stairs, and the whistle gradually died away in the distance, until it sounded only faintly upon his ears, convincing him that the stranger had gone into some of the rooms on the ground floor.

Jacob Gray now slowly descended the ladder, and pronounced the name of Ada in a low, anxious tone.

"I am here," she replied.

"Ada, our situation is now perilous and awkward in the extreme. The persons who were here have left one of their number behind them."

"Indeed!"

"Yes. They suspect I may return to this house."

"Are we then to starve here?" said Ada.

"Starved?" echoed Gray. "I—I did not think of that. God of Heaven! what shall we do?"

"Jacob Gray," said Ada, "you are caught in your own snare. This place which you imagined to be one of safety, has now become your prison. Remain here, if you please; I have no such urgent reasons as you may have. If he whom you tell me is keeping guard in the house, be an enemy to me, as well as to you, I will rather trust to his mercy than abide here the horrors of famine. Such a death would be dreadful! Jacob Gray, I will not remain here."

"You will not?"

"I will not."

"I am armed, Ada. You forget that I can force your obedience by the fear of death."

"You can murder me," replied Ada, "but I cannot perceive that it is your interest to do so."

"Why not?"

"Let me go freely, and I promise not to disclose the secret of your place of concealment. He who is waiting, if he be an enemy to me as well as to you, may be satisfied with my capture, or perchance my death, and leave you undisturbed to pursue your own course. If he prove a friend to me, which from my heart, Jacob Gray, I verily believe, for the voice I heard address me by name carried in its tones truth and sincerity, then you will have less to fear, for I here promise not to betray you,"

Gray was silent for several moments after Ada had spoken. Then bending down his mouth close to her ear, he said in a low, agitated voice,—

"Ada—there is another resource."

"Indeed?"

"Yes—but one man keeps guard above."

"I understand you. You will risk a contest with him?"

"No—no—no!"

"What mean you then, Jacob Gray?"

"To kill him."

"But should he prove the stronger or the bolder, which he may well be, Jacob Gray, you might be worsted in the encounter."

"It shall not be an encounter," said Gray.

"You speak in riddles."

"Listen to me. He is walking uneasily from room to room of the house. He does not suspect any one to be concealed here—that much I can gather from his talk. At sunset I will creep forth, and hiding somewhere in perfect security— watch my opportunity, and shoot him dead."

"What!" cried Ada indignantly—"murder him?"

"I—I—only act in self-defence—I cannot help it—he would murder me. Hush—hush! do not speak so loud—you are incautious, Ada—hush—hush!

CHAPTER XLIX.

THE PROJECTED MURDER.—THE ALARM.—THE DEATH-SHOT.—ADA'S ANGUISH
AND INDIGNATION.

ADA was so much shocked at the proposal of Jacob Gray to commit a deliberate and cold-blooded murder, that now for several minutes she remained perfectly silent—a silence which Gray construed into passive acquiescence in his pro- position.

"You see, Ada," he continued, "we have no other hope—as you say we cannot starve here—the blood of this man be upon his own head—I do not want his life, Ada; but I must preserve myself and you. You must see all this in its proper light, Ada—you do not speak."

"Hear me then speak now," said Ada. "In all your knowledge of me, Jacob Gray, what have you found upon which to ground a moment's thought that I could be as wicked as yourself? Captivity may present horrors to you, from which you would free yourself, even at the fearful price of murder. It may be that this awful deed you contemplate would, if executed, add but another item to a fearful record of crime; but, God of Heaven! what should make me so wicked? Wherefore should I connive at a deed proscribed alike by God and man? Jacob Gray, I am weak and you are strong; I am defenceless and you armed; but as there is a Heaven above us, I will dare all—risk all to prevent this contemplated murder!"

"You are wild—mad," said Gray, in a low tone, which, from its bitterness, was evidently one of intense rage likewise. "The fear of death has hitherto acted upon your mind—let it so act still."

"It was a sufficient motive," replied Ada, "when I personally was concerned, and had to choose between captivity with hope, and death which would extinguish all but Heaven's mercy hereafter. But now, Jacob Gray, I cannot, will not perchase life for myself at the price of death to a fellow-creature."

"You will not?"

"No; I will not: not if he, whose life you seek, were the veriest wretch on earth—were he even such as you are, Jacob Gray, I would leave him to his God."

" You rave, girl—you rave."

" No, I do not rave—'tis you that with a hollow, hideous sophistry delude yourself."

" Your consent or non-consent is of little moment," said Gray ; " I hold both your life and his in my hands."

" Then you shall take mine first, for I am sickened at such villany, and would rather be its victim than its spectator. From this moment, Jacob Gray, no bond, no promise binds me to you. Take but one decisive step to commit the murder you contemplate, and this place shall echo with my cries."

Gray was evidently unprepared for the dilemma into which he had now brought himself, and he knew not what to say for some moments, during which he glared upon Ada with a fiendish expression of his eyes, which she could just discern in the dim light of the cellar, that was more worthy of some malignant demon than anything human.

" You ask me to sacrifice myself ?" he at length said.

" No, I ask no such thing," replied Ada ; " allow me to ascend from this place and see the man you say waits above. Friend or foe, I will risk the encounter, and I will not betray you."

" No, no," said Gray ; " not yet, not yet, Ada ; I cannot part with you yet. Moreover, there would still be danger—great danger. I cannot do as you wish."

" Then you shall incur a greater risk, or commit two murders."

" Hush, hush," said Gray ; " you speak too loud. Let me think again ; I will spare him if I can."

Jacob Gray remained in deep thought for about ten minutes ; then, as he came to some conclusion satisfactory to him, a dark and singular contortion of the features crossed his face, and his hand was thrust into the breast of his clothing, where he had a loaded pistol, upon which he well knew he could depend in any sudden emergency.

" Ada," he said, " I am resolved."

" Resolved on what ?"

" To take this man's life, who is here for the express purpose of taking mine if he can find the opportunity."

" Then I am resolved," said Ada, " to raise a voice of warning to that man, be he whom he may. If this is to be my last hour, Heaven receive me !"

" You shall die," said Gray.

Ada sunk on her knees, and covering her face within her hands, she said,—

" Jacob Gray, if Heaven permits you to murder me, I will not shrink. May God forgive you the awful crime !"

Gray laughed a bitter, short laugh, as he said,—

" No, Ada, you may live. I do not intend to kill you. Possibly, too, I may spare him who keeps watch above for me. Be patient while I go and reconnoitre."

" No, no," cried Ada, " I cannot be patient here ; you are going to murder."

" Listen to me," said Gray. " There is one more chance. After night-fall we will endeavour to leave the house. If we succeed in doing so unobstructed, all may be well ; but if opposition be offered, I must defend myself. You surely cannot deny me that privilege, Ada ?"

" Jacob Gray, you have not the courage to pursue such a plan," said Ada.

" Girl, are you bent on your own destruction ?" cried Gray.

" No ; but I know your nature well. The plan you propose is opposite to your usual manner of acting. A darker scheme possesses you, of which the one you have now proposed is but the cloak."

" I waste time upon you," said Gray, advancing towards the ladder.

He slowly and cautiously ascended, and then paused at the top step.

Ada bent all her attention to listen if any sound came from the room above, for she was quite resolved, let the consequences to her be what they might, to raise a cry of alarm, should Gray show any decided symptoms of carrying out his project of murdering the man in the house.

The few moments that succeeded were intensely agonising to Ada, and her heart beat painfully and rapidly as she kept her eye intently fixed upon the dusky form of Jacob Gray, as it was dimly discernible at the top of the ladder. This state of suspense did not last long, for in a very few minutes the shrill whistling of Elias awakened the echoes of the old mansion, and it was evident that he was in the room from which the panel conducting to the cellar opened.

Ada strained her eyes upwards, but still all was darkness. She knew that if Gray were to remove the panel ever so slightly she must be aware of it, by a ray of light streaming through the aperture; for that ray of light Ada waited, as her signal to raise an alarm, which she was determined to do.

Little, however, did Ada suspect that Gray had formed a plan which her very effort to save the man or watch would assist to carry into effect. Such, however, was the fact. Gray fully expected, and was quite prepared for a cry from Ada, whenever he should draw aside the panel.

The loud whistling of Elias still continued, when suddenly Gray moved the panel just sufficiently to allow Ada to see from below that he had done so, and then, as he had done once before, he slid down the ladder, and, as Ada thought, disappeared in the darkness which shrouded the further extremity of the cellar. Had she felt inclined Ada could not have stopped herself from uttering a cry, and the instant she saw daylight through the panel, her voice rose clear and loud—

"Help—help!" she cried "Help—murder!"

Mr. Elias's whistling immediately ceased, although he was in the middle of a very intricate passage, and he sprung to the opening in the wall.

With one effort he tore down the piece of wainscoting and cried in a loud voice,—

"Hilloa!"

Ada made a rush to the ladder, but an arm suddenly arrested her progress with such violence that she fell to the ground with great force.

Ada lay for a moment or two stunned by her fall, and she heard only indistinctly the voice of Elias cry,—

"Hilloa! below there. Oh, here's a ladder, is there? Well, that's what I call providential."

Elias was upon the ladder, and cautiously descending backwards, when [Ada shrieked,—

"Beware!—treachery!"

Elias paused a moment. Then there was a bright flash, a loud report, and a heavy fall, all of which were succeeded by a silence as awful and profound as that of the grave. Ada rose partially from the floor, and a dreadful consciousness of what had occurred came across her mind.

"Jacob Gray," she said, "you are a murderer—a murderer."

"I—I was compelled to do the deed," said Gray, in a low hoarse voice. "Come away—come away, Ada. Let us fly from hence—come away."

"Not with you, man of blood," cried Ada. "God sees this deed. Murderer, I cannot go with you."

"'Twas my life or his," said Gray, creeping out from behind the ladder, where he had been crouching, and through the spokes of which he had shot Elias as he descended with a certainty of effect.

"No—no. Such was not the fact." cried Ada.

"I care not," said Gray, throwing off his low cautious tone, and assuming a high shrill accent of anger; "I care not. Place what construction you will upon me, or my actions, you shall come with me now, or remain here to starve. Refuse to accompany me, and I will remove the ladder and leave you here with the dead."

Ada shuddered.

"Whither—oh whither would you lead me?" she said.

"To some other place of refuge for a short time, until my purposes are completed. Be quick, girl, do you stay or go?"

"It may be death to go," said Ada, "but it is suicide to stay."

"You consent?"

"I am in the hand of Providence. To it I commit myself. I will follow you."

"Quick, quick!" cried Gray, and he ascended the ladder with nervous trepidation, followed slowly by the afflicted and terrified Ada. The evening was fast approaching as they gained the room above, and Jacob Gray, seizing Ada by the wrist, led her to the outer door of the old house in which they had lived so long

He turned upon the threshold, and holding up his hand, cried,—

"My curse be upon this habitation. Had I the means at hand—yet stay one moment, Ada."

He knelt on the step, and struck a light with materials he always carried about him.

Dragging Ada again into the house, he opened the door of a room on the ground floor, on which was a quantity of littered straw and baskets. Throwing the light among the inflammable material, he ground through his set teeth,— ;

No. 26

"Burn, burn! and may not one brick stand upon another of this hateful place."
He then dragged Ada from the house, and took his course along the fields at a
rapid pace.

CHAPTER L.

THE RUIN AT NIGHT.—THE FIRE.—GRAY'S BEHAVIOUR.—A CHALLENGE.—OLD
WESTMINSTER AGAIN.

ADA made no remark upon these proceedings of Jacob Gray. She had made up
her mind to a particular course of action. She had wound up her feelings and her
courage to a certain pitch, and she resolved not to say another word to Jacob
Gray, until she had an opportunity of acting, as she had now considered it her
sacred duty to act.

Gray himself seemed suspicious and annoyed at her pertinacious silence, and he
addressed her in a fawning, trembling voice, as if he would fain restore her to her
usual confidence in addressing him. The calm of Ada's manner alarmed him. He
would ten times rather she had spoken to him in terms of reproach and abhorrence;
but now that she said nothing, he trembled for what might be the nature of her
thoughts regarding him.

"Ada," he said, as he crept along by her side, or rather one pace before her
towards the inner side. "Ada, all that I have often pictured to you of riches and
honour shall soon be yours. You will enjoy all that your young and ardent
imagination can hope for; but there are some few things yet to be done ere I can
place you in such a position as would make you the envy of all."

These few things, in Jacob Gray's mind, consisted in efficient preparations for
his own departure from England; the secreting of his confession, and the extortion
of a yet further sum of money from the fears of Learmont.

"You do not hear me, Ada," as she made no reply.

The young girl shuddered, and shrank from him as far as he would permit.

"You shrink from me now," said Gray, "and yet I am the only person who
can and will place you in a position to enjoy every pleasure—to gratify every taste.
Ada, you will be much beholden now to Jacob Gray."

Still Ada would not speak, and they were rapidly nearing some stairs, at
which plied wherries between Battersea and Westminster. Gray now looked
cautiously around him, and being quite satisfied that no one was within hearing,
he stooped his mouth close to Ada's ear, and said, in a voice of suppressed yet
violent passion,—

"Girl, I am a desperate man. Do not tempt me beyond what I can resist
to do a deed which I fain would not do. Hear me, Ada—I swear to have
your life if you play me false. Be obedient to what I shall command, and all
will be well; but have a care—have a care, for I am desperate, and you know
what I can do."

Jacob Gray then walked on in silence until he reached the stairs, at which there
was no one but a boy, who immediately cried to him,—

"Boat, your honour—going across, sir?"

"Yes," said Gray.

The boy ran into the water to steady the boat while Gray handed in Ada, who
submitted passively. Then he stepped on board himself, and the boy, clambering
in after him, pushed the boat out into the stream.

"Where to, your honour?" said the boy, as he settled the sculls in the rollocks,
and gave a sweep that turned the boat's head from the shore.

"To the stairs at Westminster-bridge," said Gray.

The boy nodded, and the boat, under his good management, was soon gliding up the stream in the wished-for direction.

The sun was now rapidly sinking, and tall dark shadows lay upon the surface of the Thames, making the waters look as if they were composed of different kinds of fluids of varying colours and densities. Then the last edge of the sun's disc, which had been reposing on the horizon for a moment, suddenly disappeared, and a cold wind on the instant swept across the face of the river, curling it up into small wrinkles, and giving a gentle, undulating motion to the boat.

Not a word was spoken, and the small wherry might have been occupied by the dead, for all the signs of life or animation given by Gray or Ada.

That Gray's thoughts partook of the apprehensive might have been guessed by the nervous manner in which he clutched the side of the boat, and the distracted movement of the fingers of his other hand with which he held the collar of his cloak across the lower part of his face.

Ada was pale as a marble statue ; but there was an intellectuality and determination about her small, compressed lips and commanding brow, that would have won admiration from all, and enraptured a poet or a painter. She sat calm and still. There was no nervousness, no trembling, no alarm ; and it was the absence of all those natural and feminine feelings which cast a cold chill to the heart of Jacob Gray, and filled him with a terror of he knew not what.

He could not for more than one instant of time keep his eyes off Ada's face. There was a something depicted there that while he dreaded, he seemed, by some supernatural power, compelled to look upon. Like one fascinated by the basilisk eye of a serpent, he could not withdraw his gaze ; although pale, firm, and slightly tinged with a death-like hue by the strange colours that lingered in the sky from the sunset, that young and lovely face brought to his recollection one which the mere thought of was an agony, and the name of whom was engraven upon his heart in undying letters of eternal flame.

The fresh breeze caught as it passed the long glossy ringlets of Ada's hair, and blew them in wanton playfulness across her face, but still she moved not. The night darkened, and the shadows of the buildings and shipping crossed her eyes, but she stirred not. Her whole soul, with all its varied perceptions and powers seemed to be engrossed by some one great idea that would admit of no sort of companionship, and for the time reigned alone within the chambers of her brain.

Suddenly now the boy let his oars rest in the water, and the boat no longer urged forward, moved but sluggishly. H.s eyes seemed to be fixed on something. Now he lifted one hand and shaded them, while he looked earnestly in the direction from whence he had been coming.

Gray for a moment did not seem conscious that the boat was making no progress, but in fact slowly turning broadside to the stream, and Ada, if she did notice it, preserved her silence and calmness, for she neither moved nor spoke.

"Master," cried the boy, suddenly, and Gray started as if he had been suddenly aroused by a trumpet at his ear.

"What—a—what?" he cried. "Who spoke?"

"I spoke, sir," said the boy. "There's a famous fire out Battersea way."

"A fire?" said Gray.

"Yes," said the boy, and he pointed with his finger in the direction from whence they came. "It's a large fire ; now it does burn, to be sure. Look, sir, there!"

Gray turned half round upon his seat in the boat, and he saw that the heavens were illuminated with a dull, red glare in the direction to which the boy had pointed, and in that one particular spot there was a concentrated body of light from whence shot up in the sky myriads of bright sparks, and now and then a long tongue of flame which lit up the house, the shipping, and the river, with a bright and transitory glow.

"It is—the house," muttered Gray to himself; "my work prospers. Sir Frederick Hartleton, I have but one more wish, and that is, that your flesh was broiling in yon house along with your myrmidon whom you left to his fate."

"It's a large fire," remarked the boy. "A famous fire."

"Yes," said Gray, "a famous fire; can you tell where it is?"

"I think," said the boy, "it lies somewhere over the marshes."

"Indeed."

"Yes; and I should say it was Forest's old haunted house, only nobody lives there but the ghosts."

"Forest's house," repeated Gray, in an assumed careless tone. "Indeed I should not wonder if you were right."

"I hope it is," said the boy. "It was an old miserable-looking place. You've heard about it, sir?"

"A little—a little," replied Gray.

"There was a murder there once," said the boy.

"Yes,—yes, I—know," said Gray.

"Forest, you see, sir, lived in the house. He built it, you see, sir, and he wasn't content with what he had, so he murdered a poor fellow, who they say had a thousand pounds belonging to somebody who employed him to collect rents, you see, sir."

"Yes," said Gray, licking his lips.

"Well, sir, Forest shot him."

"Shot him? oh, yes. He—he shot him."

"He was hung, though," added the boy, "and well he deserved it, too. My grandfather saw him hung on the common, not a hundred feet from his own door. After that no one would live in the house, and, in course, old Forest's ghost, and the man's ghot, that he killed, took to being there. Well, it does flare now famously."

The fire seemed now at its height, for the flames rose to a tremendous height into the sky, and the roaring and crackling of the timbers could be distinctly heard, even at that distance from the spot of the conflagration.

Now and then a loud sound, resembling the discharge of artillery at a distance, would come booming through the air, indicative of the fall of some heavy part of the ancient building, and then the flame would be smothered for a moment, and dense volumes of smoke terrifically red from the glare beneath, would roll over the sky, to be succeeded again by myriads of sparks, which would, in their turns, give place to the long tongues of flame which shot up from the fallen mass, as it became more thoroughly ignited.

Jacob Gray gazed intently on the scene for a few minutes, then turning to the boy, he cried,—

"We are in haste."

The lad resumed his oars, and struck them lazily into the glowing stream, that looked like liquid fire from the bright reflection of the sky, and once more the boat was making way towards Westminster.

Several times Gray glanced in the face of Ada, to note what effect the burning of the old house had upon her imagination, but not a muscle moved—all was as still and calm as before, and save that the reflection from the reddened sky now cast a glow of more than earthly beauty over her otherwise pale face, to look at her, she might have been supposed some thing of Heaven, summoned by the small casualties and petty commotions of this world, which she had but visited for a brief space, for some specific purpose.

The boat glided on, and so intent was the boy upon the fire, that he had several narrow escapes of running foul of barges and other wherries, some of the latter of which were pulling down the stream on purpose to look at the fire, which was causing a great deal of comment and commotion among the gossips of ancient Westminster.

Many were the oaths levelled on the head of the boy, by parties who were obliged to ship their oars suddenly, to avoid a collision with his boat, and it was not until this had happened thrice, that he began to be a little more careful, and ook warily about him.

The stairs to which Gray directed the boy, were through the bridge, and the boat now reached the ancient structure, which looked beautiful and brilliant from the reflection of the fire upon its many rough stones and jagged points of architecture.

A wherry, in which sat one person besides the rower, now came rapidly from under the same arch of the bridge, through which the boat containing Ada and Gray, was about to proceed.

"Hilloa!" cried the man, who was sitting in the boat, "hilloa there!"

"Well, what now?" said the boy.

"None of your impertinence, youngster," cried the man, showing a constable's staff, which Ada knew no more the meaning of, than if he had unfurled the banner of Mahomet.

"Well, sir," said the boy, "I only want to land my passengers.

"You may land your passengers, and be d—d," replied the man in authority.

"Thank you kindly, sir," replied the boy, promptly.

The rower in the other boat laughed at this, and the constable cried,—

"Come, come, none of this. How far have you pulled up the river, boy?"

"From Battersea."

"Oh, hem! From Battersea?"

"I told you so."

"Come, come, young fellow—no insolence. Where's the fire?"

"I can't say exactly."

"Where do you think it is? You say you have pulled up from Battersea, and the fire is at Battersea, we know."

"I think it's at old Forest's haunted house," said the boy.

"D—d if I didn't think so," cried the officer, who was no other than our old friend Stephy; "I must go and see, though, notwithstanding. Pull away, my man."

The wherries shot past each other, and in a few moments more, Ada and Gray stood on the top of the flight of stone steps conducting from the river to Bridge-street.

CHAPTER LI.

THE ALCOVE ON THE BRIDGE.—GRAY'S SPEECH TO ADA.—THE FLIGHT.—
THE HUNT.—THE LAST REFUGE.

LONDON was not so thronged with passengers at the period of our tale as it is now, and Gray stood with Ada several moments at the corner of Westminster-bridge, without more than three persons passing, and those at intervals apart from each other.

Gray appeared to be in deep thought during this time, and then taking Ada by the arm, he said in a trembling voice,—

"This way, this way," and led her to the bridge.

Ada made no resistance, but suffered herself to be conducted into one of the little alcoves which now exist. Then, after a pause, Jacob Gray spoke to her in a low, earnest tone, to the following purport :—

"Ada, the time is now fast approaching when you will be free—free in action as in thought, and with the means of giving to every thought, however wayward or expensive, the immediate aspect of reality. You will be guided implicitly by me, Ada, for the space of about one month, and no longer—then all that I promise will be fulfilled, and you will be happy. You may then forget Jacob Gray, for you will see him no more. In another country I will spend the remainder of my life. What I am about to do now is, to seek in the very heart of this populous city, a temporary abode for you and myself. I am tired of solitudes and lonely places. Ada, you must for that brief month assume in all appearance, the character of my daughter."

Ada shuddered, and shrank back as far as she possibly could into the alcove, for Gray, in the earnestness of his discourse, had brought his face in very close proximity to hers.

"For your own sake, as well as for mine," he continued, " you must pass as a child of mine. When I am gone, you may repudiate the relationship as quickly as you may think proper."

Jacob Gray then paused as if awaiting the answer of Ada, but to his great surprise and aggravation, she preserved the same unbroken silence which she had dictated to herself since the murder at the lone house.

"You will not answer me," said Gray, with bitterness. " Well, be it so. Let no words pass between us. I can construe your silence—you feel that you must obey me, and yet you cannot bring your nature to give me one word of acquiescence. 'Tis as well, Ada—'tis as well. Our conversations have never been so satisfactory, that I should wish to urge their continuance. You may preserve your silence, but you must obey me. Before this time I have been placed in desperate straits, and have reflected upon desperate remedies. Now, Ada, remember that if you betray me, or even leave me, until the time I shall please to appoint, you shall die. Remember, young, beautiful as you are, you shall die."

Again Gray paused with the hope that Ada would speak, for although he affected to despise it, the silence of the young girl was an annoyance to him of the first magnitude.

His hope, however, was futile. She spoke not.

"Come, follow me," cried Gray, suddenly. " Here, place your arm in mine."

He attempted to draw her arm within his as he spoke, but Ada drew back so firmly and resolutely, that Gray saw she would not walk with him in such apparent amity.

"As you please," he said, " so that you follow me. Come on—come on."

Ada stepped from the alcove on to the bridge, and then Gray paused a moment to see if he was observed, and being satisfied that he was not, he drew aside the collar of his cloak and showed Ada the bright barrel of a pistol, to which he pointed, saying,—

"Remember—death, sudden, painful, and violent on the one hand, and on the other, after a short month, unbounded wealth, enjoyment, and delight. Come on —come on."

Side by side, the ill-assorted pair walked in the direction of Parliament-street, it being Gray's intention to pass through Westminster, and proceed towards the densely populated district north of the Strand, there to seek for a temporary lodging in which he and Ada as his daughter, could remain until he had perfected his arrangements for his own escape, and the utter destruction of Learmont and Britton.

Gray had calculated his chances and position well. He stood as free as ever from any attempt against his life by Learmont or the savage smith. Ada, even if she should suddenly leave him, scarcely knew enough to be thoroughly dangerous. Sir Francis Hartleton had but an indistinct knowledge of his person, and even should he meet him in the public streets, he could hardly hit upon him as being the man who had merely flashed across his eyes for a moment. Besides, it was possible to make sufficient alterations in his personal appearance to deceive those who were not very well acquainted with his general aspect and appearance. Then he need not go from home above four times, perhaps, in that whole month, even provided he remained so long in London, and on those occasions it would only be to creep cautiously from his own place of abode to Learmont's house and back again, so that the risk would be but small of meeting the magistrate or Albert Seyton, who were the only two persons at all interested in his capture.

His threats to Ada that he would take her life upon any attempt of hers to escape, were perfectly insincere. To Ada and her existence he clung as to his only hope of mercy, if by some untoward circumstance he should be taken, as well as for his only means of being thoroughly and entirely revenged upon Learmont.

Upon the whole, then, Jacob Gray, as he walked down Parliament-street, in the dim, uncertain light from the oil lamps of the period, and saw that Ada followed him slowly, rather congratulated himself upon his extreme cunning and the good position for working out all his darling projects, both of avarice and revenge, in which he was placed.

" There is an old proverb," he muttered, " which says, ' the nearer to church, the further from Heaven,' and I have read somewhere a fable of a hunted hare finding a secure, because an unsuspected, place of refuge in a dog-kennel. Upon that principal will I secrete myself for one short month in some place densely inhabited ; where two persons make but an insignificant item in the great mass that surrounds them, will I seek security, and then my revenge—my deep revenge !"

But few passengers were in Parliament-street ; the quantity of persons, however, sensibly increased as they approached Whitehall, and from Charing-cross the lights were just glancing when Ada suddenly paused, and Gray, on the impulse of the moment, got two or three paces in advance of her. There were two persons conversing, about where Scotland-yard stands, and laughing carelessly, while several more people were rapidly approaching from Charing-cross.

Gray was sensible in a moment that Ada had stopped, and he hurried immediately to see what were her intentions.

As he did so, Ada broke the long silence she had maintained by suddenly exclaiming, in a voice that arrested every passenger, and made the blood retreat with a frightful gush to the heart of Jacob Gray.

" Help ! help ! Seize him. He is a murderer—a murderer !—help ! help ! Seize the murderer !"

For one moment all sense of perception seemed to have left Gray, so thoroughly unexpected was such an act on the part of Ada, and it was well for him that those who were around for about the same space of time remained in a similar undecided and bewildered state, as people do always on any very sudden occasion for instant action.

Ada stood pointing with one trembling finger at Gray, while her pale face and long black hair, combined with her rare beauty, made her look like one inspired.

" The murderer !" she again cried, and her voice seemed to break the spell which kept both Gray and the chance passengers paralysed.

With a cry of terror, Jacob Gray turned and fled towards Charing-cross.

Ada's feelings had been wrought up to too high a pitch of excitement. She had felt it to be her duty to denounce the murderer, and while that duty remained to be done, the consciousness that upon her it devolved, had nerved her to the task, and supported her hitherto—now, however, the words were spoken. At what she supposed the risk of her life, she had announced the crime of Jacob Gray. The revulsion of feeling was too much, and a bystander, who saw her stagger, was just in time to catch her as she fainted, and would otherwise have fallen to the ground.

The two persons who had been talking and laughing together at the moment of Ada's first exclamation, did not seem disposed to let the accused man get off so easily as he appeared upon the point of doing. They raised the cry so awful in the ear of a fugitive through the streets of London, " Stop him ! stop him !" and they both started after Jacob Gray at full speed.

Had Gray, when he turned the corner of Northumberland-house, then walked quietly, like an ordinary passenger, the chances were that he would have escaped ; but, in his terror, he flew rather than ran up the Strand, at once pointing himself out to all as the one pursued, and tempting every person who had time or inclination to join the exciting chase.

The words, " Stop him !" sounded in his ears, and he bounded forward as he heard them, with another cry and a speed that, while it made it very hazardous for every one to oppose him, yet increased the ardour of the pursuit.

In the course of a few seconds, fifty persons had joined the chase, and yells and shouts came upon Gray's affrighted ears.

With compressed lips and a face as livid as that of a corpse, he rushed on without the smallest idea of where he was going.

"For my life—for my life," he gasped, and each cry behind him affected him like a shock of electricity, and caused him to give another bound forward in all the wildness of despair.

Of the crowd now that followed Gray, not one knew who he was, of what he was accused, or why he was thus hunted, like a wild animal, through the streets. One joined in the cry because he saw others engaged in it. The two young men who had first raised the chase were a long way off, for no one could keep up with the frantic speed of the nearly maddened Gray. Those who followed him the closest were those who had joined the hunt *en route;* although, to the fugitive's excited imagination, he seemed to be on the point of being overtaken by harder runners than himself.

Shouts, cries, hootings, groans, and every wild and demoniac noise of which the human animal is capable, were uttered by the mob, which kept momentarily increasing as each alley, court, or street, sent forth its tribute of numbers to the stream that roared, whooped, hurraed, and raced along the Strand.

Some began now to throw missiles of all kinds after Gray. Stones and mud showered upon him, and he felt faint and nearly exhausted, as he saw at some distance before him a man apparently intent upon stopping him.

Little, however, did he who thought to capture Gray reflect upon the shock he would receive from the speed of the hunted man. As Gray approached him he swerved, more involuntarily than designedly, and coming against the man rather obliquely, he shot him into the roadway with an impetus that sent him rolling over and over in the mud, as if he had been discharged from a cannon. To Gray the shock was severe, but it did not take him off his feet, and the circumstance caused some little diversion in his favour than otherwise; for the mob first trampled upon the prostrate man, and then some fell over him.

After this, none were so bold as to stand in the way of a man who was rushing along with so terrible a speed; and Jacob Gray, reeling, panting, his lips running with blood, as he had bitten them in his agony, arrived at Somerset-house.

Just beyond the stone front was a small court, and towards this temporary place of refuge from the high street Gray tottered, spinning round and round like a drunken man.

A light, agile man, who had joined the chase by the Adelphi, and who had kept very close upon Gray, now, with a shout of triumph, made a rush forward, and grappled with him at the mouth of the little court.

The touch seemed like magic to revive all the fainting energies of Jacob Gray, and he turned and grappled his enemy by the throat with fearful vehemence.

The court descended from the street by a flight of stone steps, and in the next instant with a shriek from the man, and a wild cry from Gray, the pursuer and pursued rolled down the stone descent, struggling with each other for life or death.

CHAPTER LII.

THE DARK COURT.—A DEED OF BLOOD.—THE PURSUIT CONTINUED.—THE MOTHER AND THE CHILD.

BRUISED and bleeding, Gray and the adventurous stranger who had essayed to capture him, arrived at the bottom of the flight of stone steps, and for one or two seconds it was doubtful if either of them were in a condition to make any further effort either offensive or defensive.

The fear of capture and death, however, was sufficiently strong in the mind of Jacob Gray to overcome for the moment the sense of pain arising from personal injury; and with an energy, lent to him by despair alone, he rose on his knees and felt about for his antagonist. His hand touched the man's face, and now he began to move. With something between a shriek and a shout, Gray laid hold of his head by the hair on each side. He lifted it as far as he could from the stones and then brought it down again with a sinking awful crash. One deep

hollow groan only came from the man, and again Gray lifted the head, bringing it down as before with frightful violence. The skull cracked and smashed against the hard stones. The man was dead, but once more was the bleeding and crashed head brought into violent contact with the stones, and that time the sound it produced was soft, and Jacob Gray felt that he held but loose pieces of bone, and his hands were slimy and slippery with the blood that spouted on to them.

Faltering, dizzy, and faint, he then rose to his feet, and from the open thoroughfare there came to his ears shouts, cries, and groans. Then he cast his eyes to the dim opening of the court, and he heard several voices cry,—

"He is hiding down here. Let's hunt him out. Lights—lights !"

In a state of agony beyond description Gray now turned to seek shelter further down the dark court, and in doing so he trod upon the dead body of the man he had just hurried from existence.

Recoiling then, as if a serpent had been in his path, he crept along by the wall until he thought he must have passed the awful and revolting object which now in death he dreaded quite as much as he did in life.

He then plunged wildly forward heedless where his steps might lead, so that it was away from his pursuers. A few paces now in advance of him he descried a dim faint ray of light, and hastening onwards he found himself at the entrance of a court running parallel with the Strand, and consisting of mean, dirty, squalid-looking houses inhabited apparently by the very dregs of the poorer classes.

Some of the half-broken dirty parlour windows in this haunt of poverty were converted into shops by being set open, and a board placed across in the inside displaying disgusting messes in the shape of eatables, mingled with wood, old bones, rags, &c.

Gray hesitated a moment and cast his eyes behind him. A loud yell met his affrighted ears, and lights began to flash in the direction he had left behind him. With a groan of despair, he rushed into the dark open passage of one of the houses.

Breathing hard from his exertions and the fright he was in, Gray groped his way along by the damp clammy walls of the passage until he came to some stairs—he hesitated not a moment, but slowly and cautiously ascended them.

As he crept stair after stair up the dark flight of steps the sound of pursuit seemed to come nearer and nearer, and he could hear the hum of many voices, although he could not distinguish exactly what was said. Only one word came perpetually as clearly and distinctly to his ears as if it had been spoken at his side, and that word was murder !

"They—they have found the body," he gasped. "Yes, they have found the body now. My life hangs on a thread."

The cold perspiration of fear rolled down his face, and notwithstanding his great exertions which would ordinarily have produced an intolerable sense of heat, he was as cold and chilled as if he had suddenly awakened from sleep in the open air. His teeth chattered in his head, and his knees smote each other. He was fain to clutch with both hands the crazy banisters of the staircase for support, or he must inevitably have fallen.

"This is dreadful," he whispered to himself, "to die here. They have hunted me to death—I—I feel as if a hand of ice was on my heart. This must be death."

Slowly the cold sensation wore off, and like the flame of a taper, which suddenly renews its origin most unexpectedly, when apparently upon the point of dissolution, Gray gradually revived again, and his vital energies came back to him.

With a deep sigh he spoke,—

" 'Tis past—'tis past. They have not killed me as yet. It was, after all, but a passing pang. They have not killed me yet."

Again the cry of murder echoed in the court, and, with a start, Jacob Gray set his teeth hard, and continued to ascend the dark staircase. Suddenly, now, he paused, for a sound from above met his ears—it was some one singing. How strangely the tones jarred upon the excited senses of Jacob Gray : the sound was low and plaintive, and to him it seemed a mockery of his awful situation.

He now by two more steps gained the landing, and he was sure that the singing proceeded from some room on that floor. The voice was a female's, and by the softness and exquisite cadences of it evidently proceeded from some person not far advanced in life.

Gray held by the banisters at the top of the stairs, and for some minutes he seemed spell-bound, and to forget the precarious situation in which he stood as those low, soft strains came upon his ear.

The female was evidently singing to a child, for occasionally she would pause to express some words of endearment to the little one, and then resume her song.

The few short lines of which the song was composed came fully to Gray, and there was a something about their very simplicity and innocence that rooted him to the spot, although they brought agony to his heart.

THE MOTHER'S CHOICE.

My babe, if I had offers three,
  From gentle heavenly powers,
To bless thee, who, with aching heart,
  I've watched so many hours,
I'd choose that gift should make thee great
  In true nobility—
That greatness of the soul which leaves
  The heart and conscience free.
Gold should not tempt me, gentle babe,
  It might not bring thee rest;
Nor power would I give to thee,
  'Tis but an aching breast.
But I would ask of Heaven, my babe,
  A boon of joy to thee,
To make thee happy in this life,
  From sin and sorrow free.
Nor gold nor silver should'st thou have,
  Nor power to command,
But thou should'st have a guileless heart,
  An open, unstained hand.
So should thou happy be, my babe,
  A thing of joy and light;
While others struggled for despair,
  You'd wish but to be right.

The song abruptly ceased, for the loud tones of men reached the ears of the singer, crying,—

"Murder!—hunt him—secure the murderer! This way—this way!"

Those sounds roused Gray from his temporary inaction : he started forward as if he had received some sudden and irresistible shock.

More from impulse than any direct design or preconcerted plan, Jacob Gray made towards the door of the room in which was the mother and her infant child.

At the moment, then, a sudden thought struck his mind that possibly he might convert the affection of the mother for her infant into a means of saving himself: it was a hope, at all events, although a weak and forlorn one. Time, however, was precious, and Jacob Gray, with his pale, ghastly face, torn apparel, bleeding hands, and general dishevelled look, made his appearance in the room.

By the remains of a miserable fire sat a young female scarcely above the age o. girlhood, and in a cot at her feet slept a child, the face of which she was regarding with that rapt attention and concentrated love which can only be felt by a mother.

So entirely, in fact, were all the faculties of the young mother wound up in the contemplation of her sleeping child, that Gray's entrance into the room failed to arouse her, and he had time to glance around the room and be sure that he and the mother, with the child, were the only occupants of the place before he spoke.

He then drew the pistol he still retained from his breast, and suddenly cried,—

"One word, and it shall cost you your life! Be silent and obedient, and you are safe."

A cry escaped the lips of the young female, and she stood panic-stricken by Gray's strange appearance, as well as his threatening aspect and words.

"Listen to me," he said, in a low, hoarse voice; "you love your child?"

" Love my child ?" re-echoed the mother, in a tone that sufficiently answered the question of Gray, who added,—

" I am a desperate man.   I do not wish to do you harm ; but, betray me to those who are seeking my life, and your child shall die by my hands."

" No—no—my child—no," cried the mother, in a voice of alarm.

" Hush !" cried Gray, advancing, and pointing the muzzle of his pistol towards the sleeping form of the child.   " Such another outcry, and I will execute my threat."

The young mother stood paralysed with terror, while Gray hastily added,—

" I am hunted, I tell you.   Have you no place of concealment ?   Speak !"

" Concealment ?   Good Heaven ! how can I aid you ?   What have I done that you should menace my child ?   You cannot, dare not be so wicked.'

A loud shout at this moment rang through the court, and the flashing beams of several torches blazed through the murky windows of the miserable abode of poverty.

" What sounds are those ?" cried the female.

" My pursuers," said Gray.   " Now, hear me ; I dare not leave this place.   They are on my track—your infant is sleeping—place its cot as nigh to the wall as you can, and I will hide beneath it.   It this room is entered by my enemies, you must, on the plea of not disturbing your child, prevent a search from taking place."

" I cannot."

" You must—you shall !   Betray me by look, word, or gesture, and your child shall die, if the next moment were my last.   By all hell I swear it !"

The mother shuddered.

" Quick—quick !" cried Gray ; " my life is now counted by moments !"

" Hunt him—hunt him ! Hurrah !" cried the voices of the pursuers.   " Hunt the murderer !"

" You hear !" cried Gray.   " Quick—quick !"

With a face of agonised terror the mother drew the cot, without awakening the fastly-slumbering child, towards the wall.

" Now," cried Gray, " remember—your child's life is at stake : if I escape, it escapes.   If I am taken, it dies."

" But I may not be able to save you," said the mother, in imploring accents.

" The child then dies," said Gray.

" Guard the entrance to the court well," cried a loud, authoritative voice from the outside of the house.   " Search every one of these hovels, from top to bottom."

" You hear ?" said Gray, trembling with terror, and scarcely able to speak from the parched state of his lips.

" I do," she said.

" Give me some water."

She handed him a small earthen pitcher, from which he took a copious and refreshing draught.

" Now," he said, " sit you by the fire, and sing that song you were singing.   It will seem then as if you had been undisturbed, and remember you are playing a game in which the stake is the life of your child."

" Heaven aid me !" said the mother.

" Hush!   To your seat !—to your seat !"

" Oh! even be you what you may, I will do my best to save you, if you will allow me to sit here."

She pointed to the side of the cot.

" No, no," said Gray ; " the child shall be nearer to me than to you."

" Why—oh, why ?"

" Because it will then be out of your power to prevent its doom."

" I swear——"

" Pshaw ! I trust no oaths.   Away, to your seat—to your seat, or——"

He pointed the pistol again to the sleeping babe, and with a shudder the young mother sat down by the fire-side.

The tramp of men was now heard below in the passage, and a voice cried,—

"Detain any one who attempts to leave the house. Should you meet with resistance, cut him down at once."

"The song!" cried Gray.

He then insinuated himself between the wall and the cot, so that no part of him was visible, and in a hissing whisper, he again cried to the trembling agonised mother,—

"The song! the song!"

A confused sound on the staircase now announced the approach of the persons, and once more from his place of concealment, Gray hissed between his teeth,—

"Curses on you! Will you do as I bid you, or must I do the deed?"

"Spare him! spare him!" said the mother. "Oh, spare him!"

"The song!" cried Gray.

CHAPTER LIII.

A MOTHER'S CARE.—THE PURSUIT.—A SUCCESSFUL RUSE.—THE SECOND VISIT.

WITH a faltering voice the terrified female commenced the strain which Gray had overheard her singing to her child before it was placed in the fearful jeopardy she now considered it in.

The men's footsteps sounded on the staircase, as in trembling accents she softly repeated the words,—

"My babe, if I had offers three,
From gentle heavenly powers,
To bless thee, who with beating heart
I've watched so many hours ——"

There was then a slight pause—a knock from without—a broad glare of light, and Jacob Gray's pursuers were in the room.

The mother rose from her chair, and cried,—

"What do you mean?—what is the meaning of all this?"

"We are pursuing a man, who is hiding in one of these houses," replied a stern voice. "I am an officer. There has been murder done, my good woman."

"Murder!"

"Yes. A man has been savagely murdered at the bottom of the steps, and he who committed the deed is somewhere about here. Have you heard any alarm?"

"I have heard many voices."

"I mean have you heard any one on the stairs, or has any one been here?"

"I was singing to my child. Pray do not speak so loud, or you will awaken it."

"Search the room," cried the man.

The mother walked to the side of the cot, and appeared to be regarding the features of her sleeping babe, but she was in reality endeavouring to hide the expression of terror which she felt was upon her face.

The men raised the torches they carried high above their heads, and glanced round the miserable apartment.

"Open that cupboard," said one.

It was opened and then shut again.

"Move that cot," cried he who appeared to be in authority.

"No," cried the mother, suddenly looking up, "do your duty in discovering the criminal, but do not in doing it commit a needless act of cruelty."

"Cruelty!"

"Yes; you see my babe is sleeping. Why move his cot and awaken him? He has been ill.   The fever spot is still upon his cheek.   The quiet slumber he is now enjoying, is the first he has had for many weary nights and days.   How could a murderer hide with a sleeping child ?   Some of you perhaps have little ones of your own, if you have, you will think of them, and not harm mine."

" Was it you singing just now ?" asked the officer.

" It was.   My voice, I think, soothes him, even in sleep.   Hush ! do not speak so loud, or you will wake him."

" Leave her alone," said the officer.   " My good woman, we don't want to disturb your child.   We have our duty, however, to do ; but I am quite satisfied he whom we seek is not here."

" A mother's blessing be upon you, sir," said the woman.   " You have, perhaps, saved the very life of my child by not disturbing it."

" What, has it been so bad as that ?" remarked another.

" Oh, quite, quite !"

" The turn of a fever in those young things is always a ticklish affair," remarked another.

" Come on," said the officer, " come on.   We are sorry for disturbing you.   If any strange man should walk in here, be sure you give an immediate alarm."

" Yes, yes," gasped the young mother, scarcely yet believing that her infant was safe.

In a few moments more the room was clear of the men, and then the woman covered her face with her hands and burst into such a hysterical passion of weeping, that Gray was dreadfully alarmed lest it should be heard, and induce a return of his pursuers.

" Peace, woman—peace," he said, in a hoarse whisper, from his hiding-place. " I am not yet out of danger, nor is your child yet safe from my vengeance."

" Man, man !" cried the mother, " I have saved your life.   Be grateful and depart."

" Not yet—not yet," said Jacob Gray, slowly and cautiously emerging from his hiding-place, " not yet.   This place is now the safest I can remain in for some time, because it has been visited."

" You are wrong."

" I cannot be."

" I say you are wrong.   I have a husband, and when he returns, he may not be so weak as his wife."

Gray started, and replied in accents of fear,—

" When—when do you expect him ?"

" Even now—he may be here directly."

" I must go—I must go," said Gray.   " You are telling me the truth ?   I will give you gold if you hide me here for another hour."

" My compliance with your commands," said the woman, " arose from a higher motive than the love of gold.   Heaven knows we are poor—wretchedly poor, bu gold from your polluted hands would bring with it a curse, instead of a blessing."

" You reject a large sum for an hour's safety for me ?"

" I do."

" But your husband may better see his interest in this matter."

" No—my husband is poor, but he was not always so.   The feelings and the habits of a gentleman still cling to him in the sad reverse of fortune we are now enduring.   Go, wretched man, save yourself if you can, and ask mercy of Heaven for the crime I hear you have committed."

" That crime was in self-defence," said Gray ; " I will risk all, and remain here until this house has been searched."

" I cannot hinder you.   On your own head be the risk."

Gray stood near the door, listening attentively, and presently he heard descending footsteps, which from their number, he supposed rightly to be the officers returning from their unsuccessful search in the upper rooms of the house.

He drew his pistol from his breast, and pointing to the child, said in a whisper to the weeping mother,—

" One word as they pass, and I fire."

His horror may be conceived, but scarcely described, as the door at this moment was opened, pinning him against the wall behind it, and the officer who was conducting the search, put his head into the room, saying,—

"No alarm, I suppose ?"

"None," said the mother.

"Good night, ma'am. We have not got him yet, but he cannot escape. I hope your little one will get better."

"Thank you," she said, faintly.

The door close again, and the heavy tread of the men going down stairs sounded in the ears of Jacob Gray like a reprieve from immediate execution.

His state of mind while the officer was speaking, was of the most agonising description, as one step into the room of that personage, or one glance towards him of the young woman's eye, must have discovered him, and it would have been but a poor satisfaction even to such a mind as Jacob Gray's, to have taken the life of the infant, even if he had the nerve to do it, which he certainly had not, although a mother's fears would not permit her to run the risk.

"Tell me now," said Gray, when he could speak, for his fright had almost taken away his breath, "tell me who lives up stairs in this house ?"

"I know not," replied the woman, "I am but a stranger here."

"And—and you are sure your husband would not protect me ?"

"A murderer and the threatener of the life of his child can have little indeed to expect in the way of protection from my husband. Fly, wretched man, while yet you are free to do so."

"They have left the house," muttered Gray ; "will you betray me by an alarm, when I leave you ?"

"Let Heaven punish you in its own good time," replied the young female. "Base and guilty as you are, I will not have your blood upon my head."

"You will be silent ?"

"I will strive to forget you."

"Then I go, I—I think I am safer away, as you are sure your husband will not take a hundred gold pieces to protect and save me."

Gray glanced at the woman as he named the sum of money, to see what effect it had upon her, but there was nothing but a shudder of disgust, and he gave up all hope of purchasing safety from her.

Without another word, he cautiously opened the door, and listened. All was comparatively quiet, and he passed from the room.

In a moment he heard it locked behind him in the inside, and his place of refuge was at once cut off.

"Curses on her," he muttered. "She may have no husband coming after all. What can I do to free myself from the mazes of these courts ? Ada—Ada—if ever we meet again, I will have a deep—a bloody revenge on thee. Beware of Jacob Gray !"

He shook his clenched hand as he spoke, and ground his teeth with concentrated anger. The question now was, whether to ascend or descend in the house, and after some moments of anxious consideration, he thought his better chance would be to descend, and make an effort to pass himself as one of the crowd which had come from the Strand in pursuit of the murderer.

He wiped the blood, as he thought, well from his hands, and the dust and mud from his face ; then arranging his disordered apparel, he fancied he might pass muster without much suspicion, as be was confident none of those who followed him could have obtained more than a transitory glance at him.

He then carefully groped his way in the pitchy darkness to the top of the stairs and began slowly to descend.

It was many minutes before he reached the passage, and when he did so, he felt for the wall of the passage, and glided along it towards the open doorway.

As he neared it, he heard two persons conversing, and the theme of their conversation struck a chill to his heart.

"Yes, you may pass in," said a voice; "my orders are to let nobody out. We are hunting up a fellow who has committed a murder."

"Indeed!"

"Yes. If the people in the parlour here know you, you can pass."

"I live in the house," said the other speaker, "they will recognise me directly." Some little bustle now ensued, and a third voice inquired,—

"What's the matter?"

"Do you know this person?" said the person who was keeping guard,

"Oh, yes," was the reply, "he lives up stairs."

"Very well. Sorry to have detained you, sir."

"Never mind that; I hope you may catch the scoundrel."

Jacob Gray shrank as close to the wall as he could, and some one brushed quite against him in passing along the passage, without, however, noticing him, although the imminent danger almost made him faint upon the spot.

CHAPTER LIV.

THE STAIRCASE.—THE OLD ATTIC.—A FRIEND IN NEED.—FAIR PLAY.—GRAY'S DESPAIR.

FOR several moments now Gray stood in the passage quite incapable of thought or action; his only impulse was by a kind of natural instinct to stand as close to the damp passage wall as he possibly could, to decrease the chances of any one seeing him or touching him in the act of passing.

His brain seemed to be in a complete whirl, and many minutes must have elapsed before he acquired a sufficient calmness to reflect with any degree of rationality upon his present very precarious position.

When he could think, his terrors by no means decreased; for what plausible course of action was there now open to him, as he could not leave the house? The thought then occurred to him, that if he could make his way into the cellars, he might have a chance of lying concealed until the guard at the door was removed, and with this feeling he crept along the passage, with the hope of finding some staircase leading to the lower part of the premises.

He was still engaged in this task when the door of a room leading into the passage suddenly opened, and a flood of light immediately dissipated the pitchy darkness of the place.

Fortunately for him, Gray was within one pace of the bottom of the staircase he had so recently descended; and, with the fear of instant discovery upon his mind, from the person who was coming with the light, he bounded up the staircase, nor paused till he reached the first landing, from whence he had entered the room containing the mother and her child.

There he stopped; but, to his extreme fright, the flashing of the light evidently indicated that its bearer was coming up the stairs. With a stifled groan Gray cautiously ascended the next flight, and again paused on the narrow landing.

Still the light came on, and he could not conceal from himself the fact that the person was still ascending, and that he had no other resource than to continue his flight to the very upper part of the house. The next flight of stairs was steep, narrow, and crazy, so that, tread where he would, they wheezed, creaked, and groaned under the pressure of his feet.

There was, however, no resource, and onward he went, until he was stopped by a door exactly at the top; he pressed it, and it yielded to his touch, allowing him to enter a dark attic.

Further progress Jacob Gray felt there could not be, and he stood in the doorway, listening attentively if he could detect any sounds of approaching feet.

A gush of blood to his heart, and an universal tremor of all his limbs, seized him as he saw the light coming, and felt convinced that the destination of the person approaching was one of the attics, if not the very one he had sought refuge in. All hope apycared to die within him. There was no time for the briefest reflection. With his eyes fixed upon the door, and the pistol in his grasp, he

retreated backwards into the room as the footsteps came nearer and nearer to the door.

Then there was a slight pause; after which the door was flung open, and a tall, heavy, coarse-looking man entered the room, carrying in his hand a light.

One glance convinced Jacob Gray that the man was by far his superior in strength—his only chance lay in the loaded pistol he had, and that he was

No. 28.

resolved to use should he not be able to bribe the man to connive at his presence, and aid his escape.

It was a moment before the man observed the figure of Jacob Gray with his back to the wall opposite to the door, and the pistol in his grasp. When he did, he by no means betrayed the emotion that might have been expected; but shading the light with his disengaged hand, he cried in a loud voice,—

"Hilloa! Who are you when you are at home?"

"Do you love gold?" said Gray.

"Rather," replied the man.

"Will it tempt you to assist me to escape from this place? If so, name your price."

"That's business like," said the man. "I suppose it's you they are making all the rout about below there?"

"It is. They are hunting me, and, with your assistance, I may yet escape."

"The devil doubt it. Curse me if I don't actually love you. Why, I have been poking about for this half hour to do you a good turn."

"Is that possible?"

"To be sure. Why that fellow, whose crown you have cracked so handsomely below there, was the pest of all the cracksmen in the neighbourhood. I love you, I tell you."

"Then you are ——"

"Jem Batter, the cracksman."

"Then you will befriend me?"

"In course—though hang me if I know you. I thought I knew all the hands on town; but I never clapped eyes on your paste-pot of a mug before."

Gray replaced his pistol, as he assumed a sickly smile, and said,—

"Then I have really found a friend?"

"A friend! Ah, to be sure you have. I say, I'll tell you what we'll do. We'll wait till the enemy is gone, and then I'll poke you out on the roof, and you can get in at Bill Splasher's attic. It's only across a dozen houses or so. He'll let you out then by the cellars of Somerset House, and you'll be as safe as any gentleman need wish to be."

"I thank you," said Gray. "I am now faint and weary."

"Sit down then," cried the man. "Don't stand upon ceremony here. I suppose you've been at some fakement of value—eh?"

"Yes, yes—a robbery," said Gray, who thought it best to fall in with the humour of his new friend.

"Plenty o' swag?"

"A trifle, a mere trifle."

"Never mind, better luck next time," cried the man, dealing Gray an encouraging blow upon the back that nearly took his breath away.

"Thank you," said Gray.

The thief, for such indeed he was, now proceeded to a cupboard, and handed to Gray therefrom a bottle covered with protective wicker-work, saying,—

"Drink; you'll find that the best stuff."

Gray took a hearty draught of the contents, which consisted of exceedingly strong raw spirit.

"Don't you feel better?" said the man.

"Yes," replied Gray, "a great deal better."

"Very good. Now, you see, short reckonings make long friends."

"What do you mean?"

"Oh, you know the reg'lar terms of business. It's share and share alike with all who help a lame dog over a stile."

"I am quite willing," said Gray, "to award ——"

"Oh, bother award," interrupted the other; "I'm above it. Do you think I'd take anything but my rights of lending a hand to help a poor fellow when the bull dogs are on his track? No, sink me!"

"You are very kind," said Gray, "but still ——"

"Still, nonsense. There's you, me, and there will be Bill, and Bill's young woman—that'll make four of us. Share and share alike's the plan."

"Share?"

"Yes—the swag. Come, honour bright, now; produce it, will you?"

"Really, I—I ——"

"Do you doubt my honour?" cried the ruffian. "If you do, why don't you say so, you sneak? Take my life, but don't doubt my honour!"

Gray's hand mechanically moved towards his breast for his pistol, but before he could reach it the brawny hand of the man was upon his throat, and holding Gray as if he had been an infant in his herculean grasp, he himself took the pistol from him and put it in his own pocket, saying,—

"Thank you, I'll mind it for you."

"Let me go," gasped Gray.

"Then you don't doubt my honour?"

"No, no—certainly not."

"Oh, very well, I thought you didn't mean it."

Gray was then liberated from the grasp which came within one degree of suffocation, and he said,—

"I will be candid with you. I have forty pounds with me, which I will divide as you propose."

"Forty? Humph! it's d—d little; but I hate all grumbling. We can't have more than a cat and her skin, say I."

"No, certainly," said Gray. "I didn't understand you at first you see, or I should never have for a moment hesitated."

"Oh, it's all right—it's all right. Never say die, sink me."

"That'll be ten pounds each," remarked Gray, who really, as we know, had a very large sum about him—a sum so large indeed, as materially to have inconvenienced him in his race down the Strand.

"So it will," replied the man. "Now, you know the rules, my covey, as well as I do, I dare say?"

"What rules?"

"Why, you must strip and let me examine, for myself and Bill and Bill's young woman, all your togs, to see whether you haven't forgot a stray five pound note or so. No offence, my covey; but you know rules is rules all the world over, and fair play *is* a jewel o' very great lustre, my rum 'un."

CHAPTER LV.

THE ESCAPE OVER THE HOUSES.—MANY PERILS.—GRAY'S GREAT SUFFERINGS.—
THE GUIDE ROPE.

GRAY was silent for some moments, then, with a deep groan, he dropped his head upon his hands, and gave himself up to a bitterness of anguish that must have both alarmed and melted any heart but the stubborn one of the man who now had him in his power.

"All I have struggled for," thought Gray—"all that I have dipped my hands in blood for is about to be wrested from me for the mere doubtful boon of existence."

At that awful moment of misery he did indeed feel that he had chosen the wrong path in life, and the gaudy flowers which had lured him from the right road of virtue to the intricate one of crime and deep iniquity, were but delusion, and had vanished, now leaving him a wanderer in a region of dissolution and gaunt despair. Oh, what would he have not given in that awful moment, when busy memory conjured up all his crimes before him in frightful array, to have been the veriest beggar that ever crept for alms from door to door, so that he could have said, " I am innocent of great wrong—I have shed no man's blood !"

It might be that the evident mortal agony of Jacob Gray really had some effect even upon the hardened and obdurate heart of his companion, for it was several minutes before he spoke, and then when he did, his voice was scarcely so harshly tuned as before, and it is probable he meant to offer something very consolatory when he said,—

" Snivelling be bothered. I have cracked never so many cribs, and I never guved up to the enemy yet. Keep up your heart, old 'un, you'll light on your feet yet, like a cat as is shied out o' a attic window."

Gray only groaned and shook his head.

" Now, I tell you what I'll do for you," continued the man, " you shall go into partnership with me, and we'll do a lot o' work together. You've got a good sneaking sort o' face that'll gammon the flats. You can poke about and insinivate where family plate and such like things is kept, and then I'll go and crack the cribs. Don't be groaning here."

The robber then gave Gray another encouraging blow upon the back, which effectually prevented him from groaning for some minutes, by leaving him no breath to groan with. Gray then looked up, and, glancing in the face of the man, he said,—

" I will own to you that I have about me a larger sum than I at first named."

" I know'd it," cried the man, " I know'd—you white-mugged fellers always has larger sums than they names."

" In one word," said Gray, " I have two hundred pounds. Will you take one hundred and leave me at liberty to go from here when the ardour of pursuit has abated ?"

" Without the search?"

" Yes. Without the search. You talk of your honour—why not rely upon mine ?"

" Cos I'm a known gentleman, and you isn't," replied the fellow. " My word's respected all through the profession. If I say, I'll crack that crib, I goes and cracks it."

" Exactly. You will agree to my terms ?"

" Why, you see, I'm rather awkwardly sitivated just now. It isn't safe for you to go out by the way you came in. You may think it is, but I can tell you it isn't. The people down stairs have had a cool hundred offered for nabbing you, and aint they on the look-out ?"

" A hundred ?"

" Yes. You see that's all you offer me. Now there's Bill's attic to pay for, and Bill's young woman·"

Gray replied by a groan.

" There you go, now, groaning away. It's well for you that you've fell among people with fine feelings, and all that sort o' thing. Some folks now, as know'd as much as, I'm pretty sure, I know, would put a knife in your guts."

" What—what—do—you know ?" stammered Gray, shivering at the very idea of such a process.

" What do I know? Why, I know you are trying to deceive a gentleman. You've got more money then you'll own to, you know you have."

" You wrong me. Indeed you do."

" Well, well, I'll take Bill's opinion. He's better nor all the lawyers in London, is Bill. If he says as it's all right and we are to take the hundred only, I consents. Now, my covey, I'll trouble you to come with me to Bill's attic."

" But can we go without danger? The people down stairs, you say, are on the watch."

" Let 'em watch—we aint agoing down stairs. The window's the thing for us."

" Is it the next house ?"

" No, it isn't—nor the next arter that either—but it's all the safer for that. You've got a few roofs to get over, but I know 'em as well as I know my own pocket."

The man then opened the small lattieed window of the room and looked out for a moment. Then, with a satisfied tone, he said,—

" It's a regular dark night. There aint a shadow o' fear."

" You think I shall escape."

" I know it. I've said it. Think o' my honour."

He then took from an old chest, a coil of very thick rope, in one end of which he busied himself in making a noose, which, when he had completed, he advanced with it to Gray, saying,—

" Just pop your head through."

" Gracious Heavens !" cried Gray, starting up. " What do you mean ?"

" Mean ? Why to take care of you to be sure ; I know the way over the roofs, but you don't. You'll smash yourself in some of the courts without a guide rope, you will."

" A guide rope ?"

" Yes. Don't be making those faces. Do you think I'm going to hang you ?"

" Oh no—no," said Gray, with a nervous smile. " No—certainly."

" I wouldn't do such a ungentlemanly thing. Poke your head through."

The man accompanied these words by seizing Gray by the hair and thrusting his head into the noose, which then he passed over his shoulder down to his waist.

" There you are now," he said, " as safe as if you was a diamond in cotton. Now, mind you, I go first, and you follow arter. You keep coming on in the line of the rope, you understand, as long as you feel me tugging at it ; you are sure to be safe if you follow the rope, but so certain as you don't down you'll go either into some of the yards o' the houses, or into some o' the open courts."

" I understand," said Gray, " who felt anything but pleasantly situated with a thick rope round his middle, by which he was to be hauled over roofs of old houses. There was, however, no alternative, and he strove to assume an air of composure and confidence, which sat but ill upon him, and the ghastly smile which he forced his face to assume, looked like some hideous contortion of the muscles produced by pain, rather than an indication that the heart was at ease within him.

The housebreaker now took the coil of rope in his hand, leaving a length between him and Jacob Gray, of about three yards merely, and then he nimbly got out at the window.

" Follow," he said to Gray, " and mind ye now, if you say anything until you are spoken to by me, I'll let you down."

Trembling and alarmed, Gray scrambled out at the window, and found himself standing, or rather crouching in a narrow gutter, full of slime and filth, and only protected from falling by a narrow coping, which cut and scratched his ancles as he moved.

His guide crept on slowly and cautiously, and Gray followed guided by the rope, which every now and then was pulled very tight with a jerk, that at first very nearly upset him over the parapet.

There was a cold raw air blowing over the house tops, but Gray's fears produced a heavy perspiration upon him, and he shook excessively from sheer fright at the idea of a false step precipitating him to a great depth on to some stone pavement, where he would lay a hideous mass of broken bones.

Tug, tug, went the rope, and now Jacob Gray felt the strain come in an upward direction. He crawled on, and presently found that the rope ascended a sloping roof of slates, which at the first dim sight of it, struck him he would have the greatest difficulty in ascending. He was not, however, left long to his reflections, for a sudden tug at the rope which brought him with his face in violent contact with the sloping roof, admonished him that his guide was getting rather impatient.

With something between a curse and a groan, he commenced the slippery and difficult ascent, which, however, by the aid of the rope, he accomplished with greater ease than he had anticipated.

It happened that Gray, in the confusion of his mind, did not at all take into consideration that the sloping roof might have a side to descend as well as one to ascend, so that when he arrived at its summit, he rolled over and came down with great speed into a gutter on the other side, and partially upon the back of his guide, who, with a muttered accusation of an awful character, seized him by the throat and held down in the gutter upon his back to the imminent risk of his strangulation.

It seemed that Gray's fall had given some kind of alarm, for in a moment an attic window at some distance was opened with a creaking sound, and the voice of a female cried,—

"Gracious me, what's that?"

"Hush, for your life, hush?" whispered the man in Gray's ear.

"Well, I never did hear such a rumpus," said the woman's voice. "It's those beastly cats again."

She had no sooner uttered this suggestion, than Gray's companion perpetrated so excellent an imitation of a cat mewing, that Gray was for a moment taken in it himself.

"Ah, there you are," said the woman; "I only wish I was near you. Puss—puss—puss."

This call from the woman was a hypocritical one, and evidently intended to deceive the supposed cat or cats to their serious personal detriment should they venture to the window allured by such pacific sounds.

There was a pause of some moments, then the woman exclaimed,—

"Oh, you artful wretches; I declare these cats are as knowing as Christians."

The attic window was then shut with a very aggravated bang, and Gray's companion took his hand from his throat as he said to him,—

"Curse you, what the devil made you come down the slope with such a run?"

"I—I didn't know it," said Gray.

"Come on and mind what you are about. I didn't think you were so precious green as you are; come on, I say."

The fellow crept on ahead, and a tug at the rope caused Gray to follow, which he did; so weak from terror and exhaustion that he could scarcely contrive to keep up with his guide, and numerous were the falls he received, as a sudden pull of the rope rebuked his tardy progress. Altogether, it was, to Jacob Gray, an awful means of safety, if safety was to be the result of it.

They proceeded along the gutter they were in until they came to the corner house of the court, to turn which was no easy matter, from the circumstance of the coping stones ceasing each way, at about a foot from the absolute corner, down to which the roof came with a point. Round this point the housebreaker stepped with ease, but to Gray, oppressed as his mind was with fears and terrors, and weakened and exhausted as he was from his recent unusual bodily exertion, it was a task of the greatest magnitude and terror.

There was, however, no time to deliberate, and it was, perhaps, better for Gray that such was the case, for his mind was not in that state to reason itself out of nervous apprehensions.

A sharp tug of the rope settled his cogitations, and clinging with his hands to the angle of the roof, he placed his leg round the corner. It was then a moment or two before he could find, with his foot, the coping stones on the other side, and those few moments seemed to him hours of intense agony. At length he gained a hold with his foot, and rubbing his very face against the roof for fear of overbalancing himself in the outer direction, he contrived to get round.

For a moment a deadly sickness came over him, when he had accomplished the, to him, difficult feat; then he felt as if he could have nothing else to fear, and a feeling of congratulation sprang up in his mind, that after all he might not only escape, but preserve the greater part of the large sum he had about him.

CHAPTER LVI.

THE ROBBERS.—THE DRUGGED WINE.—VISIONS OF THE MIND DISEASED.

The path over the house tops now continued for upwards of a quarter of an hour, without presenting any very extraordinary difficulties to Jacob Gray, and he was about to congratulate himself that really the worst was past. when the rope suddenly slackened, and in a few moments his guide was by his side.

" You can jump a bit, I suppose ?" he said.

" Jump? jump ?"

" Yes, jump. What the devil do you repeat my words for ?"

" I—am no greater jumper," said Gray. " Where am I to jump ?"

" Across this court."

" Across a court ? I cannot—I cannot.'

" You must."

" I am lost—I am lost," said Gray, wringing his hands ; for the feat of jumping across a court at the risk of a fall into the gulph below, appeared to him to be totally impossible.

" Well," cried the man, " if ever I came near such an out-and-out sneak in the whole course of my life. Why you are afraid of what you know nothing about. You've only got to jump off a parapet of one house in at Bill's attic window opposite."

" Only," said Gray, trembling exceedingly. " Do you call that easy ?"

" Yes ; and if you don't jump it, I must just ease you of all you have got in the money way on the roofs here, and leave you to your luck."

" Gray looked despairingly around him. There was no hope for him. He stood in a drain between the two roofs, and he was as ignorant of the locality of his position as it was possible to be. With a deep groan he sunk grovelling at the feet of the man in whose power he was, and in imploring accents he said,—

" Take me back, and let me run my chance of escape from the house you live in. Oh, take me back, for I am unequal to the fearful task you propose to me. I am, indeed—I should falter and fall—I know I should. Then an awful death would be my lot—a death of pain and horror. Oh, take me back—take me back ! "

" I'll see you d—d first," cried the man. " Come on, or I'll cut your throat where you are. Come on, I say, you whining hound, come on, and look at the jump you are so scared at afore you know anything about it. Come on, I say. Oh, you won't ?"

" Spare me—spare me !"

The man took a large clasp knife from his pocket and opened it with his teeth

" I'll go—I'll go," cried Gray. " Put up the knife—oh, God ! put up the knife—any death but that ! "

" Oh ! any death but that. Then it's my opinion you've used such a little article yourself. Speak !"

" I—I—have," gasped Gray. " Take it out of my sight, I cannot bear to look upon it."

" Oh, your a tender-hearted piece of goods, certainly. Well, well, we all have our little failings. You've had a precious fright about this jump, and now I tell you it's no jump at all."

" Indeed ?"

" No. These houses are so built that each story as they go up projects outwards, so that I'm cursed if you couldn't shake a fist with a pal from some of the opposite attic windows. Come on, now, spooney, and you'll curse yourself for a fool for being afraid of nothing,"

" Is it indeed as you say," muttered Gray, who still could not get over his great terror, although he well knew that hundreds of houses in narrow thoroughfares in London were so situated that the attics had scarcely a couple of yards of open space between them.

"Come on," was the only reply, accompanied by a jerk of the rope, and presently one of the roofs ceased upon one side, and turning an angle, Gray, by the very dim light that was cast upwards from the street, saw that he was opposite a row of dirty, squallid-looking attic windows, from some of which lights were streaming, while others were obscured by old clothes hung up in the inside. A very few steps further now brought them to a part where, as the housebreaker had told Gray, the upper story of the house, on the top of which they were, projected considerably across the narrow court; here Gray's guide paused, and pointing to an attic immediately opposite, he said,—

"There—that's not much of a jump."

"No, no," said Gray. "I could do that."

The distance was scarcely more than a long step from parapet to parapet.

The robber now slackened out some of the rope in order that by suddenly jumping across the chasm he might not drag Gray from the slight standing he had. Then, with the remainder of the rope on his arm, he sprung across, and alighted in safety in the gutter of the opposite house.

"Jump now," he said to Gray.

The distance was too insignificant to give occasion for fear, but still Gray barely cleared it, and fell in the drain where the housebreaker was standing.

"Well," said the latter, "of all the awkward hands at business that ever I saw you are the most awkward. It's well for you there's somebody to look after you."

He then undid a fastening on the outside of the attic window, and at once jumped into the room, whither he was followed by Gray.

"You remain here," he then said. "Don't stir for your life, while I go down stairs to speak to Bill."

"You will not keep me here long?" said Gray.

"Not five minutes. Make no noise; but enjoy yourself as well as you can."

The man now left Gray to his meditations after carefully locking him in the room, and these meditations were very far from an agreeable or pleasant charae.

Gray's first idea was that he would hide the money he had about him with the exception of the amount he had averred to, namely, two hundred pounds, but then it naturally occurred to him how extremely improbable it was that he should ever have an opportunity of repossessing himself of it.

"Still," he answered, with his usual selfish cunning; "still there may be a remote, although a very remote chance; and, at all events, if I never see it again myself, I may prevent these men from having it."

Deep groans then burst from him, and he smote his breast as the hought came across him that all the gold he had wrung frm the guilty fear of Learmont, and hoarded so carefully; might now be about to pass from him in a mass never again to bless his sight.

"They will rob me—they will rob me," he thought, and compared with that, it appeared to him preferable to know that it was hidden from them and undisposed of, although inaccessible to himself.

How and where to conceal it then became the object, and he felt about in the dark to discover some loose board, or other means, of placing his ill-gotten money out of sight—where, for all he knew, it might remain until the coins of which it was composed, became blackened into curiosities.

Such, however, was not to be the fate of Learmont's gold, for while Gray was still feeling about in the attic for a place of security in which to deposit it, the door was suddenly opened, and his former companion appeared, along with a shorter man, in whose countenance nature or education had taken especial pains to stamp villain!

"Here you are," said the man who had guided Gray across the roofs. "This is the gentleman, Bill. He was in an awkward fix, but now we mean to do the thing handsomely by him, eh, Bill, don't we?"

'I should think so," replied Bill. "Your sarvant, sir."

"Thank you," said Gray. "Is the coast clear, now? Can I go?"

"Lor bless you, no!" replied the man who was named Bill. "You must not venture for an hour yet. There's a watchman put at the end of this court to apprehend any strange gentleman going out of it; but in the course of an hour we can dispose of him."

"Indeed?" said Gray.

"Oh, yes. When Jim Binks comes home, he'll go and be booked, as safe as a gun."

"I don't understand you."

"Why, this is it," continued Bill. "Jim Binks can make himself look so uncommon suspicious a character, that if he likes he is sure to be taken up, if there's been any regular kick up about anything such as your murder."

No. 29.

Gray started.

"Well, well," continued the ruffian, "damme, it was well done, you needn't now look as if you couldn't help it."

"I begin to understand you," said Gray.   The person you name will allow himself to be taken for me?"

"Exactly. They know him well at the watchhouse, and will let him go directly again, because it's well known you are a stranger, as half a dozen officers can swear to."

"Then in the interval I can leave the house," said Gray.

"You can. But Jim must be paid."

"Oh, certainly. I have two hundred pounds, gentlemen; I hope you will accept of one of them for your very great kindness, and leave me the other."

"What do you say to that, Bill?" cried the man who had come with Gray.

"I think it's fair," said the other.

"Well, then, that's agreed."

"Thank you, gentlemen," said Gray, breathing a little more freely at the idea of getting off with nearly all his money.

"Now then," said Bill, "come down stairs, as all business matters are settled, and have a bit of supper."

"I shall be grateful for it," said Gray, "for I have tasted nothing to-day."

He did not perceive the wink that passed between his new friends, but at once followed them from the attic to the lower part of the crazy tenement.

In an old wainscoted room on the first floor, there was a bright and cheerful-looking fire, and such scanty articles of furniture as were absolutely requisite for the personal accommodation of three or four persons.

A table, on which were several plates, mugs, bottles, and other evidences of some recent meal, stood close by the fire.

Bill, the proprietor of all this display of dirt and dinginess, took up the poker from the fire-side, and beat it heavily against the floor, observing at the same time—

"It's a d—d sight better than a bell is a poker—the wire never breaks."

"You speak like a oracle, Bill," remarked the other man, throwing himself into a seat, and giving Jacob Gray a pull towards him to undo the rope that was still round his middle.

"What will you both drink?" cried Bill; "I have something of everything here, I do believe."

"Brandy for me," cried the other man.

"I should prefer wine," said Gray, "if you have some at hand."

"I believe you—I have," rejoined the host. "As fine a drop of wine as ever you tasted in your life, on my honour."

The door now opened, and an old wrinkled hag appeared, who, in not very courteous terms, demanded,—

"What now?"

"What have you got to give a strange gentleman to eat?" said Bill.

"Nothing," replied the woman.

"Then go and get something. Here's a guinea. Be off with you, and do you bring a bottle of our best claret for the gentleman. He prefers wine, because it shouldn't get in his head. Do you hear?"

The old woman fixed her keen, twinkling eye upon Gray, and then, with a chuckle which quickly turned to a cough, she left the room on her errand.

"We'll settle all business after supper," remarked Gray's entertainer. "Then I should advise you to lay by very snug for some days. You can't stay here, though."

"No—no," said Gray, "who had quite as much objection to remaining there as the thieves had to permitting him to do so. "I will find some place of refuge without doubt."

"Do you know the man whose head you so handsomely settled in the court?"

"No," said Gray. "It was in self-defence. He would have taken me."

"Self-defence be d—d," remarked Gray's first acquaintance. "He's a good riddance: his name was Vaughan, and a pest he was to all the family in London."

"Tell us what lay you had been on," said Bill, "that made the runners so hot after you?"

"Oh, only a—a robbery—a little robbery," said Gray, with a sickly attempt at a smile.

"Oh, that was all ?"

"Yes; a robbery of two hundred pounds, of which you are to have one, you know, and to leave me the other."

"That's quite agreed."

The door was now again opened, and the old woman appeared with a tray containing sundry viands from neighbouring shops dealing in ready-cooked victuals. Wine and brandy likewise formed a part of her burthen, and in a very few moments the table was spread, and Gray, who really, now that he felt himself comparatively safe, began to be tormented by the pangs of hunger, fell to with a vigorous appetite, upon a cold tongue of ample dimensions.

"How do you like it ?" said Bill, with a wink to his comrade.

"'Tis excellent," replied Gray, glancing towards the bottles.

"You will take wine now ?"

"If you please."

A bottle was uncorked, and Gray relished the wine very much, along with the other items of his repast.

The confederates drank small quantities of brandy from another bottle, and encouraged Gray by never allowing his glass to be empty to make great progress with the wine.

Glass after glass he drank with a kind of recklessness foreign to his nature, but the liquor was drugged, and the very first draught had made a confusion in the intellect of Jacob Gray. Up to his brain the fumes mounted, awakening a desire still for more, and lighting up his eyes with a strange wild fire.

His two companions now nodded and winked at each other openly, for Jacob Gray was too far gone in intoxication to heed them.

"He'll do," remarked Bill in a whisper.

"Of course," said the other, "you may depend he has something worth while about him."

"No doubt—no doubt."

"Gentlemen—gentlemen," said Gray, pouring himself out another glass, "here's to—to—our better—ac—acquaintance."

"Hurrah !" cried Bill, "that's yer sort."

"And—confusion to Andrew Britton," added Gray, dealing the table a heavy blow with his fist. "Confusion, death, and damnation to Andrew Britton.

"Bravo! bravo !"

"You'll take a hundred. Mind only a hundred. Don't rob me—no—no, don't rob me. It's been too hard to get, with the—the curse of blood clinging to it. The curse of blood."

"Oh, that's it, old fellow," cried Bill.

"She—she to betray me," muttered Gray "she of all others; I might have killed her—I will kill her. Some slow and horrible death shall be her's. I'll hack your flesh from your bones, Ada—I will—I will—one word and you die. I must shoot him—he seeks my life."

"Here's a beauty,' remarked Bill, to his comrade, who had very calmly lighted a fire, and sat listening to Gray's revelations with all the composure in the world, as if he had merely been present at some ordinary dramatic entertainment.

"Three thousand pounds would be enough," said Gray, tossing off another bumper of the drugged wine, and smashing the glass with the vehemence with which he replaced it on the table. "Three thousand. Yes, yes; enough to lead a life of—of riot somewhere else. Not here—not here. Then I should read of his execution, of both their executions, and—when I was dull, I would bring out the newspaper that had the account, and I'd read it over and over again. I'll wash my hands in her blood. I'll smash her face till—till there's not a lineament remains to horrify me by reminding me of her."

" 'Pon my soul," remarked Bill, " we have hit on an out-and-outer."

" Rather," said the other, without taking the pipe from his mouth.

" Don't look at me !" suddenly cried Gray, springing to his feet. " Don't glare at me with your stony eyes ! Clear away—clear away. Do you want to stop my breath—I—I—must go—go—from here—there—there—help—save me. What do you do here—one—two—three. Why do you point at me ? You would have your deaths. You—you—why do you not remain and rot in the Old Smithy ? Save me from him. His wounds are bleeding still. Will the damp earth never soak up all the blood ? You, you I shot. Don't grin at me. Away—away—I am going mad—mad—Ada—Ada—Ada—pray—pray for me !"

He reeled round twice, and fell upon the floor with a deep groan.

CHAPTER LVII.

ADA'S ESCAP.—THE MAGISTRATE.—ADA'S IGNORANCE OF LONDON LOCALITIES —LEARMONT'S FRIGHT.

WHEN Ada sunk insensible into the arms of a stranger, after denouncing Jacob Gray as a murderer, she was conveyed into a shop by Charing-cross, when her rare and singular beauty, and the peculiar circumstances under which she had fainted, were the themes of every tongue. Such restoratives as upon the moment could be procured, were immediately brought into requisition, and after a quarter of an hour she gently opened her eyes with a faint sigh and looked inquiringly about her.

Then she clasped her hands, and as she gazed upon the throng of curious, yet compassionate faces that surrounded her, she exclaimed,—

" What has happened ? Oh, speak to me ; where am I ?"

" You have fainted," cried four or five voices in a breath."

" Fainted—fainted ?"

" Yes ; I brought you in after you had called after the man as a murderer," said the person who had caught Ada before she was brought into the shop.

For the space of about another minute then the young girl looked confused ; after that a gush of recollections flashed across her mind, and the feeling that she was really at last free from Jacob Gray, came across her heart with so much happiness and joy, that covering her beautiful face with her small slender hands, she burst into tears and sobbed aloud in her fulness of heart.

Those who stood by seemed to feel that there was something sacred in the tears of the young thing before them, for they stood silent, and no one attempted to insult her by the usual common-place remarks of vulgar consolation. There were tears in almost every eye, and when Ada withdrew her hands from her face, and a smile, beautiful as a sunbeam after an April shower, illumined her expressive countenance, it seemed as if some universal joy had been awakened in every breast, and murmured blessings upon her beauty, burst from several of the persons who had crowded, from motives of curiosity, into the shop.

Then Ada looked from face to face, and oh, how different were those honest sympathising countenances to the dark ever shifting expression of the lineaments of Jacob Gray, where avarice, cruelty, and fear were ever struggling together for a mastery.

" Thank you all—thank you all," she cried ; " I am very happy now."

This was not a very comprehensible speech to those who had not gone through the scene of misery and woe, that the young heart of Ada had known, but still there was a deep truthfulness and sincerity in the tone in which it was uttered, that sensibly affected every one.

" Shall I take you home?" said the person who had supported her in the street.

" Home—home?" cried Ada.

"Yes; you are not well enough to go home by yourself; I will see you safely home."

" I have no home," said Ada.

" No home?"

" None—I never had a home."

The people looked at each other in amazement, and several of them significantly touched their foreheads in confirmation of their belief that the beautiful young girl was not quite right in her head.

" Where are your friends?" said one.

"Alas, I know not," cried Ada, mournfully. " Tell me, is he whom I denounced in the street, taken prisoner?"

" No, not that I am aware of," said a man. " There has been one here who says he ran up the Strand like a madman and escaped."

Ada shuddered as she said,—

" Let him go now; his own conscience must be punishment enough. Let him go now."

" What has he done?" said several voices at once.

" Murder," said Ada. " My eyes were shocked with the sight of blood. He is a murderer."

" A murderer?"

" Yes—I saw him do the deed."

" What's his name?"

" Jacob Gray."

The people glanced at each other, and then several left the shop, considering Jacob Gray as the more interesting person of the two to make inquiries about.

" Where will you go, my dear?" said the owner of the shop.

" I have but one friend," said Ada, " to whom there is any hope of sending. He has called himself my friend, and his voice was sincere. I will believe that he sought me with kindly feelings. His name is Hartleton—he is a magistrate."

" Sir Francis Hartleton?"

" Yes—the same."

" If he knows you and is your friend," said one, " you need look no farther, for he is a good man, and universally esteemed."

" I thank you for those words," cried Ada. " And—and tell me—do any of you know Albert Seyton?"

All shook their heads, and one man remarked,—" That he knew an Albert Brown, which was the nearest he could come to it."

" I will take you to Sir Francis Hartleton's," said the man of the shop.

Before Ada could reply, the door was opened, and a stranger walked in, saying,—

" Where is the girl?"

" Here, here?" cried many voices.

The stranger stepped forward, and upon seeing Ada, he said,—

" My lass, you must come with me before a magistrate, and tell us what you know of this man who has led us such a pretty race up the Strand."

" Is he caught?" cried several.

" No," replied the officer, for such he was; " we nearly had him by the court next to Somerset-house, but he killed the man who laid hold of him."

" Another murder!" exclaimed Ada.

" Yes; I never saw such a sight as he left the man."

" Take me to Sir Francis Hartleton," said Ada.

" That I will," said the officer.

Ada sprung to her feet, and then, turning to those in the shop, she said,—
"Accept my heartfelt thanks. I am poor in all else."

Then, taking the offered arm of the officer, who, though rough and uncouth, meant to be quite kind and considerate in his way, she left the shop, and the strangely-matched pair proceeded down Whitehall towards Sir Francis Hartleton's house.

"That fellow as you was with, my dear," remarked the officer, "is a reg'lar out-and-outer; down as fifteen hammers, and a touch above nothing."

This speech was about as intelligible to Ada as if it had been spoken in Chinese, and she replied mildly,—

"I don't know what you mean."

"Bless your innocence!" said the officer; "I means as he's the most downiest cove as we've come across lately."

"Indeed," said Ada, who was quite as wise as before.

"Yes; he went up the Strand like twenty blessed lamplighters rolled into one."

"Where's the Strand?" said Ada.

The officer stopped short at the question, and looked hard at Ada for some moments to assure himself that he was not, in his own phraseology, being "regularly done;" but there was something so very innocent and guileless in the face of Ada, that he very reluctantly came to the conclusion that she really did not know where the Strand was, and from that moment he looked upon her as a natural phenomenon, and spoke to her with a curious kind of considerate voice, such as he would have addressed to a person not quite right in her mind.

"Why, the Strand," he said, "runs from the Cross to the Bar, you see."

"Does it?" said Ada.

"This here is Whitehall."

"Whitehall? I have read of Whitehall. Cardinal Wolsey held great state here once."

"Well, I never," thought the officer, who had never heard of Cardinal Wolsey in his life. "She's wandering in her mind, poor thing."

"What building is that?" inquired Ada, as they came opposite to the Horse Guards.

"That 'ere is the Horse Guards, and leads into the Park."

"St. James's Park? I have been there," said Ada. "That too is full of recollection."

"I believe ye," said the officer. "Don't you know as Bill Floggs, who was called the 'Nubbly Cove,' robbed Lord Chief Justice Bones by Buckingham Gate?"

"No," said Ada, who, if there had been a Newgate Calendar in those days, had never seen one.

"Oh! you doesn't?—nor Claude Duval, the ladies' own highwayman, who robbed a gentleman of his gold watch, while he, the gentleman, was complaining of being stopped the very night before by him on Kennington Common?"

"Indeed?"

"Lor', bless you, yes. The ladies used to take a drive out of town on purpose to be robbed by Claude Duval."

"A strange fancy," said Ada.

They now proceeded for some distance in silence, until they came to a large mansion, every window of which was blazing with light, and from the interior of which came the sound of music.

Ada paused, and looked upon the illuminated windows as a sensation of pleasure came across her mind, arising from the sweet sounds of melody that came wafted to her ears from within the house of revelry.

"Ah!" remarked the officer, looking up at the house, "they do keep it up finely. Almost every night now for a week there has been nothing but feasting, dancing, and music in th t house. They say its master don't like to be left alone, and that he is never satisfied unless the house be full of company, and himself in the very midst of it."

" Indeed !"

"Yes, he is an odd-looking fellow; but they say he is so rich he might pave his great hall with guineas."

" And yet shrinks, as it were, from himself, that he dare not be alone !"

"Why, atween you and I, there's Tyburn written upon his face."

" What upon his face ?"

" Tyburn."

" What's that ?'

" Why—why—you don't mean all to go to say as you never heard o' Tyburn?"

" I have lived a lone and solitary life," said Ada; " and, although so near the haunts of thousands of my fellow-creatures, I have seen but one, except rarely. The names of places in this great city, the habits, the thoughts, and actions of its myriads of inhabitants, are all strange to me. For all I know of the familiar things of life—those every-day events and materials of life that make up the sum of most persons' existence—I am as ignorant as a child cast upon some desert shore."

There was a mournful pathos in the tone of voice in which Ada uttered these words, that gave them their full effect upon the rough man she was with. Nature spoke in every soft melancholy word that fell from her lips ; and, although her language was to him as strange and incomprehensible quite, as his to her, he understood sufficient to reply to her,—

" Then, whosoever shut you up, and purwented you from going about and amusing yourself, my dear, was a big brute, and only let him come across me, that's all."

" Whose house is this?" said Ada, listening, at the same time, to a beautiful melody which was being played as a prelude to the commencement of a dance.

"Squire Learmont they call him," replied the man; " but, if he lives a little longer, it's said he'll be a lord, or something of that kind."

Ada placed her hand upon her brow, and repeated the name of Learmont, as if its sound conjured up some long-forgotten images in her brain. Then she shook her head, as memory could shape to her nothing tangible in connexion with the name, which yet, as she again pronounced it, came upon her heart as something far from new.

" Learmont—Learmont!" she murmured, as if pleased with the repetition.

" Yes, that's his name," rejoined the officer. " Nobody knows exactly where he got all his money from ; but got it he has, and he knows how to spend it too."

At this moment the doors of the mansion were flung open, and a splendid carriage dashed up to the entrance.

" There's somebody coming," remarked the officer to Ada. " Let's have a look at them.'

Ada and her companion now crossed the road, and stood close to the step of Learmont's house, as a lacquey shouted to those in the hall,—

" Lord and Lady Brereton, and the Honourable Georgiana Brereton." '

A blaze of light shot from the interior of the mansion, and just as the guests were alighting, Learmont himself descended the steps of his house to receive them.

He was attired in a splendid suit of moreen velvet, and a diamond of great lustre sparkled in his sword hilt. His fingers were covered with rings, profusely studded with precious stones, and, take his appearance altogether, he looked, indeed, like the man who could pave his hall with gold.

A bland and courtly smile was upon his face, and he handed the occupants of the carriage up the steps, with the air of a sovereign prince, graciously condescending to an act of rare and unexampled courtesy.

From the moment that he had appeared, Ada had never taken her eyes from off his face ; she seemed like one fascinated by the basilisk eyes of a serpent, and, with a wild rush of mingled feelings, which she could neither define nor understand, she watched each varying expression of that cold, pale, haughty countenance, that wore upon its surface so hollow and so artificial a smile.

Learmont was one step below the Honourable Lady he was handing by the extreme tips of her fingers, into his house, when the officer, in what he thought a whisper, said to Ada,—

"That's him."

The guilty heart of Learmont throbbed even at this trifling remark, for it did reach his ears, and he turned suddenly to see who had uttered it, when his eyes met Ada's, and for the space of about one moment they looked full at each other.

The look on Ada's part was one of intense and indescribable interest and curiosity, but on Learmont's, it was that concentrated soul-stricken glare, with which a person might be supposed to regard for about a breathing space, some awful blasting spectre, ere nature gathers strength to scream.

A wild unearthly cry burst from his lips, and he stretched out his hands towards her as he ascended the steps backwards, crying, or rather shrieking,—

"Off—off—off—"

Then as he reached the top he reeled into the hall of his house, and was caught by his servants as he fell insensible from the over-wrought agony of his mind.

CHAPTER LVIII.

AN ANECDOTE.—SIR FRANCIS HARTLETON'S HOUSE AT WESTMINSTER.—THE RECEPTION.—ADA'S CONDUCT AND FEELINGS.

ADA was both astonished and alarmed at the sudden emotion of the man who, her reason told her, was a stranger to her ; but who her imagination seemed notwithstanding to recognise as one who she must have seen before. Her memory concerning him was like one of those sudden strange feelings which occasionally come over us all, as we meet particular people who we are quite sure we have not met before, but who, nevertheless wear not the aspect of strangers to us ; people whom we could almost imagine we had been intimate with, for good or evil, in some other state of existence long antecedent to this.

On occasions of this singular nature too, there will always be a dim perception in the mind concerning the person so strangely recognised, which enables us to say, with certainty, whether the circumstances connected with him or her, quite unremembered, though they may be, were of a pleasing or a disagreeable character. To Ada, the full sight of Learmont's face brought a sensation of shuddering horror, which assured her that wherever or whenever she and he had ever taken part together in the great drama of human existence, he was an enemy to be at once loathed and dreaded.

As for the officer he was so astonished and confounded at the whole affair, that after rubbing his eyes twice, he looked a long way down the street, with the full expectation of seeing something coming which might, in some measure, account for Learmont's sudden and extraordinary fright. That the mere sight of the face of the beautiful girl, who was with him, could cause such an excess of terror, he could not imagine, and when a servant came from the hall, and said to him,—

"What was it ? What scared him ?" he replied—

"I'll be hanged if I know. He was going up the steps, like Claude Duval at a 'minuet, when he was taken aback by something."

"It's very odd," said the servant.

"You may say that," remarked the officer.

"Come away—come away," said Ada, faintly, " to Sir Francis Hartleton ; come, come."

"Certainly," said the officer, " but this here is, out of all hand, the rummiest go ever I seed in all my life."

"Come, come," repeated Ada. "I would not see that man again for worlds."

"No wonder he's frightened you. My own very hair nearly stood a end. I'm afeared he's done something queer, and wants to be found out, that's what I am. I supposes as he seed some sort o' ghostesses as made him take on so."

Ada sighed.

"Don't you mind it," said the officer. "You may depend as he's a victim o' conscience, he is. I once before seed a face very like that as he made when he staggered up the steps."

"Indeed ?"

"Yes. As like it as one pea is like another."

"Where saw you it ?"

"In the condemned cell."

"The condemned cell ; where is that?"

"In Newgate. It's where we stow a fellow afore his execution. There was a man named Rankin, who had committed a murder, and he was regularly tried and condemned. Well, he carried it off with a high hand, swearing and blustering

No. 30.

away, as if he didn't care a bit, and roaring out as he'd die game, which I knew very well he wouldn't, for the noisy ones never do."

"Well, you see he was put in the cell, and we promised to wake him in the morning, in answer to which piece of politeness he swore away at us like a house o' fire.

"At half past six, I and another went to get him up, and when we went in, he never said not a word, and I cried out, 'hilloa.' Still he never spoke, and I held up his light, and there he was, a standing straight up against the further end of the cell with his eyes half an inch out of his head, and some such a face as that Learmont puts on."

Ada shuddered and the officer continued.

"When we went up to him, what do you think we found?"

"I cannot tell."

"He was stone dead and stiffened up against the wall of his cell, and our chaplain said as how he must have seen the devil all of a sudden. But here we are at Sir Francis Hartleton's."

Ada cast her eyes up to the house, and a pang shot across her heart as the doubt crossed her mind, that Jacob Gray might by some innate possibility have spoken the truth, when he described Sir Francis as her enemy; but still she hesitated not, but silently commending herself to the care of Heaven, she entered the house along with the officer.

She was left for some time in a handsomely-furnished parlour, for this was the magistrate's private, not his official residence. Each moment that passed now appeared to Ada an age of suspense and anxiety. She could hear the beating of her own heart in the silence of that room, and as she sat with her eyes fixed upon the door, she thought that she had scarcely suffered ss much anxiety, even when, in the dreary cell with Jacob Gray, a spirit of resistance to him and all his acts, supported her and prevented her mind from sinking beneath the oppressive circumstances which then surrounded her.

Ada's mind was of that rare and high order which rises superior to circumstances, and the energies of which become more acute and more capable of vigorous action, the more necessity there exists for the use of such qualities.

Now, however, when there was no iniquity to denounce, no wickedness to resist, but when her heart was only oppressed with a faint doubt of whether she was to receive from Sir Francis Hartleton kindness or not, she did feel faint, weak, and sad, and all those trembling sensibilities of her nature she had suppressed from native energy of mind, and pride of innocence, when with Gray, now that she was free from him, arose from the recesses of her pure heart, and forced her to feel, that, although a noble-minded heroine, when surrounded by great peril, yet in real nature she was but a timid shrinking girl, such as her fragile and beautifully delicate appearance would indicate.

Then when her anxiety had almost grown into a positive pain, the door opened and a tall, gentlemanly-looking man, with an intelligent countenance, entered the room.

Ada rose, but for a moment she could not speak. He who had come in, evidently saw her emotion, for he said in accents of the greatest kindness and tender consideration to her,—

"Sit down, and don't be alarmed—I will listen to you with patience."

It was not the words, but it was the tone of genuine heartfelt kindness in which they were spoken, that went direct to the heart of Ada.

Once, twice, she tried to speak, but what all the threats, and all the harshness of Jacob Gray had failed to produce, these few simple words kindly spoken, at once accomplished, and she burst into tears.

Sir Francis Hartleton had merely been told that a young girl wished to see him, and he had not the remotest idea of who she was, or upon what errand she came.

"I pray you to be calm," he said, "I have no doubt you have something to tell me that afflicts you very much."

" No, no," cried Ada.

" No!"

" It is joy—the joy of meeting a kind heart, that forces these tears from me—I am, sir, but too—too happy now."

" God forbid I should speak otherwise than kindly to you."

" Oh, sir," said Ada, dashing aside the long clustering ringlets of her hair, that in her deep emotion had veiled her face. " You do not know me, but I have pondered over your name till hopes and fears of who or what you were, have made my heart sicken. Though young in years, it seems to me that in the small space of time which has seen my existence, I have lived an age of sorrow, of persecution, of horror. I am a harmless, friendless, and for all I know, a nameless thing. Debbarred from all that to the young is beautiful, I have passed the dawning of my life the victim of another's crimes, although how connected with him and his great sinfulness, I cannot tell. My spirit has been worn by incessant rebuke, until death would have been a relief. A murderer's hand has been lifted against me while I slept—I have seen blood shed before my eyes, and could not stay the unrighteous hand of the murderer—I have had none to love me but one— no mother ever smiled upon me—no recollection of a father's caress warms my heart. To you, sir, I came for succour, for protection—a fugitive—a homeless wanderer—a thing of blight and desolation ; when I hoped, there has come despair —when I wept I have met with mockery—when I trusted I was betrayed—you called upon me once when I dared not return you one answering cry—you proclaimed yourself my friend—I am she whom you called in Forest's ancient house. I am Ada, the Betrayed !"

Sir Francis Hartleton during this speech had stood before Ada with one of her hands clasped in his, and shewing by his earnest attention, and the deep sympathy depicted in his countenance, that he was far from an unmoved listener to her words. When she had concluded, a fervent " thank Heaven !" burst from his lips, and he cried with animation,—

" Ada, I have for many months now, sought you throughout this great city—not one day has elapsed without some effort upon my part to find you, and offer you friendship, protection, and a home ; my poor girl, you have suffered much—I know it—have known it long, and it has been a shadow on my heart, to think that I could not aid you ;—your trials—your persecutions are all over now, and once more I from my heart thank Heaven that I see you under my protection, safe from that awful man, who I ever dreaded would in some wild moment, sacrifice you to his fears, or to his revenge. Ada, you are safe and free! I have both power and will to shelter you, and while Sir Francis Hartleton lives, whoever would harm you, must do it through his heart."

When first Sir Francis had commenced speaking, Ada had fixed her large pensive eyes upon his face, and appeared to drink in with her soul every word he uttered ; but as he went on, and his own voice became a little broken by the depth of his emotion and the sincerity of his sympathy, she, in all the guileless innocence of her heart, pressed his hand within hers, and tears gushed from her eyes ; but when he told her that she was now safe for ever from Jacob Gray, and that his home should be her's, her joy and gratitude became too much for her, and she laid her head upon his breast and wept, as she would have done upon her father's heart.

Sir Francis Hartleton was himself scarcely less affected than Ada, for brave, noble, and gifted natures such as his, are easily melted by the softer feelings of human nature.

When he spoke, which was not for some minutes, for he could scarcely command his voice sufficiently, he said,—

" Ada, you shall rest till to-morrow before you tell me all your history—I have likewise much to tell you, and to-morrow we will have a long conference."

" Yes," said Ada, " oh, what can I say to you to make you know how my heart thanks you ?"

" Nothing—say nothing, Ada—Heaven will help me to do what I am now doing

—it is but my duty, Ada, to protect you.   Remember now you are at home—you are no guest here, mind, but one of ourselves.   These, I hope, are the last tears I shall ever see you shed."

" Ah, sir, they are far different from those I have shed in the silence and solitude of my various prisons.   Those were wrung from me by despair.   These come from a heart too full of gratitude."

Sir Francis Hartleton now rung a small hand bell, which was immediately answered by a servant, to whom he said,—

"Tell your mistress to come to me here;" then turning to Ada, he said, with a half-smile upon his face—"Now, my dear Ada, I shall have nothing to do with you till to-morrow.   I am but recently married, and my wife will love you for your own sake as well as for mine.   She knows what of your history I know, and is well prepared to give you welcome."

At this moment a lady entered the room, and Ada cast her eyes upon her face. That one glance was sufficient to assure her she had found a friend, for it was one of those faces that cannot conceal the goodness of the owner's heart.

" Emilia, this is Ada," said Sir Francis Hartleton.   " I will not say make much of her, and I don't think you can spoil her."

CHAPTER LIX.

JACOB GRAY AND HIS KIND FRIENDS.—THE PLUNDER.—THIEVES' MORALITY. THE DRIVE TO HAMPSTEAD.

WHEN Jacob Gray fell upon the floor in a state of utter insensibility in consequence of the powerful narcotic drug infused into his drink by his two kind n d considerate friends, those two gentlemen looked on with the utmost composure for a few moments, and then Bill remarked in a careless voice,—

" I think he'll do now, Moggs?"

" In course," responded the other, withdrawing the pipe from his mouth, and knocking out the ashes very deliberately upon the hob of the grate.

" He's precious green," remarked Bill.

" Very," said Mr. Moggs.

" Doesn't you know who he is?"

" I hasn't the slightest idea.   Never clapped eyes on the fellow in my life before, but to my mind he's a new hand as has been and done something strong in the murder line for an ample consideration."

" Very likely—what's the caper concerning him?"

" Honour, Bill—honour."

" In course."

" Vun o' the rules is, that if a regular out-and-out prig or cracksman comes to vun o' us, and says, 'I'm in trouble—the runners are hard on me. Guv us a share.' Why, then we shares the swag all round equal."

" Spoke like a oracle."

" Very good.   Another o' the rules is, 'If the prig aforesaid,' as the lawyers say, 'gammon us, or tries all for to gammon us, as to the exact waley o' the swag, we takes it all."

" Never vos a truer vord spoke," responded Bill, with a look of intense admiration at his companion."

" Well, if so be as this fellow has but what he said, two hundred, we takes one, and leaves him one."

" That's the way."

" But if so be as he has more we takes it all in course; and I'll wager my blessed nose off my face that he has a precious sight more."

Bill nodded knowingly.

" Well then," continued Mr. Moggs, " in either case we gets the shay-cart, and takes him somewhere far enough off."

Bill nodded again, and then taking from his pocket a large clasped knife, he knelt down by the side of Gray, and with a neatness and dexterity that were evidently the result of practice, he ripped open every one of his pockets, and in a few brief moments Jacob Gray was despoiled of every guinea of that sum of money he had gone through so much pain, suffering, and crime, to procure.

The sum when collected from all his pockets, was in notes and gold so much larger than the thieves had any idea of finding, that when they had it fairly lying before them on the table, they looked at each other for some moments in mute surprise.

" Bill," cried the other, "this is a regular set up, it is. I'm blowed if we maydent and must retire from business with all this."

" Don't be proud," said Bill. " You always was ambitious. Take it easy, can't you. This card will be uncommonly useful. How many a poor fellow has been scragged at the tree for want of a few pounds over the blood money, to give a officer as had a warrant agin him. Tom, what I propose is, for us to take a cool hundred or so only, out o' all this here, and lay the remainder by for bad times."

" Bill," remarked the other, after a pause of intense thought, " you should have been Lord Chancellor, that's what you should ! We'll do it, my boy. Forty pounds is the blood money for hanging a poor fellow, and it's very well known a chap never will get taken by the officers so long as he can make it guineas to let him go, except we comes across that d—d Sir Francis Hartleton, and he wouldn't let a chap go for nothink or the whole world, he wouldn't. What business has a beak to be poking as he does, instead of sitting quiet in his arm-chair, and leaving the business to be settled atween such as us and the receivers? It's a iniquity, and no good can come of it."

" Very true," said Bill. " You hide the money somewheres, while I go and get the cart, for we must start this chap somewhere afore daylight."

" Bill," said the other, "you wouldn't like to cut his throat?"

" Not exactly."

" Well, well. I only mention it. I'm afraid he's a sneak, but let him do his worst. Get the chaise-cart, and bring it round to the corner by Jem Medbourn's."

Bill nodded, and went to execute his errand, and during his absence, the other carefully concealed the money beneath the floor of the room, excepting about two hundred pounds, which he reserved for himself and companion. Then lighting his pipe, he again sat down very composedly by the fire-side.

" Well, well," he said, suddenly, as if he had arrived at some mental conclusion that he could not help, and yet did not like. " Bill may have it his own way, but I would never have let that chap," nodding at Gray, " have a chance o' being venomous. He's cut out for a sneaking lump o' evidence against others he is, and I shouldn't a bit wonder if he gets into trouble himself, but he speaks agin us about the money just out o' a nasty bit o' revenge."

He then resumed his smoking as if he had been reasoning upon some very common place affair indeed, and in about ten minutes more Bill made his appearance, saying,—

" It's all right—they have guved up the search for to-night, and we shall get on famously."

" Where do you mean to take him?" said he, " who had suggested the notion of cutting Gray's throat."

" I should say somewhere a little way out of town, and shoot him out o' the cart into some blessed werdant spot," replied Bill. " He's rather a queer one, himself, so he'll find as he's all right, when he wakes up and finds as he's amusing the butterflies and daisies."

" I'm blessed if you aint a out and out good un," replied the other.

" Supposes then," suggested Bill, " we takes him up to Hampstead, It's an odd little out o' the way place enough."

"Very good," said the other. "You are quite sure there's nobody about?"

"Quite."

"Come along, then."

As he spoke the man stooped, and lifted Jacob Gray from the ground with as much ease as if he had been an infant, and followed his comrade down stairs with his burthen, which seemed in no way to distress him.

The court they passed out into was one of those kind which now are exceedingly rare in London, but which the wisdom of our ancestors took good care to make very common and infest the town with. At the period of our tale there was an immense wen, as it might be termed, of various pestiferous courts at the back of the Strand, where thieves and vagabonds of all kinds lived in a sort of community of their own, quite undisturbed by the authorities, who then could boast of very little authority indeed. Another mass of such courts was to be found where Regent-street now stands, and the vicinity; another at the bottom of St. Martin's-lane, and another close to old Fleet-market, so that the city of London was as well provided with haunts of blackguardism and vice as the mouth of the Thames is with mud banks.

Along the narrow court in which was Bill's mansion, the confederates pursued their way until they came to what any stranger would have supposed a mere door-way, but which was in reality an entrance to another court; into this they dived, and after proceeding for a small distance ascended a flight of wooden steps, at the bottom of which stood a dirty, mean chaise-cart.

Into this vehicle, without the least ceremony or consideration for what bruises he might receive, Jacob Gray was flung. There was nothing at the bottom of the cart but some littered straw, upon which he laid more like a dead body than anything living and breathing.

The two men then climbed into the frail and crazy vehicle, and Bill taking the reins gave a shrill whistle, which the horse seemed perfectly to understand as a signal to go on, for he started immediately at a smart trot.

There were no policemen then promenading the streets, who might have looked with an eye of suspicion upon the proceedings of Bill and his comrade, and the lazy watchmen having just signally exerted themselves by squalling out the hour, with the supplementary information that it was a cold night, betook themselves again to their watchboxes, leaving the community over whose lives and property they were supposed, by a fiction which lasted many years, to watch, to the care of Providence and the mercy of thieves and housebreakers.

The chaise-cart rattled and bounded along through divers very intricate lanes and bye-streets, until at length it emerged into the Strand, near Arundel-street. Then dashing across the wide thoroughfare, it entered a congeries of dirty streets on the other side, and finally emerged in a curious and complicated place close to the British Museum. There were bye-roads across the Pancras-fields, and Bill having dismounted and taken down a bar which impeded his progress, drove across a meadow which now forms part of the ground occupied by that compound of pride, bloated arrogance, and humbug, the London University. Another quarter of an hour passed, and they were rattling up the Hampstead-road, which then had tall tress on either side of it.

Camden Town was then a small village, with not above forty little whitewashed houses in it, with here and there sprinkled a few edifices of somewhat more pretensions, which had been built by well-to-do citizens, who repaired there on a Sunday to see the phenomena of a cabbage growing, and admire the sweet pea blossom as it thrust its pretty leaves in at the windows.

The most famous house of entertainment then in Camden Town, was called the Queen's Head, and has long been levelled with the dust; it was then even an old-fashioned house, and spoken of as a curiosity. It could boast of but one story, and its projecting sign hung so low that any one riding by quickly, and not aware of it, ran the risk of breaking his own head against the queen's, with no very agreeable momentum.

The entrance was adorned with oaken carved pillars, to the designs on which a great deal had been added from time to time by bread and cheese knives, rapiers' penknives, and all sorts of cutting instruments, the door posts of an inn being considered as much public property, and open to defacement, as are wooden seats in Kensington gardens.

To enter the house, you had to descend two steps, which generally at night caused a strange visitor to fall on his nose in the passage, when the hostess would come out, hearing the clatter, and probably a few oaths, and trim a lamp; so that after the mischief was done, you had the pleasure of seeing the steps quite clearly and beautifully.

At this house Bill drew up, and without getting out, called lustily,—

" Mother Meadows ! Mother Meadows !"

" Well, what now ?" said a shrill female voice from the interior.

" A shilling's worth of brandy," said Bill, and the coin he threw rattled down the steps.

The liquor was brought to the chaise-cart by a boy, with a head of hair resembling strongly one of the now popular patent chimney sweeping apparatus.

Bill took his half to a nicety, and handed the remainder to his companion, who then bumped the little pewter measure upon the boy's head till his eyes flashed fire.

Bill whistled to the horse, and with loud laughter, the two ruffians galloped up the Hampstead-road, which was then as innocent of " Cottages of Gentility" as is the Lake of Windermere.

Up the hill they went with but slightly lessened speed, nor stopped till they were quite clear of all the little suburban houses that here and there dotted the road, and within about half a mile of the village of Hampstead itself. They then turned down Haverstock Hill, which was quite free from buildings, and by a route which avoided the village, they came upon the verge of the heath.

" I think this will do," remarked Bill.

" I think so too," said the other. " How precious dark it is, to be sure."

" You may say that. I'm blowed if I can see the horse's head. Woa! woa!"

They both now alighted, and led the horse towards a thick hedge, skirting a plantation, near the large house lately occupied by Lady Byron. Then Bill let down the tail-board of the cart, and laying hold of Jacob Gray by the heels, he dragged him out, and letting his head come with a hard bump against the ground, which was by no means likely to improve his faculties.

They then pushed him along with their feet, till he lay completely under the hedge, and could not come to any harm from a chance vehicle or horseman.

" Well," remarked Bill, " I think we have done that job handsomely."

" Uncommon," replied his companion ; " I'd give something to see his stare when he wakes up to-morrow."

" He will look about him a bit, and then, when he finds his money gone, won't he put up prayers for us in that blessed little old church, as is now striking two."

Hampstead church was striking two as he spoke, and the echo of the sounds came sweetly and solemnly upon the night air.

Bill whistled to the horse, and, at a rapid pace, the thieves took the road homewards again.

CHAPTER LX.

ADA AT SIR FRANCIS HARTLETON'S.—THE PHILOSOPHY OF A YOUNG HEART.—A
CONFESSION.—THE PLEASURE OF SYMPATHY.

WHAT pen shall describe the happiness that gleamed now in the heart of Ada
as she sat with Sir Francis Hartleton's young wife on the morning after her
introduction to her, in a neat and prettily-arranged room, overlooking the park.

The air was fresh and balmy—the birds were flitting past the windows, and filled
the atmosphere with music. Crowds of gaily-dressed persons were idly sauntering among the trees ; enlivening strains of martial music came wafted to her ears
as the guard was changed at the Palace. The perfume of flowers, the kind words
of Lady Hartleton, and kinder looks—the harmony of the household—the gay
laughter from children who were chasing each other in a neighbouring garden,
and last, though greatest of all, the consciousness of freedom from Jacob Gray,
so filled the heart of Ada with delight, that she suddenly threw herself into the
arms of Lady Hartleton, and with a flood of tears, said,—

"Oh, I am too happy ! How can I bv a life's long duration ever repay you a
tittle of the joys you have filled my heart with ?"

"My dear Ada," replied Lady Hartleton, "you must not talk so. What you
are now enjoying, and for which you are so thankful, is no more, and probably
much less than what you ought always to have enjoyed. 'Tis the contrast of
this and what you have suffered, which makes you overlook all the disadvantages
and fancy that to mix with the world, and enjoy its routine of existence, must be
unalloyed happiness."

"Can any of those be unhappy ?" said Ada, pointing to the gay throngs in
the park.

"Alas ! my dear," said Lady Hartleton, "how very few of them are happy."

"Indeed, madam ?"

"Aye, indeed, Ada. Our joys and our sorrows are all comparative. You, in
your pure innocence, my dear Ada, have yet to learn how many an aching heart
is hidden by wreathed smiles."

"'Tis very strange," said Ada, musingly. "'Tis very strange that we should
be unhappy, and the world so beautiful. To live—to have freedom and liberty—
to go wherever the wayward fancy leads me, seem to me a great enjoyment. The
birds—the sunshine—the flowers—ay, each blade of grass trembling and
glistening with its weight of morning dew, is to me a source of delightful contemplation—I am sure all might be happy, the green fields and the sunny sky
are so very beautiful."

"There are evils, Ada."

"Yes—sickness, pain, the loss of those we love, are all evils," said Ada. "But
then we have a thousand consolations even from them, in the ever fresh and never
dying beauties of nature around us."

"Ada, with your feelings, death, pain, and sickness of ourselves, of those we
love, may well appear the greatest evils of existence. Yet strange as it may seem
to you, such is the peversity of human nature, that these are the very things that
affect it least."

"You surprise me."

"And well I may. The cares, the anxieties, the awful horrors of existence to
the many, arise from their artificial desires, and the mad riot of their own bad
passions. Avarice affects some—ambition, and the love of power, others ; and
many who could, without a pang, see rent the natural ties of love and kindred, will
lay violent hands upon their own lives, if they fail in some mad effort of their
own wild passions."

"Oh," cried Ada, "I think that I could be so happy without power—without wealth—my own ambition is is to be surrounded by kind and loving hearts, and happy faces—tongues that knew no guile, and breasts that harboured no suspicion. Surely then, enough of variety might be found, in watching the wonders of the changing seasons—enough of joy in marking the many charms which He who made us all, has cast around us for our pleasure."

‘ You, my dear Ada, have the elements of happiness in your heart ; but now that

we are alone, have you sufficient confidence in me, to tell me at length all your history ?"

"Confidence," said Ada. "Oh, yes ; and in whom could I have confidence, if not in you ?"

"Then sit here by me, and tell me all. We will be mutually confidential, Ada, and have no secrets but in common. Now tell me, is your happinesss quite perfect. Have you no secret yearning of the heart yet ungratified, Ada?"

No. 31.

"My happiness," said Ada, "is perfect with hope—a hope that must surely ripen into a dear reality.'

"Then you have a hope—a wish that lives upon hope—an expectation yet ungratified?"

"Madam," said Ada, gazing without the least timidity into the eyes of Lady Hartleton, "when I was quite friendless and oppressed, there was one who loved me—when no other human heart spoke a word of consolation to me, there was one that beat for me, and bade its owner whisper to me words of dearer hope and joy, than ever before had lingered in my ears. Wonder not then, that even now, when I have so much to be thankful and grateful for, my heart yearns for him to share its new born joy."

"And his name?" said Lady Hartleton.

"Is Albert Seyton," said Ada, with a sigh.

"Is he handsome, Ada?"

"I love him," replied Ada, emphatically.

"Maidens seldom avow their preferences so very boldly," said Lady Hartleton, with a smile.

"They who have felt as I have felt," said Ada, "the pangs of solitude and the horrors of a persecution, surely never paralleled, would learn to set a high value on the heart that loved them in their misery, and to cherish as something holy, the words of comfort, hope, and kindness, that were breathed to them in their despair. You wonder that I can avow without a blush my heart's fond love for Albert Seyton. Oh, lady, it has been the only light that shone upon me through years of gloom. Can you wonder, then, that I thought it beautiful—I am as one who had been confined for many, many years, in a dungeon. I read the legend in a book that Albert lent to me. For many years, then, this poor fated being had not seen the light of day—had heard nothing but the harsh grating of his dungeon door—the hideous rattle of his chains, until at last one day there came struggling like a sunbeam upon his soul, a strain of music. 'Twas a common air, and played unskilfully, but to him it was indeed divine.

"The prisoner lived to bid adieu to his dungeon, and he came abroad into the great world. He heard music in its excellence—music that seemed borrowed from Heaven, and he praised, admired, applauded it. But one day, some wandering minstrel, with a careless hand, struck up from a rude viol the strain that in his dungeon had so sweetly greeted htm. Oh, how his heart bounded, like a bird, within his breast—how a joy unequalled danced through his brain. He wept, he sobbed aloud in his happiness. What music greeted his rapt senses like that! He hung upon the minstrel's neck, and his prayer was—'Oh, stay ever near me, and when I am sad or weary, play to me that strain that I may thank God for my happiness.'"

Ada ceased speaking, and Lady Hartleton caught her to her heart, as she said,—

"My dear Ada, I did but speak for the pleasure of hearing you reply to me. I am too richly repaid."

"As that lonely prisoner loved the strain of melody that greeted his dreary solitude," sobbed Ada, "so let me love him who sought me out when I had none else to love me, and told me how to hope."

"Your pure and noble feelings, Ada," said Lady Hartleton, much affected, "do you infinite honour. "I am proud of you, my dear Ada, and hope to have the second place in your heart."

"You have the first," said Ada. "I cannot make distinctions between those I love. I open my heart freely to you. There is room, dear lady, for you and Albert both, and for Sir Francis too."

There was a beautiful and earnest simplicity in Ada's manner, that perfectly charmed Lady Hartleton, and she encouraged her to open her heart thoroughly to her; and she was perfectly astonished at the rich store of poetry, beauty, and virtue which lay garnered up in the breast of the persecuted and beautiful girl— stores of feeling, thought, and imagination which required but the sunny influence of kindness to bring forth in all their native purity and beauty.

Ada how gave Lady Hartleton an animated description of her whole course of life with Jacob Gray, commencing at her earliest recollection of being with him in various mean lodgings, and coming down through all the exciting and dangerous scenes she had passed to her denunciation of him at Charing Cross.

Lady Hartleton listened to her narration with the greatest interest, and when Ada had concluded, she said,—

" And you have still no clue, Ada, to your birth?"

" None—none. The mysterious paper addressed to your husband by Jacob Gray, most probably contained some information, but I fear that is lost for ever."

" A more strange and eventful history I never heard," remarked Lady Hartleton. " I have very sanguine hopes that the activity and exhaustless energy of Sir Francis will soon clear up some of the mysteries that surround you."

" Heaven grant it may be so," said Ada.

" There is one circumstance that must not be lost sight of, as it may afford some clue or corroborative evidence of your birth—that is, the necklace you sold to the Jew."

" It might, indeed," said Ada. " I was foolish to part with it."

" Should you know the shop again?"

" Certainly I should, and the man likewise. My intercourse with the world has been so very slight that I am not confused with a multitude of images and occurrences. Everything that has happened to me, and every one who has ever spoken to me, stand clear and distinct in my memory."

" Then the necklace may be recovered."

" Indeed!"

" Without doubt ; Sir Francis will get it back for you."

Lady Hartleton rang the bell, and when a servant appeared, she said,—

" Is Sir Francis within?"

" Yes, my lady," was the reply. " He has just returned from the Secretary of State's office."

" Ask him to come here."

The servant bowed and retired, and in a very few minutes, Sir Francis Hartleton entered the room with a smile.

Ada arose and welcomed him with evident pleasure, and he said,—

" Well, Ada, are you happy here?"

" Too happy, sir," she said, with emotion. " It requires all my reason to convince me it is real."

Lady Hartleton then related to her husband the story of the necklace, to which he listened with grave attention.

At its conclusion, he said,—

" I need not trouble Ada to point out the shop. The description is sufficient. The Jew who keeps it is well known to the police. I have no doubt of getting back the necklace if it be still in this country. It may be an important link in the chain of evidence concerning Ada's birth."

" Have you any thought of who I am?" asked Ada, with eagerness.

" I have," said Sir Francis, " but believe and trust me when I tell you it is for your own peace of mind and happiness that I would rather tell you nothing until I can tell you something which has a firmer basis than conjecture."

" You are right," said Ada ; " I should but be giving my imagination play, and torturing my mind with perhaps futile fears, and too sanguine hopes."

" Hope all and fear nothing," said Sir Francis. " The mere adventitious circumstances of your birth need not affect your happiness, Ada. If you can make this a comfortable home, we shall be much delighted."

" I cannot speak to you as I ought," replied Ada, " time may show my deep gratitude, but never can I hope to repay you."

" And appreciation of kindness, Ada," said the magistrate, "is its dearest reward. I will now leave you for a little time to call upon your very doubtful friend, the Jew."

" He who bought my necklace. In sooth I know little of money, but from what

I have read, it should be worth a much larger sum. I heard Gray call it real pearl.'

"No doubt—no doubt—I will go myself. You will see me again very soon, and it will go hard, but I will make the hoary robber disgorge his ill-gotten prey."

So saying, Sir Francis bade Ada and his wife a temporary adieu, and hurried to the shop of the Jew, who had taken such an unworthy advantage of Ada's want of knowledge of the value of a really costly pearl necklace.

CHAPTER LXI.

ALBERT SEYTON'S DESTITUTION.—A LONE AND WEARIED SPIRIT.—THE APPLICATION TO LEARMONT, AND THE MEETING WITH SIR FRANCIS HARTLETON.

WE have been compelled for a long time to leave the gallant and noble-hearted Albert Seyton to follow out his fortunes unchronicled, in order to depict the various changing scenes in the life of Ada, who, now that she is conducted to a haven of rest for a while, we can leave in calm contentment, although not yet, fair persecuted girl, are thy trials done! The sunshine of peace and joy that now surrounds you is but a prelude to a storm. We will not, however, anticipate but allow the events of our tale to flow on in their natural course like a mighty river, which, as it nears the ocean, which is the goal of its destiny, sweeps onwards with it every little tributary stream and murmuring rivulet that has borrowed a brief existence from it.

After the death of his father the scanty means of support which the elder Seyton had arising from the tardy justice of the government, ceased at once, and no answer was returned by the corrupt minister to Albert's application, not for a continuance of his father's pension, but for honourable employment.

One by one he was compelled to part with the several remnants of convertable property which his father had left behind him. His whole time was occupied in searching for Ada, until hope sickened into despair and a deep gloom began to spread itself like a vapour before the sun over his heart, which in happier circumstances would have throbbed with every free, noble, and generous emotion.

Twice he had called upon Sir Francis Hartleton, but had not been so fortunate as to meet with him, and the second disappointment, although it was purely accidental, Albert took seriously to heart, and in the gloomy confusion of his imagination, arising from the grief that oppressed him, cemented it into an intentional slight, and never called again. The consequence of this was, that at the time of Ada's introduction to the house of the kind and humane magistrate, she was entirely ignorant of Albert's place of abode and condition in life.

Several times since his father's death the young man had shifted his residence, for he could not bear that his rapidly decreasing means should become a subject of remark, even although a pitying one, and now he tenanted a small room in a narrow court, near the Savoy steps in the Strand.

Absolute destitution was now rapidly approaching, and he felt that the time was quickly coming when he would have had to bid adieu for ever to the most distant hope of ever again beholding Ada; and to save himself from starvation, enlisted as a private soldier in the army in which his father had held a commission.

On that very morning that Ada was sitting in the little room commanding so delightful a view of the park, and conversing with Lady Hartleton, poor Albert sat in his cheerless apartment with his head resting upon his hands in a deep reverie composed of gloomy and heart depressing thoughts and anticipations.

"Alas! alas!" he cried, " my beautiful Ada, thou art lost to me for ever. Oh, why did I leave you for one moment to the mercy of that man? I am rightly punished.   Having by the merest accident—by one of those happy chances of fortune that rarely occur twice, met you, Ada, when you were wandering in this great city, I madly allowed you to go from me.   Oh, what blindness was that—why did not some good spirit shriek ' beware' in my ears ?   Ada—Ada, I have lost you for ever !"

He remained for some moments silent, and suddenly rising he cried,—

" 'Tis in vain to struggle with my fate.   My lot in life is cast, and I must stand the hazard of the die.   Ada, farewell for ever, I must take a step now which will sever us for ever—a step which, while it takes from me my freedom of action, places me in a situation that will separate me from you, Ada.   There is a regiment ordered, I am told, to the West Indies.   It wants recruits—with it will I go, and bid adieu to England, hope, and Ada."

With a saddened heart, and yet a fixed and determined aspect, he now proceeded to collect and pack into a small compass such few papers and small cherished articles as were in themselves valueless, but dear to him as the words of his father.   There was one book, too, in the inside of the cover of which Ada, when quite young, had written the name of " Harry"—and underneath " Albert." This one word of her whom he loved so well he placed next his heart, with a determination that death should alone part him and it.   He then destroyed a number of letters which would have encumbered him, and which possessed no very peculiar features of interest.

For a moment he paused over one of those notes, as he was about to tear it across, and as he read it it suggested one last hope to his mind.

The reader will recollect that previous to his long and dangerous illness, Albert Seyton had applied to Learmont, whom he knew but as the reported richest commoner in the kingdom, for the situation of secretary to him, and had received not a distinct, but certainly an encouraging reply.

Before, however, Albert could follow up the application his illness had placed so long an interval between the first proceeding and that which would have been the second, that not doubting Learmont was long since suited, he had taken no further steps in the matter.   It was Learmont's note dated far back which now caught his eye, and made him in the present desperate state of his fortunes adopt the sudden notion of calling with it in his hand and explaining the cause of the long delay, which might interest the rich and powerful squire to give him a recommendation to some one else, if he could not himself employ him.

" A drowning man," exclaimed Albert, "they say, will catch at a straw, and upon the same principle I will cling to this one slender hope."   He read the letter carefully, which ran thus :—

" If Mr. Seyton will call upon Mr. Learmont at his house any morning before eleven he will oblige him, and they will converse on Mr. Seyton's application."

This was very brief, but still amply sufficient to found a call upon, and Albert placing it in his pocket, and trimming up as well as he could his faded apparel, donned his hat, and with a quick active step proceeded towards Learmont's house.

What an estimable thing to youth is hope, and from what a small tiny plant will it grow in the human breast to wondrous size and beauty.

The freshness of the morning, the sunshine and the feeling that there was yet another chance for him, slight as it was, chased many of the phantoms of gloom and despair from his mind.

He was not long in arriving at Learmont's house and entering the hall, for it was the fashion then of many of the wealthy to keep their outer-doors open, and trust to the throng of servants they kept in their halls, to defend them from any improper intrusion.   He inquired for Learmont.   He was replied to by a question concerning his business, when luckily recollecting his letter, he produced it, saying,—

" I have a note from the squire, requesting my attendance upon him,"

" Oh," said a servant, " if that is the case, young sir, I will take your name in, Pray follow me."

Albert followed the man, and was conducted into a small, but magnificent apartment, with an exquisitely painted roof, and hung with crimson damask.

He had not waited long when the servant re-appeared to say,—"that his master had no sort of recollection of the affair, and wished to see his own letter which the stranger said he had."

"Here is the letter," said Albert; "but his worship will see by the date, that the time therein mentioned scarcely authorises my present visit. Be so good as to add that long illness and the death of one near and dear to me, accounts for the delay."

The man took the note and was away for some time, when he entered and requested Albert Seyton to follow him, for that his master would see him.

He was then conducted through a magnificent suite of rooms, until the servant paused at a door which was a little way open. At this he knocked gently, and a deep-toned hollow voice from within said,—

"Come in."

The servant motioned Albert Seyton to enter the apartment, and in the next moment he was in the presence of Learmont, who fixed his keen searching eyes upon the young man's face for several moments before he spoke. Then he said in a low tone,—

"Young man, your application now can scarcely be considered as encouraged by me. The note you have bears date a long time back."

"It does, sir," replied Albert; "but I have been on a bed of sickness myself, and am now bereft of the parent who then——"

Albert's feelings would not permit him to say more, and he paused.

"Are you an orphan?" said Learmont.

"I am."

"And poor and friendless—and, and very nearly driven to despair? Have you found out what a hollow cheat the care of Providence is? are you one of Fortune's foot-balls, kicked here and there as the jade thinks proper? Have you met with ingratitude where you should have had succour? contempt where you trusted upon honour—derision where you went for sympathy—are you, young man, one of those who have seen enough of misery to retaliate upon the world? Speak, young man, are you such as I have described?"

There was a kind of subdued, snarling tone of vehemence in the utterance of these words by Learmont, that surprised Albert Seyton as much as the words themselves were unexpected. After a moment's pause he replied,—

"Sir, I scarce know how to answer you. I am, it is true, poor, friendless, and an orphan; I have met with ingratitude when I should have met friendship; cold indifference instead of ardent sympathy; but, sir, I thank Heaven that poor, nearly destitute as I am, my heart is light as thistle-down in its innocence of wrong, and from my inmost soul do I look up to and acknowledge that Providence that watches over all. You have jested with me, sir."

"In truth have I," said Learmont; "it is my custom with a stranger, heed it not. When I want a moral, religious, and light-hearted secretary, you may be assured that I will send for you, young man."

A pang of disappointment shot across the heart of Albert Seyton as Learmont spoke, and he replied sadly,—

"Farewell, sir, you will send for me in vain. This day, if unaccepted by you, I enter the ranks as a soldier."

"Indeed, are you so hardly pressed?"

"Heaven knows I am indeed. For myself, sir, I care not, but in my fate is involved that of another."

"What other?" said Learmont.

"Alas, sir, the tale is long, and its telling useless."

"Young man," said Learmont earnestly, "there is a matter in which I could give you good employment, but it is one requiring secresy, prudence, and deep caution."

"If it be honourable, sir," said Seyton, "I will freely undertake it were it beset with dangers."

"'Tis a reach above honourable," said Learmont. "The object is absolutely pious."

This was said in so strange a tone that Albert was puzzled to make up his mind if it were sincere or honourable, and he remained silent, expecting Learmont to go on with what he was saying.

"It is a trifling service," said Learmont, "and yet by trifles I ever estimate good service. I fear me, much, young man, that in this great city there is great wickedness."

"No doubt," said Albert, "and I should not object to any service that had for its end a righteous object."

"Sagely and wisely spoken, young sir," said Learmont; "I give away large sums to those who are in want, and some days since there came to me a man who told a piteous tale, in which there were, however, some glaring discrepancies. I relieved his wants, real or pretended, and sent a servant to follow him home for two objects; first, to ascertain if he had given his true place of abode to me, and secondly, to enable me to make inquiry into his real condition, in order that I might expose him as an impostor, or grant him further relief. You understand me?"

"I do, sir."

"Good. The man I sent was foiled. He did not succeed in tracing him to his home. With much doublings and windings he eluded all pursuit. This man then I wish you to track to his abode. Have you tact for such an enterprise?"

"Methinks 'tis very easy," said Albert.

"And you will do it?"

"I will, sir; I hate impostures, I hate that which puts on the garb of virtue or religion for base purposes."

"Ah, you have a right feeling of these things, young man," said Learmont "Execute this matter to my satisfaction, and I will entertain you as my secretary."

"When, sir, may I have an opportunity to prove my zeal?"

"I think to-morrow. A week seldom passes but he comes here craving for alms. You shall see him and follow him. Track him like a blood-hound; it will be esteemed good service by me. 'Tis a mere trifle, but succeed in it, and I will make much of you."

"I shall do my utmost, sir. There may be difficulties that I wot not of; but I will strive to overcome this, and do you satisfactory service."

"Here's money for you," said Learmont, handing him a purse. "Amuse yourself to-day: I shall not require your services until to-morrow, but attend me then at an early hour—say nine."

"I will be punctual, sir."

"And secret?"

"If you wish it."

"I do wish it. Hark ye, young sir, it is a rule in this house, that, if the slightest occurrence be made a subject of discourse out of it; if the lightest stray word be repeated elsewhere, he who so reports never enters its portals again."

"I will obey you, sir; I have no taste for babbling, and, indeed, in all this city I have not one that I can call an acquaintance."

"'Tis better so—'tis better so," said Learmont; "you will do me good service. Farewell, young sir, until to-morrow."

"Then I may consider myself as so far honoured by you, sir, as to call myself your secretary?" said Albert Seyton, scarcely believing his good fortune.

"You may—you may," said Learmont. "We will talk more at large to-morrow."

He touched a bell as he spoke, and, when a servant appeared, he said,—

"This gentleman has access to me. Good morning, young sir."

Albert bowed himself out, and scarcely recovered from his bewilderment till he found himself out of the house.

Then, as he began to consider all that had passed in his interview with Learmont, Albert began more and more to dislike his service, and to suspect that his employer was not by any means the high-minded and charitable gentleman he would fain assume to be. The manner of Learmont was so much at variance with his words, that Albert irresistibly came to the conclusion that there was something more than had been explained to him connected with the service he was asked to perform of watching to his home an unfortunate beggar.

"Still," he thought, "I may be mistaken, and blaming this man for faults of nature. He may be benevolent and just, as he reports himself to be, but still afflicted with as roguish and villanous a face as ever fell to the lot of mortal man. It will not do always to trust to appearances, and I should be foolish indeed to forsake an honourable employment for perhaps a mere chimera of the imagination. I can leave him when I please; and at least, while I remain, dear Ada, I will please myself with a belief that I am near thee."

When Learmont was once more alone, and the echo of the retiring footsteps of Albert Seyton had died away, he muttered indistinctly to himself for some moments. Then, as he grew more confident in the success of some stratagem which he had connived, he spoke with a tone of exultation.

"Yes," he said, "fortune has favoured me with the best chance yet of discovering the hiding place of Jacob Gray. This youth must be unknown to him, and surely will succeed in dogging him to his haunt. That once discovered, and an hour shall not elapse without witnessing his dissolution. I can set this young man too upon Britton. The grand difficuty in circumventing these fellows has always consisted in the want of unsuspected persons to mingle with them. This youngster looks bold and capable : he will surely be successful in taking him; and, should his curiosity grow clamorous, he is easily disposed of. What matters it to me a few more lives!—I am already steeped in gore—steeped—steeped ; but then I have my reward—wealth—honours—and—and enjoyment, of course. Ha ! what noise was that?"

Some slight creaking of an article of furniture sent the blood with a frightful rush to his heart, and he remained for several moments trembling excessively, and clutching the edge of the oaken table for support. Then, with a deep sigh, he again spoke,—

"'Twas nothing—nothing. I have grown strangely nervous of late. I was not wont to be so tremblingly alive to every slight alarm. Is it age creeping upon me, or the shadow of some impending evil upon my heart? Learmont—Learmont, be thyself. Shake off these vapours of the brain. I—I have been ten times worse since I saw that face upon my door step. God of heaven ! how like it was to one who sleeps the sleep of death. I—I cannot stay here. This room seems peopled with shapes. Hence—hence—I am going—I am going—going."

He slowly crept to the door, and kept softly muttering unintelligible words with his cold, livid lips, till he had passed out, and closed the door after him.

Laughter at this moment reached his ears from the servants' hall, and he smote his forehead with his clenched hand, as he exclaimed,—

"Why can I not laugh ? Why has no smile ever lighted my face for years ? Am I a thing accursed ? Others have spilt blood as well as I, and they have not been thus haunted. I will go out. There seems in the house to be ever close to me some hideous, unfashioned form, whose hot breath comes on my cheek, and whose perpetual presence is a hell. Yes—I—I will go out—out."

CHAPTER LXII.

JACOB GRAY IN THE HAMPSTEAD FIELDS.—THE PLACARD.—THE REWARD.

THE birds were singing merrily, and skimming over Jacob Gray's head long before he awoke from the effects of the drugged wine that had been administered to him by the considerate friends he had met with. The morning sun was shining

upon his pale, haggard face, lighting even it up with some appearance of less ghastliness, and yet there he lay motionless, as if dead. It is a favourite theory of dreams with some philosophers, that such visions of the fancy never occur but at the moment or two before awakening, or at the moment of losing consciousness by going to sleep, or in other words that we dream only when not fully slumbering.

No. 32.

It would appear that this was the case with Jacob Gray; for, as the birds sung above him, and the sun gleamed upon him, while a crow would occasionally flap his face as it flew over him, his perception appeared half to return, and his face became bedewed with a heavy perspiration, as some fearful images of his past life came across his mental vision.

His thoughts were evidently wandering back to the fearful night of the fire at the Old Smithy, and his busy fancy was enacting over again that dreadful drama of blood.

He tossed his arms wildly to and fro, and groaned and uttered the half-stifled screams which came from a disturbed stupor, in the agony of his mind.

"Save—save her," he said. "The child of she dead! I cannot do the deed. Help, oh, help me, my heart is burning—charring in my breast."

He then, in his intense mental suffering, bit his under lip till the blood trickled on to his breast, and with the actual pain he awoke, crying—

"Spare me—spare me! Oh, do not scorch my eye-balls so—my brain is on fire! Oh, God, have mercy—mercy—mercy."

He opened his eyes, and the full glare of the sunlight fell upon them, blinding him for the moment. Then he opened them again, and glanced around him in speechless wonder as to where he was.

His first impression was that he was dead, and in some other world. Then he clasped his hands over his face and then tried to think, but a confusion and want of images in his brain quite rendered such an effort vain, and at length he became only alive to so horrible a sensation of thirst that he shrieked aloud,—

"Water—water—water!"

He rose to his knees, and glaring around him with his parched tongue hanging from his mouth, he saw a shining sheet of limpid water at some distance before him. Then, still gasping the word "water," he attempted to rise, but so confused was his head from the effects of the opiate that had been s o unstintingly administered to him, that, after tottering a step or two, he sank to the earth again. His awful thirst was, however, unbearable, and with a dizzy brow and aching eyes, he crawled on his hands and knees towards the pond.

He was long in reaching it, for he deviated from the strait track largely; but when he did, oh, what an exquisite pleasure it was to lie by the brink and dash his head in, drinking up huge quantities, and causing the cold stream to bubble in his mouth and ears.

Not till his breath was exhausted did Jacob Gray raise his head from the pond, and then, when he did so, recollection returned to him up to the point when he had sat down to supper with his two suspicious friends in the court. With a cry that had something unearthly in it, he hurriedly thrust his hands into all his pockets, then with a wild shriek, he grovelled on the ground, dashing his head upon it, and clutching the grass with his hands as he cried,—

"Gone—gone—all gone—that I have toiled for—beggared, ruined, gone—gone."

Then he lay on his back, panting, as he looked into the clear, quiet pool before him, reflecting, as it did, the face of Heaven in its glassy surface, the thought came over him of plunging in, and at once ending a life of never-ending misery.

"Is it easy to drown?" he asked himself; "or are there unknown hours of maddening torture, after we think, by the cessation of all movement, life is gone?"

He crawled towards the bank of the stream, and leaning over it, he gazed, long and earnestly into its clear blue depths. It seemed miles down in the immensity of space, for now the ripples he had created had all subsided, and there was scarcely the slighest trembling of the reflected visage of the sky in the glassy stream.

Then with a shudder he withdrew, slowly.

"I dare not—I dare not," he moaned. "It is for those of more unstained souls than mine to take the awful leap from here to eternity, and hope to be forgiven——not for me—not for me—I dare not. Yet where is now my philosophy?

There is no eternity—no, no—we are all here but to play our parts in a great drama. What have I to fear? Nothing—nothing. I—I—believe in nothing."

Oh, how the abject terror depicted in his countenance belied his words. He was striving to cheat himself by the lying effusions of his own tongue, while his heart was a haven of despair.

Suddenly his attention was arrested by a man singing, as he ascended to the high ground, upon which Jacob Gray was lying. The strain was a merry one, and jarred strangely upon the half-maddened ears of Gray, who had just sufficient prudence left him to feel the necessity, in his present position, of not giving any clue to suspicion, for he felt that, in his weak and abject condition, a child might have arrested him.

He accordingly rested his head upon his arm, in as unconcerned an attitude as he could assume, and awaited the coming of the man who was now within few paces of him. He was coarsely and roughly attired, and evidently belonged to a very low grade of society. He did not notice Jacob Gray till he apparently came full upon him, then he cried,—

"Hilloa, friend, you rise betimes. I call it over work getting up so early."

"Yes," said Gray, "I—I am up soon. I like the cool air of the morning."

The man looked very earnestly at him, and Gray's heart sunk within him at the thought that he was about to be recognised and taken. He made one effort to save himself by quietly adding,—

"It's nothing to me to be in the fields early or late. I am well armed."

The man stepped back a pace at this intimation, and Gray saw that whether or not the man had any criminal designs against his liberty, he had succeeded in awakening his fears.

"No offence, sir," he said—"no offence, I hope—I'm a poor fellow, come upon business from Westminister."

"Oh! from Westminister," said Gray. Then he paused, and fixed an earger searching glance upon the man, who added,—

"Have you heard of the murder last night, sir, of Mr. Vaughan?"

"No," said Gray, "I have not been in London for some time, although I have very nearly wandered out of my track."

A clock at this moment chimed some quarters, and the man said,—

"The clock of the old church at Hampstead sounds clearly across the fields."

"At Hampstead," muttered Gray, gazing earnestly around him, for he was as ignorant as possible of the locality in which he rightly surmised he had been left by those who had eased him of all his wealth.

"Yes, there's the church peeping among the tree, sir," added the man.

"I know it well," said Gray, "my family all lie buried in its humble graveyard."

"Oh, indeed, sir," said the man, and then he went with a slow step towards a tree, and takihg a little tin can and a brush from his pocket, he began lathering it with paste.

Gray watched his proceedings with intense curiosity, for he could not surmise what he could possibly be about to do. All wonder and conjecture were, however, speedily set at rest, for the man took a large printed bill from his hat, and the first word that struck Jacob Gray was the awful and ominous one of "Murder," in large letters on the top.

The man pasted the bill on to the trunk of the tree carefully and evenly, and then he paused for a moment, and in a low, mumbling voice, read it.

Jacob Gray was in such a position that he conld not see the smaller print of the bill with sufficient distinctness to read it. The one word at the top—murder, only came out strongly and clearly to his eyes. That the placard concerned him, he never for a moment doubted, and now his agony became intense, at the thought that the man was most probably then engaged in mentally concerning his Gray's, personal appearance, with a description of him in the bill.

His anxiety while the man was reading, became so intense, that he could neither speak nor move, and it was not until the man turned to him, and said,—

"A horrid murder, sir, it seems," that he found breath to answer him, in a confused manner.

"Yes—yes," he said, "a very horrid murder. Have you caught the murderer?"

"No, sir—but there's a hundred pounds reward offered for him, and bills are being stuck all over London, and within ten miles, with a description of him."

"Indeed," said Gray, a violent trembling coming over him. "I am glad I am so well armed, that I hold several men's lives in my power; so, you see, should I meet him, I am safe from him."

The man again went back a few paces upon hearing this declaration, and said with an appearance of fright,—

"Certainly, sir—oh—of course, good morning, sir."

"Good morning," said Gray.

In a moment the man turned, and walk downed the hill at a pace which Jacob Gray could see he was momentarily increasing, as he placed a greater distance between them.

"He suspects me! he suspects me!" gasped Gray. "He has only gone to get assistance to capture me. Whither can I now fly? I can purchase no more safety, for I am penniless. Die I dare not—must I be taken—oh, horror—horror! The scaffold dances before my, eyes, and I seem even now to hear the shouts of the multitude as I am dragged out to die."

He shook for several moments fearfully, then with blanched lips and tottering limbs, he rose and approached the tree on which was posted the placard. For a minute or more, the letter seemed to dance before his bewildered gaze, and he could read nothing but the one word "Murder," which appeared as it were to stand out from the paper with a supernatural distinctness.

Gradually, however, this nervous delusion vanished, and the letters arranged themselves like living things in their proper places. Jacob Gray then read the bill, which offered a reward of one hundred pounds to any one who would apprehend and lodge in any gaol the perpetrator of the murder. The placard then went on to give but an imperfect description of Gray's person, and concluded by the name of one of the magistrates of the metropolis.

There were two things that surprised Gray in this placard. One was, that his name was not mentioned, and the other was, that no reference was made to any other real or supposed crime than the murder of the man Vaughan, in the court leading from the Strand.

Through Ada, who had so fearlessly denounced him, he had made sure that his name would become public, and that his other crime of recent date, namely, the murder of the officer Elias, in the house at Battersea, would have become known, and form as direct and distinct a charge against him as that of Vaughan, which was the least criminal act of the two. Moreover, Sir Francis Hartleton's name did not appear to the document, which was as great a surprise to Gray as anything, for he conjectured that to him, Ada would make her first appeal for protection.

Altogether the bill tormented and puzzled Jacob Gray, and he continued gazing at it, until again the letters danced before his fevered brain, and calm reflection became lost in a whirl of contending fears.

CHAPTER LXIII.

GRAY'S PROCEEDINGS.—A NARROW ESCAPE.—THE NIGHT VISIT TO LEARMONT.

THE necessity for some immediate movement, in order to insure his personal safety, now came strongly across the oppressed and wavering mind of Gray, and hastily tearing down the bill from the tree, he clasped his throbbing temples with his hands, and strove to reduce his thoughts to order and consistency That the bill-sticker had gone to get assistance to apprehend him, was the frightful notion that never for one instant left his mind, and without any definite notion of where he was going, he went round the declivity of the hill, until he arrived completely on the other side. The only means of concealment that there presented itself was a thick hedge, but then he thought how very insecure a place of refuge would that be, in the event of an active search being made for him.

The country before him was level for a considerable distance, with only here and there a small clump of trees. After some minutes more of painful thought an idea suggested itself to him, which was very much in accordance with his usual complicated habits of thought. That was, to leave some portions of his apparel on the bank of the pond, to induce a belief that he had drowned himself in its waters, and then to scramble into one of the trees, and hide till nightfall among the branches.

This was the only feasible plan of escape that suggested itself to him, for with his utter ignorance of the localities of the fields, an attempt to cross them to the village would most probably be seen, and but a short race in his exhausted and sickly state would ensure his capture. " At night," he thought, " I will venture to Learmont's—it is my only chance. I will then offer for a thousand pounds to deliver up Ada to him, and he still supposing, probably, that nothing material has happened, may consent, when I will find a means of leaving England for ever, and mature at my leisure plans of revenge against them all. But now most of all, Ada, will I mark you well. You, who have reduced me to my present state, my bitterest malediction light upon you. I would, I could have made you great and wealthy, but now I will devise some finely woven scheme to revenge myself on those I hate, without missing you."

He then laid several articles of his clothing by the bank of the pond to which he had walked, while the reflections we have worded were passing through his brain. Then hastily repairing to one of the clumps of trees we have mentioned, he with much difficulty and pain, for he was sadly bruised, contrived to ascend it, and although the pangs of hunger began even now to harass him, he resolved that the shadows of evening should shroud all things before he ventured from his retreat.

From his elevated position he now commanded a good view of the surrounding country, and far down the hill he had first ascended, he saw the forms of three persons rapidly approaching.

At that distance he could not see their forms distinctly, but as they neared the brow of the hill, he felt no doubt that one of them was the man who had stuck the placard to the tree. Now he saw them pause and point forwards, then with an accelerated pace they all three advanced towards the tree near which the bill sticker had left them. They now paused, and appeared to be consulting upon their next step, when one apparently saw the articles of clothing which Gray had left by the bank of the pond, and they all came to the spot using gestures to each other of astonishment.

They remained for several minutes in close consultation now, and then as if in accordance with an arrangement they had just made, one of them remained by the pond while the others commenced carefully peering into the hedges and bushes.

After satisfying themselves that he they sought was not immediately at hand, they both ran up Traitor's-hill, and from its summit took a long searching glance at all the surrounding fields. One of these men, Gray could see now to his intense fright, had a gun in his hand, and that fright was increased to absolute abject terror when he saw him level it at one of the trees in the vicinity, and fire among the branches, awakening many echoes and starting from their covert many birds who flew twittering and screaming from among the branches.

Then to his agony he saw the gun again loaded, and the man pointed it a another tree and fired. The sharp report went through Jacob Gray's excited brain like electricity, and it was only by twining his feet round an arm of the tree in which he was, and clutching another with his hands, that he saved himself from falling in his agitation to the ground.

The two men now conversed for some minutes in an undertone. Then one raising his voice, said in a tone that came clearly to Jacob Gray's anxiously-straining ears,—

"Oh, don't give it up yet—it's worth a try."

"So it is, but it's a bore to fire away so much powder for nothing," said the other.

"Oh, nonsense, blaze away," said the first, "I call it good sport."

"Well, here goes then," remarked the man with the gun, as he deliberately rammed down another charge

Jacob Gray now trembled so excessively that had the men been near at hand the shaking of the branches of the tree must have at once betrayed him; but fortunately for him they were too much occupied with the trees they were firing into to heed any other at a distance, however short.

As they came sauntering on, Jacob Gray with a deep groan that he could not repress, saw that a very few minutes more would bring the tree in which he was, under the aim of the man with the gun.

Bang went the piece again, and another flight of screaming birds flew from the tree fired at, and along with a number of crows took refuge in the one occupied by Gray. The men were now within a few paces of the tree, and he could hear in his elevated position with painful distinctness every word they said.

By a great effort, he in a great measure stilled the trembling which would have betrayed him, and lay along a thick branch nearly breathless from terror.

"You may depend he's off," said the man with the gun. "He wouldn't wait for you."

"Unless he's drowned himself," remarked the other, who was the bill-sticker.

"No fear of that," remarked the other with a laugh, "these kind of fellow never cheat the hangman that way. He has had time to run across the field to Sighgate or Hampstead, or even to skulk into town you may depend."

"Well, I'd take my oath it was him as was mentioned in the bill," said the man who had brought all this danger upon Gray. "I was thankful I got off scot-free from him, I can tell you. He would soon have blown my brains out if I had said half a word."

"Oh, bother you," cried the other, "you were too faint-hearted, you mean to lay hold of him."

"It's all very well for you to talk with a gun in your hand, but what odds was I with a paste-pot against a right down regular murderer, I should like to know?"

"Upon my faith," said he with the gun, "I should have enjoyed seeing you sneak off—I really should."

As he spoke, he commenced reloading his gun with deliberation. Oh, what a horrible process that was to Jacob Gray. Each moment gave him a pang of fear that nearly stopped the beating of his heart. How he watched the action of the ramrod as the powder was pressed down. Then the rattle of a number of small shot as they went down the barrel, came upon his ears with dreadful distinctness. Again there was a piece of paper pressed into the muzzle of the piece, and as the ramrod forced it home with a dull sound upon the charge, Jacob Gray perspired in every pore, and with difficulty kept himself from shrieking, mercy! mercy!

"That's an old tree," remarked the man, as he primed the gun, and stepping back a pace or two levelled it among the branches. "I recollect it when I was a boy."

"Fire away," said the other, who seemed quite to enjoy the sport.

"Now—now," thought Jacob, "now to fall a bleeding wounded man to the ground—now for pain horror, capture, death."

He closed his eyes, and clung to the branch on which he lay with pure desperation. All thought of a consistent character became lost in abject terror. It seemed to him an age ere the man fired into the tree. Then suddenly a loud report reached his ears. Small branches of the tree fell about him, and he uttered a deep groan, as he felt a shock upon his face, and along one arm, which assured him he had been hit by some of the shots. The pain of a gun-shot wound is not immediate ; the first effect is rather as if sensation had been suddenly stunned, but when the shock subsides, and the blood again resumes its wonted channels, the agony of the wound commences. Such was the case with Jacob Gray, and although but very few of the shots had struck him in the face, the neck, and on one arm, he could have screamed with pain in the course of a few moments, and it required all the counteracting influence of the master feeling of his mind—fear— to prevent him from discovering himself. Clinging still to the branch desperately he endured the pain in silence, for he durst not even moan. His first groan had been drowned in the report of the gun, but now that the echoes had died away, and all was still, the least sound of pain from his lips might be his utter destruction.

The men were silent for some moments after the discharge of the gun—then he who had fired it remarked in a disaffected tone,——

"He aint there. It's no use. He must have given us the slip."

"No, he could not stand that, I'm sure I couldn't," said the billsticker. "I never saw so many birds fly out of a tree in my life."

"That's because we have hunted them from all the others, and they took refuge in this one blockhead," cried the man with the gun, whose temper did not seem at all improved by the non-success of his expedition.

"Well, you needn't get in a passion," suggested the other.

"Who's in a passion? How do you know I'm in a passion? I don't believe you saw the man at all, and there's an end of it."

"Upon my conscience——"

"Bother your conscience—you've got none."

"Why, now you saw his things lying by the side of the pond yourself. What —suppose now he's drowned himself really. How you'd look then. Why don't you have the pond dragged—you know nobody will drag it for me."

"Why don't you get in and feel about for him?" suggested the man with the gun.

"What?"

"Get into the pond and see if he's there, I say."

"And put my foot on him perhaps. I'd sooner go to Jericho. I should never recover it. Suppose I was to go in, and put my foot on his very face Oh, oh!

"You are a coward, that's what you are, and you may hunt the fellow your-self for all I care."

"Don't go away," cried the billsticker. "Why—why——"

"I shan't stay here to be fooled any longer," said the other.

"Will you lend me the gun, then ?"

"Lend you my gun ?"

"Yes."

"I'll see you particularly well—never mind."

So saying, he of the gun marched off in very great dudgeon, leaving the bill-sticker gazing after him.

"Well," he muttered, "there's an air and a grace, I never knew he was so hasty before. I—I think I'll have a hunt for the fellow myself, and—yet he might master me, and I think I won't. It's all very well to take a prisoner, but when the prisoner takes you, it ain't near so pleasant."

Having come to this sage conclusion, the billsticker rapidly walked away, glancing every now and then around him in terror, lest Gray should make a sudden dart at him from behind some tree or hedge.

"Here ! here," moaned Jacob Gray, as he smeared the blood from his face with his hand, "here I must remain in hunger and pain till night, and then my only pe now is to crawl to Learmont's !"

CHAPTER LXIV.

THE CHEQUERS.—BRITTON'S CORNER.—AN ALARM.—THE MYSTERIOUS STRANGER
—A QUARREL.—A FIGHT AND A LITTLE ANATOMY.

WHILE all these important circumstances are taking place, intoxication was doing its fell work upon even the iron frame of Andrew Britton, and each day saw him more coarse, bloated, and wayward in his various fancies. He was but as an infant'in the interval, between his fits of drunkenness, and it was never until he had taken enough ardent spirits to kill any ordinary person that he felt his energies increase and his blood course through his veins with its accustomed activity. The fearful excitement of drink was deluding him with its present support, at the same time it was sapping the very springs of his life, and weakening the foundations of his strength.

He had already expended a small fortune at the Chequers, and yet his gold, to the surprise of the landlord and the frequenters of the house, appeared to be inexhaustible. Endless were the conjectures of who and what he was; and one person had actually called upon Sir Francis Hartleton to mention his strong suspicions that all was not right as regarded Britton; but we know that the magistrate had ample and judicious reasons for not alarming Learmont by a useless interference with Andrew Britton; and although he received the communication with politeness, he replied that he saw no reason at present to take any steps as regarded the drunken smith, who held his nightly orgies at the Chequers; so that the party left his office rather discouraged than otherwise, and Britton pursued his career unchecked.

On the very night which had witnessed the denunciation of Jacob Gray by Ada at Whitehall, and the various harrowing incidents, directly and, indirectly arising therefrom, Britton had been holding high revel in the parlour of the Chequers.

He had that morning visited Learmont, and was now freely lavishing around him the gold pieces, which appeared to have no limit, but to be produced by him as freely as if he had discovered the much coveted secret of the transmutation of metals.

There was one man who lately Britton had taken much to, and that was on account principally of his wonderful capacity for drink, in which he vied with the smith himself. This man was a butcher, residing in the immediate vicinity, and in every respect he was indeed a fit companion for Britton. Brutal, coarse, strong, and big, he combined in himself all that Britton admired; and as he had no money, and Britton had plenty, which he was, moreover, willing to spend freely, they became quite great cronies and friends.

On this occasion Britton and the butcher, whose name was Bond, occupied two seats near the fire-place, and were indulging in a bowl of hot arrack punch, which steamed before them, and from which they dipped large quantities with pewter measures.

The rest of the room presented its usual mostly appearance. There were persons of all kinds and conditions below the respectable, and a steam of hot breaths, vapour of mixed liquors, and all sorts of villanous compounds, to which was added copious volumes of tobacco smoke, which ascended to the roof.

All was boisterous, rough mirth and roaring jollity, the only distinguishing feature of which was that Britton took care his voice should be heard above all the surrounding din, and if any one presumed to laugh as loud as he, or raise his voice to as stentorian a pitch, he either commissioned the butcher, or went himself, to nob the said person on the head with the pewter measure. Britton was in one of his treating humours, and he had just ordered jugs of strong ale all round when the landlord came in, and said,—

"Gentlemen all, there's some rare news—most rare new!"

"What is it?" cried a dozen voices in chorus.

"Hilloa!" roared Britton. "Peace, I say, peace! am I a king or not? Damme, if I was a cockchafer instead of a king, you couldn't behave worse; curse you all!"

"Ha, ha, ha! a cockchafer," laughed a man whose back was towards Britton, but who was just within his reach, and he accordingly received from Britton such a stunning blow with the pewter measure that he had not a laugh in him for an hour.

"Now, silence all," cried Britton, and when comparative stillness was procured, he turned with drunken gravity to the landlord, and said,—

"Now, idiot, you come into my presence, and say,—'Here's news!'"

"Yes, your majesty."

"If you interrupt me, I'll brain you. No, not brain you. You can't be brained, having none; but I'll do something else that I'll think of. Now, what's the news?"

No 33.

"May it please your majesty," said the landlord, "there's news of a fire and a murder."

The smith half rose from his chair, and his face assumed a tinge of deep red as he shouted,—

"Who dare say so much? Think you I am crippled and cannot use my fore hammer still—the—the fire was accidental."

A murmur of astonishment passed among those present, and the landlord added,—

"I—I—was only told of it, your majesty, and thought you'd like to hear, that's all. No offence, your majesty, only they say that there's been a murder, and the old place where it was done burnt down to destroy the dead body."

"Liar!" cried Britton, making a rush at the landlord. "Who—who dare say half as much? Show me the man, and I'll take his life! Show his face, and then I shall find his throat!"

Everybody rose, and the landlord made good his retreat to the door, where he stood looking at Britton aghast, for he had never seen him in so genuine a rage before.

"What do you mean," growled the butcher, "by coming here and wexing him? Slaughter me if you deserve such a customer. Hands off there, leave him alone, will you?"

"It's a lie," cried Britton; "there is nobody there to burn, none—none. That woman, that hag, Maud, has trumped up the tale. She is mad, but full of malice —quite full of malice at me, for what I don't know. Who talks of the body? Who beards and flouts me, I should like to know? Beware, I am Britton, the smith— Beware, I say!"

The veins upon his forehead were swollen almost to bursting, and rage imparted to his voice a vehemence which soon destroyed it, for his last words were hoarse and broken, and still muttering only—"Beware!" he suffered the butcher to lead him back to his seat and fill for him a measure of the hot punch, which Britton drank as if it had been so much water. Then he drew a long breath and exclaimed,—

"The—villain—to—to—come to me with such a tale. His life—curses on him! His life should be worth more to him than to risk it."

"Be calm!" said the butcher, in a voice that almost shook the rafters of the house. "Be calm; give care the go by, and drown all sorts of disagreeables in drink. There is nothing like it, you may depend, whether you're a butcher or a king. Take another glass, by boy, and swear away. That's one o' the comforts of life too, gentlemen. Now I'm a butcher, and as humane a individual as is in all Westminster; and if anybody says I isn't, I'll put my slaughtering knife in his inside."

Britton was quiet for a few moments, partly from exhaustion and partly because he was nearly choked with another measure of punch which he threw into his throat rather heedlessly, and the landlord, when the butcher had done speaking, took the opportunity of throwing in a word of personal justification, for he was quite alarmed at the riot he had created, as he supposed, with such very slender materials.

"Your majesty," he said, "will humbly excuse me, but there is a fire at Battersea, and they do say there's been a murder."

"At—at—where?" cried Britton.

"At Battersea. From the back window of the room up stairs, adjoining your gracious majesty's, you may see the sky as red as—as—anything."

"Oh—at Battersea—to-night?"

"Yes—even now. It was one of Sir Francis Hartleton's men who said there had been a murder."

"Indeed!—Oh, indeed?" said Britton, breathing more freely. "I—I—What's it to me? What have I to do with it? Here's a toast, gentlemen, all. A toast, I say."

People are always ready to drink toasts at another's expense, and it is really very extraordinary what very out-of-the-way and singular sentiments many well-

THE MURDER AT THE OLD SMITHY.

meaning and harmless people will solemnly pledge themselves when they come before them in the shape of toasts ; and every glass and tankard was filled to do honour to the proposition of Britton, when the landlord, whose back was against the door, was nearly pushed down by the sudden entrance of a man, who, after one glance round the room, cried,—

" Now's your time."

At the words, there arose two men from among the guests, and nodded to him who had just arrived. What the three were about to do seemed involved in mystery, and likely to form an endless theme for conjecture, for before they could make any movement indicative of their intentions, another man appeared at the door, and nearly breathless from the haste he had made, he cried in a loud voice,—

" No !"

The two men who had risen looked at each other in amazement, and then at the stranger, who cried, " No !" in a tone of such authority. For the space of about a minute no one spoke, and a general feeling of alarm seemed to be produced by this strange proceeding, a clue to which no one could possibly imagine.

Then he who had last made his appearance said, in a lower tone,—

" You know me ?"

" Yes, sir," replied both the men in a breath.

" Enough—follow !"

He then turned on his heels and walked away. The two men as well as he who had just come in so mysteriously made a bustle to leave the room, but by this time all the indignation of King Britton was thoroughly aroused, and he roared out,—

" This is pretty ; I'll let you know who is king here. You follow him if you dare, ye hounds. What's the meaning of all this ?"

He rose from his seat and sprung to the door as he spoke, but he had no sooner got there than he found himself face to face with the man who had cried " No," so lustily, and who hearing some objections made to his orders, had come back.

There was an unflinching boldness about the man, that for a moment staggered Britton, and they stood face to face for a few moments in silence.

" Well, bully," cried the man, " what now ?"

The only reply of the smith was a straightforward blow, which was, however, so skillfully parried by the stranger, that it was not only quite innoxious to him, but gave Britton a severe wrench of the elbow.

" What now ?" again cried the man.

" Let me get at him," roared the butcher.

" No," screamed Britton. " D——e, let him have fair play. It's my quarrel, and I'll smash anybody that interferes."

All now rose, and a more strange collection of excited faces could scarcely have been seen, than was presented just then at the Chequers in expectation of a serious battle between the smith and his antagonist, who, although not near so stout a man, was fully as tall, and a great deal younger looking than he.

" What do you want here ?" said Britton.

" I shall not tell you," replied the man.

" You can fight ?"

" A little."

" Where I came from," added Britton, " we wrestle a little."

" So do we where I came from," replied the other, calmly.

" Do you," cried Britton, and then confident in his own strength and skill, even half intoxicated as he was, he sprung upon the man, and seizing him fairly by the shoulder and waist, he made a tremendous effort to throw him, but he produced no more impression upon the stranger than as if he had laid hold of the corner of a house.

After a few moments' exertion, he ceased, panting, from his endeavours, and at that moment the stranger put out his arms, and threw Britton so heavily upon his back that the room shook again.

"Foul play! foul play!" cried the butcher, half rising.

"You lie, sir," cried the stranger, in a tone that made the butcher fall back into his seat again with surprise.

"Follow," cried the stranger then, addressing the men who had waited patiently until the result of the combat. He then strode from the house, being immediately followed by those who appeared to know him, and under so implicit an obedience to his commands. Britton was picked up by the butcher, and laid with a thwack, as if he had been some huge joint of meat, upon one of the oaken tables.

"I hope there's no bones broke," said the landlord.

"Bones broke, be bothered," replied the butcher; "I think I ought to know something about bones and meat too."

"So you ought, Master Bond," cried a man; "so you ought. Only I should say you knew most about bones."

"Should you, spooney—and why?"

"Because you never send me a joint that isn't at least the best part bones."

There was a general laugh against the butcher at this sally, who, glaring ferociously at the speaker, exclaimed, —

"When you come to my shop again, look after your own carcass that's all, and now for what I calls *judgmatical atomy.*"

"What?" cried several voices.

"Judgmatical atomy," roared the butcher. "It means knowing whether bones is broke or not."

"Oh, very good, Master Bond," said the landlord. "Pray attend to his majesty, bless him. I hope he aint hurt—a d—d fool."

This last sentence was uttered very low by the landlord, and Bond, the butcher, at once commenced a ludicrous examination of the various limbs of Britton

"He aint hurt in the fore-leg," he remarked. "He aint damaged nowhere from neck to loins. He'd cut up as nice as possible, and nobody be no wiser. Pour a glass of brandy into his mouth, and hold his nose."

This operation was duly performed, and as recovery or strangulation were the nly alternatives nature had, in the case of Andrew Britton, she embraced the ormer, and he opened his eyes.

CHAPTER LXV.

AN   INTERVIEW   WITH   A SECRETARY   OF   STATE.—SIR   FRANCIS   HARTLETON
DIFFICULTIES.

In order to explain the cause of the singular interruption which occurred to the festive scene at the Chequers, we must glance at the proceedings of Sir Francis Hartleton for the preceding two days.

We have before hinted at the very awkward position in which Sir Francis Hartleton was placed as a magistrate, having suspicions of the very strongest nature for suspecting some foul crime on the parts of Learmont, Andrew Britton, and the man Gray, of whose existence and identification with the third in the iniquitous proceeding he had only lately had good reason to believe, and yet such suspicions not assuming a sufficiently tangible form to enable him to found a charge upon him.

At the same time, working as he was in the dark in trying to unravel a plot, the intricacies of which seemed to him to increase instead of diminish as he dived into it, he never knew but what some false step of his—some effort of over zeal might put the guilty parties not only on their guard of him particularly, but might set them to work to take more effectual steps than they had hitherto done for the suppression of every particle of tangible evidence against them, but might likewise induce deeper and blacker crimes than any they had yet attempted or committed for the preservation of secrets essential to their existence.

Thus it was that although Sir Francis Hartleton had a strong perception of the main facts of the case he had in hand as regarded the guilt of Learmont, yet he felt that he could not be too cautious in what he said or did consequent thereon, until some circumstance should arise to give a direct clue to such a chain of evidence as should enable him at once to pounce upon them all, and insure their condemnation on irrefragible proofs.

After his first interview with Albert Seyton, he had carefully made a narrative of all the circumstances connected with the affair, and as it will be recollected that by that interview he was enabled to place together the names of Gray, Britton, and Learmont, in such a manner as to be certain that they were then, or had been, engaged in some great act of villainy together, he was in a much better situation for arriving at a correct conclusion with regard to the various circumstances that came crowding upon his recollection.

That some crime, most probably a murder, had been committed so many years ago when he, a young man, having more passion and impetuosity than discretion, resided in the village of Learmont on the night of the fire at the Old Smithy, he never entertained a doubt, and the probability that had he been a private individual and not an open enemy as it were of Learmont's, he would have made some effort of perhaps a hazardous and illegal nature to obtain satisfaction on the affair.

Sir Francis, however, was one of those who felt deeply the responsibilities of the situation in which he was placed as one of the ministers of justice, and he would have considered himself as quite unfit for so onerous an office had he acted from impulse instead of reflection in the prosecution of evil-doers. Thus, although ferretting the while, he waited until something should occur to point him a clear and consistent path in the investigation.

His own suspicions were simply these. That Learmont had, by the assistance of the savage smith, and the man who had rushed from the burning house with the child, committed some great crime for the sake either of stilling for ever some evidence of preceding criminality, or for some then present gains or pecuniary advantage, and hence Andrew Britton's constant visits to Learmont were for probable claims upon his purse.

That Jacob Gray was the man who had so rushed from the burning smithy, and that Ada was the child he had in his arms, Sir Francis, after what was related to him by Albert Seyton, felt almost assured of, and that both Gray and Britton were now preying upon Learmont, he felt convinced.

All this, however, did not amount to much, and although greatly strengthening his own previous suspicions of foul play somewhere, afforded him no information as a magistrate. He could make no specific charge against Learmont. He had nothing to say to Britton, and Gray he had never been able to catch hold of, or he would have made an attempt to possess himself of the papers addressed to him, which he thought more than probably contained ample information.

He was likewise moved strongly by the picture Albert Seyton had drawn of the persecutions endured by Ada, and setting apart all other considerations, he was most anxious to rescue her from the ills by which she was surrounded.

Thus he wanted to discover two things principally. The one was what crime had been committed at the Old Smithy; and the other was, presuming Ada to be the child seen on that memorable occasion—who was she?

To neither of these questions could he give himself a rational answer, and he was therefore forced to endeavour to comfort himself in the affair by setting a watch over Britton, another on Learmont, and making what exertions he could himself to ferret out the abode of Jacob Gray, without exciting the suspicions of Learmont.

Several times the thought of an active search in the ruins of the Old Smithy at Learmont had suggested itself to his mind, but had been rejected upon the conviction that such a proceeding would be very public, and could not be undertaken by him as a magistrate, without some valid previous excuse.

On the day, however, that he considered himself so fortunate as to have unearthed Jacob Gray, and to have him all but in his grasp, Sir Francis Hartleton resolved to bring affairs to some sort of crisis, and adopt reluctantly the only plan that presented itself to him, of securing the safety of Ada and the punishment of two out of three criminals, and that was to arrest Britton on that day, and, confronting him with Gray, induce a clear confession from one or the other of them, under a promise of relief from capital punishment.

He, acting upon this feeling, procured ample assistance, and previous to starting for Gray's house in the marshes of Battersea, he instructed one of his experienced officers to make sure of the capture of Britton before night.

His disappointment at Forest's house we are aware of, and immediately upon his return, he was careful to countermand the order for Britton's arrest. This countermand, however, was given to an officer who was seriously hurt in a common street affray before he could communicate his message to him; who had the particular charge to capture the smith. Hence it arose that Sir Francis Hartleton was not aware that measures were taking to apprehend Britton, until it was almost too late to prevent it. He, nevertheless, made the attempt, and was, as we have seen, just in time personally to stop the arrest, for it was he himself who cried " No," in the parlour of the Chequers, being this time effectually disguised from the observation of Britton.

Sir Francis then immediately returned to his own house, where he had not long been, when he heard rapidly, one after the other, of the two astounding events of the fire at the lone house by Battersea, and the denunciation of a man, by a young and beautiful girl, near Charing Cross, as a murderer.

The thought immediately flashed across his mind that this man must be Jacob Gray, and his accuser the persecuted Ada. A very short time, as we are aware, convinced him that his suspicions were well-founded, and his main cause of anxiety being removed, he now resolved to lend all his energies to discover who Ada was, and bring home the crimes of Learmont and his associates to them.

The whole affair had now assumed so new and troublesome an aspect, that Sir Francis Hartleton thought it necessary to apply to the Secretary of State for sanction to the proceedings he might wish to adopt.

His wish was that the pursuit after Jacob Gray might not be active, but that he should be rather left alone for a time, under a strict surveillance, to see what he woud do, and how far he might commit his associates by visits and communication with them. He likewise wished the case of Andrew Britton to be entirely left in his hands, for the violent proceedings of the savage smith had begun to excite the attention of others of the local authorities, and he, Sir Francis Hartleton, was fearful that some imprudent step might be taken by some other magistrate concerning Britton and his mysterious wealth, which might alarm Learmont before he wished him to be at all alarmed.

With these views and feelings, Sir Francis Hartleton repaired to the Secretary of State, with whom he had an immediate interview, and to whom he carefully detailed all the circumstances which were within his knowledge, concerning Ada and her fortunes, from the night of the fire at the Old Smithy at Learmont, to the time when he had taken refuge at his house, concluding by saying,—

" Sir, I have, from a record of all the circumstances, the strongest reason to believe that this young girl is the same, who, when an infant, was carried from the burning ruins by the blood-stained shrieking man, but still I have no proof; I believe that Jacob Gray is that man, but still I have no proof; I believe that a murder was committed that night at the smithy, but still I have no proof; and moreover, by Gray's subsequent crimes, we are now entirely cut off from offering him any merciful consideration for a full and free confession of the whole of the circumstances, and Britton, I fear, is not the man to confess at all ; if he were, he is most probably awfully and deeply implicated. Therefore, what I wish of you, sir, is authority to stop proceedings against Gray, for the present, and to leave him at large until I procure some more tangible information concerning all these mysteries, always promising that I can arrest him at any time I please."

"Upon my word," said the secretary, scratching his chin, "it's a very disagreeable and awkward affair. This Learmont has promised us no less than seven votes in the Commons."

" Has he, sir ?"

" Yes, and you see—really seven votes—are—are—in point of fact, seven votes."

"He procures them of course by nominating members of his properties?"

"Yes, of course."

" Then, sir, should all that property be wrested from him by a conviction for felony, those votes and qualifications must revert to the crown."

" Upon my word that's true ; I dare say he's a very great rogue ; don't make a disturbance for nothing, Sir Francis, but you can take the authority you require. Of course, the votes are more useful to us in our hands than coming through his ; but the family may not be extinct."

" Still, sir, we cannot smother this affair ; justice must be done."

" Of course, I know all that ; the majesty of justice must be upheld ; only, you see, seven votes are something, and I only mentioned how awkward it is—I may say confoundedly awkward—for we have scarcely a majority ; but, however, you may take your authority, Sir Francis."

CHAPTER LXVI.

GRAY'S VISIT TO LEARMONT.—THE DISAPPOINTMENT.—A WEEK OF TERROR.—THE STREET NEWSVENDER.

EVENING was casting its broad shadows across the Hampstead fields, and the air was varied with the songs of thousands of birds retiring to roost, when Jacob Gray with pain and difficulty began his descent from the tree which had afforded him so hazardous and painful a refuge for so many hours.

Stiffened and benumbed as he was in every limb, he found it no easy matter to crawl down from his high perch; and it was only after many minutes of uneasiness and terror that he at last reached the ground ; then he leaned against the trunk of the tree, and with dizzy eyes and a bewildered brain looked anxiously around him. A death-like silence reigned around, broken by nothing but the twittering of the sparrows, and the occasional chirp of a grasshopper. He put his hand up to his wounded face, but the blood had ceased to flow, and he only now felt a heavy, deadening sensation about the region of his wounds. After a time, then, he ventured to leave the tree, and with a slow, uncertain, and tottering step he walked towards the pond.

The direful pangs of hunger, which in his recumbent position in the tree had not greatly afflicted him, now began to make themselves felt in earnest, and Jacob Gray groaned in his agony.

"Oh," he cried, "for a crust—the hardest morsel that ever a dainty beggar cast from him as unworthy of his wallet—I shall die of hunger ere I reach Westminster !"

Still he tottered on towards the pond, and when he reached its grassy brink, he lay down as he had done before, and drank largely at the clear water.

Then he bathed his face, and washed away partially the stains of blood that had hardened into coagulated masses upon his cheeks ; and he was again somewhat refreshed, although still terribly faint from want of sustenance.

To abate, if possible, the aching, racking pains in all his limbs, he strove to increase his rate of walking, but that expedient, by increasing the languid circulation of his half-thickened blood, caused his wounds from the shot to burst out bleeding afresh, and the horrible faintness that came over him for want of food made him reel along like a drunken man.

It might have been the lingering effects of the opiate that had been so freely administered to him, or it might be his huge draughts of water upon an empty stomach, but, from whatever cause it arose, a deadly sickness came over him just as he neared some cottages at the base of the hill, leading to what is now a pretty collection of suburban cottages, which was then a swampy hollow, with a few miserable huts, occupied by people who sold bundles of dry sticks for firewood ostensibly, but who were in reality bad characters, not averse to anything, so that it promised the smallest gain.

Jacob Gray held, with a shivering, nervous grasp, by one of the palings which divided the patch of garden ground belonging to one of these hovels from the waste common, and was dreadfully sick—sick until what little strength had been left to him was frustrated, and he fell, a breathing, but scarcely animate mass, by the side of the palings.

His situation was an unfavourable one for attracting the attention of any person who might be in the hut, for the palings hid him, and he had not strength, had he the inclination, to cry for help. How long he remained there he knew not, but it was quite dark, when, the awful sickness having subsided, he made an effort to rise again. With much difficulty he gained his feet, and the moment he did, the horrible feeling of hunger—maddening hunger—came across him with twice its former intensity of pain.

"I—I can go no further," he gasped. "I shall die on the road side if I attempt to reach London from here with—without food. I—I cannot—cannot."

He staggered along the palings till he came to a wide gate which had no fastening, and there, with a feeling of desperation, he crawled through, determined to isk all by craving charity of the cottagers.

As he went on by the inner-side of the wide palings, which he was obliged to cling to for support, he struck against some projection which threw him down and very much bruised his knee. As he lay there he put up his hands to feel what it was, and by the shape of the projection, as well as dipping his hand into its contents, he thought in a moment what it was, and he rose with alacrity to eat greedily from a pig-trough the loathsome remainder of the last meal that had been given to the swine.

What will hunger not induce persons to do ? Jacob Gray thought he had never so much enjoyed a meal in his life, and when he had devoured the remnants of the mash in the trough, he sat down by the palings, and in about half an hour was sufficiently recovered to make his project of proceeding to the house of Learmont at Westminster not so wild and impracticable.

The night was now fairly set in, and there was not much chance of Gray's ragged, wounded, and emaciated appearance attracting the notice of any one along the dimly lighted road from Hampstead to London.

Although his strength was now a little restored, he still felt very ill at every step of his progress, and his only hope became entirely founded upon the chance of finding Learmont within, and inducing in him a belief that his, (Gray's) strange and disordered appearance, arose merely from some accident on his road, and not from any circumstances which had put it out of his power to be half so noxious and dangerous as he had been.

"Oh," he thought, "if when I see Learmont he did not know how harmless to him I am without Ada—without a written scrap to leave behind me, to point, the finger of suspicion against him—how his fingers would close upon my throat and what music to his ears would be my death rattle. But I must deceive him—I must beard him still—still defy—still taunt him."

It was some hours before Jacob Gray, travelling at the unsteady pace he did, contrived to reach the first houses in London ; and when he did so, what would he have not given for but one of the pieces of bright gold he had been so long hoarding, and of which he had been robbed so speedily, in order that he might, ere he adventured to see Learmont, take some means of improving his appearance, and nourishing his wearied frame, in order that a suspicion might not arise in the breast of the crafty squire that all was not as usual with him.

Then there was another view of his condition, that when it occurred to his mind,

brought a tumult of distracting thoughts into the brain of Jacob Gray ; and that view was based upon the uncertainty that beset him with regard to Ada's actions since denouncing him at Whitehall. Had she gone to Sir Francis Hartleton's, and so far added to his suspicions of Learmont, as to have induced some step against the squire ; or, had she made her name and story so public that the whole of Westminster had rung with it, coupled with the fact, that it was he, (Jacob Gray,) who had been hunted up the Strand ; and that Learmont, residing as he did, within

No. 34.

almost a stone's throw of the whole occurrence, heard sufficient to let him know how innoxious Jacob Gray now probably was in his death, and how impolitic it had now become to let him live again to surround himself with those precautions which had been so suddenly and so strangely torn from him in the course of a few short hours.

Whenever all this occurred to Jacob Gray, his steps faltered, and the perspiration of mortal fear broke out upon his brow, for he knew not but that he was hurrying to his destruction, and making powerful efforts to be earlier at the place in which he was to be sacrificed.

Still, what other hope had that miserable guilty man. Learmont alone had the power to aid him, Learmont alone held him in dread, and might still fancy he could even in death leave a sting behind him which might topple him from his haughty height of power, and dissipate to the winds of Heaven all his dreams of wild ambition.

"Yes, yes," he muttered, "I must run this awful risk—I must go to Learmont and procure enough gold for my present necessaries, and then concoct some scheme for the dark future."

With a face as pale as monumental marble, save where a few livid marks and streaks of blood showed where he had been wounded, Jacob Gray now turned into the dense mass of houses about St. Giles's, for the purpose of wending his way as quietly and as far from the public thoroughfares as possible towards Charing-cross.

Skulking along by dark places, and shunning anywhere that presented a light aspect, he pursued his route towards the upper end of St. Martin's-lane. A crowd was there collected sufficiently dense to stop his progress, and he dare not, like a man of clear conscience and open heart, push his way through the motley assemblage. In vain he tried to get up one of the side streets which would not take him far out of his way. He had no recourse but to go back some hundred yards or more, or endeavour to get through the mass of persons, the cause of whose assembling he knew not nor cared, so that they would let him pass unobstructed and unquestioned.

As he neared, in his efforts to pass, the centre of the throng of persons, he found that they were collected around a man who was, in the loud conventional voice of street singers and proclaimers of news, attracting his auditors by some narrative of deep interest, apparently. In another moment, Gray, nearly lost all power of motion as he heard these words :—

" Here, my masters, you have a full account with all the particulars of the most horrid murder in the Strand of Mr. Vaughan, together with a copy of verses made on the occasion, and addressed to all young persons, warning them against dice, cards, drink, and Sabbath breaking."

The man then in a loud nasal voice, commenced his verses.

Jacob Gray only paused to hear the first line, which consisted of an appeal to young mothers nursing tender babes, and then unable any longer to remain in the throng, he pushed his way through them like a madman, and despite the kicks and cuffs he received, succeeded in passing on and arriving nearly breathless, heated, and alarmed at Charing-cross.

CHAPTER LXVII.

THE DISAPPOINTMENT.—THE LAST RESOURCE.—A STRANGE MEETING.—THE
CONFESSION.

THE clocks were striking ten as Jacob Gray came within sight of Learmont's house, and then so strongly did all his former fears regarding the possible results of his interview with the squire came across him, that it was many minutes before he could summon courage to ascend the steps of the mansion. There was, however, no other course ; and, although his fears were of a nature rather to be increased than diminished, by the feverish nature of his reflection, he reluctantly at length slunk up the steps and knocked at the door, for at that hour it was always closed.

The few moments of suspense till the door was opened, were agonising to Jacob Gray in the extreme, and all his former faintness, and some of exhaustion came over him as the ponderous portal opened, and a servant stood in the gap and demanded his business.

" You know me ?" said Gray.

The man looked at him doubtingly, for what with his wounds, and the pain, misery, and anxiety, he had gone through, he was sufficiently altered to make his recognition doubtful for a moment, even to those who had seen him often. A second look, however, let the servant know that he had seen him before as one of his master's very mysterious visitors, and he replied—

" Yes, sir, I do know you."

" Tell your master I am here."

" He is not within."

" Not within."

" No, sir. We do not expect him home to-night ; he has gone to a party at the Earl of Harrowdon's, in the Palace-yard."

Gray stood for a moment leaning for support against the doorpost—then by a strong effort he spoke—

" Thank you—I—I will call to-morrow," and he descended the steps stupified and bewildered by the cross accidents that seemed to conspire against him.

He heard the door closed behind him, and he walked on mechanically for about a hundred yards, when he sat down upon the step of a door, and leaning his face upon his hands, he nearly gave himself up to despair.

What could he do ?—What resource was open to him ?—Where could he go for food and shelter ? A starving fugitive !—with a price set upon his capture. Could there be yet a degree of horror, and misery beyond what he now endured.

" Yes—yes," he suddenly said, " I—I can beg. Till to-morrow I can beg a few pence to save me from absolute starvation ; but yet that is a fearful risk, for by so doing I shall challenge the attention of the passers by, instead of evading it. I cannot starve; though I must beg—if it be but a few pence to keep me alive until the morning."

Jacob Gray's appearance was certainly very much in favour of any tale of distress he might relate for the purpose of moving the charitable to pity and benevolence. A more miserable and woebegone wretch could scarcely have been found within the bills of mortality.

The first person upon whom Jacob Gray made an attempt in the begging way was a man who was slowly sauntering past, enveloped in a rich and handsome coat, but the moment he heard Gray say,—

" I am starving," he drew his cloak closer around him, as if by so doing he shut out his appeal to humanity, and hurried on at a rapid pace.

Gray had not been begging long enough to have learnt humility, and the bitter curses he muttered after the man with the cloak would have made his hair stand on end, had he have heard them.

As he was then upon the point of rising from the step, and crawling to some more public thoroughfare, in which he might have a more extended sphere of operation, a strange wild noise smote his ears, and he drew back into the shadow of the doorway with a feeling of alarm.

The sound seemed to approach from the further end of the street, and now he could distinguish a voice addressing some one in imploring tones, which were replied to by a harsh voice. The words spoken Gray could not distinguish, but a strange presentiment came over him that he was somehow connected with the persons approaching, or the subject matter of their discourse.

Back—back—he shrunk into the doorway, until he was completely hidden in the shadow of the house.

The disputants rapidly approached, and then he could hear the rougher voice exclaim,—

"There is no harm meant you. You are a foolish woman. I tell you, over and over again, that you are wanted for your own good."

"Murderer, away, away!" cried a voice that struck to the heart of Jacob Gray, for he knew it to be the woman he had seen at the public house by Vauxhall, when he ran so narrow a chance of capture by Sir Francis Hartleton.

"Will you come quietly?" cried the man.

"No.—no—not with you," cried Maud, "not with you. Look at your hands, man, are they not dyed deeply with blood? Ha! ha! ha! you shrink now. No —no—Maud will not go with you; but I will tell you a secret. Listen—Do you know Andrew Britton, the savage smith?"

"No, nor don't want," said the man. "Come now, listen to reason. Sir Francis Hartelton wants to see you particularly."

"Aye, aye!" said Maud, "that's a fine device. Tell me where the child is, will you?"

"Come now,—it aint far," said the man. "Here have I been hunting all over London for you nearly nearly a day and half now, and when I find you, you won't come. I tell you Sir Francis means to do something for you."

"Can he restore the dead?"

"Not exactly."

"Ah! ah! ah! He can—he can. So now I know you are no messenger of his. You come from Andrew Britton,—why? to kill me; but it is of no use—of no use, I tell you. You, and he, and everybody know well that he is to die before I do."

Maud now laid ho'd of the rails of the hous   d resolutely refused to move The man spoke in a perplexed tone as he said,—

"Come—come now, don't be foolish. I must get some help to take you, whether you like it or not, if you won't come now quietly."

"Beware," said Maud.

The man gave a start, as the poor creature showed him the glittering blade of a knife she had concealed in her bosom. There was a pause of a few minutes, and then Gray heard the man say,—

"Very well. Just as you like. I always look after number one first, and I'll be hanged if I have anything more to do with you."

Maud laughed hysterically as she sat down upon the step, and still kept a clutch upon the iron rail.

"Foiled! foiled!" she exclaimed. "Ha! ha! ha! Tell him it is in vain. He may hunt me, but it is written in the book of the Eternal, that Britton, the savage smith of Learmont, is to die before I. Go—go. Ha! ha! ha! You will never wash the blood-stains out. Never—never—never!"

The man made no answer, but walked away at a very rapid pace, no doubt for the purpose of procuring some assistance; for he was an officer who had been ordered by Sir Francis Hartleton to seek for the poor deserted creature, and bring her to him, when he would take measures for placing her in some asylum where she would be free from any violence on the part of Andrew Britton, should he accidentally meet with her.

Maud continued to mutter in a low tone after the man had left, but Gray could not closely distinguish what she said, and he remained for some time perfectly quiet, rsolving in his mind what he should do. As he communed with himself the deadly spirit of revenge against all whom he imagined to be in any way accessary to producing his present destitute state came over him, and he ground his teeth as he muttered,—

"I could kill them all. I could exult in their agonies. I will, I must have revenge. This hag was the cursed cause of all the horrors I have been compelled to wade through, and shall I now suffer her to escape, now that she is in my power?"

He cast a rapid glance up and down the street as he added,—

"And no one by. Oh, that I had some weapon that silently and surely would do its work, and leave her here a corpse. She shall be one offered on the altar of my revenge! I must, I will work the destruction of them all, and she will be the—the first."

A deathly languor came over Jacob Gray even as he spoke, and he groaned audibly.

Maud started at the sound, and turning she fixed her eyes upon his dusky form as it lay hid in the shadow of the doorway, from which, for more than a minute his extreme weakness would not permit him to move.

"What man are you?" cried Maud. "You groan—wherefore? Have you lost all you loved?"

"I have," said Gray, with a groan, as he thought of his money.

Maud crept up the steps till she came close to him, and then laying her shrivelled hand upon his arm, she said,—

"I know you now—I know you."

"Know me?" faltered Gray, making an effort to pass her on the steps.

"Yes. Where, and how, and when we meet I shall soon think, but I know you."

Gray felt a little alarmed at this speech, and he replied,—

"You are mistaken. I am poor and destitute. We have never meet before."

"Poor and destitute? Hast ever felt the pang of hunger as I have?"

"I feel them now."

Maud opened a wallet she had with her, and took some broken victnals from it, which she laid before Gray, saying,—

"Eat—eat—and I will think the while where I have met you."

He needed no second invitation, but devoured the not very tempting viands before him, with an eagerness that could leave no doubt of the truth of his statement concerning his hunger.

Maud passed her hands several times across her brow as she said,—

"I know you, yet I know you not. Did you ever hear of a murder?"

"No," said Gray.

"Done with such a thing as this?"

She half produced the knife as she spoke, and Gray immediately said with eagerness,—

"Give me that?"

Maud drew back, and fixed her wild eye upon him as she said,—

"Are you a man of blood? Let me see your hands. Are they stained with innocent gore, or free from the damning pollution that begrimes the foul, and drag it shrieking to despair. Answer me man. Saw ye ever the Old Smithy?"

"Give me the knife and I will tell you."

"Yes, the knife! He is eager for the knife, who kuows its use. Answer me, Saw ye the fire—yes, the fire—when was it? Yesternight?"

"What fire?"

"In a house where dwelt an angel, I knew 'twas that—yes! Ha! ha! ha! and there was a body too that would not burn. There it lay black and cold, untouched amidst the charred fragments of the house. I—I have been there to look for the angel, but she had flown—up—up to her native skies, with not a downy feather of her radiant wings touched by the gross element."

"You, you have been to the house?" stammered Gray.

"I have! You knew it? It lies near sweet green fields, and the merry birds mock you as you go it. Listen, and I will tell you what I did. The early dawn was brightening, and old and young with jests and laughter, and mingling voices, went to see the ruins of the ancient house."

"And you went."

"I did. Then some bright spades and hatchets, and they dug for the body of a murdered man. Pile after pile of the blackened rubbish was removed, and then one said,—he must be burned to a cinder, but I knew he would be found. No murdered body was ever yet all burnt. The murderer himself has often tried thus to dissipate in the ashes of his victim, all traces of his awful crime, but Heaven will not have it so."

Gray clutched to the railings for support as he said,—

"Nonsense—I—I know better."'

"Ha! ha! ha!" laughed Maud. "I cannot see well the working of your face, but your voice belies your words. The man was found."

"Well, well. It is nothing to me."

"They said he had been shot," continued Maud, "and that he must have died in lingering agony. I saw them bring him forth—not a thread of his garments—not a hair of his head—was touched by those flames that had destroyed all else."

"Well—well," said Gray, "I don't want to hear more. Will you give me the knife?"

Maud had kept her hand upon the handle of the weapon, and Gray had found no opportunity of taking her by surprise, or he would have made an endeavour to destroy the poor creature, upon whose head the chastening hand of Providence had fallen so heavily. A direct attack upon her he dared not make, for first of all he could not trust his present weak state to the chances of a struggle even with her, and secondly, such was not Jacob Gray's way of doing things.

"Will you give me the knife?" he repeated.

"No!" said Maude. "I'm keeping it for Andrew Britton."

"Indeed?"

"I am—I am."

"If I thought you would use it on Andrew Britton," muttered Gray, "I would not take it from you for a hundred pounds."

'Listen—listen, I have not told you all,'' said Maud.

"All what?"

"About the fire. You shall hear—all who went there from many motives, left the" smoking mass before the sun was at its topmost height in Heaven—but I stayed."

"Why did you stay?"

"I thought the angel might come to me, but she did not. I prayed for her to come near again, and show me her pale and beautiful face, but she did not. I wept, but she came not, and then I thought I might find something that should ever remind me of her. And I did—I did."

"You did?

"Aye."

"What—what—found you? Tell me, woman."

"Twas very strange that. I should find them there," said Maud thoughtfully.

"Find what?"

"Where the murdered man had lain there was no trace of fire. The flames had burned round, but touched him not, there I found them."

"Woman, tell me what you found, or—"

"Or what?" cried Maud, her eyes flashing upon the cowardly Gray, who immediately shrunk back, saying,—

"Nothing—I—want nothing. Only I am anxious to know what you found."

"You are ? Well, well, I found some of these. Here is one."

As she spoke, she took from her breast a small torn scrap of paper and gazed at it attentively.

In an instant Gray surmised the truth. In his attempt to get rid of his written confession while standing on the ladder, previous to the murder of Elias, he had dropped many pieces, and then in the exciting scenes that followed utterly forgotten them. Once indeed, while in the tree on Hampstead Heath, he remembered the circumstance, but then he immediately assumed that they had been burnt along with the house.

He now trembled in every limb, as the thought came over him, that possibly the poor mad creature might have collected sufficient of the torn pieces to give Sir Francis Hartleton a tangible idea of the whole ; and although he felt that, next thing to his life, was the repossession of those torn scraps, he was so overcome by the circumstance of their thus coming to light, that for a few moments he thought he should have fainted.

Maud, meanwhile, spread out the small crumpled pieces of paper in her hand, and commenced reading in a low muttering voice,

" Andrew Britton"—" the temptation"—" a double murder"—" shrieking "— " the child"—" guilt—"

" Ha ! ha ! brave words, brave words !" she cried, " murder and guilt, and Andrew Britton's name of course ; where there is murder and guilt, there must be Andrew Britton."

Gray slowly prepared himself for action. He cast a wary eye around him, but no one was visible. Then he drew himself up to make a rush upon Maud, when he heard a voice some distance down the street say loudly, —

" Faster, I say, faster. Who'd be a king if he couldn't be carried as quick as he likes ? On, I say, or I'll be the death of some of you."

" Andrew Britton !" shrieked Maud, and she bounded from the step and ran down the street with amazing fleetness.

Jacob Gray sunk back against the door with a deep groan.

CHAPTER LXVIII.

BRITTON AND LEARMONT.—MIND AND MATTER PRODUCE SIMILAR RESULTS.— LEARMONT'S WEAKNESS AND FEARS.—THE CHAIR.

DESPITE the apathy endured by his habitual state of intoxication, Andrew Britton began to feel some vague sort of apprehension that there was danger at hand, and that he was watched by parties who came and sat down with apparent jollity in the old parlour of the Chequers.

When once this idea got possession of his mind, it began to torment him, and, however, after thinking to the best of his ability over the matter, he determined upon consulting with Learmont upon the subject, and leaving it to his cooler judgment to take what steps he thought fit in the affair.

According to this resolve he sought the house of Learmont, where he arrived but a very few minutes after Albert Seyton had left, and demanded, with his usual effrontery, an interview with the squire.

Learmont had latterly looked upon Andrew with mixed feelings of dread and exultation—dread that he might drink himself to death some day and leave behind him ample written evidence to convict him, Learmont, of heavy crimes—and exultation that all the money the savage smith wrung from his fears was converted into the means of his destruction by his habit of habitual intoxication.

When they now met, Learmont forgot for a moment his personal danger in eager notice of the trembling hand and generally decayed state of the smith's once hardy frame.   But he forgot at the same time that anxiety and the constant gnawing of conscience were making even more rapid ravages upon his own constitution than the utmost stretch of intemperance could have done.

Britton was plae, and in some degree emaciated ; but Learmont was positively ghastly, and had wasted nearly to a skeleton.

"Well," said Learmont, in a hallow and constrained voice, " you come, as usual, for more money, I suppose."

"Yes," said Britton,—" I don't mean to go away empty-handed squire, you may take your oath ; but I have something more to say on this visit."

"Say it ; and begone !   I—I—am busy."

"Are you?   Perhaps you will be busier still some day.   Do you happen to be thirsty ?'

"No !" said Learmont impatiently.

"That's a pity, because I am ; and if it wasn't for the look of the thing, drinking by one's self, I'd have a glass of something."

"Andrew—Britton," said Learmont, jerking out his words slowly from beneath his clenched teeth ; " I have warned you more than once before not to trifle with me.   Your errand here is specific ; you come for the means of carrying on a life of mad riot and intoxication—a life which some of these days may lead you to an excess which will plunge you, and all connected with you, in one common ruin."

"Well, is that all ?"

"And enough," cried Learmont, angrily. " Have I ever resisted your demands ?"

"No."

"Have I ever limited your calls upon my purse ?"

"No ; but how d——d moderate I've been—think of that."

"But—but Britton—there was a time when you were not deaf to all reason ; hear me now.   You cannot complain of me, so long as I freely administer to your real and fancied wants.   Wherefore, then, should I run a fearful and terrible risk daily from your excesses ?   You admit—you must admit—that I, to the very spirit and letter, fulfil my contract with you ; and yet I run a fearful risk—a risk which can do you no manner of good.   What, if you were to die, Andrew Britton ? You are a man of wild excesses ; I say, if you were to die ?   Is the end of all my compliances with your demands to be my destruction, when you can desire no more ? Speak !   How do you warrant me against so hard a condition ?"

"I don't warrant you at all," said Britton.   "Recollect you forced me to it. What was I ?   The smith of Learmont.   I toiled day and night ; and they called me ' a savage,' and why ? because I was in your toils—I did a piece of work for you that——"

"Hush ! hush !" gasped Learmont.

"Oh, you are delicate, and don't like it mentioned.   I am not so nice—I murdered for you, squire, and you know it. What was my reward ? Toil—toil—and you know that too. You taunted me with my guilt and crime. Once, squire, when I threw in your teeth, that the same halter that was made for me, would fit your worshipful neck, you told me that I flattered myself, for that the word of a right worshipful squire, would outweigh the oath of a smith, and cursed me for a fool, but I believed you, and put up with it, till that sneaking hound, Gray, came to me."

"Curses on him !" muttered Learmont.

"Ha ! ha !" laughed Britton. " I like him no more than yourself—I ha vemuc to lay at his door."

"But to my question, Britton," said Learmont, impatiently.

"Well, to your question—what care I what becomes of you ?   I have myself and myself only to look to, and you may go to the devil or anywhere else, for all that it matters to me."

"Andrew Britton, once before I told you to beware.   You may carry this matter so far that I may turn upon you, and find greater safety in a foreign land than here, and if I once determine upon such a step——"

"You will leave me to the hangman ?"

"I will, because you goad me to it."

"And what is there to hinder me from doing the same thing?"

"You cannot ! You have not the means—nor the inclination. To accomplish such an object, you must come to me for a sum of money, which would be equivalent to proclaiming your intention at once, and thus my least danger would be your destruction—you understand me?"

"I do ; and although there are two words to that bargain—pray in the name of all that's honourable, what do you want me to do, squire ?"

"As a matter of common justice between us, I ask you to destroy any written evidence you may have prepared according to the accursed and unjust suggestions of Gray against me, or that in the event of your death, I may, having faithfully fulfilled my bond with you, be then released. Stay, I know what you would say.

No. 35.

That, you would tell me, holds out a temptation to me, to take your life. I say it does not, Andrew Britton, in your case. Your avarice is not so insatiable as Jacob Gray's ; and, moreover, we never meet but as man to man, and you can take what precautions you please to ensure your own safety."

" No, squire," said Britton, " it's worth all the money, I'm d——d if it aint, to see you in such a fright. You think I'm drinking myself to death, I know you do, and so I am, but it's an infernally slow process, and if you come to that, you look half dead yourself."

" I—1 ?"

" Yes ! Mind you give me none of your nonsense, you know, in case you should pop off all of a sudden."

" I—I am very well," said Learmont, " strong and well ; I never was better."

He dropped into a chair as he spoke, and a deadly paleness came over his face, robbing it even of its usual sallowness, and giving instead a chalky appearance to the skin, that was fearful to behold.

" There, you see," said Britton, " you aint well now—you don't drink enough. Here you have been making a riot about me, and the chance of my popping off, and you have hardly an ounce of flesh on your cursed long carcase."

" I am better now !" cried Learmont, " I am quite well—very well indeed. You—you have known me long, Andrew Britton—tell me I never looked better in my life, and I will give you a hundred pounds—yes, a hundred pounds, good Britton."

" Can't be such a cursed hypocrite," said Britton, who mightily enjoyed Learmont's fright, " I never saw you look so bad in all my life !"

" I am sure you are joking."

" Serious as a horseshoe."

" Well, well, that don't matter, I never take people by their looks. Sometimes the freshest and the finest go first. You know that well, Andrew Britton."

" That's very true," said Britton, " as one we know—a tall proper man enough —you recollect—his name was——"

" Peace! Peace! Do you want to drive me mad, Andrew Britton? Where is your hope, but in me? What—what other resource have you? Fiend! Do you dare thus to call up the hideous past to blast me? Peace—peace, I say, Andrew Britton. Leave me—our conference is over."

" Not quite."

" It is—it is. Go—there's money."

He threw his purse to Britton as he spoke, and then cried, —

" Go, go. Go at once."

" You forget," said Britton, as he coolly pocketed the money, " that I came here to tell you something particular."

" What is it?"

There is danger !"

" Danger ?" cried or rather shrieked Learmont, springing from his seat. "Danger? No, no; you don't mean ——"

"I mean what I say. There's danger ; and giving you credit for a cooler head than mine, though I'm not quite sure of it, I came to tell you."

Learmont leaned heavily upon the arm of the smith, as he said,—

" Good Britton, we will stand or fall together; we will not forsake each other. I will help you, Britton. We have known each other long, and been mutually faithful, I'm sure we have. You have still the sense to—to take a life—for our own safety, Britton—always for our safety."

" If I have, it's more than you have," said Britton. " Why, you are turning silly. What's the matter with the man? Have you seen a ghost?"

" Ah!" cried Learmont, " don't speak of that ; for, by the—the powers of hell, I think I really have."

" Oh! you think you have ?"

"I do."

" Where?"

"On my very door steps, Andrew Britton, I saw a face. Young and beautiful—so like—so very like—hers who—"

"You don't mean the Lady Monimia?"

"Hush, hush. 'Twas she—I knew her—come to look at me, as she looked—now two and twenty years ago, in the spring of her rare beauty, when we—we—quenched her life, Andrew Britton."

"That's all your beastly imagination," said Britton, "I wonder at you. On your step, do you say?"

"Yes."

"Stuff—you don't drink enough to clear your head of the vapours. Some of these days you'll fancy you see your——"

"Hush, hush. My conscience tells me the name you were about to pronounce. Hush, hush, I say. Oh! Andrew Britton, you are a man rough in speech and manners. Your heart seems callous, but have there been no times—no awful moments when your mental eye has been, as it were, turned inwards on your soul, and you have shrunk aghast from—from yourself, and wished to be the poorest, veriest abject mortal that ever crawled, so you were innocent of man's blood? Britton—savage, wild as you are, you must have felt some portion of the pangs that bring but one awful consolation with them, and that is, that hell can inflict no more upon us."

"I'll be hanged if I know what you are driving at," cried Britton. "I should recommend brandy-and-water."

"No, no; I cannot drink. That vulgar consolation is denied to me. My blood dries up, and my brain inflames, but I get no peace from such a source. Besides it shortens life."

"Have your own way. All I've got to say is, that I feel as sure as that I am standing here, that some one has been watching me at the Chequers."

"No—no."

"Yes—yes, I say."

"Some drunken brawl of your own!"

"No. Do you know, I suspect that fellow Hartleton is poking and prying about as usual, curse him."

"Aye, Hartleton!" cried Learmont. "There is my great danger. He suspects and watches—Britton, he might die suddenly."

"He might."

"Well, well."

"And he will too, if I catch him."

"Good, Britton. A thousand pound for news that he is no more."

"What's the use of your thousand pounds to me? I can but lead the life of a gentleman, and that I am. Why, somebody would cut my throat, if I had a thousand shillings all at once. Good day to you, squire, good day—take care of yourself. Leave me alone if I once catch Master Hartleton at bay."

"Yes, yes; you are courageous, Britton."

"Oh! by-the-by, what do you call one of those things I see in your hall, like a watch-box with two long poles to it?"

"A sedan chair."

"Oh! then I'm d——d if I don't have one."

"You?"

"Yes, me. Why shouldn't I?—it will be rare fun—upon my life it will. Good morning to you."

So saying, Britton swaggered out of the house, and by way of showing both his knowledge and his independence to Learmont's servants in the hall, when he got there, he said pointing the sedan-chair,—

"What's that?"

"A chair," said one.

"You think I didn't know that, did you, spooney?" he replied, as he gave the unfortunate footman a crack on the head that made him dance again.

CHAPTER LXIX.

A WALK AND A MEETING.—THE VISION AT THE OPEN CASEMENT.—LEARMONT
PERTURBATION.

AN idea had struck Learmont, during the course of his conversation with Britton
which, now that the smith was gone, came still more strongly and forcibly across his
mind, and shaped itself into clearer words.

"Why should not I ?" he said, "if I find that in England there is for me nothing
but danger, disgrace, and constant apprehension, why should not I take my accumulated wealth somewhere else, to some land where I could purchase with it
dignity and power, and—what is more freedom from the terrors that now beset
my path? 'Tis worth reflecting on such a course ; I could do it most easily now.
'Tis a comforting reflection—a most comforting reflection, and—and when I am
tortured by doubts and fears, I will think of such a course. But this news of
Britton's troubles me. He thinks himself watched by Hartleton ; why doubtless
so am I. Sir Francis is no friend to me, and would gladly find me tripping some
of these days—I must crush him—I will have his life, if it cost me half my wealth.
We kill a noxious reptile, because we think it may sting us ; so will I have vengeance upon you, Sir Francis Hartleton, because I know you would sting me if
you could. I must find some means subtle, deep, and dangerous to him, but
withal to me innoxious. I must kill, and yet not seem to kill, even to the instrument
with which I do the work. Britton it is of no use attempting to employ on such an
occasion, unless I could be certain of his success, and then, his execution for the
deed. In such a case, I should be rid of two enemies ; and even Britton would
not be so wantonly mischievous as to deceive me, at no benefit to himself ;—yet
is it dangerous. I must think again. Master Hartleton—you are playing with
edged tools."

Learmont was now silent for a time, and then rose, saying,—

"Now for the life of action which shall drown thought—my wealth—my house
—my brilliant entertainments have all succeeded so far as to make me a honoured
guest with more than I can visit—but I will visit many,—it—it is time I began to
enjoy something now."

The horrible contortion which he produced upon his ghastly face, by way of a
smile, at these words, startled him, as he saw it reflected in a mirror hanging
opposite to him ; and he shook in every limb, as he hastily left the room.

His servants shrunk from before him as, in about ten minutes time, he passed
down the great marble staircase of his mansion, splendidly dressed, and enveloped
in a cloak, to make some calls.

Declining, with a haughty wave of his hand, the chair that stood in the hall, he
strode out ; and, with his lips compressed as usual with him, so closely that not
a particle of blood was left in them, he turned into the park, intending to call
upon the frivolous but noble Brereton family, who had lodgings near to old
Buckingham House.

Of all the persons intent on pleasure, on business, or on intrigue, that thronged
to the park, Learmont fancied that no one could carry so heavy a heart as himself,
and yet how successful had he been ! Had he not accomplished all that he had
grasped at ? but, like the dog in the fable, what a valuable and tangible possession
had he dropped, in grasping the shadow which now darkened his soul.

He saw not the sunshine,—for his own heart was black and gloomy ; he heard
not the merry song of the birds,—for busy thought was conjuring up direful
images in his brain. He strode along, like a tall spirit—a being belonging to
some' more gloomy and uncongenial world than ours, who heard but discord in
our sweetest sounds, and could not appreciate any of our pleasures.

And yet strange to say, all that Learmont had toiled for—all he had sinned for—all he had dipped his hands in blood for, had been that he might enjoy, in greater abundance, these very delights and pleasures that seemed to mock his grasp, and to retreat like the *ignis fatuus* of the morass—far off in proportion, as he most wishes to approach.

He walked up the principal mall, and none addressed him, although many looked after the tall, gaunt, melancholy-looking man, as he strode in silence onwards. What would Learmont not have given for a companion : one who would feel and think with him, and divide the weight of oppressive conscience.

A lively burst of martial music now came suddenly upon his ears, and he glanced in the direction from whence it came, when he saw a person standing by a seat, from which he seemed to have just risen, close to him. A second glance told Learmont it was the young man, Albert Seyton, who had applied to him for the office of secretary, and he bowed coldly and stiffly to him, which Albert courteously returned, saying,—

" The morning is inviting, sir."

" Yes—a-cold, as you say," replied Learmont, in an abstracted tone.

" Cold, sir."

" Fine—fine, I mean. Did I say cold?"

" You did, sir ; but probably your thoughts were somewhere else. I fear I intrude upon you."

" No, no ; you do not. My thoughts, young sir, never wander, but I am grateful to him who can bring them back again."

" He is like me," thought Albert, with a sigh ; " a man with a very few pleasan moments to look mentally back to."

" Have you thought further of what I proposed to you at our last meeting?" said Learmont.

After a long pause, for Albert did not well know what to say in answer to the remark last made by the melancholy squire, " I have, sir," he now said, " and adhere firmly to all I before pledged myself to ; namely, that in all honour I will do you zealous service and tire not."

" 'Tis well, 'tis well. Walk with me, and we will converse more at large as we go ; I am merely out for exercise."

Albert bowed, and walked by the side of his strange employer in silence for some minutes. Learmont then said,—

" You will call upon me to-morrow, according to our previous arrangement."

" I shall be proud to do so," said Albert.

" Well, well. Perhaps the man may be there ; but beware of his consummate art, young sir. If you would successfully track him to his haunt, you must be wary and cunning, patient and sagacious ; believe me no common man will ever succeed in circumventing him."

" Indeed, sir."

" Ay, indeed, you know him not. He has the deep cunning of the serpent. Even I—but no matter. You will freely undertake the employment ?"

" As an earnest of future service, yes, sir, I will do your bidding, and if great attention and extreme care can accomplish your desire, it shall be done."

" Persevere, yourself, young sir, in such a disposition, and you will become a thriving man."

" I hope to please you, sir."

" You will ; of course you will, you will do me zealous service. But mark me you must follow this man, who will call at my house, as you would follow some light that would lead you from the caverns of poverty to fortune. Track him home, and see him fairly housed. Then mark the place by every token that may enable you again to lay your very hand upon the door, and cry, " Here dwells that man !"

" I will, sir, and I hope you may find him more deserving than you think."

" I hope I may," said Learmont.

They now walked along the Birdcage-walk, for they had doubled the canal, and were approaching towards Westminister again.   For the space of more than five minutes neither spoke, for both were busy with reflections, although of a widely different character.

Albert Seyton was more and more suspicious of the intentions of Learmont, and he began to think him a man, most probably, mixed up in some dark political intrigues, to carry out which, he required some simple and unsuspecting agent. There was something very galling to the proud spirit of Albert, in the supposition that Learmont had pitched upon him, as thinking him weak enough to believe any- thing, and never to suspect that the employment he was set upon was far different from what it purported to be, and he longed to say, "But I am not so simple and foolish as you may imagine me, and have my doubts and grave suspicions con- cerning your conduct and the truth of words ;" but then he could not bring himself to say so much, because all as yet was merely made up of doubt and suspicion, and he considered how ridiculously foolish he would look by allowing his imagi- nation to run riot in creating apprehensions, perhaps after all, to be completely dissipated by the result, and arising only, possibly, from his young and unin- structed fancy and ignorance of the ways of the world.

Albert Seyton, therefore, prudently determined to be watchful and wary ; but to take nothing on surmise, and to believe, or affect to believe, as far as the non- expression of doubt went, all that Learmont might choose to say until some positive and glaring fact contradicted him.

While these thoughts were passing through Albert's mind, Learmont, on the other hand, was congratulating himself upon his meeting with the young man, and extracting from the whole circumstance food for more agreeable hope and re- flection than had illumined his gloomy mind for a long previous period.

" Here," he thought, " there is at last a chance of discovering Jacob Gray's place of abode—a chance too, which if it fail, commits me to no one, and does me no manner of injury.   But it cannot scarcely fail.   This young man and he being perfect strangers might, in such a city as London, follow each other about for a week without exciting suspicion.   Moreover, he looks upon discovering this man's abode as the key-stone of his future favour with me, and consequent advancement. I could not have devised a better plan, and, surely, fortune must have been desirous of favouring me when she sent this raw young man to solicit employment from me.   By the powers of hell, I would not have missed such a chance of cir- cumventing that demon Gray for a thousand pounds."

Learmont, in the momentary exultation of these thoughts suddenly raised his eyes from the ground, on which they had been bent, and uttering a cry of terror, he sprang forward several yards, and then exclaimed,—

" There—there—again—again !   Is it ever to haunt me thus ?"

He pointed with his trembling finger to the windows of a house which overlooked the park for some distance.   One of the casements was open, but there was no one at it, and Albert looked first at Learmont, and then at the window in amazement, not unmixed with a sudden thought that, after all, his new employer might be a madman.

Learmont continued pointing for a moment towards the window. Then he slowly dropped his hand, and in a low agitated voice said, half aloud,—

"Could it be fancy?"

"What saw you, sir," said Albert.

"Come—come—hither."

Albert approached close to him, when he leaned heavily on the arm of the young man, and said,—

" You were walking with me, and if it were real, you must have seen it."

" Seen what, sir ?"

" A face pass for an instant across yon window."

" That now open ?"

" Yes—the sun shines upon it as you see, and across the open space there slowly passed a face.   You saw it?"

" I did not, sir. "

"You are sure?"

"Quite."

"Then fancy must be torturing me. 'Tis very strange that she—she whom I scarce think of should be the vision to haunt me. You are sure you saw no one pass that window?"

"At the moment my eye might not have been cast in that direction," said Albert, "but certainly I saw no one."

"True you might not have been looking; but neither was I, and yet my eyes were lifted as if by some invisible hand, and then I saw a face—that—that—I fear now I shall often conjure up."

Learmont leaned against the railings that divided the entrance from the open thoroughfare of the park, and for a time his strength appeared quite prostrated.

Albert Seyton continued gazing at the house which had attracted so much attention from Learmont, and after a pause of some minutes' duration, he said,—

"I think, that house is known to me, although I never looked at it from here before."

Learmont made him no answer, for although he heard him speak, he scarcely comprehended what he said, so busy was he with his own fears.

"If I mistake not," said Albert, "it is the back of Sir Francis Hartleton's house we see from here."

The name of Hartleton struck upon Learmont's ears like a trumpet, and starting from his reverie of disagreeable images, he cried hurriedly, and violently,—

"Who spoke of Hartleton? Who mentioned his name?"

"I, sir," said Albert, amazed at Learmont's wild vehemence of tone.

"You—you?"

"Yes, sir."

"Oh, you have heard of him. He is a man, I presume, known to many. Are you sure that is the back of his house?"

"Yes, now I look again I am quite sure; I know it by some peculiar chimnies. I have gazed on it for hours with a hope now extinguished for ever."

"You—you?"

"Yes, sir. My story is a strange one; I have lost both the natural and acquired ties that bind me to life. I am an orphan, and I can never more behold her who would have filled the void in my heart."

"But you speak of this Hartleton as if you knew him. Is such the fact?"

"I am scarcely warranted in saying so much," replied Albert, "although I have seen and conversed with him."

"Indeed?"

"Yes; and he gave me hopes, which were for a time my thoughts by day, and my dreams by night—my hopes which I clung to as some drowning mariner clings to a stray spar; but alas! I have lost now the power to dream myself happy."

"He disappointed you?"

"He did. Perhaps he could not do otherwise. I have no right to censure him, but he could not know how my heart was sinking, and he cannot know how it has been wrecked, or perhaps he would have done more or tried to do more. But I am querulous upon this subject, and may blame him causelessly. It is a fault of human nature to mistake the want of power for the want of will, and to him who loves all things appear so very possible."

"You have cause to quarrel with Sir Francis Hartleton, the particulars of which you shall relate to me some other time. I, too, love him not, and I may perchance aid you in your wishes more than he, although I may promise less."

"I thank you, sir."

"Let me see you early to-morrow."

"I shall attend you, sir."

"Farewell."

Learmont walked slowly away, and Albert Seyton, with a deep sigh turned and walked pensively towards Buckingham-gate.

Had he happened to have been looking at the moment Learmont did towards Sir Francis Harleton's house, he would have seen Ada pass by the open casement.

CHAPTER LXX.

THE JEW AND THE NECKLACE.—GRAY'S TROUBLES AND SURMISES.—AN ADVENTURE.

SIR FRANCIS HARLETON found but very little difficulty in getting possession of Ada's necklace from the Jew, who had made so capital a bargain with her. The wily Israelite made a practice of never purchasing any article unless he got it at a price which always implied that it was dishonestly come by, or, as was the case with Ada, of some party totally ignorant of the value of the commodity.

Another rule of his business, was to keep his greatest bargains some years, if he thought it necessary so to do, before he brought them into the market, so that if the jewel or the gold were stolen, all the excitement concerning it had subsided, and the very person from whom the property had been filched, had long since given it up as quite hopeless.

In this manner, he had acted with regard to Ada's necklace, which was really worth a much larger sum than either Jacob Gray or the Jew imagined, for the former knew only from indirect sources the value of the article, and the latter rarely came across anything so pure and costly.

Moreover, Jacob Gray had a strong motive for perserving the necklace, because, as we know, he always looked forward to a day when it might be necessary or agreeable to him to declare Ada's name, birth, and lineage ; and thus how important might any corroborative evidence become upon the subject.

As for the Jew, he had been in a ceaseless wonder ever since he had purchased the valuable trinket of the young girl, and in vain he puzzled himself to account for her possession of it, and form some idea of who she could possibly be that was wandering about alone with such valuable propery ; and it is more than possible that his great bargain was as great a source of disquiet to him, as it was of congratulation, for he reasoned with himself,—

" If sho be hash she had such a necklace, and didn't know fot it wash worth, sho help me, she might have had something else petter still."

This was a sore reflection to the Jew, and on the whole afforded a fine commentary upon such motives as his who rate their losses by their gains, in the same manner as the man who found half-a-guinea, and upon being told that two had been lost on the same spot, sunk the fact of his good fortune in finding the one, and bemoaned to everybody his loss of the other.

It was a sore blow to the Jew, when Sir Francis Hartleton walked into his shop, and at once announcing himself as the much-dreaded, because active and irreproachable, magistrate, demanded the necklace, giving a description of it, and of Ada, which rendered any kind of shuffling out of the matter of no possible use.

The necklace was therefore produced, and Sir Francis left the Jew fully impressed with a belief that he would immediately be prosecuted, although such a step was still far from the magistrate's intentions, who, as we are aware, was taking every means he could to keep matters quiet, and awakening no public curiosity concerning Ada.

It was after another conversation with his beautiful young guest that he issued an order to find poor mad Maud, intending to make some permanent provision for her benefit, not at all expecting that she really possessed sufficient pieces of Jacob Gray confession to enable him to form a much nearer estimate of the merits and demerits of the whole affair, than he had hitherto been able to do.

From Ada's description of Gray, he was now enabled to set a watch upon Learmont, who, from all the circumstances, he felt certain Gray visited to get money.

Sir Francis's object now was to give Jacob Gray time to provide himself not only with means, but to fully again write out those papers which he believed would unravel every mystery connected with the affair.

That Andrew Britton was assailable in the same way he never suspected, and he merely waited now until Gray should commit both Learmont and the savage smith in writing to take some active step in the business.

Jacob Gray little imagined that he was quite free in London to go whither his fancy might lead him, and that the man he most dreaded, namely, Sir Francis Hartleton, had taken a great deal of trouble to prevent his arrest.

No. 36.

Had he guessed he was being so angled with his terror would have killed him ; but as he sat on the step of the door near to Learmont's, he concocted in his mind a line of proceeding, which, but for various circumstances, he could not know of might have been successfully carried out.

He would see Learmont in the morning, and affecting to be wearied of his present line of life, to offer for two thousand pounds to surrender to him the living object of his fears, as well as his, Jacob Gray's, own confession, and leave England for ever. Learmont might see him on board a vessel even if he pleased. He might see him leave the shore, when he would give him any address purporting to be where he would find Ada ; and then, at the first port he stopped at, he would send a letter to Sir Francis Hartleton, containing sufficient to destroy Britton and Learmont ; but not sufficient to be of any service to the persecuted Ada.

By this means he thought to gratify his revenge against them all ; and, at least, secure to himself safety, and the means of living in comparative luxury in some cheap continental state.

If Learmont should refuse such a compromise, he could adopt some other couse of action to be resolved upon after his next interview with him ; but, upon the necessity of leaving England, and that quickly too, he was quite clear and decided.

One would have thought that Jacob Gray had met with sufficient disappointment in his various arrangements to dishearten him from attempting further to create circumstances, and philosophise upon their results ; but it is a fixed principle in those natures which are fond to excess of plotting, that no experience will deter them from concocting the hair breadth schemes and chances which would, combined, make up a satisfactory result, but which all possess the one alarming feature, that the whole fabric must topple down upon the displacement of a single brick.

He rose from the step of the door, and walked onwards, he knew not whither, for some time ; but, at length, he found himself in Parliament-street, from the immediate vicinity of which he shrunk quickly, for he dreaded the glare of the lights, and feared that some one might recognise him as the fugitive of the Strand.

There were in his mind some strange and singular contradictions with regard to his present situation, which, as calm reflection came to his aid, he found it very difficult indeed to reconcile.

That Ada had sought refuge with Sir Francis Hartleton, he could scarcely permit himself to doubt for a moment ; but then the consequences which she had always dreaded from such a step on her part had certainly not increased so rapidly if they were to occur at all, as he would have sworn they would. He anticipated so active, so persevering, so energetic a hunt from him throughout, not only the metropolis, but the whole kingdom, when once Ada should be in a condition to possess Sir Francis Hartleton of the events of the five years of her life with him, Gray, that safety and freedom for four and twenty hours was a thing not to be thought of; and yet here he was, without much disguise, without the means of taking that care to avoid suspicion which he would fain have done, free and unquestioned hitherto in the public streets.

His name seemed in no one's mouth. There was no hue and cry—no bills of any particular moment concerning him, save the meagre one he had seen at Hampstead, and which had evidently not emanated from Sir Francis Hartleton. In fact, the affair did not at all present the alarming aspect to him he had ever expected it would.

Jacob Gray was, therefore, under those circumstances thrown back upon several suppositions—none [of which, however, to his mind bore the stamp of much probability.

One was that Ada had not taken refuge with Sir Francis Hartleton, but by some means had fallen into other hands, who did not feel so interested in her story or had not the power or the inclination to act upon any of the surmises it must naturally call forth.

Another supposition was, that from some lingering feeling of pity towards him or from some dark and haunting suspicion in her mind that he might be relate to her, she had, although with Sir Francis, abstained from committing him Gray sufficiently to induce a hot pursuit for him, on other grounds than the murder of Elias, and of Vaughan. Nay, he even thought it possible that Ada might have interceded for him to be left alone, or bargained in some way for his safety. But as often as these reflections began to shed some comforting influence on Gray, there came the reflection of how firmly and broadly she had denounced him as a murderer in the public streets, and he became lost again in a whirl of conflicting thoughts and emotions.

He was slowly traversing a low, obscure street, leading from George-street, as these painful thoughts were passing through his mind, when he fancied he heard a footstep behind him, which seemed accommodating itself to his in a manner that excited at once his suspicion that he was watched.

All Gray's dreams of security immediately vanished, and a cold perspiration broke out upon him, as he fancied he was upon the point now of being arrested when his fate would be certain; for what account could he give of himself that would not at once strengthen and confirm suspicion.

He still heard the footstep, but he feared to lock behind him, and after a few moments of confused thought he resolved to try a simple experiment to ascertain if he were really followed, and he paused suddenly to see if the stranger behind him would pass on.

The whole mass of Jacob Gray's blood appeared to him to curdle in his veins, as he felt sure, whoever it was behind him, had stopped likewise.

CHAPTER LXXI.

THE PURSUIT—A SUCCESSFUL RUSE.—THE LONG NIGHT.—GRAY'S TERROR.

The little strength that Jacob Gray had left now all at once seemed completely to have left him, and he trembled so that he could scarcely stand. Walk on he could not, and yet what was he to do? Did the person know who he was, or did he only suspect? Was there a remote chance of escape, or was he fairly in the toils?

As these distressing thoughts passed rapidly through his mind, he heard the stranger step up to him, and in a moment, a voice said,

"A fine evening, sir."

Gray stretched out his hand, and held by an iron rail, while he turned slowly and with pallid features, and his tongue cleaving to the roof of his mouth with fright, faced the speaker.

He was a man about the middle height, with sharp small grey eyes, which twinkled upon the terror-stricken Jacob as much as to say, "I am a cunning, cautious fellow, and you won't escape me."

It was full a minute before Gray could command himself sufficiently to speak, and the stranger during that time had repeated his remark of,—

"A fine evening."

"Yes—yes, very," stammered Gray.

"You don't seem very well, sir?" said the stranger, twinkling his eyes designedly upon Gray.

"Yes, quite well, thank —— I—I haven't the honour of knowing you. Good evening—good evening."

"I may be mistaken," said the man; "but I think I have seen you somewhere."

Gray would have given anything at that moment to say " Where?" but he lacked the courage, and merely muttered something about it being unlikely they had ever met, a she was a stranger in London.

The man kept peering at him in a very disagreeable manner, and after a few moments, he said in a careless tone,—

"Heard of the murder?"

"What murder?" gasped Gray.

"In the Strand—Vaughan's murder I mean—strange affair, very!"

"No—I know nothing of it," said Gray.

"Odd, that—the whole town knows of it. It's crying about the streets, and what's the strangest thing of all, nobody seems to know who did it."

"Indeed?"

"No, the fellow was a complete stranger, and the only man who gives anything like a description of him, is a fellow whom he knocked down near Arundel-street."

"Yes—indeed," was all Gray could find breath to say, for he expected each moment that the man would pounce upon him, crying, "You are the murderer—I have been only amusing myself a little with your fears."

"It's odd altogether," continued the man, " and there's fifty pounds reward now offered by Vaughan's relations for the man, which, together with what government will give at his conviction, will make a good round sum."

"Exactly—yes," said Gray, quite mechanically, for his senses were in a complete whirl.

"You see that's worth looking after," said the man.

"Yes. Good evening—good evening," said Gray, and he tried to pass on.

"Are you going my way?" said the man.

"Which is your way?"

"Oh—why, really I aint at all particular, and I'll walk with you, if I am not intruding upon you?"

"I am going home," said Gray. "Good evening—I live just here."

"You haven't lost your way?"

"No—no—this place is quite familiar to me—I have known it long."

"Oh, I thought you said you were a stranger here."

Gray changed from pale to red, and from red to pale again, as he replied,—

"You misunderstood me, sir."

"Oh, did I? very likely."

"Good evening."

"You had rather walk alone, would you?

Gray summoned courage to say with tolerable firmness,—

"I would."

"Certainly—certainly. Mind if you see anybody that looks suspicious, lay hold of him; it may be the murderer, you know, and it would be a prime evening's work for anybody to nab him. -He is about your height—thin and pale, stoops a little, shabbily dressed. Look out—look out."

"I—I will. Are you an officer?"

"No, I'm a shoemaker, but I've a great fancy for catching thieves and those kind of. people."

"Curse your fancy," thought Gray.

"I couldn't sleep to-night without taking what I call a prowl just to see if the fates would place in my way the murderer."

"Oh, indeed!"

"Yes, and I don't despair yet. Good evening—good evening."

"Good evening," replied Gray; and he walked on with a faint hope that after all the troublesome shoemaker, whom he devoutly wished dead and buried, did not suspect him sufficiently to annoy him any more with his following.

To ascertain this point, after he had left him, was a great object to Gray. as it would afford him an idea how to act, and accordingly after he had proceeded some distance, he just glanced over his shoulder to see if the man had gone, and he supposed such was the case, for he could neither see nor hear him.

Jacob Gray, however, was] reckoning without his host, for not only did the troublesome shoemaker, who was the pest of Westminster, from his love of meddling with the duties of the police, strongly suspect that he had hit upon the right man, but he determined not to lose sight of him, and had merely ensconced himself in a door way until Gray should have got some distance off, when his intention was to follow him very cautiously till he saw him housed somewhere, when he would bring the officers upon him, for he did not like exactly to run the risk of attempting the capture of so desperate a character as a murderer, who had already taken one man's life merely because he made an attempt to capture him.

"Who knows," thought the shoemaker, "he is a desperate chap, and may be a great deal stronger than he looks; he might smash me just as he smashed Vaughan, and that would be no joke. I'll dog him till I see him fairly housed, and then be down upon him."

Cunning, however, as was the troublesome shoemaker he was scarcely a match for Jacob Gray, when the latter had a little time to collect his faculties, and was not flurried. There were ineded but five persons who could have succeeded in dogging Jacob Gray without his knowing it; and althuogh the shoemaker had in his mind concocted the artful scheme of letting Gray turn a corner, and then running after him, and keeping him in sight until he had turned another, he did not know his man, for that was the very course which Jacob Gray took good care to provide against by himself popping into a doorway round the first corner he came to, and waiting patiently to see what came of it.

The result confirmed his suspicions, for he had not been above two minutes in the doorway, than the shoemaker arrived at the corner at the top of his speed, and peered around it with what he considered amazing cleverness and cunning.

The street was a long one, and he felt not a little surprised at missing Gray in so very sudden a manner.

"Lost him, by——," he cried. "He must have gone into some house here—that's flat. I'll get a constable to come with me, and will call at every one. I'd wager my head he's the man."

The amateur officer now darted off at a quick rate to procure a real one, and when he had gone, Jacob Gray emerged from his hiding-place.

He paused a moment in the street, and then with bitter malignity, he muttered,—

"Beware! I am not a man to be tempted too far."

He then hastily walked in an opposite direction to that taken by the shoemaker, although he had no definite idea of where he was going, or what he meant to do until the morning should afford him a chance of seeing Learmont. As the excitement of the last half-hour began along with its danger to wear off, Jacob Gray felt dreadfully fatigued, notwithstanding he had been much supported by the broken victuals he had received from poor Maud, and he thought of proceeding to the sheds of Covent-garden, and lying down to rest himself till morning's dawn.

The rotten wooden stalls and sheds of Covent-garden-market, at the period of our tale, were the nightly resort of many who had no other place in which to lay an aching head and wearied body. There, among potato-sacks, baskets, vegetable refuse, and all the mass of filth for which that now handsome market was then so famous, the weary, the destitute, and the heart-sore would find a temporary solace from their cares, in the oblivion of sleep.

But not alone were the humble sheds of the market occupied by the sons and daughters of misfortune and want—a number of the worthless and abandoned characters who nightly prowl about the theatres had no other places of refuge; and many a thief and, in some instances, criminals of a higher grade in the scale of iniquity, were pushed out by the officers from among the market lodgers, when he happened to be particularly wanted; and when a housebreaker, or thief of any description, was compelled by necessity to lodge there, he was tolerably sure to be particularly wanted, because such a step augured a state of his finances which was far from enabling him to fee the officers—a system which, although now so very rare, was a hundred years ago flourishing in all its iniquity and glory.

To the sheds, then, of the market, Jacob Gray resolved to go, but by many foruitous accidents, he was doomed not to get there.

CHAPTER LXXII.

THE RETURN OF LEARMONT.—THE INTERVIEW.—DOUBTS AND FEARS.

IN his way Jacob Gray passed Learmont's house, and he had scarcely got half a dozen yards from the door, when he was compelled to step aside, to allow a cavalcade to pass him, consisting of some half-dozen footmen bearing links, followed by a chair containing their master.

One of the curtains of the sedan was but partially drawn, and Gray, at a glance, saw that Learmont himself was the occupier of it. His resolution was formed in a moment. He would risk whatever construction the squire chose to put upon such a visit, at so singular an hour, and procure some money from him at once for yresent pressing exigencies.

He could easily frame some lie to account for his visit at such an hour; and whether Learmont believed it or not, it must pass current, for who could contradict it?

He watched the haughty arbiter of his fortunes get out of the chair, and ascend the steps of the mansion. Then, before the door could be closed, he stepped forward; and being just behind Learmont, he said,—

"I have waited for you."

Learmont turned suddenly, and looked perfectly astonished to see Gray. For a moment neither spoke. Then the squire said, in a low tone,—

"To-morrow morning, early."

"No," said Gray. "My business is urgent and important. I must see you to-night.

"Must?"

"Yes—must!"

Learmont bit his lip, and passed into the house, which Gray taking as a passive permission to follow him, did so, until Learmont paused in a room devoted to the purpose of a library, and which was but dimly lighted. Then turning to Gray, he said,—

"Well?" in a brief stern voice.

Gray had hastily concocted in his mind what he should say to Learmont, and after carefully closing the door, he replied in nearly his usual low and cautious tone, although his voice shook a little,—

"It is not all well, Squire Learmont, methinks I should have a better reception for coming some distance, and waiting long, to tell you news of more importance to you than to me."

Jacob Gray was unconscious that he touched a chord in Learmont's heart, which had vibrated painfully ever since his interview with Britton; but he saw, by the nervous clutching of a back of a chair with his fingers, that Learmont was alarmed, and that was what he wished.

"What—what—mean you?" said Learmont.

"I mean this," replied Gray, "that Sir Francis Hartleton— "

"Hartleton again!" cried Learmont, clenching his fist. "By all that's damnable—that man is born to be my bane—my curse—I will have his blood."

Gray saw that he had struck the right chord, and he added,—

"I fear he is plotting and planning some mischief?"

"You only fear?"

"Nay, I am almost certain."

"State all you know."

"I will. And it is because I know so much that I come to you at so unseasonable an hour."

"Heed not that," said Learmont. "All hours—all times by night and by day—are alike to me, for they all teem with alarms. The shadow of some dreadful coming evil seems to press upon my soul. Bad tidings crowd upon me. Say on, Jacob Gray, I am prepared too well."

"What I have to tell you," said Gray, " consists more of a certain knowledge that there is something to discover than that something itself."

"Say on—say on."

"Before I speak, will you, for the first time, let me have a cup of wine, for I am very—very faint."

"Help yourself," said Learmont, pointing to a bouffet at the further end of the room, on which were refreshments.

Gray eagerly poured himself a glass of rich wine; and as he felt the generous fluid warm him, his blood seemed to flow easier through his veins, and he appeared to have lifted half of his cares from his heart.

"Now—now," said Learmont, impatiently. "Tell me all."

"I will. Early this evening, I went into a small hostel, in Pimlico, near to the public office of this Hartleton—"

"Yes—yes."

"And there was one," continued Gray, lying with a volubility that would have taken any one in,—"there one belonging to the magistrate's office, who had already taken more drink than his brains would stand."

"You—you—plied him well."

"I did when my suspicions were awakened. He was talking loudly, and amongst other things, he said. ' His master had an eye upon a certain squire, not a hundred miles from Westminster, who bid fair for Tyburn."

"The knave !—what—what more ?"

"On that I thought, of course, on you," said Gray, with a sneering malice in his tone.

"Well—well—what followed ?"

"Why, knowing no other squire in Westminster but yourself, with whom I could couple the allusion to Tyburn, I called for more drink and brought him to converse with me."

"And—and—what ?"

"He dwelt but in obscure hints," contined Gray, " and at last dropped off into a drunken sleep, which smothered all his faculties."

"And you heard no more ?"

"No more."

"'Tis not much."

"Enough for apprehension," suggested Gray.

"Ay ; but not enough for action."

"True—but you can think of it."

"There is the curse ! I can think of—thought is my hell !"

"Such thoughts lured unpleasnt images ; but 'tis better to have such slender information of coming danger than to dream on of safety, but to be roughly awakened by it when it comes to your doors."

"No—no. Apprehension is a fiend of far more awful aspect than danger. It only suggests the terrible; and leaves to the shrinking, trembling fancy to fill up the ghastly picture. Show me danger, and I have nerve to face it. Only tell me it is coming, and in some unknown shape, and I—I—do quail before it. Yes I—even I do quail before it !"

He sank into a chair as he spoke, and turned deathly white.

"Arm yourself with fortitude," said Gray. "You may yet triumph."

"There is but one course open," said Learmont, in a low earnest tone. " Among us we must find a means to lay the troublesome spirit of this Hartleton, Jacob

Gray, where is all the deep cunning that would enable you to circumvent hell itself? I say, where is it now, if you cannot summon it to your aid, to rid us all of this man, who will otherwise destroy us?"

"You may yet triumph," muttered Gray, with a meaning look. "Hear me Squire Learmont: I am sick and weary of the life I lead, an would fain now lend an ear to some proposal from you, which would enable me to feel more peace here."

He struck his breast as he spoke, and fixed his keen eye upon Learmont, who in his turn, from beneath his knitted brows, peered anxiously into the face of Gray.

"You understand me," continued Gray; "I am willing, if I could do so with safety, to leave you at peace—to secure you from the worst evils that can befal you—to deliver you from your greatest feelings of apprehension."

"Say on, Jacob Gray," said Learmont, in a low indifferent tone.

"Nay, I would now hear from you," remarked Gray, "what proposal you would make to me for surrendering to you your worst foe."

"The child?"

"Ay; but a child no longer," hastily interrupted Gray. "Years have now rolled on, and the child that was, has in the due progress of time passed that age and become a dangerous enemy to you. An enemy only controlled by me. I am as one holding in my grasp the thunderbolt which, were I for a moment to let loose, would rush with fearful certainty at your devoted head. I—but I want your proposal, squire—I am willing to accede to some terms, but they must be, to me, both safe and profitable."

Learmont was silent for some moments, then he said,—

"Tell me your demand, Jacob Gray, and at large particularise your proposal."

"Nay, squire, I repeat I have no proposal—none whatever—but I have bethought me that danger threatens around us, and that some day when the horizon of our fortunes may appear unclouded, a storm may come which will sweep us to destruction."

Learmont groaned, and then fixing his eyes upon Gray, he said with a fearfu and intense earnestness,—

"Jacob Gray, you are a man of crimes—you have shed blood more causelessly than I—and I would ask you if ever in your solitude, when none have been near you, you have seen or heard——"

Gray licked his parched lips, as he said with trembling apprehension,—

"What—what mean you, squire? I—I have seen nothing—heard nothing. 'Twas Andrew Britton struck the blow—he—he did it."

"Peace, peace!" cried Learmont; "nor with a hollow sophistry try to cleanse your soul of the deep spots that eat, like a wild splash of burning lava, to its inmost part."

Gray shrank and cowered before the frightened looks of Learmont, and after a pause he said,—

"What have you seen—what heard?"

"Twice now I have seen a face which, to look upon, has nearly turned my heart to stone."

"A—a—face?"

"Yes—'Tis an angel or a devil. Listen to me."

"I—I will—I will."

"Once on the steps of this my mansion, at an hour when my heart was lighter than its wont, and I was far from dreaming of such a sight, a face appeared before me. It seemed that of a young girl, but so like—oh, so like him—who sleeps in that dread spot which ever rises like a spectre before my affrighted eyes."

"The smithy?" said Gray.

"And once again," continued Learmont, not heeding Gray's interuption, "once again I saw it. Then another was with me, and I know it was not of this world because he saw it not."

"The same face?"

"The same."

"And of a young girl, say you—pale and noble, with a look of gentleness, yet pride—a—brow of snow—long raven hair?"

"'The—the same—you have seen it, Jacob Gray—you have seen it—you are cursed as well as I."

"In a dream," muttered Gray.

"Only a dream? I saw it on a bright morning when all was light and life around."

"Was that recently?" said Gray.

"This very morning."

Gray would have given much at that moment to be able to ask with unconcern where Learmont had seen Ada, for that it was she he did not entertain a shadow of a doubt, but it was several minutes before he could command his voice sufficiently to say,—

No. 37.

"Where saw you this appearance ?"

"Where all my fears are concentrated—where my worst foe resides—I saw it at the window of Sir Francis Hartleton's house from the park."

Gray drew a long breath as he thought, "So my worst fears are confirmed. She is with the magistrate." He then said, with a more assumed and confident air than he had hitherto assumed :—

"These fancies would leave you were you more at ease—I grieve that you should as yet have missed the enjoyments which your wealth should have brought within your grasp."

"Enjoyment !" said Learmont, with a deep groan—"you mock me, Jacob Gray —what enjoyments have you and Andrew Britton left me ? Have you not between you surrounded me with danger and suspicion ? I have been tempted, for the great favours I owe you both, to take some day a step that should rid me of you for ever."

"Indeed !"

"Yes—but we will talk more another time—the hour waxes late—shall we meet in the morning ?"

"The—the night would suit me better," said Gray, who by no means relished in his present dangerous circumstances a morning visit.

Learmont, with a forced air of unconcern, cried,—

"Pho—pho—let it be the morning—say at half-past ten."

"I will take money of you now," said Gray, evading the point, "in earnest of the sum which shall separate us for ever."

"There is my purse," cried Learmont, giving it to him. "'Tis moderately full —take it, and let me see you to-morrow by the hour I have named."

"Squire Learmont," said Gray, "for three thousand pounds I will rid you of the young object of your fears—of myself—and, perchance, of Andrew Britton."

"Three thousand pounds ?" said Learmont.

"Yes—a small sum you must own—a very small sum."

"You will bring me here——"

"No—no—I will do this—on ship-board, I will hand you an address written on the back of my confession."

"I will consider," said Learmont, "and in the meantime bethink you of some means of ridding me of Hartleton. While that man lives, I stand as it were upon a mine, and—and—you will be here in the morning by half-past ten."

It would have been a curious study for any deep theorist on human nature to have remarked these two men, Learmont and Gray, at this moment, watching each other's countenances, and yet endeavouring to avoid seeming so to do, and mutually suspicious that every word covered some hidden and covert meaning.

"What change has taken place, that Jacob Gray is so anxious to compromise with me for a sum of money at once ?" was Learmont's mental interrogatory.

"Why does he want me here by half-past ten so particularly ?" thought Gray; "I will not come."

Thus they parted, mutually hating and mutually suspicious of each other.

CHAPTER LXXIII.

THE TROUBLESOME SHOE-MAKER.—GRAY'S AGONY AND DANGER.—THE FLIGHT

JACOB GRAY no longer was necessitated to take a temporary lodging among the sheds of Covent-garden market, for upon, by the dim light of a lamp, examining Learmont's purse, he found a sum nearly approaching to twenty guineas in it, and ghastly smile came across his face, as, by the mere possession of money, he felt, or fancied he felt, considerably stronger and better than he had been for many days.

He walked with a firmer step and an air of greater self-possession than before. One of his first acts was to dive into a back street, for the purpose of finding some place in which he could lodge for the night, and he had not gone far before he saw a small dingy-looking public-house, where he thought he might find all he wanted in the way of rest and refreshment without risk.

It is strange how intense mental anxiety will overcome and smother almost entirely the consciousness of bodily pain. So it was with Jacob Gray—for although he had been suffering much pain now for many hours from his wounded face, his great anxiety of mind had thrown such mere physical annoyance quite into the shade ; but now that he had money in his pocket, and fancied he saw light in the darkness of fate, he began to experience great agony from the wound, and previous to seeking refreshment or rest he wished to procure surgical assistance lest any shots should be remaining in his face. With this intent he walked on until he came to a chemist's shop, near Westminster-hridge. On entering the little door-way, for a very little mean shop it was, he asked of a man behind the counter to examine his face.

" You have been wounded, and had better go to some hospital," said the surgeon, who was one of the self-taught and self-dubbed medical men who flourished up to within the last thirty years.

" I have wherewithal to pay you for your services," said Gray, taking out Learmont's purse and laying down a guinea.

Upon this the surgeon, with a good deal of practical skill, carefully examined Gray's face, and extracted several of the shots which had remained just beneath the skin.

" How did this accident happen to you ?" said the surgeon.

" A careless boy was shooting sparrows," replied Jacob Gray.

" Ah ! people never will be careful in the use of fire-arms. You will do very well now ; a little dry lint is all you require, but wash your face freque ntly with diluted milk."

" Thank you," said Gray, receiving fifteen shillings out of his guinea ; " should I feel any uneasiness, I will call again."

" That fellow has been robbing somebody, I'll be sworn, and been shot at for his pains," remarked the surgeon when Gray had gone. " Well—well, it's all one to me, from a peer to a pickpocket."

Gray felt very much relieved by the manipulation of the surgeon, and he re traced his steps towards a small public-house he had before noticed, and which from its plainness and obscurity, he thought would furnish him a tolerably secure retreat till he could venture out again.

He was dreadfully weary, and the stars were beginning to disappear, while a faint sickly light was slowly spreading itself over the eastern horizon.

A very few minutes' walk brought him to the door of the house, and he dived down a steep step to enter it. A dim light only was in the bar, although it was one of those houses that keep open the whole of the night, under pretence of accommodating travellers, but really to accommodate thieves, watchmen and police-officers.

" Can I," said Gray, to a man who was yawning in the bar,—" can I have a bed here, and some refreshment ?"

The words were scarcely out of his lips, when he heard a noise behind him ; and turning hastily around, his eyes were blasted by the sight of his tormentor, the amateur officer and shoemaker, who, with a glass of some steaming beverage in one hand, and a pipe in the other, stood glaring at Jacob Gray as if he was some awful apparition.

" Bless me," he at length found voice to say, " is it you ?"

" I have no knowledge of you, sir," said Gray, while a cold perspiration bedewed his limbs, and he glanced uneasily at the door, between which and himself th e troublesome man.

" I—I—you—you," stammered the shoemaker, " you met me you know about two hours ago, and you said you was a going home."

" Well, sir."

" It's a odd time of night to be out."

" Then why don't you go home?" said Gray, summoning all the presence of mind he could to his aid.

" Ah—yes—exactly, that is, a—hem !" said the shoemaker, feeling very much confused, for he was afraid to promote hostilities with Gray, and equally reluctant to let him go.

" Can you accommodate me," said Gray, turning to the woman, " and two friends ?"

" Three of you !" groaned the shoemaker.

" Yes," said Gray, " I have two friends waiting for me."

" There'll be a great deal of danger in having anything to do with him," thought the shoemaker ; " but I'd wager ten guineas he's the man that killed Vaughan."

" I can't accommodate you all," said the woman. " You can stay here, if you like ; and your friends can get a bed at the King's Arms at the bottom of the street."

" Thank you," said Gray, " I will speak to them ;" and he moved towards the door.

The little shoemaker, however, was not to be so easily cajoled, but gulping down his glass of hot liquor, with a speed that nearly choked him, and brought the tears into his eyes, he moved to the door at the same time as Gray, resolved to stick to him now as long as there was no actual bodily peril.

Gray paused at the door, and gave the man a look which caused him to recoil a step or two within the house. Then he walked out into the street ; but the shoemaker, although daunted for a moment, was not quite got rid of, and with a hurried whisper to himself of,—

" It would be the making of me to take him single-handed, and get all the reward," he bustled after Gray, with the intention of watching him.

In this, however, the amateur officer was disappointed ; for Gray, after proceeding half-a-dozen paces, turned sharp round, and caught the shoemaker just coming out of the door of the public-house.

Gray was trembling with fear, but he had sense enough to feel that a bold face very frequently hides a shrinking heart, and he endeavoured to throw as much boldness as possible into his voice and manner as he said,—

" Do you want anything with me, sir ?"

" Oh no, no, nothing," said the shoemaker, "only I thought you might be curious in old houses, as you had popped into this one. It's a most ancient house, and I was going to tell you that twenty-three years ago, to-day, my father apprehended the famous Jack Sheppard at the bar of this very house. Now that's curious—what I call very curious."

" Indeed," said Gray, walking on and inwardly cursing his tormentor.

" Yes," continued the shoemaker, keeping up with him, " my father took him ; one of his ladies was with him, and she got my father's finger between her teeth, and wouldn't leave go till she had bit it to the bone. Well, sir, my father took Jack to the watch-house in Great George-street, and what do you think happened there ?"

" I cannot say."

" When they got to the door, my father knocked, and the moment it was open, Jack seized hold of him like a tiger, and pitched him in right upon the stomach of the night-constable saying,—

" Take care of him. Good night, and off he went."

They had now reached the corner of the steeet, and Gray turned to his companion, saying,—

" Sir, I do not wish your company."

"Past four and a cold morning," growled an asthmatic watchman, from some distance off, at this moment.

"I'll stick by him," thought the shoemaker, "and when we come up to the watchman, I'll call upon him to help me to take him. I must have him somehow."

"Oh, you don't want company! well, sir, I'll only walk with you till you meet your two friends."

Had Jacob Gray, at that moment of goaded passion, possessed any weapon that would have noiselessly and surely put an end to the ambition and the life of the troublesome shoemaker, he would have used it with exquisite satisfaction ; but being quite unarmed, he considered himself powerless ; and as is the case in many contests in life, the affair resolved itself simply to one point, namely, which should succeed in frightening the other. But then the watchman might be a powerful auxiliary to his opponent, and Jacob Gray screwed his courage up to the sticking place, to endeavour to get rid of his companion before such aid should arrive. He therefore turned abruptly and cried in a fierce angry tone,—

"How dare you, sir, intrude yourself upon me ?"

The shoemaker started back several paces, and in evident alarm, cried,—

"No violence—no violence."

"Then leave me to pursue my walk alone," said Gray. "In a word, sir, I am well armed, and will not be intruded on ; your design may be to rob me, for aught that I know."

"Far from it—far from it," said the man. "I am a respectable tradesman."

"Than you ought to know better than to force your company upon those who desire it not," said Gray.

"Very well, sir ; very well. No offence ; I'll leave you. Good evening, or rather morning."

"Past four, and a cold morning," said the watchman again, and while the shoemaker paused irresolute for a moment, Gray walked hastily past the guardian of the night.

He felt then how impolitic it would be to look back, but he could not resist the impulse so to do, and saw the watchman in earnest conversation with his late companion, while the eyes of both were bent upon him.

The danger was great, but Gray felt that he should but provoke it to wear a still worse aspect by exhibiting any fear; so, although he kept all his senses on the *qui vive*, and every nerve strung for action, he walked but slowly away, with something of the same kind of feeling that an adventurous hunter might be supposed to feel in some Indian jungle when retreating before a crouching tiger, who he feels would spring upon him were he to show the least sign of trepidation, but who it is just possible may let him off if he show a bold front.

Jacob Gray reached in a few moments the corner of a street, and then he ventured another glance over his shoulder at the motions of the enemy. His heart sickened as he saw the watchman give a nod to his companion, and then commence running after him (Gray), at full speed.

With a spasmodic kind of gasp, produced by a choking sensation in his throat, as his extreme danger now rushed upon his brain, Jacob Gray dived down the narrow turning, and fled like a hunted hare.

CHAPTER LXXIV.

ADA'S HOME.—A HAPPY SCENE.—THE SERENITY OF GOODNESS.

SIR FRANCIS HARTLETON on that same evening was immersed in deep though, on Ada's prospects and affairs. So multifarious and complex had even what he knew concerning her and her fortunes become, putting aside all that he surmised, that now he had repaired to his own quiet little room, in which he was never interrupted

and sat down, as much for the clearing of his own mind upon the subject, as fo"
any other considerations, to write in detail all the various circumstances connected
with the history and fortunes of Ada.

When he came fairly to separate what he knew from what he only surmised
he felt much disappointed at the limited facts that really appeared upon paper,
and as we have before intimated, he found himself in the disagreeable position of
suspecting much and knowing little—able to surmise much more than he could
prove, and morally certain of many things which he despaired of ever finding the
means of making clear by proof.

The connection of Learmont with the same crimes in which Gray and Britton
had been participators was very clear, but could he specify those crimes ? It was
not enough to say—" So and so is a criminal," but it was necessary to tell and
define such a charge ; and Sir Francis Hartleton felt keenly all the advantage which
such a man as Learmont would have over him, were he to make a loose and un-
supported attack against him.

Having finished his narrative, Sir Francis sat in deep thought for more than an
hour, but yet could not form any satisfactory conclusion, nor determine upon any
course of action which would not be attended with what he considered the worst
consequence of all, namely, putting Learmont thoroughly upon his guard.

He foresaw that he could not persevere, for a very long period of time, upon the
unwilling and rather unprecedented power given to him by the Secretary of State,
but that Jacob Gray must shortly be apprehended for the murder of Vaughan, when
it was more than probable that all chance of discovering Ada's real history
through him would be lost ; for what inducement could be offered to such a man as
Gray to do an act of justice, when his own life could not by any possibility be spared,
but must be taken by the hands of the law for a clear and distinct murder,—not
to take into consideration the assassination of Elias, in the lone house at Battersea.

It had more than once occurred to the mind of the magistrate to search the
ruins of the house in which Gray had resided, but then, as often, the extreme improbability of such a man leaving anything behind him of a character to criminate
him in any way, saving the dead body of the murdered officer, came so strongly
across him that he rejected as useless the attempt.

The smithy, too, at Learmont he longed to search effectually, but how could he
do so without observation in such a place ; and should such a proceeding come to
the ears of Learmont, he might well complain of a trespass upon his own premises,
for the purpose of endeavouring to get up some charge against him of a secret and
undeclared nature.

" No," exclaimed Hartleton, with disappointment, as he rose from his chair, " I
must not.   There is no resource but patience, and, for a short time, this man Gray,
with all his crimes upon his head, must be suffered to remain at large, unless some
meddling person apprehends him upon suspicion merely, in which case the law
must take its course ; for although I can and may take no steps to make him a prisoner, I dare not discharge him if once taken.

As we have mentioned, it was mere humanity which induced Sir Francis Hartleton to order poor Maud to be brought to him.   He was very far indeed from suspecting her possession of the important scraps of Jacob Gray's written confession
which she had rescued from among the charred rafters of the house at Battersea
and he received the report of the officer, who had been commissioned to find her
to the effect that he had not yet been able to take her, without much feeling upo
the subject, engrossed as his mind was with other matters.

After thus turning the whole affair over in his mind, and, for the present resolv-
ing to do nothing, but wait and see what the chapter of accidents would bring forth
Sir Francis left his study, and sought the society of his young and amiable wife and
Ada.

During the very short residence of Ada with Sir Francis Hartleton and his lady,
she had endeared herself greatly to them.   Her love of truth—her earnest depre-
ciation of every wrong, and the sweet simplicity of her character had placed her so
high in their esteem, that they had resolved she should never leave the friendly

shelter of the roof, unless circumstances should arise to place her in a happy home of her own.

From all these circumstances and conclusions, it will be seen that not one of our characters, variously situated as they are, have great cause for congratulation on their prospects, with the exception of Ada, to whom it was a new and beautiful existence to be free from the persecutions of Jacob Gray. There was but one sad spot in the young girl's heart now, and that was, that loving, respecting, and admiring as she did Sir Francis Hartleton and his lady, she did not feel for them what she felt for Albert Seyton ; and many, very many of the gushing feeling of her heart were constrained to calmness and mere courtesy, because she felt that to the ears of a lover would they alone seem other than the enthusiastic dreams of a young and ardent imagination.

Sir Francis's wife, as we have remarked, sympathised much more with Ada concerning the probable fate or circumstances of Albert Seyton, than her husband could be expected to do; and it was at her solicitation that he now gave directions to some of his most active officers, to spare neither expense nor trouble to discover if the young man was in London or not.

CHAPTER LXXV.

BRITTON IN HIS GLORY AGAIN.—THE SONG AND THE LEGAL FUNCTIONARY.—THE SURPRISE.

THE deadly hatred which Learmont felt for Sir Francis Hartleton was a mild feeling in comparision with that of the same nature which began to engross the entire mind of Andrew Britton. Learmont he did certainly, from the bottom of his heart, dislike; Jacob Gray he detested and hated most cordially; but under the circumstances in which he was placed, he had come to consider them both as out of reach of any species of revenge he would feel gratified in having upon them. Besides he looked upon them both as mixed up with himself in the various occurrences that had shaped the whole of his existence, and he began to think Learmont a poor creature, useful only to supply his extravagancies, and Jacob Gray as a kind of necessary or, at least, inevitable evil to be endured, as far as his existence went, with much the same feelings as he would put up with the disagreeables of the changing seasons, or some other bodily ailment it was in vain to fight against.

But Sir Francis Hartleton what had he to do with the affair? and yet was he not perpetually thrusting himself forward in the most disagreeable manner, and thwarting him, Britton, at the most inauspicious moment, and in the manner calculated, of all others, to aggravate him—namely, by an exercise of personal strength.

When Britton was in that intermediate stage of intoxication which influenced his passions, he would dash his fist upon the table, and call down curses upon the head of his enemy, as terible and fierce in their language, as they were violent and outrageous in manner. Bond, the butcher, was his great companion on all such occasions, and no one was better calculated than that individual to second Britton in any word or deed of violence.

Britton had his usual large party at the Chequers, while Jacob Gray was being hunted through Westminster by the extremely officious shoemaker. His friend the butcher sat by his side, and whenever Britton roared out an oath, Master Bond was sure to cap it by some other of the most unique character.

The time was past midnight, and yet there was the rattling of glasses—the thumping of tankards—the shouts—screams—laughter and oaths of the motley assembly, proceeding in full vigour.

The landlord, when Westminster Abbey chimes struck the half hour past twelve, rushed into the room with a bland smile, after relieving his mind at the door by a hearty curse, and approaching Britton, he said,—

"Might I be so bold as to remind your most worshipful majesty that it is now half-past twelve?"

"No, you might not," roared Britton; "what's time time to me, I should like to know? Are you king of the Chequers, or am I?"

"With humble submission to your majesty, of course your majesty is king of the Chequers, but your highness must be aware that the magistrates are dreadfully jealous of a poor fellow keeping his house open so late."

"I suppose you may open as early as you like?" roared Britton.

"Certainly, your highness's grace."

"Very well; if any one comes to say a word, tell him you shut up at twelve, and open again at half-past. Do you hear, noodle, eh?"

"Do you hear his majesty's suggestion?" said the landlord, "was there ever such a head piece?"

"No, never. Hurrah!" shouted the guests.

"His gracious majesty's health," said a man rising at the further end of the room; "and may I be butchered if he aint a out and outer."

"What do you mean by may you be butchered?" said Bond.

"No reflection upon you, good Master Bond," said the man; "I only——that is, I meant nothing."

"Then don't do it again," said Bond, making three strides towards the man, and knocking his head against the wainscot till the lights danced again in his eyes.

That was just the kind of thing to arouse Britton, and he roared with laughter at the faces the man made.

"Is a man," remarked the butcher, "to have his trade, let it be ever so respectable, throwed slap in his face?"

"Bravo!" cried Britton; "well, landlord, bring us another bowl. Quick!"

"Yes, your majesty. Oh, he's a wonderful man—I mean king. What a headpiece, my masters—if there's any difficulty to be overcome, ask King Britton, and you have an answer pat at once—a most astonishing monarch he is, to be sure."

"Well, who the devil are you?" said Britton, as a stranger entered the room.

"An' it please you, sir, a serving man."

"A serving man! Whom do you serve—eh?"

"The worshipful Sir Francis Hartleton, hard by."

"Take that then," said Britton, flinging a pewter measure at the poor fellow's head, which luckily missed him; "how dare you come here, you sneaking spy?"

The man made a precipitate retreat, and when the landlord came with a steaming bowl of punch, Britton with an oath exclaimed,—

"Haven't I told you that I would have none of that Hartleton's people here?"

"Your majesty certainly was so gracious as to say so, but he whom your grace has so very judiciously turned out, tells me he has only been for a day in his service, so, your highness, I knew him not as he passed in."

"Sharpen your wits, then," said Britton, throwing the remnants of the butcher's flagon of strong ale in the landlord's face.

"Oh, what a wit he has!"

"Curse Hartleton—curse him!" growled Britton.

"So say I," said the butcher. "He has twice sent some one to condemn my scales."

"Sing us a song, somebody," cried Britton. A song I say, I say. Do you hear!"

"Gentlemen—gentlemen—a song from some of you, if you please," cried the landlord, bustling among the guests. "You hear that his majesty is musically inclined."

"Well, gentlemen,' said a small man, with a twisted lace coat, "I don't mind if I try my hand at a stave."

There was a great thumping of tankards upon the tables, and cries of "Bravo!" in the middle of which the man who had volunteered the song commenced in a wheezing tone as follows:—

THE TRIPLE TREE.

"Of all the trees that's in the land,
There's none like that I wot of;
The blossoms big upon this tree
Ne'er hang until they rot off.
But if it bloom at morning's dawn,
The fruit's so ripe and brown,
That when an hour has passed away,
We always cut it down,
　　　　Hurrah, boys!

No. 38.

> " The tree—the tree—the tripple tree,
>   None with it can compare ;
> Such heavy, goodly nuts it has,
>   But in an hour is bare.
>   Hurrah, boys !"

"Silence !" roared Britton, as the man was about to commence the second verse of his song.   " What the devil's song do you call that ?"

"The Triple Tree."

" And what may that be ?"

" The gallows," said the man, emphatically.

"Then who the devil are you ?"

" The hangman !"

All shrunk from the man as he announced his calling ; and for a minute or two a ghastly sallow paleness came over Britton's face.

"Very well, gentleman," said the hangman, " if you don't like my song, you needn't have the remainder of it I, am sure."

Britton rose from his seat in a menacing attitude as he said,—

" Now, may I be smashed if ever I met with such assurance in all my life.   You horrid —you infernal——"

" My good fellow, don't put yourself in a passion," said the hangman.   " I've come all the way from Smithfield to see you."

" See me ?"

" Yes.   I heard of you, and I came to take your weight in my eye—you understand.   It will require a good piece of hemp to hold you up.   You are bony, and that always weighs heavy.   Good night—I'll drop in again some evening."

With these words, the functionary of the law was off before Britton could make a rush at him, which he was just recovering sufficiently from his surprise to enable him to do.

As it was, when he found the hangman had fairly escaped him, he looked round him like some wild animal just turned out of a cage, and glaring about to seek for some enemy upon whom to wreak his pent-up vengeance.

"He aint far off, I'll be bound," cried the butcher, " I dare say he's waiting outside."

Britton upon this suggestion rushed from the room, and was at the street door in a moment.   There was a man shrinking just within the door-way, and without further examination,   Britton seized him with both hands, and found himself face to face with Jacob Gray.

CHAPTER LXXVI.

THE OLD ASSOCIATES.—GRAY'S FEARS.—THE OLD ATTIC AT THE CHEQUERS.

THERE was a light in the passage, which shed a strong full glare upon the pallid care worn features of Gray ; and Andrew Britton, as he held him at arm's length, turned nearly as pale as he was with the intense surprise of the meeting.   He was sobered by the shock, and in a husky whisper he muttered the name of Jacob Gray.

Such awful and abject fear seemed to take possession of Gray that had not Britton held him, he must have fallen at his feet.   All his presence of mind and cunning appeared to have deserted him, and it was not until Britton had again pronounced his name that he gasped,—

"Is—is it you, Andrew Britton?   I—I am glad to see you look so well."

" Yes, by God," said Britton, " it is me.   What wind from hell blew you here ?"

" I—I, you are looking very well," said Gray, with a sickly smile.

"Curses on my looks, and yours too. I say again what brought you here?"

"To—to see you, of course. I thought as we had been old friends, I would come and—and see you. You rather hurt me, Britton."

"You canting, whining villian," said Britton, "I will know what brought you here, or I will smash your head against the door-post."

"Violent, Britton, still violent to poor Jacob Gray, who comes to do you good. You know, my dear Britton——"

"Just say that again," cried Britton, "and I'll——"

He tightened his grasp upon Gray, who had just breath sufficient to gasp out,—

"Remember—my—confession! The gallows!"

Britton relaxed his hold, and a slight tremor passed over his frame as he said in a lower tone,—

"Jacob Gray, you must have something damnable to say or propose to me!"

"Not exactly, Britton. But I think there is danger abroad to us both!"

"Danger?"

"Yes, Britton. Of course when I thought any danger threatened, I said to myself, shall I not warn good, kind, peaceable, inoffensive Britton."

"You infernal liar!" cried Britton.

"So having," resumed Gray, not heeding any interruption, "so having placed my written confession where, in case I return not soon, it would be easily found, and forwarded to Sir Francis Hartleton, I came, you see, here at once."

"Sir Francis Hartleton!" cried Britton; "if you have anything really to say, it is of him, I'll be sworn. He has been hunting me, but I will have his heart's bood, I will!"

Gray caught at the suggestion, and immediately replied,—

"Yes—yes, Britton, it was of Sir Francis Hartleton I came to warn you."

"Indeed, on your soul?"

"On my soul it was. He is hatching some mischief against us all, Britton, and do you think I will let an old friend fall into danger, and not warn him? so, as I say, after placing my full and carefully written confession——"

"Now, Jacob Gray," said Britton, "if you say another word about your d——d confession, I will brain you on the spot."

"I only wished you to understand our relative positions, my good Britton," said Gray, who was rapidly overcoming his first fright, and with his usual fertility of invention scheming to overcome Britton by cunning.

"There, there, that will do. Let me hear no more of it," said Britton. "Come in."

Gray hesitated a moment, and Britton, bending his brows upon him, said,—

"Why, you are as safe in the Chequers at Westminster, as you were at the Old Smithy at Learmont. Why do you shrink, man? You know, and I make no secret of it, that I would as soon dash out your brains as look at you, if I could do so with safety. Come in, I say."

"I am quite sure," muttered Gray, "I may depend upon such an old friend as Britton."

He followed Britton as he spoke, and the smith, crossing the bar, ascended two flights of stairs to his own sleeping room, into which he ushered Jacob Gray.

"I have company down stairs, and be cursed to them," he said. "Wait here till I come back to you."

"You—you won't be long, Britton?"

"But five minutes.

Britton left the room, and after proceeding down about three stairs, he came back and, to Gray's dismay, locked the door of the room.

"So—so," murmured Gray, playing his fingers nervously upon the back of a chair. "Here I am hunted through Westminster, and forced at length to take refuge with Andrew Britton—he who has avowedly sought my life, and would take it now, but for fear of my confession. Have I ever been in such desperate straits as this before? Yes—yes—I have, and yet escaped. Surely he will not kill me. He dare not. Yet he drinks largely, and may remember then his revenge and hatred against me, while he forgets his own safety. Oh, if Andrew Britton knew how safe it now is to murder Jacob Gray, I should never see another sunrise. I am in most imminent danger—very imminent danger, indeed, and locked in too. What will become of me? What have I toiled for, what committed crime upon crime for, what dipped my hands in blood for, if I am to be hunted thus, impoverished, and a price to be set upon my head?"

Jacob Gray leaned his head upon his hands, and groaned aloud, in the bitterness of his despair.

Then after a time he rose and carefully examined the door with a forlorn hope, that he might be able by some means to escape by it, and slinking down the staircase leave the house ; but it was quite fast, and although his strength might have been sufficient to break it open, that was a mode of operation attended with far too much noise to answer his purpose.

"I am a prisoner here," he said,—"a prisoner to Andrew Britton, and my only chance of safety consists now in acting upon his fears, and arousing his anger more against Hartleton. He is long in coming,—what can be detaining him? Has he gone to Learmont's, and are they together hatching some plot for my destruction? Am I safe, or—or am I on the very brink of the grave? My heart sinks within me. Surely he has been gone an hour. Shall I alarm the house? No—no. I am then taken for a thief; and, perhaps, dragged before Hartleton, who would not fail to recognise me. There is no weapon here to protect myself,— no means of escape."

A sudden thought seemed to strike Gray, and he took up the candle which Britton had brought from the bar, and left with him.

"Does Britton," he muttered, "keep his confession here with—my knife? Oh, if I could find those,—if I could, 'twere worth all the risk I now run. I would sell him to Learmont for a goodly sum."

With a stealthy step, and a damp clammy perspiration of fear upon his brow. Jacob Gray crept about the room, which was at the top of the house, peering into every hole and corner in search of the much-dreaded confession of Andrew Britton.

His search was in vain—there was no paper to be found of any description, and he sat down at length in despair.

" 'Tis in vain—'tis in vain," he groaned. " I am the victim of some contrivance of Britton's to destroy me, or he would have returned ere this. I am lost— lost—lost."

Jacob Gray wrung his hands, and wept like a child, as he thought his hour was come.

A long, straggling ray of light came in at the window now, and he started up exclaiming,—

" There is one hope more—the window—the window."

The casement was one of those with diamond-shaped panes, held together by thin slips of lead, and Jacob Gray saw that immediately under it was a filthy gutter.

"One hope—one hope," he muttered; and cautiously drawing himself through the window, he closed it again, and stood in the gutter. On one side of him was the high sloping roof of the attic, and on the other was a narrow crumbling parapet.

With a shudder, he looked down into the street. An itinerant breakfast provider had taken up his station immediately below, and several early passengers were hurrying onwards to different employments.

A boy looked up, and said,—

" There he goes !"

Gray could have cut his throat with pleasure, but he could only curse him, and creep on, while the urchin pointing him out to the saloop dealer, who, shading his eyes with his hands, said in a voice that came clearly to Jacob Gray's ears,—

" It's some thief, I'll be bound, but it's no business of mine—saloop !"

CHAPTER LXXVII.

THE SMITH'S PLOT AGAINST GRAY.—AN ACCOMMODATING FRIEND.

WHEN Britton left Jacob Gray in his room, he descended but to the first landing-place of the stairs, and then paused to consider what he had better do under the circumstances so new and so strange as Gray taking refuge with him from some danger to himself, or coming to consult with him upon some common danger to them both. This latter supposition was, however, too extravagant for Britton to believe; and when he came to consider all the circumstances,—his finding Gray skulking by the door, and his evident confusion and fear when he was seized and seen, Britton with a blow of his clenched fist upon his hand exclaimed,—

"I see it now—the sneaking villain was acting the spy upon me. He wants to take my life—it's all a d——d scheme of his, but I will be even with him, or my name aint Andrew Britton. Let me consider—I'll get Bond to watch him home from here—a capital plan—he don't know Bond, and will never suspect he is followed. Then when he finds out where he lives, we can go together, Bond and I, and knock his infernal brains out. That'll do."

Having satisfactorily to himself settled this line of operations, and considering Gray perfectly safe till he chose to release him, Britton made his appearance again in the parlour of the Chequers.

"Come on," cried Bond, "there hasn't been no time lost while you was gone for I've been drinking for you."

"I thank you," said Britton—"landlord, do you hear me, never open your door to a hangman again."

"It was a piece of great impudence," said the landlord, "of such a wretch coming here." Then he added to himself, "Bless me, if he don't seem quite sober all of a sudden, and he was a going it finely a little while ago. I do wonder now if he will recollect how much liquor he has had."

"Hurrah!" cried Britton's guests—"hurrah for King Britton! we'll drink his health again."

"D—n you, then you'll do it at your own expense," said Britton. "What do you mean by sotting here at this time, eh? Clear out with you all, will you?"

"Well, I do think it's—it's nearly time to go," hiccupped one man.

"Off with you all!" cried Britton. "Clear the house, landlord."

The motley assembly, who among themselves could not have mustered the price of a jug of ale, rose in obeidence to Britton's commands, and avowing their intention of coming to see him on the morrow evening, they, with much noise and boisterous clamour, took their departure from the Chequers.

In a very minutes none were in the parlour but the landlord, Britton, and the butcher. The smith then turned to his host, and said,—

"Bring me some spiced canary, and keep every body out of here."

"Yes, your majesty—most certainly—oh dear yes!"

The spiced canary was soon set before the precious couple, and then Britton, after a hearty draught, handed the liquor to the butcher, who with a nod that might imply any toast that his companion liked to translate it into, nearly finished the beverage.

"Bond," said Britton, "I want you to do a little job for me."

"I'm your man," said the butcher. "What is it?"

"In my bedroom up stairs is a man."

"A thief?"

"He is a thief, and be cursed to him! for he has robbed me for many years of my due."

"You want him thrown out of window?"

"No, not exactly. I am interested for many reasons in finding out where he lives. When he leaves here, which I will take care he shall do soon, you follow him .

" I see—I see."

" You comprehend. He must not know you are after him, for he is as wily as a fox, but track him home, Bond, like a blood-hound!"

" Eh ?" said Bond, rather astonished at the vehemence of Britton.

" I say you must follow him closely, and not let him escape you, on any account."

" I tell you what will be the best plan," said Bond; " you don't want to lose him nohow?"

" Dead or alive I will never let him escape me !"

" Then I'll take my cleaver with me ?"

" Your cleaver ?"

" Yes ; then, you know, then if he should turn round I can easily bring him down with that."

" Yes—yes; but he has something at his home that I want."

" Oh, very well. Then we must let him go home first, I suppose. But I'd rather have my cleaver with me, in case of anything handy and delicate being wanted."

" You may have the devil with you if you like, so that you dog the fellow home, and come back with accurate news of where he lives. I hate him, and must have his life !"

" May I make so uncommon free as to ask what he's done ?"

Done ! He has swindled me out of my own. You know I am a smith? Well, for ten long years I beat the anvil, when I ought to be a gentleman, all through him. For ten years by myself—shunned by every one. I was forced to live by myself—work by myself—drink by myself."

" That was d—d hard."

" It was ; and all through this man. Hilloa there—more canary."

Britton was fast relapsing into his former state of semi-intoxication, and he struck his fists repeatedly upon the table as he continued,—

" He has been my bane—my curse—and he is so now ! He boasts of his cunning, and calls me a muddle-headed beast. I'll muddle his head for him. Curse him —curse him."

" A precious rogue he must be," said the butcher.

" He is a sneaking, cowardly villain. He is one of those who won't do his share of an ugly job, and yet wants more than his share of the reward."

" Humph ! An ugly job."

" Yes—I said it—drink—drink."

" What's his name ?" said the butcher.

" His name is Jacob Gray."

" A nice name for a small party. Well, we'll settle his business for him— humanely, you know, Master Britton, always humanely, say I. My cleaver is the thing—there ain't no sort of trouble with it, you may depend."

" Bond," whispered Britton.

" Britton," said Bond.

" If there should be any occasion, which I think there will be, to smash this fellow, do you mind lending me that same cleaver of yours ?"

" Sartinly not."

" Thank you—thank you. Keep a look out now, by the door, and when you see a pale, ill-looking scoundrel walk out—no, sneak out, I mean—follow him. He will be the proper man. I wait here your return, good Master Bond, and then we can take what steps, after you have found out where he lives, we may agree upon. More canary there !"

Britton kept taking huge draughts of liquor as he instructed the butcher, in what he wished him to do, and now his voice began to thicken, and he had but a very confused recollection of what he had confided to him, and what he had kept sceret.

"D—n the Old Smithy," he cried ; "who cares? Not I. I'd live there again although there is some strange sights and sounds."

The butcher looked confused, and then in his peculiar elegant phraseology he asked Britton what the h— he meant.

"What do I mean?" said Britton ; "why, I mean what I say, to be sure. You know what I mean well enough—I tell you this infernal thing that's now up stairs, kept me at the anvil for years, when I ought to have been, as I am now, a gentleman."

"Oh," said the butcher, "I suppose he gave you an amazing lot of work and wouldn't pay for any of it till it was all done?"

"I suppose you're a fool," said Britton.

"Thank you," replied Bond; "you may abuse me as much as you like, I'm your best friend, and can stand it. You know you'll go far afore you can find another fellow as can drink as much as me."

Britton seemed struck with the force and truth of this remark, and he took another huge draught of liquor before he replied,—

"That's true—you are a good fellow ; neer mind me—I—I shoul like to see the Old Smithy again before the last drop goes down my throat.'

"The old who?"

"The Old Smithy at Learmont. I've had some pleasant hours there and some unpleasant ones, just as it happened. In for a penny, you know, and in for a pound, so I wasn't going to say nay to the squire, you understand, and be d——d to you."

"Yes, I understand, that is to say, I don't exactly comprehend," said Bond, trying to look very knowing.

"Then you're a fool," again cried Britton.

"Very well," said Bond, with tipsy gravity, "very good—this here's the state of the case :—You've got an animal up stairs, you says—very good. You wants me to take my cleaver, and see what's to be done."

"That's the thing."

"Then what the deuce do you mean by keeping the creature waiting for, eh?"

"Because I know him," laughed Britton. "It's Jacob Gray, you know."

"Oh, is it? It may be Jacob anything else for all I know about him."

"I tell you it's Jacob Gray," reiterated Britton, striking his fist on the table."

"Very well," roared the butcher, dealing a much louder blow than Britton, and making the glasses dance again.

"Then I know he's trembling—groaning with fear. He thinks his last hour is come—I know he does. He suffers now more than as if we were to go up now and cut his throat."

"Stop a bit," said the butcher, "always knock creturs on the head afore you cuts their throats—mallet 'em first—always mallet first—it's so very humane, it is."

"Come on," cried Britton ; "you know wnat you have to do. Follow him closely and surely, and bring me word where he lives. Then we can go to-morrow night, and you may mallet him till he has no head to mallet—hurrah!"

"A d——d fool!" muttered the butcher, as he immersed a considerable portion of his immense red face in the bowl of liquor before him, nor took it out while there was a drain left.

The bar was not half-a-dozen paces from the door of the room in which Andrew Britton and Bond had been sitting, and half drunk as the smith was, he fancied, when he had his hand upon the door, that he heard the scuffling of some one's feet running away from it. This circumstance raised his ire wonderfully, and the suspicion it gave rise to, that the landlord was playing the spy upon him, nearly choked him with rage.

He paused a moment and glanced towards the bar, but no one was to be seen by the lamp which cast a tolerable light over the many bottles and bright measures there collected. Britton muttered a curse, and was about to pass on towards the staircase, when he saw from the other side of the bar a head slowly rise and then suddenly pop down again.

An exclamation of anger was upon his lips, but he repressed it, and a strong desire to perpetrate some practical joke upon the landlord for his cunning propensities occurred to him. After a few moments' thought, he returned to the room he had just left, and arming himself with a massive poker, he winked mysteriously at the butcher, who followed him in silent amazement, wondering against whom the powerful weapon was about to be used.

When Britton reached the bar, he placed his finger on his lips, as an invocation to Bond to keep silence, and then he stationed himself with the poker in such a position, that if the head should protrude again, he could by a lateral sweep of the heavy bar of iron, for such it was, make sure of dealing upon it a tolerable rap.

In point of fact, the landlord had been listening to the dialogue between Britton and his friend the butcher, and then had scampered into his own bar, and with an excess of cunning for which there was no sort of occasion, had stooped down behind his own bar, where he might have showed himself boldly, with far less suspicion attached to him.

Britton had taken his measures well, for in less than a minute the top of the landlord's head appeared, but before his eyes got to the level of the bar, the smith dealt what there was of his head such a terrible thwack with the poker, that he fell down in the bar with a deep groan.

Britton's delight at this achievement knew no bounds, and without caring in the least whether the landlord's skull was fractured or not, he sat down on the stairs and laughed till the tears ran down his cheeks.

"Here," he then cried to the butcher, "take this back," throwing the poker to him, which Bond caught very dexterously in one of his immense hands, "I haven't been so amused for a long time; keep watch, and I'll send the fellow down stairs in a minute."

"That Britton is certainly a clever man in some things," remarked the butcher, quite confidently to himself, as he lit his pipe calmly by the lamp.

Britton was in a remarkably good humour as he ascended the staircase to liberate Jacob Gray, who, he had not the least idea, had made his escape in the manner we have related. He had had plenty of drink. Jacob Gray, as he imagined, was in his power, and he had been just most amazingly amused by the little affair of the poker.

"Who says Andrew Britton is a fool and a thick-headed brute?" he muttered as he ascended the stairs; "I will be one too many for cunning clever Jacob Gray yet. I have him now safe—I have him. He cannot escape me—though what the devil brought him here, I can't guess. That's all a lie about coming here to warn me of anything; he must have been set on to watch me by Learmont, and yet would he venture? I must make him tell me before he goes."

Britton paused a moment and took a clasped knife from his pocket. Then he added, coolly,—

"I'll cut off one of his ears if he don't tell exactly what brought him here. Besides that, it will be a good plan, for he'll then be identified wherever he goes."

Britton stopped at the door of the attic to laugh before he unlocked it.

"Jacob is in a horrid fright—I'm sure he is," he muttered; "d—n me, I'll— I'll alarm him a bit."

Britton applied his mouth to the key-hole, and made an unearthly kind of noise, that had Jacob Gray been there, would have gone far towards frightening him into fits. Then he dealt the door a bang with his fists, that made the whole attic shake again.

"He's half dead, I know he is," he cried; "upon my word I haven't had such a pleasant evening for a long time."

The smith then, after several efforts, for he was not in the steadiest condition, succeeded in unlocking the door. There burnt the light, nearly expiring, and Jacob Gray was gone.

For a moment Britton could scarcely believe his eyes. He then rushed to th open window, and the truth flashed across his mind. After all Jacob Gray had escaped him. A torrent of curses burst from his lips, and he sunk upon chair quite exhausted by his ungovernable passion.

CHAPTER LXXVIII.

GRAY ON THE HOUSE TOPS.—SPECIMENS OF THE RISING GENERATION.—THE OLD ATTIC.

GRAY's situation on the house tops was as far from being safe as it was far from pleasant, for the rapidly advancing daylight, he felt conscious, would very soon make him a prominent object to the whole liberty of Westminster, if he found not some means of descending

No. 39.

His standing upon the parapets, and in the gutters, along which he crawled, was insecure in the extreme, and his nervousness, from repeated slips which nearly precipitated him into the street, increased each moment, so that he began to feel that, unless he got refuge speedily somewhere, he should meet with a fatal and disastrous accident.   His idea was to get in at some attic window, and so make his way into the street through the house ; but this, although the only possible means that he could think of, for rescuing him from his very precarious situation, was fraught with dangers and difficulties ; for who would allow a man to get in at an attic window, and walk undisturbed through their house into the street ?

Jacob Gray groaned as he thought of this, and wrung his hands in despair.

" I cannot fight my way out," he muttered.   " There is but one remote chance for me, and that is to get into some house where there are no men.   I may succeed in alarming females, so that they may be glad to let me go in peace, but what a slender hope is that."

" There he goes !" shouted a baker's boy at this moment, looking up and pointing at Gray, who nearly fell into the street with the suddenness of the alarm.

Several chance passengers now stopped, and pointed Gray out to others ; so that his situation was becoming every moment more precarious.

" Stop thief! there he goes !" shouted the boy again, setting down his basket of bread, and resolved, as boys always are under such circumstances, to see the affair out.

" Who is it ?" cried several.

" Guy Fawkes," said the boy.

There was a laugh among the crowd, which was rapidly increasing ; and now an old lady put her hea out of the window of the house on the parapet of which was the trembling Jacob Gray, and inquired, in an angry tone, what was the matter, and particularising the baker's boy as a young ruffian, wanted to know how he had collected the crowd opposite the house.

The boy with the peculiar wit of his " order," placed his hand to his ear, affecting not to have heard the old lady, upon which, to the great amusement of the crowd, she screamed out—,

" Oh, you villain, I heard you call me a guy, but I'll speak to your master, I will, you wretch."

" You'll make yerself ill, mum," said the boy, " if ycr hexerts yer old lungs so."

The old lady shook her fists at him, and the crowd roared with laughter.

Jacob Gray could see that the mob was very much amused at something, but what it could be he had no means of knowing, for the same obstacle, in the shape of a projecting parapet, which prevented the old lady from seeing him, also prevented him from seeing her.   He endeavoured to crawl round an angle of a roof and escape observation, while the altercation was going on ; but neither the baker's boy nor a sweep who had joined his persecutors, would permit such a thing for a moment, and they at once called out,—

" There he goes—there he goes !"

" What do you mean ?" screamed the old lady to the sweep.

" There's a poll parrot, mum, a-top o' your house," replied the sweep.

" A what !" screamed she, leaning as far out of the window as she could, and looking up.

" Mind yer eye, mum," shrieked the baker's boy, and amid a perfect roar of laughter, the old lady withdrew her head in a moment.

" You—you little abominable miscreant," she cried, " I'll come down to you !"

" Thank you, mum."

" There's a man on the roof," said some one near.

" A man ?"

" Yes ; just on the corner of the parapet."

" Preserve us," cried the old lady, leaning out of the window again and looking.

" Lean out as far as you can, mum," cried the sweep.

" I am," said the old lady.

" A little further, then, and you'll see him."

Here was another laugh, and Jacob Gray, with a great effort, succeeded in turning the corner of the roof just as the old lady produced a tremendous rattle, which she began springing violently at the window, to the rapturous delight of the crowd below.

"He's gone into Smith-street," cried several of the throng, and a rush round the corner was made to keep Jacob Gray in sight.

When he got round the corner of the roof which had cost him so much trouble, the first thing that poor Jacob Gray did was to fall over a pail that was set out at an attic window, into a dirty drain full of black slimy mud, interspersed here and there with delicate streaks of green and blue. When he recovered from the shock of his fall, his first thought was to rise as quickly as possible, but his second was to lie where he was, as by so doing he was hidden by the parapet from the gaze of those in the street.

But Jacob Gray was not at all aware of the ready invention and cunning of boys in the streets of London, and it was with a curse that, if curses were effective as implements of death would have destroyed both the sweep and the baker's boy he heard the latter suggest,—

"Oh, he is in the drain—I know he is—give us a stone, and I'll hit him."

"If ever," muttered Gray, "I come across you, and I shall know your confounded cracked voice again, I'll wring your neck."

The words were scarcely out of his mouth, when a good-sized stone came down upon him with a very disagreeable plump. It had been thrown by the boy with that accuracy that boys acquire in throwing stones from the abundance of practice that they have in that polite accomplishment.

"Well, my covey, did it hit you?" cried the boy then in a very insulting tone.

Gray looked up from among the mud, and he saw that the attic window was open. It was very low, and he thought he might crawl in without being seen; at all events it was better than being pelted with stones in a gutter,—and having satisfied himself that the attic was empty, he partially rose from the gutter, and had the satisfaction, such as it was, of gliding over the window-cill without being seen.

This was one object gained at all events, and he stood the picture of misery and wretchedness, gazing around him upon the scantily-furnished room, in which there was nothing but a small bed made upon a board laid across trussels, and one rickety chair.

Exhausted, dispirited, and weak, Jacob Gray sat down upon the chair, but it seemed as if in small matters as well as in great, the fates would never have done persecuting him, for he had not noticed that his chair was minus a leg, and the consequence was that Jacob Gray came down on the floor with a great noise, which was more than sufficient to alarm anybody in the house.

He in an agony of apprehension rose instantly, and flew to the window, but then the risk of traversing house tops in broad daylight, which it now very nearly was, came across him, and he recoiled from the window, feeling that in all probabilty, his least danger lay in remaining where he was, and endeavouring to excite by some spurious tale the compassion of the persons of th house.

His heart, however, felt sick and faint as he waited in trembling expectation of some one coming; and as minute after minute rolled onwards, leaving him still alone, he felt it would be a relief to his mind if they would come at once, and not leave him on the rack of apprehension.

His senses became powerfully acute to the least noise, and once or twice he fancied he heard a creaking noise upon the staircase, as if some one was coming cautiously up to capture him. This feeling grew each moment until it became awfully intolerable, and he trembled so excessively that he could not, as he wished, open the door to see if any one was upon the stairs.

A dreadful apprehension came across his mind, that whoever was coming might be armed with, perhaps, a blunderbuss, which might on the moment of his appearance, be discharged in his, Jacob Gray's, face, and so finish his career at once by a death of agony. The moment this apprehension began to haunt him he looked around him for some place of temporary concealment, and observing a cupboard at one end of the room, he glided cautiously towards it, resolving to take refuge within it until he should hear, by the voices of those who might be coming, what might probably be their station in life and their intentions.

The cupboard door was only fastened with a button, and Jacob Gray turned cautiously. The door, from the pressure of something inside, immediately came wide open. A cry of terror burst from Jacob Gray, as a dead body apparently frightfully mangled, fell at his feet.

CHAPTER LXXIX.

THE INTERVIEW BETWEEN ALBERT AND LEARMONT.—THE PROMISE, AND ALBERT'S RELATION.

ALBERT SEYTON was punctual to his appointment with Learmont, and after waiting for ten minutes, was ushered into the small room in which the miserable squire usually sat.

Days seemed to be doing the work of years upon Learmont. His coal-black hair was tinged with grey, and there were deep furrows on his cheeks, which were of that dead ashy-looking white colour, if colour it could be called at all, that the former sallow tint of his complexion had recently given way to.

Take his appearance altogether as he there sat in a chair, the back of which was placed against the wall with a table and writing materials before him, he looked a man to be shunned or pitied, according as the observer might translate his looks to imply disease of body, or that worse disease of the mind resulting from a perturbed conscience.

He slightly started as Albert entered the room, and then, in reply to his bow, he said in a hollow voice, which sounded as if it came from the lips of a corpse risen from the grave,—

" Good day, young sir."

" Good day, sir," replied Albert. " I am here in obedience to your command."

" Yes—yes," muttered Learmont, leaning his head upon his hand. " You are here, and punctual—very punctual." He then seemed to fall into a fit of abstraction, and added, " He is not here. Can he have taken alarm? or he will be here anon?"

" Sir," said Albert.

Learmont started, exclaiming,—

" Who spoke?"

" I thought you addressed me, sir?"

" No—no—I—I—said nothing. You are very young, and yet have known trouble, you say?"

" There has been much trouble, sir, crowded into the brief space of my existence," replied Albert. " I have lost all that I loved."

" All?" echoed Learmont.

" Yes, sir, all," sighed Albert.

" You have no ties then to bind you to the world, and make you pause in any undertaking? You are like me, a lone man. I am lone, and quite desolate; but I pride myself upon my isolation. I would not be surrounded by what the mass of mankind rejoice in, in the shape of connexions, for worlds."

Albert said nothing, and, after a pause, Learmont added, hastily,—

" You bear in mind our conversation of yesterday?"

" I do, sir, and am ready to perform the honourable service you mentioned to me."

Albert laid some stress upon the word honourable, and Learmont replied, coldly,—

" Well, sir, it is honourable service."

" I know it is, sir."

' You know it is?"

" Yes, sir—I know it is so, or, as the son of a soldier and a gentleman, I should never have had it proposed to me by you."

A sneer passed over Learmont's face as he said,—

" My young friend, soldiers, and gentlemen, and their sons, are not all as particular as you."

" I am sorry for it, sir."

" Nay, why should you be? Among stars would you not wish to shine the brightest? 'Tis well that some soldiers and gentlemen are not so very scrupulous; for don't you see, young sir, that it makes your great virtue shine with double lustre."

Albert did not wholly relish the tone of irony in which this was said, and his cheek slightly flushed as he replied,—

" It were unbecoming in me to dispute with you, sir."

There was a silence of some moments' duration, and then Learmont said, abruptly,—

" You will follow the man home upon whose track I will put you. Awaken in his mind no shadow of doubt, or all—I—I mean much is lost. He is crafty; but bear this in mind through life—to outwit the crafty, you have but to be simple."

" I will do my best, sir."

" Do so, and your reward will be commensurate with your deserts. Surely he will come."

" I hope you will find him honester than you suppose him to be," remarked Albert.

" You hope I may find him honest! May all the torments of hell consume him!"

" Sir?"

" I—I don't mean him. No matter—I am not quite well. Young man, beware, whatever you may see, hear, or surmise in this house, must remain locked in your own heart."

" Sir," said Albert, shrinking from the basilisk glance of Learmont, " my duty is simple. I have but to obey your honourable orders, and I shall do so to the utmost of my humble ability. It were, indeed, a poor return for your kindness to me, to babble of you or your affairs."

" Well, so it would—you are right there," said Learmont. " I would fain bind you to me and my interests by kindness—such substantial kindness as you would appreciate; and never forget I am rich—have some power, and am willing to use my wealth, and exhert my influence. Can I serve you in any matter? You hinted that you had a source of trouble."

Albert's heart beat tumultuously at these words, and his first thought was,—

" Will he exert his wealth and influence in assisting me to discover Ada?"

Learmont saw his agitation and said,—

" Speak freely. But should the man whom I wish you to follow arrive here during our converse, you must finish your story another time. I wish you to speak freely, and if I can bind you to me by benefit conferred upon you, I shall think myself well repaid."

" Sir," said Albert, " were—were you—you——"

" What?"

" Ever in love, sir?"

" I love?—I in love?—I?"

" Pardon me, sir, for asking the question; but the sadness that has hung like a leaden weight upon my heart for so long has arisen from the deep sympathy I felt for the forlorn condition of one who even then seemed, by some mysterious influence, creeping around my heart.

Learmont leaned back in his chair with a slight yawn, but Albert was too much interested in his own subject to notice the contemptuous impatience of his auditor.

"When my poor father died," he continued, "I felt great grief; but that was a grief that time would assuage. It left nothing to the imagination to work upon, and continue building up unavailing sorrow. On the contrary, when the first shock of parting with those we love—when death has robbed us of them, is over, and when reason resumes her reign—we should rejoice that they have left such fleeting and uncertain joys as this world affords for that which is eternal and knows no change; but where I loved, where I gave my whole heart's affection, sir, there indeed I have much cause for sorrow, and there is far too ample food for dreamy fancy to work upon."

"Indeed," said Learmont.

"I fear I tire you, sir."

"Not at all, not at all, go on."

"A considerable time since, sir, and I believe before your worship came to London, my father and I lodged in a mean house not very far from here, for we were poor. My father was waiting for his just remuneration for services rendered to ungrateful people. I was but a boy, sir, but from the time of my residence in that house, I may date the commencement of a love which, although I knew not then its existence, became a part of my nature, and will accompany me to the grave."

"Oh," said Learmont. Then he muttered to himself, "what can detain Jacob Gray?"

Albert continued :—

"In the same house, sir, lodged a strangely matched couple. The one was a man of wily and sinister aspect, ever crawling instead of walking—insinuating, rather than saying, what he wished to convey—a man that had villain stamped upon his face."

"I rather think," said Learmont, "I could match you such a man."

"Let us hope, sir, there are few such," added Albert, "but of such a character was he, who daily slunk in and out of this house, living apparently in great poverty. With him dwelt a young girl."

"Ah," thought Learmont, "love and poverty, the old story."

"Oh, sir, she was beautiful—beautiful as Heaven, and her face was as a speaking mirror in which you might read all the pure and noble feelings of her soul. She must have been of noble and high origin, for the seeds of every high virtue were implanted in her breast, and even then were budding forth in beauty.

"The soft blush of an Italian dawn, sir, was not more beautiful than were her eyes. Her brow, of snowy whiteness, rivalled the rarest sculpture, and her mouth——"

"You may describe her to me some other time," said Learmont, with a slight tone of impatience. "I should like to know how I can serve you."

"I have lost her, sir."

"Oh! you have lost her. Well, I presume she is to be found?"

"By your influence and means, sir, she may; but alas! I scarcely know in what direction to commence the search."

"Did you wed her?"

"No, sir; had I done so, a world in arms should not have separated us."

"The father then, I presume, was adverse to your suit?"

"She had no father, sir—no mother—no relations—no friend in the world but me, and I left her in peril ; and never saw her more—never—never!"

"Go on with your story."

"He who was with her, or rather held her in durance, was a mysterious man. I have often thought, sir, some great crime weighed heavily upon his heart."

"Perhaps so," said Learmont, in a hollow voice. "Perhaps so. His life might have been one long mistaken, and he bartered for gold that which was priceless. Go on—go on."

" He seemed, sir, ever wakeful to some great danger, and if ever there was a miserable man, it was that man."

" Well—well," said Learmont.

" Time passed, and still I fondly, dearly loved. She would have left him, or denounced him for his cruelty, but then she always had the dread upon her spirit that he might be what he appeared to be—her father; so, sir, she bore with much, and with a noble spirit would not sacrifice him, by which I much fear she has sacrificed herself. Still are they living in some dark obscurity in London, or—or he has killed her! Alas! alas! my poor Ada!"

" Ada was her name ?"

" It was, sir."

" Why does this cold shudder come over me ?" muttered Learmont as he trembled in his chair.

" But the most strange circumstance of all," continued Albert, " connected with the affair, was that this man Gray——"

A cry arose from Learmont that startled Albert to his feet in a moment, and with pale, ghastly features and distorted lips, the squire stood opposite to him, glaring in his face with distended eyes and such an awful expression, that step by step, the young man went backwards towards the door, for the thought flashed across his mind that his patron was a madman.

CHAPTER LXXX.

THE UNFORTUNATE CONFIDENCE OF ALBERT SEYTON.—LEARMONT'S PROMISES AND TREACHERY.

WHEN Albert Seyton got near the door, Learmont cried in a harsh voice,—

" Stop, stop—'twas only a passing spasm, I am subject to them, very subject to them. Come back, young sir, come back."

He reeled a step or two as he spoke, and then sunk into a chair, muttering,—

" I—I have not strength now to bear me up against these sudden surprises. Can it be really he, and I, listening with so much indifference to what touched me so nearly, and yet it cannot be—I dare not question him."

" Are you better, sir ?" said Albert.

" Yes—yes, better now. Ring yon bell, and order wine."

Albert rung a lusty peal upon the bell, and an attendant promptly answered the summons, standing respectfully for orders.

Learmont rose and approached the man, who became evidently much frightened lest his imperious master was for some real or imagined fault going to execute summary vengeance upon him.

" Mercy, sir, your worship," he cried.

" Fool!" growled Learmont, as he reached the door; and then inclining his head close to the man's ear he said :—" If Jacob Gray should come while this young gentleman is with me, show him into a room, but do not announce him."

" Yes, yes, your worship."

" Make no mistake, or I will have you hung, fellow."

" No—no—no, your worship, I won't make any mistake, I aint to announce Jac——"

" Silence, and begone," cried Learmont, in a loud voice, and the man precipitately retired in a great fright.

" Oh! I forgot the wine," said Learmont, as he turned from the door, " ring again if you please."

Albert rung, and with a pale face the servant just came to the threshold of the door.

"Wine," cried Learmont, and the man disappeared immediately with a jirk, as if he had been pulled away by some wire.

"You will continue your marration," said Learmont, trying to impart some moisture to his parched lips—"you—you—named Gray, I think, as the man's name?"

"I did, sir—— Jacob Gray."

Learmont was prepared for this, and he only gave a slight start, as the familiar name came upon his ears.

"Go on—go on," he said.

"I was about to tell you that he kept a mysterious written paper in his room, addressed on the outside to Sir Francis Hartleton, the magistrate."

"Addressed on the outside to Sir Francis Hartleton, the magistrate," muttered Learmont—"then, then, it was true."

"Sir!"

"Go on—go on."

"This paper he always charged his young and beautiful companion to repair with herself to Sir Francis Hartleton, should he on any occasion not return or send to her within three clear days of the time he had limited his absence to extend to."

"Indeed. 'Twas very strange."

"It was, sir, and I always believed that the paper contained some particulars concerning the gentle girl he had held in such cruel and unjustifiable bondage."

"No doubt—no doubt; well what happened next? Go on.'

"From that place one day they mysteriously removed, leaving behind them only an old trunk in which this strange paper used to be kept, and it was long ere I saw them again."

"But you did!"

"I did, sir—I should, however, have informed you of another circumstance, but I fear, sir, I weary you—you are not well, sir."

"Yes, yes—quite well."

"Some other time when you may feel disposed to listen to me, sir—I——"

"Go on, now—go on—it amuses me much—very much—I have not been so interested in anything for a long time—I beg you will go on."

"You are very kind, sir. Then as I was saying I forgot to tell you that this young girl was, when I first knew her, disguised in the dress of a boy, and called Harry Gray."

"Disguised as a boy?—humph—an artful, very cunning trick."

"Yes, sir, but objectless surely—I thought her a boy, and then she was beautiful, and I could have lived or died for Harry Gray; but when after that, I saw her in the clothing more becoming to her sex, and knew her as my own beautiful Ada, how different were my feelings—I passionately loved her."

"And she?"

"Returned my heart's devotion with all the frankness of her noble nature."

"Where was she when you saw her last?"

"I met her in St. James's Park—she had fled from the house to which this man Gray had hurried her, and where he had kept her a close prisoner for a weary space of time. Then I madly parted with her, as I thought but for an hour, and I have never seen her since."

"Where was the house?"

"A ruined condemned house by South Lambeth—a wretched den."

Learmont drew a long breath, as he said,—

"You say she has escaped from him? How was that?"

"Some men had sought his life, she told me, and he had assured her that his only chance of preservation lay in their not finding her with him; and moreover, as they supposed her a boy, she might escape and so preserve herself and him by attiring herself in the proper habiliments of her sex."

"Yes—yes—she did?"

"She did, sir, on the mere doubt that he might be her father."

"Well, and after that?"

" After that I never saw her. I have searched in every place in London. I have wearied myself with a long and useless hunt. I have inquired until I met with insolence from some, and mockery from others. Oh, sir, if indeed you will aid me in this matter, I do from my heart, believe that while you make two beings happy who will ever bless your name,—you will likewise be unmasking some monstrous villany which this man Jacob Gray has been concerned in."

" Bless my name," muttered Learmont, with a shudder.

" With your means, and your influence with the authorities, we surely must succeed," continued Albert. " Oh, then, sir, consider what a glorious reflection it will be to you to see our happiness, and tell yourself that it was all your work."

" The—the wine, sir," said the trembling servant, coming into the room.

Learmont motioned it to be laid before him, and then filled a bumper that quite astonished Albert, and tossed it off at one draught.

No. 40.

"Drink," he said, as he pushed a decanter across the table to Albert. "It will raise your spirits to tell me the remainder of your strange eventful story."

Albert drank a small quantity of the generous fluid, and then he said,—

"I have nearly told you all, sir. Everything else with me must be conjecture. I should, however, mention that I called upon Sir Francis Hartleton, with the hope of interesting him in the affair, but he took but little heed of it."

"Indeed !"

"Yes; he was but lukewarm as regarded all I told him, and I believe did nothing in the matter."

"And yet you told him all you have related to me," said Learmont.

"All, sir ; but there are some men who will not step out of the beaten track of their duty for any consideration."

"True, true, Mr. Seyton. I believe this man to be an overpraised man. Indeed, I am far from having the high opinion of him he seems to have obtained from most persons. I should advise you to shun him. Do not call upon him ; and, should you even by chance meet him, avoid any conversation concerning this matter. I am chary of interfering with men's reputation, but I know sufficient of this Sir Francis Hartleton to beware of him as a hollow friend."

"In truth, sir, I believe," said Albert, "that I shall have but little trouble in shunning him; for I was denied admittance to him twice when I called, since my first interview."

"Ay, that shows you the man. He found that there was difficulty, and perhaps danger, in the affair, and no immediate profit or reputation ; so, you see, he treated you coldly."

"He did treat me coldly."

"Then you rely upon me. If needs be, I will become such powerful assistance for you, that you must succeed; and, should you by any means discover the abode of this Jacob Gray, I think you had better bring me word, without adoping any mode of action of your own, and then we can consult upon some safe and effectual means of serving you."

"I feel your kindness, sir, most sensibly," said the grateful Albert, "and——"

"Well, well," interrupted Learmont—"I am sure you will be grateful. I have no service for you to-day, for it is long past the hour this man should have been here ; but attend me here to-morrow morning at the same hour."

"I shall be punctual, sir," said Albert rising.

"Good day—good day," said Learmont.

Albert bowed, and left the room.

CHAPTER LXXXI.

LEARMONT'S IMPROVED PROSPECTS.—THE PARK.—ADA'S RECOLLECTIONS.—THE MEETING.

WHEN Learmont was once more left alone, a dark scowl of triumph came over his face, and he breathed more freely than he had done for many a day.

"So," he said "many mysteries are suddenly cleared up now ; I—I am myself again. A weight is lifted off my heart. Several things are now clear and plain to me that I have been tortured with for many days. This being who has been my bane, and is now my greatest danger, is a girl, and not a boy, as Jacob Gray would always fain have made me think. He has lost her too ; and it must have been she whom I saw at my door step and at the window of Sir Francis Hartleton. So far all is clear ; and Gray's confused manner, wretched appearance, and offer to compromise with me when last we met are now accounted for. He has lost his great stronghold upon me, losing the child of—of—I cannot name him, No—no—his name shall never pass my lips."

He rose and paced the room for a few minutes with unequal strides, then suddenly pausing, he muttered,—

"All must be safe. This girl, Ada, as she is called,—and now I recollect me, it was the name of her mother—she must know but very little, too little evidently to, enable Sir Francis Hartloton to annoy me in any way, or he would have swooped upon my devoted head like an eagle on its prey. He may surmise much, but he can know nothing; and now for some plan of operation in which this lover can play his part, and when all is done, should he suspect anything or prove troublesome, it is but another deed, and he is gone to his last account. He leaves no clamouring confession behind him, to enable him to have a posthumous revenge upon those whom he hates. Perhaps after all my hopes and fears, a greater triumph than any I have experienced is at hand for me. My wealth may, after all, insure me some, if not all the advantages I so much coveted, and I may, really free and unshackled, attain the high station my panting soul has longed for."

For the first time for many a day, Learmont gazed proudly around him upon the many articles of rare magnificence that crowded his chamber.

"I shall triumph yet—I shall triumph yet," he exclaimed. "I must mature some plan of operations now that will result in the possession of this girl, the destruction of Gray and Britton, and the recovery of all papers of a dangerous tendency. Methinks it will be easy now. This hair-brained boy, Seyton, if I tell him I can put him on the track of Gray, will surely hunt him down; and then my prey is in my grasp, for he has not now two safeguards, as he had before. I will to the park, and there, beneath the grateful shadows of the trees, mature my plans. Tremble, Britton, Gray, Hartleton—you have one to deal with that will yet triumph over you."

He hastily wrapped himself in his cloak, and with a haughtier stride, and a prouder and more confident mein than he had worn since his first arrival in the metropolis, he left his lordly home, and took his way to the great mall of St. James's Park.

Leaving Learmont to pursue his walk, and to congratulate himself upon what he considered his improved prospects, we will, with the reader's permission, present ourselves at the breakfast table of Sir Francis Hartleton, where sat the magistrate himself, his lady, and Ada.

Sir Francis had passed nearly a sleepless night in reflecting, over and over again, upon the various circumstances connected with the fortunes of his beautiful guest. His great object was, if possible, to decide upon some regular course of action, which might be safely and perseveringly pursued with a prospect of an ultimate result of a successful nature.

After much thought, repugnant as he was to any step which savoured of trespassing upon the undoubted rights of another, he determined secretly and quietly, unknown to every one, to make a visit to the village of Learmont, and explore the old Smithy, with a faint hope that he might find there some indications of what had occurred on that fearful night of the storm and the fire, which he could never forget.

He had slept calmly after making this resolve, and arose more refreshed than he expected from the anxious night he had passed, and now his object was, before he undertook his journey, to have some conversation with Ada, in order by leading her mind to the occurrences at the Old Smithy, to discover if her memory, young as she was, retained any traces of the event; for that she was the child brought from the burning ruins, and that Jacob Gray was the man who so brought her, he entertained but a very faint doubt indeed.

"Ada," he said, "does any event of very early life come ever to your memory?"

"Since I have been here," replied Ada, in her clear and sweet liquid tones, "and so very happy, it seems to me as if my mind had assimilated itself to some circumstances that must have happened long since to me, so long that I can hardly believe that I am now in the same state of existence. Kind words seem now as familiar as they are grateful to me, and it seems to me that memory, wavering from the shock of years of harshness and misery, is beginning to pour forth the hidden stores and crushed remembrances of kind and gentle words, and friendly, loving smiles which guided me before I knew Jacob Gray."

Lady Hartleton could not suppress a tear as Ada spoke, and Sir Francis listened with eager pleasure to her words.

"My dear Ada," he said, "if you will endeavour to tell me in your own gentle, admirable way, what these recollections consist of, they may be of the greatest service in enabling me to unravel the mysteries that now surround you."

"Sometimes," said Ada, " I fancy I recollect some one who used to weep over me and kiss me fondly ; and when, yesterday, your dear lady," turning to Sir Francis's wife, " took me to the ancient tower, it seemed to me that some of the large ships and the cries of the seamen were not altogether strange to me."

"Do you recollect anything of a fire ?" said the magistrate.

" A fire ?"

" Yes—do you ever recollect a fire, and loud screams and much confusion ?"
Ada shuddered.

"I have always fancied that a dream," she said, "but it has haunted me so often that I have feared to find it real. I have dreamt of a wild, dark place, and then bright flames have lit it up, and cries and shrieks have filled the air, and my heart has sunk within me, for it seemed as if some one had torn me from all I ever loved. Then snow would dash in my face, and it seemed to me as if I was borne onwards by some one with terrific speed, and such dreadful shouts and cries as have made me awaken in horror, and pray to Heaven to spare me such another dream."

" And in the midst of all this could you never recognise any well-known form, or face, or familiar voice?"

" None but Jacob Gray's. His pale hideous face seemed ever turned towards me, and I used to fancy that being in so solitary a mode of life with him, put such fancies in my sleeping brain."

" Well, Ada and you, my dear," said Sir Francis Hartleton, " must endure my absence from London, I think, for about a week."

" A week?" said Lady Hartleton.

" Yes, I must endeavour to get leave to go for that time. It is upon business of the utmost importance."

He rose as he spoke, and his wife looked at him regretfully, as she said,—

" You are not going to-day, Francis ?"

" No, nor to-morrow," he replied, smiling; " and when I do go, I have not quite made up my mind that I shall not take you both with me."

" Then you may go as soon as you like, Francis, if Ada will accompany us."

A tear started to Ada's eye, as she said,—

" What other friend, save Heaven, have I but you to cling to now, for he——"
She thought of Albert Seyton, and paused.

Sir Francis Hartleton took her hand gently, and said,—

" My dear Ada, I mean to find Albert Seyton, and make him my clerk."

Ada looked up in his face, and thanked him by a glance that spoke more eloquently than words could have done. The magistrate then smiled an adieu, and left his house to proceed to his office by Buckingham House across the park.

He entered the park by the back of his house, which, as the reader is aware, opened into and near to the Birdcage-walk, and with an easy step, for he had plenty of time in which to go the distance, Sir Francis walked on, nor observed that any one was looking at him, until he by chance glanced round and saw Learmont regarding him with a fixed gaze, while a sneer of ill-concealed triumph sat upon his mouth and curled his lip.

CHAPTER LXXXII.

LEARMONT'S SNEERS.—THE SPY.—THE AMATEUR CONSTABLE.

SIR FRANCIS HARTLETON paused a moment in doubt whether he should speak to the gloomy squire, whom he so much suspected of many crimes, or pass on his way without meeting him. Before, however, he could decide upon any course of action, Learmont settled the question by walking up to Hartleton, and saying,—

"Good morning, Sir Magistrate—you are early afoot."

"I own Sir Squire," said Hartleton, rather amazed at the confident tone and manner of Learmont, "my duties take up as much of my time as other people's crimes do theirs."

"No doubt, no doubt," said Learmont; "yours is an onerous position. 'Tis well criminality is not contagious, for otherwise, coming in contact with so many troublesome thieves, and disagreable characters, London would lose her fine-spirited, upright, and noble magistrate."

"You are right," said Hartleton, determined not to take offence, "I can even speak to worse than thieves, and yet, thank Heaven, escape contamination from them."

Sir Francis Hartleton's words were barbed, but Learmont was quite as resolved as his opponent not to understand any insinuations, and he merely replied,—

"You are a judge of human nature, sir."

"As far as my opportunities go, I am," replied Sir Francis.

"I trust," added Learmont, "that, notwithstanding I am but a poor squire, you will do me the honour of visiting me in my London abode."

"That I am willing to do," said Hartleton, "forgetting all disagreements, Squire Learmont, of course."

"Disagreements, sir,—I really am not aware of any. You were at one time, if I remember rightly, subject to bad dreams, from which I hope you have now quite recovered—I should think it a most grievous and affecting malady."

Sir Francis felt that Learmont had rather the better of him in the dialogue, and with a smile he bowed and passed on.

The squire looked after him with a smile of bitterness, mingled with contempt.

"You have entered, most sapient magistrate," he said, "into a war with me. You shall abide the issue, and pay the penalty of defeat—I swear it by all the powers of heaven and hell, that you shall have my life, or I will have yours. He who thrusts his hand into a fire, cannot be expected to withdraw them unburnt. Beware, Sir Magistrate,—I will have vengeance upon you when I am safe in some important matters—but first as to Jacob Gray—ay, there is the great difficulty—. Jacob Grey."

He sauntered among the then ancient trees that adorned the park, and continued muttering to himself for more than an hour before he came to any firm resolve, and then he suddenly quickened his pace, and proceeded homewards.

When Sir Francis Hartleton reached his office, his first act was to summon the man named Stephy, and to tell him to prepare to accompany him, at a short notice, some distance in the country, for he resolved to take him with him to Learmont village, whether or not he should upon mature consideration think it desirable that Ada should accompany him there.

This matter being settled, he received a report from a man whom he had set to watch the house of Learmont, who deposed to the effect that a man who he was sure was Jacob Gray, by the description given of him by the magistrate, had visited the squire. He then detailed the whole of Gray's proceeding during the night, concluding by saying, that when his watch was relieved, Gray had been left as the Old Chequers, and that his further progress would be reported by the man who had taken his place.

"That will do," said Hartleton ; "he must not be lost sight of for a moment, unless fairly housed, and then the house must be carefully watched, and above all things, do not let him suspect he is in any danger."

"The greatest trouble, sir, during the night," said the spy, "has arisen from a shoemaker in Westminter, who is smitten with the notion of his cleverness in apprehending criminals. He has been following Gray about, and but for his cowardice would have apprehended him."

"And so spoil all," said Sir Francis Hartleton. "It is of the greatest importance that this Gray should remain at large for some time. He is in possession of information which, I fear, would never be got from him after his capture, for no kind of promise could possibly be held out to him of mercy in this world. If once taken, his trial and execution for the murder of Vaughan must ensue. And then too," added Sir Francis, in a low tone to himself, "Ada would be dragged from her present retirement forward as a witness against him, and so seal his lips for ever against any disclosure for her benefit."

A knock at the door announced some one near, and when Sir Francis cried "Come in"—one of his officers appeared, saying—"that a man of the name of Bruggles, wished to see him, on very particular business."

"Bruggles, I don't know him."

"Your worship," said the spy upon Gray, "it is the troublesome shoe-maker."

"Oh, admit him."

The amateur constable was ushered into the presence of Sir Francis, who said,—

"Well, sir, your business ?"

"My business is private, confidential, and most important."

"Will it take long in the telling ?"

"Why, no, not very long."

"Then leave us," said Sir Francis to his officer, "and mind that I have regular reports about the man. Of course your former instructions hold good. On any attempt to leave by boat or vessel, an immediate arrestment takes place."

The spy bowed and retired.

"Now, sir, if you please," said Sir Francis to the shoemaker, "my time is precious ; pray tell me in as few words as you can what you want."

The manner of the magistrate rather damped the ardour of the shoemaker, and he replied—

"Your worship, I thought it but right to call upon you to say that I have seen ——"

Here he looked about him mysteriously, to assure himself that they were alone.

"What have you seen, sir ?" cried the other.

"The murderer of Mr. Vaughan."

The shoemaker, as he said this, leaned forward in a confident manner, and then threw his head back with a jerk, to see what effect it had upon the magistrate, who, to his surprise, merely said,—

"Have you ?" and did not seem at all put out of the way by such an astounding piece of information.

"I—I have spoken to him, sir—your worship, I mean."

"Then, why didn't you say so at once ? You have got him outside, I suppose ?"

"Got him outside, your worship ?"

"Of course."

"Why—why—I—haven't exactly got him at all."

"What ?—Saw him, and spoke to him, and not got him ?"

"Why—why—your worship he looks a powerful villain."

"Sir, I'm afraid you are a great coward," said Sir Francis. "What do you mean by coming to me, and saying you have seen and spoken to a criminal ? I don't know but it's my duty to commit you for aiding, abetting, and comforting a man accused of one of the most heinous crimes in the calendar."

"Commit me ?"

"Yes—you."

"I come here to—to—ask your worship to—to—let me have an officer to go with me to try to find him."

"Sir, my officers will find him themselves, only some caution is requisite, as he belongs to a gang who have bound themselves by a solemn oath to barbarously murder any person who may be at all instrumental in the capture of any of their body."

"Eh? You—you—really—then I should have been murdered?"

"I dare say you would; but I hope when you see him again that you will take him; and when you are dead, the reward shall be paid to any one you may appoint in your will, which I think you had better make here at once in my office, in case of accidents. Two of my officers shall witness it."

"No—no—I—I—God bless me. What danger I have been in, to be sure. Gracious! If I see him again, I shall knock at some door, and ask to be let in till he is gone. I—I—I'll run into a shop—I'll leave London till some one else has taken him."

"What!" cried Sir Francis, hardly able to control his laughter. "Do you shrink?"

"Shrink! I should think I do. I'm all over in a cold perspiration, I am."

"Then you'll never do for an officer, sir. I'd advise you to stick by your last, and not interfere with other people's affairs. Leave thief-takers to catch thieves. You'll get all the danger, my friend, and none of the profit, in travelling from that you know to that you know nothing about."

"I will—bless me! Make my will indeed! The very idea is dreadful. I—I wish you an uncommon good morning."

"Good morning, Mr.—a——"

"Bruggles, your worship."

"Bruggles—good morning."

Sir Francis Hartleton enjoyed a hearty laugh at the shoemaker's expense after he had left, and was shortly afterwards fully immersed in the active duties of his office.

CHAPTER LXXXIII.

GRAY'S PERIL.—A PEEP INTO DOMESTIC AFFAIRS.—THE CORPULENT LADY, AND THE MAN WHO WAS HUNG ON MONDAY.

JACOB GRAY was so horrified at the awful sight that met his eyes, upon opening the cupboard in the old attic, that for some moments he could neither think, move, nor speak; and it was only the strong present dread of some one coming upon him suddenly from the lower part of the house and taking his life, upon finding he was aware of the murdered man being in the cupboard, that aroused him from the absolute lethargy of fear he was rapidly falling into.

The body lay on its face at his feet, and it appeared to have been propped up in the cupboard, merely by the shutting of the door quickly, so that it had fallen out the moment Gray had, by opening the door, removed the support.

He felt that there was no chance for him but putting the loathsome object back again into its receptacle, and our readers may imagine what a terrible job it was to such a man as Jacob Gray to raise that hideous mass of death, and replace it in the cupboard. He stooped and laid his trembling hands upon the neck. He dragged it up—the head hung about in that strange loose manner which indicates a certain stage in the progress of decomposition.

Gray shuddered, and bungled much over what he had to do, because his object was to get the dead body into the cupboard without looking at the face ; and he, therefore, sedulously turned his head away.

The weight was very great, and after many fruitless efforts, Gray found it impossible to get the body fixed for one instant, so as to allow him to close the door. Once he caught in one of the ghastly hands between the door and the side-post. Then, by not being quick enough, the body leaned forward, and he caught the hideous distorted face in the same way.

A cry of horror burst from his lips, as his eyes inadvertently fell upon the horrible visage, and now that he had once looked he could not turn his eyes away, had he been offered a world for the effort.

"Horrible ! horrible !" he moaned, and then letting go the door, the body fell as at first, with a heavy lump upon its face, at his feet.

"I shall be murdered here," thought Gray, "and must leave at all hazards. I—I had better risk being again seen, and hooted by the mob, than remain here to certain death."

He approached the window as he spoke ; but to his horror, he found by the shout that at once greeted him, that his tormentors were still there.

"What can save me now?" he groaned. "I am lost—lost."

He sunk upon the miserable chair that was in the room, and groaned aloud in the bitterness of his despair.

Then he began to wonder that no one came to the attic, and from that he thought it just possible there might be nobody in the house, and that his own fears had converted some casual noise into the sounds of footsteps on the stairs.

There was hope in this conjecture, and he crept cautiously to the door, and standing at the stair-head, he listened attentively, but could hear no noise.

"I wonder," he muttered to himself, "if I could venture down stairs. There might be no one between me and the street door, and possibly I might not be recognised by the gaping crowd outside, and so escape my present most dangerous situation."

It was some minutes more before he could make up his mind to venture down the stairs ; and when, at length, he did, he went step by step with such extreme slowness and caution, that it was a long time before he reached the bottom of the first flight. The least creaking sent the blood to his heart with a frightful gush, and by the time he had reached the floor below the attic, he was in a state of terror and nervousness that would have alarmed any one to behold.

He sat down upon the bottom stair, and as far as he was able to command them, he bent all his faculties to discover if there was any one in the rooms opening from the landing.

One door was ajar, and he now felt satisfied there was no one there, but another door was close shut, and it was with the greatest difficulty that he could command his nerves to crawl past it. His foot now was upon the first stair from the top of the next flight of stairs, when he nearly fell headlong from top to bottom, as he heard a man's voice below say,—

"Thomas—I shall want you in your attic, presently."

Then a step sounded up the stairs, and Jacob Gray had just time to crawl backwards into the room with the door ajar, before he must have been seen.

But he thought whoever is coming here, may enter this room, and he glanced hastily around him for some place to hide in.

A large handsome bed was in the room, with the curtains drawn, and Jacob Gray advancing cautiously, peered in between them, when to his horror and consternation, he found the bed occupied.

An elderly female, with a red termagant face, who by the mountain she made of the bed clothes, must have been of most ample proportions, lay sleeping in the bed.

The slight noise he made, appeared to have disturbed the lady, for a long-drawn snore proclaimed that her easy slumbers were about being disturbed.

Gray heard two or three hard blows given to the bed, and then the lady muttered,—

"Take that, you wretch—you'll disturb me, will you, again," and then evidently fanycing she had silenced her supposed bed-fellow, the corpulent lady, with a sin

gular imitation of a bassoon by means of her olfactory organ, she again resigned herself to sleep.

The same man's name that Gray had heard already, now said at the door,—

"You're asleep yet, are you! Oh, you are a beauty—well, there is some peace in the house early in the morning, for all who like to get up, and enjoy—because you are too lazy to be among us so early. If ever a man was cursed—ah, well, it's no use complaining."

No. 41.

"Oh, you disagreeable beast!" shrieked the lady, who had only been in what is termed a dog-sleep, and had heard the remarks of the man at the door.

"You wretch—you warmint. So that's the way you goes on, is it? You ugly lump of wretchedness?"

"What do you say, my dear?" remarked the man in so altered and humble a voice that Jacob Gray could scarcely believe it came from the same individual.

"What did I say, you unnatural villain—I say I heard you talking about peace in the house."

"Really my love, I———"

"Don't try to escape out of it, you wretched little villain—wait till I get up, that's all."

With a sigh the unhappy husband, for nobody but a husband ever puts up with a woman's tongue, and by some strange fatality, he who is the only person having a legal right to control it's wagging, never, or very rarely, does so—turned away.

"Who's down stairs?" cried the lady, peremptorily.

"Only Thomas, my dear."

"Isn't that lazy slut, Deborah, up yet?"

"Oh dear yes, my love."

"Oh dear yes, indeed answered the lady; "I'll box your ears and hers too when I get up. You've been winking at her again—I'll be bound you have."

"Really, my love———'

"Go away, sir, and don't aggravate me. It would make folk's hair stand on end to know what I suffer—it would."

The lady now turned round on the bed with such a bounce that Jacob Gray thought for a moment it must eventually come down on the top of him.

"What shall I do now?" thought Gray; "this is a strange house. They do not seem at all the kind of persons I suspected. How could that dead body have come into the cupboard in the attic? Perhaps they don't know it's there at all, and if I should be seen, it will in some way be laid to my charge."

He now remained for some moments in painful thought. Then he came at length to a conclusion that he must venture down stairs before the lady got up, as his only chance of getting out of the house.

"Only Thomas down stairs," he repeated to himself, "and a servant girl I presume? I must make the attempt as circumstances direct me—at the back or the front of the house, I may be able to leave it."

He made now a very slight movement in an endeavour to crawl from under the bed, and make towards the door, but the corpulent virago heard him, and cried,—

"I thought I heard somebody a moving. I shall get up and ring for Deborah. Lor a mighty—I'm all of a tremble."

"If I let her get up and have assistance here, I am lost," said Gray.

It took him a moment or two more to screw up his courage, and then he suddenly rose up at the side of the bed, and said,—

"If you stir or speak for the next half hour, I'll cut your throat from ear to ear."

The corpulent lady gave a loud scream, and Jacob Gray sneaked under the bed again.

"Beware," he said, "beware!"

"Oh! Mr. Murderer, spare my life," she gasped.

"What's the matter?" said the husband, who had come scuffling down stairs, upon hearing the scream.

"Beware!" whispered Gray.

"N—n—," gasped the corpulent lady, with the fear of having her throat cut, "nothing—only a—a dream."

CHAPTER LXXXIV.

THE MYSTERY EXPLAINED.—THE ESCAPE.—JACOB GRAY'S NEW LODGING.

JACOB GRAY was almost distilled with fear as this little dialogue proceeded, and it seemed as if a mountain was taken off his breast when he heard the husband go away, muttering something tnat was not intended to meet his lady's ear.

The corpulent lady then commenced a series of groans, which, however, Jacob Gray soon put an end to, by appearing at the bedside, and saying,—

"If you don't be quiet this moment, it shall be your last."

"W—w—what do you want?" stammered the corpulent female.

"No matter," said Gray; "tell me what dead body that is you have in the attic?"

"Job Magnus," said the lady, shaking the bed with trembling.

"Who?"

"Job Magnus—he—he was bought."

"Bought, woman!"

"Yes—he—he was hanged last Monday, and my—my wretch of a husband bought him."

"What is your husband?"

"A doctor."

The truth in a moment now flashed across Gray's mind, and he cursed himself bitterly for allowing his fears to cause him so much uneasiness and terror as they had done. He, then, on the instant, thought of a scheme which might serve him to escape from the surgeon's house without molestation, and turning to the lady, he said in a solemn voice,—

"Do you know me?"

"No—no"

"I have just come down stairs out of the cupboard. I am Job Magnus."

"Mercy upon us!" cried the lady—"Oh! have mercy upon us—our Father which art in heaven."

"Hush!" cried Gray, "don't be mumbling there, but listen to me. If you so much as speak one word, or stir from whence you are for the next hour and a half, I'll come down the chimney and strangle you."

"Please, Mr. Ghost, spare my sinful life, and I won't move. I'll confess all—Thomas aint that wretched husband's of mine—he's—he's—I'm quite sure——"

"Hush," said Gray, with a menacing gesture, "do you imagine I want to hear what, as a spirit, I know already?"

The corpulent lady groaned as she said,—

"Then you know all about the barber?"

Gray deliberately turned up the cuffs of his coat, and said calmly,—

"I am going to strangle you, if you open your lips again."

The corpulent lady held up her hands in mute supplication, and after a glance at her, and a contortion of his visage that nearly froze her blood, Jacob Gray crept from the room, and commenced descending the staircase.

He had not got half way down, when he heard some one coming. He paused in very great trepidation and laid hold of the banisters to await the comer. His only chance now lay on his own firmness, and that was nearly deserting him.

It was a young lad of about seventeen or eighteen, who was coming up stairs, and when he saw Gray, he waited a step in surprise.

"Thomas," said Gray, "I am Job Magnus—will you——"

Thomas did not stay to hear the remainder of what the apparition of the hanged man, as he fully believed Gray to be, had to say, but turned round, and made but ne jump down the stairs again, never stopped till he was in the kitchen, where he upset Deborah and a tray with the breakfast things, just as she was emerging from the culinary department.

"So far successful," muttered Gray, as he descended the remainder of the stairs, and then passed through the door which opened into a little parlour.

Hanging on a peg behind a door was a handsome cloak, and on another a hat, both of which Gray made no hesitation in borrowing for the occasion. Hastily attiring himself thus, he opened a small glass door, and passed into the shop.

There was a little girl in the shop, knocking perseveringly on the counter with the edge of a penny piece, and the moment Gray made his appearance she commenced,—

"Oh, please sir, my mother says do——"

"Silence !" cried Gray—and he passed out into the street, leaving the little girl with a full impression that the doctor had gone mad.

Jacob Gray's first glance was towards his persecutors, and he saw that the patience of all of them had been nearly tired out, with the exception of the baker's boy, who sat upon the edge of his basket and told the story of a man being on the roofs of the houses to all comers.

"You wretch," muttered Gray, "I should like to brain you."

"Hilloa—here comes the doctor," cried the boy, "why, you've got up wrong end first, old cove."

"Take that," said Gray, as he dealt the boy a box on the face that sent him sprawling backwards into his own basket, to the immense amusement of all the other boys there collected, who, not to be behindhand in asserting their right to the name of human beings, immediately made at the fallen hero, and commenced hauling and pummelling him to their heart's content.

With a hasty step Gray left the scene of action, and struck at once into a long narrow lane which led him among the by-streets at the back of the Strand.

His first object now was to get a breakfast, and observing a little dirty shop where every imaginable abomination in the eating line was sold, he plunged into its dark recesses, and asked of a woman, whose very appearance was enough to turn any one's stomach, if he could have some breakfast.

"That depends on what you want," said the woman.

"Some meat," said Gray ; "I will pay you liberally if you will purchase for me some meat, and let me eat it here."

The words "pay liberally" acted like magic on the woman, for she immediately unrolled her sleeves which were tucked up to the elbow, and at once, by that process, covering up all the dirt on her arms, she said,—

"Oh dear yes, certainly—his honour could have whatever he liked ; should she take his honour's hat and cloak? would his honour walk up stairs?"

"Yes—up stairs," said Gray, conceiving himself much more safe from casual observation there than below

The woman escorted him to a dismal-looking room on the first floor, and promising to be quick in procuring what he required, she left him to his meditations.

"This seems a likely place in which to conceal myself," thought Gray, "until I have rung from the fears of Learmont a sufficient sum to enable me to put my now firm design into execution of leaving England. I will ask this woman if she has a room she can spare me for a permanency—no one would think of looking for me here ; and in the darkness of the evenings I can glide out to visit Learmont, and for exercise."

When the woman returned and laid before Jacob Gray some really good and tempting meat, tolerably cooked, and had received his orders to get him a bottle of wine, he turned his small, cunning eyes upon her, and said,—

"I have but newly come from abroad, and am in London concerning some property that is left me: while I remain, can you accommodate me here ?"

"Oh, certainly," said the woman; "your honour can have any room in the house."

"I should prefer the quietest," said Gray. "An attic will suit me as well as any."

"Well, your honour," said the woman, "if you don't mind a attic, we do certainly have the best attfc, though I say it, in London. Why, 'atween two "chimbleys,' when there aint a fog, and the brewhouse isn't at work, you may see a little bit of the river from our attic."

"It will suit me very well, I dare say," said Gray; "when I have finished my meal, I will look at it."

He was not long in consuming the meat and bread, and after a glass or two of the wine he felt wonderfully refreshed, and his old quiet smile of cunning and ferocity began to linger on his face as he muttered,—

"Well, if the squire consents to my terms, and advances me a large sum of money at once, I will leave directly; and if he will not, I must increase my demands upon him as far as I can, without awakening his suspicions, and then leave him and Britton to destruction; it will go hard but I will find a means of revenge against her, who has caused me such unexampled misery and distress. Ada, beware! yet you are not safe from Jacob Gray. He is as a miner, who works in silence and secret, until some day you find what you verily considered the solid foundation on which you were treading immutable, you will find it crumbling beneath your feet. I have a plan—yes, I have a plan to wrest from you, Ada, all that would have been yours had you waited my time."

Full of these thoughts, Jacob Gray summoned the woman, and desired to be shown the chamber she had mentioned. It was a remarkable low-roofed attic, but it suited Gray well, for no one, he thought, would suspect him of living in, to him, so dangerous a neighbourhood as the Strand, where every inhabitant was full of gossip about the murder of Vaughan.

"This will do," he said. "What is the price?"

Two shillings a week were named, to which Gray assented, and paying some few weeks in advance, he said,—

"Whenever I go out I take the key of this room with me, and whatever requires to be done to it, must be done when I am at home. I make my own bed."

"Very well, just as you like."

"And mark my words, if any one should come here and ask you if you have a lodger of any description, unless you unhesitatingly answer no, I leave directly."

"Lor, sir,—suppose some friend of your honour's was to call."

"I—have no friends."

"Indeed, your honour."

"No—nor ever had any—nor ever shall—I am peculiarly situated. There are people in this city who would murder me to keep me out of my just property."

"Is there indeed, sir? Oh, the wretches."

"Yes, and the reason I come to live here is by the advice of my lawyers, in order that I should not be found by those who would take my life if they could."

"Lord, what wickedness there is in the world," said the woman.

"There is indeed," said Gray, gravely. "When I come to my property, depend upon a very handsome present from me if you obey my injunctions."

The woman curtseyed to the very ground, and Gray then signified to her that she might retire and leave him.

. Jacob Gray little imagined how actively Sir Francis Hartleton was watching him, and at that very moment that he was conversing with the woman about the necessity of denying him to every one, a man was in the doorway opposite taking the most accurate notice of the house, and revolving in his mind some means of discovering whether Jacob Gray intended remaining there or not.

The fact was, he had never been lost sight of by one or other of Sir Francis Hartleton's men, and, although they had been momentarily at fault when he got in at the doctor's attic window, one of them had remained on the spot while another went into a neighbouring house, the owner of which he knew, and clambering out on the roof, felt satisfied that Gray was housed somewhere.

He was instantly recognised, notwithstanding the hat and cloak, by the lynx-eyed officers, and quietly dogged to his new lodgings by one of them, while another went across the park to the magistrate to report proceedings, and take further orders.

CHAPTER LXXXV.

LEARMONT'S TREACHERY TO ALBERT SEYTON.—THE PLOT AGAINST GRAY.

THE guilty career of Learmont is nearly run, and the fates are hurrying him to that awful precipice down which the souls of the wicked plunge never to return ; and yet, how strange it is that in the designs and machinations of men of blood and deep iniquity, their danger is ever the greatest when they are hugging themselves in fancied security.

So was it in the strange circumstances of our story—circumstances which, with a labour we should again shrink from, we have collected from ancient resources, and time-worn family documents.

Learmont thought himself now in a far better position than he had ever been in, for although the child whose existence in the hands of Jacob Gray had always been the bane of his existence, was now, he felt sure, in the house of the man whose energy and acuteness he had most to fear, he reasoned himself into a belief that had there been contingent upon such circumstances imminent danger to be apprehended from Sir Francis Hartleton, he would ere this have heard of it, for the magistrate was prompt in action.

" I have but now," he thought, " to destroy Jacob Gray and his confession, whereas, before, by keeping his confession at one place, and the child at another, I dare not attack him with any degree of safety.'

Jacob Gray, too, as we have seen, fancied himself over his worst troubles, and hugged himself with the idea that he held as strong a hold as ever upon the fears of Learmont, and had but to exercise common caution to replace himself in as enviable a situation, as regards pecuniary resources, as he had been before.

Andrew Britton had plenty to drink, as he, too, felt in his way tolerably happy, only he would have given a great deal, or even consented to go without brandy for a whole day for the sake of an opportunity of knocking Jacob Gray on the head.

Learmont's only doubt now was, whether to set the smith or Albert Seyton upon the footsteps of Jacob Gray, when he should make his next visit ; for the same objection, namely, of personal recognition applied to both, only Jacob Gray would not be so apt to suppose Albert Seyton to be set on by Learmont.

Upon this argument, he decided upon informing Albert when he should next see him, of the identity of the man he (Learmont) wished him to watch with Jacob Gray, who held so long in durance the beautiful girl whose image held so constant a place in his heart.

By still assuring Albert of the probability of Ada being with Gray, Learmont considered that he should interest him to strain every nerve to discover his residence, and, we shudder as we write it, but the cold-blooded squire determined upon the death of Albert the moment he should cease to be of any service, or become in the least troublesome or suspicious.

Engaged in such unholy cogitations as those, the day to Learmont passed more swiftly, and more pleasantly than had done many a preceding one, and when he rose the following morning, he looked more himself than he had done since his first attempt upon the life of Gray, at the ruinous house in South Lambeth—an attempt which had so signally failed, and which, in its result, had impressed the squire with a sense of the hopelessness of ever getting rid of the cunning Jacob.

Albert Seyton, his mind agitated by a thousand hopes and fears, was punctual in his attendance upon Learmont; and, when he entered the room in which sat the squire, any one might have seen by his countenance, that he had passed a sleepless night, and that he was suffering all the tender anxieties of newly awakened hope upon a subject nearest his heart.

Learmont motioned him to be seated, and then stealing but a glance at the face of the young man, he said,—

" Young sir, I have been thinking over the story you told me yesterday."

" I thank you, sir," said Albert; "may I venture to hope that mature consideration has not in any way altered the sanguine opinion you were pleased to pronounce yesterday upon the subject ?"

" It has not."

" Thank Heaven !"

" But——"

Albert's colour came and went rapidly at this " but" of Learmont's, and the squire continued calmly,—

" You observed my agitation yesterday."

" I—I did, sir."

" Can you guess its cause—that is, can you guess what brought on the spasm I am subject to ?"

" I cannot, sir."

" Then I will tell you.   When you mentioned the name of Jacob Gray, a strange feeling came over me that I had heard it before, but I was not certain."

" Yes, sir "

" Yes.   Since last you and I met, I have taken some pains to ascertain the fact, and I find that a man of that name has applied to me, hearing of my many charities for pecuniary assistance, saying that he had an orphan child to support, and was in great poverty."

" Indeed, sir."

" Such is the fact.   His name is Jacob Gray."

" And—and sir—you have really seen him ?" stammered Albert.

" I have—he came here, and upon the spurious story he told I relieved his necessities ; but the next time he came, I refused him, when I understand he cursed me as he went through my hall, and uttered threats against me."

" The villain !"

" Yes, young sir, that is the reward generally of benevolence."

" Oh, this is most providential," said Albert, tears of joy bursting from his eyes —"it is surely Heaven's own work."

" 'Tis rather singular," remarked Learmont, coldly.

" You have then his address, sir—oh ! give it me, and let me fly to rescue——"

" Stop—I have not his address."

Albert's countenance fell.

" He left no address here.   He would allow no inquiry into his circumstances, which was the reason I refused to continue my bounty towards him."

" Then—then—nothing is gained," sighed Albert—" I am wretched as before."

" Not so," said Learmont ; " you are like all those who are easily elated—too easily depressed."

" Pardon me, sir, but this is a matter upon which my whole happiness—my whole existence, is, as it were, staked.   I do feel, perhaps, too strongly, but such love as mine is scarce, and I cannot—cannot help it, sir—pray forgive me !"

" Think not I am angry," said Learmont, " on the contrary, I have not been so well pleased for many a day : when I said you were too easily elated or depressed, I had a suggestion to offer you."

" How shall I thank you, sir ?"

" Heed not that. My strong opinion is, that this man Gray will come here again, for, after his repulse, he has written me a letter in which he begs for a small sum towards a larger one he is gathering to take him from England ; and he says, that if I felt inclined, he could tell me a secret, which he is quite sure would enable me to right the wronged, and punish those who had been guilty."

" He alludes to Ada, sir," cried Albert, with animation.   " He alludes to her of whom I told you, sir.   Oh, she is beautiful and good.   Sir, a nobler, better heart than hers never beat in woman's bosom.   It is not for her rare and unexampled beauty that I love her, sir.   Ah, no ; 'tis for her many gracious heavenly qualities —for the fine mind that, like a glistening diamond, does outshine the setting, though of purest gold."

" No doubt he alludes to her," said Learmont.   " As I say, he sent me this letter.   It was without date, without address, and stated that its writer, Jacob Gray, would call here for an answer."

Albert's breath seemed to hang upon the next words of the squire as he asked, " And has he been, sir ?"

" He has not," said Learmont.

" Ada ! Ada !" cried Albert, and then, ashamed of the violence of his feelings, he blushed scarlet, and endeavoured to apologise.

" Heed it not—heed it not !" said Learmont.   " There can be no doubt but this man will call for an answer to his letter, and your line of proceeding will then be to follow him to his home, taking care, as you say he knows you, to keep out of his sight."

" Oh, yes, sir, I will follow him were he to lead me half over the world.   Let me but once set eyes again on Jacob Gray and I will never lose sight of him except I leave him at his own home."

" I hope," said Learmont, who felt a delight in hurrying Albert's spirits down from boiling point to Zero, " that my Jacob Gray and yours are the same men."

" Surely they—they must be," faltered Albert Seyton.

" Nay, my young friend, we should arm ourselves against the disappointment if they should turn out to be different persons."

" The name is peculiar," said Albert, " and perhaps, sir, you can recollect sufficient of the personal appearance of the man to enable me at once to decide upon that doubt."

" Probably.   He is thin and pale, with an ever-shifting glance, and has a peculiar habit of continually moistening his lips with his tongue, and frequently biting the under lip."

" It is the same !" cried Albert, clasping his hands; " I should know him among a million."

" You are sure ?"

" Quite sure, sir, and Ada will be rescued.   Sir, we shall owe you a debt of gratitude we never can repay.   Heaven alone must give you your reward."

Learmont winced a little at the idea of being handed over to Heaven for judgment, and waving his hand, he said,—

" Enough ! I seek for no reward.   What I do, I do freely."

" I will never now," said Albert, " until this man comes, lose sight of the steps of your house, sir."

" He is sure to come."

" And I would not then miss him for ten thousand worlds."

" I will guard against any trifling accident; such as your missing being here when he comes, of his eluding your pursuit ; for I will give him money, and encourage him to come again."

" You are too kind, sir," said Albert, in a broken voice.

" Not a whit—not a whit.   I shall, however, exact one promise from you."

" Do but give it a name, sir."

" It is simply this: that when you have traced Jacob Gray to his home, you will come back to me at once without taking any further step.   Your precipitancy might ruin all, whereas, if I know where this young lady you mention is to be found, without a doubt I can with cooler and more extended judgment, because of my more extended resources, take measures for her recovery that cannot fail."

"I will obey your directions to the very letter," said Albert. "And now I shall be in terror of his coming each moment that I am away from here."

"On the other occasions of his visit he always came after sunset," said Learmont, "and most probably such will be the case now. I should, therefore, strongly

advise you to sleep here from this day, and never to be out of the house after darkness has fairly set in."

Albert could almost have thrown himself at Learmont's feet, so full of joyful gratitude was he, and he could not find words to express the overflowing feelings of his heart to him.

No. 42.

CHAPTER LXXXVI.

GRAY AT HOME.—THE CONFESSION.—A WALK THROUGH WESTMINSTER IN
SEARCH OF A WIG.

How well Learmont thought he had managed his interview with poor Albert
Seyton; and so he had, as far as that interview went. The results are yet to
come; but as he sat alone, after the young enthusiastic Albert had left him, a
ghastly smile played upon his attenuated features, and he muttered——

"Fortune is repaying me now for some of her unkindness. This affair could
not be managed better than it is. Jacob Gray, your doom is sealed. There is
no chance of escape now for you; for all this young man's energies will be
exerted to discover your place of abode, and it will be strange, indeed, if he succeed not. Moreover, I can give him plenty of chances, and so keep the game
alive until he is quite successful, for you must come to me, Jacob Gray, for money;
and each time you do so, you shall return with him upon your steps, until you are
fairly hunted to your lair, and then Britton—yes, Britton, then shall rid me of
you for ever."

The 'squire was silent for some time, then he muttered,—

"Yes; the suspicions of the young man once awakened, he would become most
dangerous. I must run no risks—I will run none. All shall be safe and sure;
and that it may be so, good, credulous Albert Seyton, I will find some quiet, easy
means of ridding you of the cares of this life, when you have performed your
errand in it so far as I am much concerned. How I play with these puppets!
First, Gray shall go; then Britton and this Albert Seyton; Sir Francis Hartleton,
too, when my mind is free to bestow my whole attention upon him. I will do the
thieves of Westminster a great favour, for I will find some plan of vengeance
against him, which shall cost him his life. Then the girl—ay, the girl! What
of her? Why, she falls into my power at once—a mere, nameless orphan girl.
Her safety will depend upon the amount of his information. Let her be innoxious
through ignorance of her real position, and I—I don't want to harm her. Yet she
must not be near me; because she puts me in mind of one who—who—I would
fain forget. This room gets gloomy—very gloomy. There is an awful silence in
the house. I hear no one speak or move, I—I must go out—out—out."

One of his fits of terror came over him, and he went backwards to the door,
while his limbs trembled, and his teeth chattered with an unknown dread.

Turn we now from Learmont to Jacob Gray, who was no less miserable and no
more happy in his wretched attic, than was the vile squire in his splendid
mansion.

Gray sat for a time in deep and anxious thought, and then he glided down the
stairs, for bells were things unknown in that locality, to ask his landlady to send
for writing materials for him.

His orders were very soon obeyed, and he had on the little ricketty table which
stood under the small latticed window, some ink in a cracked tea cup, several pens,
and a quire of paper.

Then he made a calculation of how long it would take him to get two thousand
pounds in small sums of Learmont, provided the squire should refuse to entertain
his proposal of a large sum at once, to insure his, Gray's, leaving the country.

Having satisfied himself on that head, and come to a conclusion as to how many
times he could call, and what sums he should insist upon having, he set about the
more serious and important job he purposed; namely, to write his confession.

The whole of the day he remained at his work, and his feelings and fears were
in a fearful state of agitation, while he was once more recording with his own
hands, events, the lightest one of which would, if known, consign him to an ignominious end.

The sun was sinking in the west when Jacob Gray had finished his labour which he had pursued since the morning with no intermission, save for one hasty meal, which the landlady had brought him, on her own suggestion, for he had been too much engrossed with what he was about to think of food.

At length, however, he finished, and with trembling hands he wrote the superscription, "To Sir Francis Hartleton," and tied the whole firmly round with a string.

A dark smile then came across his face as he muttered,—

"Ada, you know not what you have lost by your precipitancy. I have thought of a means of vengenance upon you. Here in this paper, I declare you illegitimate. The old priest who performed a marriage at Naples between your father and mother, must be assuredly dead long since, and there was no witness but myself. Ha! ha!"

He started at the hollow echo of his own laugh, and looked suspiciously around him as if he feared to see some awful visitant who had mocked his guilty exultation.

"I—I am alone," he muttered. "'Twas but an echo. These old buildings are full of them—where now shall I hide this precious and most dangerous document?"

He remained in deep thought for some time, and then he made a sudden resolution that he would keep it always about him, so that it must be found in case of anything happening to him personally, and his mind would be free from apprehension when he was from home.

He then carefully unripped part of the lining of his waistcoat, and placed the confession in between the cloth and the lining, after which, by the aid of several pins, he firmly secured it in its place.

"It is safe," he said, "security against its loss is all I wish, not absolutely concealment; and yet, should the villain Learmont ever suspect I had this document with me, I should never leave his house alive; but how should he? I have never hitherto had any cause to fear violence at his hands in his own house; and then he thinks I have the child at home. I must consider, and, perchance, change my waistcoat when I favour you with a visit, Master Learmont."

He then carefully searched his room to discover some place of concealment for the confession, should he feel disposed ever to leave it at home, and finally pitched upon the upper shelf of an old cupboard, in one corner where was stowed away a quantity of lumber.

"Yes," he muttered, "I will, whenever I suspect there may be danger in carrying this document abroad with me, place it here, it will then surely be found sooner or later, and conveyed to its address. Now let me consider what changes I can make in my personal appearance, in order further to ensure my safety from those who are still on the scent for me on account of Vaughan."

The night was by this time fairly set in, and the various objects of Gray's miserable apartment began to lose their outlines, mingling strangely together, and in some cases assuming to his alarmed imagination, fantastic shapes, that made his heart beat with fright.

"I must never be here without lights," he muttered, "darkness itself is not so bad in its intensity as this kind of dim obscurity before the night has fairly began its reign. I must never be without lights."

He crept to his door, and opening it gently and cautiously, without having any motive for so doing, he slunk down the stairs as if he were afraid of being overheard. Caution and fear had become habits with Jacob Gray now, and he could not have spoken or walked boldly had he been ever so much inclined so to do.

There was no passage into the street but through the shop, and the woman who was there gave a great start as Jacob Gray came in.

"Lar—sir," she said, "I didn't hear you."

"Not hear me?" said Gray. "I—I have come quickly down the stairs. I am going out on business, and mind what I before said to you in case any one should inquire for me."

"But I don't even know your name, sir."

"My name?"

" No, sir; you didn't tell me."

Gray paused a moment, and then he said,—

" My name is Smith," and walked out of the shop without waiting for an answer.

" Smith, is it?" said the woman, to herself; "it's about as much Smith as I'm Smith. Well, it's no business of mine, only I should like to know who he really is; but, howsomdever, as long as he pays his way, that's quite enough for me—not that I like his looks at all, oh, dear, no—I call him an ugly man, I do.—Well—well, ' handsome is as handsome does '—that's my *mottor!*"

When Jacob Gray was fairly in the street, he glanced cautiously about him, and seeing no one, he hugged himself in the notion that he had been too cunning for his enemies, and walked on, keeping, however, very close to the houses, so that he walked in their black shadows, and could not be minutely remarked by any chance passenger.

" A black wig," he muttered, " will help materially to disguise me."

<hr>

CHAPTER LXXXVII.

JACOB GRAY'S DISGUISE.—THE TROUBLESOME SHOEMAKER AGAIN.—THE VISIT.

GRAY looked now anxiously right and left for a perruquier's, where he might purchase a wig; for contrary to the general fashion of the day, he had worn his own hair and unpowdered. Time and great mental anxiety had, however, very much thinned as well as whitened his locks, and as he remarked, a black wig was certainly calculated to make a very material difference in his personal appearance.

There were several little mean barber's shops in the immediate neighbourhood, but they were not possessed of such articles as he wished to purchase—the sphere of their operations being confined to the shaving of his majesty's lieges, and particularly that portion of them who only once in a week submitted to the tonsorial operation.

Jacob Gray had, therefore, much to his dread, to wander into a better thoroughfare and more respectable street, in order to suit himself, and finally he got to Parliament-street before he could see a shop in which he was likely to get suited. t

This he would not venture into until he was satisfied there was no one there bu the master of the shop, when, more like an apparition than a welcome customer, he glided in, and asked for a black wig.

" Black wig, sir?—yes, sir—certainly, sir—black wig, sir," replied the shopkeeper, with great volubility—"should say, sir, you'll look well, sir, in black wig, sir."

" My time is precious," said Gray. " Shew me one immediately."

" Certainly, sir. Time's a precious commodity. No overtaking time, sir, no how. Lots of wigs, sir—black, brown—all sorts of shades, sir—all the gentry of Westminster wear my wigs, sir—once curled the wig of the speaker of the House of Commons, and once —"

" I am in haste, sir," said Gray, drumming with his fingers upon the counter.

" Certainly, sir. Business is business—wigs are wigs now-a-days. Here's one, sir, that will fit you to a miracle—your sized head, sir, is what we call number six. That's a wig, sir, that's a credit to me and will be a credit to you, sir."

Jacob Gray took the wig, and fitting it on his head, looked at himself attentively in a glass.

" I think this will do," he said, as he remarked with satisfaction the alteration it made in his aspect.

" You look wonderfully well in that wig, sir—upon my word you do," said the barber. " I could not have believed it, sir. You look twenty-two years and a quarter younger, sir."

"Pshaw," said Gray. "The wig will do, I have little doubt."

"No doubt whatever, sir—not a small shadow of a doubt, sir. You look uncommonly well, sir, in that wig. 'So I do in anything,' says you—but a wig is a wig, you know, and when——"

"Peace—peace," said Gray. "The price?"

"The price, sir; why I should call that wig uncommouly cheap at two guineas, si.

"There," said Gray, throwing the required amount upon the counter, and then mmediately walked out of the shop of the loquacious perruquier.

"Well, I never," exclaimed the man, after his customer had gone. "Most extraordinary man—horrid fright in that wig—must be highwayman!"

Jacob Gray did certainly look somewhat different in his wig; but no one who had ever known him well, could for a moment have doubted the identity of his strange face, with its peculiar expression of cunning, mingled with apprehension.

"Learmont," he muttered, "would have me visit him in the morning for some purpose, but I will make it night always, until I discover what can possibly be his motive for dragging me into daylight."

Little suspecting then, that he was kept in view by Sir Francis Hartleton's man, from the other side of the way, Gray walked at a rapid pace towards Learmont's.

The 'squire was within, and he gave a slight start, when Gray was announced; for, at that very moment, he had been planning his murder, when he should, through the instrumentality of Albert Seyton, discover his abode.

The wig, which Gray wore gave him a strange look, and Learmont could not for some time divine what it was that made the remarkable difference in Jacob Gray, but kept his eyes fixed upon him with a look of surprise, that the other could not but notice.

"I have thought it safer," said Gray, "to try some personal disguise, as I came a long way to visit you."

"As you please," said Learmont coldly. "I cannot, however, perceive anything you have to fear,"

"No—no—" said Gray, "but I like not being known and recognised often by the same persons."

"As you please—as you please, Jacob Gray."

"Have you considered my last proposal?" said Gray.

"To take a sum of money and leave England for ever?"

"Yes."

"If you could find some means," said Learmont, "of ridding me of Sir Francis Hartleton——"

"Who—I—I—I cannot—I dare not."

"Yet, you might, Jacob Gray."

"No, no,—I can undertake no such enterprise—what I have already done 'Squire Learmont, has scarcely met reward."

"Not met reward, Jacob Gray! Why, you must, methinks, by this time, have a goodly sum of money by you?"

Gray groaned, as he replied,——

"Yes—yes—of course; but not enough for independence; my expenses have been great."

"Is your—your young charge quite well?" sneered Learmont.

"Quite," said Gray."

"Then you refuse to aid me in the destruction of this Hartleton?"

"I do. I am content with what I have done in so far as it entitles me to your gratitude—your substantial gratitude."

"Be it so then. I will, however, consider more deeply your proposal regarding a large sum of money at once. And—and—if you will come to me, say, to-morrow, I will let you know, more at large, my thoughts upon that subject."

"I will come to-morrow," said Gray.

"In the morning?"

"I do not know—but it will be morning or evening. Give me now twenty pounds."

"Twenty?"

"Yes. 'Tis a small sum, 'Squire Learmont. Look at the enjoyments that surround you—your house—your carriages—your servants—rich wines! Ah! 'squire, you need not start at twenty pounds to Jacob Gray. Happy man!"

Learmont fixed his eye upon the mocking countenance of Gray, with such an expression of deadly hatred, that even he quailed under it.

"Jacob Gray," said the 'squire, hoarsely—"there is in me, when I am stirred by taunts, something dangerous, that even the fear of the revelations, that such as you are may leave behind you, cannot conquer. Beware, I say—beware."

Gray trembled before his master's spirit, and in silence took up the purse that Learmont threw him, and quitted the house.

When he gained the street, he shook his clenched hand, menacingly at the house, muttering between his clenched teeth,———

"Beware yourself, 'Squire Learmont; Jacob Gray will yet bring you to a gallows!"

———

CHAPTER LXXXVIII.

MAD MAUD AND THE MAGISTRATE.—THE SCRAPS OF GRAY'S CONFESSION.

"MAN proposes, but God disposes," is a saying which Sir Francis Hartleton was doomed to feel the truth of, as regarded his projected excursion to the Old Smithy, at Learmont, for firmly as he had fixed in his own mind to go, a circumstance occurred, which induced him, at all events, to put off his journey for some short time.

That circumstance was the discovery, by the officers he had commissioned to search for her, of poor Maud, apparently in the last stage of misery and sadness—she had met with some injury from a runaway horse, and it was in one of the most miserable of the many miserable courts about Drury-lane, that the poor creature was discovered almost starved, for those around her could scarcely find the roughest means of satisfying their own wants, and the hunger of their squalid children.

The fact was immediately communicated to Sir Francis Hartleton, and he, as soon as he could get time from his public attendance at his office, went himself to visit her and take measures for her comfort.

The poor creature was lying upon a miserable straw mattress, covered with an old rug, and the place she was in presented altogether a picture of wretchedness and want.

"How long has she been here?" inquired Sir Francis of an old crone, who showed him the room.

"Only last night," was the reply. "She's as mad as she can be. Just look now, sir."

The woman attempted to open one of the hands of Maud which was clutched tightly, but the poor woman burst into a scream of agony, crying,—

"No, no, no—oh, spare me that—I found it by the dead that would not burn. Help—help. Angel come and help me now."

"Do not torment her," said Sir Francis. "What has she in her hand!"

"Only some crumpled up bits of paper, sir, but she thinks a mighty deal of 'em."

"Go and fetch me the nearest medical man, and a coach," said Sir Francis. "Here is half-a-crown for your trouble."

The woman with a profusion of thanks went on her message, and the humane magistrate sat down by the miserable couch of the sufferer.

"Maud, Maud," he said, close to her ear.

"Who calls? who calls?" she muttered.

"A friend," said Sir Francis.

She shuddered, as in a low plaintive voice she said,—

"No, no—poor mad Maud has no friend. Heaven will release her when Andrew Britton is dead. He is to die before I do—yes—yes. Oh, if I could see the angel once again."

"You shall see her, if you will give me what you have in your hand."

"No, no. There spoke the cunning enemy—set on by Andrew Britton. No, no—fire will not burn a murdered corpse, and so I found the papers—most precious and rare. The angel's name is on one of them—that would I not part with for a thousand worlds."

"Where got you them?"

"At the old house on the marshes. Ha, ha—I—I saw the glare of the light—the ruddy hue of the fire, and I knew then that Andrew Britton was trying once again to burn the body—but he can't—he can't. Ha! ha! ha! he can't. Fire will not touch it—no, no—he may heap faggot upon faggot, but it will not burn. Is not that rare sport—rare—rare—and Andrew Britton too, to be before poor mad Maud."

The door now opened, and the woman approached with a medical man.

"I am Sir Francis Hartleton," said the magistrate, rising, ".will you oblige me by doing what you can do for this poor creature?"

The surgeon bowed and proceeded to examine the patient.

"She is very low," he said, "and will never get well here. The air is pestiferous. Healthy lungs can scarcely stand it."

"Can she be removed with safety?"

"God bless the angel," said Maud. "Will you come again—murder—who said murder? There—there—the flame are crawling, and like long forked tongues of snakes from the Old Smithy, because they will not burn the murdered dead. No, no, no—where are you, Andrew Britton? Ha! you are here while the murder is doing—yes, yes—and yet you will die before mad Maud."

"She raves!" said the surgeon.

"Yes, poor creature, her senses are sadly bewildered—she has known much sorrow."

"Ah, poor thing. These mental maladies are beyond the physician's skill. I will, however give her, if you please, sir, a composing draught, which will most probably throw her into a slumber of some hours' duration, and allay much of the irritability, that now evidently affects her."

"I shall thank you to do so. She shall be removed to my own house."

"You will not be troubled with her long, sir."

"I fear she is far gone on her last journey," said the magistrate.

The surgeon wrote on a slip of paper the name of the medicine he wanted, and gave it to the woman of the house to fetch it from his home.

"Oh, Heavens," said Maud, "will they murder the child—can they dip their hands in its innocent blood?—mercy—mercy."

"Maud," said Sir Francis.

"Hark—hark," she cried. "Surely I hear music. Is it the passage of the angel's wings through the sunny air, from the bright gates of Heaven—or is it human melody—ah, yes—you love me—you love me. By the moon—stars—zephyrs. Well, sing again the strain—sing, sing."

In a low mournful voice, she chanted, rather than sung, the following words,—

A HAPPY TIME—A HAPPY TIME!

" A happy time—a happy time !
   I saw a child so gay
Trip lightly o'er the shining mead,
   And laugh the hours away.
She sat beside a silver stream,
   Amid the flow'rets fair:
She laughing pluck'd the fairest flowers,
   And twined them in her hair;
They sweetly bloomed upon her brow,
   In Nature's wildness free.
Oh, happy child! oh, happy child!
   I would that I were thee.

" A happy time—a happy time!
   I saw her once again—
That laughing child, a maiden grown,
   Of wond'rous grace and mien.
She spoke—I knew again the voice,
   And blessed her beauty rare,
Once more I heard her joyous laugh
   Come ringing through the air.
I looked into her beaming eyes;
   There joy must ever be.
Oh, happy maid! oh, happy maid!
   I would that I were thee.

" A happy time! a happy time!
   She crossed my path once more,
That maiden fair; but she, alas!
   Was sadder than before.
She lingered by the silver stream,
   Where laughed the child so gay:
I longed to hear her laugh again,
   And chase the tears away.
For tears there were upon her cheek;
   Alas! that such should be.
Once happy child—once happy maid!
   I would not now be thee.

" A step came sounding o'er the mead,
   The tears were dashed aside,
A stranger clasped her to his heart,
   ' My own—my dear lov'd bride!'
I looked into the maiden's face,
   It was a happy sight:
I heard her laugh with joy again;
   Her eyes beamed with delight:
She twined young roses in her hair,
   'Twas beautiful to see.
There is no joy on earth like love.
   Ah! would that I were thee."

She ceased with a shudder, muttering :—

"There, again—there, again. There's a large murder doing at the smithy, and Andrew Britton's hands are red with human gore."

The opiate was by this time brought by the woman, and with great difficulty Sir Francis made Maud attend to him.

"Here, Maud," he said, "drink of this—'twill do you good."

"No, no, no—there's poison there."

" Indeed there is not."

" I see Andrew Britton's face scowling at me, and the dark-souled Squire of Learmont too. There—there—save the child—save it, save it. Have mercy, Heaven !"

" " Listen to me," said Sir Francis. " The angel has sent you this."

She half raised herself on the miserable couch, and looked fixedly at the magistrate.

" Your face is kindly," she said. " Did you speak of the angel?"

" Yes ; she has sent you this."

The poor creature took the cup containing the medicine in her hand, and drank off the contents without another word.

" That is well," said the surgeon, " she will fall into a deep sleep, and no doubt waken much better—see now, already."

No. 43.

The poor creature lay down, and after a few moaning expressions, which they could not hear distinctly, dropped into a heavy slumber.

"She can now be removed," said the medical man, "with ease and safety."

Sir Francis Hartleton, as we are aware, was an exceeding powerful man, and taking off his own ample cloak, he wrapped it carefully around the poor creature, and then lifting her in his arms, he carried her as if she had been a child, down the staircase, and placed her in the coach which stood at the entrance of the court.

He then courteously took leave of the surgeon, after making an appointment with him a few hours after at his own house, and got into the coach with Maud, having directed the driver to his house at Westminster.

Careful not to disturb her slumber, Sir Francis Hartleton unclosed the hand of poor Maud, and found crumpled into a hard ball, a number of small scraps of paper, on which were words and disjointed sentences. That the few words he could find were deeply interesting to the magistrate, might have been gathered from the expressions of his face as he read them. His hands trembled with excitement as piece after piece he spread open and perused.

"Here is important matter," he said, "but it is sadly out of joint. This must be some remnant of a paper containing a strange history, and here is, it seems, the name of Ada. I must more at my leisure examine these. Thank Heaven they have fallen into no other hands than mine."

He then placed the torn scraps carefully in his pocket-book; and looking from the coach window, he found that they were nearly at his house. He carefully lifted the still sleeping Maud from the coach, and carried her to a comfortable bed-room, resigning her to the care of his wife and the astonished Ada, while he hurried to his own study to decipher the mysterious scraps of paper at his leisure.

CHAPTER LXXXIX.

THE REVELATION.—LEARMONT'S DEEP DUPLICITY.—ALBERT'S GRATITUDE.

THE morning found Albert Seyton true to his appointed time at Learmont's. In fact, long before he could think of knocking for admittance, being ashamed of so much eagerness, he had arrived in the immediate vicinity, and wandered restlessly about until the hour should come.

The hope, so suddenly springing up as it had, in the midst of his despair of again beholding Ada, through the exertions of his new patron, had, in the endless mass of surmises and conjectures it had given rise to, banished sleep from his pillow, and it was not till the first faint gleam of the coming day poured in at his bed-room window, that he became conscious of the rapid flight of time.

To attempt to sleep then, he thought, was useless, and besides he might oversleep himself, and appear to be negligent of his appointment with the rich man, who had promised to do so much for him. He therefore rose, and as we have said paced about the street in the vicinity of Learmont's house, little dreaming that he was taking so much trouble and feeling so much elation for Ada's worst and bitterest enemy.

At length he thought, although he was too soon, he might knock for admittance, and with a nervous hand he seized the old massive knocker at Learmont's door.

He was speedily admitted, and his heart bounded with delight, when, in answer to his questions, he was told that Learmont was up and in his own private room. With a palpitating heart, Albert followed the servant who went to announce him. He heard the deep sepulchral tones of Learmont's voice say——

"Come in!" and he thought——

" How much now one may be deceived in estimating character. Who would suppose that voice belonged to so good a man ? And the countenance, too, of this squire, it is certainly not prepossessing, and yet what a kind heart he has !"

Albert Seyton was a far better physiognomist than he thought himself.

In another moment he was in the presence of one who, most on earth, he felt grateful to—but really the man who, most on earth, he had reason to entertain the greatest indignation at.

Learmont received his young secretary cautiously; and, turning to the servant, then he said,—

" Lay breakfast for me and this gentleman in the small morning room."

The servant bowed down to the very ground, and closed the door after him so gently and quietly, that one could hardly suppose Learmont was anything but some piece of workmanship that any sudden noise or concussion of the air would destroy.

" You are early," said Learmont to Albert, with a sickly smile.

" I fear, sir," said Seyton, " that I have intruded upon you too soon, but my great anxiety———"

" Yes, yes, I have not forgotten," interrupted Learmont. " Will it please you to describe to me this man, Jacob Gray, again, who kept the—the girl in such a state of bondage ?"

" Certainly, sir. About the middle height———"

" Humph !"

" Pale to sallowness ; a small, twinkling eye, bespeaking more cunning than courage."

" Ay—ay."

" A skulking, timid walk, as if ever afraid of question or pursuit."

" 'Tis very strange."

" Sir ?"

" I say, 'tis very strange. I think I have quite a surprise for you in store."

" A surprise, sir ?"

" Yes. You must hear it manfully. Can you stand the shock of sudden news ?"

Albert felt at this moment as if all his fond hopes were suddenly blasted. He clasped hands, and said—

" The news is bad ?"

" I said not so."

" Then—then———"

" Not to keep you longer in suspense, young sir, I will tell you of the strangest circumstance that ever I encountered. The man who came to me for pecuniary assistance—that very man who I, from charitable motives, wished you to follow———"

Albert drew his breath short and thick, as he gasped, and said,—

" Go on, sir, I pray you. That man ?"

" Is Jacob Gray."

" God of Heaven ! my heart told me so."

" Yes, he and Jacob Gray are one."

" This is Heaven's work !"

" Of course."

" Most providential !"

" Certainly."

" Oh, sir, you have indeed lifted me from an abyss of despair to a pinnacle of happiness that makes me giddy ! Thank Heaven I met with a heart like yours, and when I wish you all the happiness you really deserve, I am saying much, very much."

" Thank you," said Learmont, coldly. " I was much struck with your description of Jacob Gray—it seemed to fit the man who had called here exactly ; but before I would agitate you by vain hopes and fears, I made inquiry among my household, and found my suspicions verified, for, on more than one occasion, he has owned to them that Gray was his name."

"Oh, sir, cried Albert, " I will follow that man to the world's end !"

"Do nothing rashly," said Learmont. "Follow him you shall; for I will stir up heaven and earth to give you an opportunity."

"How can I express my thanks, sir?"

"By following implicitly my directions. You are young, ardent, and enthusisatic, moreover—in love ; now I am neither : so I condition with you, so tender am I of the majesty of the law, and my own unblemished honour, that until I point out what is meet to be done, you take no step in this matter, beyond following this man home."

"I promise all, sir—everything—anything."

"'Tis well. You will follow him home, and then come at once to me. Dog the fox to his lair ; and I'll unearth him, you may depend !"

"When is he coming, sir ?" said Albert, with trembling eagerness.

"That I cannot tell you. You must be in wait for him—I would have you now remain in this house until he comes again."

"I will not stir from the door."

"You shall have a room here ; and should this man come again, with his importunate suit, I will give him something, and, during the time I am engaging him in conversation, you can take measures to follow him."

"Sir, you have made me a new man—my blood bounds lightly through my veins—I long for you to look upon my Ada."

"I shall be gratified," said Learmont.

"Oh, she is beautiful !"

"What may be her age ?"

"I know not, sir ; but she is all perfection."

"Of course."

"The villain Gray shall pay a dear reckoning for each harsh word that he has spoken to her. Oh, that so much innocence, purity, and truth should be at the mercy, for one brief moment, of such a man as Jacob Gray."

"She shall be rescued from Jacob Gray."

"She shall—she shall! my own—my beautiful Ada, you shall not pine many more hours in your dreary imprisonment ; oh, how each moment will become to me lengthened out into an age of impatience."

"I admire your constancy and fervour," said Learmont. "Such high and rare qualities should always command success. With your own prudenc in complying with the condition I annex, as the price of my assistance, you cannot fail of accomplishing all you wish ; but any impetuosity upon your part—any sudden action that may bring things to an untimely crisis, would involve, probably, her whom you love, and yourself in difficulties from which even I could not extricate you."

"I will be prudent. When I but know where she is, I shall be happy, and will await your time to tear her from the abode of the villain Gray."

"That time shall not be long."

"Oh, sir," added Albert, "you should have seen her—watched her growing beauties—lingered on every tone she uttered as I have done, to feel for me in my present state of torturing suspense."

"I can feel for you, and I hope to see this wondrous beauty ere many days have elapsed. You must, till then, be cautious, bold, and resolute. Make this your home until Gray shall come, when I will surely let you know."

"Sir," said Albert, in a voice of emotion, "a lifetime of devotion could not express my deep sense of gratitude to you."

"Heed not that—heed not that ; I make you one promise, and that is, that while you live, you shall be my secretary, provided no better fortune arises."

"What better fortune, sir, can the poor friendless Albert Seyton have, than to enjoy your favour, sir ?"

"Well, well, enough of this. You will remain here, of course ?"

"I will, sir, if it please you; or I will haunt about the street and door, if my presence here be at all inconvenient."

"Far from it," said Learmont. "Believe me, my impatience equals yours."

Learmont now rose, and Albert Seyton, construing that into a hint to be gone, rose too. The squire rung the bell, and upon the appearance of a servant, he said,—

"See that proper accommodation is provided for this gentleman. He will remain an inmate of the house."

Albert left the room, and followed the servant into a comfortable apartment, which commanded a pretty view of the garden.

A thought now suddenly struck him that he might as well let the servant know, in case of the sudden appearance of Gray, when Learmont might be from home, that he, Albert Seyton, was to be informed of the fact, and he said,—

"Do you know a man named Gray?"

"Gray, sir?"

"Yes, a mendicant."

The servant looked hard at Seyton, and muttered to himself,—

"That's a feeler to see if I gossips about the squire's affairs."

"A thin, pale man," added Albert, who thought the servant was endeavouring to recollect.

"No; never saw him, sir—never saw nobody, sir—never mean to see."

"What do you mean?"

"We never sees nobody in this house, sir. We never talks about master's affairs, we don't."

"Oh, very well," said Albert. "I have no wish to induce you to do so, I am sure. Nothing could be further from my intention."

"No, sir," said the servant.

"I am your master's most devoted friend."

"Yes, sir."

Albert turned away, for he saw that by some means he had excited the suspicions of the man, and he determined now to say no more to him at all.

The day passed off to Albert strangely, and when the evening came, he was rejoiced that by so many hours he was nearer the completion of his hopes, for he looked upon the scheme of following Gray home as certain to bring him once more to Ada.

Sometimes he would pace his room for an hour or more in a delightful reverie, dreaming of future happiness with Ada, and fondly imagining that he was gazing on those eyes which to him were glimpses of heaven. Then again he would become despondent, and fancy her at the mercy of Jacob Gray, who to rid himself of uneasiness on her account, might at that moment be contriving her death.

The anxious lover would then torture himself awhile with this supposition, until hope refreshed sprung up again in his heart, like a phœnix from its ashes, and he smiled as, in imagination, he clasped his long-lost but much-loved Ada to his heart.

CHAPTER XC.

THE LAST MEETING.—MUTUAL CUNNING.—THE SQUIRE AND JACOB GRAY.

THE night was dark and a lowering one, and not a star appeared in the blue vault of heaven—a raw wind swept along the river, and thence up the narrow winding streets upon its banks, slamming doors, and now and then catching the hat of a too confiding passenger, and tossing it into the roadway.

Learmont sat alone in the room he usually occupied, but he heard not the sighing of the wind, nor cared for the unpropitious aspect of the night—his thoughts were all bent upon one subject, and that was the near prospect he now had of achieving the destruction of Jacob Gray. A dark malignant smile lit up his features, and as he played upon the richly-carved table at which he sat with his fingers, he muttered in disjointed sentences the subject of his reveries.

"So they say that Heaven always confounds the wicked—those who strive for power and wealth, by other than the usual channels—hard work or sycophancy—be it so : methinks that I, Squire Learmont, must have grievously mistaken my own actions, when I thought them of a fearful nature, for surely now Heaven smiles upon all my plans and projects. It would seem as if this lover, this wild enthusiastic boy, was purposely thrown in my way to be a weapon in my hands gainst Jacob Gray. The confession—ah, the confession. Dare I even trust him to bring me that? Yes—yet some damning accident might give him a glimpse of its contents, or he might be seized with some sudden whim, especially being disappointed in his main object of taking the confession to him to whom it is really addressed. No, the confession I will myself secure. Yes, myself. Britton shall do the deed of blood, and when 'tis finished, I will take the confession, and it would then be far better to take the life of Gray away from his home. Here, even here it might be done. It shall. Albert Seyton shall dog his footsteps home, and his next visit here he dies, while I proceed to his abode and possess myself of the dangerous document he leaves behind him."

How different were the reflections of Albert Seyton to those of Learmont, and yet they ran much in the same channel, and the chief personage on whom they turned was the same—namely, Jacob Gray. Perhaps never had two persons, amid the whole population of London, waited with such great anxiety for the arrival of a third, as did Squire Learmont and Albert Seyton for Jacob Gray.

It was well for the success of the plan of operations against Gray, that a part of it had been for Albert to remain in the house until Gray should come, for the crafty Jacob had made up his mind, whenever he visited the squire to take him by surprise as much as possible, by calling at odd times ; sometimes two days consecutively, and sometimes early in the evening, and sometimes very late, so that Learmont should never be able to count upon his coming, or be surprised at any long absence he should make, nor deceived into a false security, should he not see him for a considerable period.

In pursuance of this plan, it so happened that about nine o'clock, as the squire was still in deep thought, Jacob Gray was announced.

Learmont started to his feet with a suddenness that alarmed the servant, who made a precipitate retreat to the door.

"Hold!" cried the squire. "How dare you leave the room without your orders?"

"I—I—thought—your worship, that—I—I—thought, your worship."

"Fool!" muttered Learmont.

He then hastily tore off a small scrap of paper from some that lay before him, and wrote on it the words—

"J. G. is here."

"Give this," he said, "to the young gentleman, my secretary, instantly."

"Yes, sir."

"And then bring Gray to me here,"

The servant bowed and retired, leaving Learmont standing in the middle of the room with such an expression of triumph on his face, that when Gray made his appearance, which he did almost immediately, he started back a pace or two in surprise, an action which was nearly imitated by Learmont, for Gray looked so very different in his wig, that Learmont quite started at first sight of him.

The two looked at each other for several moments without speaking, then Gray, in his quick sneering tone, said,—

"Your worship will get used to my wig in the course of time."

"Probably," said Learmont, "if you live so long."

"Live so long ?"

"Ay, Jacob Gray; I never saw you look so bad in all my life. You must be nearer death than you think."

"I—I am very well," said Gray, "I hope yet to attend your funeral, and receive something commensurate with our ancient friendship through the medium of your will."

"You are kind and obliging," said Learmont, "but I don't intend to die first, Jacob Gray."

Gray smiled in his usual sickly disagreeable manner, and then drawing himself a seat, he sat down by Learmont, and said,—

"A truce to jesting, squire. Have you thought further of my proposition to you ?"

"Scarcely," said Learmont; "and yet I have a notion of entertaining it."

"You have ?"

"I have."

"Believe me 'tis the best and safest plan."

"If I understand you rightly, you offer to surrender all that may make my life now a constant source of anxiety and torment for one large sum of money paid to you at once."

"I do," said Gray.

"The child—and—the confession."

"The confession and the child that was, but you forget the lapse of years; that child is a child no longer, but at an age to be dangerous. The slightest hint from me would raise a spirit in that offspring of your ———"

"Hush," said Learmont, vehemently; "Jacob Gray, even here I will take your life if you dare to mention him you are about to revert to even now."

"I will alter my form of speech more to your liking, squire," said Gray; "I meant that one word of mine would rouse up against you a more formidable opponent than any you have ever met with."

"And for some thousands of pounds you will leave me free ?"

"I will."

"But, cunning Master Gray, you know your wit is keener than mine," sneered Learmont; "and how am I to be assured of your faith ?"

"You shall see me on ship board," said Gray; "with my own hands, then, I will hand you my confession."

"Suppose there were two copies ?"

"On my faith, squire, you are too suspicious—far too suspicious."

"Have I no cause ?"

"None whatever. It is my interest as well as yours that the past should be forgotten. What could I gain by denouncing you ?"

"Nothing but a barren triumph of man over man. I think, Jacob Gray, that I will trust you. But permit me, between this time and when we shall meet again, to consider of the subject."

"I pray you do so," said Gray, who was so elated at the idea of getting Learmont to pay him largely, for the doubtful advantage of his absence, that he almost forgot his usual caution in his extreme eagerness to induce a compliance with his wishes.

"You will feel so much at ease," he added, "when I am gone from England never to return, and many of the fears that now disturb your mind will at once terminate."

"I hope to terminate them so," said Learmont.

"Such hope is wisely grounded," replied Gray. "You have but then to get rid of the drunken sot, Andrew Britton, and a career of brilliant enjoyment will await you, unchecked by one lingering doubt of your safety."

"'Twere a blessed state," said Learmont, "and one I have much striven to btain. Now, however, I do certainly begin to see some light amid he gloom whic had surrounded me."

" Your fortunes are in your hands," said Gray; " I am tired of this mode of life. Give me five thousand pounds, and let me go in peace."

" Your demand is large."

" Nay, a mere trifle when compared with the revenues of your estates."

" Well, well, I will, as I tell you, consider; and I have a fervent hope that our next time of meeting may be our last, or, at all events, that after that, there need be but one more final interview."

" Exactly," said Gray; " it is in your own power, when you please, to get rid of me for ever."

" And the young claimant of all I am now worth ?"

" Certainly—a pistol or a knife will get you rid of all trouble upon that head, squire."

" Certainly, but you ought to do so much for me as part of your bargain."

" No, no," said Gray, confused; ." I—I cannot—my nerves will not permit me. I really cannot. If you shrink yourself from the deed, why there is Andrew Britton, the savage smith, who revels and rejoices in blood. He will do the deed for you without a murmur."

" You think then that Britton is the best man I can employ to commit a murder ?"

" I do."

" Then he shall have the job."

Gray smiled to himself as he thought, " You must first wrest your prey from the hands of Sir Francis Hartleton—no easy task !" Then he said aloud,—

" You are now on the right path, squire; you have but to pursue it, and every wish you ever nourished of pleasure and ambition will be satisfied."

" I do begin to think so," said Learmont.

Jacob Gray now rose, and said,—

" I will bid you adieu, squire, but being rather pressed for money, I will trouble you for fifty pounds."

" Fifty pounds ?"

" Ay, 'tis but a small instalment of the thousands. Agree, at our next meeting, to my terms, and I will deduct this fifty pounds from the gross sum I am to receive."

" As you please," said Learmont; " but, Jacob Gray, I will not give you so large a sum now."

" You will not ?"

" I will not."

" Know you who I am ?"

" Too well, and by this time you should know me. There are ten pounds, Jacob Gray. Take them or none."

" Has—has it come to this ?" muttered Gray.

" It has," said Learmont.

" Know you your dangers ? What if I leave England suddenly and behind me is found——"

" Pshaw ! you mean your confession," interrupted Learmont. " I know you can, if it so please you, Jacob Gray, but you prefer money to revenge."

" I do, but the money must be sufficient."

" It is most ample."

Gray looked in the calm pale face of the squire for a moment or two in silence, then he took the ten guineas which Learmont had laid upon the table, and with a bitterness of tone, which he in vain tried to conceal, he said,—

" It matters not, ten pounds or a hundred, the result must be the same; I must and will have a certain sum, and now I am resolved to have it in a certain time. Farewell, Squire Learmont, you have begun your independence too early. Farewell."

He left the room, and Learmont looked after him with such a smile as he had not worn for years, and muttered,—

"Have I begun my independence too early Jacob Gray? Humph, by some half dozen hours only, I do devoutly hope and trust. If you see another sunrise, I shall be a disappointed man."

CHAPTER XCI.

THE PURSUIT.—THE SPY.—THE THREE WHERRIES ON THE THAMES.

COULD Jacob Gray, in his wildest flight of fancy, have for one moment imagined that Albert Seyton stepped after him from Learmont's door in a few moments after he had left it, how different would have been his feelings to what

No 44.

they were—how changed would have been the expression of his countenance! Never, in the whole course of their guilty career, had he and Learmont had so strange an interview. Never had each succeeded in deceiving each, as they had done on that eventful evening. Jacob Gray departed with a smile of triumph on his face, and he left Learmont with its counterpart upon his.

The impatience of Albert Seyton after he had received Learmont's short intimation of Jacob Gray's avowal knew scarcely any bounds, and it appeared to him an age before Gray passed across the hall to leave the house.

Albert had taken his station just within a small waiting-room which commanded a view of the great staircase, and at the first sight of Jacob Gray descending, his emotions were so powerful that he was compelled to sit down to recover his composure, during which brief period, Gray crossed the hall, and passed into the street with a rapid pace.

The necessity, however, for immediate action soon roused Albert to some exertion, and being fully equipped for the streets, he made but one bound across the hall, to the great astonishment of the servants, and reached the street just in time to see Gray turn the first corner.

The emotion of Albert Seyton had now died away, and he kept but one object in view, and that was the restoration to him of his much-loved Ada, as a consequence of his successful pursuit of Jacob Gray.

He became calm, cool, and firm—every nerve seemed stretched to its utmost tension, and with a speed that was really tremendous, he cleared the distance between Learmont's door and the corner at which Gray had disappeared.

The object of his anxious pursuit was but half a dozen paces in advance of him, when Albert turned cautiously the corner, and the young man stepped into a doorway, to allow him to proceed to a safer distance.

It would have been a curious study for any one more free to make observations than was Albert Seyton, to mark the curious, suspicious manner in which Gray went along the streets. His home was really not ten minutes' walk from Learmont's house; but something on this one evening, in particular, seemed to possess him with a notion of extreme caution, and when he had left Learmont's door, instead of turning to the left, which he should have done, and then crossed Whitehall, he turned to the right, with a resolution of making a detour through the intricacies of Westminster before he reached his home.

He went on till he emerged into Parliament-street, for he had a great notion of how much he was disguised in his new wig, and he did not mind venturing into a crowded thoroughfare so much as he did before.

Crossing then by the House of Lords, he passed Westminster Abbey, and with a slow, measured step, sauntered down Abingdon-street.

Once or twice Gray had wheeled round to look behind him so suddenly upon his heels, that had not Albert ever kept at a respectful distance, and being favoured by the darkness, he must have been discovered; but Gray passed on again without suspicion, for Seyton on these occasions had not shown any signs of trepidation, or wish to hide himself, but had walked carelessly forward with a determination, however, in his own mind, of knocking at some door rather than come close up to Gray.

The wily Jacob, however, did not once wait for the listless passenger to pass him, so that Albert was not reduced to that troublesome alternative, and the pursuit continued the whole length of Abingdon-street, without any circumstance occurring to awaken suspicion in Gray's mind.

It was not, however, altogether so with Albert, for in Parliament-street he had noticed a man on the opposite side of the way to be keeping his eye upon Jacob Gray, and when they passed the abbey, the same man appeared again, and it was evident to Albert that he was not the only one who was dogging Jacob Gray to his home.

Had he but known that this was Sir Francis Hartleton's man, how much future trouble and uneasiness would have been spared him; but as it was, he only saw in the circumstance an additional cause for alarm on Ada's account, for he could no possibly divine what motive any one but himself could have in tracing Gray to his home, unless it were that the villain had been making similar applications to the one he, Albert, fully believed he had made to Learmont, and some other person was following him home with a similar motive to Learmont's, when he first requested him, Albert, to trace the man's footsteps.

This might or might not be the motive of the spy upon Jacob Gray, but one thing soon became certain, and that was, that the stranger began to regard Albert with as much suspicion and distrust as Albert regarded him, and probably never were two people engaged in one object, more angry at each other just then, than Albert Seyton and the spy of Sir Francis Hartleton.

Jacob Gray would have almost fallen down dead in the street with fright, had he imagined for one moment the predicament he was in—but, on the contrary, he went on applauding himself upon his own cleverness ; and, perhaps, never had he felt so satisfied of his superiority in point of cunning over all his enemies than he did that night.

" I shall yet, after all that is past," he thought, " receive a large sum of money, and be an independent man, while I adequately punish all who have given me uneasiness. The only men I cannot crush are the scoundrels who robbed me after my little adventure with Vaughan. I see no ready way of being revenged upon them, and my only consolation is, that sooner or later they are sure to come to the gallows."

Hugging himself with his idea, although, metaphorically speaking, he, Gray, may be said to have had the rope then about his neck, the villain passed on by the low swampy bit of ground on which the Penitentiary is now built.

He then paused a few moments, as if in doubt which way he should go next, and Albert Seyton crouched down by some timber which lay upon the ground, while Sir Francis Hartleton's man drew back into the shadow of some irregular, small, wretched dwellings which stood near to the water's edge.

Gray did not keep them long in suspense, for after a slight reflection, he determined upon adopting his favourite plan of reaching home, with, at all events, the nearest approach to a certainty of not being followed, namely, by water. He accordingly walked down to some stairs by the river side, passing within arm's-length of Albert, and jumped into a wherry in which was a boy lying fast asleep.

Gray awoke the boy roughly, and when, with a bewildered look, he gazed into the face of his visitor, Gray said,—

" Can you row me to the stairs, by Burlington House in the Strand ?"

" Yes, master," said the boy, as he began unmooring the wherry.

Gray seated himself in the stern of the boat in silence, and pulling his cravat over his chin, he with a smile muttered,—

" Humph—Squire Learmont, Jacob Gray is one too many for you. The day of independence and revenge will come for me soon."

The boat shot out from the shadow of the dark stairs, and the boy began pulling easily towards Westminster-bridge.

Scarcely had the boat got a dozen oar's length from the shore, when Albert Seyton stood upon the steps, and cried,—

" Boat—boat—hilloa, boat !"

" First oars !" cried another voice,—"quick, my man, first oars here !"

Albert turned to the speaker, and by his side, on the slippery wooden steps, was the man he had before noticed as following Gray.

For a moment they looked at each other intensely, and the officer thought to himself—

"I shall know you again, my young spark;" while Albert Seyton was quite absorbed in the exceedingly ugly face before him, further adorned as it was, for nature had intersected it by several seams from old wounds received in many a fray.

" Here you are, your honour," cried a waterman.

" For me," said Albert.

"I beg your pardon, young fellow, it's for me," said the spy.

Albert turned to him, and in a firm voice said—

"Sir, I will not be bullied out of my right by you; I called a boat first here, and the first boat I will have."

So saying, he sprung into the wherry; and not wishing the man to overhear where he really wished to go, he merely said to the waterman,—

"Pull down the stream."

The boat was pushed off, and the spy called from the stairs in an angry voice,—

"Very well, young fellow, just wait till I come across you again; you may jump better, but I'm d——d if you'll fight better than I."

"Go home to your anxious mother," cried the waterman, who, as Albert was silent, considered he was bound to take the part of his fare.

"Do not answer him," said Albert.

"He's a wagabone, sir," said the waterman,—"I knows him. He's a sort o' sneak as goes arter everybody's business but his own."

"Do you see a wherry just a-head?" said Albert.

"Yes, master."

"I want you to follow it. You shall have treble fare if you keep it in sight, and not appear to press upon it."

The waterman gave a long whistle; and then, with a nod of his head, he said—

"All's right. It's Ben's boy as is pulling; and by G—d, there comes your friend."

"My friend?" said Albert, as he looked back towards the stairs.

There was another wherry darting after them, in the stern of which sat the ugly man.

"Pull away," said the waterman with a laugh, as he took long clean sweeps with his oars,—"a stern chase is a long chase."

CHAPTER XCII.

THE CHASE ON THE THAMES.—ALBERT'S SUCCESSFUL DISGUISE.—THE OLD STAIRS
AT BUCKINGHAM-STREET.

THERE was something spirit-stirring and exciting to the young imagination of Albert Seyton in the turn things had taken, as regarded his chase of Jacob Gray Who or what the man was who seemed equally determined with himself not to lose sight of Gray, he could not divine; but be he whom he might, or his object what it might, Albert resolved he should not stand in the way of his own great effort to discover his long lost Ada.

"He may follow," thought Albert, "and I cannot, with any show of reason, quarrel with him for the same thing that I am doing myself; but he shall not, if I can help it, be foremost in the chase."

While these reflections were passing through Seyton's mind, the boat in which was Jacob Gray was shooting far a-head; and by Albert's direction, the waterman who rowed the wherry in which he (Albert) sat, moved into another channel, so as not to seem to follow Gray's boat, although he easily kept it in view.

"You quite understand me," said Albert; "I wish to follow yon wherry sufficiently close to see where it lands its passengers without being seen myself My object is an honest one, and I pray you, as you know the river, to adopt some course which will accomplish my purpose?"

"I tell you what it is," said the waterman. "The safest way in the world to ollow a boat, is to pass it."

"Rather a strange way of following," said Albert.

"I don't exactly mean following," added the man; "but finding out where it' a going to. Now, I can easily pass Ben's boy, and then all we have to do, is to take no notice, but keep on a-head for a little way till they puts in at some stairs. They won't suspect nothink then."

"That is a very good plan," said Albert; "but he I am following knows me by sight, I fear too well, to make it safe or practicable."

"Oh!—he does—does he? Then I'll tell, you what you'll do—put on my jacket and badge, and this red night-cap, and I'll be hanged if your own mother would know you."

"Row easy, then, that the change may not be noticed," said Albert.

The boatman dipped but one oar languidly in the stream, and allowed the wherry to drift among some barges when he instantly shipped his oars, and doffing his coat and red night-cap, he tendered them to Albert, who was soon attired in the very cumbrous garment, which went on easily over all his other clothing. He then gathered up all his long hair, and confined it under his red night-cap, which he pulled on nearly to his eyes.

The waterman sat for a moment, apparently lost in intense surprise, at the alteration which the two articles had made in his customer's appearance, and certainly it would have required somebody most wonderfully well acquainted with the young man to recognise him in his strange disguise. A more complete alteration of personal appearance could not possibly be conceived, and the absence of the long curled hair gave his face quite a different contour.

"Upon my word," said the waterman, "I never saw, in all my life, anything to ekal this. Why, I shouldn't have known you myself for my fare. You needn't mind running alongside of him now, for I'll be hanged if he'll guess it's you, if he eats, drinks, and sleeps with you."

"I dare say I look very different," said Albert, "but for Heaven's sake don't lose sight of him."

"Oh! I'll be up to him in five minutes. I know how Ben's boy can pull, and I know how I can pull. Hilloa—there goes your friend."

The boat, with the spy, shot past at this moment, and Albert was now the last in the chase, to his great aggravation.

Such a state of things, however, did not long continue, for the waterman, after taking a sturdy look behind him to mark the relative position of the boats, bent to his oars with such strength and determination that the light wherry shot through the water with amazing speed. At each vigorous pull of the oars the boat actually seemed to jump forward several yards, and the distance between it and the boat preceding it sensibly decreased each moment.

"I told you I'd soon be up with them, sir," said the waterman, as they came within a dozen boats' lengths of the wherry in which was Sir Francis Hartleton's man. "Now you'll see me pass 'em in proper style. I won this boat on the Thames, and you shall see as it aint thrown away upon me."

The oars were dipped cleanly into the stream, and rose with scarcely a ripple— the speed of the boat, for the space of about twenty yards, was prodigious, and Albert felt that he was moving through the water at a most exhilarating rate. Now they were alongside of the boat with the spy, who immediately, to the immense diversion of the waterman, cried,—

"Hilloa, you there. Where did you land that young fellow you had?"

"Him with the long hair?" said the waterman,

"Yes!"

"And the plum coloured coat?"

"Yes, yes—you know."

"You want to know where I landed him?"

"Of course, I do. I asked you that."

"Then find out, spooney."

"I tell you what," cried the spy, "if I wasn't busy, I'd have you taken before your betters."

"They are no acquaintances of yours, I should say," replied the waterman.

"Do you see this ?" cried the infuriated spy, as he produced a small staff with a gilt crown on the top of it.   "Do you see this, fellow?"

"Yes!"

"Then mind what you are at."

"Do you see this?" said the waterman, indicating with his fore finger the extreme point of his nose, an action which seemed to be especially aggravating to the officer, who immediately said to the boy,—

"Pull alongside of him—pull away."

"Pull away," echoed Albert's waterman, as with a laugh, he bent himself to his work, and soon left the other wherry behind, without a hope of overtaking him.

When the wherry was out of ear-shot, he turned to Albert and said,—

"You see, sir, he didn't know you."

"No, my disguise appears to be effectual.   Get now as near to the other boat as you like."

The man nodded, and in a few moments, Albert Seyton was so near to Jacob Gray that he could almost have sprung from one boat to the other.

Gray looked anxiously and suspiciously at the wherry, but as it, to his eyes, contained only two watermen, he never for a moment dreamt of any danger from it.

Albert buried his chin in the ample collar of the coat, and as his boat passed so close to the one Gray was in that the watermen had both to ship their oars, he gazed with no little emotion upon the pale sallow face of the man who he would have travelled all over the world to meet, in order to wring from him the knowledge of where to find his much-loved and cruelly-persecuted Ada.

Gray glanced for a moment at Albert, but it was evident he knew him not. Nothing was further from Gray's thoughts than a meeting with Albert Seyton; and, in fact, since Ada had left him, he scarcely regarded Albert Seyton as in any way connected with him or his fortunes, and never for a moment took the trouble to speculate upon what he would or could do or say, were they to meet accidentally.

"Where are you coming to now?" cried Gray's boatman.

"Nowhere's partiklar," was the reply of the other ; "where are you?"

"What's that to you?"

"Oh, nothink—nothink—only I'd a let you lay hold behind."

Gray's waterman, with a hearty curse, resumed his oars and gave up the parley.

"Now, I bethink me," said Gray, in a low tone, "you may put me in at the small stairs, by Buckingham-street."

"Yes, your honour.   We are just there."

"Good.   That will do."

The stairs at the end of Buckingham-street, led up to a handsome garden then, and were themselves of an ancient and decayed appearance, being worn in the centre quite into deep hollows, and withal so rickety and injured by time and rough usage, that it required some steadiness to ascend them.   Jacob Gray, however, from that very reason, thought it a safe place of landing, and when the head of his boat was moored to one of the crumbling piles, that had been rotting in the bed of the river for more than fifty years, he walked cautiously along the seats, and after liberally paying the waterman, he commenced carefully ascending the slippery time worn steps.

Albert, at this moment, was in a state of excitement impossible to be described. He paid the waterman immediately Gray's wherry turned its head towards the shore, and sat with his hands upon the coat, as ready as a harlequin in a pantomime to throw it off, and assume his proper appearance ; but then Gray might look round, and he felt the necessity of waiting until he had actually ascended the stairs.   Oh, what an agony of suspense was that brief period!

At length Gray turned sharp round to his right hand when he got to the top of the steps, and with the speed of lightning Albert Seyton threw off the coat and nightcap, and sprung after him to the intense astonishment of Gray's waterman, who stood with his mouth wide open, and his eyes staring out of his head like those of a boiled fish, for nearly two minutes before he could ejaculate,—

"Well, I never—there's ago—in all my blessed born days I never. Who the devil's that?"

"Ah, you're hit it now," said Albert's waterman, as he deliberately put on the coat.

"What do you mean?"

"I've been giving the devil a coat. Didn't you see how quick we went?"

"Yes."

"Well, he was steering with his tail all the time, so you see I'd nothing to do but to pull away."

CHAPTER XCIII.

GRAY AT HOME.—ALBERT'S JOY AND EXULTATION.—THE MEETING IN THE OLD DOOR WAY.

"MAKE way there!" roared Sir Francis Hartleton's man, as the boy who rowed him shot the wherry's nose between the other two. "Make way there—curse you all, I am on the king's business."

"Make way for his majesty," cried the man who had carried Albert Seyton. "He says he's on the king's business, but that's only his modesty. He's the king himself, I shouldn't wonder, disguised as a fool."

The spy had scrambled from the boat on to the wooden steps, but he was so annoyed at this last remark, that snatching his staff from his pocket, he turned round, saying,—

"If I lose my proper game, I'll make sure for you for obstructing an officer. You shall have a lodging in the watch-house, my exceedingly witty fellow."

The waterman was, however, a great deal too quick for him; for, as he tried to step from the stairs into the boat, by one sweep of his oars he shot the wherry out some three or four yards from the landing, and the spy stepped up to his knees in the river, and was nearly precipitated head foremost into the stream.

"Don't pison the water," said the waterman; and then he pulled steadily away.

"I'll have you another time, my man," said the spy, quite livid with rage, as he turned, and again ascended the steps.

In the meantime Jacob Gray had gathered his cloak closely around him, and smiling to himself at his own cleverness in, as he thought, thoroughly outwitting Learmont, and even when there was no danger, approaching his home in so very baffling a manner, was creeping along close to the houses as usual towards his obscure lodgings.

Albert Seyton, when he reached the top of the stairs, looked anxiously to the right, and there he saw Gray, not half a dozen yards from him. To follow so closely would have been very dangerous, undisguised now as the young man was, and he hung back, still keeping Jacob Gray in his eye, until the latter had proceeded nearly to a turning which led into the next street but one in which he lived. The moment, then, that he was upon the corner Albert walked hastily forward, and by pursuing the same system at the corner of the next street, he fairly succeeded in dogging Gray to the little mean shop above which he lodged.

Albert's heart beat high as he saw him enter the humble abode. His agitation became extreme, and the thought that he was so near Ada caused such a tumult of lightful feelings in his breast, that he forgot all passed suffering—all present cau-ions, and actually bounded forward half a dozen paces towards the shop, before his promise to Learmont came across his mind, and arrested his eager footsteps.

"Oh, oh," he said, "Ada, my beautiful and true. Even now, although so near to you, I must not rush to your rescue. My word of honour binds me, but I can gaze with rapture upon the house in which you are. I can please myself by fancying I breathe the same air with you. Oh, how cruel is this that I cannot, for my promise to the rich squire, at once rush into the house that contains my heart's treasure, and claim it as my own. I must control my impatience. Ada, your imprisonment shall now be but of short duration. Soon now shall I clasp you to my heart."

Albert now crossed over to the other side of the way, and diving into a door-way where he was completely hidden, but from whence he could command a good view of the house in which he so erroneously supposed Ada to be, he gave himself up to the delirious feeling that he had at length arrived at the end of all his troubles, and Ada would soon be his, while the patronage of the rich Squire Learmont would ensure him ease, and perhaps in time fortune.

There was no sign of inhabitants visible in the whole front of the house ; but in a few more moments, as Albert rose his eye restlessly from window to window, he saw a dirty narrow curtain moved in one of the top rooms, and fancy made him think the hand was Ada's, which he saw but partially.

"My Ada—my own Ada—my beautiful," he cried; "oh ! if I could but be sure now that you were well, and,——"

He was interrupted at this moment by some one popping into the dark door-way so suddenly as to run against him with great violence.

Albert immediately laid hold of the intruder, and cried—"Hilloa, friend ! softly here."

"What do you do here ?" cried a man's voice in no very pleasant accents.

"I may as well retaliate the question."

"Oh ! be d——d," cried the man, who was no other than the spy.

"I know you now by your voice. You are the fellow who took a boat before me."

"Then I presume," said Albert, "you are the fellow who took a boat after me."

"What do you mean by that ?"

"What I say."

"Come, come, no nonsense, young fellow—what do you mean by following that man you have made such a run after ?"

"I never explain my affairs to strangers," said Albert, coldly.

"I'm an officer."

"I don't care if you are a dozen officers," said Albert, "you have nothing to do with my private affairs."

"But I can take you up on suspicion."

"Can you ?"

"Yes, I can ; and for your impudence, I will too."

"Then," said Albert, "I'll knock you down first ;" and suiting the action to the word, he grappled with the officer before he was aware, and although much the lighter and weaker of the two, threw him upon his back in the passage with so much violence, that he lay stunned.

"I am sorry for this," thought Albert ; "but I can allow no vexatious interference with me now. Farewell, dear Ada, for a time—your lover will be with you soon—I will now away to Learmont's, and claim his proffered assistance."

"Casting then, ever and anon, lingering looks behind at the house, which he believed contained the object of his fond affections, Albert left the street; and when he had turned the corner, and could no longer see even the habitation of Jacob Gray, he started off at a pace which astonished every one he passed, towards the house of Learmont.

Jacob Gray, when he reached his room, sat down on the side of the miserable little bed, and began to think of his future plans and hopes, with a feeling of certainty, as regarded their stability, such as he had rarely before experienced. [

seemed as if Providence having now hurried him on to the very brink of destruction, was determined that his fall should be the more dreadful and full of suffering
by his having no sort of anticipation of it.   He was as one smiling and making
long calculations on the brink of the grave.

"Learmont," he said, " has seized the bait—I shall be wealthy and free, besides
satisfying my revenge.   They taunt me with being subtle—I trust that they will

find me so.   They might long ago have temporised with me, and ensured their own
safety by never awakening in my breast the dark feelings towards them that n o
possess it ; but they sought my life, and I swore revenge.   Britton and Learmon
shall fall in one common destruction, while Ada shall have more trouble to prove
her legitimacy than will last her her life, should she linger to the age of an ancient
patriarch.   Yes, I shall be revenged on her, as well as upon Britton and Learmont.'

No. 45.

He sat then for some moments in deep thought, and a feeling of anxiety began to creep over him.

"I am getting nervous now," he muttered; "of late I am fearfully subject to such gloomy thoughts. I shall be glad when this gloomy, lonely life is over. It suits not with my disposition. I—I did not feel it so much when she was with me, but now that I am quite alone, a shuddering awe creeps around my heart, and I start at—at the merest trifle. Gracious Heaven—how my heart beats now! 'Tis time I should have ease and comfort in some other land, where all things are new and strange, and there is nothing to remind me of the past—aye, then, I shall know peace."

He rose, and paced his room uneasily; but even in his mental agitation he trod cautiously, as if the very boards would proclaim to the world—there trod Jacob Gray, the murderer! Then he produced his confession, and a strange desire seized him to read it carefully through, and make some verbal corrections in it, in order that it should be still more clear and explanatory than it had been. Again, and again, he read over the document, and was satisfied that its notations were distinct and clear.

"Yes—yes—if anything should happen to me," he muttered, "this will destroy Learmont and Britton, and likewise doom Ada to poverty, while the estates of Learmont will revert to the crown, or some very distant branch of the family that will be eager to acquire them. So even I should not fall quite unavenged. In my death I should be terrible. Death?—death? I am not going to die—why did such a thought enter my brain? 'Tis strange—very strange.—I never thought of death before this night. I—I am quite well—quite. 'Tis a mere feverish fancy; a vision crossing the over-excited brain. I have had hundreds of such—such forebodings. I suppose that is what I must call the strange feeling that now oppresses me."

He was now silent for some time, and then, hastily rising, he held the confession in his hand, and glanced around his room as he said,—

"I will never again carry so important a document as this about with me. 'Tis far better—far safer in some hiding-place here; and then suppose it should not be found till some time after my death. That word again—death—death—pshaw, what have I to do with death, for many years to come?"

He, nevertheless, trembled, as he strove to reason himself out of his nervous fears, and he was some time before he could decide upon where to put his confession, so that it must eventually be found, but still where a search would be required to bring it to light. He finally ripped some of the lining from his cloak, and inserted the confession between that and the cloth.

"There it will be quite safe from any casual observation," he said, "while sooner or later it must come to light, and my vengeance would be greater by a little delay, because Learmont would be lulled into fancied security if no immediate danger assailed after my death."

He sunk upon his chair muttering.

"Death again—death again—death again—how that notion haunts me! An absurd fancy; in my case a most absurd fancy, for never was I so safe—so free—so likely to obtain all that I wish as I am now—my star is in the ascendant."

He hung the cloak on a large hook behind the door of his room, and then said,—

"How many persons would search this room, and toss this cloak about, without discovering that it contained anything so important as that now hidden in it."

He then proceeded to a cupboard, and taking from it a case bottle, he drank a quantity of raw spirits, to which he had latterly habituated himself whenever he felt any disagreeable mental qualms which he could not reason himself out of.

"Drink—drink," he muttered, as he returned the case bottle to its place. "That is the wretch's last solace. It will for a time banish care, but it is a deceitful fiend that comes at first with a semblance of great friendship, but sooner or later it will turn upon him who has been lured by it, and become a deadly foe. I—think I will sleep now—all is safe, and I am very weary; my confession will be found after my death—ah, that word again—death—death—nothing else can I think of—come, welcome sleep."

He threw himself upon his bed, and exhausted as he was by the few preceding day's actions, he soon dropped into slumber—not an unbroken or easy one, though, for the imagination, now freed from the control of reason, conjured up fearful images into the brain of the man of crime.

CHAPTER XCIV.

STRONG DRINK AT THE CHEQUERS.—THE SUMMONS TO BRITTON.—HIS MAJESTY'S
AMUSEMENTS.

BRITTON'S rage at the escape of Gray from his room, where he thought he had him so securely, almost made him sober for the next four-and-twenty hours. He was in too great a passion to drink, and it was not until his friend the butcher had generously drunk both Britton's share and his own of sundry strong compounds, that the smith, dashing his clenched first upon the table with a blow that made every article upon it jump again, exclaimed,—

"Brandy—brandy here. Quick with you."

"Your majesty shall have it in a moment," cried the landlord; "may I presume to ask if your majesty will have it raw or mixed?"

"Neither," roared Britton.

"Neither? oh dear me. Certainly—perhaps your majesty means a little of both?"

"No, I don't, fool! Bring me a pint of brandy boiling."

"B—b—b—boiling?"

"Yes."

"Without any water?"

"What do I want with water. For the future I'll drink nothing but boiling brandy."

"Smash me," remarked Bond, the butcher, "if that aint a good idea."

"Off with you," roared Britton, to the amazed landlord. "Mind you drink it in with the bubbles on it. Let me see the hot steam rising from it—like—like reeking blood, and be d——d to you—take that."

As these remarks were accompanied by a pint measure, which passed within an inch of his head, the landlord made a wild kind of rush from the room, shouting,—

"Brandy boiling—brandy boiling directly, for his majesty King Britton!"

Britton felt himself wonderfully better and much appeased in spirit after his order of the boiling brandy, and he turned to the butcher with something of his usual manner, saying,—

"Bond, my boy, I shall never be the man I was till I have taken that fellow's life."

"You don't say so?" remarked Bond.

"Yes, I do."

"Oh, be bothered; you'll be able to drink as much as ever, I know."

"Yes as to that—but,——"

"Well, what more do you wish? Don't be unreasonable—joint me with a notched cleaver if I don't think you are the most comfortable cove as I knows, and lots of money and nothing for to do but to melt it down into all sorts o' strong drinks. I calls that being in heaven, I does."

"It's something," said Britton.

"Something ? I believe you it is.   Why, if you was an angel, what more could you have, I should like to know?"

"Jacob Gray's blood."

"So you will, but you must wait your time. Now I tell you what, Master Britton; you're like a pig as is going to be stuck—he makes a squalling when he knows as it won't do no good, and here you've been a denying of yourself your proper drink when you know that'll do no good. Have patience till this, 'ere fellow as you owes sich a uncommon grudge to, comes in your way again, and when he does, don't you let him out of arm's length.   Just give him a malleter on the head to stun him, while you fetches me, and then we can cut him up quite comfortable."

"I was a fool to leave him a moment," said Britton ; "I ought to have known better. The fellow is as crafty as a dozen devils rolled and welded all into one. He has as many shiftings and doublings as a hunted fox."

"Some animals is very difficult," said Bond, " to bring to the slaughter. A ring in his nose, and a rope is the very best thing, but it's difficult to put it on."

"You are an ass, Bond," said Britton, " it aint a bullock, you idiot, but as crafty a man as ever stepped."

"Perhaps I is a ass," remarked Bond. "Birds of a feather they always flocks together, which, I take it, is the reason why us two makes such good company, Master Britton,"

The landlord at this moment made his appearence, with the boiling brandy in a punch-bowl.   At least, the landlord was supposed to follow it into the room ; for the steam that arose from the liquor hid his face in a kind of glory, such as sometimes may be seen in an old picture confounding the physignomy of a saint,

He said nothing, but laid the streaming beverage before Britton, and then he coughed, and winked, and wiped his eyes, and sneezed, all of which symptoms of uneasiness arose from the subtle particles of the evaporating spirit having nearly suffocated him.

" What do you mean by all that ?" said Britton.

" Ah, what do you mean ?" roared Bond, giving the landlord a smack on the back that nearly felled him.

" The—the steam of brandy is rather—a—chew—, a—a—a—chew. Bless me, I can't help sneezing—a—chew—strong—very—strong. I shouldn't wonder if it's very good for the eyes, it makes 'em water so. What an idea—boiled brandy !"

"Oh, you think it's a good idea, do you ?" said Britton, as he ladled up a brimmer of the scalding-hot spirit.

" Uncommonly good——chew."

" Leave off that sneezing, will you ?"

"I really can't—a—chew. Excuse me, your majesty, but we never had such a thing as boiled brandy ordered at the Chequers before."

" Oh, indeed ; then you shall have a drop. Come drink, this—drink I say."

" Really, I—I—"

" You won't !"

" I don't persume to use such an expression in reference to any command from your majesty, but the truth is—I would rather not."

" But I say you shall."

"" Spare me, your majesty ; I am rather weak in the head."

"Hold him, Bond, while I pour it down his throat," cried Britton.

The landlord groaned—" If I must take a small sip, why I would rather take it myself."

" Toss it off, then, at once ; and don't be making those faces. Come, now, off with it."

The landlord was perfectly well aware that no mortal throat could with impunity llow the scalding liquor to trickle down it ; and, in fact, he had been pleasing himself with the idea of how scalded the smith would be if, with his usual precipitancy, he should take a gulp of the liquor ; but now that it came to his turn first, the joke altered its complexion altogether, and his hand trembled as he held the ladle to his mouth.

"Quick," roared Britton; and the unfortunate landlord took a small sip, which went down his throat like a small globule of melted lead, and induced him to make such wry faces and contortions as quite delighted Andrew Britton, who, in the enjoyment of the moment, actually forgot Jacob Gray.

How long the landlord's sufferings might have been protracted it is hard to say; but fortunately for him, in the midst of Britton's high enjoyment of the scene, a boy came into the room, and screamed out, without the least reverence for the kingly dignity that the smith had assumed at the Chequers,—

"Is Andrew Britton here?"

"Halloo, you villain," cried Britton, "what do you mean?"

"I wants Andrew Britton," cried the boy.

"You scoundrel!"

"You're another!"

Britton's face assumed a purplish hue with rage, but he was silent, and then beckoning to the boy, he whispered to Bond,—

"I'll scald him from top to toe."

"Don't you wish yon may catch me," cried the boy. "hilloo, old read face. Look at your nose. I want Andrew Britton.

"Oh, you villain," cried the landlord, "how dare you behave so? What do you want with the gentleman you have named?"

"I've got a letter for him—where is he? I suppose as he'll give me a penny."

Britton slowly rose from his seat and began sidling round the table towards the boy; who, however, was far too quick and agile for the bulky smith, and throwing a folded piece of paper upon the floor, he darted to the door, crying—

"Don't you wish it, old guts; you'll make yourself ill if you exert yourself so. Good bye."

"Hold him," cried Britton to the landlord, who made a futile, and not very energetic, attempt to detain the boy, who was out of the house in a moment, and in the next a stone came through a pane of glass and hit the landlord upon the side of the head.

"Oh, the vagabond," said mine host, making a rush to the door, and fully participating in Britton's indignation now that he had himself cause of complaint; but Britton intercepted him, and being resolved to have revenge upon somebody, he knocked the landlord's head against the door-post, with a rap that made him look confused for a moment, and then retire from the room dancing with pain.

"All right," cried Bond.

"Aham!" said Britton, returning to his seat. "That'll teach him to run against me another time, and if I meet that boy, I'll wring his neck."

"What's this here?" remarked the butcher, as he picked up the note the lad had thrown down. "'To Andrew Britton,' that's large, but hang me if I can make out the rest. The first word is sensible enough, howsomdever."

"What is it?"

"Meat."

"Meat? nonsense. What the devil have I to do with meat? Give it to me."

Britton snatched the note from the hands of the butcher, and read as follows:—

"Meet me by nine o'clock to-morrow morning at Buckingham Gate.

"L."

"Short and civil—I'll see him d—d first—nine o'clock too? A likely hour—no, Master Learmont, I'll call upon you when I please, no oftener and no seldomer; but I won't meet you at Buckingham Gate, as sure as my name's Andrew Britton. Am I to be dictated to?"

"I should think not," cried Bond. "Does that come from the squire, eh, Britton?"

"What's that to you?"

"Nothing at all, but I asked you, nevertheless, and you needn't put yourself out of the way."

"You be hanged."

"Be hanged yourself."

Britton liked Bond principally because when he roared at him, he was replied to much in the same strain, and, if possble, an octave higher, so he betrayed no indignation at the independence of the butcher, but taking up a ladle full of the brandy, which had now much cooled, he poured it down his throat, and then followed it by another, after which he flung the ladle at the head of a quiet-looking man who was smoking a pipe and drinking a pint of small ale in a corner, and rising, he cried—

"I'll go out now—order my sedan chair—I'll be hanged but that's the rummest thing ever was invented ; I like it. My chair, there. Halloo—halloo; I'll have some fun to-night."

"But you needn't have thrown away the ladle, you beast," remarked Bond, as he took the bowl in his hand and finished the contents at one draught, hot and strong as they were.

The landlord's voice was now heard shouting—

"His majesty's chair—quick—quick. His majesty's chair, and right glad am I to get him out of the house awhile," he added to himself; "and if it was not that he spends every week a matter of ten or twelve guineas at the Old Chequers, I'd never let the beast cross its threshold again."

CHAPTER XCV.

THE WALK IN SEARCH OF ALBERT.—THE RECOGNITION AT CHARING CROSS.

WAS Ada happy in her pleasant home at Sir Francis Hartleton's—was there no cloud yet upon her young heart? Alas, how purely comparative are all our joys and all our sorrows. The change from her weary confinement with Jacob Grey, and the dismal habitations it was his policy to live in, to the kind looks—kinder words and happy home of the warm-hearted magistrate, was like suddenly, to some adventurous voyager to the far north, breaking the misty horrors around him, and at a moment when he felt almost inclined to lie down and die before the rigour of the season, and transporting him to some fair region, where the bright sun shone upon the trailing vine—where the orange groves were musical with the songs of birds, and the very air as it gently fanned his cheeks was in itself a delicious luxury.

To Ada, for the first few days, it seemed as if she had stepped into a new existence ; but when the novelty of the change was over—when she had done assuring herself that she was free for ever from Jacob Gray, how her heart began to yearn for him she loved ! what an instable curiosity arose in her mind, to know who and what she was—what name she should associate with the endearing one of father, and whether she should weep over another grave, or ever feel the fond embrace of a living parent.

It would have been strangely unnatural, if these active sources of anxiety had not sprung up rapidly in such a heart as Ada's, alive as it was to every noble feeling—every tender sympathy.

The companionship of the young persons of her own sex, whom Lady Hartleton often collected about her, tended probably to foster and encourage these feelings in Ada, and the ready tears—tears which she had never shed when in misfortune, and exposed to all the harshness of Jacob Gray, would start to her eyes at the mention of a father's or a mother's love, by any of the fair young beings who delighted in her company.

Sir Francis Hartleton had promised her he would have Albert Seyton sought for, and he had kept his word ; but what degree of exertion on the part of another will satisfy the heart that loves, and Ada longed to search herself for him, who had cheered her under unhappier auspices, and loved her in her gloom and misery.

Into the friendly bosom of Lady Hartleton, she poured her griefs and anxieties, and if she found no relief of a tangible nature, she there at least found ready sympathy, and Lady Hartleton would say to her,—

"My dear Ada I can do not more at present than weep with you, if you must weep, and comfort you, if you will be afflicted. Be assured, Sir Francis is doing his utmost to discover Albert Seyton's place of abode, as well as toiling hard to unravel the mystery connected with you."

Ada would then, in tears, exclaim against her own ingratitude, and accuse herself of selfishness, and Lady Hartleton frequently had the greatest difficulty to remind her, that she considered her feelings natural, and in every way worthy of her.

It was early in the day preceding that on which the magistrate had discovered poor Maude, that Ada with a trembling voice, said to Lady Hartleton,—

"I have a great favour—to—ask."

"No, my dear Ada," said Lady Hartleton, kissing her cheek, "you have nothing to ask—everything to demand. Recollect, 'tis we who think ourselves much your debtors for your company with us, and consequently we are much bound to consult your wishes."

"Ah, it is your kind heart which prompts your tongue," said Ada, "and not your judgment; but I know you will not hear me speak to you of my gratitude, although it is a theme which I could never tire of."

"Say no more, Ada, but tell me what you wish."

"Will you permit me, myself, for one day to go in search of Albert Seyton?"

"Yourself, Ada?"

"Yes. 'Tis perhaps a foolish wish; but sometimes, what great resources courage and deep knowledge of the world may fail to accomplish, the zeal of affection will be able more easily to do."

Lady Hartleton shook her head, as she said,—

"Ada, you would but, in such a place as London, expose yourself to much danger and insult. Believe me, that my husband has in his service those who will leave no spot unsearched for him you so much wish to see."

"Ah, lady, can hired zeal ever reach the height of exertion attained by that which springs alone from the true heart?"

"I grant you that it seldom can; but then, Ada, there are many cases where mere knowledge and skill will do much more than the warmest, holiest zeal that ever animated a human breast?"

"There may be; but is this one."

"It is, Ada. You are ignorant of London, and its intracicies, and would but lose yourself in a fruitless endeavour to find another."

"It may be so," said Ada, with a disappointed air, "and I must be content."

"No, Ada, far be it from me to say you shall not take a tour through London in search of him. If you accomplish no more by such a step, you may at least please your mind with the reflection that you have taken it."

"You will let me go then?" and cried

"Yes, but not alone. I will accompany you wheresoever you please to go, and some experienced officer, of Sir Francis's own choosing, shall follow us in case of need. I think then we may venture anywhere."

"Generous friend," cried Ada. "Oh, may Heaven give me words to say how much I thank you"—

"I am thanked already," said Lady Hartleton, with a smile. "The idea of active exertions has already kindled a colour in your cheeks, Ada, and lent new animation to every feature of your face."

"I shall be better satisfied, even if I altogether fail," said Ada. "I have been now for so many years accustomed to look to myself alone for resources of action, that when anything nearly concerning me has to be done, I am unhappy if I am not doing it myself. Forgive me, dear lady, for all this troublesome spirit, but recollect I am a young wayward thing, brought up in solitude and harshness, early accustomed to repress every fond emotion, and my heart's best feelings oftener checked with a blow, than encouraged by a smile."

"We will go as soon as I can consult Sir Francis about who shall accompany us?" said Lady Hartleton.

Ada could only look her thanks, and Lady Hartleton left the room in search of her husband, who gave a more ready consent to the scheme than she imagined he would, only that he said he would send with them two officers on whom he could thoroughly and entirely depend.

"You will then be as safe," he said, "as if you were in your own drawing-room, and if it will satisfy the mind of Ada, I advise you to go at once."

With this Lady Hartleton returned to Ada, and in ten minutes they were equipped for their walk, the two officers being strictly ordered by Sir Francis never to lose sight of them for a moment.

"I can adopt but one plan of operation," said Ada, "and that is to go from place to place where Albert has lived, and at each make what inquiries may suggest themselves on the moment. I think I can find my way, if put in the neighbourhood, to the first lodging Jacob Gray brought me to in London; at least, the first I have any recollection of. It stood, as I have often wearied you with telling, in a bye-street, at the back of another, the name of a which well recollect was Swallow-street."

"That we shall have no difficulty in finding," said Lady Hartleton. "Swallow-street is a well-known thoroughfare; although, I believe, none of the most select. I think I can act as your guide there; but should I be at fault those who are following us, as our guards, can no doubt set us right."

Many were the glances of admiration cast upon Ada, as she and Lady Hartleton walked along Whitehall to Charing-cross, and by the time they reached the corner of the Strand, several idle loungers had enlisted themselves in their train, with a determination to see where they could possibly be going.

"We must cross here," said Lady Hartleton, "and pass those mean rows of buildings, which are called the Royal Mews, and then we shall, if I mistake not, be in the immediate neighbourhood of the street you mention."

As Lady Hartleton spoke, she felt Ada clutch her arm very tightly, and turning to see what occassioned it, she saw one of the puppies of the day with his grining face, within a few inches of Ada's ear, muttering some of the ineffable nonsense common to such animals, when they pitch upon an apparently unprotected female as the object of their insulting addres.

A flash of indignation came from the eyes of Lady Hartleton; but before she could speak, she saw the fopling flung into the roadway, with a violence that sent him half across it; and Sir Francis Hartleton himself, who had followed after the officers, took Ada's arm within his, saying,—

"There now. If you had been quite alone, Ada, you would havbeen pestered, probably, for an hour, by that ape in man's clothes."

Ada turned to speak to the magistrate, when a cry of pleasure escaped her.

On the opposite side of the way was Albert Seyton, walking liesurely towards the Horse-guards.

Sir Francis Hartleton was just in time to stop her from rushing across the road-way, and detaining her by the arm, said,—

"Ada, do me one favour ? Go home at once, and trust to my word of honour that I will not lose sight of him for one moment. The public street is no place for you and him to meet in. For Heaven's sake, now go home!"

"I—I will—if you wish it," said Ada. "Oh! he is found—he is found!"

"Take her home through the park, by Spring-gardens," whispered Sir Francis to his wife. "I wish to have some conversation with this young man, before Ada, with her generous feelings, commits herself too far. I will be home within the hour."

The magistrate then darted across the road, and followed Albert Seyton closely, as his first object was to see where he lived, provided he was going home, a he, Sir Francis, was not quite satisfied with Albert's long absence from his office.

CHAPTER XCVI.

SIR FRANCIS HARTLETON'S SURPRISE AT ALBERT'S PLACE OF DESTINATION.—
THE WATCH ON THE SQUIRE'S HOUSE.—ADA'S DISAPPOINTMENT.

" WHEN Sir Francis Hartleton darted across the road in order to follow Albert
Seyton, his views, with regard to the young man, were to trace him to his house,
and then immediately after send for him to his, Sir Francis's office, by Bucking-
ham-house ; and, in a conversation with him, endeavour to come to a more
decided opinion than he was at present able to arrive at with respect to the stability

of his affection for Ada ; for it is not saying too much, when we assert that the
interest felt by the magistrate in the welfare and future happiness of the beautiful
girl, who was, by so singular a train of circumstances, placed in his care, was
equal to that of a fond father for a darling child of his own.
    The very romantic circumstances connected with her would have invested Ada
with a great interest, even had she been other than what she was ; but when in
    No. 46.

herself, she concentrated all the sweet feminine charms of mind and person which the warmest fancy could suggest, she became, indeed, an object of deep interest to Sir Francis—an interest which amounted to a pure and holy affection.

Her gentleness, and yet her rare courage—her simplicity, and yet her active intellect—her clinging affection and gushing gratitude to those who were kindly disposed towards her, and her utter want of selfishness, all combined to make her such a character as one might dream of, but seldom hope to see realised.

"Her future happiness," thought Sir Francis. "all depends upon this young man whom I am now following, and I think I have a right to be more careful that Ada, with all her fine noble feelings, is not sacrificed to one, who may fail to appreciate the rich treasure he may possess. I will, ere I welcome this Albert Seyton to my house, be well assured that he is deserving of the pure young heart that I am convinced is all his own. One pang is far better for Ada to endure than the years of misery that must ensue from an ill-assorted union."

Reasoning thus the magistrate followed Albert Seyton sufficiently close to be certain he could enter no house without his observation; and yet at the same time, at such a distance as to run no great risk of recognition should the young man turn round.

Little did poor Albert, whose mind was, at the present moment, so full of recollections of his Ada, that he scarcely knew whither his footsteps led him, imagine that he had not only passed her within twenty paces, but was now actually kept from her because there was a doubt of the sincerity of that passion which was at once the bliss and the bane of his existence.

Sir Francis could not hear the deep sighs that burst from the labouring heart of the young man, as he whispered to himself,—

"My Ada—my beautiful and true! Oh, when will kind Heaven bless my eyes by permitting me to gaze upon thy face again? The summer's sun may shine brightly for others, and the green earth look beautiful, but there is a cloud upon my spirits, and all is dreary, bleak, and desolate to me without you, my beautiful Ada!"

Alas! poor Albert—if already Sir Francis Hartleton, from your long absence from his office, entertains a lingering unwelcome doubt of your feelings for Ada—what harsh suspicions are you not about to subject yourself to within the next quarter of an hour. How near are you to the completion of your fondest hopes, and yet how distant—long sought for as you have been, you are now found but to be avoided.

The young dejected lover passed onwards in his sorrow, and Sir Francis, whose anxiety was increasing each moment, followed with his eyes fixed on him alone, and totally unobservant of the many curious glances that was cast upon his animated and anxious looking countenance by the passengers.

They passed the Horse-guards—the low mean building which was then devoted to other purposes, and which is now the treasury—and still onwards went Albert listlessly as before. Now he turned down a small street behind Parliament-street. Then another turning led him into a large handsome thoroughfare; his steps quickened and he, at length, paused by the steps of a large mansion. Sir Francis Hartleton stopped, but kept his eyes rivetted on the young man. He saw him ascend the steps—could he believe his eyes? Yes—it was—it must be Learmont's house. Then magistrate walked forward. He was not mistaken—Albert Seyton had entered the house of Learmont. The surprise of the magistrate was intense in the extreme. Here was the lover of Ada on visiting terms, if not on more intimate ones, with her worst foe. What was he to think? Had gold had its influence upon the young man—and had he sold himself to the wealthy squire, changing from a lover of Ada to one of the conspirators against her peace? Was such conduct possible? or had the professions of Albert Seaton been from the first those of a hyppocrite? Had he always been a creature of Learmont, and only deputed to perform the part he had played in order the more easily to entangle the young pure girl into an inextricable web of villany?

As these painful reflections passed rapidly through the mind of Sir Francis, he saw a livery servant descend the steps of Learmont's house, bearing a letter in his hand.

"I will question this man," he thought. " He is going on some message in the neighbourhood, and I dare say will be communicative enongh to satisfy me with regard to the position held by Albert Seyton in Learmont's house."

The man came down the street towards Sir Frnacis, who, when he came sufficiently near, said in a careless manner,—

" Was that Mr. Seyton who just now entered your master's house ?"

" Yes, sir," was the reply.

" Ah, I thought it was he. I have not seen him for a long time. He is intimate with the squire, I believe."

" He is his worship's private secretary, sir."

" Oh, yes, to be sure. Good morning, friend."

" Good mording, sir."

The servant passed on, and Sir Francis Hartleton stood a few moments in deep thought.

" So," he said, " this lover of Ada's turns out to be Learmont's private secretary. The private secretary of a villain should be like his master, and if the young man be a faithful servant, he is no fit match for Ada. He must be in league with Learmont in all his atrocities, else would he, occupying the situation he does, be a sore encumberance to such a man as the squire. The facts speak plainly—a confidential servant of a man like Learmont can only be one degree removed from his principal in villany, and that degree must be one deeper still. Is it possible that this young man, who spoke so fairly—who looked so frank and candid, and in whom I, with all my practice of human nature, could discover nothing but what was manly and interesting in his first interview with me—is it possible that he can be one employed to do the dirty work of such a man as Squire Learmont? Alas! alas! such is humanity. Surely some sort of presentiment of this—some special interposition of Providence in favour of the good and pure—must have induced me, for Ada's sake, to follow him thus, instead of permitting a recognition in the streets. A fine tale would this private secretary have had for the ears of his master—that the simple, easily-duped Sir Francis Hartleton had in his care the object for some reason of his bitterest hatred, and that he, the sweet-tongued, honied-accented, private secretary was welcomed as the accepted lover, and had free ingress and egress to the house in which she lived—could concert what plots and plans he liked—nay, could take her very life for a reward sufficient. Thank Heaven, for unmasking so much villany."

Sir Francis Hartleton's face was flushed, and there was resentment at his heart, as he walked with hasty steps past Learmont's house.

He had not, however, proceeded far when he heard his name mentioned by some one behind him, and suddenly turning he saw, within a few paces of him, the object of his present angry thoughts—namely, Albert Seyton, who had left Learmont's house upon seeing the magistrate from a window of the little room by the hall.

" I may as well," thought Albert, " see him—not that I have any hopes beyond those that at present possess my mind, through the interposition of my generous patron, Squire Learmont."

" Well, sir?" said Sir Francis Hartleton, in no very amiable voice.

" Do you not recollect me, sir ?"

" No, sir."

" You do not?"

" I know nothing of you, sir, and desire not your acquaintance."

" Sir Francis Hartleton, you are labouring under some error. You mistake who I am."

" There can be no mistake, sir. Good morning. If you have any business with me, you may probably know my office, and the hours of attendance at it."

" One moment, sir."

" Not half a one," said Sir Francis as he walked away, leaving Albert bewildered. After a few moments' thought, he said,—

" Now I have not one lingering doubt. What Learmont hinted of this magistrate is true. I have but one friend, and that is the rich squire."

" The impertinent scoundrel, to accost me !" said Sir Francis, striding homewards in a great fume. " I was never so out of temper in my life. I have no doubt now whatever, but that he is a mere creature of Learmont's. Thank Heaven ! Ada, you are saved."

Sir Francis proceeded home as quickly as he could ; but as he neared his own door, the thought came over him of how he was to inform Ada of the discovery he had made ; for although his own suspicions were strong against Learmont, and the scraps of paper he had procured from poor Maude had supplied some wanting links in the chain of his conjectures, he had abstained from fully explaining to Ada sufficient to make her now comprehend why Albert's engagement with the rich squire should place such an insurmountable barrier between them.

" She must now know all," he thought, " and perhaps it is far better that she should, as at all events she will, in her own thoughts, be better able to separate her friends from her enemies. I will now, however, plan another watch upon the squire's house, in order to ascertain if this young spark is in any communication with Jacob Gray, or only an agent of the squire's. He may be playing some complicated game of villany that, after all, may assist me."

CHAPTER XCVII.

THE VISIT TO GRAY'S HOUSE.—LEARMONT'S EXULTATION.

WHILE Albert Seyton was absent on his errand of following Jacob Gray, Learmont was a prey to the keenest anxiety, and he could neither sit nor walk for any length of time, such was the exquisite agony of mind he suffered at the thought that, after all, the young man might fail in his mission, either from want of tact or from over-forwardness. The first supposition of failure presented itself to the squire's mind in by no means such disagreeable colours as the last ; for, even admitting that the wily Jacob Gray should on this one occasion succeeed in eluding Albert's pursuit, there would arise many other opportunities for renewing the same plan of operations with greater chances of success, because with greater experience; but should Jacob Gray once catch a glance of Albert Seyton, all hope of successfully tracing him to his house, through the means of the young lover, wo be at an end.

As minute after minute winged their heavy flight, Learmont's mental fever increased, until it became, at length, almost insupportable. He strode to and fro in his apartment with hasty steps ; then he threw himself into a chair ; then he would raise a cup of wine to his lips, but to lay it down again untasted, as he thought to himself,—

" No : I must keep my mind now clear and active ; for should he be successful, I shall have need of my mental energy to turn the occasion to advantage. Jacob Gray, even when discovered, is not destroyed. It is one thing to track the fox to his lair, and another to kill him. There will yet remain much to be done, even if my most sanguine hopes are realised through the instrumentality of Albert Seyton."

The thought then crossed his mind of parading through the various rooms of his mansion in order to divert the anxiety that was preying upon him; and taking a light in his hand, he commenced a tour somewhat similar to the one he had undertaken when first he arrived in London, only that he was now alone, and the freshness of his enjoyment of all the glitter and splendour which surrounded him on every side was worn off.

In the double action of walking and constant change of place, Learmont did find some little relief.

" He will be successful," he muttered, " and Jacob Gray will be destroyed. He must be successful. Why should he not ? There are a thousand chances to one in his favour. Then I shall breathe freely : the heaviest load that ever pressed upon my heart will be lifted from it ; I shall no longer totter and turn sick and giddy on the brink of the precipice which has so long, as it were, yawned at my feet ; I shall know peace, peace of mind, and, by cultivating the enjoyment of the present I shall, in a short time, learn to forget the past. Forget—forget—can I ever forget? Even now a voice seems to ring in my ear with a fearful cry. Blood—aloud it shrieks; can blood ever be forgotten? Can the cry of the dying man? can the wail of the fatherless child ever fade from the memory of him who has heard them as I have? Can I ever be happy? Was I ever happy? Yes, once; I was a child once, and my heart was spotless as a pearl within its shell. Oh, could I recal the past! but that is madness. The past is gone, and may not be beckoned back again. If man could undo the folded scroll of events which have, in the course of years, taken their progress, it seems to me that human nature would reach some few brief years of its onward march, and then be ever toiling back again to undo what was done. Which of us, if we could live again from earliest infancy the same life, would do as we have done? I am no worse than others. The wisest, the best have felt as I feel now. The blood—blood—the curse of blood! Who whispers that to my heart? I did not do the deed; it was the savage smith; my hands reeked not with the gore. No, no, no. Hence, horrible shadows of the soul, hence, hence—I—I am not, I will not be your victim."

His whole frame trembled; and as was usual with him, when conscience whispered with its awful voice his crimes to his shrinking soul, he felt an utter prostration of every physical energy, and could scarcely crawl to his room.

At the same moment that he reached the door, Albert Seyton, flushed, excited, and nearly breathless, reached it likewise.

Learmont darted towards him, and clutching his arm with frantic eagerness, shrieked, rather than said,—

"Found—found?"

"Yes, yes," cried Albert.

"You—you have traced the villain to his lair? You know where you could lay your hand upon his throat as he sleeps? You could tear his heart out? He—he saw you not, you are sure? Swear by heaven and hell you have found his home!"

"I have, sir," said Albert, amazed at the vehemence and wild excitement of Learmont; "with some difficulty, but still with complete success, I have traced him, and know at this moment where to find him."

"So, so," said Learmont, with a sickly smile, "I—I much rejoice for your sake —for your sake, Albert Seyton, I do rejoice. Let—let me lean on you a moment; a sudden faintness——"

"Shall I summon your attendants, sir?" said Albert, much alarmed at the ghastly looks of the squire, who tremblingly held him by the arm.

"No, no," said Learmont; "'tis nothing, I shall be better presently; I felt so much for you that it made me over anxious, and—and so, you see, as I am of a nervous temperament, I tremble for you—for you, you understand. There is wine upon the table."

Albert led the squire into the room, and then poured out and presented to him some wine, which he drank with eagerness, after which, drawing a long breath, he said,—

"I am much better now;—and so you found him. Do you not rejoice?"

"Indeed I do, sir," said Albert, "and much I long for you to remove all restrictions from me, and allow me to proceed at once to the rescue of her I love."

"All shall be speedily accomplished," said Learmont; "have but a little patience, and all shall be as you ask. Not many days shall elapse when you shall have your heart's desire."

"Sir, you bestow upon me a new life."

"Yes, yes. Let me consider a moment. To-morrow—to-morrow—yes, to-morrow is now at hand. Midnight—aye, midnight. Call upon me here on the morning after to-morrow, not sooner—no, not sooner—midnight is a good hour."

"I scarcely understand you, sir," said Albert, who really thought the squire must be a little insane, he talked so strangely.

"Not understand me, sir?" said Learmont. "Surely I speak clearly—I mean the morning after to-morrow. By then I shall have matured some plan—but say —stay—God of heaven I had forgotten."

" Forgotten what, sir ?"

" You have not told me where he lives."

" 'Tis near at hand, although to reach it he traversed thrice the space he needed to have done."

" 'Tis like him," said Learmont. " Most like the man."

" I know not the name of the street, but I could guide you there, sir."

Learmont sprung to his feet.

"Now, now. On the moment," he cried. " My hat—my sword. You shall show me now."

Then suddenly speaking in a subdued tone, he added,—

" You see, Mr. Seyton, that I am an enthusiast, and what I take an interest in possesses my mind most fully. You perceive that having promised you to stir in this matter, I am inclined to do so well, and amply so ; you shall show me the house in which this man lives, and then I will mature some plan which we can jointly put in execution when we meet again. You understand me quite, Mr. Seyton ?"

" I do, sir, and am most thankful to you."

" You shall have cause to thank me," said Learmont—then as a servant appeared in answer to the bell he had sounded, he cried in a loud voice,—

" My hat and sword. Quick—my swor !"

Both were instant y brought to him, and he commenced hastily descending the stairs with his sword in his hand, and a flush of excitement on his brow, that made him look widely different to the pale trembling man he was but a few short minutes before.

" Pray Heaven," thought Albert, " his wits be not deranged. It would be sad indeed if my only friend were t turn out a madman."

They were soon in the street, and Learmont taking Albert by the arm, said,—

" Remember your promise, and make no sort of demonstration of your presence, until I shall permit you. All now depends upon your discretion. Lead me now as quickly as you can to this man's abode."

" I owe you too much, sir," said A bert, " to quarrel with your commands, whatever restraint they may put upon my own inclination. I shall control my impatience until the time you mention."

" Do so. Then as a reward, I will contrive some means of providing for you, so that you shall never know again what care and trouble are. You shall have a happy destiny."

These words were uttered in a tone so strange, that Albert looked in Learmont's e, to see what expressions accompanied them, and there he saw a lurking smile, which brought a disagreeable feeling of suspicion to his heart for a moment, but no longer, for he chased it away again by reflecting what possible motive could Learmont have for first raising his hopes and then crushing them ; if, indeed, he had not already gone too far to be of any detriment, if he was of no assistance, by enabling him, Albert, to discover the abode of Jacob Gray, and as he fondly imagined that likewise of his beloved and deeply regretted Ada.

" No," he thought, " I am wrong in my suspicions. He who has done so much for me already is entitled to my confidence, beyond the casual feeling of suspicion that may arise from a smile or a particular tone of voice. I will obey him."

" Is there," said Learmont, " any dark and secret place in the vicinity of this man's dwelling from which we may view it securely without being seen ourselves ?"

" There is a door-way, deep and gloomy, opposite the very house he inhabits," replied Albert. " If it be now unoccupied, which it was not before, I should name it as a good place for observation."

" Was it occupied ?"

" Yes ; and by one who seemed as much interested in watching Jacob Gray as I was."

" Indeed ?"

" Aye, sir. A man followed him closely, even as I did, and took up a station nally in the very door I mention."

"That is very strange!" said Learmont, with a troubled air.

"It is ; I cannot account for it, unless some person like yourself is watching him to discover if he be what he seems or not ; or, perchance, some one may have seen Ada, and have been so smitten by her wondrous beauty, as to set a watch upon his house, with the hope that she may come forth."

"I like it not—I like it not," said Learmont musingly. "A watch upon Jacob Gray ! Tis very strange! Bodes it good or evil?"

They had by this time arrived at the corner of the street, in which was situated the obscure shop above which Gray slept, as he supposed, in security, and Albert turning to Learmont, said,—

"This is the street, and yonder is the doorway I mentioned to you."

CHAPTER XCVIII.

ALBERT'S LOVE AND DETERMINATION.—THE SQUIRE'S DREAM.

"LET us cross to it," said Learmont, in a low husky voice, which betrayed how deeply he felt himself interested in the affair.

In a moment they both stood in the dark entry. Learmont's spy was not there for conceiving justly that Jacob Gray was housed for the night, he had, by way of solacing himself after his quarrel with Albert, betaken himself to a neighbouring public-house, where by that time he was deep in a second jug of old ale.

"There is no one here," remarked Learmont.

"No," said Albert; "but I left one here. However, his following Gray might after all have been from mere curiosity, seeing me follow him so closely.

"The house—the house," said Learmont; "which is the house ?"

"Yon dingy-looking dwelling, with that mean shop upon its basement floor."

Learmont looked long and eagerly at the miserable dwelling ; then he muttered,—

"I should know that house again were I absent from it a hundred years. Yes—found—found—at last! The game is played ! Jacob Gray, with all your cunning—with all your art of trickery—you are at last found! Sleep on, if you can sleep, in fancied security ! You know not that your career may soon be ended !"

"You will recollect the house, sir?" said Albert.

"I may forget my own name," said Learmont, "but not that house. Young sir, here is money for you ; let me see you on the morning after to-morrow, and I will have news for you."

He gave Albert his purse as he spoke, and then, without waiting for a reply, he strode from the spot, leaving the young man in great astonishment at his singular behaviour.

"Till to-morrow and then the morning after that," said Albert, "is a precious ime to control my impatience. If I could but catch the merest glance of Ada, it would help me to sustain my impatience. Oh, what a Tantalus-like state is mine, to be even now within so short a distance of her I love, and yet unable to make my presence known to her. My very voice would reach her were I to raise it above its ordinary compass, but I dare not. I have bound myself on my word of honour, and that must not be broken—farewell then, for a time, dear Ada ! To-morrow, during daylight, I will try to sleep, so that when the sun has set, and I may, without fear of being seen by Jacob Gray, take up my station here, I may be able to watch the house you inhabit, and please myself with the thought of being so near you, even though I cannot see you, or speak to you. Truly I am glad the squire has left me here, for here will I remain until the morning's light warns me of the danger of recognition by Jacob Gray if I longer tarry."

With his arms folded on his breast, and his eyes fixed upon the window, which he pleased himself by imagining belonged to Ada's room, Albert Seyton kept possession of the doorway.

In the meanwhile, Learmont, with feelings of exultation at his heart, strode with a hasty step towards the Chequers at Westminster.

"I have him now—I have him now," he muttered; "I will stir Andrew Britton, to destroy him, and as for this Albert Seyton, from whom, were he to live, I should prophesy much trouble, I will give him on the morning that he calls upon me, a subtle poison, in a cup of wine; but not enough shall he have to leave his body within my doors. No—the dose shall be skilfully graduated, so that some hours shall elapse ere the wild excitement passes through his system. Then he may lie down and die in the public streets or where he lists, so he is out of my way—'tis a deep skill I have obtained in poisons, and it shall do me good service."

He then paused, and tearing a leaf from his pocket-book, he wrote on it the words which we are aware were on the note Britton received in the midst of his drunken orgies at the Chequers, and which Learmont got conveyed to him by means of a boy who was wandering houseless about the streets.

Satisfied, then, that he had everything in train for the destruction of Jacob Gray, Learmont bent his steps homewards in a more satisfied state of mind than he had ever been in before, and resolved to attempt immediately to procure some sleep, before he should thoroughly mature his yet but projected plan of murdering Gray on the next evening.

The difficulties in the way of executing the deed safely and securely were very great; for not only was Gray to be destroyed, but his written confession was to be secured before its superscription should be perceived by any one who might officiously communicate to the magistrate that such a document had been addressed to him.

To accomplish all this required skill, courage, caution, and a favourable train of circumstances; but, wearied as was Learmont then, as well by the violence of his alternating passions, as by want of anything in the shape of refreshing sleep, for some nights he felt himself unequal to the details of a plan which should command success, if no very extraordinary obstacle presented itself in his way. He therefore hurried home, and giving directions to be called at an early hour in the morning, he threw off some of his upper clothing, and wearied as he was, soon sunk into a slumber—not, however, a calm and easy one, for he was, as usual, tortured with frightful dreams, and images of terror flitted before his mental vision. Sometimes he would fancy himself in the midst of the fathomless ocean, tossed about at the mercy of every surge, while each wave that burst over him seemed crusted with blood. Ravenous monsters of the deep would stretch their long tendril-like arms from deep vallies in the ocean's bed, and strive to drag him into their insatiate maws; then suddenly, "a change would come o'er the spirit of his dream," and he would lie upon the burning sands of Africa. For hundreds of miles there would be nothing but sand—sand hot and scorching to the touch as the fire-ash of a glowing furnace—then a fearful drought came over him, and he shrieked for water, and thought what a heaven it would be to be once more dashed madly to and fro by the surging waves—then a caravan would appear in sight upon the pathless desert— he heard the tinkle of the camel's bells—he saw the weary men, with bronze complexions and travel-worn apparel, come slowly on, and he saw that they had water, for all were drinking deep draughts of the delicious beverage. One then asked him if he too would drink, and then he could not speak. His tongue seemed glued to the roof of his mouth, and, one by one, as they passed him by, they asked him to drink, and he could not say yes. Then the caravan slowly faded away, and when the last man was far across sandy the plain, his voice came again, and he shrieked for water—for but one drop to quench for a passing moment the burning fever of his throat.

The dream was horrible, but the vision that followed was more terrible, because the suffering was mental as well as physical.

Learmont fancied he was at the foot of a high winding staircase. He commenced slowly ascending, and then he heard behind him a sound like the rushing wind, and looking back, he saw linked, in an awful companionship, three livid spectres, as if fresh from the reeking corruptions of the tomb. The flesh hung rag-like upon the yellow moistened bones, and huge drops of green and sickly corruption fell dashing like the preludes of a thunder storm, upon the stairs. Worms and moist things were crawling in and out the sightless eyes—the rattling lips grinned horribly, and

amid the havoc of the grave, Learmont could recognise the features of those whom he had driven to death. Slowly they came after him, and a voice seemed to ring in his ears, saying,—

"They will catch you, and fold you in their dreadful embrace, ere you reach the top of those stairs. Fly, Learmont, fly!"

Then he tried, with a scream of terror, to ascend the staircase like the wind, but

No. 47.

his feet seemed glued to the steps, and he could ascend but slowly step by step, while he felt that his pursuers were gaining on him momentarily, and that he must in another moment be in their grasp.   He heard the chattering of the fleshless gums —he smelt the rank odour of the grave, and yet he could proceed but at a funeral pace.   Now they were upon him—now they gibbered in his ears—they clutched him by the throat—the long skeleton fingers press upon his throat—he his lost! One moan bust from the agonised sleeper, and he awoke shrieking,—

"Help—help! save me yet, Heaven—oh, save me, I do repent!   God have mercy upon me!"

He sprung from his bed, and, with dishevelled hair, eyes starting from their sockets, and a face livid with agony, he sunk upon his knees, just as the terrified domestics, hearing his cries, knocked loudly at his chamber door.

Then succeeded a death-like stillness, and Learmont, in a deep sepulchral voice, said,—

"God of Heaven, was it a dream?   Dare I ever sleep again?".

The knocking continued at his door, and he rose to his feet.

"Peace—peace!" he cried.   "Away, I did but dream."

The servants retired from the door gazing at each other in mute terror, for Learmont's cries had alarmed the whole house, and filled them with superstitious fears.

"So—so," said the squire, when he trimmed his light, and recovered a little from his state of mental excitement; "that was a dream—how terrible—how terrible. Can I ever sleep again in peace? Dare I lay down my weary head upon my pillow with the hope of repose? no—no. And yet there are potent drugs that I have heard wrap the soul in oblivion, or else in the slumber they create, visit it in gorgeous shapes, and present rare phantasies to the mental eye. I will try them. To-morrow—to-morrow, I will try them. I may find peace then; but I must not tempt sleep again. 'Tis too terrible—too terrible."

CHAPTER XCIX.

ADA'S FAITH IN ALBERT SEYTON.—THE CONFIDENCE OF A GENEROUS HEART.

SIR FRANCIS HARTLETON was never so much vexed in his life as he was at the supposed treachery of Albert Seyton.   He revolved in his mind over and over again, how he should tell Ada of the scene that had occurred between him and her lover, and of all his suspicions concerning him, and at length he resolved that Lady Hartleton should be the medium of communicating the unwelcome intelligence of Albert's defection from his love and entertainment by Ada's worst enemy.

For this purpose it became necessary that Ada should be put in possession of more facts concerning herself than the humane and considerate magistrate had, as yet, thought proper to burthen her mind with.   This he much regretted, because he had hoped that before he had occasion to mention Learmont's name particularly to Ada, he should be able to couple with it something more than mere surmises, however well founded such surmises might be.

While he was in his own private room, considering deeply and painfully this matter, a note arrived to him, which was immediately another source of vexation, inasmuch as it hurried on the events which he would have been glad to see develop themselves a little further before he actively interfered in them.

The letter was from the Secretary of State, intimating that the charges confidentially made against Learmont, by him, Sir Francis Hartleton, must either be abandoned, or speedily proved, for that a dissolution of Parliament was about to take place, and it was absolutely necessary to know in whose hands the Learmont property was.

"This," said Sir Francis, as he laid down the minister's note, "must bring affairs to a crisis. I must apprehend Jacob Gray now, and Britton, and trust to one or other of them committing Learmont ; a slender hope, I am afraid, since no mercy can be offered to Gray on account of Vaughan's business, and Britton is the last person to expect a confession from."

Sir Francis then took from a secret drawer the small scraps of paper which he procured from mad Maude, and read them again attentively.

"These are interesting to me," he said, "as leading me on in my chain of conjecture ; but they are no evidence, for, first of all, who is to prove they were ever written by Jacob Gray, or in his possession ; and secondly, they are too vague in themselves to be of any importance, unless merely used as evidence corroborative of facts which can be nearly proved without them. The question now is, has Gray written a full disclosure of who Ada is, and what crime has led to her being placed in so singular a position, or not? Well, I will crave of the minister another week, and then consent to withdraw my charges against Learmont for the present. He must triumph, I suppose, and I cannot help it."

He then sought Lady Hartleton, and informing her of what he had discovered concerning Albert, begged her to communicate the same to Ada as carefully as she could, so as not to shock her sensitive mind too suddenly with the news of the bad faith of him to whom she had given her heart.

Lady Hartleton was so much accustomed to rely upon the judgment of her husband, that, although she was not without some lingering doubts, after all there might be some possible explanation of the conduct of her lover, she consented to the task which was set her, and immediately went to Ada to communicate the sad intelligence.

"My dear Ada," said Lady Hartleton, "there are circumstances which have induced Sir Francis not to ask Mr. Seyton to come here."

Ada started, and with a heightened colour she said in her soft gentle voice,—

"Lady, you have already done too much for the poor and friendless girl whom chance threw in your way—I ought never to have accepted——"

"Now, Ada, you mistake me," interrupted Lady Hartleton, "the cause which prevented Sir Francis from bringing Albert here with him, has no reference to anything but the young man's want of worth."

"Albert Seyton's want of worth?" said Ada.

"Yes—my dear Ada. You have a great enemy in London—an enemy who would take your life, and when I tell you that Albert Seyton is in the confidential service of that enemy, there is good cause of suspicion."

"Suspicion of what, lady?"

"Of his want of faith."

Ada shook her head. "No," she said, "there is no want of faith in Albert Seyton. Where I can give my heart and my faith, I never suspect. You do not know him, dear Lady Hartleton."

"But he is with your enemies."

"Still he is true."

"He may have sold himself to them, and be even now plotting destruction."

"Albert Seyton loves me," said Ada.

"But you are open to conviction."

"No, no—there are some things that the heart will cherish, despite all reasoning. You suspect Albert Seyton, my dear Lady Hartleton ; but, let appearances be what they may, he can and will explain them all. He may be, from his own honest, unsuspecting nature, the dupe of villains, but he is not one himself."

"Then you preserve your good opinion of him, Ada, despite all unfavourable appearances?"

"I do, as Heaven is my judge. He is innocent of all wrong—my heart tells me he is. I must go to him myself."

"Nay, that were, indeed, to court destruction—for where he is, is a fatal place for you."

"He will protect me."

"But, admitting all your confidence to be well grounded, he may may not have the power."

"But I must see him," said Ada ; "he must have an opportunity of clearing himself from the suspicion that surrounds his name in the mind of you and Sir Francis, my dear and only friends. Oh, why did I not follow him myself, when Providence threw him in my way ? Then all would have been well, and perhaps, with a few brief words, he would have explained every seeming contradiction in his present and his past conditions."

"I will not deny to you, Ada," said Lady Hartleton, "that such a thought crossed my mind when Sir Francis first spoke to me on this point. 'Tis said that suspicion breeds suspicion, but in this case it is not so; for your generous and noble confidence in your lover has imbued me with much of your own feelings."

"You believe, then, he may be innocent ?"

"I certainly do."

"Bless you, lady, for your noble confidence. You have given me more pleasure by that word than you gave me pain by hinting disparagement of Albert—that never reached my heart, for it was proof against it; but your confidence is kindred with my own feelings, and shares their place. As I have faith in the reality of my own existence, I have faith in Albert Seyton's constancy and truth. Oh, tell Sir Francis, your noble husband, that he is mistaken. I implore him, for my sake, to seek him once more, and to question him, when he will meet with no guile— no evasions—but the honest truth will flow from his lips, and his innocence of purpose will be apparent."

"Ada, a heart so full of dear emotions, and so replete with noble confidence, as yours, deserves, indeed, a happy fate. Be you tranquil, and I will urge my husband to the step you now propose ; and if my earnest prayers can make you happy, you will never know another care."

Ada could only thank Lady Hartleton with her eyes, and the kind-hearted wife immediately left the room in search of her husband, much shaken in her own mind with respect to Albert's supposed faithlessness—so infectious is generosity and confidence among noble spirits.

While this conversation, so painfully interesting to Ada, was proceeding between her and Lady Hartleton, Sir Francis was informed that the spy he had set upon the house inhabited by Gray wished particularly to see him, and upon the man's admittance, he informed Sir Francis of his hunt after Gray the evening before, and his fears that some person was after him for some other purpose.

"A light and active young fellow," the man said, "kept as close upon his heels as I did ; he would not lose sight of him a moment, and once or twice nearly baulked me in keeping my man in sight. Thus, when I had traced him safely from the rich squire's house to his lodgings in Buckingham-street, this fellow popped himself in the very same doorway from which I and the other officers have, from time to time, watched Gray come and go."

"What kind of young man was he ?" said the magistrate.

"A light active fellow of the middle height, with a clear blue eye and long hair. A slight moustache is on his upper lip."

"'Tis Seyton," thought Sir Francis. "Thank you; keep an eye on him, and, should anything particular occur to Jacob Gray, mind you lay hands on this young man you mention."

"We shall want assistance, then, sir."

"That you shall have. Take with you some one on whom you can rely to-night. You go on duty at eight, do you not?"

"Yes, sir. Philip Lee is on the watch now."

"Very well. Go now, and take your rest. Your duty in watching this man will not last much longer, for he must be arrested within a week. Did you leave this young man you mention on the spot when you came away?"

"No, sir. We had a sort of scuffle who should stand in the passage, and he ran away."

"Ah, that is not in his favour," thought Sir Francis. "My poor Ada! your best affections are thrown away. You may go now, but let me see you in the morning with a report of your night's work."

The man departed, and Sir Francis Hartleton remained for some time in melancholy thought.

"Before the week expires," he said, "I must go myself and arrest Jacob Gray, ostensibly for the murder of Vaughan. I may find some written paper of importance. Well, well, it must be so. Ada, your fortunes hang upon the events of the next four or five days."

CHAPTER C.

LEARMONT'S VISIT TO THE CHEQUERS.—THE SLEEPING SMITH.

By nine o'clock, according to his appointment with Andrew Britton, Learmont was in the park. His face was dreadfully pale—his limbs shook under him as he gladly availed himself of one of the wooden seats on which to rest his wearied and exhausted frame.

"When will this end?" he muttered. "Four nights now without repose—I am sinking into the grave; yet this last night, with its feverish dreams, and awful spectral visitations, has been much the worst I ever passed. Surely it must have arisen from my great anxiety just now concerning Jacob Gray, and when he is dead I shall have some peace. Yes, then, surely, I shall feel much relieved, but not till then—not till then. 'Tis the time, and yet Andrew Britton comes not. Dare he refuse to obey my summons? or is he sleeping off some deep drunkenness of last evening, and deaf to time? The sot! I cannot do without him in this matter, for Gray may be armed, or he may even procure assistance. We must be in force sufficient to make sure work. Let me think. Yes—yes. 'Twere far better to kill him in his own abode than in mine. Of what use is his confession to him, unless placed somewhere where it may be easily found? None whatever. I shall be able easily to lay my hand upon it, and, when I have that document once fairly in my grasp, I shall feel myself again. I and Britton will go at midnight, and make our way into the house as best we can. No lock can stand the practised skill of the smith; and, from the ancient grudge he has to Jacob Gray, he will enter into this affair with a good will. I am sure he will. Moreover, I can inflame his passion ere we go."

Learmont began to get very impatient, as Britton did not make his appearance; and, after waiting a full hour beyond the specified time, he rose from the seat, and, with a bitter execration on his lips, he walked slowly in the direction in which Britton must come in proceeding from the Chequers.

Still the squire met him not, and finally, he left the park, by Storey's Gate, and walked on until he came within sight of the ancient hotel in which the unconscious Britton was lying fast asleep, with no great prospect of arousing himself for some hours to come.

Learmont paused as he said,—

"Now, if I thought there was no chance of being known, I would call upon the savage smith, and at once ascertain the cause of this broken appointment. Let me consider—I have not seen him for a week—perchance he is ill—perchance dead. The latter would be a blessed release, if Jacob Gray preceded him, and he left no damning evidence behind, a matter in which I have always had my doubts as regarded Britton. Surely none at this low pot-house can know me? I think I may venture—the stake I have in hand is worth the risk. Yes, I will make inquiry, for if Jacob Gray die not to-night, I shall have another night of misery—oh! I shall sleep well when I am assured that he sleeps never again to awaken."

Learmont, however, still lingered, ere he could make up his mind to call upon the drunken smith, at the Chequers, for he was most fearful that such an act, trifling as it was, might form a link in the chain of evidence against him, should any accidental circumstances occur to fix suspicion upon him, after Gray's murder should have been achieved.

"And yet," he reasoned, "what can I do? stay, a thought strikes me—I can send some one with an inquiry, and then shape my own conduct by the answer. Ah, yon poor beggar-woman, with her squalid children, will, for the promise of an alms, do my errand.

He walked up to a miserable looking object,, who was shivering upon a door-step, with some wretched-looking children around her. The moment he shewed an intention of speaking to her, she commenced a piteous appeal for charity.

"Oh, sir—kind sir," she said, "bestow a trifle upon a starving widow, and her wretched children—my husband was a waterman, sir, he was murdered on the Bishop's walk, at Lambeth, and since then, we have been starving."

Learmont reeled from the woman as she spoke, and he felt that him she spoke of, was the man who had met so cruel a death from his hand.

"Not her—not her;" he muttered. "I must go myself—a cursed chance to meet her—now I shall dream of that, too, I suppose—curse on the dreams—me-thinks I hear that man"s gasping screams, as he fell upon the snow, after I had run him through; but I must not torture myself thus—I will to the Chequers—a sudden faintness has come over my heart—I will take a cup of wine there, and make my inquires cautiously."

The woman's voice sunk into a low wail of anguish and despair, as she saw Learmont turn away, and then bursting into tears, she sobbed over her famishing children, in all the bitterness of a mother's grief.

"God help us—God help us," she cried, "and Heaven have mercy on your father's murderer."

Learmont walked hastily towards the Chequers, and early as it was, sounds of mirth and revelry were issuing from it. Bond, the butcher, was waiting for Brit-ton to rise, and amusing himself by chanting Bacchanalian songs the while, and drinking deeply. His roaring voice arrested Learmont's steps, and he wondered who it could be that so rivalled even the lungs of Britton, as he heard the follow-ing strains :—

> " Up, to the skies
>   Let the goblet rise,
>   We heed nor wind nor weather ;
>   We moisten each lip
>   With the wine sip,
>   And we clank our cans together.
>   Clank—clank—clank.
>
> "Drink, drink to the vine,
>   'Tis a goddess fine,
>   There ne'er was such another ;
>   Its fruit rich and rare,
>   Will banish all care,
>   And all bad feelings smother.
>   Clank—clank—clank.
>
> " Fill, fill to the brim,
>   A bumper to him,
>   Who leaves in his glas no drain ;
>   He knows not a strife,
>   But so calm his life
>   Glides on without a pain.
>   Clank—clank—clank."

Learmout stepped into the dingy, dark passage, and making his way up to the bar, he, in an assumed voice, said,—

" A cup of your best wine, landlord."

The wine was placed before him, and then he said in a careless tone,—

" Has Master Britton risen yet ?"

" Oh, dear, no, your worship," said the landlord. " He won't be up for a good hour or two yet. He went out in his chair last evening, and came home all over bruises from a tumble. Oh, such a man as he is—but perhaps your worship knows him ?"

" No, but I have heard of him."

" Ah, all Westminster has heard of him. He drinks hugely. He is fast asleep now in his attic. He won't be in any other room, because he says he should have to murder somebody for treading heavy over his head, if he was lower down in the house. A strange fancy, your worship—a strange fancy."

" Indeed it is."

A violent pull from the parlour bell now induced the landlord to rush from his bar to answer it, with the exclamation of,—

" That's Master Bond, I'll warrant. He's as bad as Britton, every bit, only he helps him to drink a vast quantity of liquor."

" In the attic," muttered Learmont to himself, as he glanced round him, and saw that he was alone, and the staircase leading to the upper part of the house immediately before him. " I will go and see him. My business brooks no delay."

He accordingly ascended the stairs, and was half way up before the landlord came back.

" Well, I never," exclaimed the host ; " fairly done out of a cup of the best wine in the house. He looked a very respectable man, too, though no beauty. Who would have thought he'd have gone off without paying in this minute ? The villain !"

The landlord walked to the door, and looked up and down the street ; then he came back, shaking his head, as he said,—

" How he must have run, too, for he aint to be seen anywhere. Well, if I catch him again, I'll be even with him, though he is a lanky. Two yards of bad stuff, he is—a vagabond. To cheat me ! He might as well rob a church !"

Learmont had just about as much idea of bilking the landlord out of payment for his wine as he had of robbing a church ; but his mind had been by far too intent upon his own object to think of the money at all.

With hasty strides he ascended the dark, narrow staircase of the old Chequers, and seeing a half-open door on the topmost landing, he pushed it wide open, and entering a room saw Andrew Britton, perfectly dressed, lying in a deep sleep across the bed.

CHAPTER CI.

THE SEARCH.—THE ASSIGNATION.—BRITTON'S SURPRISE AND EXULTATION.

LEARMONT stood for some few moments gazing on the bloated swarthy countenance of the smith, without making an effort to awaken him from his slumber. Dark thoughts chased each other through the mind of the 'squire, and he said, through his clenched teeth,—

"Sot !—Villain !—But that you are useful to me still, I would strangle you as there you lie in your drunken sleep ! If Jacob Gray was dead, this moment should be your last, Andrew Britton ! But I have use for you, and the opportunity which now occurs, may never occur again. Still I may do something even now ; I may search to see if I can find any papers or documents in this room. He may, notwithstanding my suspicions to the contrary, have left behind him some record of the crimes he has been engaged in !''

Learmont walked carefully about the room, and peered into every probable place, in the expectation of being repaid by some discovery of importance to his interests, but there was not a scrap of writing in the chamber that he could discover.

" Where can he have put the papers he always boasted of having found upon the body of him who met his death on that eventful night, at the old Smithy ?   He said there was a pocket-book, in which were family documents touching me very nearly ; and Jacob Gray, of his own knowledge, confirmed the tale, regretting the while that his own fears would not allow him to rob the dead of those important papers. If Britton has them, they must be here somewhere.''

Eagerly again did Learmont examine the room, but there was nothing to be found of the character he wished, and he was fain, at length, to give up the search in despair.

Then he half-drew his sword and thought he would kill Britton, but a second thought told how much safer he might do so on some of his visits to his own house, and he sheathed his sword again, muttering,—

" The time will come—the time will come. I will first use him, and then he shall die. Now to awaken this slumbering clod.''

He seized Britton by the collar, and shook him very roughly, crying,—

" Britton—Andrew Britton, awake !''

" You be d—d !'' muttered Britton.   " Ale all around ; I think I see it—it's a lie !''

"Andrew Britton awake,'' cried Learmont in his ear.

" Con—con—confusion to Jacob Gray,'' growled Britton.   " Curse everbody !''

Learmont now shook him so violently that he opened his dull heavy eyes and fixed them on the 'squires face, with a stare of such astonishment, that it was doubtful to Learmont if he were in his senses or not.

" Do you know me, Andrew Britton ?'' he said.

" I should think so,'' said Britton.   " It's a rum dream, though I could almost swear I was awake.''

" You are.''

" Am I ? That's a lie.''

" Feel my hand. 'Tis flesh and blood.''

" You—you don't mean to say, 'squire, that you are here,'' cried Britton, starting from the bed.   " What's the matter? What have I done ?''

" Nothing ; but I wish you to be up and doing. I have discovered the abode of Jacob Gray, and he says that poor silly Britton will never cope with him. He says that Andrew Britton's muddle head is only fit for the pillory, and that he has more cunning in his little finger than you have in you whole composition. So says Jacob Gray.''

" Now curse him, I'll have his life,'' cried Britton.

" You shall, if you will be guided by me ; I can take you to the house he is in ; I can make you sure of him now, Britton.''

" You can 'squire ?''

" I can.''

" Then I'm your man—drunk, or sober, I'll cut Jacob Gray's throat, with pleasure. The only disagreeable thing will be, that when he's dead, one can't taunt him about it.''

" It will be revenge enough to kill him,'' said Learmont.   " Will you be ready this night ?''

" This minute if you like.''

" No—it must be at midnight—we must be very careful yet, for Gray is cunning, and moreover, he does not now reside in a lone house, where no cries would be heard. He lives now where there may be many people, and it would detract from our triumph over Gray to be hanged for his murder.''

" It would rather,'' muttered Britton ; " we must be cunning then. I think I'm quite as cunning as Gray any day.''

"Be guided by me, and all will be well."

"What is your plan?"

"That you meet me to-night at twelve o'clock, and bring with you tools to open locks."

"Yes, I have them."

"Then we will make our way to Gray's chamber, and silently, if possible, kill him."

"Silently or not, he shall die; but where is the young scion of——"

"Hush—that is now no obstacle; meet me to-night at twelve."

"I will 'squire. You have brought me tne most welcome news I've heard yet for a long time."

"Now promise me, Britton, solemnly, that you will drink nothing till this enterprise is concluded?"

No. 48.

"Drink nothing ? Why I live upon strong drink. How do you suppose I am to exist till twelve o'clock at night without anything to drink ? I must drink, and there's an end of that, Squire Learmont."

" If you must drink, let me beg of you to do so then in moderation."

"Never fear me, when there's actual work to be done. Where shall we meet ?"

" At the steps of my house," said Learmont. "Be punctual and sober, and remember, Andrew Britton, how much depends upon the proceedings of this night. You yourself daily and hourly incur danger from Jacob Gray greater than you dream of. Suppose him suddenly off by sickness, and we, not knowing of it, sleeping in fancied security, while his damning confession of his passes from hand to hand until it reaches him who is panting to destroy us--I mean Sir Francis Hartleton. Think of that and tremble, Andrew Britton. Then again, who knows a day when his insatiate avarice may induce him to fancy he has accumulated gold enough to live independently in some other country, and leave England for ever after. Mark my words, Andrew Britton, after taking measures for our destruction by leaving behind him documents which too many will be willing to believe and act upon. He has used language which, translated into plainer terms, would expressly signify such an intention ; and more than once has he smiled to himself, and chuckled over the imaginary account of the execution of the sot—the ass—the clod-brained Andrew Britton. Do you mark my words ?"

" I do, 'squire—say no more—he dies, if he had twenty lives. Curses on him —he dies, I say. Be assured I shall not fail to meet you at the hour your name. If there be one thing I live for above another it is to slaughter Jacob Gray. He calls me a sot does he, because now and then I take a glass too much ? Why, he would be drunk himself morning, noon, and night, if he had the courage."

" Certainly," said Learmont. "He hoards his money."

"By-the-bye, 'squire, when we've knocked him on the head, we'll find where he keeps this same hoard of money."

" We will—we will, Britton, and you shall have an ample share of it for your pains. Be sure you are punctual. Be secret and vigilant."

" Never fear me, 'squire, I'll only take enough drink to steady my nerves, and as the clock strikes twelve to-night, I will be at your door."

" Adieu," said Learmont, as he stalked out of the attic. " Adieu, Andrew Britton, this night makes or mars your future fortunes. The idiotic sot," muttered Learmont to himself, as he descended the stairs, " he falls easily into the trap, which will eventually prove his own death, so shall I be free of both my enimies."

" There goes a vagabond," said Britton, when the 'squire had left him. " He thinks to gammon me, does he ? but I'm deeper than he thinks for. Curse that Gray ! I will kill him for my old grudge against him, but I'll not only have all his money, but, if I lay hands on his confession, the squire must be a stouter fellow than I think him if he gets it."

Meanwhile Learmont, full of dark thoughts, proceeded slowly down the stair-case until he reached the door opening into the passage, which, although wide open when he passed through, was now closed ; and on the outer side was the back of mine host himself, who was supporting his corporeal substance against it, while, with many flourishes and amplifications of his arm, he detailed to some of his gossipping neighbours how grievously he had been cheated, by a tall pale man in a cloak, out of a flagon of the best wine the Chequers could afford.

" My masters," he said, " the villain had an odd look, you will understand, but not a poor look; for a ring sparkled on his finger that was worth many pounds, as sure as I'm a sinner, and we are all sinners."

" Ah, that's true as regards us all being sinners," said one. " Now there's Mr. Sniffler, the godly minister, who preached at Paul's ——"

" Hear me out—hear me out," cried the landlord, to whom the pleasure of tell-ing the story was almost an indemnification for his loss. " As I was a saying, I was a standing, with my back against the cupboard in my bar, as I might stand now, when all of a sudden comes ———"

At this moment Learmont gave the door so vigorous a push that the landlord fell forward on to his hands and knees, with a cry of wrath, as he supposed some one of his household was the cause of this *malapropos* accident.

" Do you block up your doors," said Learmont, haughtily, " and hinder your guests from going forth at their own pleasure ?"

" Well, I never!" cried the landlord, scrambling to his feet. " You—you haven't paid me for my wine; you know you have not."

Learmont took from his pocket a piece of silver, and threw it on the floor; then, drawing his cloak tightly round him, he stalked from the house with a word."

" Well now, neighbours," said the landlord, " did you ever see the like of that ? That's the very man who went away without ing me for my wine."

" Are you quite sure he hasn't been up stairs, and stolen something ?" suggested one.

" Gracious me!" cried the landlord ; " I never thought of that. Hilloa—hilloa ; there's mur—"

"So you won't be quiet," cried Britton, suddenly appearing, and giving the landlord a knock on the head that made him stagger again ; " who do you suppose will live here to be annoyed by your noise, eh ?"

" But your majesty," said the landlord, " here's been a long thief here wih a cloak."

" There hasn't," said Britton.

" An, it please your majesty, these worthy neighbours saw him, and—"

" They didn't," roared Britton ; " bring me brandy, and whoever says they saw or heard anything that I say nay to, I'll make him eat the measure."

The landlord now merely cast up his eyes, and made a movement with his hands, as much as to signify it's no use saying anything, let us be wise and silent, and then hurried into his bar, to execute the imperious smith's order.

When Britton entered the parlour, he was vociferously welcomed by Bond, but the smith beckoned him to one of the windows, and when the bulky butcher obeyed the summons, Britton whispered in his ear :—

" Bond, you promised to lend me your cleaver, in case I wanted it."

" So I did."

" Well, I do want it."

" You shall have it, my boy—is it to smash that fellow with, who you mentioned ?"

" It is ; but mum's the word. Let me have the cleaver some time before twelve to-night."

" I'll give it a sharpen, and bring it you, you may depend."

" Thank you," said Britton, " upon my soul I wouldn't miss using it to-night for a thousand pounds."

CHAPTER CII.

THE HOUR OF ELEVEN.—GRAY IN HIS SOLITARY HOME.—THE LOVER'S WATCH.—
THE EVE OF THE MURDER.

THE night set in dark and lowering, and heavy masses of black clouds piled themselves up in the southern sky long before the hour appointed by Learmont for the attempt upon the life of Jacob Gray. A cold wind swept round the corner of the streets, and occasionally a dashing shower of rain would sweep horizontally along for a moment, and then cease, as the cloud, from whence sprang the shower, swept onwards on the wings of the wind through the realms of space.

Many of the lamps were extinguished by the sudden gusts of wind, and the watchmen wisely betook themselves to their various boxes, comforting their consciences with the conviction that no decent foot-pad or house-breaker, had any right to be out on such a disagreeable night.

People who had homes to go to, and warm fire-sides to sit down by, and happy smiling faces to welcome them, hurried through the streets in search of such dear enjoyments, while the poor houseless creatures who had no home—no kind kindred, no friend to warm the heart with a soft cheering smile, crept into old door-ways and covered courts, and half-built houses, huddling themselves up with a shiver, to try by the unconsciousness of sleep to forget for awhile their miseries.

There was one though who heeded no wind nor weather—one to whom the cutting blast, the dashing rain, and the general discomfort out of doors was nothing, for his heart and brain were too full of brighter, fairer objects, to allow the smallest space for a consideration of the more external face of nature—so for him the elements might wage what war they liked—he heeded them not, for his heart was crammed with fire from Heaven, and the sunshine of his soul made its own beauty in his breast.   That one was Albert Seyton, who, as soon as the shades of evening had made it safe for him to do so, had silently and cautiously ensconced himself in the ancient door-way immediately opposite to Gray's house, determining there to watch until the morning's dawn over the house, which he fondly believed contained his dearly-beloved, lost Ada.

One by one he saw the lights put out in the house, with the exception of two, and one of those he pleased himself by imagining lit up the chamber of Ada. Now and then a shadow would flit across the blind at the window of that room, and the fond lover, in his ardent creative imagination, endeavoured to trace in it the beauty of form, the sylph-like symmetry of her he loved.

"Yes—yes," he said, "she is there, my beautiful Ada. Oh, could she but guess how fond, how true a heart was beating for her here. How vigilant a sentinel was watching lest harm should come to her through the long hours of the night.   Could she but dream of much—were some kind angel to whisper to her as she slept that her lover was near her, that he watched over, and blessed her as she slept, what smiles would kindle on her face, what flashing tenderness, would beam from her, and what a new-born joy would spring up in her, perhaps, heavy heart."

Albert crossed his arms upon his breast, and waited more than an hour without the least interruption, and then, just as the only other light in the house, besides the one which he pleased himself by fancying burned in Ada's chamber, was put out, and the entrance to the deep door-way in which he was became darkened by a human form, and Sir Francis Hartleton's spy stood for a moment or two muttering to himself, without observing Seyton, who drew back silently, resolved to wait a few moments to see if he intended a stay or not.

"A nice night," muttered the man. "I think I see myself waiting here. All's right, I dare say. If I come once an hour, it will be ample time enough There's a gust of wind. It's enough to make a fellow's marrow feel cold."

With these words he cast another look up at the house inhabited by Gray, and then struck off to a public-house, which was at the corner of the street.

"A good riddance," said Albert, "although I wonder what on earth he can be watching Gray for. A few hours though must end all my suspense and restore her to me. No doubt even now the rich squire is maturing some plan to aid me effectually. I am well guided by his wisdom, for he says truly that Ada would never be perfectly happy without knowing what those papers contained which Gray sets such store by, and any rash attempt to rescue Ada might involve their destruction. I must be patient—I must be patient."

The light which Albert Seyton took such interest in came from Jacob Gray's room ; he had not stirred out the whole of the day, and the tempestuous state of the evening induced him to abandon all intention of leaving his home. About sun set he had crept down stairs to the shop, and desired his landlady to procure him some refreshment, carefully locking his room door even for the few moments he was absent from it in making his request. Then, when he returned, he paced to and fro until the viands he had ordered were brought to him, when, with an attempt at a smile, he said—

"A bad night—the wind howls fearfully."

"Ah, you are right, sir," said the woman; "there's ever so many tiles blowed off of our house, and I'm sure I don't know what I shall do, for there the chimney in the next room smokes, and the people as lived there is gone."

"Indeed—then your next room is untenanted."

"Yes, sir, it is—more's the pity."

"Aye—more's the pity," said Gray. "'Tis far better."

"Better, sir?"

Gray started, for he had uttered his thought loud enough to be heard.

"Nothing—nothing," he said; "good evening—you can leave these things; I am going to rest."

"Good night, sir; I do hope as the wind won't go on howling in this way. It hasn't come down our chimnies in such a schocking way since we had a death in the house,"

"A death!" cried Gray; "don't talk to me of deaths, woman—don't croak to me; I—I—good night—good nght."

"Well I never," muttered the woman to herself, as she left the room; he is a very odd man to be sure. One never knows w it to say to him."

"How dare she talk to me of deaths in the house?" muttered Gray, "there is no death in the house—a croaking hag—I am very well—I—I never was better— death—death—I hate the word. Curses on her for putting it in my head. I am exceedingly well to-night—quite strong and well. Let the wind howl—if any one dies it will not be me. No—I am so very—very well."

He sat down now, and fixed his eyes intently on the clock, between the lining and outer cloth of which he had hidden his confession.

"There—there hangs what would be more than a nine day's wonder," he muttered, "for all the gaping fools in London. There hangs what would bring the high, the proud, the mighty Squire Learmont to a scaffold; and Britton, too the savage smith, whose hands so itch to be imbued in my blood. Ha! ha! I have them, when I like—but I bide my time—I bide my time. Yet why do I feel this horror—why do my hands shake, and my lips stick together for want of healthful moisture? This is what they call nervousness—mere physical weakness. I shall get rid of all this when I am far from England—yes, I shall be quite well then. Now, I really wonder if ever, in after years, I shall come to believe what priests prate about. Is there a Heaven? and—and, more awful question still, is there a hell? What am I saying? I shall drive myself mad if I think thus. I wil hope nothing—fear nothing—believe nothing—nothing—nothing."

The disturbed state of his mind deprived him of all appetite, and he forced rather than enjoyed his meal, of which he scantily partook. Then folding his arms upon the table, he leant his head upon them, and fell into a disturbed and harrassing slumber—a slumber that brought with it no refreshment, but weakened both mind and body by allowing the imagination to prey unchecked upon the nervous system.

Eleven o'clock boomed forth sullenly from the church clocks, now sounding clear and startingly loud as a gust of wind took the sound, and then sinking to the faintest indication of a sound, as the fickle element whirled in some contrary direction, destroying its own conducting power. Learmont was standing, like a statue of melancholy, in his own chamber, and he heard the hour from the clock of Westminster Abbey, as well as from a French timepiece in his room, which, as if in defiance of the dark and bloody thoughts that ran through his brain, struck up one of those light waltzes which such toys are made to play. With an oath Learmont dashed the clock to the ground, and the gay scenes which had been so little in accordance with his humour ceased.

"Some meddling fool must needs put that gilded annoyance in my chamber, he muttered, as he spurned it with his foot, "Time speeds not with me in such lively measures; I would have the hours tolled forth now by a funeral bell, for each one comes more closely to the knell of Jacob Gray. Eleven—eleven—in another hour—it will soon pass away. I have saved myself some occupation for that hour."

He took a key from his pocket, and, unlocking a cabinet, took from it a brace of pistols, the loading and priming of which he carefully examined.

"These may be useful in case of need," he muttered; "it may be we may have more foes to encounter than Jacob Gray. Oh that I could leave the smith alone to do the work! but then the confession—that I must secure myself; I dare not trust Andrew Britton with that—and it were unsafe for me to go alone. It were to risk too much—when I consider, I will run no risks—my victim shall be overpowered—will Britton stab him—or—or will he strangle him? Some quiet mode were best. I will take with me this poniard—its point is dipped in poison—the merest scratch is instant death. Should Britton fail, I must do the work myself; for, come what may, this night shall witness the death of Jacob Gray."

He stood now for some moments in the room in deep thought; then he walked to the window, and gazed upon the black sky.

"The night is wild and boisterous," he muttered; "and yet such nights are congenial to me. I will walk the streets until the hour of twelve. Britton will be sure to come—yes, he will be sure to come."

CHAPTER CIII.

FROM TWELVE TO ONE.

HEEDLESS of the dashing rain which ever and anon came in soaking showers upon the wind, Learmont paced up and down by his door. Never before had he made up his mind to risk so much by one act as he was about to do by taking the life of Jacob, for after all there clung to him like a shrieking fiend, which he could not shake off, the horrible thought the confession might by some means elude his search, and so fall into the hands of others to his destruction. To rid himself of such dire forebodings, Learmont was in no state as regarded the powers of reason, for his mind was so wrought upon now by the near approach of the hour of action he had waited for with such a feverish impatience, that when doubts assailed him, he could only resist them by muttering his fixed determination that Gray should die, and that upon this state he would risk all.

Now a dark heavy figure was approaching Learmont's house—was it the smith? The squire crept up his own steps, and stood in the shadow of his doorway. The figure came on. It was—yes, it must be he!—Now he pauses!—It is Britton!—He has kept his word. He glances around him—mutters a malediction—and ascends the steps! Then Learmont went forward to meet him. He drew a long breath and placing his trembling hand upon the smith's shoulder, he said,—

"You are punctual, Britton—most punctual! I am glad to see you! Welcome—welcome! What have you there?"

Britton took from beneath the flap of his coat, whither he had hidden it, a large bright cleaver, and holding it up before Learmont's face, he said, with a bitter laugh,—

"Will that do, squire? I say will that do?"

"For—for Gray?"

"Yes—curses on him! I think this will make sure work! I've borrowed it on purpose. One blow with it, and Jacob Gray, will trouble us no more!"

"True—true! and now, Britton—good Britton, I should tell you that the child of him who lies in the Old Smithy, has left Gray, so that there need not be the same scene enacted over again which once baulked our vengeance."

"Left him, squire, and without knowing?"

"In complete ignorance, or we should ere this have heard of it. Of that, be assured, for I am quite sure Britton, where we are going to night, there is nothing to apprehend if we can secure Gray's confession."

"That will do. He dies, or my name ain't Andrew Britton! Come—come —'tis time;" and they walked slowly toward's Jacob Gray's mean lodging.

Learmont spoke not as they went, but now and then Britton, when he thought of Jacob Gray, with all his deep cunning, being circumvented, would laugh to himself, and striking his thigh with his disengaged hand, would mutter, with the accompaniment of some fearful oath, his extreme satisfaction that he had borrowed the cleaver of Bond, and was in a fair way of trying it upon the skull of Gray, who he so cordially hated."

"Hush—hush!" Learmont said, as they neared the street; "hush, Britton! We must be cautious, for to all appearance the house in which Gray lives is filled with inhabitants. Even I do not know the room that he inhabits, except by guess, and that the guess of another."

"That's awkward," said Britton: "but we'll have him, squire, if he's in the house. If I have to go from room to room, smashing somebody in each, have Jacob Gray at last!"

"Hush! this is the street. Have you the means of opening doors?"

"I have. Just hold the cleaver."

Learmont took the weapon, while Britton diving his hand into his pocket, produced a bunch of skeleton keys, saying,—

"I ll warrant with these to get at him even behind fifty locks."

"Then understand me clearly," said Learmont, in a low, husky voice; "I have arms about me should they be required; but you shall take Gray's life while I secure you from all interruption, by keeping guard at the door. Whatever money is found you shall possess yourself of, while I take possession of the confession, which must, surely, if at all in existence, come easily to hand. See here, I have a light.

Learmont produced from his pocket a small lantern as he spoke, and showed Britton, that when he drew the slide he could cast a strong ray of light upon any object.

"Very well, the money is of more use to me than the confession; because you know, squire, I can confess myself whenever I've a mind that way."

"True—true, that is the house. Now, Britton, we must be firm, and by all the powers of hell, I swear that, let who will interrupt me this night shall meet his death."

"Oh, that's the house, is it?" said Britton, as beckoned by Learmont, he stood with him on the verge of the narrow pavement and glared up at it.

"There is but one light," whispered Learmont.

"And that," said the smith, "I'd wager a thousand pounds comes from Gray's room. He told me long ago, when we had some talk, that he never could bear to be without a light."

"'Tis more than probable. The keys—the keys! Ha, what was that?"

It appeared to Learmont as if a footstep had sounded on the opposite side of the way, but upon hastily turning, all was still, and he could see no one. His ears, however, had not deceived him; for Albert Seyton, when he saw two figures pause opposite to Gray's house, had stepped forward, intending, by walking past them, to ascertain, if possible, who they were, and had recognised the squire as soon as he had emerged from the deep doorway where he held his solitary watch. For one instant only Albert paused, and then recollecting his solemn promise not to interfere in the business until the time appointed, he shrunk back again, convinced in his own mind that Learmont was adopting some safe and sure means of rescuing his Ada. Nay, he might even see her brought from the house under the protection of his generous friend.   Could he then keep from rushing to her side? No.   He felt that then he could not ; but now was not the time.   He shrunk far back into the passage, but kept his eyes fixed with a painful and absorbing interest upon the proceedings of Learmont and his companion.

Then the smith took Learmont's lantern, and after carefully examining the lock of the outer door, he took from among the keys he carried, one which in a moment turned it.   Still, however, the door resisted all attempts to open it, and Britton whispered to Learmont that there was a bar.

"What are we to do?" gasped the squire.

"Pull it off," said the smith ; "but wait a minute."

As he spoke he made a great rummaging in one of his capacious pockets, and then producing a flat case bottle, which was capable upon a moderate computation, of holding about a pint and a half, he uncorked it, and placing it to his lips, took a hearty draught of the contents.

"Now, by hell," muttered Learmont, "cannot you go on without drink, and if so, why stop at such a juncture as this?"

"Go to the devil!" said Britton.   "Here's as choice a drop of brandy as ever was drunk.   It's no use offering you any.   Now, I'm ready again ; give me the cleaver."

Britton took the cleaver, and by great pressure succeeded in inserting its blade partially between the door and the joint; then he gave it a sudden wrench, and with a sound that went to the heart of Learmont and filled him with alarm, a wooden bar, with which the door had been made fast, fell into the shop, being forced from its place by the wrench given by the cleaver.

"You will ruin all by your haste and want of caution," muttered the squire; "some one is sure to be alarmed by that noise."

"That's just what I intend," said Britton.   "Whoever comes, we can ask them for a certainty where Gray is."

"Such a scheme would be madness," said Learmont.   "Britton you will ruin all."

"Come in," said the smith, and grasping Learmont by the arm, he dragged him into the little shop, and closing the door after them as well as he could.

All was utter darkness, and for a moment or two, Learmont stood listening painfully to hear if the bar had created any alarm, or had passed off without notice. Then, to his horror, he heard a footstep in some room contiguous to where they were ; a gleam of light shot from under a door, and just as Learmont with a deep groan strode towards the outer door to leave the place, believing that the house must be thoroughly alarmed, Britton, in a whisper said,—

"Stoop down, squire, and leave me to manage it."

Learmont mechanically obeyed him.   The door from whence the gleam of light had issued, opened, and the woman of the house entered the shop.

"There's that bar down again, I declare," she said.   "It's always a slipping down, just as I am going to bed too."

A faint scream burst from her lips as Britton suddenly placed his hand over her mouth, saying—

"Make any noise, and I'll smash your brains out.   Be quiet and I won't."

Terror then kept the woman from screaming, and when Britton released her, she sank upon her knees, with the candle she carried in her hand.

"Mercy—mercy, sir," she faltered.   "Oh, have mercy."

"Hush," said Britton.   "How many people are in this house?"

"Three—three—sir, your worship.   Oh! spare my life."

"Do you see this?" said the smith, holding the cleaver within an inch of her face.

"Yes—yes—yes," gasped the terrified woman.

"Very well, then, if you don't answer truly all I ask of you, and remain quite quiet for the next hour or more, I'll dash your brains on this floor, and your skull shall be picked up in damnation little bits by some one to-morrow morning."

"Oh, mercy, sir—mercy.   I'm a poor lone woman.   Spare my life."

"Answer, then, who else is in the house besides you?"

"Poor old Mrs. Garnett, sir, and—and—Muster Gray, sir—if you please, sir."

"Humph! and where does Muster Gray sleep?"

"In—in—the three pair front, sir."

"Very good. Now, my good woman, I shall just tie you up when I've refreshed myself a little."

Then with a nod at the woman, and a wink, towards Learmont, who was crouching behind a pile of baskets, Britton took another draught from his case bottle, a process which he seemed resolved upon repeating at every stage of the business he had in hand.

He then took the light from the woman's trembling hand, and seizing her by the hand, he pushed her into the room from whence she had come, and in a few moments tied her securely to the post of a bed which was there.

No. 49.

"Now, if you so much as mutter a word, or attempt to make any alarm till I see you again," he said, "you know what you have to expect. Look at this cleaver.

"I—I—won't, sir. Have mercy, sir—I won't; I—I—suppose as you are Muster Gray's relation as he's afeared of?"

"Yes, I'm his uncle."

"Good gracious!"

"Silence, I say. Another word, and—"

Britton made a fearful demonstration with the cleaver round the head of the terrified woman, and then went back to the shop, where Learmont was standing, looking awfully pale, and his eyes emitting an unnatural brilliance from the great excitement under which he was labouring.

"What do you think of that, squire?" whispered the smith. "D—n him, he's in the three pair front, and nobody to interfere with us. Now that's what I call pleasant. There's only two women in the house. Oh, won't I have some fun with Master Jacob. Cunning Master Gray,—Ha! ha! ha! Artful, clever Jacob."

"'Tis well," said Learmont, "as it has turned out; but you run great risks. Let us secure the door now."

"I can lock it," said Britton, as he did so. "Now we are all right, squire. How cunning Gray is, and what a clod that Britton is. A sot am I. We shall see, Master Gray, with all your cunning, how you will wriggle out of the pleasant circumstances you are in to-night."

"Now, Britton, let me implore you to drink no more. Wait, at least, until our enterprise is concluded."

"Why, it's only brandy, squire. It's cooling and pleasant when one's at work. I used to drink it at the old smithy till I made the anvil ring again as anvil never rung before beneath the strokes of a fore hammer. Come on—come on. I'm the better for the drink."

"We must succeed—we must, surely, succeed," said Learmont, as Britton holding the candle above his head, glanced around him a moment and then said,—

"Here is the staircase: it's at the top of the house. Come on, squire—come on."

They ascended the staircase slowly on their awful errand; and, oh! what a whirlwind of dark passions filled the heart of Learmont! Fear, rage, hate—all were struggling for pre-eminence; and now that he was so near the accomplishment of his much cherished scheme of vengeance upon Jacob Gray for the horrible uneasiness he had made him suffer for so many years, his mental suffering was probably greater, because augmented by the most intense anxiety, than ever it had yet been.

The stairs creaked beneath their footsteps, and the wind blew about the flame of the candle, making the shadows of themselves, and of the balustrades, dance in wild disorder upon the walls. Then the storm without appeared to have increased, for the rumble of distant thunder came upon their ears; and, as they reached a narrow window on the staircase, a bewildering flash of lightning for an instant lit up everything with its fearful lustre, and then left behind it comparative pitchy darkness.

CHAPTER CIV.

THE MURDER.

DID any perception of his great danger haunt the brains of Jacob Gray as he slept in his miserable abode? Did the shadow of the grave rest upon his soul? Was there no fiend to whisper in his ear suspicions, and to aggravate his suffering by the horrors of imagination? Yes. Although Gray slept—although the corporeal part of him was still—the mind knew no repose. The sweet oblivion of sleep was not for him, and as he sat, with his head leaning upon the table, deep moans, and now and then a gasping sob, like that of some drowning wretch, who sees the waters closing above his head, and shutting out the last glimpse of hope with the last glimpse of light, burst from his labouring breast. Busy fancy was carrying him on its airy pinions from earliest infancy through all the chequered scenes of chicanery and crime. From the happy stainless hours of childhood he wandered in thought through every scene of robbery, of murder, of pain, terror, and despair which he had acted in and endured. Again he rushed from the burning ruins of the smithy, with the child of the dead in his arms ; again he was hunted from house to house by the squire and by Britton ; then followed his denouncement at Charing-cross by Ada, and his wild run up the Strand—the murder of Vaughan— his own danger as he tremblingly crossed the roof-tops—his agony in the field near Hampstead—his hunger—his pain, misery, destitution, and wretchedness—all were enacted over again in frightful distinctness, and Jacob Gray could not awake. The perspiration, cold and clammy, stood upon his brow in bead-like drops ; tried to shriek, but his tongue clove to the roof of his mouth—he tried to struggle, but his limbs were powerless. The man of crime was dying a thousand deaths in his deep, mental agony.

Meanwhile, slowly approached his executioners. Step by step up the creaking staircase they came—the smith with a dogged resolution, and his bloated face inflamed with passion and the quantity of raw spirits he had already drunk. Learmont followed him, twining his arm round the crazy balustrade of the staircase to steady himself as he proceeded on his awful errand. Now they had reached the second landing, and the flight of stairs leading to the floor on which was Jacob Gray's room presented themselves, steep and narrow, winding into dimness and obscurity, and scarcely permitting more than one person to ascend them at once.

The smith did not speak, but he pointed up the stairs, and then, with a grim smile, held up the cleaver threateningly.

" On, on," whispered Learmont ; " let it be done quickly now—this suspense is terrible."

" Take a little of this," said Britton, producing the brandy ; " it will warm you ; for you tremble as if you had got the ague," and Learmont, in his heart, felt thankful for the offer. He took the bottle with a trembling hand, and drunk deep of the contents. He might as well have drunk as much water, for, in his present state of mind, the ardent spirit had no power over him, nor could any artificial excitement equal the fearful one which possessed him already.

Britton himself took a draught from the bottle, and then placed it in a corner by the staircase, as of no further use, being empty, and without another word he commenced the ascent of the attic staircase. Learmont followed him closely, and, when they were half way up, he laid his hand upon Britton's arm, and said, in a whisper that sounded like the hissing of a snake,—

" Britton, Britton—kill him—at once—do not delay—kill him at once."

" What ?" muttered Britton, " and scarcely let him know that there are people as cunning as himself. If I do kill him at once, may I be ——"

" Hush, hush—remember that we must secure the confession. Without that, we are but forging a bolt for our own destruction. Perhaps I had better see him first myself."

" That you may do as you like, squire, but give me the pleasure of using this cleaver on his skull when I please."

" You shall, you shall—I will see him first, and, by practising upon his fears, endeavour to procure his confession from him by a quicker means than searching for it. Go on, Britton—go on. Should his door be locked, you can open it ; and do you keep guard at the head of the stairs while I enter his room."

" As you please, squire. First or last, I care not, so as I'm in at the death, and have a few minutes talk with my old friend, Jacob, first."

" Hush, hush. We are there. See ye not yon streak of light from beneath that door ? It must be his chamber. Now, Britton, now—remember if he be awake, he must die at once, for the opening of the door will alarm him, and he may raise some cry that may bring help ; but if I succeed in entering his room without his knowledge, do you wait, and when you hear me utter the words, ' The hour has come,' do you enter and kill him—but do not have a struggle, Britton—kill him at once—kill him at once."

" There's something inside over the key-hole," whispered Britton ; " it's all the better, for it will deaden the sound of unlocking the door."

With the slightest possible noise consistent with the performance of the opera-tion at all, Britton unlocked Gray's door. A faint light issued from the room.

Learmont paused a moment, and pressed his hand tightly upon his breast—then placing his finger on his lips, and waving his hand to Britton, he glided into Jacob Gray's apartment.

The door slowly shut to within an inch or less—all was as still as the grave. The candle shed but a faint light, for Gray had been asleep long enough to allow the snuff to grow gigantic. In a moment Learmont saw Gray sleeping in the uneasy position he had chosen, and he stood with his feelings wrought up to the highest pitch of excitement, gazing upon his victim. Soon a low moan came from Gray, and he muttered the words,—

" Oh, God—oh, God !"—in such awful wailing accents, that even Learmont felt sick at heart to hear them.

" I must awaken him," he whispered, " I must—not delay."

Thrice did Learmont try to raise his voice to awaken Jacob Gray, and thrice did his tongue refuse its office, producing but a faint whisper, which failed in its purpose. Then, as if a ton of lead had been appended to each foot, Learmont crept towards the table and stretched out his hand. The long white fingers shook like leaves agitated by the wind—his heart beat with fearful violence—his lips were drawn back with a painful spasm from his teeth—he breathed short and hurriedly ; the effort to lay his hand upon the sleeping man was great, and it was more than a minute ere he could do so. Then nearer, nearer, still he crept, and by a desperate effort he touched his shoulder, as in a hollow, spectral voice he said,—

" Awake, Jacob Gray."

One cry escaped Gray's lips as he lifted his head, and that cry seemed to arouse Learmont from his lethargy, for he seized Gray by the throat, and held him as with a face distorted by excitement, he said,

" Another cry, and it is your last, Jacob Gray."

" Learmont," gasped Gray, and then they glared into each other's faces like two spirits of evil, conscious of the other's power, yet prepared for some awful struggle for life or death.

Gray put up his hands and held Learmont's arm, while he shook the chair on which he sat by his trembling, and thus in awful silence did these two men regard each other for more than a minute, each enduring mental agony, such only as the wicked are doomed to suffer. It was an awful picture—ghastly and dreadful to imagine—a scene to haunt the brain in sleep, and people vacancy with horror. The dim spectral-looking light, lighting up the distorted features of these two men, whose souls seemed to be concentrated in their dilated eye-balls, as they glared at each other with the fixedness of marble statues. Then there was the huge bulky form of the smith, at the crevice of the door, which he had enlarged, to allow himself a view of what was passing in the room, with the bright shining instrument of death clutched in his grasp, and gloating over the prospect of the blood which was to be shed—the crushed bones and the mangled flesh he was to exult over—the prayers for mercy choked in gore. Oh, it was horrible !

Learmont was the first to speak, and when he did so, his voice was hoarse, and for want of breath his words came strangely disjointed from his lips.

" The confession—the confession—the confession," he said.

Then Gray seemed to feel that death was at hand, and he slid from the chair on his knees, crying,—

" Mercy—mercy—mercy."

"Hush," said Learmont, dwelling upon the word till it became a long hissing sound. "Hush! The confession—the confession. Speak above your breath, and you die—the confession."

He still kept his grasp of Gray, and shook him to and fro as much from his own nervousness as from design.

It was awful then to hear Jacob Gray, in a husky whisper, pleading for his life —praying for that mercy he had never himself shown, and appealing to feelings which had no existence in the breasts of either Learmont or himself.

"Spare me—spare me," he said, "and I will go far away from you. Oh, spare my life, and that mercy you now show to me will plead with Heaven for you, while I have no such hope. Oh, spare me."

"The confession—the confession."

"You will kill me—you will kill me if I give it to you. Oh, relent—take me now away—place me on ship board—take all I have of money back again ; you shall have the confession, too, if you will spare my life. Oh, God! if you want revenge against me, let me live, for life to me is horrible enough. Yet I dare not die. Learmont, if you have one lingering hope of grace hereafter, spare me now. I am beaten—conquered—I admit all—you shall triumph over me as you may, but do not—oh, do not kill me."

"The confession—the confession," was Learmont's only reply.

Gray then wrung his hands and wept hysterically, and Learmont let go his hold of him, for he saw he was incapable of resistance.

"God help me—God help me," he said. "You, Learmont, made me what I am ; you tempted me—oh, spare my poor worthless life ; why should you kill me —I, poor Jacob Gray, your slave—one who has done so much for you —who will do anything you please. Think again, Learmont, think again."

"Time is flying—I must have the confession."

"Then, you would kill me—you would—you would—let me go into the street, and I will tell you where to find it ; but you would kill me here, Learmont. I swear I will tell you where it is if you will but let me go. I will never trouble you more—you shall never hear of me. Oh, why kill me—it may bring you danger, but can give you no safety. I tell you you shall never look upon my face again, and you will have the consolation of reflecting that you overcame without soiling your hands with my blood. You relent—I can see you relent, Learmont. You will not kill me—you will not kill me !"

"Peace—peace," said Learmont. "I must have the confession. Give it me, and you shall live."

"Can I—dare I ? Oh, let me be assured, Learmont. Let me go first—I cannot denounce you without condemning myself ! Let me leave here, and when we are in some public place, I will tell you where to find it, as well as swearing ! I will trouble you no more ! I will for ever be thankful to you for my life ! Oh, think what a great gift is life to me, and yet how small an one it is for you to give. It gives me all—takes from you nothing ! Spare me—you see I am abject !— You hear my sobs !—See I am clasping your knees—I am kneeling to you !—I, who never even knelt to Heaven !—Look at my tears !—Life—life—life !—Oh, let me have life !"

He grovelled as the feet of Learmont—he sobbed—wept—prayed—implored for mercy ! He crawled after him as the squire shrunk back ; he seized him by his cloak, and when that was wrenched from his hands, he clasped them above his head, and with an awful spasmodic action of the throat, he kept repeating the one word,—

"Mercy ! mercy! mercy !"

Learmont was getting each moment more and more enraged at Gray's pertinacity in refusing him the confession, and he made one last effort to induce him to produce it to him.

"Give me the confession," he said, "and you may go from this room now while I remain here."

" We will go together," said Gray. " My cloak—God bless you, "squire !—We will go together !—My cloak—my cloak !"

Learmont shook his clenched hand, and uttering an awful curse, he added,—" The hour has come !"

In a moment Andrew Britton stood before the terrified gaze of Gray, who seemed perfectly paralysed with terror, for although his lips moved, he uttered no sound, but stretching his arms out before him, as if to keep off the smith, he still knelt in the room where Learmont had left him.

The smith stepped up close to the horror-stricken man, and then his sides shook with demoniac mirth as he said—

" Ho ! ho ! cunning Jacob Gray is in the toils at last—clever, artful Jacob—run down at last by the drunken son with the middle brain. Ho ! Ho ! Ho !—why don't you laugh, squire—why don't you laugh, Jacob ? you may as well, you know—it's all the same."

Gray appeared from the moment of Britton's entrance to give himself up for lost. With one gasping sob he let his head sink on his breast, and the only sign of life he gave was in the nervous twitching of his fingers which played with each other convulsively.

Britton then stepped up to him, and producing the cleaver from behind his back, he held it close to Jacob Gray's face, saying—

" Artful Jacob, what do you think of that ? Look at it—it is sharp and bright —fancy it crashing through your skull till it comes to the brain ; and then, even then, you may have still life enough to feel the cracking of your own bones and the crushing agony."

" Oh no—no," cried Gray, suddenly. " Save me from him, Learmont—oh, God, save me from Andrew Britton ! Learmont—Learmont—make me your slave—maim me—inflict daily, hourly pain upon me—but save me from Andrew Britton ! Off, off, off—Oh, Heaven, have mercy !"

Britton made a chop with the cleaver, purposely, so near Jacob Gray's face, that it passed only within a hair's breadth of him, and excited his utmost terror ; a scream burst from his lips as he fell over on one side, and held up his hands to avert the blow.

" Andrew Britton," cried Learmont, " do your work. This will ruin us—quickly —quickly."

" Hark ye, Jacob," said Britton ; " make as much noise, or half as much again, and I'll smash you. What would you give to live a little longer ?"

" Oh, worlds ! worlds !" said Gray.

" Be quiet, then, and you shall have a few minutes more, to think how cunning you have been, and what a sad, muddle-brained fool Andrew Britton is. Ho ! ho ! Jacob Gray ! Think fast, as you will not have time to turn over in your mind all your cleverness."

" Britton—Britton !" said Gray. " Triumph over me, but spare my life. I have done much for you."

" Must for me !" exclaimed Britton, and his face became more inflamed with rage. " Much for me ? Now, curses on you ! you kept me working at the forge for ten long year, all because you were too much of a coward to strangle a young brat you had in your power. Yes, you have done much for me, Jacob Gray, and I will do something for you. I'm going to hack you to pieces with this cleaver."

Learmont, during this awful conference, was busy about the room laying his trembling hands upon everything with a hope of finding the confession of Gray, and each moment as his search was unproductive, he became more dreadfully anxious and excited, until his very brain seemed on fire.

" The confession," he said, turning to Gray. " Give me the confession, and you may yet live."

" Not here—not here !"

Learmont came close up to him, and laying his hand upon his shoulder, he said,—

"Jacob Gray, a thought strikes me, there is no confession—this has been a creation of your own fancy, to alarm me. There is no confession."

"There is," cried Gray. "God knows it. There is—there is!"

As Gray spoke, he crept towards the window; a wild hope had occurred to him, that he might open it suddenly and dash out into the gutter, which was under it, and possibly escape.

"Produce it, then," said Learmont to him.

"One moment for thought," said Gray. "Spare me a moment—I will think —keep Britton off me—keep him away—his looks kill me—I shall go mad if he keeps so close to me."

Gray then suddenly pushed a chair between himself and Britton and fled to the window. Learmont turned his eyes away as he saw Britton step over the obstruction with the cleaver uplifted. Scream after scream burst from Jacob Gray as he stood with the back of his head against the window.

There was an awful crashing sound, one gurgling shriek, and a noise of broken glass.

"Kill him—kill him!" gasped Learmont. "Keep him not in agony!"

The cleaver descended again, a heavy fall succeeded, and then all was still. Something cold fell on the back of Learmont's hand. A glance told him it was blood; but before he could utter the cry of horror that rose upon his lips, a tremendous knocking at the street-door awakened every echo in the house.

CHAPTER CV.

AFTER THE MURDER.

THE knocking continued without intermission for several seconds, and each blow seemed to Learmont as if it was struck upon his own heart.

"Britton, Britton," he cried, "you hear. There is some alarm. Hasten, hasten, or we are lost."

Britton turned his excited face towards the squire, and the dim light of the candle fell upon it. Learmont could not but be struck by its awful expression. The smith had at length succeeded in gratifying the long cherished desire of his heart, namely, to be in some dreadful manner revenged upon Jacob Gray. Wild excitement had caused him to do the deed which he had just committed, and every evil passion of his nature was peeping forth like a bold fiend from his countenance. Crimson spots of human gore were likewise upon his face— horrible evidences of the work he had been about.

"Who knocks?" he said, in a low, earnest voice. "Who is mad enough to interfere with me?"

He raised in his hand the cleaver as he spoke—with a dull heavy splash there fell from its blade on to the floor "gouts of blood," and Learmont turned away his head, sickened at the sight.

"Who dares, I say, to interfere with me?" repeated Britton. "Squire, Jacob Gray won't trouble you any more."

"Name him not—oh, name him not," said Learmont. "Hark—hark!"

As he spoke, it appeared that whoever had been knocking at the outer door of the house, had grown impatient, and burst it open, fraily as it had been fastened after the violence that had been used towards it by Britton, for there was heard a loud crash, and then a sound of rapid footsteps approaching.

"Flight—flight," gasped Learmont, as he sprung towards the door.

"Flight be d—d," said Britton, as he flourished the cleaver above his head. "I'm not going to be scared now because some one is coming."

He then walked deliberately to Gray's cloak, in which it will be recollected the confession was concealed, and wiped the reeking blade of the instrument, by which he had put Gray to death, upon it.

"For my sake, and your own," said Learmont, "leave this room. What enemy to us can he be who is coming, unless we make him one?"

As he spoke, he seized the reluctant smith by the arm, and dragging him across the narrow landing pushed open another door-way on the same story, and entered an empty room.

Now that the savage smith had dipped his hands in Gray's blood, he would, with wild ferocity, have defied the world; and it would have given him far greater pleasure to have been hindered in his retreat, and to have had to fight his way out of the house with Bond's cleaver, than to escape easily and without a struggle.

In order now to explain the cause of the violent knocking at so terrible a moment at the door, we must carry the reader back for a brief space to Albert Seyton and his lonely walk. Filled with surprise, as we know he was, to see the squire at such an hour making a clandestine entrance into the house in which Gray resided, he remained upon the tip-toe of expectation waiting his re-appearance, accompanied by Ada, in which case he felt that he could no longer restrain his impatience, but must fly across to her, and welcome her to freedom, even if it cost him the reproach of breaking his word, and his future friendship of the rich squire.

But as minute after minute passed languidly away, and no re-appearance took place, Albert's impatience and anxiety became excruciating, and he could no longer stay within the deep door-way, but scarcely knowing what he did, he walked to the very middle of the road, and keeping his eyes fixed upon the door, with but now and then an occasional glance at the window, which he had all along pleased himself with the idea was that of Ada's room, he trembled again with impatient excitement.

The profound stillness of everything surprised him, and more than once he was almost tempted to believe he must have been dreaming, when he supposed he saw Learmont enter the house at all. Suddenly, however, the silence was broken by a loud crash at the windows, and, by the dim and uncertain light, Albert saw some object apparently dashed through the glass, and then withdrawn again.

That object was the head of Jacob Gray, for then had Britton given him his death blow in the manner we have recorded.

Excited as he was, this maddened Albert, and the idea seizing him that Ada must be in some danger, he, on the impulse of the moment, knocked loudly at the door, and finally with one vigorous rush against it, burst it open, and fell himself into the shop.

It was some moments before, in the dark, he could find the staircase; but, when he did, he ascended it as rapidly as he could, resolved, when he reached the top, to make himself known by his voice.

"Ada—Ada," he cried in a tone that rang through the house, and fell with a disagreeable chill upon the heart of Learmont, who immediately recognised in it the voice of Albert, and could not divine how, at such a moment, he should happen to be at hand.

"Ada—Ada," again cried Albert, and then Learmont laid his hands on the smith's arm, and whispered,—

" Britton, there is but one man there, let us kill him and escape."

"I'm willing, but where is Master Jacob's money, and his confession, I should like to know?"

" The money I will make good to you, and I am quite convinced of what I always suspected, that there is no confession but what lay in Gray's own brain."

" Then it don't lay in his brain now," said Britton, " I'll be sworn."

" Hush—come on."

"Ada—Ada," cried Albert, pausing upon the staircase, with the hope of hearing some answering sound, and more alarmed at the dead silence which prevailed in the house, than had he encountered noise, tumult, and evident danger.

"What the devil is he shouting in that way for?" muttered Britton.

"Hush—hush," said Learmont. "Some cursed chance has brought him here: Let us descend, and, as you pass him, Britton—you understand me?"

"I do," said Britton. "Come on, then. Where's your light."

"We need none. I would not be seen by him. What you have to do, you can easily do in the dark—kill him or maim him, I care not which."

"Well, squire," muttered Britton, "you certainly do leave me all the work to do; but when one's hands in, it aint much matter."

No. 50.

Albert, in the excitement of his feelings, when he got as high as the second floor, paused, uncertain whether or not he had arrived on a level with the room of which the window had been broken so violently, and he stood for several minutes calling upon Ada, his voice, each time that he uttered her name, betraying the great anxiety which he laboured under, and which was momentarily increasing.

Suddenly, then, a voice answered him faintly, and guided by the sound, Albert pushed against a door, which, yielding to his touch, presented a dark room, into which he stepped, saying,—

"Whoever you are here, for Heaven's sake, let me have a light."

"Oh, spare a poor old creature, who hasn't long to live," said a voice.

"I intend you no harm," said Albert, "but for God's sake get me a light."

There was a great creaking of an old crazy bedstead, and then the voice said, in the tremulous accents of old age,—

"Are you the man that lives up stairs ?"

"No, no," said Albert; "but get a light quickly."

The old woman, after stumbling over every article of furniture in her room, at length found a tinder-box, and commenced striking a light with a particularly small bit of flint, which, produced, upon an average, one spark to every half dozen blows.

Albert Seyton, in his impatience, little suspected that the very circumstance of, the old woman not being able to get him a light quickly, saved his life, for while she was endeavouring to procure one, Learmont and Britton were creeping down the staircase with the expectation of meeting Albert and taking his life.

As they passed the door of the room in which Seyton was, and heard the hacking of the flint and steel, Britton muttered,—

"There's some one getting a light, squire. We may as well move on, or shall I go in and smash whoever it is ?"

"No, no; come on—come on," said Learmont. "I know what it is, and there will come a time for rendering him innoxious. Come on—come on."

They passed the door, and Albert was saved. In a few moments more the old woman procured a light, and then peering at Albert from her deep sunken eyes, she said,—

"And who may you be, young gentleman? I don't know you, I'm sure."

"Ask no questions," cried Albert, as he took the light from her, "but on your soul, tell me in which room of this house resides a young girl, by name, Ada ?"

The old woman was alarmed at his vehemence, and tremblingly muttered, that she did not know who he meant, for there was no such person to her knowledge there.

"One Gray lives here?" said Albert.

"Oh, yes," said the woman, "I've heard there's a Mr. Gray up stairs."

Albert waited not another moment, but bounded up the staircase with the light in his hand.

"Ada—Ada. 'Tis I—Albert," he said, as he reached the top landing.

The echoes of the old house were the only sounds that replied to him, and shading the light with his hand, he walked into Jacob Gray's room, the door of which was partially open. Everything appeared in confusion, and the first article that Albert trod upon, was the cloak, which had fallen from its hook at the back of the door. A feeling of awe crept over him, which he could not account for. His blood seemed to creep through his veins, and there was an anxious flutter at his heart, as he again, but in a lower tone, pronounced the name of Ada.

All was silent as the grave. Albert stood a few paces only within the door-way, and his heart misgave him, that something dreadful must have happened to her he loved.

"Ada—Ada!" he cried, wildly. "If you live, speak—Gray—Learmont. Where are you all? Am I dreaming, or is this awful silence real ? Ada—Ada—God of heaven? Where, oh, where are you, my Ada?

He felt something soft and slimy under his feet. He stooped with the light—deadly sickness came over him—for a moment all objects swam before his eyes;

he was compelled to hold the back of the chair for support—he was standing in a pool of coagulated blood !

How long it was then before he recovered full consciousness he knew not, but gradually his perceptions returned, and then he shrieked the name of Ada, with a tone of anguish, that would have saddened any heart, and lingered in the ears for months like a death shriek.

" They have killed her—they have killed her !" he cried. " Ada—Ada—I should have flown sooner to your aid—God help me, I am heart-stricken now for ever—she is dead—she is dead. My beautiful Ada—oh, God—oh, God !"

He reeled further into the room, and when he had passed the bed, which partially concealed the window, he stood like one suddenly transformed to stone ; for there lying in a ghastly heap, in a pool of blood, the features horribly disfigured, and scarcely a trace of the upper portion of the skull visible, his eyes fell upon what once was Jacob Gray.

All his air-drawn schemes—his deep resolves—his cunning—his cruelty—his avarice, and his ambition—where were they now ? What had he reaped as the reward of his great selfishness ? A death of horror. May Heaven have mercy on his soul.

Albert Seyton felt like one fascinated by the hideous glare of a serpent. He could not withdraw his eyes from the ghastly spectacle for many minutes, and while he so gazed, his very heart seemed to shrink within him, and a feeling of horror crept up—up to his brain, till a clammy perspiration broke out upon his brow, and hung there in heavy drops, while each breath he drew, was laboured and heavy.

It was frightful, but by the crushing blow of the cleaver, one of Gray's eyes had been forced from its socket—it hung by a bleeding filament—round—glassy and fixed—it seemed to glare upon Albert like a thing of life—he could almost fancy it moved. The young man covered his eyes with his disengaged hand, as he said,—

" This must be a dream—God of heaven, this cannot be real—when oh, when shall I awake ?"

Distinct sounds, as of many voices, now suddenly came upon his ears, and he started, as if the tones of a human voice had removed some spell from off his faculties. Louder and louder the sound came upon his ears. There were evidently several voices. Then he heard a confused trampling of feet—heavy footsteps were approaching.

" Thank God," said Albert, with a feeling of inexpressible relief, as he felt sure now that some human beings besides himself were at hand. He withdrew himself with difficulty, from the awful spectacle in Gray's room, and proceeding to the head of the stairs, he said,—

" Help—help—murder—murder—murder."

CHAPTER CVI.

THE ARREST.

THE sound of his own voice seemed now to conquer all the nervous feelings which had oppressed him, and Albert Seyton continued shouting for aid, until lights flashed up the narrow staircase, and several voices cried,—

" Hilloa there, what's the matter ?"

" Murder !" cried Albert, " quick here. There has been murder done—this way—quick, whoever you are."

Several men now made their appearance on the stairs, and in a few moments the landing was crowded with a party bearing lights, some of whom were likewise armed.

" This way," said Albert, pointing to the door of Gray's room; " a man has been barbarously murdered—his corpse lies there."

" Oh! it's you, my spark, is it?" cried a man stepping up to Albert, who at a glance he recognised as the spy upon Jacob Gray, who had caused him so much uneasiness.

" For God's sake," cried Albert, " forget all but the necessity of securing the perpetrators of the horrible crime which has been committed in this house to-night. A man, I tell you, has been murdered."

" Very like," said the spy, as he took a constable's staff from his pocket. " You are my prisoner, my light-heeled gentleman. Till we catch somebody else more more suspicious, we may as well have you."

Another officer who had gone into Gray's room now came with a face as pale as a sheet, and trembling in every limb.

" It's true," he cried, " I never saw such a sight in my life, and hope never to see such an one again."

" Do with me what you like," cried Albert, " but take, for Heaven's sake, some measures for securing the murderer."

" It's my opinion, young fellow," said the spy, " that you know about as much of this affair as most people—keep a strict eye on him, my men. Why, you look as scared as if you had seen a ghost. Give me your light. If there is a dead man there, I'm not afraid of him."

All but one constable, who kept a firm hold of Albert, went into the room, but hardened as these men were to scenes of terror, a cry of unmingled horror escaped them as they saw the ghastly spectacle under the window, and they quickly retreated to the landing again.

" You see I have spoken the truth," cried Albert; " God only knows whether those I suspect are guilty or not, but to any magistrate I will communicate all I know with regard to this night's dreadful proceedings."

" You are, out of all hand, the most hardened ruffian I ever came near," said the constable who held Albert; " why you'll be hung for this as sure as you are now a living man."

" I," cried Albert, the dreadful circumstances of suspicion in which he was placed for the first time darting across his mind, for in the excitement of his feelings he had scarcely noticed what was said before. " I? why you rave, man—I did not do the deed."

" The less you say the better," remarked the spy; " comrades, this will be no bad night's work for us—I can give evidence that this young fellow has been dogging the man who is murdered for some days past. Here we find him actually in the very room, or on the very threshold of it. It was a lucky job we happened to see the door wide open, and came in."

" A clear case," said another.

There's been many a man hung on half the evidence," remarked a third.

Albert looked from one to the other for a few moments, perfectly bewildered at this new turn things had taken; then he said,—

" You do not—you cannot suspect me. Good God, 'twas I who called you here. I burst the door open below but a short time since."

" Hear him—hear him," cried the spy; " he will own to it all in a minute."

" Unhand me," cried Albert; " I am as innocent of this awful crime as you yourselves—I——"

He struggled to free himself from the grasp of the officer, but a couple more of them immediately closed with him, and in a few moments he found himself hand-cuffed and a prisoner.

" One of you stay," cried the spy, " and don't let any one come near the body. By Heaven, this is as ugly a job as ever I heard of!"

Albert clasped his manacled hands together, and a feeling of despair came over his heart—a prison—a scaffold, and an ignominious death seemed to be staring him in the face. How was he to extricate himself from the fearful circumstances by which he was now surrounded? where now were all his fond hopes of once more seeing his Ada? The rush of wretched feelings across his mind was almost too great for mortal endurance, and had it not been for the stern, unpitying men by whom he was now surrounded, he could have shed tears in the bitterness of his despair."

"Take me where you like," he cried. "Do with me what you like—accuse me of what you please—but, as you are men and Christians, search this house, I implore you, for a young maiden, whose name is Ada. She must be here somewhere. I entreat you to search for her—I implore you. Moreover, there are papers in the room, most probably, of yon murdered man, which are directed to Sir Francis Hartleton. Find them, and take them to him. Then do with me what you please, and in my heart I believe the kindest hand would be that which took my life."

The accent in which these words were uttered was so despairing—so full of exquisite grief and abandonment of all hope, that even the officers, blunted as their feelings were, looked affected by what they heard.

There was a moment's silence, and then one said,—

"Bring him along at once before Sir Francis. He never minds being knocked up on real business."

"But you will do what I ask you," said Albert; "you will search for her I have mentioned to you?"

"We cannot," was the reply; "we must lose no time—come on—come on."

"With a deep sigh Albert dropped his head upon his breast, and suffered himself to be led down the staircase in a state of great dejection.

When he reached the foot of the topmost flight, he summoned all his energies, and once more cried,—

"Ada, Ada!"

Echo only answered him.

The officers paused themselves involuntarily to listen if any voice responded to Albert's frantic call, but when all was still again, they urged him forward, saying,—

"We can wait no longer—come to the magistrate's."

"Once more hear me," cried Albert; "some of you must have hearts to feel for the unfortunate. Here, I swear to you that there are papers in yon room, where lies the ghastly remains of the murdered man, which it much imports Sir Francis Hartleton to have. Oh, search for them—search, I pray you—I will attempt no escape. You shall find me patient—most patient; but as you love justice, find those papers."

The vehemence and earnestness of his tone was not without its effect even upon those rude men, and they looked in each other's faces for a moment or two, irresolute, when something came down the staircase with a rustling sound, and the man who had been left above to keep guard on the door of Gray's room, called to his companions below, saying—

"Ask the prisoner if that's his cloak—it was lying half in and half out of the door way."

One of the officers lifted the cloak from the floor, and turning to Albert said—

"Is this yours?"

"No," replied Albert, "it must be his who lies above in death. It is not mine."

"I more than suspect it is, though," said the officer, as he held his light close to it, "why it is smeared with blood. We must take this with us, comrades. It's a dainty piece of evidence against the prisoner. Come on—there hasn't been such a famous murder as this since Mr. Vaughan was killed in the Strand."

"But the papers. You forget the papers," cried Albert.

"Hang the papers," was the reply. "There are none. We cannot waste time with you."

The unhappy young man resigned himself to his fate, and accompanied the officers in silence. Evil fortune seemed to be expending all her malice against him; a tide of circumstantial evidence was rushing over him more than sufficient to overwhelm him in the consequences of a crime of which he was innocent. Ada appeared lost to him for ever now that Gray was dead, for what clue had he to find her now ; and the conduct of Learmont was mysterious, if he were not the actual murderer of Jacob Gray. A confused whirl of thoughts and conjectures passed through the brain of Albert with frightful rapidity. The strange and most unexpected events of the night were completely bewildering. At one moment he thought of accusing Learmont of the murder ; at another he almost doubted if he was correct in fancying he had seen the squire at all—so strangely disjointed—so full of mystery—so redolent of horror had been the night's proceedings, that the unfortunate Albert could scarcely be said to be in a sufficiently collected frame of mind to form a just conclusion, or hazard a practicable conjecture respecting them. His brain seemed to grow into fire with the agony he endured, and more like one dead than alive, he was passively led by the officers towards the residence of Sir Francis Hartleton, to be there accused of the awful crime of murder.

As the party neared the house of the magistrate, a feeling of utter despair crept over Albert's heart, and he was conscious but of one thought ; that was, that he would be glad when he was dead, for then all his miseries would be over, and he should perhaps in some happier state, see Ada, who, with an awful shudder, he thought must have been murdered long since by Jacob Gray.

CHAPTER CVII.

THE INTERVIEW AND THE EXCULPATION;—SIR FRANCIS HARTLETON'S CAUTION.

WHO in this world can safely calculate his true position, or say what circumstance is fraught with woe and what with happiness, when we are more frequently upon the point of obtaining our most glorious and delightful aspirations, while we fancy the cloud of adversity is thickening around us, than when, to our limited perceptions, we are emerging into the sweet sunshine of felicity. Situated as Albert Seyton now was, even hope was a stranger to his heart—he could see not one ray of sun-light amid the dreary gloom by which he was immured—all was blank despair. Like some wave-tossed mariner, who, after struggling with the remorseless seas for a long dreary night, looks with lack-lustre eye along the world of waters as the first streak of the morning light enables him to do so, and sees no hope—no distant land—no sail, and feels that to struggle longer is but to protract death which is certain, Albert gave way to the circumstances by which he was surrounded, and as he entered the magistrate's house, the expression of deep dejection on his countenance was remarked with significant whispers and glances by the officers, who looked upon it as a sign of conscious guilt, and entertained no more doubt of the fate of their prisoner, than they did of their own existence, so confident were they that he was, in truth, the murderer.

Oh, could he have guessed at that moment, that he was under the same roof with his Ada—could he have dreamt that he was breathing the same air which she breathed—what bursts of glorious sunshine through the murkiest sky that ever frowned upon the world, could, in its contrast, have equalled the feelings that would have possessed his breast, in lieu of the twin-hags grief and despair, which now possessed it wholly.

And Ada—the beautiful and good—the pure of heart—the noble—the gifted Ada—she was sleeping, all unconscious of the events of that fearful night ; little imagined she, that her great enemy had died so awfully, or that he who loved her lived in such great jeopardy.

The morning was rapidly approaching now, and Albert was taken into a room facing the east, in the residence of Sir Francis, and closely guarded, until the magistrate should make his appearance, which, in a few moments he did, having been awakened with the news that a barbarous murder was committed, and the criminal was in his house.

Albert stood facing the window, and it was partly the dull reflection of the early morning light, and partly the death-like paleness of his face, from the state of mind he was in, which made him look more like a corpse than a living man, and for a moment prevented Sir Francis from recognising him.

Albert flinched not from the magistrate's earnest gaze, but looking steadily at him, he said,—

" Sir Francis Hartleton, I am brought here accused of murder—I am innocent, but I cannot say more—do with me what you will, for I am tired of life."

" Mr. Seyton!" cried Sir Francis.

" The same," said Albert—" the unhappy Seyton."

Sir Francis remained a moment or two in deep thought, then he said :—

" Officers what is the charge against this young man ?"

" Murder, your worship," replied one.

" Leave the room, all of you, I will hear the evidence one by one."

" Oh, sir," said Albert, " there is evidence enough—fate has marked me for destruction. You may send me now to prison, and spare your labour—I am innocent, but yet submit ; you see I am patient, sir."

" You speak from the bitterness of your heart," said Sir Francis. " I am here to do my duty, without favour or affection. My previous knowledge of you I now wholly discard from my mind. You come before me as an utter stranger, accused of an awful crime—you shall have justice, and were you my own son, I could say no more. Now, officer, let me hear what you have to say."

Sir Francis himself swore the officer, who remained in the room, and who was the principal spy upon Jacob Gray.

" Your worship," he said, " is aware that my duty has been to keep watch on a man named Gray."

" Which duty you must have to-night neglected," said the magistrate.

" I beg your worship's pardon, Gray don't need any more watching."

" What do you mean ?"

" He is dead."

" Dead—Gray dead? It surely is not his murder—but go on—go on."

Sir Francis reclined back in his chair, and partially shaded his face with his hand while the officer proceeded in his narrative.

" It was nearly half-past one o'clock, your worship, when, upon passing the door of the house where this man Gray lived. I saw it open, and upon examination, saw that it had been forced by some one. Not knowing then how many persons might be there, I ran to the round-house in Buckingham-street, and got assistance, when I and several officers, with lights, entered the house. The first thing we heard, was the moaning of a woman, who we found tied to a bedstead, in the room adjoining the shop, and immediately after, we proceeded up stairs, when we heard the prisoner calling out to some one—"

" Who did he call to ?"

" The name was Ada. When we got to the top of the house, we found the prisoner on the landing, in a state of great excitement, and upon going into the first room we came to, their lay murdered, and dreadfully mangled, the man Gray—your worship had told me to watch."

" He was quite dead?"

" Quite, your worship—we picked up this cloak stained with blood, which we believe belongs to the prisoner."

" That is all you have to say ?"

" It is, your worship, except that the prisoner has been dodging Gray about as closely as I have, for a day or two now."

"Do you wish to ask any questions of this witness?" said Sir Francis to Albert, in a cold tone.

"None," said Albert. "He has spoken the truth, and yet I am innocent."

"What further evidence is there?" said Sir Francis.

"The other officers can swear to what I have said, your worship," said the officer, "and I have left one to see that no one meddles with the body."

"That was right," cried Sir Francis, with sudden animation, "I will go there myself at once. There may be some papers."

Albert immediately spoke in a tone of such deep emotion, that Sir Francis paused as he rose from his chair, and listened to him with an interest and a growing doubt of his guilty connexion with Learmont, that it would have given him the sincerest pleasure to verify.

"Sir," said Albert, "I implore you for the sake of one for whom I have suffered much—one who I have loved, who I still love more fondly—more fervently than I love life itself, to search for the packet which long ago I told you was directed to yourself. How Jacob Gray came by his death as I hope for God's mercy I know not."

"Know not!" said Sir Francis. Then turning to the officer he said, "Wait without," and in a moment he was alone with Albert. There was a pause of some minutes' duration, and then Sir Francis said,—

"You may, or you may not, as it may please you, give me an account of this affair."

"For the sake of the name I bear and the memory of my dear father," said Albert, "I will declare my innocence, and although you may judge me wrongfully, shall die happy, if you will do justice to one who is dearer to me than myself. That one is the persecuted Ada, who, if she be still living, I implore you to succour. Oh, sir, you do not know her—and—and I have no words to paint her to you."

"But about this murder?" said Sir Francis, uneasily.

"I will tell you all I know. Being some time since destitute, I applied to one Learmont for employment, and was by him entertained as his secretary."

"So have I heard. Go on, sir."

"The first confidential employment he put me on, was to follow a man home, who he thought was imposing upon his benevolence, but before I could proceed upon that employment I had related to him the secret of my heart—my passionate love for Ada, even as I told it to you, sir—my long and weary search for her—my bitter reflections concerning the cruelty of Jacob Gray—I told him all that, and his generosity seemed much worked upon. He proffered me unbounded assistance. His wealth—his power—all he said should be exerted to do justice to the innocent."

"And you believed him?"

"I did, and was happy in the thought that Ada would be rescued from her miseries. Then by a strange chance it turned out that this very man who he had commissioned me to watch to his house, was Jacob Gray."

"Indeed?" said Sir Francis, in a peculiar tone.

"Yes, and then I thanked Heaven for its great goodness, and believed myself on the road to happiness. I did watch Gray home and flew to Learmont with the news. He then enjoined me by a solemn promise to allow him the whole management of the affair, which, from gratitude to him, I could not refuse, but I lingered ever round the house where I believed Ada to be. I could not deny myself the delight of fancying myself near her. It was joy to look upon the house that I thought contained her—to watch a passing shadow at a window, and fancy it was her's ; during that watch I encountered your officer, whose motive in being a spy upon Jacob Gray I could not divine.

"Last night I commenced my watch, and being hidden in a deep door-way, immediately opposite the house, which engrossed all my attention, I saw between the hours of twelve and one, two men approach and pause at the residence of

Gray. By some means they quickly opened the door, when, partially emerging from my place of concealment, I saw that one of them was Learmont."

Sir Francis Hartleton slightly started and changed his posture, so that Albert could not see his face.

"The other," continued Albert, "I know not."

"What kind of man was he?"

"A tall bulky man."

"The smith—the smith," thought Sir Francis to himself.

"The door was closed when they had entered the house, and in an agony of impatience I waited for their re-appearance, expecting to see Ada with them, for I doubted not but the squire was rescuing her from Jacob Gray."

"Well, well," said Sir Francis, in a tone of deep interest, "what followed then?"

No. 51.

"One o'clock had struck, and no one came forth, nor could I hear any commotion in the house—my agony of impatience was growing exquisitely painful—my eyes were fixed upon the only window which showed a light, and I was on the point of forgetting all promises and rushing over to the house, when with a crash a considerable portion of the window was forced outwards, and a faint scream caught my ears;—maddened by apprehension for Ada, I rushed across the road and knocked loudly at the door. Then scarcely waiting for an answer, I burst it open, and shouting the name of Ada, I rushed into the house."

Sir Francis rose from his chair and in a voice that echoed through the room, he cried,—

"Young man, on your soul is this all true?"

"On my soul," said Albert.

"As you hope for Heaven's mercy?"

Albert stretched out his arms, as he said solemnly, "May the curse of God be upon me evermore if what I say be not the truth. I am innocent—I am innocent."

Sir Francis sunk into his seat again, and drew a long breath-before he said,—

"You shall have justice. Be assured you shall have justice—go on, I pray you."

"I have little more to add, save that I obtained a light of a female in the house, and that still calling upon Ada, I ascended to the room where lay awfully mangled the ghastly remains of Jacob Gray. Upon my descent, your officers seized me, and accused me of the murder."

"And that cloak?"

"Is not mine."

The natural feelings of Sir Francis Hartleton's heart would have prompted him on the instant to tell Albert that he fully believed what he said, but while he never, when acting in his magisterial capacity, forgot that he was a man, he now felt the necessity of remembering that a sworn deposition had taken place. With some difficulty then he mastered his feelings, and said,—

"I shall proceed at once to the house where the deed in question has been committed, and be assured that all shall be done to discover the truth. Till then you must remain here in custody. As a magistrate I can only act upon sworn evidence."

Sir Francis now went to the door, and giving one of the officers whispered instructions to allow no one to see the prisoner, nor suffer him to leave the room, he left him as a guard over Albert, while with hasty steps, and accompanied by one of his most trusty officers, he proceeded to the house of Jacob Gray.

CHAPTER CVIII.

ALBERT'S DESPAIR.—THE TESTS OF TRUTH.

WITH far pleasanter feelings as regarded Ada and her fortunes, than he had ever experienced since his opinion of the unworthiness of Albert Seyton, Sir Francis arrived at the house where so awful a scene of bloodshed had taken place. He was immediately saluted with respect by a constable who had remained in charge of the shattered door, and upon entering the house, the first person belonging to it he saw was Jacob Gray's landlady, who sat in her parlour wringing her hands, and lamenting the death which had taken place under such horrible circumstances in her house, and which as she feelingly remarked, was "a uncommon wicked thing, considering she was a lone woman, and lived principally by letting her lodgings, for nobody wouldn't come and live in the house now, because Mr. Gray's ghostesses would, as a matter of course, haunt the attic and the staircase, so it would."

"Now, my good woman," said Sir Francis Hartleton, "I am a magistrate, so tell me now how all this happened."

" Lord love you, sir, if you was six magistrates, I couldn't tell you. All I knows is, as I am a ruinated woman."

" Well, well, something must be done for you, but I want to know what you heard about this murder."

" Oh ! dear me, sir, Master Gray was such a great man, he was, and his relations must be wretches."

" His relations ?"

" Yes, sir. When he comed to live here, he says, says he, my relations would take my life if they could. That's what he said. Well, I didn't think much of that, but last night—no, it was after twelve, for I recollect I'd heard the Abbey clock strike, cos the wind blowed in that quarter. Well, I was a listening to the rain, when I heard never such a smash in my shop. What's that ? says I, and without more ado, I gets a light, and I goes out."

" Well, and you saw the young man ?"

" No, I didn't sir. There was two villains, sir—one was a amazing tall villain, and the other was uncommon big, only the amazing tall villain looked so in consequence of being so desperate thin, he did. Well, sir, the other villain, not the amazing tall one, he asks where master Gray lives, and I tells him ; then he says as he's his uncle, and desires me to say nothink, and ties me to my blessed bed post and laughed in my face. The idea, sir, of laughing at a lone woman."

" Seyton has spoken the truth," said Sir Francis ; " Learmont and Britton have murdered Gray."

" Sir," said the woman.

" Nothing—nothing ; is there any one else in the house ?"

" Yes sir ; there's an old lady up stairs, and she says as she gave a light to one of the murderers."

" All confirms his statement" thought Hartleton ; " all that now remains for me to do is to secure Gray's confession." Turning then to his officers, he said,—

" Shew me to the murdered man's room, and following them up the narrow stair-case, a few minutes brought him to the presence of the awful remains of Jacob Gray. Sir Francis shuddered as he looked upon the dreadful spectacle, and turning away his eyes, he said,—

" Do not allow the body to be moved. There will be an inquest on it, but search every hole and corner of the room for any papers, and should you see any, give them into no hands but mine."

The search which took place was the most energetic and active that could possibly be made ; but it was, of course, quite unsuccessful ; so after a full hour being spent in it, Sir Francis Hartleton most reluctantly turned towards the corpse, saying to his men—

" You are not afraid of a dead body ? The papers I spoke to you about are most important, and as they may be about him, I wish you to search the pockets."

Hardened as those men were, and callous to most scenes of horror, they approached the remains of Gray with evident reluctance, and made a brief search of his pockets. Nothing was found but a small sum of money and a wedge-shaped steel instrument, which was then commonly used by housebreakers to wrench open doors with.

" There are no papers here, sir," said the men.

Sir Francis Hartleton turned from the room with a look of great disappointment. He entertained now not a moment's doubt, but that the object of Learmont's murder of Gray was to get possession of the packet addressed to him, Sir Francis, and there was every reason to believe that in that object the 'squire had succeeded.

" Ada's name and birth," thought Hartleton, " seem ever doomed to remain mysterious—well, she may still be happy, and as for Learmont and Britton, they must, at all events, expiate this crime upon the scaffold if it is brought home to hem."

Full of these mingled reflections, Sir Francis hurried back to his house, and sought the room in which sat poor Albert Seyton, melancholy and solitary for he could not make up his mind whether his tale, truthful as it was, was believed by the magistrate or not; and when Sir Francis appeared again before him, he rose with a saddened countenance to hear what he had to say to him.

"Mr. Seyton," said Hartleton, "what you have told me has been confirmed, as far as it could be, by the parties in the house I have been to; but tell me now how it was that you, after communicating to me the singular facts you did concerning this Ada, stayed away from me so long?"

"I called upon you, sir," said Albert, "and not seeing you, I fancied you had cooled upon the matter. The 'squire Learmont had prejudiced me against you, representing you as cold and selfish."

"Mr. Seyton—you have yet to learn that those who say the least are often the most to be trusted. I am convinced of your innocence of this murder."

Albert clasped his hands as he cried—

"Thank Heaven! thank Heaven! I shall not die the death of a felon. In some battle for right against might, I am content now in a foreign land to lay down my life. Something tells me that Ada is lost to me for ever. The villain Gray must have taken her life, and I am desolate."

"You jump, perchance, too hastily at that conclusion," said Sir Francis. "You may yet find her. She may even some time since have escaped from Gray."

"Oh if I could but think so."

"Why should you not? Besides, do you mean to give up your friend, the squire?"

"I do—from the first I have had my suspicions of that man. It is not for me to say he killed Jacob Gray, but I will see him no more. His ways are crooked and mysterious."

"Why, he certainly is not the most open and candid character in the world, Mr. Seyton; but were I you, I would not yet give up all hope of discovering Ada."

"Oh, sir, if I could find the smallest foothold for hope to rest upon, I should be again, as I have been, sanguine; but my heart is very sad, and full of despair."

"Being now at liberty, as you may consider yourself, what may be your intentions."

"I shall pursue a course," replied Albert, "that I marked out for myself before I entered the service of this Squire Learmont. I shall, in the capacity of a common soldier, join the army, and hope to find an early and an honourable grave."

"But your testimony will be required on the inquest, which will be held on Jacob Gray."

"I cannot help it. I tell you, sir, I am as one weaned now from the world, and all its uses and companionships; Ada, I feel is lost to me for ever! Farewell, sir. For what exertion you have made, and for what consideration you have shown me, I thank you. Farewell, sir."

"Do you intend now to enlist?"

"I do."

"Well, then, I wish you a happier fate and brighter destiny than you have sketched for yourself. If such be your determination, it is not for me to prevent it."

With a heavy heart Albert rose, and bowing to Sir Francis, who followed him to the room-door, and gave orders for his free egress, he passed out of the house, sick and weary at heart.

Albert then paused in the street a moment, and the idea came across him that it was just possible he might by calling upon Learmont, procure some hint or information of the fate of Ada; but he rejected the proposition almost as quickly as he formed it, and the ghastly corpse of Gray rose up before his imagination, mutely, but strongly accusing Learmont of the murder.

"No—no," he said, "that man is a man of blood! For some cause unknown to me, he has made me a mere tool in his hands, to aid in the destruction of Gray. I will leave him to his conscience, and to the laws. I will see him no more."

The unhappy young man then turned his steps towards the park, and sauntering down the Birdcage-walk, till he came to the old barracks, he accosted a soldier who was lounging by the gate.

Albert had never once glanced behind him, or he might have seen Sir Francis Hartleton, who had, resolving to be perfectly assured in Albert's truth and faith, permitted him to leave the house in the manner we have recorded, but followed him as closely as consistent with ordinary caution. Had Albert gone to Learmont's, new suspicions would have risen up in the mind of the magistrate, and choked like noxious weeds the kindly feelings which he was beginning to entertain towards him ; but now that he saw him enter the park, and proceed towards the barracks, Sir Francis felt all the pleasure which a noble mind always receives from getting rid of suspicion and doubt.

Albert and the soldier passed into the barracks, and then Sir Francis Hartleton immediately stepped up to the gate, and addressing another soldier, said,—

" I must see that young man who has just passed in. My name is Hartleton ; I am a magistrate."

Sir Francis was well known by reputation, and upon his announcement of who he was, the soldier ran after his comrade and Seyton, and brought them both back to the gate again.

" What does this young man do here ?" said Sir Francis.

" He offers to go in the army," said the soldier, " and I was conducting him to my officer."

" I have something to say to him first," remarked the magistrate. " Will you follow me home, Mr. Seyton ?"

" No sir," said Albert, proudly ; " I wish to give you and myself no further trouble with each other."

" Nay, but I have something to communicate."

" You are too late," said Albert. " I came to you in my agony of mind, and implored you to assist in righting the wronged, and saving the innocent from oppression ; you received my suit coldly. You have done, for aught that I know, nothing. Leave me now, sir, for my own course ; I want no cold friends."

" You are angry with me for no cause," said Hartleton, who was secretly pleased at Albert's independence of spirit. " If I have appeared luke-warm in your affairs, I beg you will not attribute it to indifference."

" You may call it what you please, sir," said Albert. " Good morning."

" But I want you to come back with me."

" I hope your honour don't mean to persuade our recruit off?" said the soldier, who was in apprehension that he should lose his gratuity, for bringing so unexceptionable a soldier as the handsome Albert Seyton to the regiment.

" If I do take your recruit away, my friend," said the magistrate, " you shall lose nothing by it if you will call upon me to-morrow."

" Thanks to your honour."

" This is as idle as it is insulting," said Albert. " Am I to be made a thing of barter between you ? I tell you, Sir Francis Hartleton, that you shall not, were you twenty times what you are, interfere with me. When your activity is implored, you are cold and most indifferent, but now when your presence is quite unlooked for and unnecessary, you come after me, as if merely to perplex and annoy me. Take me to your officer, soldiers ; I will serve the king despite of this mocking magistrate."

" But I have not done with you yet," said Sir Francis, with provoking coolness ; " I have an affair in hand in which you must assist me."

" This is insult, sir."

" No ; I have a young friend who I think would make a very good match for you, as you are a likely-looking young man."

Albert's cheek flushed with indignation, as he cried,—

" Sir Francis Hartleton, you came to insult me. Unworthy is it of you, who are revelling in the amplitude of means and power, to deride the unfortunate. You are——"

" Come, come, be calm," interrupted Sir Francis. " You must come with me."

" I will not."

" Then I must make you.   I shall have you taken into custody.   Ho, there !"

The magistrate turned and beckoned to his officers, whom he had directed to follow him, and when they sprang forward to the gate, he said,—

" Take this young man in custody to my house."

" This is the very wantonness of power," cried Albert.   " How dare you thus abuse your office."

" Take him away—I will follow."

Albert was immediately seized, and burning with rage, conveyed to Sir Francis's house again, while the magistrate followed with a smile upon his face.

CHAPTER CIX.

THE MEETING OF THE LOVERS.

SIR FRANCIS HARTLETON's officers paid but little heed to the loud and angry remonstrances of Albert Seyton, but hurried him the short distance between the park and the magistrate's house, at which in a few minutes they arrived, and in obedience to their orders fastened him in the same room from where he had come so recently.

As Sir Francis stood for a moment on the threshold of the apartment, Albert turned to him and said—

" Sir Francis Hartleton, for the treacherous and ungentlemanly conduct of which I have been the victim, I will now denounce you as a disgrace to the office you hold.   I look upon you as——"

" Nay, nay—hold," cried the magistrate, " I will hear no more.   The less you say, the less you will have to retract and ask my pardon for."

" Your pardon?" cried Albert ; " I——"

" Shut the door, he is raving," interposed the magistrate, and in a moment Albert was alone.

The young man stood in the middle of the floor, in deep disgust with Sir Francis, and revolving in his own mind what he should do in the situation he was now placed in.   He walked to the window which overlooked a garden, but there were iron bars across the frame-work, which appeared too firmly let into solid oak to be removed without appropriate tools.

" I will not, however, be caged here if I can help it," thought Albert ; and he seized one of the bars, and exerted all his strength to move it, but it was in vain, for it showed no signs of giving way.   Albert then glanced around him for some weapon, but none such was in the room.   He then threw himself into a chair, and after a few hasty expressions of indignation, relapsed into melancholy silence.   Suddenly, then, he recollected a small knife that he had in his pocket, and he thought he might possibly be able to cut away sufficient of the wood-work to wrench out one of the bars from the window, which, could he accomplish it, would leave a space sufficiently large for him to get through, and drop into the garden, which was at no very great depth, although amply sufficient to make any one, not labouring under the excitement of mind that Albert was, pause ere they adventured the leap.

He found the job of cutting away the wood-work at the window a long and a tedious one, for he could only get the oak away in small pieces, and the iron bars were very deeply imbedded.

" I have heard," thought Albert, " of these things being done with more inefficient tools than a tolerably good knife, aided by perseverance.   I shall rejoice to give this tricky magistrate the slip, even if I walk directly to another, and claim an inquiry into the causes of my present most unjustifiable detention."

"When the heart is in any work, it makes good progress," says Lord Bacon ; and so it seemed in the present instance, for Albert was rapidly getting towards the end of the bar, when an unhappy circumstance retarded his labours. In getting out a large piece of the wood, he struck the blade of the knife on one side, and snapped it short off by the handle. In the excitement, then, of the moment, he seized the bar, and did what, at a cooler time, he could not have done, namely, wrenched one end of it from its hold. The powerful leverage he now had, soon enabled him to free it at the other extremity, and a prospect of escape seemed on the instant opened to him.

In a moment he threw up the window, and glancing into the garden, he was upon the point of springing out, when he saw that there were some iron rails covering some underground part of the premises, upon which he must have fell, had he adventured the leap. Albert paused for a moment, and then a sudden thought struck him that he could make a means of descending in safety. He took Gray's cloak, which had been left hanging on the back of a chair, and firmly tying one corner of it to one of the remaining bars of the window, he let the remainder hang out, intending to slide down by it.

"Now, Sir Francis Hartleton," he exclaimed, "with all your power I am able once more to defy you ; and lest my flight should give occasion to surmises of my guilt, on account of Jacob Gray's murder, I will betake me to the nearest magistrate, and allow him to hold me in custody if he pleases."

He flung himself out at the window. His weight cut the cloak across, and there fell at his feet a folded paper. The young man lay stunned for a moment by his sudden fall. Then he slowly rose, and his eye fell upon the paper ; it was addressed—"To Sir Francis Hartleton, with speed."

Albert clasped his hands, and a cry of surprise escaped him. He knew the endorsement—it was Jacob Gray's confession.

We must now leave Albert for some few moments to his mingled feelings of surprise, and joy, and grief, for such were all struggling in his breast, in order to follow Sir Francis Hartleton to his own private study, whither he instantly repaired after seeing Albert, as he thought, properly secured for the present.

He sat down, and covering his eyes with his hands, a habit he had when he wished a steady communion with his own thoughts, he remained silent for some time. Then he spoke in a low voice, and with a confident tone.

"This young man's honesty and honour," he said, "has been sufficiently tested, and the noble confidence of Ada in his love and sincerity is, thank Heaven, not misplaced. The mystery that envelopes Ada's name and history, I fear now will never be disclosed ; but I must make these two young people happy, and they will be foolish to torment themselves about the past, when the present will be so dear to them, and the future so full of hope. There shall be no sense of dependence, for I will exert all my interest to procure Albert Seyton some honourable employment ; and although the solution of the mysterious conduct of Learmont and his strange connection with Gray and Britton, may go to the grave with him, yet she, the long suffering, persecuted girl will be happy with the object of her heart's choice. I must see her and prepare her for the interview which she shall have with him. How will his anger at his detention here change its complexion when he knows its cause."

Sir Francis then summoned an attendant, and desired that Ada might be requested to come to him as soon as possible. The message was duly delivered, and in a few moments our heroine, to whose fortunes we have clung so long, and who holds so large a place in our hearts, glided like a spirit of beauty into the magistrate's study.

Sir Francis Hartleton, when he had offered her a seat, looked with kindly interest in her face, and said—

"Ada, you look unhappy ; you are paler than you were."

A slight increase of colour visited Ada's cheek, as she replied in her sweet, low musical voice,—

"I am all unused to cloak my feelings, either of joy or sorrow; I am not happy. I have told myself often that I am most ungrateful to you, for your great kindness to me, by being unhappy; but the heart will not be reasoned with, and the subtlest logic of the mind will fail to stop a tear from dimming the eye, when the full heart says 'weep.'"

"You are full of regret, Ada, that I think harshly of young Albert Seyton."

"I am, I am," said Ada. "Oh, sir! you do not know him as I know him, or you would seek some other cause for his conduct than faithlessness."

"Hear me, Ada," added Sir Francis with emotion. "Since I last saw you, I have had occasion to alter my opinion."

A half suppressed cry of joy escaped the lips of Ada, and then she clasped her hands; and while the rapid beating of her heart testified to the emotion occasioned by Sir Francis's words, she fixed upon his face her beautiful eloquent eyes, and eagerly dwelt on every word he uttered.

"Believe me, Ada," he said, "my deep concern for your happiness alone made me anxious that he who was to make or mar your happiness in this world, should be proved pure as virgin gold, ere with joy I could see you become his. I have tested him."

"And—and—" said Ada.

"And believe him true," continued Sir Francis, "although the victim of as strange a series of circumstances, as ever fell to the lot of mortal man."

Ada burst into tears, and sobbed for very joy, while the magistrate turned his head aside to conceal his own emotion.

"My dear Ada," he said, after a pause, "I have much, very much to tell you that concerns you mostly, but I will not now detain you to listen to me. Take this key; it opens the little eastern room which looks into the garden. Release the prisoner you will find there.'

"It is Albert," said Ada.

"It is—"

She rose, and placed both her hands in those of Sir Francis Hartleton's, and smiling upon him through her tears, she said,—

"Dear friend; can I ever thank you—can the poor Ada ever hope even in words to convey to you the full gratitude of her heart?"

"Let me see you happy, Ada," said Sir Francis, "and I am more than repaid. Go to your lover, who is, I fear, a very impatient prisoner, and tell him, from me, that I will never interefere with him again, let him do what he may."

Ada could not understand what Sir Francis meant by his last words, but at that moment she was not much inclined to ask explanations, but taking the key while her hand trembled, and her lustrous eyes seemed swimming in an ocean of tenderness as she glided from the room to rescue her lover.

Ada knew the room well to which Sir Francis had directed her, and her eager footsteps in a few moments brought her to the door. For one brief moment then she paused to recover herself from her state of agitation. In the next she had opened the door—the room was tenantless. Ada flew to the window—there hung the torn cloak.

"Albert, Albert," she cried, and sunk upon the floor in an agony of grief.

Sir Francis Hartleton heard the cry of Ada, and hastening from his room, the truth shot across his mind in a moment when he saw the cloak hanging by the iron bar.

"Who could have imagined this?" he cried. "Ada, Ada, be of good cheer; all will be well. He cannot leave the garden."

"Oh, Sir Francis," cried Ada; "For Heaven's sake explain to me the meaning of all this—what could induce him to fly thus strangely?"

"Think nothing of it, Ada, all will be well. I meditated giving Albert Seyton an agreeable surprise, and he has given us a disagreeable one, that is all—hark!"

As Sir Francis spoke, there arose a confused noise in the garden, and upon his going to the window, he saw Albert in the grasp of two of his officers. Without any remark concerning what he was to say, he turned to Ada and said,—

"Leave all to me. Do you remain here, Ada, until I come to you. I pledge you my word all shall be explained to your satisfaction within this present hour."

Sir Francis then hurried from the room, leaving Ada in a greater state of bewilderment than ever, and, hastening to the garden, he met the officers who had recaptured Albert.

"So, sir," said Sir Francis, "you have, methinks, a small amount of patience."

"Patience, sir," cried Albert. "Why should I have any under a tyranny as unexampled as it is despicable. In plain words, sir, tell me what you mean by detaining me?"

No. 52

"Young man, it is for your own good. Let me advise you now, for your own benefit. I shall send some one to you, to talk you out of your unreasonable humour."

"I warn you, Sir Francis Hartleton," said Albert. "I am now upon my defence, and, if you send any of your myrmidons to me, they may chance to regret coming within the reach of my arm."

"Indeed! Now, I will wager you my head, that you will be in a more complaisant humour shortly. Bring him in, and confine him in my parlour."

Resistance against the powerful men who held him, Albert felt would be quite absurd, and merely wasting his energies to no purpose ; so he suffered himself, although boiling with rage, to be led into a room on the ground floor.

"Now, my young friend," said Sir Francis, "I shall send some one to you to tame your proud spirit."

"I defy your utmost malice," cried Albert.

"Oh!—let him rave—let him rave. Shut him in," said Sir Francis calmly.

The moment the door was closed upon the prisoner, he drew from his breast the confession of Gray, and was upon the point of opening it, when his high sense of honour forbade him breaking the seal of a communication addressed to another, and he dropped it on the floor, as he said,—

"No, no! Although this magistrate, from some inexplicable cause, is my enemy, I must not forget that I am a gentleman."

The words were scarcely out from his mouth, when he heard the door unlock gently, and arming himself then, with all the indignation he felt, he cried in a loud voice,—

"Whoever you are, advance here, at your peril !"

The door opened very slowly, and when it was just wide enough for one person to enter Ada glided into the room.

"At my peril, Albert ?" she said.

The colour forsook the cheek of Albert, and he stood gazing at her for a few moments, incapable of thought or action ; then, with a gush of joy, he flew towards her.

"Ada, Ada! my dear Ada, are you in life or am I mocked by some vision? My Ada, speak !"

"Albert."

He clasped her to his heart. He kissed her cheek, her brow, her hands. Tears gushed from his eyes, and mingled with those of the long-lost, fondly cherished idol of his heart. They could neither of them speak, and nothing was heard for many minutes in that room, but sobs of gushing joy, such as make the heart leap in extacy, and give humanity a glimpse of heaven.

CHAPTER CX.

THE LOVERS. — THE INTERVIEW OF SIR FRANCIS HARTLETON WITH THE SECRE-
TARY OF STATE.—THE BALL.

ALBERT SEYTON first broke the silence, and as he clasped Ada's hands, and gazed into her beaming eyes, he said,—

"Ada ! my own beautiful Ada ! Am I, indeed, so blessed? Do I once again see you in all your beauty, smiling on me ? Am I dreaming, or are you; indeed, and in truth, my own dear Ada ?—the dream of my boyhood, the cherished idol of my heart."

"Indeed, and in truth," said Ada.

"Oh! I am too, too, happy. Heaven forgive me all my sinful repining. Does not this moment's joy repay me for all. My darling—my true and beautiful——"

What a heavenly light shone from the eyes of Ada! What a sunny smile played around her cherry-mouth, dimpling her cheek with beauty.

"We will part no more, Albert," she said. "After many, many trials, we have met at last to part no more. God has blessed us in each other's love, and we will not cast from us the pure bright gift of heaven!"

"We will not," cried Albert. "Bless you, my own true-hearted Ada! At the very moment of my despair, I have been, as it were, lifted to heaven. 'Tis foolish of me, Ada ; but, even now, so great is my happiness, I can scarce believe it real."

He drew the blushing girl again to his throbbing heart. He kissed the raven tresses of her silken heart. He looked into her eyes, sparkling with dewy tears, and saw the happiness that shot from every radiant glance. Her cheek, gentle and soft as a rose-bud's inmost leaf, touched his—was there ever so much happiness. Could all the ills of life concentrated, poison the rich fragrance of that one cup of overflowing joy?

We will not attempt to record the gentle confidences of the happy lovers—the broken sentences—the speaking glances that filled up the pauses which the faltering tongue, too much oppressed by the heart's gushing eloquence, could not choose but make, the tones upon which memory in after years lingers like the shade of a loved one long hidden in the tomb, nor the thousand purest vows breathed by Albert, nor the thousand smiles with which they were all believed by Ada. Suffice it to say, that they were very happy, and those of our readers who have felt a sympathy with the trials of the lone maiden, will be pleased to leave her for a brief space, knowing that her heart is dancing with joy, and that even the memory of the past is emerged in the pure and heavenly enjoyment of the present.

Sir Francis Hartleton's first step after seeing Ada enter the room in which Albert was, was to communicate to his wife all that had passed, and commission her to explain all to Albert, if such explanation should be sought for before his return, for he felt it necessary, in consequence of the extraordinary events which had transpired, to communicate to his impatient friend, the home secretary, before even taking steps to apprehend Britton and Learmont for the murder of Gray, which upon Albert's testimony he felt was what might be safely ventured upon.

The magistrate accordingly left his house, and proceeded on foot to the secretary's office, where he was fortunate enough to find the great man disengaged.

"I have come," said Hartleton, "to state to your lordship some strange circumstances with relation to the person named Learmont, concerning whom I have before had the honour of conversing with you."

The secretary put on a face of alarm as he replied—

"Really, Sir Francis, you must drop this matter—his majesty has only this day, in council, determined upon a dissolution of the present parliament—of course I tell you in confidence—and this Learmont's votes in the Commons may be of the greatest consequence."

"But, my lord," said Hartleton, "there is good reason to believe that no later than last night he committed a most awful murder."

"Dear me," said the secretary, "he might as well have waited till the general election was over. It is really such a very awkward thing to hang a man who can command several votes in the Commons."

"It may be so," said Sir Francis, with a smile, "but when people who command votes will commit murder, what is to be done?"

"Ah that's very true ; but uncommonly disagreeable."

"I thought it my duty," continued Hartleton, "to let your lordship know before I arrested him."

"Bless my heart," said the secretary, "now I recollect there has been a record here to-day, containing an invitation to a masked ball, which this very man is going to give on Friday."

"Indeed, my lord."

" Yes. I sent a civil acceptance of the invitation of course, because I meant to sound him in the course of the evening about his votes. Now really, Sir Francis, you must let the ball be over before you come in with your charge of murder, and so on."

" I will if your lordship pleases ; but the property of Learmont, provided he be convicted of murder, will revert to the Crown, in which event you will have his votes,"

" Ah, but, my dear Sir Francis, the Crown, in common decency, must waive its right to the property in favour of the next of kin."

" I believe there can arise no claimant," said Sir Francis ; " therefore there can be no delicacy on the subject."

" Well, that's lucky—but you will let the ball be over. I'm told it's to be a splendid affair, and really so many of our political friends intend to make it a complete rendezvous, that it would be a thousand pities not to let it go off with some eclat."

" I shall, of course, not interfere, my lord ; but should anything occur to force a magisterial duty, I trust your lordship will not expect me to shrink from performing mine."

" Well, I suppose not, but don't be provoking, Sir Francis, if you can possibly avoid it. By-the-by, I quite forgot to ask who he had murdered. It's nobody of any consequence, I presume ?"

" He certainly had no vote."

" No vote ?"

" No, nor was likely ever to have one."

" Indeed. Well, I do hate people who have no vote most cordially, and I should say there can be only one class of people more abominable, and that is the class which votes against one. I don't at all see the use in this world of people without votes. How uncommonly silly Learmont must have been, really."

" Silly enough, my lord, to put his neck in jeopardy, for a jury will most naturally bring him in guilty, and the king cannot very well spare a murderer."

" Why no, not exactly ; but at all events don't say a word about it till after the ball."

" Unless there should arise an absolute necessity I will not, but the inquest upon the body of the murdered man may interfere with your lordship's wishes."

" Bless me, yes—what's to-day ?"

" Wednesday."

" Oh, well, I must speak to the coroner about it, and the inquest must just be put off till Saturday. In fact, I don't see the use of an inquest upon a man who had no vote, Sir Francis ; but I suppose these things must be done to please the common people."

" They must indeed," said Sir Francis ; " any tampering with what Englishmen consider their liberties, will ever be a dangerous task for a minister."

" Ah, well, we must do the best we can, but you know it would have been much better if this Learmont, while he was murdering, had murdered some one with a vote who was opposed to us. It might have made a difference of two votes you see, Sir Francis."

" So it might, your lordship ; but when people murder, 1 am afraid they think more of their own private quarrels than of votes."

" Ah, no doubt. You are quite right—good morning, Sir Francis, good morning."

" Good morning, your lordship."

Sir Francis Hartleton could not help laughing as he walked homewards at the curious morality of the secretary, who measured everybody's importance by their number of votes, and he thought to himself surely this system of representation will be some day done away with, and Englishmen will be permitted to exercise their franchise and their conscience freely.

Absorbed then in meditation concerning the important steps which required to be taken previous to the Friday evening, beyond which time Sir Francis Hartleton was quite resolved Learmont should not remain at liberty, he sauntered home from the minister's.

Believing, as the magistrate now did, since Jacob Gray was dead, and no written papers could be found about his person, or in his lodging, that no overt act as concerned Ada could be brought home to Learmont, he resolved to have a warrant made out for the 'squire's apprehension, on the charge of murdering Jacob Gray, a crime which upon the testimony of Albert could be brought as nearly home to him as strong circumstantial evidence could bring it.

"It may be then," thought Sir Francis, "that when he sees his mortal career closing, he will do one act of grace, and declare who and what Ada is, detailing his reasons for persecuting her so strangely, and for taking the life of Jacob Gray. That now seems to be the only chance of arriving at a solution of the mysteries which still envelope this whole strange transaction."

When Sir Francis reached home a letter was put into his hands, which, upon opening, he found to contain these words,—

"Mr. Learmont presents his compliments to Sir Francis Hartleton, and begs specially to request his company on Friday evening, to a masked ball and supper."

"Well," said Sir Francis, "of all the cool pieces of assurance that it was ever my lot to encounter, this is the coolest. But I can well understand Learmont's feelings now; he fancies himself rid of some great danger by the death of Jacob Gray, and this is the very mockery and insolence of security in inviting me, who he hates so cordially, to his entertainment. Well, be it so, I will be there, Learmont, and it shall go hard but your masked ball shall have a far different conclusion to what you imagine. Let me see, this ticket admits Sir Francis Hartleton and friends—friends. Yes, that will do—that will do. A plan of operation occurs to me, which on the surprise of the moment, may wring from the guilty heart of Learmont something of importance to the interests of Ada. She shall go with me to this masked ball. Yes, Learmont shall be surprised from his usual cold caution by her sudden appearance, which, conjoined with his arrest, may so disturb his faculties as almost to induce a confession of all we wish to know. It shall be tried— it shall be tried."

CHAPTER CXI.

THE CONFESSION.

WHILE Sir Francis Hartleton was still engaged in these reflections a low knock sounded on the door of his room, and when he cried, "come in," the happy face of Ada appeared like a beam of sunshine in the entrance.

"Ada," he said, "come in."

There were the humid traces of tears upon her cheek, but they were like the pearly drops of dew which hung upon the rose leaves, speaking not of sorrow or decay, but giving new beauty to what before seemed matchless. They were tears of joy, and the magistrate saw that they were so. He held out his hand to Ada, as he said with a smile,—

"Will you forgive me for tormenting Albert a little?"

"He will scarce forgive himself," said Ada, "and sends me as his ambassador."

"He had a right to feel a little angry, Ada. But has he told you that your old enemy is dead?"

"He has," said Ada. "Much as I had to complain of against Jacob Gray, I would that he had come to some gentler death. Heaven have mercy upon him!"

"He has need of heaven's mercy, Ada. But are you not much disappointed that all chance of discovering your name and station seems now faded away?"

"I scarcely know how to answer you," said Ada, "for hope that it may not be so, has within the last half hour disturbed me more with anxious doubts and fearful surmises than ever agitated my breast before. This paper ——"

As she spoke, she handed to Sir Francis the confession of Gray still sealed up as Albert had picked it from the garden.

"Gracious heavens!" said Sir Francis, as a sudden flush of colour to his face showed the interest he felt in the document, "where got you this, Ada?"

"When Albert, impatient of his temporary detention in the room overlooking the garden," said Ada, "made an attempt to escape from it, he tried to descend from the window by the aid of a cloak, which rent with his weight, revealing this packet of papers addressed to you."

"Thus heaven works its wonders," said Sir Francis; "and the very circumstances that at the moment of their occurrence fill us with regret, bring us to the dearest of our wishes. You know this handwriting, Ada?"

"It is Jacob Gray's."

"Then there can be no doubt," said Sir Francis, as with fingers that trembled with eagerness he broke the seals by which the packet was fastened—"there can be no doubt that these are the papers, or similar ones to those long ago addressed to me by Jacob Gray, and said to be concerning you."

"Albert thinks with you," said Ada, "and longs to penetrate the mystery of their contents."

"Will you leave me?" said Sir Francis. "I would fain read this alone, Ada. Will you grant me that indulgence?"

Ada rose as she said,—

"Dear friend, a wish of yours shall ever be a command to me : but remember that, let these papers contain what they may, I can bear to hear all."

"Nothing shall be concealed from you, Ada," said Sir Francis, "but—but my own deeply interested feelings would not permit me to read these documents aloud to you at first."

Ada saw his extreme excitement and agitation, and instantly leaving the room, she gave him an opportunity of reading alone the long sought-for confession of Jacob Gray.

Sir Francis's first step was to lock himself in his room, and then, with a flurry at his heart, and a total abstraction of mind from everything but the papers which lay before him, he tore them open and read as follows:—

"TO SIR FRANCIS HARTLETON.

"I, Jacob Gray, address the following confession and statement of facts to you, because, from circumstances within your own remembrance, you will the more readily believe what is here recorded. May the bitterest curse of a dead man fall on you and yours, if you do not take instant means to bring to an ignominious end those who I shall accuse of crimes which shall far exceed any that I have committed. By the time you receive this, I shall most probably be dead, or have left England for some distant land, where all search for me would be in vain. I leave, however, behind, whether dead or absent, this legacy of vengeance, and so fulfil a promise I made to my own heart to destroy those who would long since have murdered me, but that I had fenced myself round with safeguards which they dared not despise.

"In the year 1737 I was staying at Genoa, where I had been discharged from the service of an English family for matters of no consequence to my present narrative. For some months I could procure no employment, until an English gentleman, by name Mark Learmont, was taken ill at one of the hotels in the city, and the proprietor of the establishment, fearing that his guest was dying, sent for me as a countryman of the sick gentleman, to attend upon him. I nursed and tended him with anxious care, and I soon learnt that grief was his only malady.

He told me he had left England in consequence of the death of his wife and child, and that he could never more with pleasure look upon his ancient home again, which he had left in the care of his brother. Time, however, seemed in some measure to assuage his grief; and when he got well enough again to travel, he retained me as his permanent attendant, liberally rewarding me for the services I had rendered him. We went from city to city of the Italian states until we came to Rome, where an attempt was made by some hired bravo to take the life of Mr. Learmont. He was saved, however, by the gallant interposition of a young Italian nobleman, named Geronimo Madelina; and my master became in a short time on terms of the greatest intimacy with the family of his preserver, who had a sister so surprisingly beautiful that even Mr. Learmont forgot his grief for her whom he had loved so fondly, and became attached to Ada Madelini with a pasionate fervour that knew no bounds. Learmont was handsome, brave, and accomplished. The young Italian returned his passion. A child was born—an illegitimate child—which Ada Madelina died in giving birth to.

"Mr. Learmont was again plunged into the most excessive grief. Rome became more hateful to him than the home in England he had left; the very language of Italy was ever reminding him of the beautiful being who had gone to an early grave through her love for him. In vain he travelled from city to city. His grief knew no reduction, until at length, wearied with travel, and sick at heart, he resolved upon once more revisiting his native land, taking with him the child of Ada Madelini, who had been named after its mother, and who had begun to exercise a strong control over his affections.

" A letter was written to the brother, who had been left sole master of the estate of Learmont, signifying the intention of the widowed man to return, and once more assume the control of his own property for his young daughter's sake. When we reached Dover, that is, Mr. Mark Learmont, myself, and his infant child, a letter was awaiting my master from his brother. That letter I by chance saw. It said that peculiar family circumstances, which the writer would explain when they met, rendered it necessary that their first meeting should be a secret one, and quite unknown to any person connected with the property. It named as the place of rendezvous, an old deserted mansion, the lower part of which was converted into a smithy, and had been long occupied by a man named Andrew Britton.

" Full of wonder at this letter, and yet never doubting that there were, did he but know them, full and reasonable grounds for it, Mr. Learmont wrote to his brother, according to his request, and promising to be at the Old Smithy with his child, by the evening of a particular day, which he named.

" He sent me beforehand to apprise his brother of this. I was the bearer of the answer, and when I reached Learmont's house, he that is now called Squire Learmont, and who resides in your immediate vicinity, received me most cordially. He spoke to me of the advantages of wealth—of the luxuries of independence—of the delightful feelings of those who could scorn the world's utmost malice—secure in the haven of independence—but it is idle to dwell upon the deep temptation that he held out to me. I consented to the murder of my master and his child !

" The day of his arrival came. · It was one of alternate storm and sunshine; but, as the evening approached, the elements seemed to have broken loose, and to have united to shake the very earth with terror. The wind howled, and the forked lightning shot from earth to heaven, while peal after peal of thunder shook the habitations, of the peasantry, convulsing the stoutest hearts with fear, and destroying all the produce of their industry.

" It was on such a night, that, leaving Learmont, and the smith Andrew Britton in the smithy, I started to meet my doomed master.

" From obscure hints the smith had dropped, I was satisfied that Mr. Learmon's first wife and child had been murdered by him and the brother, and even after I had consented, I shuddered at the awful crime I had pledged myself to assist in committing—but it was too late to retract. I had already received some of the wages of crime—I could not recede. But surely I was innocent compared with him who would shed a brother's blood. Let him suffer the penalty of his crimes —let the rich Squire Learmont dangle on the gallows tree—spare him not, nor Andrew Britton—you will find him at the Old Chequers—let him too die a death of pain and ignominy—so shall I have my revenge—my deep, long-cherished revenge.

"I met Mr. Learmont. He alighted from the carriage, which he left at a distance of a mile or more from the appointed place of meeting with his brother. He gave me the young child to carry—the infant Ada, and we walked under cover of the darkness of the stormy evening until we reached the smithy. I was to kill the child, while Britton took the life of the father ; but one thing they had not told me namely, that they intended to burn down the Old Smithy after the deed was done, in order that the two bodies should be consumed in the ruins, and no suspicion should arise of their untimely fate.

" It was an hour to me of horror—Mr. Learmont entered the Old Smithy unsuspectingly, and I followed with the child. He took his brother kindly by the hand, and I heard him say,—

" Well, brother, what is amiss, that we cannot meet in my own home !"

" Come this way, Mark," said he who is called the squire, as he opened a heavy door at the further end of the smithy. " Come this way, and you will know all."

" Mr. Learmont followed him, and I went after them with the child. It was clinging to my neck, and as I gazed upon its features, by the occasional flash of lightning, all strength seemed to desert me, and I felt I had not power to take its life,—I thought I should have sunk into the earth—a fearful timidity came over me, and the cold perspiration of terror bedewed my brow.

" I scarcely know then what happened, but the storm without increased to tenfold fury ; and while the smithy was being set fire to by Learmont, the squire, I saw by the dull red glare that began to spread itself around, and light up everything with its ghastly lustre—I saw my master stagger back, as if from some sudden blow, and the smith, Andrew Britton, faced my gaze, armed with a forge hammer, with which he had already struck one blow at my master.

" Mr. Learmont then tried to wrestle with his opponent' and he screamed, Murder—murder. He called too on me to help him, but I could not move. I saw another blow given, and I heard the sickening crushing of his head, as the hammer sunk into his brain—then he fell, with one shriek that wrung in my ears, for many months, scaring me from sleep, and causing me to start in horror from my bed.

" The fire had spread with greater rapidity than had been calculated upon, and at the moment of my master's murder, a portion of the roof fell upon me and the child—I was hurt, but the infant was not—alarm and horror took possession of my faculties, and I fled, shrieking, through the house, seeking for some outlet to escape by—I got confused in a labyrinth of rooms—burning flakes fell upon my flesh—I cried for aid, but no voice answered me, and I felt a conviction that I was purposely left there to perish. Despair lent me strength, and with the child still in my arms, I leaped a burning staircase—I saw a crowd of faces before me, and, with frantic cries, I rushed from the building with the child.

" Who, then, snatched the infant from me, I know not, for I was suffering much pain ; but certainly it was taken from me by some of the villagers, and I, frantic with the terrors I had received, and believing that the hand of Providence was upon me, fled I knew not whither, until I sunk exhausted from fatigue, in a wood a short distance from the village on the road to London.

" The cool night air assuaged the pain of my burns, and after resting for some hours, I found myself sufficiently recovered to think upon what I should next do. Return to the smithy, I dared not, for I dreaded the vengeance of the squire, not only on account of my failing in what I had to do, but I could not dispossess myself of the idea that my death had been determined upon, between him and the smith, so soon as I had killed the child, and was no longer useful to their purposes. I had received, in advance, a sum of money from my tempter, Learmont, and after some thought I resolved upon proceeding direct to London, and there endeavouring to forget the horrors I had gone through, in the varied amusements of a great city. I turned my back upon the village of Learmont, and all its ter-

rible recollections, taking my route to the capital by the quickest means I could find.

"It was on the second day that I arrived, and resolving to husband my money until I could procure some other employment, I took an obscure lodging, and kept my expenses as small as possible.

"It was the fourth evening after my arrival in London, that a woman, who was sitting upon a step, with a child in her lap, implored my charity. I refused her,

No. 53.

and was about to pass on, when a glance told me that the child with her was the young Ada Madelini, the child of Mr. Learmont; I paused, and questioned her. She told me her name was Tattan, and said she had fled from the country with the child, to save its life, which had been threatened by a man, wicked and powerful. All this confirmed me—I snatched the child from her arms, for I thought it an admirable possession, since it would give me the means of making my own terms, at some future time, with the Squire of Learmont.

" The woman screamed and ran after me, crying for help. No one was near us, and with one blow I silenced her, and she fell to the ground. What became of her I never knew, but I took the child home with me, and the next day I changed my lodging, passing the infant as my own.

" From house to house I shifted my residence, always thinking myself suspected by some one, until I went to reside at a low house, kept by a woman, by name Strangeways, who resided in the neighbourhood of Swallow-street. Before going there, however, I bought boy's clothing for the girl, as I thought it safer to make her appear as a boy than let her real sex be known. Nearly ten years had elapsed, and I was falling fast into poverty, for a concern in which I had placed some money, under tempting promises, proved a failure. Then I bethought me of some means of improving my condition, and recruiting my empty coffers.

" After much thought, I resolved upon going to the village of Learmont, and forming a coalition if possible, with the smith, Andrew Britton, for the purpose of extorting money from the rich squire. But previously to going I wrote a paper, containing all the particulars I here relate, and sealing it, I left it with Ada, who I had named, in conformity with her male attire, Harry, charging her to let it reach the hands of yourself in the event of my not returning by a stipulated time.

" I went on my errand. It was in the winter, and the snow lay thickly in the valley of Learmont; as I reached the village inn, I inquired if the smith, Britton, was still alive; I was told he was, and heard then the clank of his forge-hammer, the same most probably that had taken the life of Mr. Learmont. I sought him, and suffice to say, that I not only convinced him of the inexpediency of attempting aught against my life, which, as I guessed he would be, he was much inclined to do, but succeeded in inducing him to join with me in extorting large sums from the guilty squire.

" Britton, too, I persuaded to search the body of the murdered man, when, as I told him, he found papers of great consequence to the squire—papers which he would gladly have redeemed at any price, but which were of infinitely more value as a source of permanent income to their fortunate holder.

" I had lent the smith a knife of mine at his own request before the murder, and when I visited him he produced it, stained with human gore, taunting me with the fact, that my name was on the handle, and that it would ever prove a damning evidence of my guilt.

" Thus were we three men in each other's power. Either Britton or myself could bring the whole three to destruction, and the squire was but too glad to ensure his own safety, by paying large sums to us from time to time. He came to London, and we followed him. Andrew Britton led a life, as he now leads, of riot and extravagance, at the public-house called the Chequers, Westminster. The Squire Learmont lives in splendour, as you must be aware, in your immediate vicinity. I have led a life of dangers and terror. My existence has been continually threatened by Learmont, who, could he at any time have laid his hands upon Ada, who he believed to be legitimate, and likewise have secured my written confession, would have murdered me.

" I repeat, I may be dead, or absent from England, when you arrive; but be it which way it may, if you want proofs of what I assert, search the ruins of the Old Smithy at Learmont, and you may still find some traces of the murdered body of Mr. Mark Learmont. Apprehend Andrew Britton, and search for the knife, I mention, as well as for any papers that he may have taken from the dead body. Among them will be found the letter from the squire, begging his brother to meet him at the Old Smithy, instead of coming direct to his own mansion. .

"It will be understood by you, then, clearly, that I accuse these two men, Squire Learmont and Andrew Britton, of the murder of Learmont's elder brother, and the projected murder of his illegitimate child. She, Ada, left me some time since, after an attempt made by you to take me into custody at the old house a Battersea Fields, among the ruins of which I believe you will still find some articles that belonged to Ada when her father's death occurred.

"Let, then, these men be brought to an ignominious end. Remember that the Learmont family will become extinct with the present squire, for the girl Ada, I repeat, is an illegitimate child. The elder Learmont and Ada Madelini were not married. The large estates, then, must revert to the crown, and my vengeance will be complete. If I am living, I shall hear of the execution of Learmont and Britton; for who can doubt their guilt? If I am dead, and the spirits of the departed retain any shadow of the feelings which agitated them in this world, I shall still rejoice that I have had my revenge.   "JACOB GRAY."

CHAPTER CXII.

THE CONSULTATION WITH ALBERT AND ADA.—THE ARRANGEMENT FOR THE BALL.

WHEN he had finished the confession of Gray, Sir Francis Hartleton looked up and drew a long breath. An inexpressible feeling of relief came over him, and he cried,—

"It is as I partly expected. Ada is related to this squire nearly. With regard to her alleged illegitimacy, I do not believe it for a moment. The malice of Jacob Gray, for denouncing him in the open street, is fully sufficient to account for his making such an assertion. That, however, is a fact which can be very easily ascertained; and I have not a shadow of doubt but my beautiful young friend, after all her severe trials and persecutions, will become the possessor of the splendid estates of Learmont, and will be able to reward the constancy of her lover with a princely income. Oh, what a relief it is, after all, to find that Jacob Gray cannot claim the least shadow of kindred with Ada. Well, he has gone to his account; and, although I have no moral doubt in the world of the guilt of Britton and Learmont as regards Ada's father, yet this paper would be very insufficient evidence to proceed upon. If they suffer the penalty of the law for murder, it will be for that of Jacob Gray himself."

Sir Francis Hartleton then left his room, after locking up Gray's confession, and hastened to where he had left Albert. The good-hearted magistrate will be excused by our fair readers for forgetting that in all probability Ada, when she had left him, had gone back to Albert, and that, consequently, when he, Sir Francis, opened the door very abruptly, the beautiful girl was just, to the smallest possible extent annoyed, to be seen with Albert's hand clasped in her own, and such a smile of joy on her face, that her lover thought himself in heaven, and, at all events, would have challenged any one to produce a heartfelt joy equal to that which then filled him with thankfulness.

"My dear Ada," said Sir Francis, "I have to apologise."

Ada rose, and while a blush spread itself over her face, she said,—

"Sir Francis Hartleton, how can Albert and myself find words to tell you how much we owe to you, our noble, considerate, generous friend. What would have become of the poor destitute, desolate Ada, but for you?"

"And I, sir," said Albert, while a tear glistened in his eye, "I'm afraid I have offended you past all forgiveness."

"No such thing," said Sir Francis. "You know I was very provoking indeed,

Mr. Seyton; but Ada, my dear, go and fetch Lady Hartleton, for she must hear what I have to tell you."

Ada looked in his face a moment, to read by his expressive features the character of the intelligence he had gleaned from Gray's confession; and the magistrate shaking his head, said playfully,—

"Now, Ada, that is too bad;" but the smile with which he accompanied his words assured her that what he had to say was not the worst that could be under the circumstances anticipated, and she flew to Lady Hartleton to come and join the group.

When they were all assembled, Sir Francis said,—

"What I now tell you must remain in our own breasts until Saturday. Ada, I shall commence with one piece of intelligence, which will not displease you, and I am sure remove one occasionally disagreeable thought from your mind—Jacob Gray is not in the remotest degree connected with you by the ties of relationship."

"Thank Heaven!" said Ada.

"Now then, my dear Ada, I counsel you to bear, with a patient resignation, the will of Providence, when I tell you you are an orphan."

One sob burst from Ada's breast, for she had always pleased herself with the idea of some day finding a dear mother or father. That dream was now dispelled, and it was with some difficulty she could say,—

"Heaven's will be done! I should not mourn, for have I not found all the love and care of dear parents from you, my kind friends?"

"Your father," continued Sir Francis Hartleton, "was a noble, honourable gentleman—your mother, a lady of wealth and family."

"Go on—go on," gasped Ada, while Albert Seyton and Lady Hartleton looked the intense interest they felt in Sir Francis's words.

"Will you not, Ada," he added, "be now content with knowing so much, and seek not to dive deeper into the past."

"Tell me more of my father and mother," she sobbed; "oh, leave me not to conjecture. The mind will ever conjure up from the realms of fancy tenfold horrors. Tell me all—oh, tell me all."

"I cannot refuse you," said Sir Francis, "because you have a right to demand to know all. Your mother, as far as I can rely upon my information, died in giving birth to you. Your father——"

Sir Francis paused, and Ada, clasping her hands, cried—"my father—what of him—oh, speak."

"Your father fell a victim to the avarice of one whom he trusted. His own brother murdered him."

Ada shuddered, and as the tears rapidly coursed each other down her cheeks, she said, in a low, plaintive tone,—

"Tell me all now. Surely I have heard the worst. My poor father!"

"Returning with you, when you were an infant, to his native land, and his ancient home, his life was taken by three men. One was his brother, the other a smith, by name Andrew Britton, and the third——"

Sir Francis Harleton paused, and Ada filled up the blank with the words,—

"Jacob Gray."

"True," said the magistrate; "Jacob Gray was, it appears, by his own confession, a confidential servant of your father's, and was suborned by your wicked and most unnatural uncle to commit the crime, or, at all events, aid in its commission, which, for so many years, plunged him in all the miseries of a guilty conscience, and placed you in the singular circumstances from which you have been but so recently rescued."

"And—and—my name?" said Ada.

"Your name is Learmont."

"Learmont!" cried Albert. "God of Heaven, can this be possible? Then he who I have fancied my friend—he who so speciously taught me to believe he was doing me such great service, is the uncle of Ada!"

"He is, and her father's murderer."

" The assassin, too, of Jacob Gray ?"

" The same."

" And he, the stout bulky man, whom I saw enter Gray's abode with the squire ?"

" He is Andrew Britton, the smith, the associate in guilt of the Squire Learmont. You were made a mere tool to assist in the destruction of Jacob Gray, who, no doubt, was troublesome on account of his rapacity, and dangerous on account of the written confession he kept by him, and which has so providentially and strangely fallen into my hands."

Albert Seyton looked perfectly petrified with astonishment for a time. Then, in a voice of emotion, he said,—

" Oh, Heaven, how near was I proving your worst enemy, my Ada, by too credulously becoming a victim to the arts of the man, who, of all others in the wide world, you had most to dread."

" I can scarcely understand all this," said Ada. " You must relate everything to me, Albert, in a more connected manner. Is this Learmont a tall, dark man, with a face of death-like paleness ?"

" He is," said Albert.

" And he is my father's brother ?"

" I grieve to say that such is the fact," said Sir Francis Hartleton. " The law must take cognisance of Jacob Gray's murder, and that will most probably be the only one of Learmont's crimes that can be satisfactorily proved against him. A word with you, Mr. Seyton."

While Ada sat with her hand clapsed in that of Lady Hartleton, who was striving to soothe the agitated spirits of the gentle girl, Sir Francis took Albert to the window, and said,—

" Gray, in his confession, asserts the illegitimacy of Ada, but from all that I have ever heard of the character of the elder Learmont, as well as from the evidently anxious manner in which Gray has repeatedly stated the circumstance, I much doubt its truth. It is quite necessary, however, that such a point should be satisfactorily set at rest, or we shall have difficulty in procuring for Ada her father's property, which has been so long withheld from her by this squire, as he has falsely called himself. The family of Ada's mother can surely be easily found, and I think some one must be instantly despatched to Italy, where Ada was born, in order to prosecute the necessary inquiries."

" Oh, Sir Francis," said Albert, his countenance beaming with pleasure; " let them say what they like of Ada, she is to me the whole world. With her I can be happy as the day is long, and I am sure we shall never sigh for the wealth, the possession of which could not make our hearts more true to each other than they are now."

" Yes, my dear sir," said Sir Francis, with a smile, " I quite agree with you that you may make yourselves very happy indeed, in a humbler station of life than that in which I have hopes of placing Ada ; but it is but common justice that she should possess what is hers of right. The Learmont property is immense."

Albert sighed.

" Why, what's the matter now ?" said Sir Francis, good humouredly.

" Can I expect," said the young man, " that Ada Learmont, the rich heiress, should give her hand to the poor, destitute Albert Seyton ?"

" Oh, I have nothing to do with that," exclaimed the worthy magistrate, " you must settle all that between you. Ada, I wish you to give an opinion on a very knotty point raised by Albert Seyton."

Before Albert Seyton could interpose, Ada approached the window, and Sir Francis added,—

" You must know, Ada, that Mr. Seyton is of opinion that if he were to get immensely rich, his feelings would alter as regards his affections for one poor and dependent,"

" Good God, Sir Francis," said Albert, " I never said any such thing !"

" Then it was Ada's feelings which were to alter, provided she was rich and you poor."

Albert looked abashed, and Ada said in a gentle voice to him,—

" Is this kind, Albert ?'

"No, Ada," he said. "It is foolish and wrong. Forgive the scruple that rose up in my mind of still urging my suit to you when, as I hear from Sir Francis Hartleton, you are likely to become very wealthy."

"And did such a thought cross your mind, Albert," said Ada, sadly, "when you stood between little Harry Gray and him who is now no more—when you spent days and nights of anxious toil in searching for me—did then a thought of that affection which sprung up in my heart for the only human voice which had spoken kindly to me—the only heart that had felt for my distresses—cross your mind ? Are persecution, distress, danger, misery, all to fail in shaking our faith, to leave the gold the triumph of doing so? Albert, is this well done of you ?"

Sir Francis quietly walked away from the window, leaving Albert to make his peace how he could ; which it is to be supposed he did, as, after a few moments, Ada, with her usual frank candour, gave him her hand, and shaking her head said, with a smile, something that made his eyes glisten with joy.

CHAPTER CXIII.

LEARMONT AND BRITTON AFTER THE MURDER.

HAVING devoted so large a space to the hopes, the fears, the surprises, and the joys of those in whose happiness and freedom from the distresses and persecutions which surrounded them, we are so largely interested, we turn with a sensation of sickening gloom to the two men of blood, Learmont and the savage smith, after they had sated themselves with gore, and like ferocious tigers of the jungle, came slinking from the feast of blood which they had sought with avidity, and tasted of so greedily.

Neither of them spoke after they reached the street door of Gray's house, until they had placed several streets between them and the one in which the awful deed was committed.

There was a dogged, apathetic kind of movement and manner about Britton, as with a heavy tread he slowly walked by the side of the squire, which more resembled the gross serenity of some overgorged reptile than anything e'se. Never before had the smith's appetite for destruction been so throughly sated— never before had he accomplished a darling wish of his heart so fully and so completely. His hatred to Jacob Gray had been one of his chief passions for years, and he had always pleased himself with the notion of some day having a revenge which should be in accordance with his savage nature, and full of terror. Yet in his wildest dreams—in his most fanciful imaginings of what he would like to do to Jacob Gray, he had fallen short of the scene of horror and blood he had that night gone through. Yes ; Andrew Britton was satisfied—quite satisfied, as regarded Jacob Gray, and he felt all the ennui and satiety which was sure to arise, when the great object which he had always pleased himself he should one day be able to accomplish, was done. Jacob Gray was dead. He had died by his (Britton's) hands an awful death, such as rejoiced him to inflict, and which was only disagreeable because it was done, and could not be repeated.

Now and then he would cast a scowling glance upon the squire, as if he longed to strike him down with the cleaver he still held in his grasp. He felt like man, the great object of whose existence has slipped away from him, leaving the mind no fixed point upon which to fall back in thought.

" Curses on him !" he muttered. " He's dead," and Britton felt himself almost injured that Gray could not be brought to life again, in order to give him again the pleasure of dashing Bond's cleaver into his quivering brain.

But what were these thoughts of the coarse-minded, brutal animal, Britton, in comparison with the whirlwind of frightful feelings that made a hell in the teeming brain of Learmont. If he looked up to the sky, huge gouts of blood seemed to intercept his view of the blue vault of heaven ; if he cast his eyes downwards, he could not divest himself of the idea that he was treading in ensanguined pools of human gore. He ground his teeth together till he produced a resemblance of the crashing sound which the clever wielded by Britton had made as it came in contact with the crunched bones of Gray's skull. His last despairing cry of " Mercy—mercy—mercy !" was still ringing in his ears ; and, finally, such was the intense excitement of his feelings, that he was compelled to lean upon the arm of Britton as he gasped,—

" I—I—shall go mad—I shall go mad. Andrew Britton, get me some water to cool my brain. I shall go mad !"

" Water be d—— !" growled Britton ; " have some brandy, why, what's the matter now ?"

" Do— do you not hear, Britton ? Gray is still screaming for mercy—does not the sound rush like burning lava through your brain—hark—hark—he still shrieks mercy—mercy—mercy."

Learmont held the smith by the arm as he spoke, and trembled so especially that he shook the bulky form of Britton to and fro.

" Why what's come over you, squire ?" cried Britton, " curse you—you are not going to make a die of it now, just as that canting thief Gray is put out of the world."

" Oh, Britton—Britton, was it not horrible ?"

" No, it wasn't. When you knock a fellow on the head with a cleaver, you do for him at once, and all you get out of him is a kick or two. Come this way, and don't be shaking here. Come and have some brandy—d—n water, I'm as thirsty as I can be, and water always makes me worse. Come on—oh ! you are a beauty, Master Learmont—you used not to be such a fool. Time was, since I've known you, when you'd have thought nothing of this. Don't you remember ?"

" Oh, hush—hush—hush," said Learmont ; " do not call to my recollection things which have already left their brand upon my soul."

" Ha—ha—ha," laughed Britton, " now I will have some fun with the squire. Don't you recollect knocking your brother Mark's first baby on the head, squire ?"

" Peace—peace—fiend," gasped Learmont.

They had now reached the door of a small public-house, which was kept open usually all night for the convenience of thieves and watchmen, when Britton pulled Learmont across the threshold to the little bar, where a man sat smoking with imperturbable gravity and placidity.

" Brandy !" cried Britton, as he reached over the bar, and snatched the pipe from the man, throwing it into the street.

The man was one of those slow thinkers, who are some time comprehending anything—so he merely stared at Britton, out of two exceedingly small eyes, that were nearly buried in mountains of flesh.

" Brandy !" again cried Britton, as he gave the front of the bar a clanging blow with the flat part of the cleaver, that made every bottle dance again, and so astonished the potman, that he slid from his chair, and sat on the ground, looking first at Britton, and then at Learmont, with as much alarm depicted in his countenance, as it could depict, considering it was by no means well calculated for pourtraying human feelings.

If the potman's mind was rather overcome by the sudden abstraction of his pipe, the blow upon the bar with the cleaver completed a mystification which, to all appearance, looked as if it would last a considerable time ; so Britton, perceiving a little half door leading within the   on the swing, entered without any ceremony, and laying violent hands on the first quart pot he saw, he drew liquor from every tap in succession that came to hand, until he had filled the measure with a combination of strong spirits, of which he took a long draught, and then handed it across to Learmont, who stood holding himself up by the bar, and but slightly conscious of where he was, or what Britton was doing.

"Here," cried the smith, "drink some of that."

Learmont took the quart measure, and lifted it to his lips mechanically, he drank some of the contents, and then handed it back to Britton, who, after pouring the remainder on the fat landlord's head, gave him a thump with the measure, saying,—

"That's to clear your wits, and if you say that two gentlemen have been here with a cleaver, I'll come back some day, and smash you."

With this Britton hustled Learmont out of the house, and in about three quarters of an hour the fat landlord said,—

"Bless us, and save us!"

Learmont was half intoxicated with the draught of spirits he had taken, when he reached his own door-step, to which he was conducted by Britton, who said to him,—

"Now, squire you are home again, and that job's jobbed ; Jacob Gray won't trouble you any more, and as for his confession, why I begin to think as you do, that there never was one."

"Ah, the confession—the confession !" gasped Learmont. "We are lost—we are lost, Britton ! if, after all, there should be one found."

"Go to the devil," said Britton, as he shook himself free of the squire, and flourishing the cleaver proceeded on his way to the Chequers.

The first person that Britton encountered on his road home was a particularly slow-moving watchman, whom he levelled at once with a thwack between the shoulders, inflicted with the flat part of the cleaver. Then, when he reached the Chequers, it was a great satisfaction to him to find the door shut, because it gave him an opportunity of taking the heavy cleaver in both hands, and bringing it down with a blow upon the lock that on the instant smashed it, and burst the door wide open to the great consternation of the landlord, who immediately hid himself below the bar, and only peered up when he heard Britton's voice exclaim,—

"Curse you all!—where are you? Boil me some brandy, I say, or I'll smash everything in the place."

"Oh, dear, your majesty! so you're come home," faltered the landlord ; "dear me !"

Britton's only reply to this conciliatory speech was to throw the cleaver at the landlord's head, who only escaped it by ducking in time, when it flew over him, smashing some dozens of glasses, and producing a noise and confusion within the bar that was quite gratifying to Britton's feelings.

"Hilloa!" cried Bond, when he saw Britton enter the parlour. "Here have I been waiting for you, I don't know how long."

"Who told you to wait?" roared Britton.

"Nobody," shouted Bond, in as high a tone. "Where's my cleaver?"

"In the bar. Didn't you hear it?"

"Ha! ha! ha!" laughed the butcher. "I did hear a smash. You are a great genius, Britton. I say, have you settled that fellow, eh?"

"What's that to you?"

"Oh, nothing. I only asked. I suppose he was one too many for you?"

"Too many for me ! I've smashed him !"

"Very good," said Bond, resuming his pipe with an air of great composure.

In the meanwhile Learmont was lighted by his wondering domestics to his own chamber. They had never before this seen him in such a state of physical prostration ; and, but that they were in too great fear of his violence to offer him even a kindness, they would have assisted him up the staircase, for they saw that he was scarcely capable of ascending alone, and had to clutch to the banisters nervously for support.

When he reached his chamber, he sank into a chair, and after a few moments, he said,—

" More lights—more lights! Let me have more lights here. The place is dark."

One of the servants lit the wax candles which were in silver sconces on the mantel-shelf, and then humbly inquired if his worship had any further orders to give.

"None—none!" said Learmont, "none! Why do you stare at me so? Is—is there blood upon me? How dare you look upon me with eyes of suspicion?"

No. 54.

The servants looked at each other in surprise and terror, and slowly slunk to the door.

"Let me have wine—wine!" cried Learmont. "Wine to give me new blood, for, by the God of heaven, what I have is freezing in my veins. Wine—wine, I say!"

They brought him wine, and a massive silver goblet to drink it from; but when they did so, they found him resting his head upon the table, and apparently half-asleep, for he was moaning occasionally, and muttering the words,—

"Mercy—mercy—mercy!"

None dared to arouse him, but lifting up their hands in silent terror, they gently closed the door, and crept softly down the staircase, leaving him alone with his dark and awful thoughts.

The sun was lighting up the east, and the dim clouds of night were rapidly changing their inky hue for the glorious tints of day; but there sat Learmont still with his head upon the table, and the glare of the many wax lights he had ordered, strangely mingling with the roseate tints of the coming day.

Oh, what awful images of horror and despair came marching in dismal troops through the brain of the blood-guilty man. Over and over again was the fearful tragedy he had been an actor in, exhibited to his shrinking imagination. Then he fancied himself alone with the mangled body of Jacob Gray. His feet were rooted to the floor of the room, and he thought the body rose, while Gray, with his long, ghastly-looking fingers dabbled in blood, strove to hold his eyes in their sockets —to replace the splintered pieces of his fractured skull, the while he glared at him, Learmont, with such a look of stony horror, that with a shriek the squire awoke, and stood in his chamber a picture of guilty horror, staring with blood-shot eyes at the wax-lights and the morning sunshine with a racking brain and a fevered pulse.

CHAPTER CXIV.

ALBERT'S VISIT TO LEARMONT.—THE SQUIRE'S TRIUMPH.

AFTER a time Learmont became more conscious of his situation, and a feeling of exhaustion coming over him in consequence of the fatigue, both of body and mind he had undergone, he partially divested himself of his apparel, and throwing himself upon the luxurious bed which was in the room, he soon dropped into a deep sleep, which was not visited and rendered hideous by any of the frightful images which had before been conjured up by his oppressed brain.

It was some four hours or more before he again awakened, and then he found himself much refreshed both bodily and mentally. He ran over in his mind accurately all the circumstances of his present position, and now that his cooler judgment had sway, and the horror of the recent events he had passed through was beginning to subside, he inclined more and more to his previously expressed opinion, that Jacob Gray had not really written any confession, but had merely pretended to have such a document always at hand, for the purpose of aweing him and saving his, Jacob's life, from any attempt on the part of either of his great enemies.

Learmont rose and paced his room in deep thought, and then, while he stood as it were upon a mine, which, did he but know it, was ready to explode beneath him, and hurl him to destruction; a feeling of self-satisfaction began to creep over him, and he re-assured himself into a belief that he must have materially bettered his situation by the destruction of Gray.

"It must be so," he muttered. "There is no confession written, and Gray was not only a heavy expense, but would, no doubt, some day have played some serious trick in payment for the attempts which, to his knowledge, had been made against him. 'Tis well, then, he is dead—exceedingly well, for my worst enemy is gone. Britton will drink himself to death, surely; and as for the pretended papers he has, of such great consequence to me, as he and Gray ever affected they were, I now begin to think that like Jacob Gray's written confession, such a tale is merely invented as a bugbear to my imagination. Yes, I must be now in a better, a far better position, and the day will come, when I shall have no further fears of the stability of my fortunes."

Reasoning thus, he argued himself into a more placid mode, and then the dark feelings of hate, revenge, and gloomy triumphs, which, for a time, had been over-powered and forced to hide their diminished heads in consequence of his great excitements, once more rose, phœnix-like, from their ashes, and the wild scheming, blood-stained villain smiled, as he glanced round him upon the magnificence with which he was surrounded, and which he thought would soon be all his own, without the shadow of fear being cast over them.

"By the powers of hell!" he cried, " I will still let them see that I can live right royally in my noble halls. When last I met the Minister of State, methought he looked strangely at me, and he certainly did, upon some most shallow and slight excuse, put me off when I spoke of my baronetcy, promised as it has been for so long. That magistrate too—that Hartleton, who I so deeply hate. There was a sneer, too, upon his face when I saw him last, as if he would have said,—

'Learmont, your fate is hurrying on, and I shall triumph over you.' Ha! ha! my best sense of security lies in the fact that he leaves me alone. Could he but get up the shadow of a charge against me, how gladly would he strive to blacken me and my fame in the eyes of those who, despite him, will yet heap honours on my head. Sir Francis Harleton, I know you well as my active enemy, and while I am unmolested by you, I am safe indeed. I will persevere, most certainly, in my intention of giving a fete on Saturday, which shall surpass, in rich-ness and magnificence, any that have yet been vaunted highly by my crowds of visitors—visitors whom I despise, but yet find useful as tools to work out my great scheme of ambition."

Learmont then rung for his servants, and with a malignant pleasure caused the cards of invitation to his grand masked ball for the Saturday to be sent to Hartleton and to the minister.

"I will vex the very soul of this Hartleton," he said, "by the gorgeous display of wealth I will make."

A shade of care then suddenly came across his brow, as for the first time since his departure from the house of Gray, he thought upon the promised visit of Albert Seyton.

"Ha," he cried, "my young secretary, I had nearly forgotten him. Will he prove troublesome? Did he catch a glimpse of me at Gray's? No—no—that he did not—and if he did—well. The shortest plan of operation with regard to him is to give him more hopes, no matter how slenderly based; and along with them a cup of wine, which shall contain an insidious drug. Yes, I will poison him, and then send him some long errand to a distant part of the country, which he will never live to return from—a safe way—a most safe way. So shall I be rid of him without the—the—horror (Learmont shuddered as he spoke) of seeing such an-other death, perhaps, as that I would fain blot from my memory for ever, but which rises gaunt and bloody ever before my mental eye. I must not think of it. My fete—my brilliant fete—my baronetcy—ah, those are grateful ima-ginings."

The receipt of Learmont's card of invitation to Sir Francis Hartleton we are already aware of, and in the course of the day its presence, as it lay before him, gave the magistrate an idea, which, if it could be successfully carried out, would save some time in the apprehension of the guilty squire, as well as, in all probability, force some sudden recognition of Ada and her rights. Besides, it was, at all events, important, that as he, Sir Francis Hartleton, had given his promise to the Secretary of State that Learmont should not be molested until after the Saturday's fete, the squire should not be led to suspect that any of his plans had failed, or that any immediate danger beset him.

For the purpose of preventing such a thing from occurring, Sir Francis Harttleton proposed to Albert Seyton that he should see Learmont on that evening, in pursuance of the arrangement which had been entered into between him and the squire.

Another difficulty, or rather a doubt, beset this line of proceeding, however, and that was to know whether the squire was aware, or not, of the fact of Albert having been present at the house in which Gray was murdered on the night, or rather morning, of that event. To solve this question, or, at all events, to render it an innocuous one, Sir Francis Hartleton advised that Albert should take with him to the squire's an exact copy of the confession of Jacob Gray, and hand it to him, admitting that, seeing the door of Gray's house open, he had entered and become possessed of the document by the accidental tearing of a cloak in which it was concealed.

"Such a step on our parts," said Sir Francis, " must have the effect of thoroughly disarming Learmont of all suspicion of his danger; and since his friend, the Secretary of State, has him so much under his special protection, on account of his parliamentary influence, I should like very much to let him see, personally, what a beautiful protege he has, and make the masked ball the scene of his apprehension."

"I am quite willing to act upon your advice, said Albert; "and indeed, I am not a little curious and anxious to know what Learmont can possible say to me this evening, when I call upon him, and demand Ada, according to the solemn promises he made me."

With this understaning Albert and the magistrate repaired to the study of the latter, where they took an accurate copy of the confession, which Albert placed in his pocket, while Sir Francis charged himself with the preservation of the original.

"Return as soon as possible," said Sir Francis, "and, above all things, be mindful of treachery,"

"I think I am more than a match for the squire," said Albert, smiling.

"Be that as it may," said the magistrate, "remember that during your stay at his house there will be a force within hearing of you should you require any assistance. We must trust this man of many crimes as little as we possibly can."

Without saying anything to Ada of his intention, for he knew that her anxiety would be very great if she knew that he was venturing into the house of Learmont Albert, just as the shades of evening began to fall upon the streets and house-' left the residence of the magistrate, and proceeded at a sharp pace towards Learmont's splendid abode.

He was readily admitted, and upon being shown into the room, where he usually saw Learmont, he found him seated with a multitude of papers before him, apparently very busily engaged. He started as he saw Albert, and yet he felt intensely gratified, for it tended much to assure him of his safety. His only difficulty consisted in his want of knowledge of whether Albert had seen him or not a Gray's.

"You are true to your appointment, Mr. Seyton," he said, after a few moments thought. "Have you heard any news of Jacob Gray?

"He is murdered," said Albert.

Learmont turned a shade paler as he said,—

"So I have heard this morning, and that has, I fear, placed an obstacle in your way."

"I found that he was murdered," continued Albert "at an early hour this morning. Being anxious concerning her whom I loved I passed the house in which

Gray resided, when I saw the door ajar. That excited my curiosity, and I entered from an impluse which I could not control."

" He did not see me," thought Learmont ; " he suspects nothing."

" I called aloud upon Ada" continued Albert, " but no one answered me. Procuring, then a light from a woman in the house, I proceeded to search it, and found Gray a mangled horrible corpse."

Learmont drew a long breath as he said,

" I heard so much this morning from a casual visitor, and I was intending before now to take with me a warrant from the Secretary of State which would have been granted upon my application, to take Gray into custody, and offer the young girl, in whom you have made me feel a strange interest, an asylum under my own roof, until your arrival to-night."

" You are very considerate, sir," said Albert, " By the accidental rending of a cloak which I presume belonged to Jacob Gray, a packet of papers——"

Learmont uttered a loud cry, and rising, he stretched out his hands ,saying, while his face was livd with apprehenson,—

" You—you have them. The—the confession—this instant—on your life give it to me. You have not dared to read—you will take some wine—you will—this—this goblet will refresh you. The papers—give me the papers."

He shooklike an aspen leaf as he pushed the cup of wine of he had drugged, in case he should wish to get rid of Albert, towards him, and his voice grew hoarse with anxiety as he continued to say,—

" The papers—the papers !"

Albert handed him the copy of Gray's confession, which Learmont snatched with the most frantic eagerness.

" You see, Mr. Seyton," he said, " I am most anxious about the welfare of yourself and this young maiden—I pray you drink. The wine is good. Yes, this is addressed to Sir Francis Hartleton, but it is far better in my hands. She would fare badly, you know, in the tender mercies of such man as he. Drink—you—you do not drink."

There was something about Learmont's extreme eagerness to induce him to drink that excited the suspicious of Albert, and he resolved that he would not touch a drop of wine, but having executed his errand, would get out of the house as quickly as possible.

Learmont rose as he spoke, still grasping the document Albert had given him in his hand, and said,—

" Wait for me a short time ; I will read this most carefully, and then communicate to you the result. Drink Mr. Seyton. I pray you do not spare the wine. You look fatigued."

With an expression of triumph upon his brow, and a haughtier, firmer tread than he had used for years, Learmont left the room, with, as he supposed, the confession of Jacob Gray in his possession. Albert Seyton disposed of, as he thought he would be, by partaking of the drugged wine, he then considered he should have no further trouble concerning Ada, except what might easily be overcome.

Before he returned to Albert, the latter had cast the wine from the window, and when Learmont glanced at the goblet, and saw it was empty, he said,—

" Mr. Seyton, I have read the paper; it says that your Ada, your much-loved Ada, is an orphan, and that you will find her at—at—Chatham."

" At Chatham, sir ?"

" Yes, off with you. You must inquire for the residence of a Mr. Henderson. He is well known, and will conduct you to Ada. Off with you, and come back to me—when you can." These last words were uttered after Albert, who was disgusted with the scene, had hurried from the room

Then Learmont drew himself up to his full height, and cried,—

" He will be dead within an hour ! I triumph—I triumph !"

CHAPTER CXV.

THE MASKED BALL·

How singularly different the various actors in our eventful drama of real life passed the Thursday and the Friday preceding Learmont's masked ball. To the squire himself it was a period of restless inquietude, for even in his moments of self-exaltation, and triumphant congratulation, there was bitterness at his heart, and he could almost fancy a voice said to him in a hissing whisper—This is not real. Had it not been for the great preparations he occupied himself in making and superintending for the approaching entertainment, his imagination, having more leisure to brood upon the past, would have brought upon him greater suffering than he really endured, but, as it was, each hour that had winged its flight, he told himself that he was safer still, and that he had now little more to do than enjoy the discomfiture of his enemies. That Albert Seyton had died of the poison which he, Learmont, thought he had taken, he entertained no doubt. The only circumstance that surprised him much was, that he had not seen Britton, but having ascertained, upon inquiry, that the smith had not been one degree removed from helpless intoxication since the Wednesday morning, he felt satisfied, and rather pleased than otherwise, at the speedy destruction which Britton must be making of his powers of existence.

Oh, with what malignant satisfaction he read and re-read, as he supposed, the only document which could have hurled him from his high estate to destruction, to death, to infamy! How he laughed with a wild demoniac mirth at the simplicity of Albert Seyton in handing him the confession, and being so easily put off from a knowledge of its contents. With what a proud air he trod his splendid saloons, and how haughtily he reasoned with himself about that Providence which he in his wild excitement of fancied success almost considered he had circumvented.

"This ball," he muttered, "shall be the scene of my triumph and the discomfiture of my enemies—envy shall become more envious, humility and sycophancy more humble and cringing—for all shall see that the star of Learmont is in the ascendant. Then, this confesson, addressed to Sir Francis Hartleton, shall make assurance doubly sure; I will totally confound him by handing to him a document of my own contrivance similarly addressed, but with contents most widely differing from this! Yes, it shall be done. With seeming candour and simplicity the subtlest plots are carried out, the deepest designs concluded successfully. What will be the result? All that I can wish—I will write a supposed confession of Jacob Gray, and hand it to this active magistrate."

For some moments Learmont was so delighted with this plan that he paced the saloon in which he was in silence, while a grim smile lit up his face, giving him a c ose resemblance to some of those strange old carvings, which modern fashion, if not modern taste, is rescuing from the dust and oblivion of centuries at the present day.

In silent meditation he concocted his plan, which he considered would either place Ada in his power, or force the magistrate in a very disagreeable position, for the mock confession he meant to write, and hand to Sir Francis Hartleton, as having been brought to him by his secretary, he intended should merely contain an appeal to his, Learmont's, charity in favour of the orphan girl.

While triumph was thus setting on the brow of Learmont—while Heaven was inflating his heart with the vanity of success. as if but to make his fall more awful, Ada, who we have followed through her various fortunes so long, [was indeed happy in the best, the purest, acception of the term. Her joy was not the feverish excitement arising from successful machinations. It was the heavenly serenity—the sunny happiness of a heart which knew no guile, and was only too much blessed in being permitted uncoerced and unpersecuted to follow out the dictates of its own ennobling feelings.

The whole household indeed of Sir Francis Hartleton, seemed to share in the satisfaction that there abounded, from what cause they knew not, but they were satisfied, from the smiles of Ada and the returning colour on her cheek, the evident happiness of Albert Seyton, and the pleasure which sparkled in the eyes of their master and mistress, that something must have happened to bring great joy among them.

It was the Saturday morning before Britton had the least interval of sobriety, and then so stultified were his faculties with the debauch of the last two days, far exceeding as it did any that he had previously indulged in, that he was some time in comprehending what Bond the butcher meant, when, after repeated howlings in his ear, he heard him say—

"Britton, curse you, you beast, the squire, your rich friend, is going to give a ball to-night, I hear, and all the people are to go, they tell me, with masks. Do you hear, you brute?"

"Yes, and be hanged to you; you are as drunk as you can be, and you know it," responded Britton. "More brandy—more brandy! Damn Jacob Gray—no, curse it, it's no use damning Jacob Gray any more now: he's damned already—damn everybody."

"Ah, Master Britton," exclaimed a man who had just entered the Chequers with a determination of enjoying a pipe, and a quart of ale, and a grumble—"we live in hard times, Master Britton—are we to have our heads smashed—are we to have our throats cut—are we to be murdered in our beds—are we——"

"I tell you what," said Bond, "if you come any more of your 'are we's,' I'll just throw you out of the window."

"Throw me out of the window? pooh! I sit here on the liberty of the subject, and what I mean to say is, that everything is smothered now-a-days. Here's been two murders, and they've both been smothered up. There was poor Mr. Vaughan's murder—who ever heard anything of that, I should like to know? Then there's been the murder of Mr. Gray, a most mysterious affair; and Sir Francis Hartleton, who prides himself so much upon his being such an active magistrate, he does nothing—nothing, my masters, I may add, nothing."

"Smash him!" said Britton, and Bond, immediately rising, would have probably done some serious mischief, had not the man, who, by good luck was near the door, taken alarm in time, and rushed out crying, 'Murder!' until he was met and pacified by the landlord, who persuaded him to sit down in the bar while he sneaked into the parlour to fetch his pipe and ale.

Just as the landlord entered the room, Britton shouted to him in a half-drowsy tone,—

"Hark you; mind my sedan-chair is ready to-night. I'm going to Squire Learmont's ball."

"Bless your majesty—are you really! I never!"

"Didn't you," said Britton, as he flung the fire-shovel at the landlord's head, who made a precipitate retreat without the ale and the pipe, which articles, rather than again venture into the parlour, he again supplied to the talkative man.

* * * * * *

By one hour after sunset, Learmont had the various lamps and chandeliers lit in his splended mansion, and with feelings somewhat akin to those with which he had first made a tour from room to room, he glanced around him upon the rare magnificence with which he was completely surrounded.

"'Tis well—exceedingly well," he muttered. "I have suffered much to bring about such a night of triumph as this. Within some few brief hours three hundred of the highest and the noblest in this country will be assembled in my halls, while I, the observed of all observers, do the honours of my costly home. To-night I will claim a fulfilment of the minister's promise concerning the baronetcy To-night, in soft whispered accents, will I once more essay to win the hand of the proud beauty whose ancient patrician name will add a lustre to my own too new nobility. This is indeed a night of triumph! I ought to be happy." Even as he spoke, such a pang shot across his heart, that he absolutely reeled again, and when he could speak, he said in faltering accents,—

"What—what means this emotion? Why do I tremble now? What have I to fear?—Nothing—nothing !—What can happen ?—Oh nothing !—I am safe— very safe! I wish my company would come. I like to hear the hum of life in my glorious abode !—I like to see the moving plumes !—I like to note the diamonds glittering presence !—I wish they would come. I wonder where and how Albert Seyton died ?—The poison he took was subtle !—He could not escape—that was impossible—quite impossible ! He might have been a dangerous enemy !—I wish my halls were full !"

One of those disagreeable feelings came over Learmont now to which he had been frightfully subject of late, namely, a fancy that some one was constantly behind him, turning as he turned, and ever keeping so far behind him as never to permit him to catch a glimpse of what it was. This terror always for a time reduced him to a pitiable state of nervous weakness, and the only resource he could ever find was to sit in a chair, the back of which was close to a wall. Trembling, therefore, and slinking along like one accursed, he sought the small room he usually sat in, and there remained for some hours in the position we have described, awaiting the coming of his guests.

Soon after nine o'clock, the street began to show signs of animation ; ancient lumbering coaches drawn by sleek, fat horses, bore precious freights of rank and beauty to Learmont's doors, which were thrown wide open, the steps being lined by lacqueys, many of whom bore flaming links. Some gentlemen came on horse- back, concealing their costumes with ample cloaks, and before ten o'clock (for our ancestors began their amusements earlier, and left off sooner than we do) the thoroughfare was nearly blocked up with chairs.

Then ensued a scene of squabbling among coachmen, linkmen, chairman, &c., a faint imitation of which sometimes is exhibited at a modern rout. Learmont's saloons presented a most dazzling appearance ; the richness and variety of the costumes—the immense looking-glasses—the brilliant lighting—the glitter of diamonds—the waving of countless plumes—the music now coming in wild crashes of melody, and then sinking to a plaintive measure above the soft tones of which could be heard the hum of voices—the merry laughter of the young, and the shuffle of the dancers' feet, as now and then a space would be cleared for a giddy couple, who ere the regular ball began would extemporise a dance.

Learmont too was marching among his guests for some time, like a spirit of evil. There was a cloud upon his brow, but he wrestled with the dark spirit that clung to his heart, and soon his countenance became wreathed in smiles, and he had a word of welcome, of gaiety, or of friendship, for every one of his guests. Some- times he would pause, and cast his eye about him, to note if all had arrived,—a fact he could only judge of by the thronged state of the rooms, for being a masked ball there was no announcement of names. Learmont, however, had provided against the contingency of not knowing those parties to whom he wished to speak privately, by leaving orders in his hall that as their tickets were taken, an accurate account of their costumes should be brought to him.

He had already been told that the minister had arrived, and was enveloped in a purple cloak, embroidered with silver lace, and that Sir Francis Hartleton, like- wise in domino, had come with a small party in his company, he having a black velvet cloak, and a hat with white feathers.

The Brereton party Learmont was well aware he would have no difficulty in recognising, for they were too much impressed with their own dignity to hesitate in throwing off all incognita as soon as possible.

The dancing was to commence at eleven o'clock, but before that hour Learmont saw that the principal saloon was uncomfortably crowded, and he immediately ordered the folding doors conducting to the next apartment, which was deliciously cool to be thrown open, and the ball to commence. Directing his eyes to the musicians, and clapping his hands, they struck up a lively measure, when he advanced to the haughty Lady Brereton, the younger, and offering her his hand, begged the honour of opening the ball with her, at the same time slightly removing his mask to assure her who he was, although such a measure was needless, for there was not one of his guests who had ever seen him before, that failed to recognise him. A large space was cleared for the dance, and Learmont led the

proud beauty to perform one of those elaborate and tedious minuets now so properly exploded. When it was over, Learmont led the lady to a magnificent seat, and while the band struck up a lively measure, and one of those laughter provoking dances which a hundred couple might engage in was proceeding, making the very lights dance in the chandeliers, he stooped to the lady's ear, and whispered,—

"May I presume to hope that my devotion to your beauty will ensure me

No. 55.

success in my suit for your hand? My income is immense, and I have nearly half a million of ready money. The other half you see around you in the decorations of this house."

There was surely some fatality about Learmont's money, for at that moment a trembling servant stepped up to him, and said,—

"An it please you, sir, there's a—a row in the hall; and, and—an please you, sir, it's—him."

The man tendered to Learmont a dirty scrap of paper, on which he read,—

"The King of the Old Smithy, and friend."

CHAPTER CXVI.

THE DEATH OF LEARMONT,

IT was well Learmont's face was partially concealed by a mask, or even the Honourable Georgiana Brereton might have had her fine aristocratic nerves shocked by the death-like hue of his features, as he gasped,—

"Damnation!"

A slight scream burst from her ladyship's lips, and then a general clapping of hands caused Learmont to look around, when he saw Britton attired in his garments as a smith, and wearing an enormous nose, executing a grotesque dance with Bond the butcher, who had disdained all concealment, and came in his usual, not very elegant, costume.

Up the centre of the saloon, the guests making way for them, they came like two bears at play, stamping, waving, whirling round, treading on each other's toes, and then cuffing each other with boisterous mirth, till they reached the place where Learmont stood, when, rushing forward with a shriek of rage, the squire clutched Britton by the throat with desperate energy, and said—

"Villain—wretch! How dare you?"

"Hands off, squire," cried Britton.

"And eyes on," added the butcher, recollecting that these were the words of an announcement he used to append to the fattest meat.

"Bravo! bravo!—capital!" cried many of the guests, thinking that the whole affair was got up as part of the evening's amusement. Even the minister smiled, and wondered to a mask who stood next him, if the two strange creatures had votes.

"Andrew Britton," growled Learmont, in the smith's ear, "are you mad?"

"You be d——d!" was the elegant rejoinder. "Hurrah! Come along, Bond, now for it."

Upon this the butcher took from one capacious pocket the same cleaver which had been the instrument of Jacob Gray's murder, and from another a large bone, with which he executed such a lively tune upon the flat of the weapon, that Britton roared again with mirth, and after a wild dance sat down on the floor, and shouted like a wild animal. Then he caught hold of the Honourable Georgiana Brereton's foot, and her white satin slipper coming off in his hands, he fell on the flat of his back, while shouts, screams, roars of laughter, and the clapping of hands, sounded through the saloon.

Learmont made a rush from the rooms, and summoning all the servants he could meet with, he brought them back with him, in order that they might eject Britton and Bond; but by this time the smith had arisen from the floor, and turning to the squire, he said,—

"Honour bright, and no nonsense. D——n it, squire, a joke's a joke. Were off again. I've had my fun, and there's an end of it. Ladies and gentlemen you may all be d——d ! Strike up, Bond."

The butcher again played the marrow-bone and cleaver, and with many whirls, shouts, and singular gyrations, he and Britton left the saloon.

Learmont stood for some moments trembling with rage ; then, suddenly, h e cried,—

" Music—music—the dance—the dance—a mere jest. Music, I say."

A crash of melody followed his call, and he was looking for the lady he had left when a domino in a black velvet cloak met his eye.

The domino bowed and unmasked.

" The rooms are warm, squire."

" Ha ! Sir Francis Hartleton," cried Learmont.

Then a sudden thought struck him, that he would efface all recollection of Britton's drunken vagary, by calling public attention to the forged paper he had intended to give Sir Francis privately. He waved his arm to the musicians, and they suddenly paused in the midst of a lively air, which had the effect of preparing the guests for something unusual. As many as could, crowded round Learmont and Sir Francis Hartleton, while the former said, in a loud voice, —

" I have had placed in my hands a packet addressed to Sir Francis Hartleton, which I am informed has been found at the lodgings of the man who, you have all heard, was murdered on Wednesday morning early, in this immediate neighbourhood."

Sir Francis Hartleton looked astonished ; and taking off his mask, he glanced round him anxiously. A murmur of curiosity rose among the guests. Many mounted upon chairs, and some few even upon the tables. A more curious scene than Learmont's saloon then presented could scarcely be imagined.

" Read—read !" cried many voices, as Sir Francis took a sealed paper, which was handed to him by Learmont, and put it in his pocket. The shouts to him to read the document increased each moment, and then a sudden thought crossed the mind of Sir Francis, that the squire might be caught in his own snare. In the same pocket in which he had placed the packet Learmont had given him, Sir Francis had the real confession of Jacob Gray, which he had brought with him to show the minister, should an opportunity present itself.

" Shall I read that, and confound the guilty squire at once," thought Sir Francis. " I have plenty of assistance at hand for his capture."

He hesitated a moment, and then said aloud,—

" His Majesty's Secretary of State is present. If he will sanction my reading the paper aloud, I will do so, but as it may possibly criminate some one, I demand that the door be secured."

" Aye," cried Learmont. " Secure the door. Let no one pass in or out."

He then cast a triumphant glance at the magistrate, for he felt so very sure how disappointed he would be. The minister now took off the mask, and said,—

" Well, well ; it can't be helped. Go on, Sir Francis."

There was now a breathless silence, and Sir Francis Hartleton drew from his pocket the real confession of Jacob Gray. Learmont was in far too great a state of excitement to notice any difference in the aspect of the documents, and waving his arm, he cried,—

" Silence, friends, and welcome guests. We may find some secrets here worthy our attention."

Sir Francis cast his eyes upon Learmont with a look of peculiar meaning as he said,—

" You will, I think, in this instance, squire, turn out a true prophet."

He then opened the confession, and while every sound was hushed, and all eyes bent upon his, he, in a clear full voice, read,—

" TO SIR FRANCIS HARTLETON,

" I, Jacob Gray, address the following confession and statement of facts to y because, from circumstances within your own remembrance, you will the more readily believe what is here recorded. May the bitterest curse of a dead man fall upon you and yours, if you do not take instant means to bring to an ignominious end those who I shall accuse of crimes which shall far exceed any that I have committed. By the time you receive this, I shall most probably be dead, or have left England for some distant land, where all search for me would be in vain. I leave, however, behind, whether dead or absent, this legacy of vengeance and so fulfil a promise I made to my own heart to destroy those who would long since have murdered me, but that I had fenced myself round with safeguards which they dared not despise.

"In the year 1737, I was staying at Genoa, where I had been discharged from the service of an English family for matters that are of no consequence to my present narrative. For some months I could procure no employment, until an English gentleman, by name, Mark Learmont——'

The guilty squire seemed absolutely stupified until the magistrate had got thus far, and then with a cry, that struck terror to the hearts of all who heard it, he drew his sword, and with the wildness of dispair, dashed through the throng of masks around him, shouting,—

"'Tis false—'tis false—false as hell. I did not do the deed—make way—who stays me dies upon the spot. Help—help! A plot—a plot."

He had wounded several persons before, in the universal panic, they could get out of his way, and then Sir Francis Hartleton raised his voice above all other sounds, shouting—

"Seize the murderer."

In an instant some half dozen of the maskers threw off their dominos and masks, presenting to the astonished eyes of the guests, roughly attired, well armed men, who immediately darted after Learmont.

Two other persons, likewise threw down their masks. One was Albert Seyton and the other was Ada; but by this time the half-maddened squire had fought his way to the further end of the saloon, and dashing against some folding doors, they flew open, disclosing a flight of steps leading to a conservatory filled with rare plants; waving, then, his sword round his head, he sprang up the steps.

"Surrender or we fire," cried Sir Francis Hartleton.

Learmont turned, and said something that was not heard in the confusion—blood was streaming down his face, for he had bit his lips through, and he made repeated lunges with his sword, as now with frantic voice and gesture, he cried,—

Off—off—tear me not to hell—fiends, off—why do you glare at me—off—off—'tis false—false, I say—a plot—a plot!"

"Seize him," cried the magistrate, as he himself sprung upon the first step.

"Yield, monster," said Albert Seyton, as passing Sir Francis, he flew up the staircase.

At the sight of him, Learmont uttered a cry of despair; but when Ada, fearful for Albert's safety, was by his side in a moment, and Learmont met her gaze, his sword dropped from his grasp, and he could but totter backwards towards the conservatory, shrieking,—

"The dead—the dead—Gray next—and then—my brother—my murdered brother—"

With a heavy crash he fell just within the door of the conservatory, and was immediately seized by the officers of Sir Francis Hartleton, who himself turning on the steps, said,—

"I much grieve to have marred the mirth of this noble company, but I apprehend 'Squire Learmont, as a murderer—an assassin—a persecutor of the innocent—a reveller in the wealth of another. This young maiden, I here proclaim as heiress of the estates of Learmont."

Ada shrunk back, as Sir Francis pointed to her, and leaning upon the arm of Albert, she sobbed as she said,—

"Oh, tell me, Albert, what is the meaning of all this fearful scene."

"I have proof of the marriage of this lady's mother with the elder broth r

Learmont, now in custody, from the Austrian ambassador," said Sir Francis Hartleton. "His predecessor was present at the ceremony."

"Ada," cried Albert, rapturously. "Look up—my own Ada."

"This," said Sir Francis Hartleton, addressing her, "is your house. It is for you to make the company welcome or not."

Ada burst into tears, and was led down the steps by Albert and the magistrate, but scarcely had they entered the saloon, when the officers who captured Learmont, appeared at the top of the stairs with him. All eyes were fixed upon his face, which was livid and ghastly. He offered no opposition, but came down step by step with an awful calmness, like one going to execution, who had long since bid adieu to hope. When he reached half way, he paused, and extending both his arms, while his fingers pointed to Sir Francis Hartleton, he burst into such a frantic howling laugh, that the officers shrunk from him aghast. Then an awful spasm came across his face, and like a log, he fell upon the stairs.

When raised, he was found quite dead. A small phial, which was afterwards picked up in the conservatory, and which contained yet a lingering drop of deadly poison, told his fate. The erring spirit had flown to its Maker, there to render up that awful account, which we may shudder at, but not define.

CHAPTER CXVII.

THE PURSUIT FOR BRITTON.

A SHUDDER ran through the gaily attired guests, at this awful and most unlooked for termination of the fete they had come to witness. Many pulled off their masks, and Ada, as she clung convulsively to Albert, said,—

"Oh, that I had remained unknown, poor and nameless, rather than have acquired what they say I have, by such awful steps as these."

Sir Francis Hartleton then spoke aloud, saying,—

"This man has poisoned himself, to escape the just penalty of his crimes, but another act of justice yet remains to be done. Officers, hasten to the Old Chequers, at Westminster ; living or dead, arrest Andrew Britton."

There was a wild shriek at this moment at the door of the principal saloon, and in another moment, brandishing a knife in her hand, mad Maude rushed forward.

"Who spoke of Andrew Britton?" she cried. "Who talks of him? Tell me where he is, that I may hunt him. That I may see his blood flow like a rivulet. Heaven has kept life in me yet that I may see Andrew Britton die. Ha, ha, ha! He is to die before poor mad Maude, who was hooted and pelted through mud and mire, till the good angel pitied her. The good angel—bless you, Heaven bless you—look kindly on poor Maude, who has come to see Andrew Britton die."

The guests huddled together in groups, and looked in each other's faces with fear and amazement, while each wondered what next would occur to fill them with terror, ere they could depart from the splendid mansion, which they had approached with such widely different feelings.

Sir Francis Hartleton, observing the officers pause, as if waiting for some orders concerning Maude, who they all knew, and felt assured, as was indeed the fact, that she had strayed from his house, called to them in a loud voice,—

"To the Chequers—to the Chequers, and secure your prisoner. Hasten, or he may receive an alarm from some one, and yet escape us for awhile. I will see to this poor creature's safety."

"Who stays me must have a charmed life," cried Maude, springing to the doors and holding above her head the glittering knife, while her eyes beamed with a scarcely inferior lustre. "To the Chequers—to the Chequers. Ha, ha, ha! to the Chequers!"

Her voice was harsh and grating to the ear, and she was heard, as she left the house still shouting—"To the Chequers—to the Chequers," till distance drowned the fierce, maniacal cry.

Sir Francis Hartleton then sheathed his sword, and turning to the Secretary of State, said, with a low bow—

"As a higher authority by far than my humble self, I will leave your lordship to take what steps may seem to you proper in this house, while I pursue my proper vocation in attempting the arrest of as great a criminal as London at present possesses."

"Who, I?" cried the minister. "Bless my heart, I really don't know what to do; but before you go, Sir Francis Hartleton, be so good as to introduce me to your charming young friend there, who, you say, is to inherit the Learmont property—I wish just to ask her which way she means to make her tenants vote at the next election."

Before the minister had finished this speech, Sir Francis Hartleton had left the saloon, being perfectly sure that Ada was safe with Albert Seyton, in order to assist at the capture of Britton, whither we will follow him, being equally well assured that Ada was in good hands.

The officers had made good speed, and when Sir Francis reached the street, he found more than fifty of the youngest and most active of Learmont's guests hastening towards the Chequers; their strange motley dresses producing a singular effect, as they were mingled with boys bearing links, and many stray passengers who joined the throng in intense curiosity to know whither they were going.

CHAPTER CXVIII.

THE CHEQUERS AGAIN.—BRITTON AND BOND AT THE OLD QUARTERS.

WHILE all the foregoing parties are making such haste to the Chequers, endeavouring to outvie each other in speed and in the capture of Britton, we may as well take a cursory glance at what is taking place there.

As soon as Britton and Bond had quitted Learmont house, they made their way back again the Chequers with as much haste as they could, excessively enjoying the chagrin they had caused Learmont.

When they entered the Chequers, the landlord of that very respectable house was quietly serving a person at the bar, and not observing "his majesty," that worthy personage, to make his august presence known to his disrespectful subject the landlord, quietly took the marrow-bone and cleaver out of Bond's hands, and threw then with all his might at the landlord's head, taking off the customere's hat in their flight, and dealing the landlord such a tremendous blow that he fell stunned to the ground.

"That's a beauty," said Bond.

"Hilloa," cried Britton, "why don't you move when you see a gentleman coming? A dozen quarts of brandy, I say, do you hear?"

"Yes, yes, your majesty," stammered the landlord.

"Be quick then."

They were about to push against the parlour door with such force as almost to send it off its hinges, when a little man in the parlour, who had been enjoying a pint of half and half and a pipe, suddenly opened the door, intending to go out ; thereupon Britton fell on his nose, with Bond the butcher on him.

The little party collected in the parlour could not repress a hearty laugh at the unbecoming situation of his Majesty King Britton.

Bond being uppermost received no hurt, and was up again in no time ; but Britton lay for a moment writhing in pain, rage and mortification.

" What are you lying there for ?" cried Bond.

" What's that to you. D——n ! who opened the door— I'll smash him."

This threat seemed to frighten the man who had been the cause of the catastrophe, and forthwith he rushed past Bond, and alighting on Britton's chest was out of the house in a moment.

" Curse him," muttered Britton, panting for breath.

" Come, up with you," said Bond.

" You be d—d, you fool," said Britton, as he slowly rose from his recumbent position. " Why didn't you stop him ? I would have murdered him."

" No doubt of it, and so would I, if I had caught hold of him. But your fat carcase being in the way, I was afraid of making a pancake of you."

" You're a humbug."

" Very likely," said Bond.

The butcher having acquiesced in the assertion of Britton, the latter muttered something about blood, which was unintelligible to the former, and seated himself comfortably in the chair devoted solely to himself, while Bond immediately took the next place to him.

Just at this pause in the interesting scene that had just been enacted in the little parlour of the Chequers, the landlord entered with two pots of brandy, and two ale glasses, and placed them before Britton without a remark.

" Well I'm d—d," said Britton.

" What did your majesty pleased to say ?" asked the landlord

" What did I order ?"

' A dozen quarts of brandy."

" Where are they ?"

" I thought——"

" Who gave you leave to think upon what his majesty chooses to order ?" interrupted Bond.

" Go and fetch the other ten directly," roared Britton as he took up one quart pot full of brandy, and threw it at the landlord ; while Bond took up the other, and drank with such vigour that it appeared as if he were determined to drain the pot.

Suddenly Britton pulled his arm, and down went the pot, and the remainder of the liquor went on the floor.

Bond looked black.

" How much longer did you intend to be swilling that brandy ?" inquired Britton.

" I hadn't above half finished," said Bond.

" You should have been quicker then."

" I never hurry."

" So it seems."

The landlord and waiter now entered with the remainder of the brandy ordered by Britton, and both made a safe retreat.

" Here's a blow out," said Bond, as he took a pot in each hand.

Britton took one up.

" This is good," he said.

" I believe you," said Bond.

Britton now invited the parties assembled in the parlour to help themselves, and the liquor was very soon dispersed.

" We played the tune well at Learmont's," said Bond.

" Yes, we did," said Britton.

Britton then seemed to fall into a quieter mood while Bond continued to drink as fast as the burning liquor would flow down his throat, and in a short time all in the parlour were in a complete state of intoxication.

CHAPTER CXIX.

THE CAPTURE OF BRITTON.—HIS AWFUL DEATH AND THAT OF THE OFFICER.— THE DEATH OF MAD MAUDE.

NONE of the officers had thought proper to interfere with mad Maude, for there was nothing to be got by running the chance of an ugly wound with the knife she carried, and the consequence was that she outstripped every one in the race to the Chequers, being the unconscious cause of giving an alarm of danger to Britton, which he otherwise would not have received. He was still sitting with Bond, exulting over the success of his visit to Learmont's, and regretting that, before he left, he had not gone to greater lengths in his wild spirit of mischief, when a scuffle at the door of the Chequers attracted his attention, and then he heard the voice of Maude—a voice he knew full well, shrieking in its loudest accents,—

"Andrew Britton! Andrew Britton! I have come to see you die! Savage Britton, come forth! murderer, I have come to see you die."

"Now, by all the foul fiends," cried Britton, "I will be troubled by that croaking witch no more."

He rose from his seat, and despite the remonstrances of Bond, rushed into the passage to execute summary vengeance upon poor Maude, when he was seized by one of the officers, who had been quicker than his fellows, and who cried,—

"Andrew Britton, you are my prisoner."

For one instant Britton was passive, and then drawing a long breath, he seized the unlucky officer round the waist, and with one tremendous throw he pitched him through the open doorway into the street, where he fell with a deep groan, for a moment obstructing the passage of his comrades, and giving Britton time to dart up the staircase, which he did as quickly as his unwieldy bulk would let him. In another moment the voice of Sir Francis Hartleton—the only one he dreaded—rung in his ears as the magistrate cried—

"A hundred pounds for the apprehension of Andrew Britton! After him, men —after him! follow me!"

Maude stood screaming with a wild unearthly glee in the passage, and clapping her hands while Sir Francis and his officers rushed up the narrow staircase of the Chequers. As for Bond, he just looked out at the parlour door; when he saw how affairs were proceeding, he went back, and drunk up all Britton's liquor, after which lifting one of the low parlour windows, he stepped out, and walked leisurely down the street with his pipe in his mouth, as if nothing particular had happened, except that when he reached the corner he knocked the ashes out of his pipe against a post, and remarked,—

"That's a smasher!"

Britton was not much intoxicated previous to the arrival of his enemies, and the shock of finding himself thus openly sought for by his worst, or at all events, his most dangerous foe, completely sobered him. What has happened to Learmont? was the question he asked of himself as he reached his attic and bolted the door, in order to gain a moment's time for thought. It was but a moment, however, that he had to spare, and while the confusion and terror of his mind were each instant growing stronger, he opened the window and clambered out into the gutter, along which he crawled a few paces, and then commenced the ascent of the sloping roof of the old house, knowing that upon its other slope it abutted so closely upon some other houses, that in the darkness of the night he would have a chance of escape. For the first time, however, in his life, a mortal fear crept over Britton's heart, and when a shout arose in the street from the maskers, some of whom saw his dark figure crawling up the roof, he was compelled to clutch desperately to it, to save himself from rolling down headlong.

One glance behind him showed him the officers on the gutter, and preparing to ascend the roof.

"Come down, or we fire!" cried one.

"No—no," shouted Sir Francis, "take him alive; he cannot escape."

"Cannot escape?" groaned Britton as he made frantic efforts to reach the top of the roof, but each time foiled by his own too powerful struggles, for the small flat tiles kept coming off in his hands, which were already torn and bleeding from his recent exertions.

Some flambeaux were now elevated on long poles, borrowed from a neighbouring shop by the maskers, and a broad red glare was cast upon the roof of the Chequers, bewildering the eyes of the smith as well as making him visible to all his enemies. Then shouts, hoots, screams, and all sorts of discordant cries burst from the rapidly increasing crowd below, while several of the officers began to crawl up the roof after Britton, who by the most tremendous efforts had nearly sncceeded in gaining the summit.

" Come down, men," cried Sir Francis to his officers—" he is in our power—down, all of you."

The magistrate had sent one of the officers along the gutter with instructions to ascend the roof as rapidly as possible some distance on, and getting upon the other slope meet Britton, when he should reach the top; and seize him. This manœuvre was executed with adroitness and despatch, for what to the terrified and half-maddened Britton was a task of immense difficulty, was nothing to the cool and determined officer, whose head exactly rose up and faced Britton's as he reached the summit of the roof.

With a cry of rage Britton clutched the man by the collar, at the same moment that the officer made a desperate attempt to push him down the sloping roof into the gutter. Then all the devil in the smith's nature seemed to revive—fury kindled his eyes, and with a yell more like that of a wild beast than a human being, he dragged the officer over the pinnacle of the roof, as if he had been a child, and dashing down with them tiles, mortar, and rubbish, the two rolled with tremendous speed into the gutter.

There was a shout from the crowd below, for Britton's capture appeared certain, when a large piece of the flat stone which formed the street side of the gutter, gave way with the shock of the two rolling bodies, and fell into the street with an awful crash. A shriek then arose from a hundred throats—one half of either Britton's body or the officer's, no one could tell which, hung over the abyss. There was one plunge of the feet, and many of the crowd turned away their eyes, as before the officers above, or Sir Francis Hartleton could get a hold of them, both Britton and his captor fell over, and locked in an embrace of death, reached the pavement, with a dull, hideous sound. There was then a rush forward of the crowd, but it was found in vain to attempt to unlock the death clutch of the two men—both were dead. Britton's face was terribly disfigured, and when, with a wild terrible cry, Maude sprung to the corpses, it was only by seeing that the one whose face was discernible, was not Britton, that she could guess the other to be the savage smith, who had worked her so much woe. She did not exult—she did not scream or laugh with her usual mad mirth, but a great change came over her face, and in a low plaintive tone she said,—

" Where am I—is this my wedding-day—what has happened?" She then clasped her head with her hands, and appeared to be trying to think—reason had returned, but it was to herald death.

" He who loved me is no more," she moaned—" the savage smith took his life —God bless——"

Her head sunk upon her breast—lower—lower still she drooped. Then, some tried to raise her—they spoke kindly to her, but her spirit had fled.

CHAPTER CXX.

CONCLUSION.

OUR eventful history is nearly ended, and yet we would fain linger by Ada and her fortunes. We would fain follow still through the various scenes of life, the hil which was brought from the blazing smithy—the enthusiastic girl, who, in the majesty and might of innocence, defied Jacob Gray,—the pure beautiful being, who in maturer years denounced him as a murderer—she who still clung to her first, her only love, and when the dearest friend that fate had given her, Sir Francis Hartleton even doubted, still asserted her confidence in his devotion, his integrity, and his love. We would like to follow her into domestic life, to see how the budding graces of the girl reached the glorious meridian of their charms, and how then they mellowed into a graceful autumn, but already we have been seduced beyond our limits, by our beautiful Ada and her strangely varied fortunes, and we must leave to those readers who have gone with us heart and hand thus far, to imagine for themselves much that we would fain record. Something, however we cannot refrain from stating, and first and foremost we may say, that Ada became Mrs. Seyton just one week after the eventful ball at Learmont's house, and that the Secretary of State came to the marriage, and wanted to give the bride away; but Sir Francis Hartleton claimed the privilege, and reconciled the minister to his disappointment, by assuring him that Ada meant to let him have all the parliamentary interest connected with her property.

The ladies at the period of Ada's marriage wore immense state dresses, which "would stand up of themselves," and Ada's, still well preserved, is considered a kind of heir-loom in the author's family, who, by-the-by, may as well state at first as at last, that he is a lineal descendant of the persecuted girl, and more proud of his ancestress than if she had been a throned queen.

For the satisfaction of his lady-readers, the author begs to state that Ada's wedding dress was, and is of silver grey satin, on which are wrought roses in white silk, with here and there so delicate a roseate tinge, as to give quite an air of reality to the mimic floral adornment. She wore no ornaments in her hair, but a rare and costly lace robe, presented to her by Lady Hartleton, was confined to her forehead by a single diamond, from whence it hung down to the very ground.

Then Albert Seyton looked extremely well in the uniform of a captain in the guards, to which rank he had been immediately presented by the minister; of course not on account of his votes—oh, no. Lady Hartleton, we find by an old letter before us, was foolish enough to cry at the marriage, but Ada was quite ob-durate, and would not shed a tear, saying in her quiet way,—

"Why should I weep when I'm happy?" and as nobody knew why, she left the church with a smile.

We dislike interfering in family affairs, but we must say, that we would have proposed Ada's first little one to be called Albert, as it was a boy, but she would have it named Francis, after the worthy magistrate, who stood godfather to it. The next was a girl, and that Albert would have named Ada, and after that came—but our readers may imagine all that, when we tell them that Ada was the happy mother of as happy a family as ever lived.

*　　*　　*　　*　　*　　*　　*

Sir Francis Hartleton went himself down to the Old Smithy, and upon digging carefully among the ruins, a skeleton form was found, which from the remnants of clothing still adhering to it, was proved to be Ada's unhappy father. In the nearest churchyard, the remains were, with all proper solemnity, consigned to the tomb, but Ada was not informed of the circumstance for some years after she had been in full enjoyment of the Learmont estates.

It would appear that ritton had never run the risk of having a written confession in London with him, but upon a careful search in the smithy, a bag was found, in which was a knife with the initials of "J. G." on the handle, and several letters, likewise odd papers, one of which was a certificate of the marriage of Ada's mother at Rome; another proved clearly that Learmont, who had lived so badly, and died so terribly, was really illegitimate, so that his claim to the estates was not good under any circumstances.

Those documents and papers Sir Francis handed to Albert Seyton, and by him they were, as time and occasion served, shown to Ada.

Dame Totten was diligently sought for by Ada, and finally found in a wood she. She said that soon after the fire at the smithy, Learmont and Britton called at her cottage, and with bitter threats, insisted upon her bringing the child to Learmont House in the morning, and that she fearing for its life, fled from her cottage with it, and reached London, where she subsisted for some time on charity, till a man robbed her of the child, leaving her insensible from the effects of the blow he gave her. The aged woman, for she was nearly ninety, shed tears of joy upon Ada making herself known to her, and need we say, that the remainder of her life was assisted with every comfort by Ada.

Bond the butcher was hanged at Tyburn for a highway robbery, attended with brutal violence, within one year after the death of Britton. As for the landlord of the Chequers, he lost his licence, and the last that was heard of him was his selling a liquor called snap, then in vogue, at Bond's execution.

Thus, despite all her grievous trials and all her dangers, was Ada the Betrayed happy, and, in course of time, she thought with chastened sorrow upon the fate of her father, and learned to regard with patient resignation as one of the decrees of Heaven, the Murder at the Old Smithy.

THE END

London: Printed and published by E. Lloyd, 12, Salisburysquare, Fleet-street.

www.ingramcontent.com/pod-product-compliance
Lightning Source LLC
Chambersburg PA
CBHW080946020726
47505CB00009B/2150